BIRTH OF A MONSTER

There was his hand, her father's strong hand ... There was then a shadow behind him in the murk and spume, a tall man who touched a staff to her father's head. The fingers slackened. A surge tore her from them ... She saw him lean forth, reach after what he had lost. A torrent swept her away ...

A shape heaved into view, timbers afloat, fragment of a ship ... A roller cloven by a rock sent it from her.

She was among the skerries. Fury swirled around them, fountained above them. Never could she reach one, unless as a broken corpse. Billows crashed over her head.

Dazed, the animal warmth sucked from her, she did not know the last of them for what it was. She was simply in the dark, the time went on and on, her lips parted and she breathed sea. The pain was far off and brief. She spun down endlessly through a whiteness that keened.

At the bottom of that throat was not ... rth into somewhere ... neone waited. Trans-

The "King of Ys" series:

ROMA MATER
GALLICENAE
DAHUT

THE KING OF YS:
THE DOG AND THE WOLF

POUL AND KAREN ANDERSON

THE DOG AND THE WOLF

This is a work of fiction. All the characters and events portrayed in this book are fictional, and any resemblance to real people or incidents is purely coincidental.

A Baen Books Original

Baen Publishing Enterprises
260 Fifth Avenue
New York, N.Y. 10001

First printing, April 1988

ISBN: 0-671-65396-2

Cover art by David Mattingly

Printed in the United States of America

Distributed by
SIMON & SCHUSTER
1230 Avenue of the Americas
New York, N.Y. 10020

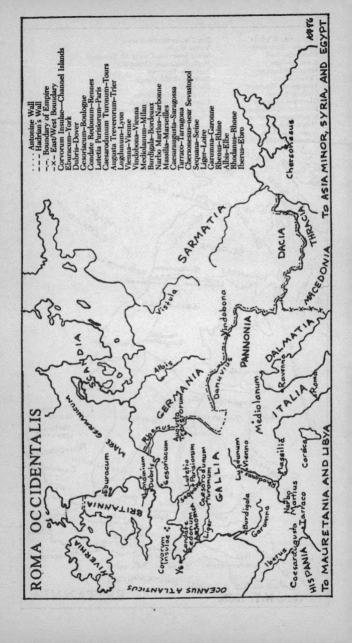

ROMA OCCIDENTALIS

.... Antonine Wall
--- Hadrian's Wall
-..-. East/West Boundary
—— Boundary of Empire
—x— East/West Boundary
Corvorum Insulae—Channel Islands
Eburacum—York
Dubris—Dover
Gesoriacum—Boulogne
Condate Redonum—Rennes
Lutetia Parisiorum—Paris
Caesarodunum Turonum—Tours
Augusta Treverorum—Trier
Lugdunum—Lyon
Vienna—Vienne
Vindobona—Vienna
Mediolanum—Milan
Burdigala—Bordeaux
Narbo Martius—Narbonne
Massilia—Marseilles
Caesaraugusta—Saragossa
Tarraco—Tarragona
Chersonesus—near Sevastopol
Sequana—Seine
Liger—Loire
Garumna—Garonne
Rhenus—Rhine
Albis—Elbe
Rhodanus—Rhone
Iberus—Ebro

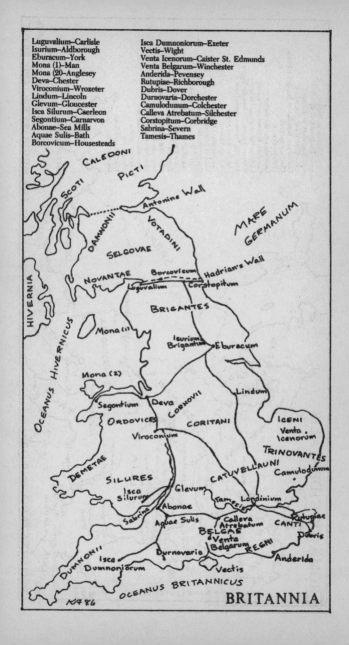

Luguvalium–Carlisle
Isurium–Aldborough
Eburacum–York
Mona (1)–Man
Mona (2)–Anglesey
Deva–Chester
Viroconium–Wroxeter
Lindum–Lincoln
Glevum–Gloucester
Isca Silurum–Caerleon
Segontium–Carnarvon
Abonae–Sea Mills
Aquae Sulis–Bath
Borcovicum–Housesteads

Isca Dumnoniorum–Exeter
Vectis–Wight
Venta Icenorum–Caister St. Edmunds
Venta Belgarum–Winchester
Anderida–Pevensey
Rutupiae–Richborough
Dubris–Dover
Durnovaria–Dorchester
Camulodunum–Colchester
Calleva Atrebatum–Silchester
Corstopitum–Corbridge
Sabrina–Severn
Tamesis–Thames

BRITANNIA

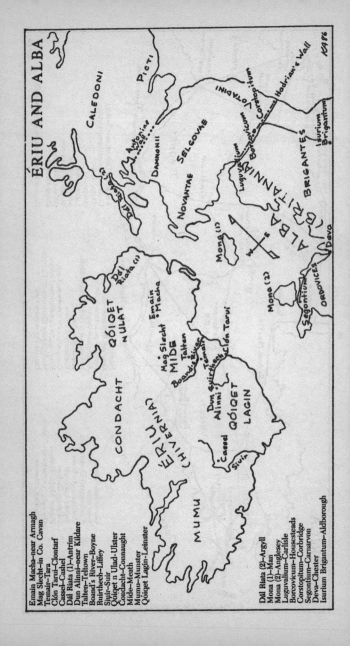

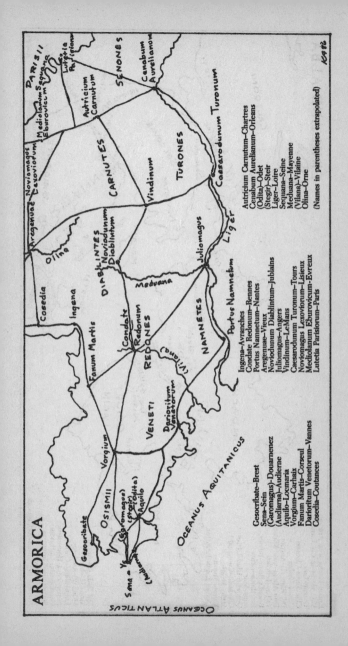

ARMORICA

Ingena—Avranches
Condate Redonum—Rennes
Portus Namnetum—Nantes
Aregenuae—Vieux
Noviodunum Diablintum—Jublains
Juliomagus—Angers
Vindinum—LeMans
Caesarodunum Turonum—Tours
Noviomagus Lexoviorum—Lisieux
Mediolanum Eburovicum—Evreux
Lutetia Parisiorum—Paris

Autricium Carnutum—Chartres
Cenabum Aurelianum—Orleans
(Odita)—Odet
(Stegir)—Steir
Liger—Loire
Sequana—Seine
Meduana—Mayenne
(Vilana)—Vilaine
Olina—Orne

(Names in parentheses extrapolated)

Gesocribate—Brest
Sena—Sein
(Garomagus)—Douarnenez
(Audierna)—Audierne
Aquilo—Locmaria
Vorgium—Carhaix
Fanum Martis—Corseul
Darioritum Venetorum—Vannes
Cosedia—Coutances

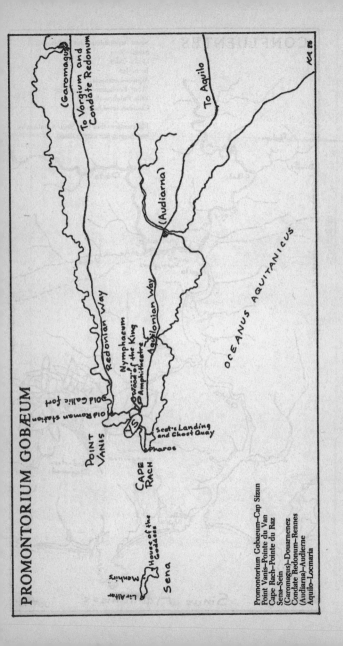

PROMONTORIUM GOBÆUM

Point Vanis

Old Roman station

Old Gallic fort

Redonian way

Nymphaeum
Wood of the King
Amphitheatre

Aquilonian way

To Vorgium and
Condate Redonum

(Garomagus)

(Audiarna)

To Aquilo

OCEANUS AQUITANICUS

CAPE
RACH

Pharos

Scot's Landing
and Ghost Quay

Sena

House of the
Goddess

Menhirs

Lia Altar

Promontorium Gobaeum–Cap Sizun
Point Vanis–Pointe du Van
Cape Rach–Pointe du Raz
Sena–Sein
(Garomagus)–Douarnenez
Condate Redonum–Rennes
(Audiarna)–Audierne
Aquilo–Locmaria

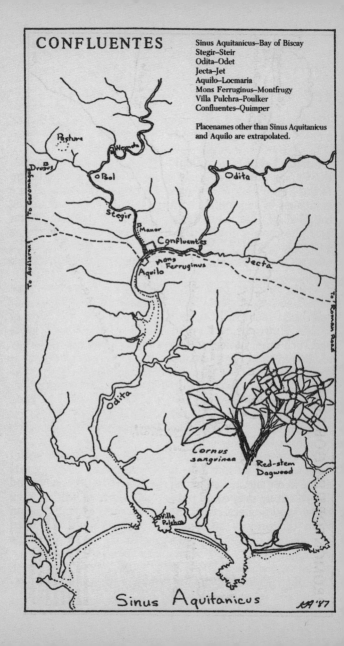

CONFLUENTES

Sinus Aquitanicus–Bay of Biscay
Stegir–Steir
Odita–Odet
Jecta–Jet
Aquilo–Locmaria
Mons Ferruginus–Montfrugy
Villa Pulchra–Poulker
Confluentes–Quimper

Placenames other than Sinus Aquitanicus
and Aquilo are extrapolated.

Pasture

To Cornouge

Drusus

To Audierna

O Bel

Wenade

Stegir

Odita

Manor

Confluentes

Mons Ferruginus

Aquilo

Jecta

To Roman Road

Odita

Cornus
sanguinea   Red-stem
Dogwood

Villa
Pulchra

Sinus Aquitanicus

WHAT HAS GONE BEFORE

Gaius Valerius Gratillonius, born in Britannia, joined the Roman army at an early age and rose to be a centurion in the Second Legion Augusta. Distinguishing himself in a campaign to stop a barbarian onslaught from overrunning the Wall of Hadrianus, he was chosen by Magnus Clemens Maximus, military commandant in the island, for a special mission. With a small detachment of soldiers he was to go to Ys, at the western end of the Armorican peninsula.

That city-state, originally a Phoenician colony, had always been mysterious. Since the days of Julius Caesar it had been technically a foederate, a subordinate ally, of Rome. However, he never mentioned it in his writings, and such other notices of Ys as chroniclers made had a way of becoming lost in the course of time. Gradually it withdrew entirely from the affairs of the troubled Empire. Gratillonius was now supposed to fill the long vacant position of Roman prefect, an "advisor" whose advice had better be followed. With this power, he was to keep as much of Armorica peaceful as he could in a difficult period soon to come.

Unspokenly but clearly, the difficulties would result from an effort by Maximus to overthrow the co-Emperors of the West and make himself supreme. Gratillonius hoped such a strong man could put an end to the corruption, civil strife, and general weakness that were leaving Roman lands the prey of barbarians. His assignment was given him despite his being of the dying Mithraic faith, in an age when Christianity had become the state religion.

Having marched across Gallia to Ys, he was stunned by its beauty. Then suddenly he found himself in single combat.

1

Battles of this kind, held in a sacred grove, determined who would be King of Ys. That man was required to answer all challenges and to spend the three days and nights around full moon in the Red Lodge at the Wood of the King. A new winner was immediately married to the Gallicenae, the nine Queens. These were recruited from among children and grandchildren of their Sisterhood. Such a girl must serve as a vestal virgin until age eighteen—unless first, at the death of a regnant Queen, the Sign, a tiny red crescent, appeared between her breasts. If it did, she was consecrated a high priestess and married to the King. Otherwise she had to remain a maiden until her term was ended, at which time she became free. A Queen conceived only when she chose; to avoid it, she need but eat a few flowers of the Herb ladygift, blue borage. She bore only daughters. Most Gallicenae in the past had possessed strong magical powers, but in later generations these had been fading away.

All this had been ordained by the three Gods of Ys, Taranis of the heavens, triune female Belisama, and inhuman Lir of the sea. Other deities could be honored if so desired, and under Roman pressure Ys maintained a Christian church serving a minuscule congregation. Aside from the ritual combat, the city was highly civilized. For the past five years the King had been brutal Colconor. When the Nine could endure him no longer, they cast a curse on him and a spell to bring yet another challenger. This they did on the island Sena, out among the rocks and reefs beyond the headlands, reserved to them alone. Except on special occasions, one of them must always be there, holding Vigil.

They conspired to get Colconor drunk and pique him, so that when Gratillonius arrived he gave the Roman a deadly insult. Nevertheless Gratillonius should not have lost his temper and gotten into a fight. Afterward the centurion wondered what had possessed him. By that time, to his astonishment, he was victorious, proclaimed King and wedded to the Nine.

Of these, the youngest was beautiful Dahilis. He and she fell deeply in love. He must also consummate his marriage to the rest, except for the two who were past

2

childbearing age. It was fortunate that one of these, Fennalis, was, because she was the mother of another Queen, Lanarvilis, and his Mithraic principles would not have allowed him to sleep with both. He found that a King was always potent with any of the Nine, and impotent with all other women.

Gratillonius's faith caused more conflicts, but did not prohibit his carrying out his duties as high priest and avatar of Taranis and also head of state. And his was the ceremonial task of locking and unlocking the sea gate.

In the days of Augustus Caesar, Brennilis, foremost among the Gallicenae, had had prophetic visions. She foresaw that rising sea level would drown the city unless it was protected, and got Roman engineers to build a rampart around it. The Gods demanded that this be of dry-laid stone, so that Ys would lie at Their mercy. Floats operated to open the seaward gate as tide ebbed; it closed of itself when waters rose. In times of storm, when waves might swing the doors wide and come raging in, a heavy bar kept the portal shut. Counterweighted, it could be raised or lowered by a single man. The King did this at need, except when he was elsewhere. The key to the securing lock was an emblem of rank that he must always carry on his person while in Ysan territory.

Ys believed that Brennilis had inaugurated a new Age, and that the city's often helpful obscurity, despite its brilliance, was due to its Gods—the Veil of Brennilis. Its manufactories, trade, and ships had made it the queen of the Northern seas; but the troubles of Rome inevitably affected it too.

Unlike many past Kings, Gratillonius took vigorous leadership. Besides influencing the Roman authorities in Armorica to stay neutral in the civil war as Maximus wanted, he sought to cope with the Saxon and Scotic pirates whose seaborne raids had devastated the coasts. His measures brought on a certain amount of controversy and opposition among the magnates of Ys. Its institutions founded in paganism, the city felt doubly wary of a Rome now officially Christian; yet without the Empire, it could scarcely survive.

In Hivernia, which they called Ériu, the Scoti were

3

divided into tuaths, not quite the same thing as tribes or clans, each with its king. Such a king was usually subordinate, together with others like himself, to a stronger lord. The island as a whole held five Fifths, not truly kingdoms though as a rule one man dominated each. They were Mumu in the south, Condacht in the west, Qóiqet Lagini in the east, Qóiqet nUlat in the north—and Mide, which an upstart dynasty had carved out of Condacht and Qóiqet Lagini. The high Kings in Mide centered their reigns, if not their residences, on the holy hill Temir.

Niall maqq Echach now held that position, a mighty warlord and the mastermind behind the assault on Britannia that Maximus had turned back. Smarting from this, he plotted fresh ventures against the Romans, beginning with an attack on Gallia while they lay at war with each other. He would steer wide of Ys and its witch-Queens. His son Breccan, young but his eldest and most beloved, persuaded the King of Mide to take him along.

Fearing that sort of event, Gratillonius made preparations. At his urging the Nine conjured up a storm (it was the last time they were ever able to do so) which blew the Scotic fleet onto the rocks outside Ys. Survivors who made it ashore were mostly killed by Roman soldiers, Ysan marines, and the mobilized seamen of the city. Niall escaped but Breccan perished. Grief-stricken and furious, Niall vowed revenge on this folk who had done him such harm when he intended them none.

Among the Romans lost was Eppillus, Gratillonius's second in command and fellow Mithraist. Fulfilling a promise, the King buried him on Point Vanis, the headland he had defended, though the Gods of Ys had long since decreed that burials be at sea unless well inland and the necropolis on Cape Rach now crumbled unused. Further religious conflict arose when Gratillonius unwittingly initiated another legionary, Cynan, into the woman-banning Mithraic faith, in a stream sacred to Belisama.

This happened near the Nymphaeum, which the vestals and minor priestesses tended in the hills. Dahilis, who had gone there with Gratillonius to get a blessing on their unborn child, came upon the ritual and was appalled, but continued to love him. On the whole, the rest of the Nine

4

were also anxious to keep him. One among them, Forsquilis, still had some of the magical powers that few Queens did any longer. She could do such things as send her spirit forth questing in the form of an eagle owl, or sometimes take omens. Her arts seemed to show that the Gods would be reconciled with unrepentant Gratillonius if, among other acts, a Queen with child took Vigil on Sena at midwinter. This had to be Dahilis, very near her time.

Gratillonius insisted on accompanying her. It was forbidden him, a man, to betread the island, but he could wait on the dock. When a storm came while she was off on her sacral duties, and she had not returned to the house there by dark, he defied the prohibition and went in search. He found her crippled by an accident—if it was an accident—and dying of exposure. Yet labor had begun. At the moment of her death, he cut the child free.

In the morning a fishing smack arrived to take them back. It belonged to Maeloch, who lived in the hamlet Scot's Landing below Cape Rach.

Numbed by sorrow, Gratillonius broke with custom and named his daughter Dahut as a memorial. Then with indifference he married the young woman on whom the Sign had come. On a later night, the knock of an invisible hand summoned the fishers of Scot's Landing to ferry the souls of the newly dead out to Sena for judgment, as their fathers had done for centuries. It was believed that some spirits returned as seals, to watch over those they had loved.

For two years thereafter, things went generally well in Ys. Gratillonius adored Dahut. Among the Queens, he was especially fond of scholarly Bodilis and witchy, passionate Forsquilis; but all had their virtues, and Lanarvilis in particular was a valuable political counselor to him.

Maximus had forced a settlement which made him an Augustus, ruling over Gallia, Hispania, and Britannia, with his seat in Augusta Treverorum. He summoned his prefect to report to him. On the way there with his legionaries for escort, Gratillonius rescued a party of travelers from a band of Bacaudae. These men were more than simple brigands; mostly they had fled Roman oppression and developed a loose organization. As the leader of this group,

5

Rufinus, negotiated with Gratillonius, they felt a sudden liking for each other.

Later Gratillonius encountered Martinus, bishop of Caesarodunum Turonum and founder of a monastery near that city. Again there was quick mutual respect and friendliness. Martinus had been seeing Maximus in an effort to win clemency for certain heretics on trial. Soon after he reached Treverorum, Gratillonius became a victim of the general hysteria—after all, Ys was pagan and he had dealt with sorceresses—and was interrogated under torture. However, Maximus could not dispense with him and hence released him with an adjuration to promote the Christian faith. Actually, Gratillonius sought out a surviving Mithraic congregation and got himself elevated to the rank of Father, so that he could found and lead a temple of that religion in Ys.

Time passed. Children were born to him and grew. The Nine took turns caring for Dahut. Physically resembling her mother, she was often aloof and moody, though well able to charm when she chose. Men as rough as the legionaries or the skipper Maeloch became her slaves. There was always something strange about her—Forsquilis read signs of a destiny—and occasionally she was seen in company with a particular female seal.

On the whole, Gratillonius's reign was highly successful. His naval, military, and political measures brought safety from the barbarians, which in turn revived industry and commerce. He gave justice to rich and poor alike. Even his defiances of the Gods from time to time did not shake his popularity. Among these was his sparing the life of Rufinus. Driven desperate and not knowing who really was the King of Ys, the Bacauda came and challenged him. Gratillonius disarmed Rufinus in combat, then refused to kill a helpless man. Rufinus became the King's devoted henchman, coming and going widely on his behalf, gradually recruiting Bacaudae to settle in the largely unpeopled interior of Armorica, give up their banditry, and serve at need as scouts and irregulars for Ys. This was violation of Roman law, but Gratillonius saw no alternative.

He had to replace the Christian minister, who had died. With Martinus's advice and consent, he picked Corentinus, whom he had come to know as a hermit in Osismia, the tribal territory adjacent to Ys. Despite the difference in faith they became friends and worked well together.

Another Christian friend whom Gratillonius made was Apuleius Vero, a senator and the tribune of the small Gallo-Roman city Aquilo. He likewise grew fond of Apuleius's wife Rovinda and their children Verania and Salomon.

Maximus invaded Italy but was soon defeated and killed. With the help of such influential Romans as Apuleius and Martinus, Gratillonius arranged for Maximus's veterans to be resettled in Armorica, where they could provide a leaven in the civilian reservists and ill-trained native regulars. The old legionary units were depleted, and modern heavy cavalry had not yet been much seen in the West.

It seemed the Gods would nevertheless chastise Gratillonius. The oldest Queen died, and the Sign came upon a daughter of Bodilis by an earlier King. Thereafter the mother and her royal husband could only be as brother and sister, much though that pained them. But in time he and the new Queen, Tambilis, became a loving couple.

Rufinus secretly bore another kind of love. Forceful Queen Vindilis ferreted out the fact of his homosexuality, which was abhorred in Ys, and thus had a hold on him.

Hoping to win back the favor of the Gods, the Queens raised Dahut to be Their fervent worshipper. The girl early showed immense promise as a witch, and got the idea that she was destined to inaugurate a new Age, now that the Age of Brennilis was clearly ending.

Time had also been at work in Ériu. Niall's foster-kinsman Conual Corcc became a mighty king in Mumu. He did not have Niall's implacable hatred of Ys, and eventually received envoys from Gratillonius (or Grallon, as the Ysans often rendered the name). Rufinus went on some of these missions, and in the course of doing so became friendly with a well-born young Scotian, Tommaltach.

Niall had been fighting in Ériu. He defeated his enemies the Lagini and demanded a huge tribute. At the parley, Eochaid, a son of the Laginach King Éndae, flared up and insulted Naill's master poet Laidchenn. Laidchenn's son and student Tigernach immediately composed a satire

7

which, unexpectedly, raised scarring blisters on the face of Eochaid and thus forever debarred him from becoming a king.

Niall went on to overrun territories allied to the Ulati, against whom his grand design lay. He had not forgotten his curse on Ys, but must first complete his conquests in northern Ériu.

While preparations for this were in train, he made a massive raid on Britannia. In his absence, resentful Eochaid entered Mide at the head of an army and plundered it widely. Niall gathered his forces next year and broke the Lagini, ravaged their lands, and collected the ruinous Bóruma tribute. He also took back Eochaid and other high-born young men as hostages, and kept them harshly confined. This was contrary to his usual practice. He treated very well those from the north whom he had as sureties. They had earned him the nickname Niall of the Nine Hostages.

Gratillonius in Ys was maintaining an ever more uneasy balance, trying to keep his subjects content despite religious and secular conflicts, to build up the strength of Armorica despite Roman laws forbidding or Roman bureaucracy discouraging what he saw as necessary actions, and at the same time to keep from provoking the Imperium into ordering an invasion of the city. He made a number of domestic enemies, notably Nagon Demari, Labor Councillor.

As she grew toward maturity, Dahut became the belle of Ys, her frequent strangenesses overlooked for the sake of her beauty and vivacity. The death of her seal cast her into deep grief until her father offered her what consolation he could and vowed he would never forsake her. Thereafter, under the tutelage of Forsquilis, she cultivated more and more of her magical powers. It heightened her arrogance. Yet she bedazzled young men. Among these were three foreigners now resident in Ys, Tommaltach, the Gallo-Roman Carsa, and the legionary Budic.

By then Niall had invaded the country of the Ulati and subjugated much of it. While he was there, Rufinus came to Mumu and proceeded to Mide, ostensibly carrying a peace feeler, actually in the hope of stirring up trouble for

Gratillonius's great enemy. He made the acquaintance of the wretched hostage Eochaid and engineered the latter's escape. On his way home, driven half mad by hardship, Eochaid met and killed Tigernach. The slayer of a poet could not remain in Ériu, even in his native Fifth. Eochaid got some followers and went into exile as a pirate. Tigernach's father Laidchenn satirized the Lagini for a year, bringing such a famine on them that for long afterward they were nearly powerless. These events sharpened both Eochaid's vengefulness toward Niall and Niall's toward Ys. The King began to prepare himself by learning the language and customs of the city.

There certain matters came to a head. Gratillonius brought criminal charges against Nagon Demari and got him dismissed. Doubly embittered, Nagon moved to Turonum and won somewhat the confidence of the provincial governor Glabrio and the procurator Bacca. These men saw renascent Ys as a threat to the shaky Imperium and Gratillonius himself as a threat to their careers. They conspired with Nagon.

Gratillonius had also made mortal enemies among the Franks at Redonum, Germanic barbarians who had forced Rome to let them settle there as laeti, responsible for much of the defense. They had hesitated to send challengers against him at the Wood, since he had always won, but Nagon persuaded them to come in a large body and pit a new man against the King every day. Eventually one must prevail. Glabrio and his colleagues arranged that the Ysan armed forces, who would have denied the Franks entry, would be off on joint maneuvers with the Romans.

Gratillonius overcame his first opponent but was hurt. Dahut again proved her powers by healing him with a touch. He then organized a band of Ysan civilians and his legionaries to attack the Franks, few of whom escaped. Otherwise, after his death, the city would have been occupied by them and suffered horribly. Nevertheless, this was another defiance of the old law, the old Gods. A further one occurred when, in fulfillment of a battlefield vow, he made a bull sacrifice to Mithras at the grave of Eppillus.

He overrode the magnates who considered this a sacrilege, and the people remained on his side, but it seemed the Gods were now determined to break his spirit. Old Fennalis died, and the Sign came on Dahut.

Jubilant, she hastened to him. This would begin the new Age, of which she would be the new Brennilis. The union of King and daughter was not forbidden; there had been cases in the past. She was aghast, then enraged when Gratillonius refused. His faith forbade.

It brought a crisis in Ys. Under Vindilis's leadership, most of the Nine refused themselves to the King unless he should give Dahut her rights. The one who did not suffered a disabling injury; yet he continued intransigent. Dahilis attempted to trick him into taking her, but failed. All omens that Forsquilis could read were evil. She even appealed to Corentinus; but he could only pray for God's mercy, he who in the past had more than once worked a miracle.

It began to seem that Dahut might try something desperate. Rufinus sought her out and warned her against it; if necessary, he would kill to protect or avenge his King. Dahut in her turn got Vindilis to blackmail the Gaul into leaving. He was to go down to the South and be an observer and spokesman for Ys at the court of Emperor Honorius—or, rather, Stilicho, the half-barbarian Roman general who had become the effective dictator of the Western Empire. Though this would be a genuine service, Gratillonius was reluctant to let Rufinus depart, since the latter was still more valuable to him in Armorica; but the other man insisted, without really explaining why.

Certainly Gratillonius needed advocates. The Franks had failed to dispose of him for Glabrio, but the heavy casualties he inflicted on those laeti, "defenders of Rome," gave the governor an opening to press any number of charges against him—illegal actions, dereliction of duty, outright treason. Apuleius helped him get prominent citizens such as Martinus to write testimonials on his behalf.

Meanwhile, with Rufinus out of the way, and with no word of her intentions to anyone, Dahut set herself to bring about her father's death. A new King would wed her and so carry out the will of the Gods. First she secretly seduced Tommaltach. He challenged Gratillonius, who

10

killed him in the Wood. Carsa met the same fate. Suspicions of Dahut were voiced to Gratillonius, but only infuriated him—that anyone dared slander the child of Dahilis! Later she took him aside and assured him of her love, despite the unhappy matter dividing them. He believed her. And all the while she was seducing Budic.

This took a long time, he being a devout Christian as well as loyal to his centurion. Meanwhile she bedded Gunnung, a sea rover from Scandia who happened to come visiting in Ys. He promised to fight Gratillonius, but instead slipped away. She finally won Budic over. He challenged, and also died. Now Gratillonius, heartsick, could no longer pretend that suspicions of Dahut were totally unfounded.

Plans for an investigation, which he hoped would clear her name, were interrupted by a summons to Treverorum, to answer the accusations against him. He did to the satisfaction of the praetorian prefect, Ardens, who even promoted him to the rank of tribune. However, the journey there and back went slowly in the dreadful weather of that winter.

Hardly had he left when Niall arrived, in the guise of an aristocratic Hivernian trader looking for new markets. He soon met Dahut, and soon thereafter was in her bed. She fell wildly in love with him. At last she brazenly gave a feast in his honor and lodged him in her house.

Deeply troubled, Vindilis sought out Maeloch, who had always spoken fondly of "little Queen Dahilis" and afterward of her daughter. What was going on? Could Maeloch take his *Osprey* to Hivernia and try to find out something about this Niall, who he really was and what his intentions might be? Maeloch agreed and set sail, though a monstrous storm was brewing.

Gratillonius returned after dark and heard what Dahut had been doing. He was appalled and meant to dig out the truth; but first he should stand his full-moon Watch at the Wood, for in the eyes of the Ysan magnates he was already more than enough in the enmity of the Gods.

Niall persuaded Dahut to steal the royal key as the ultimate token of her love; he said it would give him the power by which he might prevail in combat and become

11

King. She went through the storm, cast a sleep spell, and took the thing from her father. When she herself was asleep, Niall left her. He got past the guards on the wall, unlocked and unbarred the sea gate, and started back to the ship and crew he had left in the Roman harbor town Gesocribate.

A prophetic dream roused Corentinus. Leaving the many people who had sought refuge from the weather in his church and throughout the city, he went to awaken Gratillonius. The dream had told him the King must be saved. Against Corentinus's wish, Gratillonius, alarmed, mounted his horse Favonius and galloped back to Ys. A lantern, knocked over as he set forth, ignited the Wood.

He arrived just as the gate flew open and the sea came in. Barely did he stay ahead of the flood. Now his one desire was to save Dahut. He found her fleeing up a street and was about to draw her onto the saddle. Corentinus came striding over the waters and told him not to, lest the weight of her sins drag him down as well. He would have anyhow, but the holy man gave him a vision of the destruction of Ys, his Queens, everything. In his agony he lost hold of Dahut and the sea swept her away.

Somehow Gratillonius and Corentinus won to shore. The miraculous powers went out of the pastor. A handful of others had likewise escaped. Gratillonius recognized that his duty was toward them. But once their survival was assured—he did not know what he could do.

I

1

There was his hand, her father's strong hand, closing on the arm she raised toward him. The waters roared and rushed. Wind flung a haze of scud off their tops. Barely through salt blindness could she know it was he and sense

12

the bulk of the horse he rode. Memory passed like a lightning flash: she had sworn she would never mount that horse again while her father lived. But he was hauling her up out of the sea that would have her.

There was then a shadow behind him in the murk and spume, a tall man who touched a staff to her father's head. His grip clamped the tighter, but he did not now draw her onward. Waves dashed her to and fro. Tide went in flows and bursts of force. The noise filled heaven and her skull.

It was as if she sensed the sudden anguish, like a current out of his body into hers. The fingers slackened. A surge tore her from them. She screamed. The flood flung a mouthful to choke her. She had a glimpse of him, saw him lean forth, reach after what he had lost. A torrent swept her away.

Terror vanished. Abruptly she was altogether calm and alert. No help remained but in herself. She must hoard her strength, breathe during those instants when the tumult cast her high and hold the breath while it dragged her back under, watch for something to cling to and try to reach it, slowly, carefully. Else she was going to drown.

The sea tumbled her about, an ice-cold ravisher. She whirled through depths that were yellow, green, gray, night-blue. Up in the spindrift she gasped its bitterness and glimpsed walls crumbling. The violence scraped her against them, over and over, but bore her off before she could seize fast. Waves thundered and burst. Wind shouted hollowly.

The snag of a tower passed by and was lost. She understood that the deluge had snatched her from high ground and undertow was bearing her to the deeps. Surf brawled white across the city rampart. Already it had battered stone from stone off the upper courses, made the work into reefs; and still it hammered them, and they slid asunder beneath those blows. Right and left the headlands loomed above the wreckage, darknesses in wildness. Beyond them ramped Ocean.

A shape heaved into view, timbers afloat, fragment of a ship. It lifted on crests, poised jagged against clouds and the first dim daylight, skidded down troughs, rose anew. The gap closed between it and her. She gauged how she

13

must swim to meet it. For this chance she could spend
what might was left her. With the skill of a seal, she struck
out, joined herself to the waters, made them help her
onward. Her fingertips touched the raft. A roller cloven
by a rock sent it from her.

She was among the skerries. Fury swirled around them,
fountained above them. Never could she reach one, unless
as a broken corpse. Billows crashed over her head.

Dazed, the animal warmth sucked from her, she did not
know the last of them for what it was. She was simply in
the dark, the time went on and on, her lips parted and she
breathed sea. The pain was far off and brief. She spun
down endlessly through a whiteness that keened.

At the bottom of that throat was not nullity. She came
forth into somewhere outside all bounds. Someone waited.
Transfiguration began.

2

Fear knocked in the breast of Gratillonius as he approached the Nymphaeum.

Around him dwelt peace. The stream that fed the sacred canal descended in a music of little waterfalls. Morning sunlight rang off it. This early in the year, the
surrounding forest stood mostly bare to the blue overhead. The willows had unsheathed their blades, a green
pale and clear if set beside the intensity of the pasture-
lands below, but oak and chestnut were still opening
buds. Squirrels darted along boughs. Certain birds started
to sing. A breeze drifted cool, full of damp odors.

What damage he saw was slight, broken branches, a
tree half uprooted. The storm had wrought havoc in the
valley; the hills sheltered their halidom.

Nothing whatsoever seemed to have touched the space
into which he emerged. Swans floated on the pond, pea-
cocks walked the lawn. The image of Belisama Mother
stood on its pile of boulders, beneath the huge old linden,
above the flowing spring. Earth of flowerbeds, gravel of
paths, hedgerows and bowers led his gaze as ever before,

to the colonnaded white building. The glass in its windows flashed him a welcome.

You did not let hoofs mar those grounds. A trail went around their edge to join one behind the Nymphaeum, which led on into the woods and so to the guardhouse and its stable. For the moment, he simply dismounted and tethered Favonius. The stallion snorted and stood quiet, head low. Despite having rested overnight at the last house they reached yesterday, man and beast remained exhausted. Recovery from what had happened would be slow, and then—Gratillonius thought—only in the body, not the spirit. Meanwhile he must plow onward without pause, lest he fall apart.

Corentinus joined him. The craggy gray man had refused the loan of a mount for himself and strode behind, tireless as the tides. He leaned on his staff and looked. Finally he sighed into silence: "Everything that was beautiful about Ys is gathered here."

Gratillonius remembered too much else to agree, but he also recalled that his companion had never before beheld this place, in all the years of his ministry. It must have smitten him doubly with wonder after the horrors of the whelming. Usually Corentinus was plain-spoken, like the sailor he once had been. With faint surprise, Gratillonius realized that the other man had used Ysan.

He could not bring himself to reply, except for "Come" in Latin. Leading the way, his feet felt heavy. His head and eyelids were full of sand, his aches bone-deep. Doubtless that was a mercy. It kept the grief stunned.

But the fear was awake in him.

Female forms in blue and white appeared in the doorway and spread out onto the portico. Well might they stare. The men who neared them were unkempt, garments stained and wrinkled and in need of mending. Soon they were recognizable. Murmurs arose, and a single cry that sent doves aloft in alarm off the roof. The King, dressed like any gangrel. The Christian preacher!

They trudged up the stairs and jerked to a halt. Gratillonius stared beyond the minor priestess to the vestals whom she had in charge. His heart wavered at sight of his daughters.

15

Nemeta, child of Forsquilis; Julia, child of Lanarvilis. Them he had left to him. Una, Semuramat, Estar—no, he would not mourn the ten who were lost, not yet, he dared not.

He found himself counting. The number of persons on station varied. It happened now to be seven, or eight if he added the priestess. Besides his own pair there were four maidens ripening toward the eighteenth birthdays that would free them from service. He knew them, though not closely. All were grandchildren of King Hoel. One stemmed through Morvanalis, by an older sister of that Sasai who later became Gratillonius's Queen Guilvilis. One descended from Fennalis's daughter Amair, one each from Lanarvillis's Miraine and Boia. (Well, Lanarvillis had been dutifully fruitful in three different reigns; she deserved that her blood should live on.) Then there was a little girl of nine, too young for initiation but spending a while here as custom was, that she might become familiar with the sanctuary and serene in it. With her Gratillonius was better acquainted, for she was often in the house of Queen Bodilis, whose oldest daughter Talavair had married Arban Cartagi; the third child of that couple was this Korai.

He hauled his mind back from the past and addressed the priestess in Ysan: "Greeting, my lady. Prepare yourself. I bear dreadful tidings."

It might have been astonishing how steadily she looked back. Most often the house mother at the Nymphaeum was elderly, seasoned in dealing with people. Runa was in her mid-twenties. However, she was the daughter of Vindilis by Hoel. You would expect forcefulness, and persuasiveness too when she cared to employ it. He had never known her well, either, and as the rift widened between him and her mother, they met less and less. He knew that after she completed her vestalhood without the Sign coming upon her she married Tronan Sironai. The union was without issue and evidently not happy. Though she did not terminate it, she re-entered the Temple of Belisama and occupied herself mainly with the activities of an underpriestess.

"We have wondered," she said low. "We have prayed. Clear it is that the Gods are angry." At you, said her gaze.

Riding here, he had thought and thought how to tell what he must. Everything that had occurred to him had dropped out of his mind. He could merely rasp forth: "I am sorry. Ys is gone. Somehow the sea gate opened during the storm. Ocean came in and destroyed the city. The Gallicenae have perished. Most of the people have. I do not know that your husband, or any near kin of any among you, is alive. We must look to our survival—"

What followed was never afterward clear in his memory. Runa yowled and sprang at him. His left cheek bore the marks of her nails for days. He fended her off before she got to his eyes. She cursed him and turned to her vestals. One had swooned, others wailed or wept; but Gratillonius's Nemeta stood apart as if carven in ivory, while Gratillonius's Julia tried to give comfort. Likewise did Corentinus, in his rough fashion. Runa slapped faces, grabbed shoulders and shook them, demanded self-control. Gratillonius decided it was best he seek the guardhouse and the Ysan marines barracked there.

That was bad enough, though they refrained from blaming him. Three among them reviled the Gods, until their officer ordered them to be quiet. He, a burly, blond young man named Amreth Taniti, accompanied Gratillonius back to the Nymphaeum.

In the end, as memory again began clearly recording, those two sat with Corentinus and Runa in the priestess's room of governance. It was a chamber light and airy, furnished with a table, a few chairs such as were—had been—common in Ys, and a shelf of books. Three walls bore sparse and delicate floral paintings. On the fourth the blossoms were in a grassy field where stood the Goddess in Her aspect of Maiden, a wreath on Her flowing locks, arms outspread, smile raised toward the sun that was Taranis's while at her back shone the sea that was Lir's. Beyond the windows, springtime went on about its business just as joyfully.

Runa stared long at Corentinus. Her knuckles whitened on the arms of her seat. At last she spat, "Why have *you* come?"

"Let me answer that," said Gratillonius. He had quelled weariness and despair for this while; he moved onward

17

through what was necessary, step by step. So had he once led his men back from an ambush, through wilderness aswarm with hostiles, north of the Wall in Britannia. "I asked him to. We deal—I suppose we deal with Powers not human, as well as our mortal troubles and enemies. You know I am a Father in the cult of Mithras. Well, Corentinus is—a minister in the cult of Christ. Between us—"

"Do you include me?" she demanded rather than asked.

"Of course. Now hear me, Runa. We need these voices of different Gods so we can agree to set every God aside. Aye, later we can pray, sacrifice, quarrel, try coming to terms with the thing that's happened. But first we have the remnant of a folk to save."

Her glance raked him, the big frame, rugged features, grizzled auburn hair and beard. "Then you deny that your deeds caused the Gods to end the Pact," she said flatly.

He tautened. "I do. And be that as it may, 'tis not worth our fighting about. Not yet."

"That's true, my lady," Amreth said almost timidly. "Bethink you what danger we're in."

Corentinus raised a bony hand. "Hold, if you will." Somehow his mildness commanded them. "Best we understand each other from the outset. I shall say naught against your beliefs, my lady. However, grant me a single question." He paused. She nodded, stiff-necked. "Ever erenow, when a Queen died, a red crescent instantly appeared on the bosom of some vestal. This marked her out as the next Chosen to be one of the Gallicenae, bride of the King and high priestess of Belisama. True? Well, the Nine are gone in a single night. Here are the last of the dedicated maidens. Has the Sign come upon any of them?"

Runa sat straighter still. She passed tongue over lips. "Nay," she whispered.

The knowledge had already seeped into Gratillonius, damping the fear, but to become sure of it was like a sudden thaw.

"I utter no judgment concerning your Gods," Corentinus said quietly. "Yet plain is to see that we have come to the end of an Age, and everything is changed, and naught

18

have we to cling to in this world unless it be our duty toward our fellow mortals."

Visibly under the close-cropped beard, a muscle twitched at the angle of Amreth's jaw. "Right that is, my lady," he said. "We marines will stand by you and the vestals to the death. But this place was under the ward of the Gods, and no raiders or bandits ever dared put us to the test. Now . . . we number a bare dozen, my lady."

Runa sat back. She had gone expressionless. Gratillonius studied her. She was tall; beneath the blue gown, her figure was wiry but, in a subtle fashion, good. Her face was thin, aquiline, with a flawless ivory complexion. The brows arched above dark eyes. Beneath her wimple, he knew, was straight hair, lustrous black, which could fall past the shoulders. Her voice was rather high but he had heard her sing pleasingly.

She turned and locked stares with him. "What do you propose?" she asked.

Halfway through, he noticed that he had fallen into Latin. She followed him without difficulty. Amreth sat resigned.

"Ys is lost. Nothing left but a bay between the headlands, empty except for ruins." He forebore to speak of the dead who littered the beach and gulls ashriek in clouds around them. "Many people died who'd taken shelter there out of the hinterland. Very few escaped. Corentinus and I led them up the valley and billeted them in houses along the way. Those who don't succumb in the next several days ought to be safe for a while.

"Just a while, though. The granaries went with Ys. It's early spring. There's nothing to eat but flocks and seed corn, nothing to trade for food out of Osismia." He could certainly not make anyone go back and pick through the ghastliness in search of treasure. "Soon all will be starving. And the barbarians will hear of this, Saxons, Scoti, every kind of pirate. Ys was the keystone of defense for western Armorica. The Romans will have more than they can handle, keeping their own cities, without worrying about us. Most of their officials never liked us anyway. If we remain where we are, we're done.

"We have to get out, establish ourselves elsewhere.

19

Corentinus and I are going on to search for a place. I am a tribune of Rome, and he's a minister of Christ, known to Bishop Martinus in Turonum, and— But meanwhile somebody has to give the people leadership, those we brought from the city and those who held on in the countryside. Somebody has to bind them together, calm and hearten them, ready them for the move. A couple of landholder Suffetes are already at it, but they need every help they can get. Will you give it, my lady?"

The woman sat withdrawn for space before she said, "Aye," in Ysan. "Between us, I think, Amreth and I may suffice. But first we must talk, the four of us. Grant me this day. Surely you can stay that long." The hand trembled which she passed across her eyes. "You have so much to tell."

—Nonetheless, throughout words and plain meals and tearful interruptions from outside, she held herself steelhard. As the hours wore on, the scheme took shape, and hers were two of the hands that formed it.

—At eventide, the vestal Julia led her father and Corentinus to adjacent guestrooms, mumbled goodnight, and left them. They stood mute in the gloom of the corridor. Each had been given a candle in a holder. The flames made hunchbacked shadows dance around them. Chill crept inward.

"Well," said Gratillonius at last, careful to keep it soft and in Latin, "we had to work for it, but we seem to have gained a strong ally."

Darkness ran through the gullies in Corentinus's face. "We may hope. Still, be wary of her, my son. Be wary of them all."

"Why?"

"A dog abandoned grows desperate. If it does not find a new master, it goes the way of the wolf. These poor souls have been abandoned by their Gods."

Gratillonius tried to smile. "You offer them another."

"Whom they will perhaps not accept, as long as the old smell haunts them."

"But the Gods of Ys are dead!" Gratillonius exclaimed. "They brought Their city down on Themselves—" down and down into the deeps of the sea.

20

Corentinus sighed. "I'm afraid it's not that easy. The Enemy never gives up, not till Judgment Day." He clapped his friend's shoulder. "Don't let him keep you awake, though. You need your rest. Goodnight."

—Gratillonius recognized the chamber assigned him. Here he and Dahilis had lodged when they came to ask a blessing on their unborn child, she who would become Dahut. He gasped, knotted his fists, and struggled not to weep. Only after he had surrendered did sleep come to him, full of fugitive dreams.

3

Southbound out of Gesocribate, Niall and his men passed within sight of the island Sena. Low it lay in the heaving seas, bare of everything but sere grass and brush, a pair of menhirs near the middle, and some stones of the building at the east end. Wind whistled as it drove smoke-gray clouds overhead. Waves ran murky, streaked with foam, bursting in white where they struck rocks. A few seals swam in them, following along with the ship at a distance as if keeping watch. Cormorants rode the surges, dived, took flight on midnight wings.

Niall nodded. "Lir was more wrathful that night than ever I knew," he said slowly.

A shiver passed through Uail maqq Carbri, and him a hardened man. "I do think the Goddess willed it too," he muttered. "That was Her house."

"Like the Ulati when they burned down Emain Macha before we could make it ours. Someday men will dare settle here again because of the fishing grounds. They will take those stones for their own use. Then the last trace of Ys on its holy isle will be gone. But I have seen the ruins. That is enough."

Uail's gaunt countenance drew into a squint as he peered at his lord. "Was it for your enjoyment you had us come this way?"

Niall straightened, taller than any of the crew, a tower topped with the silvering gold of his hair. "It was not," he said grimly. "Let no man gloat that Ys is fallen, for a wonder and a glory it was in the world. When we return home, I will be forbidding poet and bard to sing this one deed of mine."

Uail kept silence. The King had told how he destroyed Ys, then laid gess on further talk about it unless he spoke first. He could not thus keep the story from spreading, but it would take root more in humble dwellings than in high. Most likely after a few lifetimes it would be forgotten, or be a mere folk tale with his name no longer in it.

Niall's eyes were like blue lightning. "I did what I did to avenge my son and my brave men, a sworn duty," he went on. "Else would that never have been my desire. As was, at the end I must . . . force myself." He gripped the rail and looked afar. The handsome visage was briefly twisted out of shape.

"You need not have this pain, dear," Uail ventured to say. "We could have gone directly back to Ériu."

Niall shook his head. "I must see what I wrought and make sure the vengeance is complete."

The ship toiled on eastward under oars. Ahead cruised her two attendant currachs, each with a pilot who had knowledge of these waters, picking a way among the reefs. The horns of land loomed ever more high and massive in view. Between their ruddy-dark cliffs there gleamed no longer the bulwark and the towers of Ys. Remnants thrust out of the bay, pieces of wall, heaps of stone, a few forlorn pillars. Waves chewed at them. The overturned carcass of a vessel swung about like a battering ram wielded by blind troops.

With care the crew worked their way toward Cape Rach. They saw the pharos on top, as lonely a sight as they had ever seen, and lost it as they passed along the south side. Flotsam became frequent, timbers, spars, but no other sign of man apart from a fragment of quay. The storm had swept away the fisher hamlet under the cliffs.

The beach was still Scot's Landing, laughed the men. They could go ashore. Their ship was no war galley capable of being grounded and easily relaunched; in accordance with their guise of peaceful traders, she was a round-bottomed merchantman. But they could drop the hook, leave three or four guards aboard, and ferry themselves in the currachs.

Niall led them up the path to the heights. It was slippery and had gaps, demanding care. Caution was also needful when foes not spied from the water might lurk above.

None did. Only the wind and a mutter of surf had voice. Standing on the graveled road that ran the length of the cape, the men saw bleakness around, desolation below in the bay. Such homes as they glimpsed, tucked into the hills above the valley, seemed deserted. On their left were ancient tombs, beyond them the pharos, and beyond it nothing but sky. The air felt suddenly very cold.

Niall raised his spear and shook it. "Onward for a close look and maybe a heap of plunder, boys!" he cried. "It's glad the ghosts are of those who died here these many years agone."

That rallied their spirits. They cheered and trotted after him. His seven-colored cloak flapped in the wind like a battle banner.

A paved road brought them down to the bayshore. Part of the southern gateway rose there, a single turret, an arch agape, a stretch of wall which had irregularly lost its upper courses. Inland, on their right, the amphitheater appeared undamaged, or nearly so; but an oakenshaw north of it had flamed away on the night Ys died, was blackness whence thrust a few charred trunks.

No matter that Niall of the Nine Hostages was their chief, the awe of a doom fell upon the men.

Waves rushed and growled above the remains. Amidst and beyond the wreckage above the waterline lay strewn and heaped incredible rubbish. Waterlogged silk and brocade draped broken furniture. Silver plates and goblets corroded in torn-up kelp. Tools and toys were tumbled together with smashed glass and shattered tiles. Copper sheathing lay green, crumpled, beside the debris of cranes and artillery. Paint or gilt clung to battered wood. Calmly smiling, a small image of the Goddess as Maiden nestled close to the headless, gelded statue of a man that might well have stood for the God. And skulls stared, bones gleamed yellowish in the damp, everywhere, everywhere.

Smells were of salt and tang, little if any stench. In the past few days, gulls at low tide and crabs at high had well-nigh picked the corpses clean, aside from what hair and clothing clung. Many birds walked the sands yet, scavenging scraps. They were slow to flee men who shouted or threw things at them. When they did, they flapped awkwardly, stuffed fat.

That was after the hush among the warriors broke. "Ho, see!" yelled one. He bent over, picked an object up, and flourished it: a pectoral of gold, amber, and garnets. Immediately his fellows were scrambling, scratching, casting bones away like offal, wild for treasure.

Niall stood apart, leaning on his spear. Uail did likewise. Presently the King said, distaste in his tone and on his face, "You too think this is unseemly?"

"It is that," Uail replied.

Niall seized his arm so hard that he winced. "I am not ashamed of what I did," hissed from him. "It was a mighty deed. But I must needs do it by stealth, and that will always be a wound in me. Do you understand, darling? Now we shall give Ys its honor, for the sake of our own."

Again he shook his spear in the wind. "Lay off that!" he cried. The sound went above the surf to the farther headland and back. Men froze and stared. "Leave these poor dead in peace," Niall ordered. "We'll go strip yon houses. The plunder should be better, too."

Whooping, they followed him inland.

—Toward sunset they returned to Cape Rach. Besides what they had taken from the mansions, they brought firewood off the wind-demolished, nearly dry buildings that had stood outside the main land gate. Niall sent a currach party to relieve the watch on the ship, who were to bring camping gear for all with them. When they arrived, he gave them gifts to make up for the looting they had missed. "Will we do more tomorrow?" asked one hopefully.

The King frowned. "We might. I cannot promise, for it may be we shall have to withdraw fast. Soon the Romans are bound to come for a look, and they will sure have soldiers with them. But we shall see."

—He could not sleep.

24

The wind whispered, the sea murmured. More and more as the night grew older, he thought he heard a song in them. It was music that keened and cut, cold, vengeful, but lovely in the way of a hawk aloft or a killer whale adown when they strike their prey. The beauty of it reached fingers in between his ribs and played on his caged heart until at last he could endure no more. He rolled out of his kilt, stood up, and wrapped it back around him against the bleakness of the night.

Banked, the fire-coals glowed low. He could barely make out his crew stretched in the wan grass and the gleam on the spearhead of him who kept guard. That man moved to ask what might be amiss. "Hush," breathed Niall, and went from him.

Clouds had gone ragged. Eastward the moon frosted those nearby and seemed to fly among them. Time had gnawed it as the tides gnawed what was left of Ys. Dew shimmered on the paved road, wet and slick beneath his bare feet. Between the hulking masses of headland, argency flickered on the bay. As he came closer, walking entranced, wind shrilled louder, waves throbbed deeper.

He stopped on the sand at high water mark, near a shard of rampart and the survivor of those two towers which had been called the Brothers. Looking outward, he saw how ebb tide had bared acres of ruins. *When last it did I was ransacking undefended houses,* he thought in scorn of himself. By this dim uneasy light he discerned fountains, sculptures, Taranis Way running toward what had been the Forum. Across Lir Way, a particular heap had been the Temple of Belisama, and Dahut's house had stood nearby. A skull lay at his feet. He wondered if it had been in the head of anyone he knew, even— He shuddered. It was a man's. Hers would have the strong sharp delicacy of a brooch from the hand of an ollam craftsman in Ériu.

Unshod, he did not wish to go farther, through the fragments. He folded his arms, gazed at the white unrestfulness of the breakers, and waited for that which had called him.

The song strengthened. It was in and of the wind and the waves, but more than they, from somewhere beyond.

It yearned and it challenged, a harp and a knife, laughter and pain, endlessly alone. Someone sported in the surf, white as itself, like a seal but long and lithe of limb, high in the breast, slim in the waist, round in the hips, plunged and rose again, danced with the sea like a seal, and sang to him. Vengeance, it sang, I am vengeance, and you shall serve me for the love I bear you. By the power of that love, stronger than death, I lay gess on you, Niall, that you take no rest until the last of Ys lies drowned as I lay drowned. It is your honor price, King on Temir, that you owe her whom you betrayed; for never will her love let go of you.

Long and long he stood at the edge of the fallen city while the siren sang to him. He remembered how he had called Mongfind the witch from her grave, and knew now that once a man has let the Otherworld into his life, his feet are on a road that allows no turning back.

But he was Niall of the Nine Hostages. Fear and regret were unbecoming him. At the turn of the tide, she who sang fell silent and swam away out of his sight. He strode back to the camp, laid himself down, and dropped quickly into a sleep free of dreams.

—In the morning he ranked his followers before him. They saw the starkness and were duly quiet. "Hear me, my dears," he said.

"A vision, a thought, and a knowledge came over me in the night. You will not be liking this, but it is the will of the Gods.

"Ys, that murdered our kinsmen, must do more than die. Overthrown, she could yet be victorious over us. For folk will be coming back to these parts and settling. If they saw what we see, they would recall what we have heard, the tales and the ballads, the memory of splendor; and in their minds *we* would be the murderers. Shall they found a new city and name it Ys? Shall they praise and dream of Old Ys till heaven cracks open? Or shall, rather, the city of treachery die forever?

"Already, I have told you, I want no word of it bound to my own fame. Today I tell you that *nothing* of it may abide.

"Our time here is short. We cannot do the whole work

at once. But this is my command, that we leave the valley houses be—others will clean them out soon enough—and start the razing of yonder lighthouse which once guided mariners to Ys."

—Dry-laid, it yielded more readily to strong men than might have been awaited from its stoutness. They cast the blocks over the cliff. When they set sail, half was gone. Niall thought of a raid in summer, during which the rest could be done away with. Of course, warriors would require booty. Well, much should remain around the hinterland, as well as in settlements on this whole coast.

He grinned. They might find a party of Gauls picking over the shards of Ys, and rob them. In the song of the siren had been promise as well as threat.

He sobered, and men who noticed slipped clear of his nearness. She had laid a word on him. Year by year, as he was able, he must obey. Untouched thus far on Cape Rach stood the necropolis. He must level it. First would be the tomb of Brennilis.

II

1

The sun was not yet down, but the single glazed window was grayed and dusk beginning to fill the room where Apuleius Vero had brought his guests. It was a lesser chamber of his house, well suited for private talk. Wall panels, painted with scenes from the Roman past, were now vague in vision. Clear as yet sheened the polished walnut of a table which bore writing materials, a pair of books, and modest refreshments. Otherwise the only furniture was the stools on which the three men sat.

The news had been brought, the shock and sorrow

uttered, the poor little attempts at condolence made. It was time to speak of what might be done.

Apuleius leaned forward his slender form and regular features. "How many survivors?" he asked low.

Gratillonius remained hunched, staring at the hands clasped together in his lap. "I counted about fifty," he said in the same dull voice as before.

The tribune of Aquilo drew a sharp breath and once more signed himself. "Only half a hundred from that whole city and . . . and those from outside whom you say had taken refuge? Christ be with us. Christ have mercy."

"There may be two or three hundred more who stayed in the countryside, including the children. We've tried to get in touch with them."

Corentinus's fist knotted on his knee. Tears gleamed under the shaggy brows. "The children," he croaked. "The innocents."

"Most will starve if they don't soon get help," Gratillonius said. "Afterward the reavers will come."

Apuleius forced business into his tone. "But I gather you have leaders for them while you are off seeking that help. Where have you been?"

"Thus far, only Audiarna. The reception we got there decided me to come straight to you."

"What did they say?"

Gratillonius shrugged. Corentinus explained, harshly: "The tribune and the chorepiscopus both told us they had no space or food to spare. When I pressed them they finally cried that they could not, dared not take in a flock of pagans who were fleeing from the wrath of God. I saw it would be useless to argue. Also, they were doubtless right when they said our people would be in actual danger from the dwellers. Ys is—was near Audiarna. The horror of what has happened, the terror of more to come, possesses them in a way you should be free of here at your remove."

Apuleius looked at Gratillonius and shook his head in pity. The centurion of the Second, the King of Ys had lacked strength to dispute with a couple of insignificant officials and must needs leave it to his clerical companion.

"We can take in your fifty at once, of course," Apuleius

told them. "A trading town like this has a certain amount of spare lodging in the slack season. It is not a wealthy town, though. We can find simple fare, clothing, and the like for that many, but only temporarily. The rest shall have to stay behind until something has been worked out with the provincial authorities. I will dispatch letters about that in the morning."

"God will bless you," Corentinus promised.

Gratillonius stirred and glanced up. "I knew we could count on you, old friend," he said, with a slight stirring of life in his voice. "But as for the tribunes or even the governor—I've given thought to this, you understand. They never liked Ys, they endured it because they had to, and some of them hate me. Why should they bestir themselves for a band of alien fugitives?"

"Christ commands us to succor the poor," Apuleius answered.

"Pardon me, but I've never seen that order very well followed. Oh, Bishop Martinus will certainly do what he can, and I suppose several others too, but—"

"I'll remind them that people who become desperate become dangerous. Don't fret too much." With compassion: "It'll take time, resettling them, but remember Maximus's veterans. Armorica continues underpopulated, terribly short of hands for both work and war. We'll get your people homes."

"Scattered among strangers? After they've lost everything they ever had or ever were? Better dead, I think."

"Don't say that," Corentinus reproved. "God's left the road open for them to win free of the demons they worshipped."

Gratillonius stiffened. His gaze sought Apuleius and held fast. His speech was flat with weariness but firm: "Keep them together. Else the spirit will die in them and the flesh will follow it. You've been in Ys. You've seen what they can do, what they know. Think what you've gained from the veterans and, all right, those former outlaws who came to these parts. We're going to need those hands you spoke of more than ever, now Ys is gone. It was the keystone of defense for Armorica. How many troops does Rome keep in this entire peninsula—two thousand?

29

And no navy worth mentioning; the Ysan fleet was the mainstay of that. The barbarians will be coming back. Trade will be ripped apart. I offer you some good fighting men, and some more who can learn to be, and others who're skilled workmen or sailors or scribes or— Man, can you afford to waste them?"

He sagged. Twilight deepened in the room. Finally Apuleius murmured, "You propose to resettle the Ysans, your former subjects, rural as well as urban, in this neighborhood?"

Gratillonius was barely audible: "I don't know any better place. Do you?"

Corentinus took the word. "We've talked about it a little, we two, and I've given it thought of my own. I used to live hereabouts, you recall, and though that was years ago, the King's brought me the news every time he paid a visit. There's ample untilled land. There's iron ore to be gathered nearby, and unlimited timber, and a defensible site that fishers and merchantmen can use for their terminus." Apuleius opened his mouth. Corentinus checked him with a lifted palm. "Oh, I know, you wonder how so many can be fed in the year or more it'll take them to get established. Well, in part we'll have to draw on Imperial resources. I'm sure Bishop Martinus can and will help arrange that; his influence isn't small. The need won't be great or lasting, anyway. For one thing, the Ysan hinterland grazes sheep, geese, some cattle and swine. Their herders would far rather drive them here and see most eaten up than keep them for the barbarians. Then too, Ys was a seafaring nation. Many a man will soon be fishing again, if only in a coracle he's made for himself, or find work as a deckhand on a coastal trader." He paused. "Besides, the former soldiers and former Bacaudae who owe their homes to Gratillonius—I think most of them will be glad to help."

Apuleius gripped his chin, stared afar, sat long in thought. Outside, sounds of the town were dying away.

Finally the tribune smiled a bit and said, "Another advantage of this site is that I have some small influence and authority of my own. Permissions and the like must be arranged, you understand. That should be possible. The situation is not unprecedented. Emperors have let hard-pressed barbarian tribes settle in Roman territory; and Ys is—was—actually a foederate state. I have the power to admit you temporarily. Negotiating a permanent status for you will take time, since it must go through the Imperium itself. But the, alas, inevitable confusion and delay are to the good, for meanwhile you can root yourselves firmly and usefully in place. Why then should the state wish to expel you?

"Of course, first you require somewhere to live. While land may lie fallow, it is seldom unclaimed. Rome cannot let strangers squat anywhere they choose." —unless they have the numbers and weapons to force it, he left unspoken.

"Well?" asked Corentinus tensely.

"I have property. To be precise, my family does, but God has called most of the Apuleii away and this decision can be mine."

Gratillonius's breath went sharp between his lips.

Apuleius nodded, as if to himself, and continued methodically. "You remember, my friend, that holding which borders on the banks of the Odita and the Stegir where they meet, a short walk hence. On the north and east it's hemmed in by forest. Of late, cultivation has not gone so well. Three tenant families have farmed it for us, one also serving as caretakers of its manor house. They grow old, that couple, and should in charity be retired. As for the other two, one man has lately died without a son; I am seeing what can be done for his widow and daughters. The second man is hale and busy, but—I strongly suspect—would welcome different duties. God made him too lively for a serf. Can the Lord actually have been preparing us here for a new use of the land?"

"Hercules!" Gratillonius breathed. Realizing how inappropriate that was, he gulped hard and sat silent.

"Hold on," Apuleius cautioned. "It's not quite so simple. The law does not allow me to give away an estate as I might a coin. This grant of mine must employ some contorted technicalities, and at that will involve irregularities. We'll need all the political force we can muster, and no doubt certain . . . considerations . . . to certain persons, if it is to be approved. However, I'm not afraid to have the

31

actual work of settlement commence beforehand. That in itself will be an argument for us to use."

"I *knew* I could count on you—" Abruptly Gratillonius wept, not with the racking sobs of a man but, in his exhaustion, almost the quietness of a woman.

Apuleius lifted a finger. "It will be hard work," he said, "and there are conditions. First and foremost, they were right as far as they went in Audiarna. We cannot allow a nest of pagans in our midst. You must renounce those Gods, Gratillonius."

The Briton blinked the tears off his lashes, tasted the salt on his mouth, and replied, "They were never mine."

Corentinus said, like a commander talking of an enemy who has been routed at terrible cost, "I don't think we'll have much trouble about that, sir. How many among the survivors can wish to carry on the old rites? Surely too few to matter, except for their own salvation. Let most hear the Word, and soon they will come to Christ."

"I pray so," Apuleius answered solemnly. "Then God may be pleased to forgive one or two of my own sins."

"Your donation will certainly bless you."

"And my family?" Apuleius whispered.

"They too shall have many prayers said for them."

Both men's glances went to Gratillonius. He evaded them. Silences thickened.

"It would be unwise to compel," Corentinus said at length.

The door opened. Light glowed. "Oh, pardon me, father," said the girl who bore the lamp. "It's growing so dark inside. I thought you might like to have this."

"Thank you, my dear," said Apuleius to his daughter.

Verania entered timidly. It seemed she had taken the bringing upon herself, before it occurred to her mother to send a slave. Gratillonius looked at her and caught her look on him. The lamp wavered in her hand. She had barely seen him when he arrived, then the womenfolk and young Salomon were dismissed from the atrium.

How old was she now, he wondered vaguely—fourteen, fifteen? Since last he saw her, she had filled out, ripening toward womanhood, though as yet she was withy-slim, small-bosomed, barely up to his shoulder if he rose. Light brown hair was piled above large hazel eyes and a face that—it twisted in him—was very like the face of Una, his daughter by Bodilis. She had changed her plain Gallic shift for a saffron gown in Roman style.

She passed as near to him as might be in the course of setting the lamp on the table. "You are grieved, Uncle Gaius," she murmured.

What, had she remembered his nickname from her childhood? Later Apuleius had made her and her brother be more formal with the distinguished visitor.

"I brought bad news," he said around a tightness in his gullet. "You'll hear."

"All must hear," Apuleius said. "First we should gather the household for prayer."

"If you will excuse me." Gratillonius climbed to his feet. "I need air. I'll take a walk."

Apuleius made as if to say something. Corentinus gestured negation at him. Gratillonius brushed past Verania.

Within the city wall, streets were shadowed and traffic scant. Gratillonius ignored what glances and hails he got, bound for the east gate. It stood open, unguarded. The times had been peaceful since Ys took the lead in defending Armorica. Watchposts down the valley sufficed. How much longer would that last?

Careless of the fact that he was unarmed, Gratillonius strode out the gate and onward. His legs worked mechanically, fast but with no sense of vigor. A shadowy part of him thought how strange it was that he could move like this, that he had been able to keep going at all—on the road, in council, at night alone.

The sun was on the horizon. Level light made western meadows and treetops golden, the rivers molten. Rooks winged homeward, distantly cawing, across chilly blue that eastward deepened and bore a first trembling star. Ahead loomed the long barricade of Mons Ferruginus, its heights still aglow but the wrinkles beneath purple with dusk.

He should turn around, raise his arms, and say his own evening prayer. He had not said any since the whelming of Ys. There had been no real chance to.

He did not halt but, blindly, sought upward. The rutted

33

road gave way to a path that muffled foot-thuds. It wound steeply among wild shrubs and trees, occasional small orchards, cabins already huddling into themselves. Boughs above him were graven black. Ahead they were mingling with the night as it welled aloft.

He reached a high place and stopped. This was as far as he could go. He wanted in a dull fashion to trudge on, maybe forever, but he was too drained. It would be hard enough to stumble his way back down. Let him first rest a while. And say that prayer?

From here he looked widely west. A streak of red smoldered away. "Mithras, God of the sunset—" No, somehow he could not shape the words. Mithras, where were You when Ocean brought down Ys and her Queens, where were You when it tore Dahut from my hand?

He knew the question was empty. A true God, *the* true God was wholly beyond. Unless none existed, only the void. But to admit that would be to give up his hold on everything he had ever loved. But if the God was too exalted to hear him, what matter whether or not He lived outside of human dreams? A good officer listens to his men. Mithras, why have You forsaken me?

The sky darkened further. Slowly within it appeared the comet. It was a ghost, fading toward oblivion, its work done, whether that work had been of warning or of damnation. Who had sent it? Who now called it home?

The strength ran out of Gratillonius. He sank to the ground, drew knees toward chin, hugged himself to himself, and shivered beneath the encroaching stars.

2

A waning half moon rose above woodlands whose branches, budding or barely started leafing, reached toward it like empty hands. They hid the River of Tiamat, low at this season; among stars that glimmered in the great silence went the Bears, the Dragon, the Virgin. Only water had voice, chirring and rustling from the spring of Ahes to a pool in the hollow just beneath and thence in a rivulet on down the hill, soon lost to sight under the trees. Moonlight flickered across it.

Nemeta came forth. Convolvulus vines between the surrounding boles crackled, still winter-dry, as she passed through. Her feet were bare, bruised and bleeding where she had stumbled against roots or rocks on the gloomy upward trail. First grass in the small open space of the hollow, then moss on the poolside soothed them a little. She stopped at the edge and stood a while catching her breath, fighting her fear.

The whiteness of her short kirtle was slashed by a belt which bore a sheathed knife. Unbound, tangled from her struggle with brush and twigs on a way seldom used, her hair fell past her shoulders. A garland of borage, early blooming in a sheltered spot despite the rawness of this springtime, circled her brows. In her left hand she carried a wicker cage. As she halted, a robin within flapped wings and cheeped briefly, anxiously.

She mustered courage and lifted her right palm. Nonetheless her words fluttered: "Nymph Ahes, I greet you, I . . . I call you, I, Nemeta, daughter of Forsquilis. She was—" The girl swallowed hard. Tears coursed forth. They stung. Vision blurred. "She was of the Gallicenae, the nine Queens of Ys. M-my father is Grallon, the King."

Water rippled.

"Ever were you kindly toward maidens, Ahes," Nemeta pleaded. "Ys is gone. You know that, don't you? Ys is gone. Her Gods grew angry and drowned her. But you abide. You must! Ahes, I am so alone."

After a moment she thought to say, "We all are, living or dead. What Gods have we now? Ahes, comfort us. Help us."

Still the spirit of the spring did not appear, did not answer.

"Are you afraid?" Nemeta whispered.

Something stirred in the forest, unless it was a trick of the wearily climbing moon.

"I am not," Nemeta lied. "If you will not seek the Gods for us, I will myself. See."

Hastily, before dread should overwhelm her, she set down the cage, unfastened her belt, drew the kirtle over

35

her head and cast it aside. The night air clad her nakedness in chill. Taking up the knife, she held it against the
stars. "*Cernunnos, Epona, Sucellus, almighty Lug!*" She
shrilled her invocation of Them not in Ysan or sacerdotal
Punic but in the language of the Osismii, who were half
Celtic and half descendants of the Old Folk. When she
slew the bird she did so awkwardly; it flopped and cried
until she, weeping, got a firm enough hold on it to hack off
its head. But her hands never hesitated when she gashed
herself and stooped to press blood from her breasts to
mingle in the pool with the blood of her sacrifice.

—False dawn dulled the moon and hid most stars. A
few lingered above western ridges and the unseen wreck
of Ys.

Nemeta crossed the lawn toward the Nymphaeum. Her
steps left uneven tracks in the dew. She startled a peacock
which had been asleep by a hedge. Its screech seemed
shatteringly loud.

A woman in a hooded cloak trod out of the portico,
down the stairs, and strode to a meeting. The girl stopped
and gaped. Runa took stance before her. Now it was
Nemeta's breathing that broke the silence. It puffed faint
white.

"Follow me," said the priestess. "Quickly. Others will
be rousing. They must not see you like this."

"Wh-wh-what?" mumbled the vestal.

"Worn out, disheveled, your garb muddy and torn and
blood-stained," Runa snapped. "Come, I say." She took
the other's arm and steered her aside. They went behind
the great linden by the sacred pond. Hoarfrost whitened
the idol that it shaded.

"What has found you tonight?" Runa demanded.

Nemeta shook her dazed head. "I kn-know not what you
mean."

"Indeed you do, unless They stripped you of your wits
for your recklessness." When she got only a blind stare for
reply, the priestess continued:

"I've kept my heed on you. Had there been less call on
me elsewhere—everywhere, in these days of woe—I'd
have watched closer and wrung your scheme out of you
erenow. It struck me strange that you never wailed aloud

against fate, but locked your lips as none of the rest were able to. I misdoubted your tale that you snared a bird to be your pet; and tonight it was gone from your room together with yourself, nor have you brought it back. And you have crowned yourself with ladygift, the Herb of Belisama.

"I know you somewhat, Nemeta. I was nine years old when you were born; I have watched you grow. Well do I recall what blood is in you, your father's willfulness, your mother's witchiness. Each night after you went to bed, since the news came, I have looked in to be sure. . . . Ah, you were aware of that, nay, sly one? You waited. But I slept ill this night, and looked in again, and then you were gone.

"Where? And what answer did you get? Who came to you?"

The girl shuddered. "Who?" she said tonelessly. "Mayhap none. I cannot remember. I was out of myself."

Runa peered long at her. Fifteen years of age, Nemeta was rangy, almost flat-chested. Her face bore high cheekbones, curved nose, big green eyes; the mane of hair grew straight and vividly red, the skin was fair and apt to freckle. Ordinarily she stood tall, but in this hour, drained of strength, she stooped.

"You sought the Gods," Runa said at last, very low.

Nemeta raised her glance. Life kindled in it. "Aye." Her voice, hoarse from shrieking, gained a measure of steadiness. "First just Ahes. I begged her to speak to Them for us. Not the Three of Ys, though I did make this wreath to—remind—The old Gods of the land. They might intercede or—or—When she held off—has she fled, has she died?—I summoned Them myself."

"Did any come?"

"I know not, I told you." Nemeta dropped her glance anew. Her fingers twisted and twined together. "It was as though I . . . blundered into dreams I can't remember—Did I see Him, antlered and male, two snakes in His grasp? Were there thunders? I woke cold and full of pain, and made my way back hither."

"Why did you do it?"

37

"What other hope have we?" Nemeta half screamed. "Yon pale Christ?"

"Our Gods have disowned us, child."

"Have They?" Fingers plucked at the priestess's sleeve. "Forever? At least the Gods of the land, They live. They must!"

Runa sighed. "Mayhap someday we shall learn, though I think that will be after we are dead, if then. Meanwhile we must endure . . . as best we can." Sternly: "You will never be so rash again. Do you hear me?"

Stubbornness stood behind bewilderment; but: "I p-promise I'll be careful."

"Good. Bide your time." Runa unfastened her brooch and took the cloak from her shoulders. "Wrap yourself in this, lest anyone spy your state. Come along to your room. I'll tell them you've been taken ill and should be left to sleep. 'Twould not do to have word get about, you understand—now that we shall be dealing with Christians."

As she guided the girl, she added: "If we hold to our purpose and are wise in our ways, we need not become slaves. We may even prevail." Bared to the sky, her countenance hardened.

3

When the warriors appeared, Maeloch spat a curse. "So nigh we were to getting clear. Balls of Taranis, arse of Belisama, what luck!" He swung about to his men. "Battle posts!"

All scrambled for their weapons, some into *Osprey* where the fishing smack lay beached. The tide was coming in, but would not be high enough to float her off for another two or three hours. With axes, billhooks, knives, slings, harpoons, a crossbow, they formed a line before the prow— fifteen men, brawny, bearded, roughly clad. That was almost half again as many as the craft carried while at work, but these were bound for strange and dangerous bournes. At their center, Maeloch the captain squinted against the morning sun to make out the approaching newcomers.

From this small inlet, land lifted boldly, green, starred with wildflowers, leaves already springing out on trees and shrubs. Here was no bleak tip of Armorica jutting into Ocean, but one of a cluster of islands off the Redonic coast of Gallia, well up that channel the Romans called the Britannic Sea. Fowl in their hundreds rode a fresh breeze which drove scraps of cloud across heaven and bore odors of growth into the salt and kelp smells along the strand. A rill trickled down from the woods decking the heights. The foreign men must have followed it. They continued to do so as they advanced.

Maeloch eased a bit. They numbered a mere half dozen. Unless more were lurking behind them, they could not intend hostilities. However, they were clearly not plain sailors like his crew, but fighters by trade—nay, he thought, by birth. It would cost lives to provoke them.

He shouldered his ax and paced forward, right arm raised in token of peace. They deployed, warily but skillfully, and let him come to them. He recognized them for Hivernians, though with differences from those in Mumu with whom Ys now had a growing traffic. Nor were they quite like those he had fought—seventeen years ago, was it?—after that gale the Nine raised had driven their fleet to doom. Here the patterns of kilts, cut of coats and breeks, style of emblems painted on shields were subtly unlike what he had seen before. But swords and spearheads blinked as brightly as anyone's.

Maeloch was no merchant. However, he had had his encounters when boats put in to Scot's Landing or chanced upon his over the fishing grounds. It behooved a skipper to speak for his men; he had set himself to gain a rough mastery of the Scotic tongue. "A good day to yuh," he greeted in it. "Yuh take . . . hospitality . . . of us? We . . . little for to give . . . beer, wine, shipboard food. Yuh welcome."

"Is it friendly you are, then?" responded the leader, a man stocky and snubnosed. "Subne maqq Dúnchado am I, sworn to Eochaid, son of King Éndae of the Lagini."

"Maeloch son of Innloch." The fisher captain had decided before he left home to give no more identification than he must. With phrases and gestures he indicated

39

what was quite true, that *Osprey* had been blown east, far off course, by the gigantic storm several days ago. Once she had clawed her way around the peninsula, there was no possibility of making any port; she could only keep sea room, running before the wind, full-reefed sail as vital as the oars. When the fury dwindled, his vessel—seams sprung, spars and strakes strained, barely afloat because the crew spent their last flagging forces bailing her—must needs crawl to the nearest land. They grounded her at high tide, and after taking turns sleeping like liches, set about repairs.

Maeloch refrained from adding that he had not simply chanced on the haven. He had never before been so far east, but some of his followers had, and all had heard about the Islands of Crows. That name had come on people's lips in the past hundred years, after the Romans withdrew a presence which had always been slight. Pirates and barbarians—seaborne robbers—soon discovered this was a handy place to lie over. With curses and a rope's end Maeloch had forced his men to gasp at the oars and the buckets till they found a secluded bay. He hoped to refit and set forth before anybody noticed them.

So much for that, he thought harshly. The island folk were a few herders, farmers, fishers. They had no choice but to stay in the good graces of their visitors, furnish food, labor, women . . . and information. Doubtless a fellow ranging the woods up above had spied the camp and scuttled off to tell. Doubtless he got a reward.

"Scoti come far," Maeloch ventured. In truth it was surprising to find them here. They harried the western shores of Britannia and, in the past, Gallia. Eastern domains were the booty of rovers from across the German Sea.

Subne tossed his head. "Our chief goes where he will."

"He do, he do." Maeloch nodded and smiled. "We poor men. Soon go home."

To his vast relief, Subne accepted that. Had the warriors searched *Osprey* they would have found hidden stores of fine wares, gold, silver, glass, fabric, gifts with which to proceed in Hivernia should necessity arise to shed his guise of a simple wanderer.

40

He was not yet free, though. "You will be coming with us," Subne ordered. "Himself wants to know more."

Maeloch stamped on a spark of dismay. "I glad," he replied. Turning to Usun, he said in swift Ysan: "They'd ha' me call on their leader. If I refused, we'd get the lot o' them down on us. Float the ship when ye can and stand by. Be I nay back by nightfall, start off. Ye should still have a fair wind for Britannia, where ye can finish refitting. . . . Nay a word out o' ye! Our mission is for the Nine and the King."

Stark-faced, the mate grunted assent. Maeloch strode from him. "We go," he cried cheerily. The Scoti looked nonplussed. Belike they'd expected the whole crew to accompany him. But Maeloch's action changed their minds for them. Their moods were as fickle as a riptide. Also, he knew, they made a practice of taking hostages to bind an alliance or a surrender. To them, he was the pledge for his men.

He wondered if his spirit could find its way back to Ys, for the Ferrying out to Sena.

Game trails, now and then paths trodden by livestock, wound south from the brooklet, through woods and across meadows, down into glens and aloft onto hills, but generally upward. The warriors moved with the ease of those accustomed to wilderness. Maeloch's rolling gait, his awkwardness in underbrush or fords, slowed them. They bore with it. Warmth rose as morning advanced until sweat was pungent in his tunic.

After maybe an hour the party reached a cliff and started down a ravine that was a watercourse to the sizeable bay underneath. There men lounged around smoky fires. Below the height were several shelters of brushwood, turf, and stones. Some appeared to be years old. This must be a favored harbor for sea rovers.

Two galleys of the deckless Germanic kind lay drawn up on the beach, their masts unstepped. Leather currachs surrounded one. The other was by herself, three hundred feet away. She was longer and leaner, with rakish lines and trim that had once been gaudy. The sight jolted Maeloch. He felt sure he knew her aforetime.

Subne led him to the first. Those were two separate

encampments. Such bands tried to keep peace, and mingled somewhat with each other, but had learned not to put much trust in their own tempers.

Scoti sprang to their feet, seized arms, calmed as they recognized comrades, and gathered around. They did not crowd or babble like city folk; their stares were keen and their speech lilted softly. Subne raised his voice: "Chieftain, we've brought you the captain of the outland ship."

A man bent to pass under the door of the largest hut nearby, trod forth, straightened his wide-shouldered leanness. Behind him a young woman peeked out, grimy and frightened. Maeloch saw a few more like her in the open, natives commandeered to char, cook, and be passed from man to man.

His attention went to the leader. Eochaid maqq Éndae, was that the name? The king's son was well dressed in woad-blue shirt, fur-trimmed leather coat, kilt, buskins, though the garments showed soot and wear. His age was hard to guess. Gait, thews, black locks and beard seemed youthful, but the blue eyes looked out of a face furrowed and somber. It would have been a handsome face apart from what weather had done to the light skin, had not three blotchy scars discolored it on cheeks and brow.

His gaze dwelt for a moment on Maeloch's grizzled darkness and bearlike build. When he spoke, it was in accented but reasonably good Redonic, not too unlike the Osismiic dialect: "If you come in honesty, have no fear. You shall be scatheless. Say forth your name and people."

He must have visited himself on these parts before and at length, Maeloch decided; and he was no witless animal. An outright lie would be foolhardy. The fisherman repeated what he had told Subne, but in the Gallic language and adding that he was from Ys.

Eochaid raised brows. "Sure and it's early in the year for venturing forth."

"We carry a message. We're under . . . gess . . . not to tell any but him it's for."

"They know not gess in Ys. Well, if you gave an oath, I must respect it. Nonetheless—" Eochaid reached a swift decision, as appeared to be his way, and addressed a man, who sped off. "We must talk further, Maeloch," he resumed in the Gallic tongue. "The Dani over there have lately been in Ys. I've sent for their captain. First you shall have a welcoming cup."

He settled himself cross-legged on the ground. Maeloch did likewise. The hut was unworthy of a chieftain entertaining a guest, at least in clear weather. Eochaid gestured. His wench scurried to bring two beakers—Roman silver, Roman wine, loot. A number of warriors hung about, watching and listening although few could have followed the talk. Others drifted off to idle, gamble, sharpen their weapons, whatever they had been doing. All had grown restless, waiting on the island.

"You can better give me news of Ys than Gunnung," Eochaid said. "He was there two months agone; but a German would surely miss much and misunderstand much else." The marred visage contorted in a grin. "Beware of repeating that to him." His intent was obvious, playing Northman off against Armorican in hopes of getting a tale more full and truthful than either alone might yield.

Bluntness was Maeloch's wont. "What d'ye care, my lord? Foemen break their bones on the wall of Ys and go down to the eels in the skerries around."

For an instant he thought Eochaid had taken mortal offense, so taut did the countenance grow. Then, stiffly, the Scotian replied: "Every man in Ériu remembers how Niall maqq Echach won sorrow there. Will Ys seek to entrap the likes of me too? I should find out ere I again sail near."

Maeloch knew what was in his mind. Scoti had learned from the disaster and from the later strengthening of the Ysan navy to confine their raids to Britannia—until this new generation reached manhood. Would the city and her she-druid Queens avenge attacks on the rest of Gaul, as they would any on Armorica? Eochaid must be headlong, and belike driven by a murderousness he could only take out on aliens, to have ventured past it. Now, with his men turning homesick, he was having second thoughts.

His words reminded him of that which brought heat into his tones: "Not that I can ever really go back—never to my father's house. And this is the work of Niall. O man of Ys, in me you have no enemy. The foeman of my

43

foeman is my friend. Might we someday, together, bring him low?"

A thrill rang through Maeloch. "Mayhap we do have things to say one to the other, my lord."

The runner returned with the foreign skipper. Eochaid lifted a knee in courtesy to the latter and beckoned both to sit. The wench brought more wine while namings went around.

Gunnung son of Ivar was a huge blond man, young, comely in a coarse fashion. His tunic and breeks were wadmal, but gold gleamed on his arms and was inlaid in his sword haft. A certain slyness glittered in his eyes and smoothed his rumbling voice.

Talk went haltingly, for he knew just a few Celtic words, Eochaid and Maeloch no more Germanic. The runner, a sharp-faced wight called Fogartach, could interpret a little. Moreover, Gunnung had a rough knowledge of Latin, picked up when he went adventuring along the Germanic frontier and in Britannia, while Maeloch had gained about as much over the years—though their accents were so unlike as to make different dialects.

Regardless, Gunnung was happy to brag. Not many of his kin had yet reached the West. It was Juti who were beginning to swarm in, together with Angli, Frisii, and Saxons. Hailing from Scandia, outlawed for three years because of a manslaying, he had gathered a shipful of lusty lads and plundered his way down the coasts of the Tungri and Continental Belgae. Finally they settled for the winter among some Germanic laeti in eastern Britannia, but found the country dull. Defying the season, they embarked for Ys, of which they had heard so much. Piracy there was out of the question, but they did a bit of trading and saw many wonders. "Of course, ve said ve vere alvays peaceful shapmen, ho, ho!"

Eochaid had been watching Maeloch. "Gunnung tells of strife in Ys," he said slowly.

The fisher scowled, searched for a way out—it was loathsome, opening family matters to strangers, let alone barbarians—and at length muttered, "The quarrel's more 'twixt Gods than men. The King has his, the Queens have theirs. 'Tis nay for us to judge."

"They've sent challengers against the King, I hear."

"And he's cut them down, each filthy hound o' them!" Maeloch flared. "When he comes back—" He broke off.

"Ah, he is away?"

"On business with the Romans." Maeloch swore at himself for letting this much slip out. "He may well ha' returned since I left. He'll set things right fast enough."

Gunnung growled a demand which Fogartach relayed, to know what was being said. Eochaid nodded and the interpreter served him.

The Dane guffawed, slapped his knee, and cried, "*Iukhai!*" Looking at Maeloch, he went on in his crude Latin, "Vill the King then throw his datter off the ness?" He leered. "That douses a hot fire. Better he put her in a whorehouse. She make him rish, by Freyja!"

Maeloch's belly muscles contracted. "What you mean?"

"You not hear? Vell, maybe nobody but they she got killed. For I think they also first yumped through her hoop." Gunnung sighed elaborately. "Ah, almost I vish I stayed and fighted too like she vant. Never I have a gallop like on her. But I do not vant for only nine vomen till I die, haw-aw!"

"Who . . . she?" grated out of Maeloch's throat.

"Aa, Dahut, who else? She vant I kill her father and make her Qveen. I am a man of honor, but a she-troll like that is right to fool, no?"

"Hold," interrupted Eochaid. He laid a hand on Maeloch's arm. "You're white and atremble. Slack off, man. I'll have no fighting under my roof," as if that were the sky.

"He lies about—a lady he's not fit to name," the Ysan snarled.

Gunnung sensed rage and clapped hand to hilt. Eochaid gestured him to hold still. "He's told me how a princess lay with him, hoping he would challenge her father and win," the Scotian said in Gallic. "Was it true, now?"

"It was nay, and I'll stop his mouth for him."

"Hold! I think the Gods were at work in this. You yourself said we must not judge. Dare you, then? If he lies, sure and They will be punishing him. If he does not lie—I know not what," Eochaid finished grimly. "But to me he has the look of a man whose luck has run out. Yet

45

today he is my guest; and I will never spend my men on a bootless quarrel that is none of ours. Heed."

Maeloch stared around the circle of warriors. They too had winded wrath and drawn closer. Their spearheads sheened against the sun. Inch by inch, his fingers released the helve of the ax that lay beside him. "I hear," he said. To Gunnung, in Latin: "I be surprised. Hurt. You understand? Grallon be my King. Bad, bad, to know his daughter be wicked."

The Dane smiled more kindly than before. "Truth hurt. I tell truth." Wariness reawoke. "You no fight, ha?"

Maeloch waved a hand at the men. "How? If I want to. No fight."

"He's gloated about it," Eochaid said in Redonic. "That is ill done, and now here to your face. But you told me you have a task of your King's. Save your blood for that."

Maeloch nodded. He had gone impassive. "I will." He pondered. "Mayhap he can even help. There'd be rich reward."

"How?" asked Eochaid instantly.

Maeloch considered him. "Or mayhap ye can. Or both of ye. My oath binds me to say no more till I have yours. Whatever happens, whatever ye decide, ye must let my men and me go from this island."

"If I refuse?"

Maeloch drew down the neck of his tunic. White hairs curled amidst the black on his breast. "Here be my heart," he said. "My oath lies in it."

That was enough. Barbarians understood what Romans no longer did, save Grallon: a true man will die sooner than break his word. After a pause, Eochaid answered, "I swear you will go freely, unless you harm me or mine."

"Vat this?" Gunnung wanted uneasily to know.

"Scoti help me?" Maeloch replied. "You help me too? Gold. Scoti protect me."

"You no fisher?"

"I travel for the King of Ys. You not fought King. Not his enemy. You like to help? Gold."

"I listen."

Maeloch passed it on Eochaid. The four sitting men rose. Solemnly, the Scotic chief called his Gods and the spirits of this island to witness that no unprovoked hindrance should come to the Ysans from him.

"Now I can say this much," Maeloch told him. "We're bound for Hivernia . . . Ériu. The errand's about your enemy Niall and nay friendly to him. Our craft be just a fishing smack, damaged. We've nay yet got her rightly seaworthy, though we can sail in fair weather. This be a tricky season. We'd house at home were the business not pressing. An escort 'ud be a relief. We can pay well and . . . get ye past Ys without trouble."

Fogartach explained to Gunnung. "Haa!" the Dane bellowed in Latin. "You pay, you got us."

"It may be best that the men of Ériu guide you," Eochaid said.

"Yours and his together?" Maeloch suggested. "Well, settle that 'twixt yourselves. First ye'll want to see what we can offer ye." He paused. "Wisest might be that none but ye twain have that sight. Too often gold's drawn men to treachery."

Eochaid took a certain umbrage at that. Gunnung, however, nodded when it was rendered for him; he must know what ruffians fared under his banner. "He be not afraid to go alone with me," Maeloch stated in Gallic, leaving Eochaid no choice but to agree.

The Scotian did order a currach full of warriors rowed to the inlet to lie offshore—"in case we have a heavy burden to carry back," he explained. "This eventide all our seafarers shall be my guests at a feast."

He gave directions about preparing for that, sent word to the Dani, called for refilled wine goblets. When those had been drained to Lug, Lir, and Thor, the three captains set off.

Forest took them into itself. Beneath a rustling of breeze, noon brooded warm and still. Branches latticed the sky and wove shadows where brush crouched and boles lifted out of dimness. Sight reached farther on the ridges, but presently nothing was to be seen from them either except tree crowns and a glittery blue sweep of sea. Nobody spoke.

The trail dipped down into a glade surrounded by the wood. Folk said that one like that lay near the middle of

47

the grove outside Ys and was where the sacred combat most often took place. Maeloch, in the lead, stopped, wheeled about, and brought his ax up slantwise. "Draw sword, Gunnung," he said in Latin. "Here I kill you."

The big bright-haired man hooted outraged astonishment. Eochaid sensed trouble. He poised the spear he carried. Maeloch glanced at him and said in Gallic, "This be no man of yours. He befouls my King. Ye swore I'd be safe of ye. Stand aside while I take back my honor."

"It's breaking the peace you are," Eochaid declared.

Maeloch shook his head. "He and I swapped no oaths. Nor be there peace 'twixt Ys and Niall. Later I'll tell ye more."

Eochaid's mouth tightened. He withdrew to the edge of the grass.

"You die now, Gunnung," Maeloch said.

The Dane howled something. It might have meant that the other man would fall and his ghost be welcome to whimper its way back to the little slut he served. Sword hissed from the sheath.

The two stalked about, Gunnung in search of an opening, Maeloch turning in the smallest circle that would keep the confrontation. The Dane rushed. His blade blazed through air. Maeloch blocked it with his ax handle. Iron bit shallowly into seasoned wood. Maeloch twisted his weapon, forced the sword aside. Gunnung freed it. Before he could strike again, the heavy head clattered against it. He nearly lost his hold.

Maeloch pressed in, hewing right and left. His hands moved up and down the helve, well apart as he drew it back, closing together near the end as he swung. The sword sought to use its greater speed to get between those blows. A couple of times it drew blood, but only from scratches. Whenever it clashed on the ax, weight cast it aside. The next strike was weaker, slower.

Gunnung retreated. Maeloch advanced. The Dane got his back against a wall of brush. He saw another blow preparing and made ready to ward it off. As the ax began to move, Maeloch shifted grip. Suddenly he was smiting not from the right but the left. The edge smacked into a shoulder. Gunnung lurched. His blood welled forth around two ends of broken bone. The sword dropped from his hand. Maeloch gauged distances, swung once more, and split the skull of Gunnung.

A while he stood above the heap and the red puddle spreading around it. He breathed hard and wiped sweat off his face. Eochaid approached. Maeloch looked up and said, "Ye had right. His luck had run out."

"This is an evil thing, I think," Eochaid replied. "And unwise. Suppose he had slain you. What then of your task?"

"I have a trusty mate, and ye promised my crew should go free." Maeloch spat on the body. "This thing misused the name of Dahut, daughter of Queen Dahilis—or misused her, which is worse yet. The Gods wanted him scrubbed off the earth."

"That may be. But I must deal with his gang."

"Yours outnumbers them. And 'twasn't ye what killed him. Come with us to Ériu like ye said ye might."

"What is your errand there, Maeloch?"

"What be your grudge against King Niall?"

"This." As Eochaid spoke, it became like the hissing of an adder or a fire. "He entered my land, the Fifth of the Lagini, laid it waste, took from us the Bóruma tribute that is ruinous, made a hostage of me. And I was not kept in honor; he penned me like beast, year upon year. At last I escaped—with the help of a man from Ys—and took my revenge on that follower of his whose satire had so disfigured me that never can I be a king after my father. That man's father cursed my whole country, laid famine on it for a year. Oh, the women and children who starved to death because of worthless Tigernach! But he was a poet, for which I am forever an exile. Do you wonder why I am the enemy of Niall?"

Maeloch whistled. "Nay. And I think he brews harm for us too."

"How?" Eochaid laid a hand over Maeloch's. "Speak without fear. I have not forgotten that man from Ys."

Maeloch stared down at the corpse. He gnawed his lip. "It goes hard to tell. But Dahut—she guests a stranger who admits he's from Niall's kingdom. They go everywhere about together. The Queens be . . . horrified . . .

49

but she mocks them, and meanwhile the king be away. Has yon outlander bewitched her? His name is likewise Niall. I'm bound for Ériu to try and find out more."

Eochaid clutched his spear to him. "Another Niall?" he whispered. "Or else— It's always bold he was; and he has sworn vengeance on Ys. He lost his first-born son there, in that fleet which came to grief long ago." Louder: "What does this Niall of yours look like?"

"A tall man, goodly to behold, yellow hair turning white."

"Could it truly be— Go home!" Eochaid shouted. "Warn them. Seize and bind yonder Niall. Wring the truth out of him!"

Maeloch gusted a sigh. "That be for her father the King. Besides, at worst he, whoever he be, he can only be a spy. Let me fare on to his homeland and try to learn what he plans, ere he himself can return. . . . What ye say, though, bids me make haste. I'd meant going to friendly Mumu and asking my way for'ard piece by piece. But best I make straight for . . . Mide, be that the realm? We need to stop in Britannia first and finish our work on the ship. I'll send a man or two back to Ys from there—we'll buy a boat— with word for King Grallon of what I've found out here."

Eochaid had calmed. "Well spoken that is. And indeed you should not bear home at once. When the Dani learn you've killed their chief, they'll scour the waters for you— along the coast, believing you've headed straight west. If you go north you'll shake them."

"Will ye come too? We could meet somewhere."

Eochaid sighed and shook his head. "They remember in Mide. This face of mine would give your game away." Bleakly: "We've thought we'll seek folk like ourselves, Scoti, where we may be making a new home; but that cannot be in green Ériu, not ever again."

Maeloch chopped his ax several times into the turf to clean the blood and brains off it. "I'll be on my way, then."

"I'll come with you to your ship, and sign to my own men that they return. Heave anchor when they're out of sight. I must let Gunnung's men know what happened to him, though I need not tell them more than that." Eochaid grinned. "Nor need I hurry along these trails. For it may be that in you is the beginning of my revenge."

50

III

1

Rovinda, wife of Apuleius, slipped into the darkened room. She left the door ajar behind her. "How are you, Gratillonius?" she murmured. "Sleeping?"

The man in the bed hardly stirred. "No, I've been lying awake." His words came flat.

She approached. "We shall eat shortly. Will you join us?"

"Thank you, but I'm not hungry."

She looked downward. By light that seeped in from the hallway and past the heavy curtain across the window she saw how gaunt and sallow he had grown. "You should. You've scarcely tasted food these past—how many days since you came to us?"

Gratillonius didn't answer. He couldn't remember. Six, seven, eight? It made no difference.

The woman gathered courage. "You must not continue like this."

"I am . . . worn out."

Her tone sharpened. "You fought your way out of the flood, and afterward exhausted what strength you had left for the sake of what people had survived. True. But that soldier's body of yours should have recovered in a day or two. Gratillonius, they still need you. We all do."

He stared up at her. Though no longer young, she was sightly: tall, brown-haired, blue-eyed, fine-featured, born to a well-off Osismiic family with ancient Roman connections. He recalled vaguely that she was even more quiet and mild than her husband, but even more apt to get her

51

way in the end. He sighed. "I would if I could, Rovinda. Leave me in peace."

"It's no longer weariness that weighs you down. It's sorrow."

"No doubt. Leave me alone with it."

"Others have suffered bereavement before you. It is the lot of mortals." She said nothing about the children she had lost, year after year.

Two lived. Well, he thought, two of his did, Nemeta and Julia, together with little Korai, granddaughter of Bodilis. But the rest were gone. Dahut was gone, Dahilis's daughter, swept from him with foundering Ys, off into Ocean. Would her bones find her mother's down there?

"You should be man enough to carry on," Rovinda said. "Call on Christ. He will help you."

Gratillonius turned his face to the wall.

Rovinda hesitated before she bent above him and whispered, "Or call on what God or Gods you will. Your Mithras you've been so faithful to? Sometimes I—please keep this secret; it would hurt Apuleius too much—I am a Christian, of course, but sometimes in hours of grief I've stolen away and opened my heart to one of the old Goddesses. Shall I tell you about Her? She's small and kindly."

Gratillonius shook his head on the pillow.

Rovinda straightened. "I'll go, since you want me to. But I'll send in a bowl of soup, at least. Promise me you'll take that much."

He kept silent. She went out.

Gratillonius looked back toward the ceiling. Sluggishly, he wondered what did ail him. He should indeed have been up and about. The ache had drained from muscles and marrow. But what remained was utter slackness. It was as if a sorcerer had turned him to lead, no, to a sack of meal. Where worms crawled. Most of his hours went in drowsing—never honest sleep, or so it seemed.

Well, why not? What else? The world was formless, colorless, empty of meaning. All Gods were gone from it. He wondered if They had ever cared, or ever existed. The question was as vain as any other. He felt an obscure restlessness, and supposed that in time it would force him to start doing things. They had better be dullard's tasks, though; he was fit for nothing more.

—Brightness roused him. He blinked at the slim form that rustled in carrying a bowl. Savory odors drifted out of it. "Here is your soup, Uncle Gaius," Verania greeted. "M-m-mother said I could bring it to you."

"I'm not hungry," he mumbled.

"Oh, please." The girl set it down on a small table which she drew to the bedside. She dared a smile. "Make us happy. Old Namma—the cook, you know—worked extra hard on it. She adores you."

Gratillonius decided it was easiest to oblige. He sat up. Verania beamed. "Ah, wonderful! Do you want me to feed it to you?"

That stung. He threw her a glare but encountered only innocence. "I'm not crippled," he growled, and reached for the spoon. After a few mouthfuls he put it back.

"Now you can eat more than that," she coaxed. "Just a little more. One for Namma. She does have good taste, doesn't she? In men, I mean—Oh!" She brought hand to lips. By the sunlight reflected off a corridor wall he saw her blush fiery.

Somehow that made him obey. And that encouraged her. She grew almost merry. "Fine. Take another for . . . for your horse Favonius. Poor dear, he misses you so. . . . One for Hercules. . . . One for Ulysses. . . . One for, m-m, my brother. You promised Salomon you'd teach him sword- and shieldcraft when he was big enough, do you remember? . . . One for Julius Caesar. One for Augustus. One for Tiberius. You don't have to take one for Caligula, but Claudius was nice, wasn't he?"

With a flicker of wish to argue, Gratillonius said, "He conquered Britannia."

"He made your people Romans, like mine. Give him his libation, do. Down your throat. Good." She clapped her hands.

Feet thudded in the hall. Verania squeaked. She and Gratillonius gaped at the tall gaunt man in the travel-stained rough robe who entered. He strode to the bedside and placed himself arms akimbo, glowering.

"I hear you're ill." His voice was harsher than before, as

if he had lately shouted a great deal. "What's the matter? Rovinda says you have no fever."

"You're back," Gratillonius said.

Corentinus's gray beard waggled to his nod, as violent as that was. "Tell me more, O wise one. I've brought men for you. Now get out and use them, for I've reached the limit of what I can make those muleheads do."

"Sir, he *is* sick," Verania made bold to plead. "What do you want of him? Can't father take charge, or, or anybody?"

The pastor softened at sight of her face. Tears trembled on her lashes. "I fear not, child," he said. "To begin with, they are pagans, disinclined to heed me."

"From Ys—from what was Ys?"

He nodded. "We must start at once preparing a place for the survivors. The first few score have lodging here, but not for long; soon the traders will be coming, and Aquilo needs them too much to deny them their usual quarters. Besides, it could never take in all who are left in the countryside. They'll require shelter, defenses—homes. Your father has most Christianly granted a good-sized site, his farmland. Oh, you knew already? Well, first we should make a ditch and wall: for evildoers will hear of the disaster and come seeking to take advantage. I went back after able-bodied men. On the way, I thought they'd better include some who know how to fight."

He and Apuleius decided this, and he walked off . . . without me, Gratillonius thought. Inwardly he cringed. Aloud: "Who did you find?"

"I remembered that squad of marines at the Nymphaeum," Corentinus answered. "They refused to leave unless the women came too. They think it's their sacred duty to guard the women of the Temple. Well, that's manly of them. But I had a rocky time persuading the priestess in charge, that Runa, persuading her to leave immediately. At last she agreed. By then such a span had passed that I thought best we go straightaway. The marines could begin on the fortifications while I went after additional labor. But they will not. I stormed and swore, but couldn't shake them."

"Why?" wondered Gratillonius.

"In part their leader claims they must stay with their charges. I have to admit Runa's trying to convince them she and the others will be safe in Aquilo. But also, they say it's demeaning work. Furthermore, they don't know how to do it. Ha!"

Gratillonius tugged his beard. "There's truth in that," he said slowly. "It's more than just digging. Cutting turfs and laying them to make a firm wall is an art." After a moment: "An art never known in Ys because it was never needed, and pretty much lost in Gallia. I think we in the Britannia were the last of the real old legionaries. On the Continent they've become cadres at best—the best not worth much—for peasant reserves and barbarian mercenaries."

The eagles of Rome fly no more. All at once the thought was not insignificant like everything mortal, nor saddening or frightening. It infuriated him.

"So stop malingering," Corentinus snapped. "Go show them."

"Oh!" wailed Verania, shocked and indignant.

"By Hercules, I will." Gratillonius swung himself out of the blankets onto the floor. He had forgotten his nakedness. Verania smothered a gasp and fled. His blunder lashed yet more life into him. He had to make it good. Flinging on tunic, hastily binding sandals, he stalked from the room, Corentinus at his heels.

Given directions, he found the party outside of town, at the western end of the bridge across the Odita. He must push through a crowd of curious local folk. They kept well aside, though, and he glimpsed some making furtive signs against witchcraft.

It was a clear afternoon. He felt a faint amazement at how bright the sunlight was. A blustery wind chased small clouds; a flight of storks passed overhead, as white as they. Light burned along the greenness that had bestormed fields and forest. The wind was sharp, with a taste of newly turned earth in it. Women's dresses, men's cloaks, stray locks of hair fluttered.

The vestals shared none of the wind's vigor. Their trip had been cruel to soft feet, though they took turns on the four horses and had overnighted in a charcoal burner's hut. They clutched their garments and stared with eyes full of fright—and Nemeta's an underlying defiance. Korai clung to Julia's hand like an infant. Runa did seem undaunted. Her lips were pressed thin in anger. She hailed Gratillonius coldly.

The dozen marines stood together, Amreth at their head. They bore the full gear of their corps: peaked helmets, flared shoulderpieces and greaves, loricated cuirasses engraved with abstract motifs, cloth blue or gray like the sea, laurel-leaf swords, hooked pikes. Gratillonius felt relief at seeing the metal was polished; but the outfits made them glaringly alien here.

He approached the leader and halted. Amreth gave him salute. He responded as was fitting among Ysans. "Greeting," he said in their tongue, "and welcome to your new home."

"We thank you, lord," Amreth answered with care.

" 'Twill take work ere 'tis fit for the settling of our folk. What's this I hear about your refusing duty?"

Amreth braced himself. "Lord, I am of Suffete family. Most of us are. Pick-and-shovel work is for commoners."

" 'Twas good enough for Rome's legionaries when Caesar met Brennilis. Sailors born to Suffetes toil side by side with their low-born shipmates. Do you fear you lack the strength?"

Amreth reddened beneath his sunburn. "Nay, lord. We lack skill. Why not bring men off the farms?"

"They're plowing and sowing, lest everyone go hungry later. 'Twill be a lean year, with so many mouths. Be thankful Aquilo will share till we can take care of ourselves."

"Well, countryfolk who were your subjects are still back in the homeland. Fetch them, lord. Our duty is to these holy maidens."

"Aye. To make a proper place for them, not stand idle when they've ample protection waiting behind yonder rampart."

Amreth frowned. Gratillonius drew breath. "They who remain of Ys *are* my subjects," he said levelly. "I am the King. I broke the Scoti, I broke the Franks, and I slew every challenger who sought me in the Wood. If the Gods of Ys have forsaken my people, I have not. I will show you

56

what to do and teach you how and cut the first turfs with these hands that have wielded my sword." He raised his voice. "Attention! Follow me."

For an instant he thought he had lost. Then Amreth said, "Aye, King," and beckoned to his men. They fell in behind Gratillonius.

"I will take them to the site, and barrack them later," he told Runa. "Let Corentinus lead you and the vestals to your quarters now, my lady."

She nodded. He marched off with the marines, over the bridge, through the town, out the east gate, northward along the river to the confluence. As yet he must compel himself, hold a shield up to hide the vacantness within; but already he felt it filling and knew he would become a man again. If nothing else, he had a man's work ahead of him.

It was odd how he kept thinking of Runa. Her look upon him had turned so thoughtful.

2

Most fruit trees were done with blooming, but a new loveliness dwelt in Liguria. From mountains north, south, and west, the plain around Mediolanum reached eastward beyond sight, orchards, fields marked off by rows of mulberry and poplar whose leaves danced in the breeze, tiny white villages. The air lulled blithe with birdsong. It was as if springtime would repay men for the harshness of the winter past, the brutality of the summer to come. Even slaves went about their work with a measure of happiness.

Rufinus and Dion rode back to the city. Sunlight slanted from low on their right. The horses plodded. They had covered a number of miles since leaving at dawn. In hills northward they had had hours of rest while their riders took the pleasures of the woodland, food and drink, lyre and song, frolic, love, ease in each other's nearness. But the return trip was long. When walls and towers became clear in their sight, the animals regained some briskness.

Rufinus laughed. "They're ready for the good old stable,

they are! And what would you say to an hour or two in the baths?"

"Well," Dion replied with his usual diffidence, "it will be pleasant. And still—I wish this day did not have to end. If only we could have stayed where we were forever."

Rufinus's glance went fondly over him, from chestnut hair and tender countenance to the lissomeness of the sixteen-year-old body. "Be careful about wishes, dear. Sometimes they're granted. I've lived in forests, remember."

"Oh, but you were an outlaw then. You've been everything, haven't you? Naturally, I meant—"

"I know. You meant the Empire would bring us our wine and delicacies and fresh clothes, and keep bad men away, and be there for us to visit whenever the idyll grew a bit monotonous. Don't scoff at civilization. It's not just more safe and comfortable than barbarism, it's much more interesting."

"It did not do well by you when you were young. I hope those people who were cruel to you are burning in hell."

The scar that seamed Rufinus's right cheek turned his smile into a sneer. "I doubt it. Why should the Gods trouble Themselves about us?"

Dion's smooth cheeks flushed. "The true God cares."

"Maybe. I don't say that whatever Powers there are can never be bribed or flattered. Heaven knows you Christians try. I do ask whether it's worthwhile. All history shows Them to be incompetent at best, bloodthirsty and dishonest at worst. Supposing They exist, that is."

The Gaul saw distress rise in his servant. He made his smile warm, leaned over, squeezed the youth's hand. "I'm sorry," he said. "That was nothing but an opinion. Don't let it spoil things for you. I'm not bitter, truly I'm not. Since I became the sworn man of the King of Ys, my fate has generally been good. At last it brought me to you. That's why I praise civilization and call it worth defending as long as possible."

Large brown eyes searched the green of his. "As long as possible, did you say?" Dion's words wavered.

He was so vulnerable. But he needed to learn. His life had been sheltered: son of a Greek factor in Neapolis by a concubine native to that anciently Greek city, taught arts and graces as well as letters, apprenticed in the household of an Imperial courtier two years ago, assigned to Rufinus as a courtesy after the Gaul became a man whose goodwill was desirable, and by this new master initiated in the mysteries of Eros. "I do not want to make you unhappy, my sweet," Rufinus emphasized. "You have heard about the dangers afoot, both inside and outside the Empire. We needn't feel sorry for ourselves on their account. Coping with them is the grandest game in the world."

"*You* find it so," Dion breathed worshipfully. White with dread, he had watched Rufinus's hell-for-leather chariot racing and other such sports. The first time, Rufinus could only sooth him afterward by tuning a harp and singing him the gentlest of the songs that the envoy of Ys had brought from the North.

Rufinus blew a kiss. "Well, maybe the second grandest," he laughed.

His own happiness bubbled. Of course he longed for everything he had had to leave, but that was months agone and forebodings had faded. Here the newnesses, adventures, challenges, accomplishments—real victories won for Gratillonius and Ys—were endless, and now Dion had come to him. Oh, true, they must be discreet. However, that did not mean they must be furtive; those at court who guessed found it politic to keep winks and sniggers private, if indeed anyone especially cared. And this was no bestial grappling among the Bacaudae nor hurried encounter with a near stranger, it was an exploration day by day and night by night shared with beauty's self.

They left their horses at a livery stable and passed on foot through the city gate to a majestic street. Seat of the Emperors of the West for nearly a hundred years, Mediolanum had accumulated splendors and squalors which perhaps only Constantinople surpassed. Often Rufinus found the architecture heavy, even oppressive, when he thought of the slimnesses in Ys; sometimes the vulgarity ceased for a while to excite, the shrill contentions of the Christian sects to amuse, and he remembered a people who bore the pridefulness of cats; but this place was at the core of things, while Ys merely sought to hold herself aloof. This was where men laid snares for men, and his heart beat the higher for it.

Through workers, carters, vendors, beggars, housewives, whores, holy men, soldiers, slaves, thieves, mountebanks, provincials from end to end of the Empire, barbarians from beyond, through racket and chatter and fragrance and stench, he led the way to the home granted him. It was a small apartment, but in a respectable tenement and on the first floor. (In Ys he lived, by choice, up among winds and wings.) Dion would choose clean clothes for them both, they would seek the baths and luxuriate until they came back for a light supper the boy would prepare, and then—whatever they liked. Perhaps simply a little talk before sleep. Rufinus would do most of the conversing. He enjoyed the role of teacher.

A eunuch in palace livery sat on the hallway floor at the apartment entrance. He jumped to his feet when he saw them. "At last, sir!" he piped. "Quickly! I am bidden to bring you before Master of Soldiers Flavius Stilicho."

"What?" exclaimed Rufinus. He heard Dion gasp. "But nobody knew where I was or when I'd return."

"So I informed his gloriousness after I learned." The messenger's hairless, somehow powdery face drew into a web of lines. "He was most kind; he bade me go back and wait for you. Come, sir, let us make haste."

Rufinus nodded. "At once." With a grin: "He's an old campaigner, he won't mind dust and sweat on me."

"Oh, he has much else to occupy his attention, you know, sir. Doubtless you'll make an appointment with a deputy for tomorrow. But *come*."

"Seek the baths yourself," Rufinus suggested to Dion.

"I'll wash here and have a meal ready for you," his companion answered, and gazed after him till he was gone from sight.

Hurrying along thoroughfares where traffic was diminishing, Rufinus tugged the short black forks of his beard and scowled in thought. What in the name of crazy Cernunnos might this be? Why should he be summoned by the dictator of the West? And of the East, too, they said, now that the Gothic general Gainas was in charge there; Gainas was Stilicho's creature, and Emperor Arcadius a weakling a few years older than his brother and colleague Honorius, who in turn was one year older than Dion. . . . Rufinus had conveyed letters from the King of Ys, Bishop Martinus of Turonum, and others in the North. He had contrived excuses to linger while he made himself interesting or entertaining or useful in this way and that way to men of secondary importance at court, until by their favor his status was quasi-official. He could doubtless continue the balancing act till his term of exile ended and he went home. But how did he suddenly come to be of any fresh concern to Stilicho, so much that the great man wanted to see him in person?

Rufinus sketched a grin and swayed his head about snakewise. It might not be on its neck this time tomorrow.

Sunset flared off glass in upper stories of the palace compound. The eunuch's garb and password gave quick admittance through a succession of doors and guards. He left the Gaul in an anteroom while he went off to find the deputy he had mentioned. Rufinus sat down and tried to count the blessings of the day that had just ended. The garishness of the religious figures on the walls kept intruding.

The eunuch returned. Three more followed him. "You are honored, sir," he twittered. "The consul will see you at once."

Aye, thought Rufinus in Ysan, this year did also that title, of much pomp and scant meaning, come to the mighty Stilicho. Well, he had forced peacefulness on the Visigoths in the East (though 'twas strange that King Alaric received an actual Roman governorship in Illyricum) and had put down rebellion in Africa and two years agone had married his daughter to the Emperor Honorius. . . . Precautions and deference were passed. The two men were alone.

Twilight was stealing into the austere room where Stilicho sat in a chair behind a table. Before him was a litter of papyruses he must have been going through, documents or dispatches or whatever they were, together with some joined thin slabs of wood whereon were inked words that Rufinus suspected meant vastly more. The general showed the Vandal side of his descent in height and the time-dulled blondness of hair and short beard. He wore a robe

61

plain, rumpled, not overly clean, the sleeves drawn back from his hairy forearms.

Never himself a soldier, Rufinus had watched legionaries come to attention. He tried for a civilian version of it. Momentarily, Stilicho's lips quirked.

The smile blinked out, the look became somber. "You should have left word where you would be today," Stilicho rumbled.

"I'm sorry, uh, sir. I had no idea my presence would be wanted."

"Hm. Why not? You've been buzzing enough about the court and . . . elsewhere."

"The Master knows everything."

Stilicho's fist thudded on the table. "Stow that grease. By the end of each day, it drips off me. Speak plain. You're no straightforward courier for the King of Ys. You're at work on his behalf, aren't you?"

Rufinus answered with the promptitude he saw would be best for him. "I am that, sir. It's no secret. The Master knows Ys and its King—the tribune of Rome—are loyal. More than loyal; vital. But we have our enemies. We need a spokesman at the Imperium." He paused for three pulsebeats. "Rome needs one."

Stilicho nodded. "At ease. I don't question your motives. Your judgment—that may be another matter. Though you've shown a good deal of mother wit, from what I hear. As in finding that ring stolen from the lady Lavinia."

Without relaxing alertness, Rufinus let some of the tension out of his muscles. "That was nothing, sir. When I compared the stories told by members of the household, it was clear who the thief must be."

"Still, I don't know who else would have thought to go about it that way, and save a lot of time and torture." The general brooded for a moment. "You call Ys vital. So did the letters you brought, and the arguments were not badly deployed. But it's a slippery word. How vital was, say, the Teutoburg Forest? We don't know yet, four hundred years later. Sit down." He pointed at a stool. "I want to ask a few questions about Ys."

—Beeswax candles had the main room of the apartment aglow. Dion woke at Rufinus's footsteps and was on his own feet before the door had opened. "Oh, welcome!" he cried; and then, seeing the visage: "What's happened, my soul, what is it?"

Rufinus lurched across the floor. Dion hastened to close the door and meet him by the couch. "Stilicho told me at last," Rufinus mumbled. "He drew me out first, but he told me at last."

Dion caught the other's hands. "What is it?" he quavered.

"Oh, I can't blame Stilicho. I'd have done the same in his place. He needed my information calmly given, because he will never get it elsewhere, not ever again. Nobody will." Rufinus's long legs folded under him. He sank onto the seat and gaped at emptiness.

Dion sat down at his side and caressed him. "T-t-tell me when you w-want to. I can wait."

"A dispatch came today," said Rufinus. His words fell like stones, one by one. "Ys died last month. The sea came in and drowned it."

Dion wailed.

Rufinus rattled a laugh. "Be the first of the general public to know," he said. "Tomorrow the news will be all over town. It'll be a sensation for at least three days, if nothing juicier happens meanwhile."

Dion laid his head in Rufinus's lap and sobbed.

Presently Rufinus was able to stroke the curly hair and mutter, "There, now; good boy; you cry for me, of course, not for a city you never knew, but that's natural; you care."

Dion clung. "You are not forsaken!"

"No, not entirely. The King escaped, says the dispatch. Gratillonius lives. You've heard me speak of him aplenty. I'm going to him in the morning. Stilicho gave me leave. He's by no means an unkindly man, Stilicho."

Dion raised his face. "I am with you, Rufinus. Always."

The Gaul shook his head. "I'm afraid not, my dear," he replied almost absently, still staring before him. "I shall have to send you back to Quintilius. With a letter of praise for your service. I can do that much for you before I go—"

"No!" screamed Dion. He slipped from the couch and went on his knees, embracing the knees of Rufinus. "Don't leave me!"

"I must."

"You said—you said you love me."

"And you called yourself the Antinöus to my Hadrianus."
Rufinus looked downward. "Well, you were young. You
are yet, while I have suddenly become old. I could never
have taken you along anyhow, much though I've wanted
to. It would make an impossible situation."

"We can keep it secret," Dion implored.

Again Rufinus shook his head. "Too dangerous for you,
lad, in the narrow-minded North. But worse than that, by
itself it would destroy you. Because you see—" he searched
for words, and when he had found them must force them
forth—"my heart lies yonder. It's only the ghost of my
heart that came down here. Now the ghost has to return
from Heaven to earth, and endure.

"Someday you'll understand, Dion," he said against the
tears. "Someday when you too are old."

3

Osprey came to rest on a day of mist-fine rain, full of
odors sweet and pungent from an awakening land. Maeloch
had inquired along the way and learned that this was
where the River Ruirthech met the sea, the country of the
Lagini on its right and Mide, where Niall of the Nine
Hostages was foremost among kings, to the left. He steered
along the north side of the bay looking for a place to stop,
and eventually found it. Through the gray loomed a great
oblong house, white against brilliant grass. It stood a short
distance from the water, at the meeting of two roads
unpaved but well-kept, one following the shore, one van-
ishing northwesterly. "Belike we can get hospitality here,"
he said. His voice boomed through the quiet. "Watch
your tongues, the lot o' ye." Several of his men knew a
Hivernian dialect or two, some of them better than he.

They made fast at a rude dock. By that time they had
been seen, and folk had come from the house or its
outbuildings. They were both men and women, without
weapons other than their knives and a couple of spears.
The compound was not enclosed by an earthen wall as

most were. A portly red-bearded fellow trod forward. "Welcome to you, travelers, so be it you come in peace," he called. "This is the hostel of Cellach maqq Blathmaqqi. Fire is on the hearth, meat on the spit, and beds laid clean for the weary."

Such establishments were common throughout the island—endowed with land and livestock so that their keepers could lodge free all wayfarers, for the honor of king or tribe and the furthering of trade. "Maeloch son of Innloch thanks yuh," he replied ritually. "We from Armorica." That much would be plain to any man who knew something of the outside world, as they surely did here.

"A long way you've come, then," said Cellach.

Maeloch beckoned to a crewman who had been on trading voyages to Mumu and could speak readily. "The storm at full moon blew us off course for the south of your country," that sailor explained. "Having made repairs afterward, and being where we were, we thought to do what had been in many minds and see if we could find a new market for our wares." That was true, as far as it went. To be caught in an outright lie would mean the contempt of the Scoti and end any chance of talking with them.

Cellach frowned. "Himself at Temir is no friend to the Romans or their allies." He brightened. "But his grudges are not mine, nor are they the grudges of my tuath and our own king. Let us help you with your gear and bring you to our board."

"Yuh no afraid enemies?" asked Maeloch on the way up.

"We are not," Cellach replied. "Do you see rath or guards? True, the Lagini were close by, but they could never have come raiding without being spied in time for men to rally from the shielings around about. And Temir is some twenty leagues off; though the King there is often away, warriors aplenty would soon be avenging. Even in days when the hostel was founded, the Lagini left this strand alone. And now Niall has reaped their land with his sword, and afterward the poet Laidchenn called famine into it, till nobody dwells across from Clón Tarui. What my wife and I fear, so long as the sky does not fall, is only that we may fail to guest our visitors as grandly as did my mother, the widow Morigel, who had this place before me."

The main house was built of upright poles with wicker-work between, the whole chinked and whitewashed, the thatch of the roof intricately woven. Windows let in scant light, but lamps hung from the beams, which were upheld by pillars, and a fire burned in a central pit. The floor was strewn with fresh rushes. Furnishings were merely stools and low tables; however, hangings, albeit smoke-blackened, decorated the walls. One side of the cavernous space was filled by cubicles. Two wooden partitions, about eight feet high, marked off each; the third side stood open toward the east end of the hall, revealing a bed that could hold two or three. "You're few enough that you can sleep alone," laughed Cellach, "the which is not needful for those among you who are lucky."

True to his promise, when the mariners had shed their wet outer garments and shoes, he settled them at the small tables. Women brought ale and food. Scoti custom-arily took their main meal in the evening, but this midday serving was generous, beef, pork, salmon, bread, leeks, nuts, unstinted salt. The one who filled Maeloch's platter was young, buxom, auburn-haired and freckle-faced. She brushed against him more than once, and when he looked her way she returned a mischievous smile. "Ah, a daugh-ter of mine, Áebell," said the landlord. He had joined the captain and Usun at their table. "It seems as though she favors you." Proudly: "If true, you are lucky indeed, in-deed. She's unwed thus far, but not for lack of men. Why, King Niall beds her and none else when he honors this house."

The eyes narrowed in Usun's leathery countenance. "When was that last, may I ask?" he murmured.

"Och, only some eight or nine days agone, though long since the time before. He came here in a Saxon kind of ship, which his crew took onward while himself and a few warriors borrowed horses of me and rode straight to Temir in the morning. That was a wild night, I can tell you. They drank like whirlpools and swived like stallions. Something fateful had happened abroad for sure. But the King would not let them say what." Cellach shook his head and looked suddenly troubled. "I talk too much." He made a sign against misfortune.

66

Maeloch and Usun exchanged a glance. It was as if winter had stolen back upon them.

Nevertheless Maeloch donned a gruff heartiness when he sought out Áebell. She was easy to find, and free for a while. He invited her to come see his craft. Poor though his command of the language was, she listened eagerly as he hacked his way through it. He could follow her responses, and his skill grew with practice. While grimness underlay his spirit, it was lightsome, after a hard voyage, to boast before a girl. When she must go back to her household duties she kissed him hard and he cupped a breast, they two out of sight in the dim rain.

That night they left the drinking after supper hand in hand, earlier than most. A couple of her father's tenants uttered a cheer, a couple of sailors who did not have wenches at their sides groaned good-naturedly. In his cubicle she slipped her dress over her head and fumbled at the lacing of his tunic. His lust made her lovely; she glowed in the shadows. He bore her down on the bed and, both heedless of anyone who might hear, he rutted her.

When she had her breath again, she said in his ear, "Now that was mightily done. It's glad I'd be if all men were like you—"

"Soon I do more," he bragged.

"—or King Niall. Is it that the sea makes you strong?" She giggled. "Sure and he was a bull from out of the waves last time, in spite of brooding about Ys." She felt his frame go iron-hard. "Are you angered? I am not calling you the less, darling."

Still he lay without motion, save for the quick rise and fall of his breast above the slugging heart. "Were you ever in Ys?" she tried. "I hear it was magical. They say the Gods raised it and used to walk its lanes on moonlit nights."

He sat up and seized her. "What happen Ys?" he rasped.

"Ee-ai! You hurt me, let go!"

He unlocked his fingers. "I sorry. How Ys? Yuh know? Say."

"Is something wrong?" Cellach called from the fireside talk of those still up.

67

"Not, not," Maeloch shouted. To Áebell, low: "I beg, tell. I give gold, silver, fine things."

She peered through the gloom at the staring whiteness of eyeballs and teeth. "I kn-know nothing. He forbade they say. But they got drunk and, and words slipped free—" Rallying her wits, she crouched amidst the tumbled coverings and whispered, "Why do you care?"

"Ys great," he said hastily. "Rich. Make trade."

"M-m, well—" She nodded. "But I am just a little outland girl. I don't understand these man-things." She smiled and brought herself against him. "I only understand men. Hold me close, darling. You are so strong."

He obeyed; but no matter what she did, his flesh had no more will toward her. Finally she sighed, "Ah, you are worse tired from your travels than you knew, Maeloch, dear. Get a good night's rest, and tomorrow we'll make merry." She kissed him, rose, pulled the gown over her, and left.

After a while the last folk went to bed. A banked fire barely touched the darkness. Maeloch lay listening to the horrors in his head. Once he thought he heard hoofbeats go by.

In the morning, which was overcast but free of rain, he told Cellach he and his crew had better be off. "Now why would you be wanting to do that this soon?" the hostelkeeper replied. "You've talked with none but us here. You've shown us nothing of your goods nor asked what we in these parts might wish to trade for them. Take your ease, man. We want to hear much more. It's close-mouthed you've been, I must say."

Maeloch felt too weary after his sleepless night to press the matter. He sat dully on a bench outside and rebuffed Usun's anxious questions. Áebell was nowhere about. Had she sought another mate elsewhere, or was she simply staying from him till he could get over his failure? He cared naught. His wife and children, the first grandchild, those were encamped in him.

Áebell returned at midday. With her rode a troop of warriors. Their spearheads rose and fell to the onwardness of the horses, like wind-rippled grain. At their head was a tall man with golden hair and beard begun to turn frosty. A seven-colored cloak fluttered from his shoulders.

The household swarmed forth. The sailors drew together and advanced behind. Their weapons were in the hostel. "Lord Niall!" cried Cellach. "A thousand welcomes. What brings you to honor us again?"

The King's smile was bleak. "Your daughter, as you can see," he answered. "She rode through the night to tell me of men from Ys."

Some women gasped and some men gaped. Cellach held steady. "I felt the breath of such a thought myself, lord, that they are Ysans," he said. "But I was not sure. How could you be, Áebell mine?"

She tossed her head. "What else, the way he turned cold? And Ys was the enemy of Niall from before my birth." She edged her mount toward the tall man.

Aye, thought Maeloch, Scotic women were free, and therefore keen and bold, as Roman women were not. As women of Ys were, in their very different way. He should have remembered.

Niall looked over heads, pierced him with a lightning-blue stare, and said, "You are the captain." —in Ysan.

Maeloch stepped to the fore. The heaviness was gone from his limbs, the terrors from his heart. It was as if he stood outside his body and steered it. Thus had he been in combat or when close to shipwreck. "Aye," he said, "and ye too ha' lately fared from my city."

"I have that."

"What did ye there?"

Niall signed to his followers. They leaped off their horses and took battle stance. "Prepare yourself," he said quietly. "Ys is no more. On the night of storm, Lir came in."

At his back, Maeloch heard Usun croak like one being strangled, another man moan, a jagged animal noise from a third. "How wrought ye this?" he asked, well-nigh too low for anybody to hear.

Niall bit his lip. "Who are you to question me? Be glad I don't cut you down out of hand."

"Oh, ye'll get your chance. Come fight me, or forever bear the name of craven."

Niall shook his head. "The King at Temir is under gess to fight only in war." He nodded toward a giant in his

69

band. "There is my champion, if you wish a duel." That man grinned and hefted his sword.

" 'Tis ye that hell awaits," Maeloch stated.

"Hold your jaw!" Áebell shrilled furiously.

A chillier wrath congealed Niall's features. "My task is unfinished until naught whatsoever remains of Ys, the city that murdered my son and my good men. Your insolence has doomed you likewise."

"My lord!" Cellach thrust his mass in front of Maeloch. "These are my guests. On my land they have sanctuary. Heed the law."

For an instant Niall seemed about to draw blade and hew at him. Then the King snapped a laugh. "As you will, for as long as you house them."

"That will be no longer than they need to take ship, lord." Cellach looked over his shoulder. "Be off with you," he spat. "It's lucky you are that there is no craft on hand for pursuing you."

"Nor harbor for you at journey's end," Niall gibed.

How fierce must his hatred be, that he stooped to mockery of helpless men? Or was it something deeper and still more troubling? Maeloch was as yet beyond all feelings, like a sword or a hammer; he knew remotely that later he must weep, but now his throat spoke for him:

"Aye, well may the memory of Ys glimmer away, for the Veil of Brennilis did ever ward her; but ye ha' gone it behind it yourself, and somehow this ill thing be your doing. Forgetfulness shall come over it also, and over everything else till folk unborn today wonder if Niall truly lived; but first we who do remember will bring ye to your death."

He turned to his crew. "Fetch your things," he ordered. "We can still catch the tide."

Behind him Áebell made fending signs against his curse. Niall reached over and touched her. She calmed immediately and smiled at the man she loved.

70

IV

1

Publius Flavius Drusus, old soldier, came in from his farm and took over as taskmaster in making wall and ditch for the new settlement. Work went fast, once the marines and the refugee laborers who presently joined them had gotten the knack.

"No, no," he explained to a man who had brought a turf; the spade wielders were beginning predictably to cut standard thirty-pound pieces out of the topsoil. "You lay it grass side *down*. That holds better, and we can smooth and level the dirt for the next course."

Amreth, who knew some Latin, translated for him and asked why the wall wasn't being raised more than breast high. A deeper or broader fosse would provide the material, together with added protection.

"We're doing this like an old-time legion setting up camp," Drusus answered. "We don't need anything else, at least not right away. Only two sides; we've got the rivers for the other two. The idea is simply to slow down an attack enough that men will have time to rouse, arm themselves, and take their stations. You see, meanwhile they'll have gotten their sleep, because they won't have needed but a few on sentry-go. They'll be fresh, ready for combat."

"What when the colony gets too big?"

"Well, we can lengthen this work. If the growth still keeps on, we'll build a proper wall, high, with timbers and stones in it. But first start begetting some youngsters, eh?"

71

Drusus's jape drew no smiles from those who heard and understood. Most had lost all but their own lives, mere days ago.

It was nevertheless fortunate that he could spare the time, as busy as Gratillonius became with shepherding people from the Ysan hinterland. At the outset he billeted them in Aquilo. When all free spaces there were filled, he must find shelter round about in the countryside.

After the first time he did this, he stopped at the confluence to inquire how things were progressing. Time pressed. Before long, trade goods would start arriving up the Odita and overland, and their conductors require those roofs in town that now covered his folk.

He found the defenses completed. They enclosed tents for workers and guards. Houses were going up, the wood for them taken from the nearby forest. They were rude Celtic shielings, but quickly built, sufficient to keep off the weather until something better was ready. Rustics should do well enough in them; Gratillonius wondered how survivors from the city would fare.

Somehow the labor had spared a stand of cornel between the wall and a brook that came from the north to meet the Odita. It was in bloom. He saw, and the frail whiteness stabbed him through. Tonight the moon would be full, as it had last been over the death of Ys.

He left at sundown, knowing he could not sleep, flinching from the thought of a room that would feel as black and narrow as the grave. First he should stable Favonius— No, a day's faring around did not seem to have worn the stallion out, given a while to rest and crop. "Would you like a ramble, old friend?" Gratillonius murmured. "Tomorrow you can take your ease in a pasture." He crushed the wish that he himself might someday enjoy the same peace. A man should not whine at the Fates.

They crossed the road and followed the river road east. Ultimately it would join the highway from Darioritum Venetorum, but that ran north of here on its way to Vorgium and Gesocribate. The great hill bulked darkling on his right; for a time gold lingered on the crowns of its uppermost trees, then died as the sky deepened and the first western stars blinked forth. He left it

72

behind. The river turned north and the road went off more or less parallel to the Jecta stream though at a little distance from it and gradually climbing. High forest hid the tributary but the view south ran widely. Parts remained under cultivation—light gleamed yellow from a cluster of huts—while woods that were reclaiming the rest had not yet grown tall. Cornel, abundant in these parts, stood especially thick along the wayside. Sweetness breathed from it out of the shadows. There was hardly a sound but the clop of hoofs, occasional creak of leather, breath and heartbeat.

The moon rose, enormous at first, smaller and colder as it mounted. When Gratillonius looked at its ashen face his eyes were briefly dazzled. The light washed over the world like a sea. White blossoms caught it and shone like Dahut's hair, like her outreaching hands.

Something moved afar. Gratillonius strained to see. Another rider, hitherbound from the east. Welcome, whoever you are. Bring my soul back from the flowers and the moon. He clucked to Favonius. The stallion broke into a trot.

Nearing, he saw that the other horse was exhausted. Its man must have forced it unmercifully. Of course, you couldn't gallop all the time, and now the pace was down to a shambling walk, but—

Moonlight dappled a lean form, sharp features, fork beard that might have been snipped out of the night. Could it be? It was. "Rufinus!" yelled Gratillonius.

"Cernunnos! Is that you?" croaked the remembered voice. "Oh, at last."

Both sprang from their saddles. Favonius would not stray and Rufinus's poor beast could not. The men cast arms about each other.

"How did you know?" Gratillonius babbled. "How could you get here so soon?"

He felt Rufinus tremble and clutch him more tightly. That was distasteful, much though you had to allow for weariness and grief. Gratillonius disengaged himself and took a step backward. Rufinus stood for an instant alone before he mastered his shivering and teeth glinted in the old crooked grin.

"Word came to Mediolanum by special courier," he

said. "Stilicho granted me postal privileges for my return. He didn't know I'd arrive at each relay point with my mount ready to drop and commandeer the next. In Venetorum I learned where you'd gone to. I didn't expect to meet you already, though. Don't tell me you had a vision or cast a horoscope."

"No, I was restless. Gods, man, how did you hold to that speed? You can't have slept more than half of any night."

Rufinus shrugged. "I was in a hurry."

His coolness broke apart. "O master, King, Ys is gone!" he cried. Moonlight runneled through tears. He stretched out his arms. "Who lives? Bodilis, the other Queens, your daughters, our friends, who's left?"

Gratillonius's words fell like thuds of a sledge hammer. "Two of my daughters and a grandchild of Bodilis. Maybe three hundred fugitives, nearly all rural. Otherwise none. Nothing."

"How did it happen? How could the Gods let it happen? Why?"

"Nobody knows, unless it be Corentinus, and he won't answer my question. I'm certain it was the work of an enemy. The Key was missing from my breast when Corentinus woke me that night—worst storm ever known— and the gate stood unlocked to the sea."

A wildcat might have screamed. "We'll find him! We'll get you your revenge! I will, I swear it!" Rufinus sank to his knees and embraced Gratillonius's. His sobs, raw and unpracticed, shook him as a hound shakes a fox it has caught. "Tell me how I can serve you, master. Only tell me."

2

Beneath wolf-gray heaven, wrack flew. The north wind drove it, clamoring shrill, fanged with cold. Spindrift hazed the waves. They roared in their wrinkled hordes, green-black where foam did not swirl, until they burst and fountained on rocks or against mainland cliffs. All birds were gone from sight. The skerries were empty of seals.

Osprey rolled, pitched, yawed, wallowed along on oars. Often the rowers missed a stroke. They kept looking shoreward. Nobody could tell if the salt that stung and blinded them was of scud or tears.

Maeloch stood in the bows, hunched into his leather jacket, legs braced wide. Now and then he signalled Usun, who had the helm. These waters were as ravenous of ships as always. Yet he too must glance over and over at the land, a league off. Within the hood, his face might have been cast in iron. The white-shot beard might have been too, as drenched as it hung.

Ys was gone. Naught but wreckage remained, snags of wall and pillar around which billows ramped. As he watched, a piece gave way. The splash when it fell was lost in surf. Even above highwater mark, where King and Queens and the wealthy had dwelt, ruin littered a naked strand. He could see beyond to a few blackened spires; fire had consumed the royal grove. Mansions still clung to the hills, tiny at their distance, but surely their folk were dead or fled. The Gods of Ys had ended the Pact of Brennilis, and with it her city.

Out to Sena itself— He and his crew had descried a heap of stones at the eastern end of that island. There he had left Bodilis, dearest of the Queens since little Dahilis died so long ago. There, maybe, her bones abided. He had not risked putting in to search.

But how could it be that the pharos on Cape Rach was also broken, barely half of it left? Could Lir reach that high, or had Taranis cast His hammer in the hour of the whelming?

Maeloch knew he could not sanely seek answers today. He must go on to some unharmed haven, Audiarna or mayhap the Odita mouth and upriver to Aquilo. King Grallon had had friends in Aquilo.

Osprey struggled on south. Once she rounded the headland, wind and seas ought to be less wild. Maybe he could raise sail and let the men rest. If not, he'd have to pull far out and heave to, because they couldn't keep on like this much longer.

Easement or no, Maeloch dreaded that part of the passage. It would go by the place under the cliffs where

Scot's Landing had been. And there would be emptiness. More than once, lesser storms than the one that drowned Ys had destroyed the fisher hamlet. But its dwellers had first taken refuge in the city and afterward returned to rebuild. Not ever again.

Faint through the wind, a shout came to him. He turned, saw a crewman point from his bench, bent his own gaze to the port quarter and squinted.

Well he knew that reef and the rocks around it. Waves crashed across them, fell back in monstrous whirls and rips, whitened the wind with spray through which death grinned black. Usun was steering well clear. What was it that lay on the back of stone, entangled with weed torn from the bottom, not yet altogether broken and strewn? A splintered curve rose across the sullenness of Cape Rach, up into the wind: the prow of a wreck. No man could live whose craft went yonder. Well, this was a cruel ground, where none but the mariners of Ys had ever been at home.

"Nay!" tore from Maeloch's throat. " 'Tis *Betha!*"

He knew that high stempost, carved at the top into a Celtic spiral. Red paint still clung to clinker-laid strakes. It had been a fine, unusually shaped boat he bought while *Osprey* rested under repair on the Dumnoniic shore, and named for his wife, and sent off with four of his men to bring to Ys the tale of what he had learned in the Islands of Crows. Now the sea had reaved away both *Betha* and Betha.

"How?" he groaned. "Ye were bonny sailors, all o' ye. Why, Norom, ye were my own crewman. How often did I give ye the helm, Norom, aye, on crossings when we ferried the dead to Sena? How could ye go astray like this?" The wind snatched his words from him and scattered them over Ocean.

A sudden flaw of the air? But any Ysan pilot would give himself plenty of room. Did a gale threaten, too quickly for him to make harbor, he would beat out as far as he was able and cast a sea anchor. Fogs did sometimes rise to blind men. Maeloch himself had been thus trapped in the past, and once would have come to grief were it not for a certain seal. However, you could hear from afar where these rocks were, the brawling and hissing and grunting of the waters. Wherever else they blundered to, it should not have been here that a skilled crew perished.

They had come without warning upon the remnants of Ys. Had grief so greatly dazed them? Maeloch felt it rise anew in himself. He thought he had done with weeping, that night ashore in Hivernia on the way back; he and his men had howled like hounds. And mayhap that had been all the tears he would ever shed. What he felt now was the end of hope. There came to him dimly a memory of what Queen Bodilis had chanced to tell him one day, how the folk of distant Egypt used to ready their dead for the tomb before they were Christian. It seemed to him as though someone had lifted the heart and entrails out of him too. Hollow, he would soon blow away on the wind. Would it ever let go of him?

Something stirred on the reef by the wreck. He heard men cry aloud, they saw it themselves. White it glimmered amidst the spindrift. No seal sacred to Belisama—it stood upright, sweetly curved, clad in naught but fair hair that tossed banner-free around its beckoning to him.

"Thunder me down, 'tis a woman!"

A survivor? How? Or a spirit, or the Goddess Herself, Our Lady of Mercy, calling Her sailors to Her? Come, come and be comforted, you who are weary and weighted. So had voices sung through dreams, such dreams as bring a man awake laughing in sunrise. She sang, she called, she promised and summoned.

Oh, you who must wander the wind-way and never
May rest by the woman who once was your bride,
Be gladdened by knowing it is not forever.
To you shall come peace with the turn of the tide.
You are not forsaken, but all that was taken
From you on the earth shall wing homeward to me.
Beloved and lonely, fear not. Here is only
An end to your sorrow, the gift of the sea.

The men bent to their sweeps. Usun put the helm over.

And Maeloch saw past her beauty to Ys that was dead, and back to the skerry whereon she stood with the waters furious at her feet; and he cast forth the joy that had begun to warm him within his breast. "Ha' done!" he shouted. "Would ye steer into yon rocks?"

77

Still the crew rowed, and Usun stood staring before him.

Maeloch whirled, bounded the length of the deck, smote fist into his mate's belly. Usun whoofed out his breath, doubled over, sagged to the planks. Maeloch seized the tiller. Usun scrabbled at his ankles and started to rise. Maeloch kicked him in the ribs. *Osprey* came around.

The rowers could have overridden the steering oar, but they were lost in their dream. "Stroke, stroke, stroke!" Maeloch bellowed, and, mindless, they heeded. A wave swept over the rail, cold dashed into their faces. Surf snarled close by. It fell aft as the vessel clawed off. Maeloch thought he heard a scream, as of a beast that had missed its prey. He cast a glance over his shoulder and saw no more than tumbling waters, the reef and the wreck.

Usun clambered to his feet. "What got into me?" he choked. "Skipper, if 'twasn't for ye—"

The crewmen were likewise back in the mortal world. Bewildered, terrified, they rowed like lubbers; but they were safe for this while, till they got their full wits again. *Osprey* plowed on by the headland.

"A mermaid, who'd lure us to our deaths." Usun shuddered. "I've heard o' such, but off the shores o' witchy lands afar. I never thought to meet one."

"Ys stood guard athwart the gates of the Otherworld too," Maeloch said starkly.

"How did ye hold out, skipper? What gave ye the strength?"

"I know nay. Unless—unless 'twas remembering that we do yet have much to live for—if naught else, avenging Ys, and our kin, and poor little Dahut."

3

Seventeen persons crowded the atrium of the Apuleius home. They sat on what stools could be found, or on the floor, or stood. All stared toward Corentinus. Clad as ever in shabby robe and wayworn sandals, he loomed against the wall whereon was painted the Chi Rho. The symbol seemed to obscure delicate floral patterns elsewhere, as if

78

giving back the darkness of a rainy day which filled the windows; and yet it was traced in gold.

"Thank you for coming," the chorepiscopus began in Ysan. "Well do I know what a hard time this is for you. Natheless we've reached a need that your folk consider their morrows; and I think you whom I asked hither are their natural leaders."

His look ranged across them. Most were men. Two women—no, a woman and a girl—sat in front: Runa, priestess at the Nymphaeum when Ys perished, and the vestal Julia, daughter of Gratillonius and Queen Lanarvilis. The King's other daughter, Nemeta, by Forsquilis, had seemingly chosen to spurn the invitation. Well, she was a strange one, like her mother before her.

The rest of the vestals no longer had any special status. The sole additional person from the sanctuary was Amreth Taniti, captain of its small guard of marines. He stood behind Runa and Julia, arms folded, face dour.

Three more women were on hand. Two were widows of Suffete family who had been managing their late husbands' acres in the hinterland. The third, Tera, stout and sunburned, was a commoner and unwed, though she had had many lovers and commanded a certain awe among herdsmen; for she had been—not quite a priestess—ritemistress to their heathen God Cernunnos and His consorts.

The others were male: a few rich landholders, several small but once prosperous yeomen, some merchants and skippers, three who had belonged to the Council of Suffetes: Bomatin Kusuri for the mariners, Ramas Tyri for the artisans, Hilketh Eliuni for the overland transporters. They had all chanced to be in the countryside or, in four cases, to have escaped when Ys went under. Though he had no official standing, Maeloch should have been present too, once a Ferrier of the Dead—crucial to the old religion—and still surely a spokesman for his kind; also, he had just arrived from Hivernia and must have much to tell. But he and Gratillonius had gone off together, heedless of anyone or anything else.

Most here were drably or raggedly clad. A few bore a salvaged robe or jewel. Gone was the splendor of Ys. The pride lived on, though, in nearly every countenance that regarded him. Arrogant had Ys always been, sinful, worldly, until at last God gave her into the hands of those demons she had served for so long. Yet Corentinus could not but mourn for her and humbly offer his love to such of her children as remained.

Again and again the Suffete face met his eyes, the lean high-boned mask of lost Phoenicia. It had been uncommon in the city; too much blood of Egyptian, Babylonian, Greek, Roman, above all Celt had flowed in throughout her centuries. But it had been a sign of her being, as much as the towers agleam above clouds or the sea gate opened and shut by Ocean itself. Soon it must vanish, drowned in foreignness. Maybe once or twice in generations hence it would be reborn, and parents wonder what had given an alien look to their offspring; but that would happen seldom, and finally never.

Already four of the clans were gone, destroyed entirely in the whelming: Demari, Adoni, Anati, Jezai. Each of the thirteen took its name from a month of the lunar calendar. Was it mere chance that those four were at the quarters of the year? God could thus be showing how the false Gods were fallen. The calendar that had set Their rites must give way and be forgotten before the calendar of Julius, like the pagan moon before the Sun of Christ.

"What have you to say to us, priest?" demanded Bomatin Kusuri in his blunt fashion.

Corentinus overlooked the incorrect title. He had business far more grave. "I wish less to speak at you than with you," he answered. "My power is only to give counsel and, yea, in certain matters, warning. You set your course for yourselves. My prayer is that it be the right one."

"The King should lead this meeting," Amreth said.

"He meant to," Corentinus explained, "but troublous tidings came suddenly upon him. We having already set the day, I felt it best to abide by it. Naught that is said will be binding on anyone."

" 'Tis well he's absent anyhow," blurted Evirion Baltisi.

Attention sought him in surprise. He glared back, a large and powerfully built young man, dark-haired, bullet-headed, snub-featured. No matter his lack of the aristocratic lineaments, he was a grandson of Hannon Baltisi, who had been Lir Captain and bitterly hostile toward Christ. Like the old man in his younger days, Evirion was a seafarer, boldly trading and sometimes slave-raiding from Mumu to the Germanic coasts, beyond the Imperial bounds. It was rumored that he had also had dealings, not always peaceful, in places claimed by but no longer under any real protection of Rome.

"What mean you?" asked Runa sharply.

"That far from heeding Grallon, we should erenow have slain him and left him to the ravens for a traitor. Who else called the wrath of the Gods down on Ys?"

A whisper sibilated around the room, half appalled, half enraged—at whom?

Julia sprang to her feet. "That's not true!" she cried. Blood beat in her round young face. She struggled for breath. "My father, he upheld all of you. He saved more than anybody else could have."

Evirion slitted his look on her. "In those last months when King and Queens were sundered by his denial of her holy rights to Dahut—where were you, Julia? With your mother."

"Oh, but I—I—" The girl fell back onto her stool, bent head into hands, and wept. She was fifteen years old.

Evirion stood challenging the assembly with his glance. "Never did Grallon honor the Gods of Ys. His lips alone did, while he bowed down before his Mithras and made this agent of Christ his foremost counselor. It was Grallon who finally broke the Pact and so brought doom. Then he led you to the Romans and their Church, as a bellwether leads sheep to the slaughterer."

"Why did you keep silent?" Hilketh inquired.

"None would have heeded, earlier. And certes we had necessity to bring survivors to safety and let them regain some strength of body and spirit. I did my share or more in that work. 'Tis time to exact justice and seek freedom."

"Where 'ud you seek it?" gibed Tera the shepherdess.

"Will you sink your neck under the yoke, you who knew the Stag-Horned One?" Evirion retorted.

"That's as may be. I've my brood to think of first. We'll see what Gods do best by 'em."

"The great Three are surely done with us," Runa said slowly, "or we with Them. Nor can we afford feuds among ourselves. Go back to our former lands if you will, Evirion, and wait for the barbarians."

The seaman scowled but kept still. Corentinus sensed a lessening of tension in the air. It had felt like the moments before a lightning storm breaks; now rain ran softly across the windowpanes. She was shrewd, that woman, and fearless, a leader born.

"You are founding a colony, a new community," reminded the chorepiscopus in his most level tone. "Or may I say that we are, together? I have come over the years to feel myself one among you, a man of Ys. I grieve for Ys the beautiful even as you do. But we have our lives to live. We have children with us and children yet unborn. Tera has right, their welfare is our first earthly duty.

"Those who choose can in truth withdraw. Outlands are still pagan, wilderness is well-nigh unpeopled. But do you think you can thus preserve the ways of your fathers, or any memory of your city? Nay, in your waking hours you will grub for a bare living, while your sons grow up to be unlettered backwoodsmen and your daughters to be brood mares in huts they share with the pigs. Friends, in my time I've been sailor, vagabond, laborer, and hermit off in the woods. I know whereof I speak."

He had their entire heed. Quickly he went on: "Here at the confluence is the ground for a city—not a sleepy provincial town like Aquilo but a city real and great. The location is excellent. 'Twas mere accident of history that settlement began downstream of it, when ships can reach it on a flowing tide. The hinterland is rich, timber, iron ore, fertile soil. The neighbors are solid Osismiic tribesfolk leavened by Maximus's veterans, always admiring of Ys and ready to welcome everything you can bring to them. For above all you have yourselves. You bear the learning, the traditions, the loyalties; you are Ys. Keep well your heritage."

"Never will her towers rise anew," said old Ramas Tyri low.

"I fear you speak sooth." Corentinus looked toward Bomatin Kusuri. "But new ships can venture forth. Salt and surge were ever in Ysan blood. Let them now run in Armoricans for aye."

Again Runa took the word: "Ramas meant that whatever we build here, it cannot be like that which is lost."

Corentinus shook his head. "Nay, my lady, it cannot. If you would work upon Armorica, you must let Armorica—Rome—work upon you." He paused. "The city you build must be a city that avows Christ."

An ugly expression passed across Evirion and a few others. The rest seemed resigned or, some of them, half glad. Runa stayed impassive as she nodded and answered, "That is clear. What will you have us do?"

"Why, listen to the good news," Corentinus told them in a rush of happiness. "Open your hearts. He will dry your tears, heal your wounds, and welcome you into life eternal. In return He asks no more than your love."

"Then He wants everything," said a new voice.

Corentinus looked that way. A young man had spoken, shyly—slender, blond, blue-eyed, with thin straight features. The pastor recognized Cadoc Himilco, son of the learned landholder Taenus by a Gallic leman but raised like an heir. His father lay dying of a sickness in the lungs caught during the trek hither.

"I d-do not call this wrong," Cadoc went on. "We served the old Gods as our forebears did . . . because they did . . . but what were the Three, really? Nobody ever knew. Can you tell us about Christ?"

"With my whole heart." Corentinus refrained from pointing out how he had tried to, year after year, and ears were deaf until God had brought Ys into the abyss. The salvation of one soul was infinitely more important than any niggling resentment. There had been ample punishment.

There had been thousands drowned in their sins and error—that a few score be saved? He crossed himself as he veered from the forbidden question.

Forcing a smile: "Stand easy, brethren and sisters. Today you shall be free of sermons. Let us instead talk about the worldly matters around us and how to cope with them. Daily will I preach in my wonted spot for such as care to listen, and ever will I be ready to talk with anyone in private. Nor will I rant or scold. My Master awaits you, but His patience is without bounds."

Julia, who had sat head bowed, staring at the hands clenched together in her lap, glanced up. He thought that through the parching tears he saw a flash of hope.

4

While the meeting used his home, Apuleius had taken his family and slaves out to the farmstead he owned, on the edge of the land he had granted the colony. Toward evening Corentinus found him there in a room alone with Maecius, chorepiscopus at Aquilo. "I'm sorry, I didn't mean to intrude," Corentinus said. "Rovinda told me you were in here. I supposed she meant you were by yourself."

Apuleius smiled in the gathering dusk. "I was only taking the opportunity for prayer and spiritual counsel, on this day when nothing else is happening to me. The pastor was kind enough to come." His manner was unaffected, even cheerful; the growing devoutness of his later years left him as comfortable as before with his God. Sometimes Corentinus felt envy.

"How did discussion go?" Apuleius continued. "Unless you want to keep that confidential."

Corentinus folded his lanky length onto a stool. "It went quite well, on the whole. We arrived at some practical plans. The flock should soon have a better notion of what to expect and what each member ought to do . . . or keep from doing."

"And did you win any to the Faith?" asked Maecius. He was aged, bald and dim of sight; the years when he, like Bishop Martinus, had made efforts to evangelize the countryside were long behind him.

Corentinus shrugged. "It'll take a while."

"Well, you are the man for that holy work. Proceed, surely with the saints at your side and the blessing of the Lord upon you."

"It's more difficult than that, Father," replied Corentinus, turning earnest. They said Maecius had always been too innocent; some said too simple.

84

Apuleius nodded. "M-hm. Language; how many of them know Latin? Folkways, customs, ideas of what is legal and moral. A tribe of foreigners, whom we can't properly assimilate while this generation is alive. They'll start marrying among our people, though. What then? Can we allow it?"

"If they confess Christ, of course we can." Doubt wavered in Maecius's voice.

"The means of that we must prepare, and soon," Corentinus told them. "A pastor who can serve their special needs. A church, not just a building—yours in Aquilo will be too small—but the whole underlying organization. Proper instruction. Baptism. In Ys I heard that much is changing in the Church these days; but away off there among pagans, I could not very well follow or understand it. Can you enlighten me?"

Maecius sighed. "At best, I was never a gifted teacher. And all these disputes about doctrine and liturgy— My poor wits might as well be at Babel."

"We need counsel and we need support." Corentinus regarded Apuleius. "Have I your leave to go seek them?"

"Where?" asked the tribune.

"Where else but to Bishop Martinus in Turonum?"

Apuleius nodded again. "The soldier of God." After a moment: "Make haste. He can't have much time left in this world. Who shall carry the light he has kindled?"

Darkness deepened. Rain stammered on the roof.

V

1

Titus Scribona Glabrio, civil governor of Lugdunensis Tertia, received Quintus Domitius Bacca, his procurator, in that room of the basilica of Caesarodunum Turonum which they generally employed for confidential meetings. Today not even an amanuensis was present.

"Ah, welcome. Come in, my dear fellow, and make yourself as comfortable as possible," Glabrio greeted. "Beastly weather, eh?" Outside, wind blustered cold, herding clouds and quick, hard rainshowers before it. Occasionally windowpanes flickered with a moment's sunlight, otherwise the saints and angels painted on the walls stared out of a gloom wherein their eyes seemed phosphorescent. "We'll have something hot and spiced to drink after our business is done."

Bacca folded his robe, which the walk here had rumpled, about his gaunt frame and took a stool opposite his superior's. "I get the impression the business itself will be of that nature," he said. A smile cut creases under his swordblade of a nose.

Glabrio nodded so vigorously that jowls and double chin wobbled. "A pleasure too long deferred. You have guessed what it is?"

"Considering what intelligence you've had me gather for you, and how quietly—"

"I have now digested the material."

Bacca glanced at Glabrio's paunch and raised the eyebrow the governor could not see.

"I took my time," Glarbrio went on. "You know how prudent I am. Albeit God's vengeance has at last fallen on wicked Ys, the powers of evil may still have resources. I had to feel sure. But today we can begin planning in earnest. Our task is to complete God's work for Him and bring Gratillonius, whom surely none less than Satan rescued from the destruction—bring him low. Do you agree?"

"Well, it'll feel good," said Bacca in his desiccated fashion. He need not add: After he resisted and circumvented us for years, raised his power and honor in Armorica above ours and Rome's own, slew the Franks who were supposed to rid us of him and demoralized their survivors, met our charges before the praetorian perfect in Augusta Treverorum and not only got them dismissed but won elevation to tribune . . . indeed he has rankled in our flesh.

"It is right," Glabrio insisted. "It is vital. It is holy. Let this village he is founding grow, and the same evils will flourish afresh. Insubordination. A corrupting example before the entire province. Paganism. Black sorcery."

"Do you truly consider a few miserable fugitives such a threat?"

"Not in themselves, perhaps. But with Gratillonius as leader— No, we must make an end of his insolence."

Bacca stroked his chin. "That presumably means terminating the Ysan colony, the basis of whatever strength he may gain."

"I believe so. The people can then be redistributed."

"Scattered, you mean."

"That will be wisest, don't you think? Put them into their proper stations in life, teach them humility, save their souls. A holy work, I tell you."

Bacca frowned into the middle distance. "A difficult work, at least," he murmured. "Gratillonius has gotten himself rather firmly ensconced. He and his followers do have temporary permission to settle. Quite legal; Apuleius, the tribune of Aquilo, arranged it behind our backs, with praetorian prefect Ardens. He's also a senator, Apuleius, you know, and has the ear of other important men too. Application for permanent status is in train, and I doubt very much it can be blocked. My inquiries indicate Stilicho himself will be partial to the Ysans."

"How can that *be?*"

"Oh, all right, they're deluded, those men; Satan has whispered to them in their dreams; but the fact remains. Moreover, we'd better not forget a good many lowly people. Maximus's veterans, who owe Gratillonius their homes. Former Bacaudae, who could take up their old trade again if provoked. Osismiic tribesmen, who remember pirates and bandits kept off their necks, trade revived. We're going to have troubles enough without stirring up revolt . . . which could, among other things, cause the Imperium to question *us.*"

"I am no fool, thank you," huffed Glabrio. "I realize we shall have to proceed carefully. But we do have instruments to hand. Taxation—"

"The most obvious, because the most pervasive. As well I know."

"You should!"

"I do. My knowledge includes technique. A levy by itself may prove insufficient to destroy, or impossible to

87

collect, or productive of the very resistance we wish to prevent. First we had better plan ways and means suited to the project. That includes making preparations for the next indiction, two years hence. We will want to have an influence on it."

Bacca's look speared the purple-veined face before him. "I anticipated this," he continued. "When you sent for me today I guessed why, and took the liberty of bringing a man of mine along. He's waiting in the anteroom. Shall I have him called?"

The governor flushed. "You take a good deal upon yourself, Procurator. Who is he?"

Bacca curbed impatience. "You remember Nagon Demari."

Glabrio reddened further. "The Ysan renegade last year? I certainly do. That disaster with the Franks was his fault. I thought afterward he fled."

"I deemed it discreet that he withdraw," Bacca explained coolly. "He and his family have been living on my fundus. A few days ago, foreseeing this summons of yours, I had him brought here and lodged in my town house." He gave the other no chance to use a mouth that opened and shut and opened again. "Your indignation was quite natural. But actually it's wrong to blame him for the scheme going awry. It was an excellent idea in itself . . . as you agreed at the time. No fallible mortal could have foreseen just how tough and ruthless Gratillonius would prove to be. Now, like it or not, Nagon is the single Ysan left for us to consult—to use; and he is eager. He knows those people, their ins and outs, as we never can. We need him for our principal advisor and later, I think, our agent. A wise man does not throw away his sword because a shield stopped it once; he keeps it for his next stroke. You are nothing if not a wise man, Governor."

"Well, well—" Glabrio fumed for a while but in the end agreed. He struck a small gong and bade the slave who entered fetch the outsider.

Almost, Nagon stamped through the door. He halted, his stocky frame half hunched as if for a fight, and glowered before he made himself give a proper salutation.

"You have much to answer for," said Glabrio in his

sternest tone. "Be thankful to your kindly protector. He has persuaded me to grant you a second chance."

"I do thank you, sir," Nagon grated. His sandy hair stood abristle. Small eyes like glare ice never wavered in the flat countenance. "The procurator has informed me. Sir, I'm ready to do whatever is called for—anything at all—that'll bring yon Grallon to hell."

Glabrio bridged his fingers. Rings sparkled. "Really? You are quite vehement, considering what months you've had to cool off."

Nagon knotted fists that were once a laborer's. "I could wait till Judgment Day and never hate him the less."

"Ah, scarcely a Christian sentiment. True, he caused you to go into exile. But thereby he saved you and your family from perishing with Ys."

"No wish of his, that was!" Nagon barely kept from spitting on the floor. "And what brought Ys to ruin but him—he that made mock of the Gods—" After an instant: "Without owning the one true God." He swallowed. "Sir, I've asked about it. I've gone to the Aquilo neighborhood myself and talked with Osismii and such Ysans as I could come on in the woods. Ys is gone. My city, my folk, my clan. I am the last of the Demari Suffetes, do you know? I've only two children alive, both girls. The Demari die with me. What's left to live for?"

"Them and your wife," Bacca suggested. "Whatever career you can find among us."

"Oh, I'll provide for them, sir, of course. And I'll make my way as best I can. But if that could be by helping you against Grallon—" The breath staggered into Nagon and back out. "That'd be worth dying for."

"I hope we can arrange something better, including the satisfaction you want," Bacca soothed. "It does require patience."

"Say the word, and I'll catch him alone and kill him."

"He might very well kill you instead. Besides, that would be stupid, making a martyr of him, possibly angering the Imperium. No, let us undermine him, discredit him, till he is powerless and disowned; and meanwhile, let him experience it happening."

"Bear in mind, my man, this is a preliminary conference," said Glabrio. "You will provide information. If in addition your opinion is occasionally asked, do not get above yourself. I have not forgotten the consequences of your last advice. Furthermore, everything that passes between us, today and later, is a secret of state. If you reveal a single word, you will rue it. Is that clear?"

Nagon was still for a space, so still that the noise of the wind outside flew alone through the room under the stares of the saints, before he said: "I understand."

"Good. You may be seated." Glabrio gestured at the floor. "We shall proceed."

A knock sounded at the door. "What the devil?" exclaimed Bacca. "Didn't you order we aren't to be interrupted?"

"Unless for something major," Glabrio told him nervously. "Enter!"

The slave obeyed, bowed, and announced, "I beg the governor's pardon and pray I have not erred or given offense. An emissary from the bishop has arrived and demands immediate audience."

"What? From Bishop Martinus? Why, he should be at his monastery—"

"I thought, rightly or wrongly, the governor would wish to know. Shall I admit him, or have him wait, or . . . send him on his way?"

"No, no." That last would be impolitic in the extreme. "I will see him."

The slave scuttled out. After a minute during which the wind gusted louder, a man came in. Young, lean, he was clad only in a rough dark robe and sandals. His fair hair was shaved off from the brow to the middle of the scalp, the tonsure of Martinus; weather had ruffled what was left into a halo against the dimness of the chamber.

"God's peace be upon you," he said evenly. "You will not remember me. I am of no consequence. But my name is Sucat." His Latin bore a curious accent, Britannic subtly altered by years of Hivernian captivity.

"I do, though," Glabrio answered in a relieved tone. "You are the bishop's kinsman. Welcome." He pointed to a vacant stool. "Will you be seated? Will you take refreshment?"

Sucat shook his head. "No, thank you. My message is soon conveyed. It is from Martinus, bishop of Turonum. He commands you in the name of God that you show mercy to the poor survivors of Ys and afflict them no more than the Almighty has done; for what would be presumptuous, and un-Christian, and troublesome to the Church in her work among them."

Glabrio gaped. Nagon froze. Bacca stood up and spoke tautly: "May I ask why the bishop chooses . . . to advise the civil authorities?"

"Sir, it is not for me to question a holy man," Sucat replied, unshaken, almost cheerful, and beneath it implacable. "However, he did point out that there are souls to be saved; that their community may become the seed from which the Evangel will grow through a tribe still mostly pagan; but that first it needs protection and nurture."

"And exemption from the usual requirements?"

"The civil authorities can better decide such things than we religious. We simply appeal to their consciences. And, of course, to their hopes for their own salvation."

"Hm. How did you find us, Sucat?"

"The bishop bade me seek the basilica. He said the governor and yourself would be here, together with a third party who should also be reminded about charity. He said that if you want to discuss this with him, you are free to come out to the monastery; or you can arrange an appointment for sometime after he has attended to the suffering poor and conducted services in the city. Have I the governor's leave to depart? Good day, and God's blessing be upon you, His wisdom within you."

The young man strode out.

Glabrio dabbed at sweat on his face, chilly though the room was. "That . . . puts a different . . . complexion on the matter, doesn't it?"

Nagon lifted hands with fingers crooked like claws. "You'll bow down to Martinus with never a word?" he shouted. "Him, so old and feeble he can barely totter into town once a sennight? What *right* has he got?"

"Be still," Bacca snapped.

He paced the floor, scowling into shadows, hands working against each other behind his back. "We've small

91

choice, you know," he muttered at length. "Martinus may have no office in the government, but he stood up to Emperor Maximus, and with his influence he could break us apart and scatter the pieces. He would, too, if we made him angry enough."

"He could do worse than that." Glabrio's flesh rippled with his shudder. "He's driven demons from the altars where pagans worshipped them, and raised the dead, and talked with angels—he could bring all of them down on us— No, we'll heed him; we are good, obedient sons of the Church."

A hiss went between Nagon's teeth.

Bacca stopped before the man, looked into his eyes, and said low: "Control yourself. Bide your time. Nothing forbids us to watch, and learn, and think, and wait. Our beloved bishop is in fact very old. Soon God will call him home to his reward. Then we shall see. We shall see."

2

Again Gratillonius sought privacy on the heights, but now it was with Rufinus. At first they walked in silence. The path climbed and curved amidst leaves whose brilliant green broke morning light into jewel-glints of color on raindrops that clung to them yet after the past several wet days. Cloudlets wandered on a breeze filled with fragrances. Birds a hundredfold rejoiced. Where the view opened downward, it was across a broad western sweep of land. The rivers gleamed through awakening acres; smoke rose from the hearths of Aquilo; northward the colony site at the confluence was half hidden by mists steaming out of its newly spaded earth, white against the forest beyond.

Finally Rufinus ventured, "You can unlock your throat here, master. You've kept too much inside for too long."

Gratillonius's close-trimmed beard only partly concealed how his mouth writhed. He stared before him as if blind. A minute or two passed while they walked on, until he said, "I wanted to speak alone with you." His voice sounded rusty.

Rufinus waited.

"You've been to Hivernia," Gratillonius continued presently. "You know them there."

Rufinus winced. The expression grew into one of pain as Gratillonius went unheeding on: "It's become pretty clear what happened, how Ys was murdered and who the murderer is. What we must figure out is how to get our revenge." Laughter barked. "How to exact justice, I mean to say . . . when Corentinus or Apuleius or their sort are listening. But probably it's best if they aren't."

"I've heard little," Rufinus said with care, "and what I have heard may well be unreliable."

"Maeloch— He came back from Hivernia himself, you know. After he . . . told me . . . what he'd learned— I thought of swearing him to silence. But of course it was already too late to gag the men who'd sailed with him. And others from Ys, they have their own stories to tell. Luckily, everyone's been too busy to think much about it. Except me."

Rufinus nodded. Of late, Gratillonius had often gone away by himself, riding or striding for leagues in the rain; and he was curt among people, and bore signs of sleeplessness.

"They'll also put two and two together eventually," Gratillonius said. "The story will be in every common mouth . . . throughout Armorica . . . for hundreds of years? Dahut's name—" He did not groan, he roared.

Both halted. Rufinus laid a hand on the massive shoulder beside him and squeezed until most men would have cried out. "Easy, sir," the Gaul breathed.

Gratillonius gazed past him. Fist beat in palm, over and over. "Dahut, whore to Niall the Scotian," rattled forth. "She stole the Key from me while I slept, for him. It must have been her. We all slept so heavily in the Red Lodge, in that wild night that should have kept us awake, and I know she could cast such spells, Forsquilis told me she had a gift for witchcraft like no princess—no Queen, since— since— And before that, oh, I closed my eyes and stopped my ears and who dared warn me? He can't have been her first lover, Niall. Why else did—Tommaltach, Carsa, those young men challenge me, make me who liked them cut them down in the Wood? And that Germanic pirate—

93

Maeloch says he was lying, but I can't believe it and I don't think Maeloch really can either— Dahut! Dahilis, our daughter!"

"Are you quite sure?"

Gratillonius wrestled himself toward steadiness. "What else will account for everything we've discovered? And Corentinus, he knows. There at the end, he told me to let her go, let the sea have her, or . . . the weight of her sins would drag me down with her. Not that I cared, not that I did . . . willingly. The visions he gave me, of the Queens, how each of them died, it made me—I lost strength—" He snapped air. "Since then, he won't talk about the matter. When I've asked, he's said that's not for him to speak of, and gone straightaway to something else. Oh, he can find enough urgent business to steer me off this."

"Are you angry with him, then?"

Gratillonius shook his head. "Why? As well be angry with the messenger who brings bad news. And he did save my life, and other lives, and now when he's off to Turonum I realize through and through how much he's been doing for us here."

Suddenly, terrifying calm, he lifted his face to the blue overhead and declared: "No, this goes beyond the world. Gods have been at work. What else could have led my Dahut astray like that? The Gods of Ys, and that poor, bewildered, lonely girl; They played on her like Pan playing on pipes made from a dead man's bones. And Mithras, Mithras was too careless or too afraid to stand by us. Dahut was left all alone with the Three, and They are demons. As for the God of the Christians—I don't know. I've asked Him for an honest answer, and gotten silence. So I don't know of anything except the demons. Maybe otherwise there's only emptiness."

Rufinus, who had entertained the same idea, shivered to hear it thus set forth. He waited a bit, while Gratillonius brought his gaze back to earth and across the lands afar, before he said low, "You want to avenge Dahut—and Ys—on Niall."

"Since I cannot reach the Gods," replied Gratillonius, flat-voiced, still looking into distance. "In any event, he needs killing."

Rufinus mustered courage. "First I do."

Startled out of grief, Gratillonius swung around to peer at him. "How's that?"

Rufinus stood straight, hands at sides, and spoke fast. "Sir, I failed you. I may well have something to do with what happened. You remember my telling how I freed that prisoner of Niall's, Eochaid, the same man Maeloch found on the island. It seemed like a fine trick at the time. But it must have poured oil on Niall's fire against Ys. Certainly it made it impossible for us to send any mission to his kingdom, negotiate, try to engineer his overthrow. I was vain and reckless, I overreached, and Ys had to suffer for it."

A slow smile, with no mirth but considerable pity, lifted Gratillonius's lips. "Is that all? Nonsense. You should know the Scoti better than that. I do. They never forget what they think is any wrong done them, and anything that keeps them from having their way is a wrong. Blame me. I was the one who wrecked his fleet and his plans, all those years ago. And I don't feel guilty about that. It was a good job well done. As for you, why, you freed an enemy of his, who may yet become an ally of ours."

Rufinus hung his head. "Maybe. But I did go away, down south, just when the trouble was brewing. I should have stayed. I might have been able to warn you, or—or somehow head things off."

"You might have at that," said Gratillonius, "you, if any man alive could. I've wondered what made you go. It wasn't really necessary, and you didn't seem like simply wanting the adventure."

"I had . . . reasons," Rufinus croaked. "I thought it—might ease a conflict—I should have stayed, whatever it cost. All the way back from Italy, after the news came, I was feeling more and more certain the whelming couldn't have been an accident, it had to be some outcome of the evil I'd smelled everywhere around us."

"You did? You never let on."

Rufinus straightened, met his master's look, and grinned his grin that was half a sneer. "I'm good at putting a nice face on things." He slumped. "Now scourge me, kill me, anything to free me of this."

Gratillonius sighed. "All right, you made a mistake, but I was with you in it. I could have required you to stay, couldn't I? Are we magicians to foretell the future? I need your wits. Throw that remorse of yours on the dunghill where it belongs. That is an order."

Rufinus's words seldom rang forth as they did: "At your command, sir! What do you want of me?"

"I told you. For the present, your thoughts. And your ways of dealing with people, seducing them into doing what you want and believing it was their own idea. We'll have our hands full getting the colony established, dealing with Imperial officers, collecting intelligence about barbarian movements and making ready to meet them—everything." Gratillonius paused. "But it's not too soon to start thinking about Niall of the Nine Hostages." His tone had gone quiet as a winter night when waters freeze over. "I mean to wash Dahut's honor clean in his blood. Then my little girl can rest peaceful."

3

The day was so lovely that to sit in the murk and dinginess of Martinus's hut was itself a mortification. The door did sag on leather hinges, letting in a bit of sunlight and a glimpse of grass and river. Sounds also drifted through, from monks at their prayers—those who worked in the kitchen gardens stayed mute—all along the bottomland and up in the hillside caves which were the cells of most. But smells of loam and growth were lost in malodor; saintly men scorned scrubbing. The light picked out dust, cobwebs, mushrooms in the corners of the dirt floor. Two three-legged stools and a chest for books and documents were the only furniture.

The bishop's few remaining teeth gleamed amidst wrinkles and pallor as he smiled. "Do not pretend to virtues that are not yours, my son," he jested. "I refer to simplicity. You know perfectly well who should take leadership there. Yourself."

Corentinus bowed his head. That was never quite easy for him to do for a fellow mortal. "Father, I am not worthy."

Martinus turned serious. His dim eyes strained through the shadows, studying the visitor. "No man born of woman should ever dare imagine himself truly fit for the cure of souls. However, some are called, and must do the best they can. You are familiar with those people, and familiar to them. You get along well with their King—with him who was King. In fact, the two of you make a formidable team. Moreover, you are a man of the folk; you have known labor and hardship, shared the joys and sorrows of the humble. That includes the tribes round about. The effort to bring them into the fold has waned with Maecius's strength. You are still in your full vigor, never mind those gray hairs. Who better to take over the ministry?"

He sat still before adding, "This is more than my judgment, you understand. God has long marked you out. You are one of the miracle workers."

So lengthy a speech took its toll of him. He hunched, hugging himself against chill despite the springtime mildness, regaining breath. Eyes closed in the snubnosed countenance.

They opened again when Corentinus protested hoarsely, "Father, that was nothing— No, I repent me; of course I must not demean His mercies. But that is what they were—the fish that kept me fed in my hermitage, the ability to heal or rescue, the rare vision of warning—mercies to a wretched sinner."

Martinus straightened. Something of the old soldierly manner rapped through his tone. "Enough. Humility is not a virtue natural to you either, Corentinus. Affecting it like this, false modesty, is nothing more than spiritual pride. You have your orders from Heaven. Obey them."

The tall man gulped. "I'm sorry." After a moment, his words wavering: "Let me confess it, I'm afraid. I don't know how to handle these powers. They were such small, comfortable miracles before. Now—"

"You confront the very Serpent." Martinus nodded. "I know. All too well do I know."

He leaned forward, intent. "The divine will is often hard to riddle. We make blunders which can bring disaster. And sometimes—oh, Satan works wonders of his own. I have seen what wore the semblance of Christ Himself—" He drew the Cross before him.

97

"But the Lord is always with us," he said, "even unto the end of the world. He will help us see through and win through, if only we ask. I recall a mistake—" Once more he must stop to breathe.

"Tell me, Father," Corentinus begged.

Abruptly Martinus seemed nearly at ease. He smiled anew. "Ah, no great thing. There was a shrine not far from here which my predecessor had consecrated as being of a martyr. But I could find no believable story about his passion; even his name was uncertain. Could members of my flock be calling on a false saint? I went to the grave and prayed for enlightenment. Night fell. A figure appeared before me, wrapped in a shroud black with clotted blood; for his head had been cut off and he must hold it to the stump of his neck. I bade him speak truth, and he confessed he was a brigand, put to death for his crimes. Afterward sheer confusion among the rustics—confusion with a former godling of theirs, I think—caused them to venerate him. I dismissed the ghost to his proper place, and next day made known the facts, and that was the end of that."

"You treat it so lightly," Corentinus whispered.

Martinus shrugged.

"But that which walked in the dark around Ys—" Corentinus went on, "that which I'm afraid still haunts the ruin It made—"

Martinus grew solemn anew. "We may have terrible things to deal with," he said. "Therefore we need a strong man."

Corentinus braced himself. "I'll do what I can, Father, since you want it."

"God wants it. In Him you will find strength boundless."

Then, in the practical way that was his as often as the pious, Martinus added: "A chorepiscopus at Aquilo is no longer enough, given the changed circumstances. We require a full bishop. We can't elevate you immediately. These are indeed deep waters. You and I shall have to talk, and think, and pray together, before we can hope for any idea of how to fare in them. Meanwhile, you need instruction. A great deal has happened, a great deal has changed, also in the Church, during those years you spent isolated in Ys. We have to make you ready for your ministry. It will be harder than most, my son, and perhaps mortally dangerous."

4

Returning from Mons Ferruginus, Gratillonius sought the house of Apuleius in Aquilo. His talk with Rufinus had vastly relieved him. The pain and rage were still there, but congealed, a core of ice at the center of his being. He could turn his thoughts from them. The day must come when he let them thaw and flood forth over Niall; meanwhile, he should get on with his work.

At the moment he had in mind to discuss the organization of defense, now that construction was progressing so well that soon his colony would be a tempting target. If only Imperial law did not limit the arming of populaces to peasant reservists—but it did, and Rufinus's woodsrangers were an illegality at which the authorities might soon cease winking, as they perforce had done while Ys was their bulwark. . . .

Salomon bounded down the front steps to meet him. "Oh, sir, can we go?" he cried.

Gratillonius stopped. "What's this?"

"Why, you promised, sir, the first day the weather was dry you'd take me to your town and explain how it's guarded. I got my tutor to let me off, and I've been waiting, and—and—" The boyish voice stumbled. A tousled head drooped. "You can't?"

Gratillonius regarded him. At eleven years of age, Apuleius's son approached his father's height, though all legs and arms and eyes. Blue as his mother's, those eyes clouded over. He tried to keep his lip still. "Of course, sir, you're busy," he managed to say.

The man remembered. A promise was a promise, and this was a good lad, and he had no overwhelming urgency. "Why, no, I hadn't forgotten," he lied. "I was engaged earlier, but that's done with and I came to fetch you. Shall we go?"

Joy blazed. "Thank you, sir! Right away!"

If I had a son of my own—Gratillonius thought, and the old pang returned. But my Queens in Ys could bear nothing but daughters, and the same spell made me powerless with any woman other than them.

Am I still?

Too much else had filled him since the whelming. Desire was crowded out. He did wake erected from dreams, but the dreams always seemed to be of what he had lost, and he hastened to leave them behind him.

He started to turn around. A flash of white caught his glance. Verania had come out into the portico. "Must you leave at once?" she called softly.

"Why not?" demanded her brother.

"Oh, I have some small refreshments ready . . . if you have time, sir."

The wistfulness caught at Gratillonius. It would be unfair to make Salomon wait any longer. However— "Thank you, when we are finished," he blurted. "Uh, first, if you're free, would you like to come with us?"

Her radiance quite overran Salomon's disgruntlement. She skipped down to them with a gracefulness that recalled Dahilis, and Dahut (no). Hair, also light-brown, blew free of its coiled braids in rebellious little curls. She had her father's big hazel eyes. The face hinted at Bodilis's daughter Una, and more and more the mind at Bodilis herself; pure chance, that, no relationship whatsoever to those two who lay drowned. His stare made her redden, plain to see under so fair a skin. The faintest dusting of freckles crossed a pert nose. . . . He hauled attention elsewhere and the three of them began walking.

Their way went opposite from the bustle at the dock, out the eastern gate and up the left bank of the Odita. To reach the section between the rivers without wading, it was necessary to take a wooden bridge just above their confluence. "We're going to put one across the Stegir," Gratillonius remarked. "Save time for carters and such, once our town begins drawing them from the west."

"Won't that be dangerous, sir?" Salomon asked. "I mean, you said the streams were two sides of your city wall."

"A shrewd question," Gratillonius approved. The stuff of leadership was certainly in this boy. He wasn't fond of

100

book learning like his sister, nor as quick to master it, but he was no dullard either, and where it came to military subjects you might well call him brilliant. He shone in the exercises, too, or would when he had tamed the impulsiveness of his age. "It'll be a drawbridge, and flanked by a real wall."

"Will your city be grand like Ys?"

Verania sensed the wrenching within the man. "Nothing can every be so beautiful again, can it?" she said. "But what you make, sir, it will be *yours*."

Somehow Gratillonius could chuckle. "Well, I expect the architects will have more to say about it than this old soldier. If we can ever afford them, that is. Confluentes won't become any Rome or Athens in my lifetime. I'll be satisfied if we get it beyond these cob and log shacks we're throwing up at first."

Verania shook her head. "Confluentes. Couldn't you find a prettier name?"

"It's fine," Salomon retorted. "It means what it is."—the juncture of the rivers.

"Serviceable, anyhow, same as we want the town itself to be," Gratillonius said. There had never been any formal decision about a name. It had simply grown from the mouths of soldiers and workmen.

The walk from Aquilo was short. Having crossed the bridge, the three found themselves looking at an expanse of open ground about a mile on a side, cut by a brook. The streams hemmed it in on the south and west, the woods on the north and east. Much of it was now mud churned by rain, boots, wheels, hoofs. Log pathways were crowded with traffic. Hammers banged, saws grided, frames lifted raw against heaven. The former tenant farms sheltered workers and their tools. Toward the northwest angle, beyond the fortification, the manor house of the Apuleii remained untouched. Dwindled by distance, its white walls and red roof, outbuildings, garden, orchard had a loneliness about them, like that of an old man who watches turmoil among strangers.

"We'll go around," Gratillonius said. "No sense in mucking up our feet." He led the way to the south end of the eastern earthworks and thence north.

Peaceful was the meadow outside the ditch, before the forest rose green and white. When he stopped and was about to describe the function of the barriers, he noticed Verania gazing yonder. Her lips moved. He barely heard: *"Now leaf the woodlands, now is the year at its fairest."*

It stirred a vague memory. "What's that?" he asked. She gave him a fawn's startled glance. "What you were reciting. Poetry, hm?"

She colored and nodded. "A line from the third Eclogue of Vergilius, sir. He w-would have loved this landscape."

He attempted humor. "Kind of cold and damp for an Italian, I should think."

"Oh, but—the cornel blossoming. That's what we ought to call your city," she exclaimed. "The Meeting of Rivers Where the Dogwood Grows."

Confluentes Cornuales, he rendered it in his mind. Not bad. He'd try using it and see if it caught on. The second part, at least, might well fit this entire country. Cornel was more than bonny. It supplied excellent wood for charcoal, skewers, handles, spokes, spearshafts: the needs of men.

Watch that! he reminded himself. You're not in a real country any more. Ys is gone. You're in a province of the Empire.

VI

1

That was a chilly year, but toward midsummer a spell of heat set in and lasted a while. It brooded heavy on the day when Evirion met Nemeta. Forest leaves might have been cut out of sea-greened sheet copper. They roofed off the hard blue sky, save where beams struck through from the west to glance off boles and speckle shadows. No breeze moved, no animal scampered, no bird chirred. Silence stretched like a drumhead waiting for a storm to beat thunder from it.

A spring trickled to keep filled a pool. Insects hovered above its dark stillness. Sedge and osier choked the banks, held off only by the lichenous mass of a boulder. Nearby loomed a giant of a beech. Moss and fungus grew on its trunk and on boughs fallen to earth. Lightning had long ago blasted it, with fire hollowing a cavern higher than a man.

There stood the girl. The charred wood obscured her thin, drably clad body; face and mane sprang forth, snow and flame. She carried a stick as long as herself, around the top of which she had bound the coiling mummy of a snake.

Brush crackled. Evirion pushed his way through, saw her, stopped and wiped from his brow the sweat that stained his tunic and surrounded him with its reek. "At last!" he growled. "I thought I'd never find you. Why'd you pick this, of all meeting places?"

"Because no one else would be nigh," Nemeta answered. "They shun it, the fools. Power indwells here yet."

Evirion frowned. A hand dropped to the shortsword at his belt. "What do you mean? How do you know?"

Her eyes glowed cat-green. "When the Celts first came hither," she said low, "they piled the heads of slain foemen around this tree as an offering to their Gods. Long afterward, the Romans trapped seven fleeing druids beneath it, murdered them, and took the skulls away. Taranis killed it as you see. But spirits linger. I have felt them touch me and heard them whisper."

For all his size and strength, the young man must fight down unease. "We could have been quite alone in a mort of spots easier to reach."

" 'Twas you asked for a secret talk about an enterprise you have in mind. It put me to some trouble, slipping away without rousing questions. I had a right to set my terms."

He considered her. Quiet but intense, she revealed

103

nothing of the hoyden—mostly sullen and short-spoken, sometimes shrill in futile fury—that they knew at Aquilo and Confluentes. "There is more in you than I supposed," he murmured after a moment, "and already I understood you were the one whose help I should seek." He looked around him. The depths of the wood might have concealed anything. "Aye, you may well hope you can call on—whatever you call on—for a blessing or an omen or—what, Nemeta?"

"Say what you want of me."

"Come, shall we sit down?" he proposed. "I've brought wine." He gestured at a leather flask opposite his sword and lowered himself to the ground. Fallen stuff crackled faintly.

She shook her head. "We'll not water it from this spring. It too was once holy." Nevertheless she joined him, though hunkering and at a slight distance, as if prepared to bound away should he make a wrong move.

Evirion drank without dilution, passed a hand over his clean-shaven chin, and smiled. It livened his rugged good looks. "You are an astonishing lass. Fifteen years, is that your age? But then, you're the daughter of Forsquilis—" he turned somber— "and she was the last of the great witch-Queens in Ys."

"I'll never know what she knew." The girl's tone was stoic. "But I did learn a little from her ere the whelming. And others, like Tera—Give me the freedom to seek, and I may win back a small part of what went down with Ys." Abruptly she colored. The big eyes lowered before him. "That is my dream."

He seized the opening. "And what chance have you to make it real? What are you now, princess of Ys, but a scullion?"

"That's . . . unfair. Everybody must do whatever they're able. My father—we're his housekeepers, Julia and I. Not menials. He has no wife any more—"

"Did his Queens go to market, cook, scrub, mend, weave, hold back in the presence of men, look forward to marrying a rustic lout and farrowing for him?" Evirion gibed. "How glad are you these days, Nemeta?"

"What of you?" she counterattacked.

104

"Why, I am wretched," he said without hesitation. "I, a Suffete born of the Baltisi, I who owned my ship and was her master on ventures from the Outer Isles to far Thule—since Ys drowned I've been a laborer. Oh, one who has some skill; I shape wood, rather than grub dirt or carry it in a hod; but I take my orders and swill my ration and at night lie on a clay floor in a wattle-and-daub hovel." Rage broke free. "I've been flogged! Like a common, mutinous cockroach of a sailor, I was flogged."

"I heard about that," Nemeta said carefully, "but 'twas in snippets mixed together, and I'm not supposed to ask."

"Aye, you're among Romans and Christians, who keep their women meek. Hear the tale. Cadoc Himilco—you know him, surely, the dog who comes sniffing around the skirts of your sister—"

"He and Julia . . . like each other."

"Well they might. *They're* not ill content, I imagine. A sanctimonious pair like that should fit well into the new order." Evirion tried to check his temper. "He and I were on the same task of building. He made a stupid botch. I reproved him. He struck me. Naturally I struck back, taught him a lesson. 'Twas three days till he was fit for work. And Grallon had me triced up and given three lashes. For defending myself!"

Nemeta tensed. "My father is, is a just man. Mostly. I heard Cadoc got one lash after he was well. You two shouldn't have fought when there's so much to do. Why did he hit you? 'Tisn't like him."

"I—ah, I do have a quick tongue. I called him a son of a pig."

"With his own father newly dead. And you disabled him for three days. I wonder how stupid his mistake truly was."

Evirion swallowed. Silence thickened. At last he said, "You defend your father more than I awaited."

"We—oh—we quarrel, everybody knows we do, and of course when the Nine broke with him because of Dahut—" The stick wavered which Nemeta gripped. She rallied and challenged: "Say forth what you came to say, or go."

"I've half a mind to do that, and leave you to your insolence and misery."

105

Her tone softened. "Nay, please, abide. Let's start afresh."

His anger subsided. Eagerness rose in its place. "Hark, then. We've few skills that are of use any more, we who stood high in Ys. The commoners with us, they can doubtless lose themselves and their names in the ruck. Must folk like you and me? How shall we escape the trap? Wealth would free us, but we've lost everything that was ours."

His voice dropped. He leaned close. "*It abides, Nemeta.*"

She caught her breath.

He nodded. "Aye, in the ruins. Gold, silver, gems, coined money. The sea cannot have washed it all away—thus far—though it will erelong. Unless first we have courage to come reclaim our heritage."

She shivered and drew signs in the simmering air. "The Gods destroyed Ys. We're outcasts. 'Twould be death, or worse, to go back."

"Are you certain?" he pressed. "How do you know? Tell me that, and I'll let slip my hopes."

"Why, 'tis—Well, I—" She stared from side to side. The red hair bristled outward.

"You suppose so," he said. "Like everybody else. *I* think the dead there would welcome and aid whoever returned; for the aim is to keep alive some part of what they were. My thought is that I'll leave shortly after harvest. Then nobody will much care or heed that this pair of working hands is gone. Having won the means at Ys, I'll go on to Gesocribate and buy the best ship to be had. I'll get as many Ysans for crewmen as possible. We'll adventure forth again, our own masters again, and hell may have Rome!"

"Wha-what of me?"

"I'm not wholly reckless. I agree we know not what may haunt the desolation. I want a comrade who can sense, warn, do whatever is needful for our safety . . . amidst things of the Otherworld. This world I can handle myself."

She made a fending motion. "But I'm a child! I have no such powers."

"Mayhap you've more than you think, Nemeta. I've done my watching and my asking—more quietly, more patiently than most folk would believe me able to. You've guessed where lost objects were, and been right. Your dreams, such of them as you've spoken of, have a way of foreshadowing what happens. Ofttimes small objects fly through the air in houses where you are, though never a human hand cast them. When it seemed a prize cow of Apuleius's would die in calving, you touched her and muttered and at once the birth went easily. These and more—aye, small happenings, but they've already made you talked about, made some people look at you askance. They wonder what you do when you walk solitary in the woods. I wonder too."

"Naught, naught. I seek for Gods. M-my father lets me, he defends me in spite of—I've never really told him—" The girl straightened. "I won't help any foe of his."

"Still, you twain are not quite friends, eh? Well, he and I have been at odds, doubtless we shall be in future, but I wish him no ill."

Her gaze steadied and brooded. "Is that true? I hear you have blamed him for the fall of Ys."

He flushed. "I'll leave him alone if he'll do likewise for me. Let the Gods deal with him however he may deserve. Enough?"

Slowly, she nodded.

"Think of yourself," he urged. "Think what your share of our gains will mean to your life. Is that not worth any hazard? Afterward—aye, a woman has curbs upon her in this Roman world, but you'll have me for your friend, counselor, partner if you wish. Or even more, Nemeta."

She tensed. Her words flew quick, not quite firm, yet underlaid with steeliness. "I am a maiden. No man shall own me, never. If I fare with you, first you must swear to honor that; and I will devise the oath you swear."

The least bit daunted by her manner, he hesitated an instant, then replied: "So be it. Indeed you are your mother's daughter. Now let us talk about how we may do this thing."

2

Work being finished that had needed every hand at the colony, and repairs upon her being completed, *Osprey* could again go fishing. She left Aquilo on the ebb tide, down the Odita to the sea.

For a while the river broadened. Farther on it narrowed and twisted through such a series of bends that the crew, when they first headed upstream, had sometimes wondered if they did not have the wrong part of the waterway and had entered a mere branch. Only on oars could a craft her size or larger keep from going aground. Twice she passed a merchantman at anchor, both waiting for the tide to turn so they could proceed. Boats full of rowers stood by to tow them.

There was scant other occupation in these parts. The banks were high and mostly wooded. Where the terrain sloped more easily one might see cleared land, farm or pasture. Much of this looked new but was not. It had been abandoned and had reverted to wilderness during the evil years, then reclaimed once peace came back. "I wonder how long 'twill last, now Ys and her navy be down," Maeloch said half aloud.

At the rivermouth a fisher hamlet huddled, and on the very edge of land the ruins of a Roman villa, sacked by pirates. Little of the buildings remained; folk of the neighborhood had quarried them for stone, tile, brick, glass. That was what became of nearly all the shells left behind when civilization receded.

Osprey put to sea. Wind was from the east. Sweeps came inboard, sail rattled aloft, and the smack ran over gray-green chop toward her old fishing grounds. First she must bear southerly, to round the peninsula. Maeloch kept her closer to shore than his men quite liked. These waters were less dangerous than those around Ys, but still had their share of rocks and shoals. Toward evening, he pointed to where hearthsmoke rose from the land and said, "We'll put in yonder for the night."

A couple of mariners groaned. "Why, that's daft, skipper," Usun protested. "We'll have moon enough to fare after dark. And we ken nay the approach."

"Just the same, we go in, me lads, as we will each darkfall that we can. 'Tis wise we make acquaintance with our fellows along this coast. They can tell us a mickle about it; and should we ever find ourselves in distress, why, we'll have their goodwill."

Usun shook his head. "In the time these calls 'ull take, we could make a second voyage. We've become poor men."

"With fewer mouths to feed than erstwhile," said Maeloch bleakly.

"Ye could at least ha' taken on a pilot who knows the way."

"That would be one more mouth to . . . talk. Helm over!"

Narrowed glances dwelt on the captain, but the crew obeyed. More than once had he issued strange orders; and thus far they had stayed alive.

It was slow work, crawling forward on oars, constantly heaving the lead. The sun had gone down behind western heights when *Osprey* arrived. The village was a mass of shadows, the men who waited to meet the strangers almost as murky. Maeloch sprang from the bows and advanced with hands open. In Osismiic he declared his name and port of departure. His dialect differed from what prevailed here, but was understandable. Suspicion dissolved. Everyone was delighted to meet newcomers, and they were invited to lodge overnight. As he had hoped, Maeloch ended in the headman's hut.

"Ye're kind to a wayfarer," he said as the wife set forth a belated meal of stockfish, leeks, and roots. "Let me offer somewhat." He had brought a jug of wine. Soon he and his host were on the best of terms.

Palaver went on long after dark. Maeloch led it toward pirates. That was easy. Nightmare memories were already astir. Even these dwellings had what drew barbarians— women to ravish, youngsters to take for slave markets, men to kill and roofs to burn for the fun of it.

"They'll nay come back at once, the Saxons and Scoti," Maeloch said. "First they must hear o' what's happened, then make small, probing raids till they're sure the back of Armorica's sea defense be broken. And the north shores be nearer them. 'Tis a long beat around the headlands where Ys was. Those who sail too nigh will likely sail no more." His rumbling voice lost steadiness for a moment.

109

There had been that which sang on a reef. Boldly again: "But in time they'll reach ye, sure as death. Will ye be ready?"

Bitterness replied: "What can we be ready with? Fish spears and firewood axes—or our feet to carry us inland when we see the lean hulls."

"It could be more, my friend. Hark'ee. The Romans have nay the manpower to ward ye, yet will nay let ye arm yourselves and form a trained force, the kind that made the barbarians give Ys and her ships a wide berth. However, the Romans need nay know all that goes on in a quiet way."

The headman sat straight. "What d'ye aim at?"

"Ah, nay too fast. 'Quiet' be the word I used. But I be a man o' Grallon's, he who was King of Ys, and he did ask me to sound out those like yourself as I fared—"

3

The Sunday was clear, surely a good omen. Already at dawn, people began to gather in front of the cathedral. When Gratillonius arrived shortly after sunrise, the square was crowded. Mostly folk stood mute; those who talked did so in murmurs. The consecration of a bishop was an event of the highest solemnity.

The great building shadowed them. Brick, tile, and glass of its clerestory caught the early light, a brightness as cool as the air. Memory tugged Gratillonius's lips ruefully upward. When had he last attended a Christian service in Turonum, or anywhere else for that matter? Thirteen years ago? So little had he known then that he supposed the church was the only one in the city. Actually, the cathedral had been under repair after a fire. Today Corentinus would have a setting worthy of him.

Apuleius waited at the head of the assembly, together with a few other men of secular importance from his territory. Gratillonius went to join them. Nobody said more to him than a greeting. He felt the constraint and tried to shrug it off his mind.

Beyond the columns of the porch, the doors opened.

110

Darkness obscured the men who cried, "Come, all Christians! Come to worship!" They went down the three stairs and across the pavement, calling their summons.

The people moved forward, upward, inward. Frescos between the windows in aisles and clerestory were more plain to see than the picture of Christ the Lawgiver in the apse; but the light from the east that dazzled eyes was as a glory under His feet. At that end the floor was three steps higher, bearing altar, offertory table, and cupboard for holy things needful. Ranked in the apse were the clergy, wearing robes of white. Over these, priests had the dalmatic, bishops the chasuble, splashes of color against dusk. The bishops were three, Martinus in a carven chair flanked in lesser seats by the two colleagues whom the occasion required. Corentinus folded his long frame close to them. Priests used stools. The choir, double-ranked below them, seemed almost phantom-like. Candleflames glimmered.

The lay notables took stance behind a few benches set out for the aged and infirm. Several hundred commoners pressed in at their backs. The energumens had been led away. From the bema a deacon called for silence. The doorkeepers passed the command on to the overflow attendance in porch and square. Mumbling died out. For a minute the hush was enormous.

The deacon's voice trod forth: "Let us kneel."

Gratillonius felt a brief surprise. He was used to seeing those who prayed stand erect, arms raised in supplication. Was this a new practice, or had he forgotten, or was he still more ignorant of the Mass than he had supposed? Awkwardly, he lowered himself to the patterned stone floor.

A priest mounted the ambo on the north side and prayed, "—to God, Saviour of the faithful, preserver of the believers, author of immortality—" The congregation's "Amen" sounded deep, and all stood up.

From the cupboard a subdeacon brought a volume of Jewish scripture to the first level of the ambo, read a passage, "—Better a poor man who walks in his integrity, than he who is false in his ways and rich. . . ." and returned it. The people knelt while the priest read a second collect, and rose again. The first deacon called for silence. Another deacon brought a lavishly bound volume of the

111

Apostles to the second level of the ambo, proclaimed the title, and read. Gratillonius thought Martinus must have chosen the shipwreck of Paulus in compliment to old sailor Corentinus. The deacon took the book back.

"Oh, all you works of the Lord, bless you the Lord," sang the choir. The response, "Praise Him and magnify Him forever," had not that soaring beauty, but force throbbed in it. Gratillonius kept silence. From the corner of an eye he saw how fervently Apuleius entered into the antiphony as it went on.

Meanwhile a subdeacon had lighted the incense in the censer. A rich odor wafted from it. The second deacon took the Gospel from the altar where it lay, the subdeacon censed it, and the deacon carried it to the third and highest level of the ambo. Resting it on the lectern, he announced the title, certain verses from holy Marcus. Seated clergy rose. "Glory to God Almighty," said the congregation.

The words welled up: "—And Lord Jesus told them: Pay Caesar what is Caesar's and God what is God's. . . ."

The book was returned to the altar and the choir sang a brief anthem from the Psalms. Again the first deacon called for silence and the priest on the ambo made announcements. Gratillonius's mind wandered elsewhere. Another collect followed.

Gratillonius's attention awakened when Bishop Martinus trod to the top of the bema steps and gave his sermon. Drawing its text from the Gospel passage, it was characteristically short and pointed. Gratillonius half felt the preacher's eyes were on him. "—doing what Caesar requires, or just what is necessary to sustain life and common decency, is not enough. It can even become the subtlest of temptations. We do well to be honorable, unless we make so much of that that it turns into pride and causes us to neglect the far higher duty we owe to God—"

If he meant a reproach, he set it aside afterward, when his fellow bishops led Corentinus to him. Having signed themselves, they formally named the candidate and intoned together, "Reverend Father, the churches at Aquilo and Confluentes beg you to raise up this present chore-

112

piscopus to the task of full bishop." Corentinus genuflected. Gratillonius's heartbeat quickened.

Martinus turned to the visiting leaders. "Speakers for those whose shepherd he shall be," he asked, "do you find this man worthy?"

Faith made no difference. A bishop must be acceptable to his entire community. When Gratillonius joined in replying, "He is worthy," he found himself stammering. Why? He had been instructed in everything that was to happen.

Martinus questioned Corentinus ritually and at length about his orthodoxy and intentions. Though equally stylized, the answers rang with sincerity. In the end, Martinus said, "May the Lord return these and other goods to you, and keep you safe, and strengthen you in all good."

A subdeacon brought a chasuble for Corentinus to don. Its rich blue, with glistening gold embroidery, looked out of place on his gauntness, but it was the work of loving hands at home. He knelt. Martinus prayed that he might prove a faithful and prudent servant over his family. The three bishops laid their hands on his head. "Receive the Holy Spirit," Martinus bade, "for the office and work of a bishop, now committed to you by the laying on of our hands; in the name of the Father, and of the Son, and of the Holy Spirit. Amen." Corentinus rose, hallowed.

The first deacon cried dismissal. It was time for catechumens, penitents, and infidels to leave. Gratillonius felt on his back the looks of Martinus, Corentinus, and Apuleius, about to enter the mystery that he denied. Its secrets were ill-kept, unlike those of Mithras, and he knew more or less what would take place; but for no sound reason, his exclusion hurt.

—However, those who stayed saw practices that had changed somewhat over the years. Offerings were now taken only from the baptized, while the choir sang. Thereupon the second deacon went to the top of the ambo and led a prayer for God's mercy on sinners and the ignorant. He then took a diptych, conjoined tablets of cedarwood with heavy silver covers, and saying, "May you show mercy, Lord, on Your servant—" read out every name inscribed, beginning with that of Emperor Honorius, con-

113

tinuing through bishops present and past, the martyr Symphorianus whose holy relics rested here, on to various living and departed members of the congregation whom there was special reason to name. At the altar Martinus prayed for God to bless them, free the souls of the dead from suffering, and let "this oblation converted to Christ's flesh and blood be effective." He ended with the words "through Our Lord Jesus Christ," and the people answered, "Amen."

The Gospel was taken to the cupboard and a linen cloth spread over the altar. On it were set the chalice and a ewer of water, while fresh incense went into the censer. A brief prayer proclaimed belief in the Trinity, confessed frailty, begged for forgiveness, and ended with the mutual "Amen."

A deacon took the chalice to the offertory table and half filled it with wine; another chose some of the bread donated and set it directly on the altar cloth. Martinus poured water into the wine. A deacon covered the Elements with a napkin. Words went to and fro: Let us greet one another. Peace be with you. And with your spirit.

Martinus kissed Corentinus, they both in turn kissed their brother bishops, these passed it on to the rest of the clergy and to the laity, who exchanged kisses. Meanwhile Martinus prayed aloud for mercy, remission of sins, and "that whosoever are joined in the kiss be more bound to each other and hold with affection in the breast that which is offered with the mouth."

Congregation: "Amen."

Martinus: "Let us lift up our hearts."

Congregation: "We have, to the Lord."

Martinus: "Let us return thanks to the Lord our God."

Congregation: "It is meet and just."

Martinus: "It is meet and just to give thanks to the Lord, Holy Father, Almighty Eternal God, Whose Son was born of a virgin, through the Holy Spirit; and being made man shrank not from the shame of a human beginning; and through conception, birth, and the cradle, and infant cries traversed the entire course of the reproach and humiliations of our nature. His humiliation is the ennobling of us, His reproach is our honor; that He as God

114

should abide in our flesh is in turn a renewal of us from fleshly nature into God. In return for the affection of so vast a condescension, for which the angels praise Your majesty, the dominations adore it, the powers tremble before it, the heavens, the heavenly virtues, and blessed seraphim with a common jubilation glorify it, we beseech You that we may be admitted to join our humble voices with theirs, saying—"

All: "Holy, holy, holy, Lord God of Sabaoth. Heaven and earth are full of Your glory. Blessed are You through the ages."

While Martinus prayed onward, he and the other bishops each touched every piece of bread on the altar, and the chalice. "— This is the cup of the New Testament in My blood—" The prayers ended with the Lord's.

Martinus: "Free us from evil, Lord, free us from all evil, and establish us in every good work, You Who live and rule with the Father and the Holy Spirit forever and ever."

All: "Amen."

The choir sang an anthem as the four bishops broke up the loaves of bread. They took care that no crumbs fall on the floor; it was now Christ's body. Two subdeacons stood with peacock fans to keep away insects. The clergy took the Food and the Drink first, in order of rank, starting with Martinus; after them the choir, one at a time, while the rest sang antiphonally the Thirty-Fourth Psalm ("Oh, taste, and see, how gracious the Lord is—"); last the other laity, ending with the doorkeepers. As a communicant came to the altar, he or she held out the right hand cupped in the left, and Corentinus placed a fragment of bread in it, saying, "Receive the body of Christ." The worshipper responded "Amen" and bowed head to take it. Thereafter he or she moved to the other end of the altar, where Martinus held out the chalice and said, "Receive the blood of Christ." Again the worshipper said, "Amen," bowed head, and sipped.

When everyone had finished, Martinus said, "Restored by Heavenly food, revived by the drinking cup of the Lord, we return praise and thanks to God the all-powerful Father through Our Lord Jesus Christ."

115

"Amen," they responded.

The chief deacon called on them to bow their heads once more. Martinus prayed for the hearing of prayers and for guidance. "Amen," they answered.

Martinus: "Peace be with you."

All: "And with your spirit."

Martinus: "Go, it is sent."

All: "Thanks be to God."

—Well, Gratillonius thought, his part was done. As soon as his friends were ready, he'd start home with them.

VII

1

Westward over Ocean, mists dimmed and reddened the sun-disc, brought the edge of sight ever closer to the headlands. Elsewhere the sky was gray, already darkening above eastern hills, and shadow filled the valley that ran out of them. Cliffs on either side of the bay hulked darkling. Wind eddied between, acrid with strand-smells. Though still some distance off, surf overwhelmed its whimpers.

"Once more," Evirion urged. "Only once, while the tide is out. Tomorrow morning we'll be off."

Nemeta shook her head. Locks blew rusty about the whiteness of her face, the hugeness of her eyes. She hugged her tunic to her against the chill. "Nay," she said thinly. "We have enough. And we've dared more than we should, in this world or the Other."

"A single great find, and we're not merely provided for, we're wealthy. Powerful. We can do whatever we will— for our people, Nemeta; for our Gods." Whoever They may be, Evirion did not add.

"But I feel the menace yonder. Sharper than this breeze. A wind out of the future." Nemeta waited until she had his look directly upon her. "You trusted me to find where treasures lay buried, and I did. Now trust me when I say Stop. Best would be if we departed on the instant." She gestured with her head at the amphitheater behind them. It had been their shelter these past three days and nights since they arrived at Ys. "We can sleep in one of the forsaken houses above the vale. If first we cover our tracks." That would not be quite simple, when they had two laden mules. Evirion had earned them by toiling for an Osismiic farmer; they were so aged and weak that that was possible for him in the time since he was released from labor for the community.

He laid hand to sword, a laurel-leaf blade of Ysan make. "What is it you dread?"

"I know not. I've a foreboding. It grew on me hour by hour today." She turned her gaze left, south, where Aquilonian Way climbed the steeps before bending east toward Audiarna.

He himself squinted west. The tide had in fact turned and was flowing in, though it would not lap at the ruins farthest inland for a few hours yet. Well before then, he gauged, everything would be shrouded in fog. If aught more was to be done there, it must be done soon—or on the morrow, but he had acceded to her and promised that then they would leave at first light.

That was a pledge readily given. The city he loved had become an uncanny place, a haunting ground. Several times he had thought he glimpsed something white that danced more than swam in the waves among the rocks; fragments of song had frightened him with their allurement. He had said nothing to Nemeta about it, as uneasy as she was, and to himself insisted it must be mistake, illusion, dream giving half-life to wind and sea.

"I thought the danger all lay that way," he said. Indeed it was tricky to scramble over stones broken, tumbled, slippery with water and weed, where glass shards lurked, and to pry them apart and grope downward—though worse was turning up a human bone or a skull to which the

117

drenched hair still clung. Had you danced in those arms, traded kisses with that mouth?

But the gems and precious metals were there, the ransom of freedom. No single hoard yielded them as Evirion hoped; they were spread among what had been buildings, scattered by currents and the shifting of ruins as ground settled. Without the peculiar talent Nemeta had found herself to possess, the searchers would have needed a month to find what they amassed in days. As was, they bought every small gain with hurtful travail, hour by hour until darkness or waves made work impossible and they stumbled back to the amphitheater carrying their laden sacks, bolted cold food, and toppled into sleep through which walked nightmares.

Evirion came to think that it was as if the Gods mocked him: the Three of Ys, Taranis the Thunderer, Belisama the All-Mother, Lir of the Deeps, dethroned, homeless, become trolls. He denied it with every force he could summon, but it gnawed past his defenses like the sea undermining the foundations of the city. If not They, then Someone laired here and hated everything human.

Abrupt rage burned away doubt and fatigue. He would not surrender. If only by a gesture, he would declare his manhood.

"Well, stay behind and nurse your woman-fears," he snapped. "I'm bound on a last questing."

She stared at him, stricken. "Without me?"

"As you wish. I've no more use for your wand. Half the public coffers were in the basilica, and that's what I'll attempt."

He turned on his heel and stalked to the gateway outside which the tethered mules grazed. Within it were stored the boxes for loot—not that he used the word to himself—together with bags, spades, picks, crowbars. Grabbing up his tools, he strode down the broad path that led to Aquilonian Way. Grass had begun to thrust upward between its paving blocks.

Through wind and surf he heard feet patter. He glanced behind. Nemeta hurried after him. Her long, bare legs glimmered in the dull light. She carried another bar in her left hand. Her right clutched the forked stick, graven with signs, that dipped in her grasp to show where they should dig.

118

"Are you coming after all?" he asked with a gladness that surprised him.

"I'd not . . . have you alone . . . out there," she answered unsteadily.

Or yourself alone ashore, he refrained from saying. " 'Twill be quick, you know. Soon dark. Whether or not we've found anything, we'll come back and—and start a fire, enjoy hot food and our last wine, make celebration."

A slight smile trembled on her lips.

Desire stirred in him. She was attractive in her spare, half-grown fashion; so much life surged through her. On the coldest nights they had joined their bedrolls together, and he was hard put to honor his promise of chastity. Mayhap when they were safe—

Wreckage and remnants strewed the beach less thickly than at first. From the lack of valuables there, Evirion supposed that someone, possibly a gang or two of barbarian sailors, had picked it over. Since, bit by bit, spring tides reclaimed the debris. Doubtless the steepening of slopes helped. Without the wall for protection, the sandstone under Ys wore away as fragments rolled grinding across it. The caverns dug underneath had begun to collapse. Each time that happened, not only did whatever had rested on top fall into the hole, but earthquake-like shock brought low more of what had been standing elsewhere. The bottom dropped sharply toward depths of ten or twelve fathoms. Pieces of the dead city slid thither as currents tugged them, to be forever lost. A few decades from now, he guessed, nothing would be left save whatever was above extreme high water. Amphitheater, pharos, necropolis, the solitary headstone of Point Vanis—and even those? Somehow the lighthouse was half its olden height. . . .

Man and girl clambered over the rubble that had been High Gate. Stumps of wall lifted on either side, like teeth in a jawbone. Lir Way was almost as choked. Courses of stone, pillars still upright, statues battered nearly into shapelessness, thrust forlornly above. The same chaos reached right, left, ahead, in some places mound-high, in others roughly leveled. Wetness sheened, kelp sprawled, three cormorants wheeled black overhead. The wind whistled.

119

The Forum had been sufficiently wide that parts of it remained clear, aside from shards. The lowest bowl of the Fire Fountain stood, filled with chunks of the upper ones and with seawater that the wind ruffled. On the northeast side, the basilica was recognizable. Several of its columns rose over the detritus in the portico. The roof had fallen in but the walls mostly survived, however scarred and weakened. Hitherto, given Nemeta's guidance, Evirion had sought easier unearthing. But it should be possible to clear the outer doorway leading to the treasury. With luck, in the time that was left them they might work part of the contents free.

Nemeta drew a ragged breath. "Hark. Do you hear?" she whispered.

He squinted westward as she pointed. Lowtown was a pit of gloom into which the waves were marching, forward, back, forward again and higher. He could not see them because of the fog bank, but he heard their roar and the rattle of loosened stones. And—a voice? A song? *O wearyfoot wanderer—*

"Nay!" he answered, louder than he had intended. "Wind, water, belike a seabird. Come. We must hasten."

He led her around to the side of the building that fronted on Taranis Way. They mounted the stairs. As he had noticed earlier, the bronze door there lay wrenched off its hinges. The space beyond was piled with refuse, but that was more broken tile than it was stone or roof beams, and only about three feet deep. Nemeta halted, laid down her bar, took the forked wand in both hands, closed her eyes, soundlessly moved her lips.

He had expected to see the end of the stick lift and point ahead, yet it fired his hopes. "To work!" he said, and attacked.

Nemeta cried out.

Evirion dropped his bar and turned. Around the corner of the building had come four men. Weapons lifted ugly in their hands.

The foremost gestured. "Hem 'em in," he rapped in harsh Latin. The rest jumped, one to his right, two to his left, making a semicircle under the stairs.

Evirion's vision pounced among them. Everything registered, noonday-stark in the fading light. They were tough, dirty, unkempt, clad in tunics and breeches that had seen much wear and little washing. Each belt bore a knife. The leader was an ursine blackbeard with a broken nose. He carried a short ax. His companions were slighter, never well-nourished, but equally evil-looking. Their arms were a spear, a bill, and a nail-studded club.

"Who are you?" Evirion called in their language. No need to ask their purpose, said his suddenly lightning-swift mind. He knew this breed, waterfront toughs without tribe or ethic.

The leader grinned. "Ullus of Audiarna, at your honor's service. And you, sir, and the young lady?"

"We are here by right. How dare you invade our home and profane our shrines? Be off before the Gods strike you!"

It was a belly sickness to hear Ullus laugh. His followers leered, uncomfortably but also unflinching. "Why, I guess we've as much right as anybody else to help ourselves," he said. "There'll be plenty more later on. We thought we'd got the idea first, but we found your tracks—your animals, your stores." Again his elation boomed. "Thanks for doing so much work for us."

Nemeta lifted her wand. It trembled as she did, and her voice: "I witch. Go. Or I curse."

The schoolchild Latin actually seemed to hearten the newcomers. Ullus licked his lips. "You'll feel different pretty soon," he told her. "Me and my boys know how to break a filly for riding, hey?"

Evirion drew sword. "I am a seaman of Ys," he stated. "You're from Audiarna, you said? That's a seaport. You know what I mean. Come any closer and you're dead."

Ullus's mirth gave way to rage. His ax chopped the air. "How I do know your kind, you! Or did, afore God brought you down in your pride and sins, like the preacher always told He would. Do *you* know how it is being poor all your life, dock walloper, deckhand, ordered around, worked till you drop, fed like nobody 'ud feed a pig, paid off in nummi, and the boot or the whip if we speak up? And meanwhile your ships from Ys 'ud swagger by, with you on deck in your gold and silk. Well, that's done with,

121

fellow. The high are brought low and the low are brought high, like Christ promised. We're here to claim our share. Now drop that blade and come down slow. We may leave you your stinking life. But you got to behave yourself. Understand?"

Evirion did. They'd never let him past. They knew he might well outrun them, seize the mules, make off with the treasure. So at best, they'd hold him bound and vent their grudges on him till they were ready to leave. And then it would be safest for them to cut his throat and toss him out for the eels. As for Nemeta—

Trained in combat, he was more than a match for any of them. But they were four, two with pole weapons. Something like a plucked harpstring keened within him. He stood beyond himself and saw he was become an instrument whereon Belisama played, She in Her avatar the Wild Huntress.

He bent close to the girl. Her stare was blank, face wet with more than mist; he heard the short breaths go in and out. "Listen well," he whispered in Ysan. "I'll attack them. You run to the left at once. Hide in this jumble. After dark, slip off to the hills. Do you hear?"

He might have been talking to a noosed hare. "You can't help me," he went on. "Go home. Tell them what happened. Cast a spell against these creatures if you like. Remember me, Nemeta. Go."

"Are you coming, or must we fetch you?" yelled a man.

"Easiest to throw rocks at him," said Ullus loudly.

"Ya-a-ah!" Evirion hallooed, and bounded downward.

He saw the broken visage gape open in surprise. He was there. He stabbed. Almost, he killed. Ullus's ax met his sword in midthrust and knocked it aside. He barely kept a grip on it. His speed carried him by. The bludgeon brushed his shoulder. That threw him spinning. He lurched a pair of yards, recovered, whirled about in a crouch.

Three men milled and howled in his direction. Beyond them, atop the stairs, he saw Nemeta dash off. So, said a remote voice, that's as it should be. Let me hold them for two or three minutes till she's safely away.

The spearman poised with his weapon and cast. It flew in a long arc, upward, directly before her shins. She fell

122

over the shaft and toppled, step by step, a whirl of limbs and hair. He was off to meet her, ferret-swift. She rolled to a stop and picked herself up. He got there and flung arms around her. She screamed. He hooted.

"Good work, Timbro!" Ullus bellowed. "Keep 'er for us too!" He swung to advance on Evirion. The billman and the clubber hung back. "Move, you scuts! Hold him busy and I'll hit him from the rear."

They gathered courage. Evirion thought he saw the dawn of pleasure on them. Ullus was triumphant. He had no reason to hide his plan. It was clear and certain. He sidled across the avenue, around the Ysan.

To stand and fight would be to die, uselessly. The spearman had Nemeta down on the pavement. She struggled. His fist struck her beneath the jaw. Her shrieks dropped to a thin wailing, her movements to feebleness. Between them and Evirion were the rest of the band.

He sheathed his sword, whipped about, dodged out onto the Forum, and ran.

For a brief while he heard shouts and footfalls at his back. Then he was alone. None of them could match his fleetness; and even now, he had some knowledge of Ys. He zigzagged, climbed, slipped in and out among huge shattered remnants, until he had shaken pursuit. Still he kept on. He knew not why. It was as if the sea drew him.

Yet hard was the way he must fare. Down here the stones only saw sky when water was very low. Shells encrusted them, for hands and knees to flay themselves. Green weed wrapped them, slimy to make feet lose footing. Strange things grew, swam, scuttered in pools between. Fog swirled ever thicker and more cold. Through the blindness that it wove beat ever louder the rumble, rush, plash, smack, growl of waves. Evirion cast himself down at their verge.

He could dimly see a few feet in the wet smokiness. A rock lay fallen upon lesser ones. They were paving stones and building blocks; it was rudely hewn, if men had ever given it any of its shape—a megalith. He had come to Menhir Place, where Ys preserved a relic of an age ere ever the city was. What, had this first and last piety also been overthrown? Or was its raw mass the sign of a doom spoken at the founding of the world?

Evirion's panting faded into a sigh. He knew just that he too was broken. His emprise had enriched barbarians (aye, barbarians swarmed out of Rome as well as the wild lands; a carcass breeds maggots) and destroyed a girl. His strength had drained away with his hopes. The shoulder that the bludgeon had scraped throbbed with pain. The rent cloth around it hung sodden with blood. Water licked him, higher at every wave. The fog hooded his eyes, laid salt on his mouth, like tears.

Through the blood-beat in his skull he thought he heard a song again. Peace without end, love to enfold him as does the sea, all he need do was abide and she would come. Did the mists eddy together and form a wraith of her whiteness in the dusk? It was her lips that tasted of salt, her kiss.

Desire torrented upward. He rose, spread his arms, called into the deep noises, "Here I am. We'll go and snare the rest, won't we? I'll bring you their bones to play with out on the reefs."

A snarling gave answer, and a giggle in the wind.

The wind lifted. It blew him back shoreward. Or else he was the wind and the fog and the following sea. He flowed across rocks, poured along broken pillars, swept over tumbled roofs, a salmon bound upstream, an orca in the final shearing rush at a seal. The sword flared free.

In Taranis Way, the last man got up and belted his breeches. The red-haired girl sprawled at his feet. "Ready for another go, anybody?" he crowed. He was young, the fuzz thin across a face raddled with sores and pimples.

Nemeta stirred. Her eyes stayed shut, but she pulled at the hem of her tunic, trying to bring it down, while she squirmed about so as to lie curled tightly on her side.

"Nah," said Ullus. He cast an uneasy glance west across the Forum. Wind rumpled his beard and shrilled in his ears. Darkness advanced yonder, a wall of it from which gray tatters flew. "We've spent too much time with her as is. Might be sunset—who can tell through that stuff? Back to camp, their camp where the gold is, while we can still see what we're doing."

"Tomorrow'll be soon enough for work," agreed the spearman. He nudged the girl with his foot. "Up, you." When she merely shivered, he kicked.

"Hey, easy," said the youth. "Don't spoil that nice, tight thing. If she can't walk, gimme a hand with her."

"Ah, she can walk, all right." The clubber spat. "Stubborn bitch. I'll teach her better."

"Move!" rasped Ullus. "Never saw fog come in so fast or so heavy."

The boy and the pikeman dragged the girl half upright and shoved her along. She stumbled between them, eyes still closed. A bruise was starting to blossom on her jaw. Blood trickled down her thighs.

The vapors whirled around. Ullus swore. "Stick close. We'll have to feel our way. If anybody strays, he'll likely be lost till morning in this damned spook-hole—"

He with the sword sprang out of the brume. Steel smote. Ullus staggered, dropped his ax, clutched his belly, stared astounded at the red and the entrails that fell out between his fingers. "Why, why, can't be," he mumbled and went down on his face. There he threshed for a short while. The tall man with the sword was gone.

The three yelled fury and threats. They formed a triangle, back to back. The wind snickered and flung a deeper blanket over them.

The spearman shouted, "There!" and jabbed at a shadow. It was only a clot of mist. The tall man glided under the shaft and struck upward, into the throat. The club whirred at him but he was gone and it smote a toppled statue. That blow knocked a chip out of the sculptured mouth so that it no longer smiled but sneered.

Nemeta's eyes were open. The two who were left had none for her. They stood gaping into sightlessness. She slipped from them.

"We've got to keep moving," gasped the clubber. "You face right, I'll face left. Crabwise, got me?"

They advanced a few paces, reached a wall whose remnant top they could not see, moved along it. He with the sword leaped from above. He landed on the shoulders of the clubber, who went down with a sound of breaking spine and ribs. The clubber lay where he had fallen, for he had no movement below the waist. He flailed his arms about and ululated. The spit bubbled red in his beard.

"No!" yammered the boy. "Please, please! I'm sorry!" He dropped his bill and fled. The tall man followed leisurely.

—Evirion found Nemeta halfway up Taranis Way, resting on a wing that had fallen off a stone gryphon. His blade dripped, but the hue was pale, fog settling on the steel and running down to carry the blood away. Surf noises sounded louder. The wind had died.

He stood and stared at her, barely able to see through the murk. "How are you?" he asked hoarsely.

She raised her head. "I live," she answered without tone. "I can travel if we go easily. And you?"

"Unhurt save for this shoulder, which isn't too bad." He left off mention of scrapes, cuts, and bruises from his scramble to the sea. "Tomorrow the carrion birds will make dung of those bandits."

"How did you do it?"

"I know not. Something other than my own spirit had me. Something that laughed as It bargained—four lives in exchange for our two."

She hugged herself, bit her lip, climbed painfully to her feet. "Then the deal is completed, and we'd best depart while we can," she said.

"Aye." He gave her his free arm to lean on. "Nor ever return. Unwise was I to come. The Gods I trusted are evil, or mad. Never can I make amends to you."

She looked before her, into the unrestful gloom through which they groped. "You did not compel me," she said wearily.

"At least," he vowed, "you shall have your full share of what we did win."

She shook her head. "I'll take none of it. Cast it from you."

"Hoy? After what 'tis cost us?" He overcame his shock. "And what it means to my life. How can you say that? What knowledge have you?"

"No more than you have of what happened this eventide—" All at once she could walk no farther. She swayed, her knees buckled. He caught her.

"Poor lass," he mumbled. "Poor hurt lass." He sheathed

his sword and took her up. "Here, lay your arms around my neck. I'll carry you back. At dawn we'll leave. If you refuse the gold, well, you may always call on me for whatever else is in my gift. Always."

She nestled her head against him. "I'll remember that," she whispered.

2

Mons Ferruginus and the woods beyond the Odita blazed with autumn, red, russet, yellow under the earliest sun-rays. Dew glittered on grass, vapors curled white above the stream. It ran through an enormous silence, beneath blue spaciousness. Air lay chill but already full of earth odors.

No one else was about when Gratillonius left Aquilo. Folk were sleeping late after last night's festivities. Tables had been modestly spread, in this year when the neighborhood divided what it had with the survivors of Ys, but drink was plentiful and merriment, after a while, feverish. As early as manners allowed, he had retired to a bed in the Apuleius home. His own was too close to the noise.

Not that he begrudged the people their celebration. They had earned it. They were alive, safe, housed; more toil and hardship lay before them, but nothing they could not overcome. When Corentinus dedicated Confluentes, he simply gave utterance to the fact of the colony. It was built. Most of its inhabitants occupied their dwellings, the rest would as soon as they had finished whatever obligations they had assumed in the course of earning their keep. Well might they cheer for Gratillonius their tribune, Grallon their King.

Wryness twisted the man's mouth. He was neither, of course. If his appointment was not revoked, that was merely because no one in the Imperial administration had thought to do so. As for his throne, it was under the sea with the bones of his Queens.

He strode on. Gravel scrunched underfoot. He needed something to do, anything. Well, he had no lack. But decision, organization, leadership required others be present. He thought he'd seek the manor, where Favonius was stabled, saddle the stallion and ride into the forest. Take spear and bow along; he might have a chance at a deer or a boar. Afterward, the tension out of him, maybe he could start arranging the woodworking shop he wanted. The one in Ys had given him pleasure and, aye, peace.

Should he have become a carpenter? He might this day dwell quietly in Britannia with wife and . . . sons; oh, daughters too, the older ones married and giving him grandchildren. But he wasn't born to that station. Anyway, somebody had to keep guard over the carpenter's hearth.

At the upper bridge he lingered a few minutes. The air was so pure, the river so serene. How different from yesterday. Here Corentinus had stood and preached his sermon, while the bank and the harvested field beyond were packed solid with people, not simply those of Ys—of Confluentes but nearly everyone in Aquilo. After all, Corentinus was their bishop now, the first resident bishop they had ever had. Old Maecius had retired to the monastery at Turonum. You could sense a new order of things being born. Conversion of the pagan immigrants to the Faith would be just the beginning.

The rough voice echoed in Gratillonius's head: "—thanks to almighty God and His Son, our Lord and Saviour Jesus Christ, for Their manifold mercies. May the Holy Spirit descend to sanctify and bless these homes—" Mainly, however, as usual, Corentinus had talked to the commoners like one of their own. "—'Love your neighbor' isn't any simpering bit of goody-goodyness, you know. It's as tough a commandment as was ever laid on a man. Often you'd like to bash your neighbor's head in, or at least kick him in the butt. You Aquilonians, and I include the surrounding tribesfolk, you've been mighty kind to these outcasts; and you Ysans have been brave, and mostly done your best to make some return; but I know of quarrels, or outright blows, wrongs done on both sides, and it could get worse instead of better as time wears on. Doesn't have to, though. We're none of us saints, but we can be honest and reasonably patient with the neighbor. We can all stand together against whatever troubles come on us, in this world where Satan always prowls on the lookout for souls he can snatch. — "

Gratillonius wondered why the words stayed with him. He'd heard their like aplenty during the years Corentinus was in Ys, and they'd never been anything startling in the first place. Was it their impact on Julia that drove them into him? Lanarvilis's daughter had stood unwontedly solemn, intent, listening. Most times she was calm, even cheerful; when the memory of what she had lost struck fully into her, she didn't weep or brood or get drunk like many survivors, she grew quiet and kept extra busy. Suddenly she had seemed beautiful to him. Before, she was merely a large girl, well filled out, roundfaced, snubnosed, blue-eyed, her best feature the wavy reddish-brown hair.

Well, if she was to find consolation in Christ, good for her. Likewise had Gratillonius's mother, for whom he named the child. He hoped the religion wouldn't estrange her from him. It was a glow near the middle of the cold and hardness in him that she, after the alienation of the final months in Ys, again gave him not bare filial obedience but, he thought, some love.

As Forsquilis's daughter Nemeta had not—secretive, rebellious, runaway Nemeta. Since her vanishment in late summer Gratillonius had had no heart for revelry. They were dancing on the ground outside the ditch, beneath torches lashed to poles, when he left. Julia and young Cadoc Himilco had looked very happy together. Let them savor it for whatever short while they could.

Gratillonius shook himself. No use moping here. He crossed the bridge. It was of wood, like the one above the Aquilonian waterfront, but smaller, meant for workers on the Apuleius estate and in the forest to convey their produce. Confluentes would bring more traffic than that; something better was necessary. He found refuge in thinking about ways and means.

On the opposite shore, three sentries paced back and forth between the Stegir and the south end of the eastern earthworks. Regulars, but local, they were not legionaries nor outfitted like legionaries; that was a thing of the past. However, they did wear helmets and coats with iron rings sewed to the leather, they did carry swords, spears, and small round shields. If their bearing and movements weren't soldierly by ancient standards, at least they were alert and reasonably smart; they had learned from Maximus's veterans. The nearest of them recognized Gratillonius and snapped to a halt, thudding his spear down in salute. No law entitled Gratillonius to that, but so men did in these parts. He made an acknowledging gesture and passed on.

Confluentes lay around him, the town he and Corentinus had brought into being. A visitor from a city would find it unimpressive. It amounted to less than a hundred buildings between two streams and a breastwork with ditch, in a corner of cleared land whereof the rest would now be devoted to subsistence agriculture. The buildings were wood and clay under thatch roofs. The largest, oblongs of coarsely squared timber, held three or four rooms and had windows covered with membrane; the least were cylindrical wattle-and-daub shielings. Shops and worksteads were few, tiny, primitive. There was no marketplace, basilica, church, ornamentation; everything still centered in Aquilo. At this hour there was hardly a sign of life.

Nevertheless . . . the houses were well built, neatly kept. The streets ran in a Roman grid, with gravel on them. If men, women, children slept yet behind these walls, it was because yesterday they had rejoiced at what was done here and what might be done in years unborn.

He passed a house as long as any. It was for unmarried women, chief among them those who had been vestals of Ys. The door stood ajar. It opened, and Runa came out.

He stopped at her signal. For a moment they regarded each other. The daughter of Vindilis and Hoel wore a blue cloak over a plain gray gown. Its cowl was thrown back and the raven hair flowed free from under a headband, past the narrow face and the shoulders. "Well," she said at length, low and in Ysan.

"How are you?" he replied awkwardly, in Latin.

"Whither fare you this early?"

He shrugged.

"Restless, as often aforetime." From beneath the high arches of brow, her dark gaze probed him. The whiteness

130

of her skin made that look appear doubly intense. "I too. May I walk along with you?"

He wondered if she had thought him likely to come by and had waited. "I'd in mind to go hunting," he said brusquely.

"You may change your mind after we've talked. A private hour is rare for us."

"Well—as you wish." He set off again. She accompanied him without effort. The long skirt billowed and rustled.

"They missed you after you left last eventide," she said presently. "They wanted their King among them. It was a hallowing, after all."

"The Kingship is dead. Those Gods indwell no longer." He observed in faint surprise that he had also gone over to the Ysan tongue.

"Are you altogether sure, Gratillonius?" She seldom shortened his name as most people did. "I stayed not late myself. Drinking and dancing are not to my taste. But I'd heard the regret. You cannot abdicate."

"What do you want of me?" he growled.

"Why must you suppose I have a petition?"

He grinned lopsidedly. "From you 'twould be a demand. Ever has it been. Oh, I understand and respect. We clash, but we work toward the same end, and you've been a strong help. Shrewd, too."

Especially had she done what neither he nor Corentinus could, taken chieftainship among the women, spoken for them, found places where they could work with a measure of dignity, pressed in her acid fashion for a little of the freedom they had enjoyed in Ys. The bounds now around them were high and strait.

Runa sighed. "That nears an end. One by one they settle in, marry or find service that will endure and is endurable. Aye, you can grant me something. But 'twill be for the colony as well."

"What?"

"I suppose you've heard that I won myself paid occupation."

He nodded. "I've seen some of what you've done. Apuleius showed me."

Skilled copyists were always in demand. Runa was not

131

only literate, she could do calligraphy. Apuleius was eager to have duplicates of books on his shelves. He could trade them for volumes he did not possess—or, rather, trade the older editions and keep hers. She was well along with the *Metamorphoses* in spite of adding flourishes and figures that delighted the beholder.

"Corentinus admired it too when he returned," Gratillonius added. "I happened to be there. In fact, he asked whether you might replace the church's worn-out Gospel—I forget which one—after you've become a Christian."

"He takes much for granted, does he not, the holy man?" she murmured.

He threw her a startled glance. She gave him a look of—expectancy? "What would you of me?" he blurted.

"Apuleius has told me the family will no longer use the fundus. 'Twas never a profitable property; in the main, a retreat the children enjoyed, and they are growing up."

Gratillonius nodded. "Aye. The house lies outside the defense, you recall. Natheless, men have suggested I occupy it—for my palace? I'm content with my cabin in Confluentes. Still, I have thought—we'll hold occasional meetings, business concerning this community alone. The manor house our basilica? 'Twould be worthier than aught else we have."

"A good thought. In between, though, shall it stand deserted save for a caretaker? Nay, let me dwell there. I'll assemble a proper staff for its maintenance and for the reception of your . . . council. I'll have space and peace to carry on my work—which is more than copying books, Gratillonius."

Taken aback, he considered her proposal. It did look like having merit. True, tongues would wag. What of it? Females—widows, for instance—had commonly enough taken charge of places. "What more do you mean?" he inquired cautiously.

"Guidance," she said. "Counselling. I was a leader in Temple affairs. Let not my experience go to waste."

He harked back. After her vestalhood ended she had in fact made herself useful among the Queens until she married Tronan Sironai. Whatever happiness the pair had was brief. While no open breach occurred, most Suffetes knew she was soon ill content with the part of wife. She was much in company with the more intelligent young men of Ys; for them she put aside the dourness she bore at home. Rumor did not, though, make any of them her lovers. At last she took minor orders and busied herself in the Temple, where she handled her duties well. During the conflict between King and Queens she was wholly and bitterly of the latter party. However, since the whelming she had reconciled herself with Gratillonius. Sometimes, as today, she was outright amiable.

"Among females, I suppose," he ventured.

She frowned, parted her thin lips as if to retort to an insult, closed them again. When she spoke, it was stiffly. "Whoever may have need. 'Tis a cruel change we've all suffered. Many are worse wounded than you know." The tone softened. "Such as your child Nemeta."

He stopped in mid-stride and faced her. His heart stumbled and began to race. "You have news of her?"

Runa took his arm. "Walk onward. Folk will be astir. Best they see naught to make them wonder."

He fell into a mechanical gait. His throat felt engorged. "What can you tell me?" he demanded.

"First give me what information you have," she replied calmly.

"What? Why?"

"That I may know if any confidences remain for me to honor." After a moment she went on, against his outraged silence: "A girl can open her heart to an older woman as she cannot to her mother, or her father. Shall I betray her? Would you spill what a boy told you as he wept?"

He waged a struggle before he could answer: "Well, you recall I gave out she'd left to take a position offered her elsewhere, as nurse to the children of an honorable Gallic family. That was to shield her name."

"And yours," Runa said tartly. "Yet a clever story. With their educations, doubtless a number of well-born Ysan women will find themselves thus invited, once they're christened. Of course, Nemeta is fierce in her refusal to submit. What did she give you?"

"A scrawled note. I found it tucked into the sheath with

133

my sword, days after Rufinus and his men were scouring the woods for any spoor of her."

"They were? I was unaware. Everybody was."

"You were meant to be. Rufinus is cunning." Gratillonius sighed. "The note said she would suffer no more humiliation but had gone off to a better fate. That was all. Since then, naught." His jaw clenched till it hurt. "Now, by Ahriman, tell me what you know ere I wring it out of you."

"I've lately had word from her," Runa said. "Ask me not who bore it. She'd fain come back, but it must be on her terms. No questions, ever. A house built on a site away from these towns, which she will choose. Freedom to make her own life. That's a freedom you must stand guarantor of, Gratillonius, because 'twill defy the Church. Oh, no whoredom, naught sordid; but what Gods she serves will be old ones."

"Where is she? I'll go speak to her."

Runa shook her head. "My faith is plighted."

Again he stopped. They had passed out of Confluentes, through a gap in the north wall and a ridge of shored-up earth that led across the ditch, onto the path beyond. The sentries there had also saluted him. The manor house gleamed from behind a callous loveliness of autumnal trees. He seized her by the upper arms. "Dare you stand between me and my daughter?" he snarled.

The grip was bruising, but she held firm. "Let me go," she said: a command.

He dropped his hands. "That's better," she told him. "Henceforward give me my due respect, if you'd have any good of me; and God knows you need all the good you can find in this world, Gratillonius. My counsel is that you give Nemeta what she wants. Else you've lost her forever."

They stood a long while under the climbing sun. Finally he muttered, "I pray your pardon."

She smiled in her prim fashion. "I grant it. You were overwrought. Come, shall we seek the house, look it over, mayhap take an early stoup of wine? You'll require a span of ease ere you can realize your happiness is coming home."

He stared at her. How stately she stood. Beneath that gown was a body lithe and strengthful—

No! he cried at the sudden tide of lust. My Queens not a year dead, and she the daughter of one of them!

But likewise was Tambilis, for whom I put her mother Bodilis aside.

But that was at the behest of the Gods of Ys, Whom I have disowned.

But the law I think of is the law of Mithras. But it was never clear about this matter. Besides, I have disowned Mithras too.

But I was bound for life to my Queens alone.

The chill in that thought helped him master himself. "Aye, let's do so," he said. "And thank you."

3

Where the River Vienna joined the Liger they made a broad stretch of water always peaceful. Forest enfolded it and a small human settlement. To this place came Bishop Martinus at the beginning of winter's pastoral rounds.

He loved these journeys. They were not long and arduous, with strangers at the far end, like many farings he perforce made, as far as the praetorian seat at Augusta Treverorum; then old bones ached and thin flesh shivered for weariness. They took him from the cares of his episcopate both in the city and the monastery. Those were heavy of late. Bricius, his disciple whom he had named to be his successor, now looked on him as a crazy dotard clinging to notions of poverty which might once have brought men nearer God but surely no longer served the needs of Mother Church and her princes. In the country-side harvest was ended, weather still mild, ordinary folk and the little children had leisure to meet him on his way, listen to him talk in language they understood, receive his blessing and mutely give him theirs.

But this year trouble pursued him even there. Word had come of a vicious quarrel in the presbytery where the

135

rivers met. He would compose it if he could. With a few companions he set off down the Liger in his barge.

They arrived beneath a low gray sky. Trees raised bare arms from the banks. Water sheened dully. Fisher birds dived and bobbed back into sight. Their cries rang loud in the stillness. Martinus pointed. "Behold," he said. "The demons are like that, ravenous, never sated." He lifted his voice. "Begone!" Feeble though the shout was, they immediately took off, a racket of wings through the wet air. Once up they made a military-like formation and flew out of the watchers' ken.

"A holy omen," breathed young Sucat.

The elders received the bishop with full reverence and took him uphill to lodge at the church. His attendants found pallets in their quarters or among humble families nearby. In the next pair of days, Martinus brought the factions to amity. "Put down your pride," he told them. "For your sake, Christ let Himself be mocked and scourged and nailed to the Cross between two thieves. The least you can do is humble yourselves before one another."

Even as he labored, fever was in him. When time came to go on, he could not. He lay burning hot, lips cracked, eyes stabbed by what faint light entered the room. He allowed none to touch him, and refused straw to lie on; he would keep with his wonted sackcloth, and ashes thereto.

It was not that he wished to die. Too much remained to do. Once those who held watch on him heard the quavered prayer: "Lord, if my people still have need of me, I am ready to go to work again. But Your will be done."

In the days that followed, as word got about, a swarm arrived, monks, nuns, grief-stricken common folk. Nearly all must needs do without a roof, bleak though the season was, and live on whatever crusts they had brought along. Yet they were determined they would follow their shepherd to his last resting place.

When the presbyters saw death nigh, they asked Martinus if he would like to be shifted to a more comfortable position. "No," he whispered. "Leave me looking toward Heaven."

Then his tone strengthened. Wrath called out: "Why

are you standing there, you bloody fiend? You'll get nothing from me. I'm bound for Abraham's bosom. Go!"

He sank back. Breath rattled into silence. God's soldier departed, obedient to orders.

VIII

1

Axes rang in the forest, picks and spades grubbed at stumps, oxen hauled logs and bundles of brushwood south to Confluentes. Some land had been cleared during the summer, but that was for timber to make houses. Now men were readying a much wider ground to cultivate.

When nothing else claimed his attention, Gratillonius was there. In hard labor and rough comradeship lay healing of a sort. He did not lose prestige—Kings of Ys had been more like Ulysses or Romulus than today's Emperors— but rather gained admiration by strength, skill, and helpfulness. Besides, the faster the colony grew and began to export such things as lumber, the sooner his own position would be secure. At present he had scarcely a solidus to his name, nor any revenues to support himself in office and whatever public works might need undertaking. He could not continue much longer living on Apuleius's kindness. Indeed, the senator might find himself in trouble were it known that he put funds at the disposal of a man who had no clear Imperial standing.

Gratillonius cared little about that on his own account. The brash young centurion who had dreamed of becoming mighty and famous seemed altogether a stranger. What counted was his duty toward people who trusted him.

One day he happened to be the last homebound as the short period of winter light drew to an end. The gangs plodded quietly off, exhausted. Even Ysan commoners had never been accustomed to this kind of work; their

137

country was nearly treeless, open to the winds. Some among the loggers were of Suffete birth, too; there was scant other livelihood for them if they refused to become hirelings on established farms. Gauls bore the toil more easily, though it told on them also. Small groups of them had been arriving lately, piecemeal, not only Osismii but a few Veneti and Redones. They had heard tales of opportunities for a fresh start under leadership that bade fair to keep off the barbarian raids that Armorica once again dreaded.

Today, as Gratillonius was hewing, a man had appeared and asked that he come with him. Gratillonius recognized Vindolenus, a former Bacauda. Those who had followed Rufinus west and settled down as more or less law-abiding were generally still shy of the Roman authorities. They were apt to make their homesteads deep in the woods and well apart. There they worked tiny plots, hunted, fished, trapped, burned charcoal, to scratch out a living for themselves and whatever families they acquired. Despite their isolation, they formed a widely flung net which as King of Ys he had found invaluable for gathering information, transmitting messages he did not want to risk being intercepted, and keeping down banditry.

Thus he felt he could not deny this man's plea. "My oldest son, lord, he's deathly sick. If you'd bless him with your hands, he might live, you, the King."

"I wish that were so," Gratillonius sighed. "But whatever power of that kind ever was in Ys lay with its Queens. They're gone, the city is, and my Kingship with them."

"No, my lord, begging your pardon, but I can't believe all the magic's left you, King Gradlon that drove off the Franks." Like most Gauls, Vindolenus softened Gratillonius's name differently from Ysans.

"Well, if it'll make you happier, I'll come, but I can promise nothing—unless, if I think a physician may help, to bring one tomorrow." At least the woodsrunners did not blame Gratillonius for the whelming of Ys and hold him accursed. That was doubtless thanks largely to Rufinus.

It was more than an hour's walk along twisted game trails to the hut. The woman and the rest of her brood greeted him with pitiful joy. He needed patience, but at

138

last got from her an account of what she had tried, treatments and simples. They seemed as likely to avail as anything that anybody knew about in Aquilo. The boy lay twitching and muttering, eyes full of blankness. Gratillonius covered the burning forehead with his palm. "May health return here" was all he could think of to say.

"Won't you call on Belisama, lord?" asked Vindolenus. "She was the great Goddess of Ys, wasn't She?"'

A nasty sensation passed through Gratillonius. "It was . . . not mine to serve Her, so I ought not invoke Her." These folk must have offered to Cernunnos, Banba, whatever ancient deities they knew; they might well have added Christ for good measure. "Mithras, God of men, grant that this youth grow to manhood in Your sight." That hurt him to say, as hollow as it sounded within his skull.

Afterward he must take a little refreshment, else he would hurt feelings and give a bad omen. By the time Vindolenus had guided him back and said farewell, the sun was down.

A streak of cloud glowed furnace red to southwest. It was the single sign of warmth. Elsewhere the sky ranged from ice-green to bruise-purple. The Stegir gleamed steely through naked fields. Confluentes ahead, Aquilo more distant, Mons Ferruginus beyond the Odita were hunchings of darkness touched by fugitive light-glimmers. Nearer was a yellow hint of comfort from the windows of the former manor house, but it too seemed to huddle under the vacant sky. A low chill gnawed in the quiet.

Gratillonius shifted his ax from right to left shoulder and started across the plowland toward the path that ran along the lesser river past the house and thence to the colony and his dwelling there. A flock of rooks passed overhead; their calls were peculiarly lonesome. Abruptly he stopped and peered.

Vague in the dusk, a horseman came from the northern verge of forest, off one of the tracks that snaked among its trees and brush, out into the open. He drew rein and appeared to look around, as if to get his bearings. Alone, though that seemed like an excellent mount he had—He wasn't far. Gratillonius broke into a trot. "Hail!" he called, first in Latin, then in Osismiic. "Wait for me. I'm friendly."

Whoever this was, he'd need a roof tonight, at least. It behooved the headman of Confluentes to offer it. And a newcomer with new tales to tell should be welcome in a season when few people traveled. Through Gratillonius's mind passed a line from the Christian scriptures he had several times heard Bishop Martinus use. "Be not forgetful to entertain strangers; for thereby some have entertained angels unawares." Odd how those words stayed with him. Well, they were solid counsel, like much else he'd heard from the same lips. Where now did old Martinus lodge?

As he drew close, he thought the rider tensed. It was hard to be sure. A voluminous cloak with the hood drawn up muffled what looked like a small, slender frame. Though a wan blur in vision, the face showed fine-boned and smooth. Was this a boy? Gratillonius put down his ax and advanced with hands widespread. Any traveler might well be skittish these days, meeting an armed man by twilight. Gratillonius himself was prepared to spring aside at the first hint of treachery.

He heard a broken scream, and halted. "Father!" wailed through the shadowiness, in Ysan. "Is that truly you?"

Lightning rived. Amidst the thunder that followed, Gratillonius called, "Aye. W-welcome, Nemeta. Welcome home."

He stumbled closer. She urged the horse aside. Something like choked sobs jerked from under the cowl. "Be not afraid," he begged. "I gave my promise. Why did the messenger, whoever that was—did he really take so long to reach you? Or did you linger? Why? I'll keep faith. You shouldn't have fared without an escort. But welcome."

Control regained, she lifted a hand. How frail it was. "Hold," she said unevenly. "I pray you, stand where you are. You've . . . surprised me. I was bound for the big house yonder. Runa is there, nay? She—she and I—I hoped she'd meet with you ere—I did."

He obeyed. His own hands dangled helpless. "I know Runa's been the go-between," he said dully. "But what have you to fear from me? I'll give you all you asked for. If

140

I can't talk better sense into you. Do let me try, Nemeta. For your own sake. I plight you there'll be no scolding. Follow me to my house in Confluentes. We'll talk, unless you'd liefer go to bed when you've eaten. I've been in such a nightmare about you, but now you're home again. Naught else matters."

Starkness replied: "Your fears were well founded. Behold." She drew the cloak back. Enough hueless light was left for him to see the swelling under her tunic.

"Yea," she said, "thus it is. I fled in quest of freedom. Along the way I was caught and violated. I escaped, and in another place had a protector. He's an honorable man who never touched me save as brother might sister. After your answer to my message came, 'twas a while ere I could bring myself to leave, for by then I could no longer lie to myself about the state I was in. But at last 'twas clear that to bide where I was would be worse than my life here had been. I used some money given me to buy this horse, boy's guise, bedroll, provisions. Along byways, sleeping in thickets at night, I returned. Ask me no more—you promised—for this is everything I will ever tell."

Gratillonius had met the same glacial resolve in her mother Forsquilis. "I won't," he pledged, flat-voiced. "Of course I'm bound to wonder."

What had her hope been, the wild fancy of a girl in whom ran witch blood and soldier blood? Where had she gone? Who had forced her, and what had become of the creature? (Oh, to catch him, beat him flat, cut off his parts, gouge out his eyes, and—the Osismii knew what to do with their foulest criminals—set the hounds on him!) Where afterward had she wandered? Who was her benefactor—a Christian, maybe a cleric, hoping to win a convert or simply acting in the charity his faith enjoined? Had she any other friends?

"Seek not to find out!" she shrilled. "Leave what's happened in its grave!"

"If that be your wish." Gratillonius drew breath. "But come. All the more have we need to talk, to reason out how best we can provide for you and—" his throat thickened— "the child." My first grandchild, he thought. This.

141

He could barely see her head shake. "Nay. Let me go to Runa as I'd meant. Leave me a while in peace." She struck heels to the horse and cantered off. Night quickly reclaimed sight of her. He stood where he was a long time before he went onward.

—In Confluentes next day was much excitement. Evirion Baltisi came back. He was well outfitted and mounted, as were the several men hired to accompany him. In Gesocribate, he said, waited a ship he owned. Thence he had traveled around Armorica, assessing conditions and prospects. Here he would spend the winter, engaging and instructing crewmen. In spring they would go to the ship and take her on the first of many merchant ventures. Little more would he tell; but youth and eagerness blazed from him.

2

The new year might be more hopeful than the last. Weather grew springlike well before the vernal equinox. Corentinus took advantage of it, holding meetings outdoors whenever possible, beyond the colony wall. There he exorcised evil spirits, taught the Faith, and answered questions before large groups. Otherwise, lacking any building of size, he must needs see one or a few persons at a time, whenever it could be arranged—oftenest in their homes. He got little rest.

Rufinus perched himself atop the breastwork and observed such a gathering from that distance. When it ended and folk straggled back toward their occupations, he bounded down, across the ditch, over the field till he drew alongside Evirion. "Hail," he said in Latin, with his warmest smile. "How are you?"

The young man squinted at him. Their acquaintance was slight. "Why do you care?" he replied curtly, using the same tongue. Among the Romans he had gained full command of it.

"Oh, it's polite," said Rufinus. "However, I really would like to hear. I've been gone for some time."

Off on what errands? Maybe Gratillonius knew. "There are enough people to give you the gossip," Evirion snapped. "I'm healthy, thank you. I'm also busy."

Rufinus matched his stride. "Bear with me, please. I approached you for a reason. If you can spare an hour, I'd like to bring you to my house and pour you a cup of wine. It's decent stuff."

Evirion scowled. "You're Grallon's man."

"What, are you his enemy?"

"Well—" Evirion seized on an Ysan saying. "He and I are not surf and seal."

"Nor keel and reef," answered Rufinus likewise. Again in Latin: "Do come. You needn't respond to any questions you don't want to. And you could learn something."

Evirion considered, shrugged, nodded. Together they walked across the earthen way and through the portal. Evirion glanced at a sentry. "Why does Grallon insist on that absurd watch?" he grumbled. "If a foe was coming, we'd know in plenty of time to man the defenses."

"Not necessarily," Rufinus maintained. "Anyhow, it helps keep the men in training." They continued along the street. "I wish you'd put your hostility to him aside," he added. "What happened was not his fault."

"Whose, then?" Evirion's tone became less aggressive, as if he truly wanted to know.

"The Gods'? *I* want no part of beings that would destroy a city, Their worshippers, just because of some dispute over morals. It's worse than atrocious, it's stupid—or insane."

"I'll agree to that," said Evirion slowly.

"Me, though," Rufinus went on, "I'll put the blame where it belongs, on a ruthless man, a greedy little slut, and sheer bad luck. I notice you're turning from the Gods of Ys, like nearly everyone else. In other words, you're ranging yourself with Gratillonius, where he always stood."

"No! I only—" Evirion's words turned into a grinding noise.

"You find it expedient to join the Christians. No offense." Rufinus squeezed the shoulder beside his. "I would too, if I had a reason like yours. What difference? We may as well bow down to one nothing as to another."

143

"Are you calling me a hypocrite?"

"Of course not. My humble apologies if I misspoke myself. Here we are." Rufinus opened the door of a wattle-and-daub hut and left it thus for light. As yet, no one in Confluentes possessed a lock, nor had any been needed.

Primitive, the dwelling was nonetheless soundly built. Already Rufinus was crowding it with a jackdaw collection of oddments—carvings, curiously shaped vessels, shells, pebbles, toys, a childish charcoal drawing on a wooden slab—as well as weapons, clothes, and utensils. If not quite neat, it was clean. Rushes covered the floor around a firepit. Furniture amounted to a pallet and two stools.

At a gesture, Evirion sat down. Rufinus poured from a jug into clay cups, gave him one, and joined him. "To your fortune," said the Gaul, and drank.

"What's that picture?" asked Evirion, to clear the air.

"By Korai. The little girl who was at the Nymphaeum, you know, granddaughter of Queen Bodilis. She comes visiting whenever she can. We're great friends. I'm her Uncle Rufinus."

Evirion cast a quizzical glance at this man who had never married, but inquired simply, "What do you want of me, out of all the rest?"

"News," said Rufinus. "You've been about in places and ways I haven't, couldn't."

"Are you simply curious?"

"Of course. Wouldn't you be? But I'm not so foolish as to try lying to you. The more I know, the better help I can give Gratillonius." Sudden pain twisted the lean face more than the scar ever did. "I was ignorant before, or blind, or cowardly, and—Disasters squat all around us, waiting to happen."

Evirion sensed a guard let down and attacked. "Would you turn Christian if he did?"

Mercurial, Rufinus recovered his lightness. "That's a moot point, seeing that he isn't doing so," he said with a grin. "He takes these matters far too seriously, as I've often told him." He drank, crossed his ankles as if lounging, and drawled, "Much the most of our people are willing to be baptized—glad, many of them, I suppose. They want something to cling to. But I daresay the feeling

144

isn't unanimous. In your case, it's become necessary for your business."

Evirion stiffened. "I don't lick boots. Christ must be real, and strong. Look how He's winning everywhere. For me it's like—like being a barbarian warrior whose chief betrayed him. Another, more powerful chief offers me a berth. Very well, I'll take it, with thanks, and be loyal."

"I see. It's what I guessed about you. But others—the former priestess Runa, for instance. Tongues were clacking when I came back from the woods. She refuses, they say."

"M-m, not exactly," replied Evirion, mollified. "She's taking instruction. In fact, she's dived into what books the church has, and wrung Corentinus dry with her questions, till I heard him laugh she knows more—what's the word? —more theology than most priests. But she wants to stay a catechumen for a while longer."

"I thought that was the usual thing. I'm puzzled why you converts are to be baptized already this Easter."

"The custom has changed. Don't ask me why. The old idea, as I understood it, was that people needed time to make themselves ready. Runa says she does."

"Or less restriction than otherwise, less attention paid to her comings and goings?" Rufinus murmured. "She and Gratillonius's wayward daughter—"

"That's none of your affair!" Light from the doorway showed Evirion reddening.

"Agreed. Agreed." Rufinus raised his palm in token of peace. "Still, a fellow can't but wonder. I daresay Corentinus is unhappy about it."

"You'll find out what your master Grallon wants you to know, when he wants you to," Evirion fleered.

"He and Runa do seem to have become rather close. . . . Look, I'm a mere backwoodsman, a landlouper. How can I say which tale is true and which a lie? I wish you'd give me some guidelines."

The mariner glowered. "What do you hear?"

"Rumors. Mistake me not. I don't spread them farther. But you aren't deaf either. You must have an inkling of these notions that you and Nemeta—No, hold on, nothing to your discredit. You'd have answered to Gratillonius

145

before now if he imagined that. However, the two of you did disappear and return at about the same times. You're both close-mouthed. You visit Runa at the old manor—granted, quite a few people do, but mainly women, and Nemeta *is* staying with her. You've lent men of yours, prospective crew, to building her that house out in the forest her father's letting her have. At the least, might you be hopeful of marriage, a way around the fact she's a pagan? That's the sort of thing I hear."

"Dogs yap. It means nothing." Evirion tossed off his wine. Before he could rise, Rufinus was up and pouring him more. With almost imperceptible pressure, the Gaul's free hand kept him seated.

He stared into the cup for a minute, grimaced, and muttered without raising his eyes, "Oh, you may as well hear from me what I've told others. Then they can't garble it for you. Nemeta and I both felt caged here. She knows certain secret things and . . . advised me. For that I'm grateful, and want to make some return. But it was a strange journey I went on. You're wrong, man, about there being no Gods—or demons, or whatever it is yonder. . . . I got a pile of valuables for myself. They've asked me if I found it in Ys. If I did, what of it? Remember, though, Armorica is a very ancient land. Forgotten folk must have left hoards. Consider this a mystery I can't speak of."

"The Romans might not," Rufinus said.

Evirion looked up. "What d'you mean?"

"What do you suppose? There you arrived in—Gesocribate, right?—suddenly loaded with riches. You can't have bought your ship straightforwardly. You're not born to the navicularius class; you're not even a Roman citizen. How many purses did you have to fill before local officialdom . . . obliged you? If the governor in Turonum gets wind of this, I can imagine him following the scent. You could be charged with banditry."

"I did no crime!"

"You'd have to prove that, my friend. Certainly your illegalities in the city would come to light. An investigation might also turn up gossip about Nemeta. She must have spent those months somewhere."

146

Evirion dropped his cup. Wine drained away into the rushes. He leaped to his feet. "You'd run to them with that story?" he shouted.

"Never." Rufinus sighed. "Can't you tell a warning from a threat? You've a way of charging ahead like a bull aurochs. I'm trying to do some of the thinking you should have done."

Evirion breathed hard. Rufinus smiled. "Let me talk to Gratillonius," he said. "The two of us alone. Then with you. It's in his interest to keep things quiet—but not to stop you in your course, because you can in fact help Confluentes prosper. We're on the same side. Confess it to yourself."

"You . . . want to think . . . for him too?"

"Well, I daresay these ideas have crossed his mind. But he's had so much else on it. He needs help. We all do, you not least. And we've nobody to give it but each other."

Evirion stared at his hands, which knotted together.

"Sit down," Rufinus coaxed him. "Have a fresh stoup. I know this is a heavy weight to dump on you in a single load. But we must plan ahead. Have you, for instance, have you given any thought to the matter of pirates? The Saxons and Scoti will be coming back, remember."

"That's a landlubber's question." Therefore it acted on Evirion like a tonic. "The ship's big and fast. Her crew will be large and well-armed. I doubt whatever barbarians we may meet will care to do more than turn tail. They seldom attack at sea anyway. Land is where the best plunder and prey are."

"I see." Rufinus, who had been perfectly aware of it, nodded. "This gives me the ghost of a notion. . . . But let that go for the time being. Do sit again. We'll drink and talk and drink some more. You never really know a man till you've gotten drunk with him."

3

Candlelight glowed warm, but the hue it cast over the girl in the bed was purulent, so white she was. Only her hair had color, red waves across the pillow, streaks of it sweat-plastered to a face where bones strained against skin. Reaching for her father's hand, her fingers were like straws, her elbows like spurs. The grip felt cold when his closed on it.

"I should go now and let you sleep," Gratillonius said in his powerlessness.

"Thank you for coming," Nemeta whispered.

"Of course I come whenever I can. Tomorrow again. Be better then." He attempted a smile. "That's an order, do you hear?"

"Aye." She glanced down toward the bulge beneath the sheet. "If it will let me."

"What?"

"Yon giant leech. Is it not yet bloated full?"

"Hush," he said, appalled. He must not let her speak hatred for this thing. Not among Christians. It was innocent. He must make himself accept his grandchild when it came.

Nemeta's head turned to and fro. "If I could have shed it—"

Across the bed from Gratillonius, Runa's tall black-clad form stooped. She laid her hand over the girl's lips. "Hush," she also said. "Rail not against . . . the Gods."

"Goodnight." The man bent likewise, to kiss the wet forehead. He released Nemeta, turned, and left with Runa. His daughter's gaze pursued them out the door. The woman shut it.

In the atrium, Gratillonius took his cloak from a serving maid whom Runa dismissed with a gesture. Whey they were alone he said in Latin, "She does seem to have mended a bit since I was here last."

The dark, hawk-sharp head nodded. "I think so. Small thanks to that dolt of a physician."

148

"Hm? I heard how you sent him away—"

"He wanted to bleed her, after the convulsion nearly cost her the babe. No, I've prescribed rest and nourishment, and predict she will soon be well."

Gratillonius's eyes met Runa's. "A miscarriage would have been a liberation," he said.

"It would have. I confess to hopes, for Nemeta's sake and . . . yours."

"She had been looking more and more sick. Almost since her return, do you agree?"

"Well, it wasn't fated. Now we must do whatever we can for them both. These are not olden times, when parents could expose an unwanted infant."

He hesitated. "You've been a true friend," he said at last. "I've often wondered why."

"Who else is there?"

"What do you mean?"

"You are still our King. In spite of everything, you are he without whom we are nothing, or we die." The least of smiles flitted across her thin lips. "Besides, you remain rather an attractive man."

Bemused, vaguely alarmed, he threw the cloak over his shoulders. "I'd better be off."

She grew serious. Her voice deepened. "This must be a cruel night for you. Would you like me to walk back to Confluentes with you?"

"Huh? Oh, no—no, thanks—no need—Hard for you too, I'm sure, but best we don't talk about it, eh? Goodnight. I'll look in tomorrow. Goodnight." He hastened out.

She can be an astonishing person, he thought. Cold and strict, but like a mother to my poor torn child, and then without any warning she shows me this side of herself—Well, I do have to sleep.

His footfalls were loud on the path. Otherwise the single sound he heard was from the Stegir, purling and clucking along to his right. Some of the day's warmth lingered, but coolness rose beneath it and flowed into the breaths he drew, mingled with faint blossom odors.

Phantom white, the manor house dropped behind him. Ahead loomed the black masses of the colony town. Beyond

149

the gleam upon the river, fields stretched wan out of sight. Eastward they ended at the forest, which was darkness dappled and wreathed with silver. A full moon had just cleared those crowns. That low it appeared enormous, and its luminance drove surrounding stars from heaven.

Full moon, the first after the spring equinox. More than a solar year had gone since Ys died, but the Queens had reckoned their holy times by the moon, and tonight was the lunar anniversary of the death.

How still it was. Wind, racket, and sundering seas might never have been, might have been merely a nightmare; but then, so would all else be unreal, Dahilis, Bodilis, Forsquilis—Dahut, but he would not think of her, tormented and beguiled; he would call back to him her mother, Dahilis, to dance at his side in the moonlight or sing him a song across the years; he would not weep.

He clenched his fists till nails dug into calluses. Let him keep silence. Even rage against the Gods was unseemly for a man who had a man's work to do. Let him seek peace instead, let his lungs drink of it from the cornel flowers and in the quiet let him imagine he did hear her singing. She played on a small harp—

He stopped. Cold shocked up his backbone. Directly ahead, on the river side of the path, was a stand of dogwood. Its branches reached like snow beneath the moon. From under them rang the notes he heard, and a clear young voice.

Dahilis, I should not be afraid!

The music broke off. A gown billowed around hasty feet. As she came forth, loose hair rippled long, a net to snare moonlight. He recognized those delicate features. A tide of weakness passed through him. His knees buckled, he swayed where he stood.

But this was only Verania, Apuleius's daughter, she who used to call him Uncle Gaius. How like a woodland spirit she seemed, one of those that flitted on nights such as this around the sacred pool at the Nymphaeum. Only Verania, though. He caught hold of his strength and hauled it back into himself. "What are you doing here?" he nearly shouted.

She poised before him, gripping the harp to her breast as if it were a talisman. Yet her look never wavered from

150

his. "I'm sorry if I startled you, sir." Her tone trembled a little. "I couldn't sleep."

"A devil of a thing, you, a maiden, wandering out alone after dark," he scolded.

"Oh, but it's safe, isn't it? You keep the country safe for us."

"Ha!" Nonetheless her words somehow softened the edges of pain. At least she gave him a task. "You're a fool. Disobedient, too. Your parents certainly don't know you've sneaked out."

She hung her head. Defenselessness could always touch him. He cleared his throat. "Well, I'll see you home," he said, "and if you can slip back in without waking anybody, they don't have to learn. But you've got to promise you'll never do anything like this again."

"I'm sorry," she repeated. He could barely hear. "I promise."

"Will you keep it?"

She raised a stricken glance. "I couldn't break a promise to you!"

"Ah. Um. Very good." It made no sense, but abruptly he didn't want to return. Not at once, to a cabin shut away from the moon. Besides, he'd be wise to soothe the lass first. "What was that you'd begun to sing?" he asked. "It sounded like nothing I've heard before."

She clutched the harp tighter. "A song . . . of mine. I make them up."

"You do?" He had known she was quite musical—her father sat proudly when at his request she sang for company—but not that she was creative in this as well as in her drawing and needlework. She was so shy. "Good for you." Gratillonius rubbed his chin. The beard made that like stroking a pet animal, a small added comfort against emptiness. "Where did you get the tune? It didn't sound Roman, nor like any Gallic I know of. Could almost be from Ys."

"It was meant to, sir."

"It was? Well, well." He saw no choice but to ask her for the whole. The words were Latin, he'd caught that much; a childish ditty shouldn't be unbearable; and anyhow, she had a lovely voice. "Would you sing it for me?"

151

"Do you want me to?" Anxiety tinged the words. "It's sad. It's what wouldn't let me sleep."

Afterward, when he had bidden her goodnight and lay in his own bed, he wondered if she had known where he was going and had waited for him to come back. He did straightaway sense that, afraid, she nonetheless wished keenly for him to hear it. "Go ahead," he urged. "Get it out of your system."

She edged off, took stance beneath the arching white cornel flowers where moonlight half reached her, and struck a shivery chord from the harpstrings. Low at first, her verses lifted as they went on, and for no understandable reason would hold him long awake.

"I remember Ys, though I have never seen her,
With her towers leaping gleaming to the sky,
For a ghost once walked beneath her mighty seawall
And along her twilit streets. That ghost was I.

"In my dreams I was a dweller in the city
Where I lived and loved and laughed aloud with you.
Now that Ys is overwhelmed and lost forever,
I must pray you give me leave to mourn her too.

"Here at sunrise, when I looked along the highways
I knew well the one our couriers took to Rome
And the fading path that led to Garomagus—
But the Ysan road flew off to magic's home.

"At the eventide, the time for storytelling,
There were many ancient tales of splendid Ys
That had risen from the seed of Tyre and Carthage
And that with her very Gods had sworn a lease.

"I will shed my tears for Ys the hundred-towered,
For the city facing west against the sea,
For the legend-haunting city, Ys the golden,
For the wondrous place where all once yearned to be.

"I'll remember Ys, though I shall never see her
Shining tall where only waves are left to grieve.

When we've given this new city to our children,
Will our ghosts return to Ys and never leave?"

4

Easter Eve was clear. Green misted the plowlands; leaves were bursting forth; the rivers sparkled on their way to the sea; everywhere sounded birdsong. Soberly clad was the throng that gathered at the church in Aquilo that day, but quietly joyful the spirits of many.

Julia, daughter of Gratillonius, hardly knew what she herself felt. Fasting had left her lightheaded, for ordinarily her appetite was robust. Teachings, prayers, rites buzzed about in her head like swarming bees. The bodies packed close around her seemed from time to time to be at immense distances, their faces the faces of strangers.

The church, not meant to become a cathedral, could barely hold all the converts. There would have to be several celebrations of the Mass tomorrow, with worshippers taking their turns. On this occasion, those to be received were assembled in the street outside, with guards on the fringes to keep order. One by one they were summoned inside. First the children, next the men, last the women—it went on endlessly, Julia had stood here for centuries, nothing changed save that her feet ached worse and worse.

Then sunbeams, slanting richly out of the west and between houses, caught a blond head and came afire. Cadoc Himilco was mounting the steps to his christening. Faintness swept through Julia, and after it a rush of almost unbearable joy. Were angels aloft? Today was the day of her salvation.

Folk inched forward. She reached the front of the women. She heard her name called, saw the deaconess beckon. None of it was real. She stumbled, she floated, the angel wings whirred in her head.

Since returning as bishop, Corentinus had had a baptistry added to the stone building. It was wooden, little more than a lean-to at an end of the portico, but solidly

153

made; he had worked on it himself in rare free moments. Likewise put together in some haste was the organization he needed, priests, deacons, a deaconess, brought in from among Martinus's people at Turonum or recruited here. He cherished plans for a new, properly enlarged church and Church—to be founded at Confluentes, where sites were still available—but this required first that by God's grace the colony flourish and grow.

Julia saw the dim little room as aflicker with rainbows. Its dankness smelled musty. For her the ceremony must be different from what Cadoc had known, she being a woman. Curtains had been drawn from wall to wall behind the font, lest the priest at the back of it see her naked. Nonetheless, as she disrobed with the help of the deaconess, she felt a sudden heat. It terrified. She needed no prompting to cry out thrice, "I renounce you, Satan!"

Thereafter she stepped down into the font. It was not a fine stone basin such as she had heard of, but a barrel-stave tub. The water was holy, though, deep enough to cover her waist. Motionless once the ripples she raised had died, it yet somehow licked at her loins. She drew her hair over her shoulders, tightly across her breasts, and kept her head lowered. In Ys you had not been ashamed of your body; Ys lay drowned.

The priest's voice tolled through a vast hollowness: "Do you believe in God the Father, almighty?"

"I do," she gasped. Oh, I do.

The deaconess dipped up the first bowlful of water, gave it to the priest, and guided his hands as he poured it over Julia. She remembered a brooklet falling across an edge in the hills behind the Nymphaeum, how it flashed and chimed, bound for the pool over which watched the image of Belisama.

"Do you believe in Jesus Christ, His only Son, Our Lord, Who was born and suffered for us?"

"I do." Forswear all heathen things. Forget them. Anew the water of redemption ran down her head and above her heart.

"Do you believe in the Holy Spirit, the holy Church, the forgiveness of sins, and the resurrection of the flesh?"

154

"I do." Forgive my sin, that I don't quite understand it. I believe. Let the water wash me clean.

A hand urged her forward. She went up the steps and stood dripping. At this point, the bishop would have anointed a man; but for modesty's sake, the deaconess simply embraced her—perfunctorily, being by now weary—and helped her on with the clean white robe that was Christ's welcoming gift.

Taking her former garments, she passed through a doorway knocked out of the stone wall, into the vestibule. This she knew; as a catechumen she had stood here listening to the services until the inner door was shut on those who were not initiated. Tonight she too would partake of the Mystery.

Corentinus waited just within the sanctum. "Bless you, my daughter," he said, and signed her with the seal of the Spirit. He held his post like an iron statue, though he must have been on his feet all day at least. Nonetheless she heard the wound within him, a hurried whisper: "Go home after we are done here and beseech your father that he come too. If you love him, do it."

The chamber was already packed. Lamps and candles burned everywhere. They, the incense, the bodies made the air chokingly thick. Julia felt dizzy, drunk. She feared she might fall or otherwise disgrace herself. What when she received the Bread and Wine?

Voices gabbled. Among the converts were a leaven of lifetime Christians, chosen for their calm tempers. They took the lead in kissing the new faithful, a tender hug and a quick brushing of lips.

But the converts were mingling with each other as well. Suddenly Julia found herself in the arms of Cadoc. The Light shone from his eyes. It burned when his mouth touched hers.

"Hoy, is't not sufficient, or a trifle more?" asked a sardonic voice in Ysan. The two disengaged. Evirion Baltisi stood hard by. "I also would fain greet my sister—chastely," he said. Cadoc flushed. The look he cast was less than charitable. Evirion returned it, with the slightest sneer. Then another woman came in, and another, and the milling of the expectant crowd pulled them apart.

155

5

Tera, who had kept sheep and led rites among those folk who sparsely dwelt in the hinterland of Ys, knew she would never know ease in Aquilo. Like most survivors, at first she found a place for herself and her four children on a farm. Unlike most, after the raising of Confluentes she did not move there, but remained where she was. That happened to be the freehold Drusus had hewn for himself out of the forest. The former soldier was a Christian, but easygoing; he saw no harm in keeping a person who knew how to get along with the ancient landwights. Besides, Tera was a good, sturdy worker, and her youngsters—two boys, two girls—did as much as could be expected at their small ages.

On Easter morning, they five were well-nigh alone. Apart from a pagan man who rode watchful about the acres, everyone else had gone into town for the postbaptismal services and the festivities that would follow.

The children dashed to her from their play and squealed that a traveler was coming. She left the bench outside the house on which she had sat half adoze, went around the wall, and peered southward. Snowpeaks of cloud brooded over fields where shoots thrust from furrows and paddocks where cattle grazed the new grass. At her back reared wilderness, a thousand bright hues of green decking cavernous shadows. The farmhouse and its outbuildings made the four defensible sides of a square with a well at its middle. They were long structures of cob, thick-walled, thatch-roofed, and whitewashed. Tera and her brood slept in the haymow, a territory she had claimed for herself and defended with threats—once, a pitchfork—against fellow underlings who shared quarters with the animals.

Aquilo was out of sight, miles to the southeast. Thence meandered roads, branching every which way, scarcely more than tracks worn by feet, hoofs, wheels. On the one that led to this place, a man was bound afoot. He was powerfully built, with gray-shot black hair and beard. His rolling gait he aided with a spear used like a staff; a knife was at his belt, a battle ax slung across his shoulders. Yet the condition of breeks and tunic proclaimed him no outlaw; and the guard had let him by.

The hounds that Drusus kept, as most well-to-do Gallic landholders did, sensed the approach and gave tongue. Huge and savage, the half dozen were penned when someone who could command them was not there to order them back from tearing a newcomer apart. However, they had come to know Tera. At her word, the deep baying died away.

Recognition: "Maeloch!" She hurried to meet him and seized his free hand in both hers. "Why, what brings you hither, lad?"

"I felt restless," the seaman answered. "No haven for the likes o' me this day, Aquilo nor Confluentes. The King too, he went off aboard his stallion."

"But you'd call on a friend? Be welcome. I'm sure the master wouldn't grudge you a stoup of ale."

" 'Twould lay the dust in this gullet. Ahoy, there." Maeloch grinned at the children. The two oldest pressed close, the younger pair looked from behind their mother's skirts. "Ye await a harbor fee, I'll be bound. Well, then, how be this?" His huge hand dipped into a pouch and came forth full of sweetmeats.

"You've a chiefly way about you," Tera said.

Maeloch scowled. "A chief 'ud give gold. The day may come—"

And in the clay-floored kitchen, he said over his cup: "I've somewhat to talk about with ye."

"I thought so," Tera replied. "If your legs are not worn down, let's go walk in the woods. No ears yonder to hear us, unless they be on the elves."

He gave her a close regard. She stood before him in an oft-mended linsey-woolsey shift, on her bare feet, stocky, strong, and returned look for look. A shock of hair, sunbleached flaxen, bonneted a round, pugnosed face from which not quite all the youth had weathered away. Her eyes were small but a very bright blue. You would not have guessed she was familiar with spells, spooks, fayfolk, and maybe even the old Gods of the land.

157

"Aye, ye'd know," he said. "It be a thing I mean to ask about."

He drained his drink, she gave orders to her older boy, and they set forth. "I've scant wisdom or might," she warned. "Naught like what the Queens of Ys did; and their powers were far on the wane in our last years. I made my offerings, cast my sticks, dreamed my dreams, and sometimes it worked out aright and sometimes not."

"I know. Ye've done naught like that since the whelming, ha' ye?"

"Nay. Only a muttered word, a lucky charm, a sign seen in wind or water or stars. What else can I? What dare I, any longer?"

They left cleared land behind and were in among trees. The trail, leading to the Stegir, was packed hard by use, yet it seemed as though that use were on sufferance, perforce around great roots and mossy boulders. Brush hedged the path, boughs roofed it, boles loomed in a dimness speckled with sun-flecks. Air hung heavy. Through silence drifted the moaning of doves; now and then a cuckoo call rang forth.

"Nemeta will dare, I think," said Maeloch after a while.

"The King's wild daughter? I've heard a little."

"They're building her a house in these woods. Her wish, which Grallon grants. Scant more than that will he say about it, to me or anybody."

Tera caught his hand. Compassion gentled the hoarseness of her voice. "You fret for him—because of him, nay?"

"He be my King. And yours. . . . Look after her, will ye?"

"How can I?"

"Ye'll find ways. How many women amongst us ha' had strength to hold out against Corentinus?"

They wandered on.

"Why do ye?" he asked at length. "How can ye?"

She stared before her. "I've not wondered much about it," she answered low. "It felt like—being herded. Oh, he's a kindly herdsman, I suppose, but I was born free."

"With a God your father? I've heard that said."

She laughed. "My father can have been any man my

158

mother liked. Same for my brats. I can guess, of course."
Sobering: "Thrice I've seen Cernunnos, His antlers athwart
the moon, and once—but that may have been a dream
after I'd breathed too much of the hemp smoke." Forlorn-
ness touched her. "They're ghosts of what They were, the
Gods are. For sure, my children will go to Christ. Else
their age-mates'll mock them, and why should they suffer?"

"But ye'll abide?"

"I hope I will."

"It be a terrible thing to be old alone."

They reached the riverbank and stopped. The water
rilled so clear that they could see stones on the bottom and
fish darting across. Years ago, a tree had fallen. Moldering
away to punkwood, it had spread a place for moss to grow
thickly alongside the stream. Maeloch and Tera sat down
on what remained of the trunk. It too bore a padding soft
and cool.

"You risk the same, lad," she said. "For Grallon's sake?"

He tugged his beard. "N-nay. His God and mine never
came betwixt us."

"But you serve yet the Three of Ys?"

He heard the scorn slice through her tone, and shook
his head. "Nay after what They did."

"Nor I. But to inlanders like me, who just came to the
city on market days, They were something afar. We lived
with the wights that had always been of our land; and what
Gods we called on were of the Gauls, or the Old Folk
before them. Now you—"

"I have none left me," he said, forcing the words out. "I
might well seek to Christ—save that that 'ud mean forsaking the spirits in the sea. D'ye understand? Those I ferried
across to Sena. Where be they now? Who'll remember little
Queen Dahilis, her happy laugh and dancing feet—who'll
kindle a torch on the eve of Hunter's Moon, so our dead can
find their way back to them they loved—save it be me?"

She caught his arm. "Me too, if you'll allow. And I've
Gods for us both."

He turned his face and body to hers. "I had thoughts
about that, lass," he growled.

"Me too," she said again. " 'Tis been a lonely while."

The moss made them welcome.

IX

1

Immediately after Easter, Evirion Baltisi traveled overland with his crewmen to Gesocribate to claim the ship he had waiting for him there. Rufinus came along. He said it should be amusing, he might collect a grain or two of information, perhaps he would even have an idea or two to offer. Aquilonian men muttered that a pagan aboard was bad luck, but the Ysans, who outnumbered them, put a stop to that. Newly Christian themselves, they yet remembered how their city had been the queen of the sea.

Evirion had left the craft drydocked, which meant that upon his arrival, a couple of days went to launching and fitting. None of the company minded. This city offered inns, stews, and other entertainments such as Aquilo lacked. Rufinus disappeared into haunts he knew until they were ready to sail.

Nevertheless Evirion departed furious. He had understood beforehand that he would be unable to take on a cargo here. The guilds and authorities had barely been persuaded—bribed—to let an outsider acquire a ship. Now an official wanted to detain vessel and captain while he sent notice to the procurator of what appeared to be an illegal transaction. The tribune put pressure on him to let the matter pass, but expected compensation for the service. When he heard what sums Evirion had laid out earlier as well as this time, Rufinus whistled. "They led you by the nose," he said. "You shouldn't have paid more than half this much." It did nothing to mend Evirion's temper.

Still, he had his ship, and his hopes for the future. A beauty she was, Britannic built, her keel laid years ago but abidingly sound. He had had her worked over from stem

160

to stern, under his own eyes, until she suited his manifold purposes. She was slenderer than a Southern merchantman, her stern less high, though the castle did enclose a small cabin. A lifeboat was lashed fast amidships. At the bow was a projecting forefoot; at need, he could safely drive the vessel onto a beach. Stepped well forward, the mast carried a sprit rig. It drew less strongly than a square sail, but gave greater maneuverability, and wind was seldom lacking in Northern waters. The bowsprit bearing the artemon terminated in a carven scroll; the sternpost was shaped like the head of an enormous horse, facing forward, painted blue. The hull was black with a red stripe. Defiantly, he had named her *Brennilis*.

When he stood out from Gesocribate harbor, his intent was to proceed back to Aquilo. There he would take products of the land, with such manufactured goods from elsewhere in Gallia as were available—on consignment, since he lacked the means to buy them and could not raise a loan until he was better established. Then he would make for southern Hivernia. Dominated by King Conual, who had been friendly toward Ys, the folk of Mumu would likely give him profitable exchange. Two or three such voyages this year ought to shake ship and crew down for longer, more adventurous journeys later, to Germanic lands in quest of amber, furs, and slaves.

Evirion had meant to steer well out west into Ocean before turning south and then east. He had no wish to come anywhere near the ruins of Ys. Warnings given him should have reinforced his intent. Reports had arrived of Scoti in that bight north of the Gobaean Promontory which the Ysans called Roman Bay. They were too few to be a serious threat, save to such isolated persons as they came upon. "I suspect they've been sent to probe, to find out what strength the Empire has hereabouts these days," said Rufinus. "Where they see a defenseless village or homestead, they'll plunder it."

"Too many of those," Evirion spat, "thanks be to the Empire." The network of coastal patrols that Gratillonius wove had fallen apart as soon as Ys perished.

"*We* have defenses," said Rufinus.

Evirion stared. "What do you sniff at now, fox?"

161

"Given a large hull and well-armed men, we can rather safely go take a look for ourselves. Who knows what we may gain?"

Evirion was usually ready for a daring venture. In his present mood he leaped at the suggestion.

Brennilis spent her first night anchored off Goat Foreland. In the morning, after giving herself ample sea room, she wore east on a breeze out of Ocean, into the bay. The weather was bright and gusty. Whitecaps surged over blue. Achingly remembered cliffs showed on the starboard horizon. For the most part men chose to look ahead, where hour by hour green hills swelled out of the water. At last someone shouted, and curses went the length of the hull. Smoke was rising to stain the sky.

"We'll see about revenge," Evirion promised.

After a while they spied seven lean leather boats. Spearheads blinked where kilted, fair-skinned men went alert on sight of the stranger. Evirion sought the bows, gauged wind, currents, distances, speeds, and signalled the helmsman. *Brennilis* surged forward, a bone between her teeth.

The Scotic craft scattered. Their crews would have no chance in a fight against this ship, with her high freeboard and mail-clad sailors. Evirion chose one on which he had the weather gauge and bore down. Under sail, *Brennilis* was faster. The Scoti caught his intent and began to strike their mast. Using oars alone, theirs would be the more nimble craft. Crossbows thumped on the merchantman. Two warriors fell. Thus hampered, the rest were too slow at their work. *Brennilis* struck. Her forefoot stove in the slight hull and capsized it.

"Hard over!" Evirion roared.

Sail cracked, yard slatted, the ship came to rest. Crewmen tossed lines to the swimming barbarians. Anguished, the others circled in their boats at a distance. "Best not let them make an attack," Rufinus advised. "They'd die, but we'd lose too."

Reluctantly, Evirion agreed. As soon as the half dozen Scoti were on board, he put around and beat outward toward Ocean. The currachs followed for a while, but fell behind and finally turned south. That far off, they seemed like cormorants skimming the waves.

Pikes and bows held the dripping captives close to the poop. Rufinus approached them. "It's binding you we must be," he said in their language, "but if you behave yourselves you'll live."

A big red-haired man, who seemed to be the skipper, returned a wolfish grin. "That wouldn't matter, could we take some of you down with us," he replied. "But as is, well, maybe later we'll get the chance." He glanced upward. "We've fed your birds, Mórrigu. I hope you'll not forget."

"Bold fellow," said Rufinus. "The Latin word would be 'insolent.' May I ask your name?"

"Lorccan maqq Flandi of Tuath Findgeni," rang forth.

"That would be near Temir, would it not?" Rufinus recognized the dialect and had recollections from his visit to those parts.

"It would. A sworn man of King Niall of the Nine Hostages am I."

"Well, well. Now if you will hold out your arms—These are honorable bonds, and yourselves hostages."

The prisoners submitted, scowling. When Lorccan's wrists were lashed together and his ankles hobbled, Rufinus drew him aside and offered his own name. "I have been in your beautiful country," he added. "Sure and I understand how already you must long homeward. Let's try between us to make that possible."

They stood at the lee rail, talking quietly; the wind blew their words away. "None less than King Niall must have sent such men as you," Rufinus insinuated.

"We had meant to fare," answered pride. "But himself did speak to me and my companion leaders before we left. He must go north to put down rebellion among the Ulati, else he would have come, and today it would be you with ropes on you, unless you lay dead. Your turn will come."

"And what raiders like you have to tell will be helpful to him." Rufinus stroked his beard, twined the forks of it together, gazed afar, and after a short span said absently, "You have been to Ys, I see."

Lorccan started. "How do you know?"

Rufinus smiled. "Not by witchcraft. Around your neck is

163

a pendant of gold and pearl, Ysan workmanship. Somehow I doubt you came by it in trade."

"I did not," Lorccan replied, turning grim. "I found it there."

"Among the ruins? I hear they are dangerous, a haunt of evil spirits. You are either a brave man or a foolish one."

"I won it doing the work of my King."

"Oh? Rumor is that the whelming of the city was his deed. Is he not satisfied?"

"He is not. He laid on us what he says he will lay on all who rove this way, that we tear down some of what remains. I found this in . . . a tomb." Lorccan grimaced. He could not be entirely easy about it, however bold a face he showed.

"The rocks thereabouts are hungry."

"My party went afoot, from older ruins where we were camped."

"Ah, Garomagus. And I take it you had satisfactory pickings thereabouts?"

"Some." Lorccan stiffened. "You wield a sly tongue. In grief for friends lost, I have spoken too much. You won't be learning from me where the booty was stowed."

"It can buy you your freedom."

"And what of my shipmates?"

"We can bargain about that. Otherwise we'll take the lot of you to Venetorum for sale. They know there how to gentle slaves. Think." Rufinus walked off.

When the Scoti had been herded below and secured, he went to Evirion. The captain was back in high good humor. "We're done well," Rufinus agreed. "However, the real treasure we've gained won't go onto any scale pan."

"What's that?" asked Evirion.

"Knowledge," said Rufinus softly, "that my King will be glad to have."

2

Trees groaned in the wind that roared raw about them. Rain made a mighty rushing noise through their crowns.

Where unhindered it struck the Stegir, the river foamed at its force. Blackness drowned the forest, until lightning flared. Then again and again each leaf, twig, droplet stood luridly in the glare. Thunder rolled after on wheels of night.

In her house, Nemeta screamed. "Hush, child," Tera said. Her voice barely made its way against the racket outside. She laid a hand on the sweat-cold forehead. "Easy. Rest between the pangs."

"Out, you damned thing!" The voice was worn to a rasp by hours of shrieks and curses. "Out and die!"

Tera fingered the charm bag hung at her throat, as often before. For a mother to hate the life she was bringing forth boded ill. "Cernunnos, give strength," the woman muttered wearily. "Epona, ease her. All kindly landwights, be with us."

Flames guttered and smoked in earthen lamps. They cast misshapen, unrestful shadows which filled every corner of the room. Nemeta's face jutted from the darkness. Pain had whittled it close down around the bones. Teeth glimmered as if her skeleton strove to break free. Her eyeballs rolled yellow in the niggard light. The straw tick beneath her was drenched and red-smeared.

Her belly heaved anew. "Sit up and bear down," Tera said, and lent her arms to help. She had forgotten how often she had done this. Would the labor never end? "Not two, but three bulls to You, Cernunnos, if they both live," she bargained. "I'm sure King Grallon will give them. Epona, to whatever else I promised I lay—aye, my man Maeloch will carve Your form in walrus ivory, I can make him do that, and 'twill be there at Your rites always after. Elves, nymphs, ghosts, every dweller in woods and waters— ha, d'you want me to lead the Christian wizard to your lairs? He'll ban you, he will, he'll give your haunts to his saints, 'less you help us this night."

Lightning burst. Through cracks between shutters, it seemed to set afire the membranes that covered the windows. Thunder grabbed the cabin and shook it. Wind boomed and clamored. Between the thighs of Nemeta, a head thrust forth.

"He comes." Tera was too exhausted to rejoice. Her hands worked of themselves.

"Aye, he, a boy, the King's grandson." She lifted the sprattling form and slapped its backside. The storm overrode the first wail.

There was the cord to cut and tie, there were washcloth and towel and blanket, there was the afterbirth, and then Tera could care for the mother. She cleansed the thin naked frame, helped it stagger from the pallet of the floor to the fresh bed that waited, got a gown around the limbs where they flopped loose, combed the matted ruddy locks. "We've soup in the kettle, dear," Tera said, "but here, hold your wee one for a while. You've earned the right, so hard you fought."

Nemeta made fending motions. "Nay, take it away," she whispered. "I've cast it from me. What do I want with it?"

Tera turned, hiding the trouble on her countenance. Nemeta fell into sleep, or a swoon. The infant cried.

—Morning was cool and bright. The ground lay sodden under torn-off boughs and bushes, but drops of water glinted like jewels. A messenger arrived from Gratillonius, as one had done daily since Tera came to look after his daughter. Nemeta had said she did not wish to see anyone but a midwife, nor have any who was Christian. Gratillonius masked his hurt and spoke to Maeloch. Tera and her children now lived with the fisher captain in his house in Confluentes.

"Aye, at last," she told the runner. "A boy. Sound, though 'twas a cruel birthing. Tell my man I'll be here a few days yet, till she's on her feet." She added a recital of supplies she wanted brought on the morrow.

Alone again, the two women could rest. Tera had little to do but keep house and fire, cook, wash, tend mother and babe. Those both did as well as could be awaited; the blood of the King ran in them, and they were properly sheltered.

Nemeta's cabin was no hovel. It was stoutly built of logs, moss-chinked, with clay floor, stone hearth, sod roof: a brown-green-gray oblong nested close to a huge old guardian oak. Close by flowed the Stegir. Forest crowded around, full of life and sun-speckled shadows, while a beaten path wound toward humankind. Nemeta chose the site because it was immemorially holy, a place where folk had come seeking the help of the spirits since the menhirs first arose. Years ago, a Christian hermit actually settled here. Her workmen had heaped up the rotted remnants of his shack, and she kindled them to burn an offering.

That day passed mutely on the whole. Most sound within the walls came from the babe. "You must soon take him to your breast, you know," Tera said in the afternoon.

"Aye," Nemeta sighed from her pillow. "Nine months it sucked my blood. It may as well have my milk."

Seated on a stool at the bedside, fingers twined together in her lap, Tera said slowly, "I'm disquieted about you, lass. You've been dumb throughout, save when bearing. You stare like one blind. But at what?"

The young woman's lip flicked upward. "You told me not to waste strength crying out while the thing happened. I strike a balance, nay?"

"You do wrong if you blame the child."

"Do I? Four beasts begot it; and it would not go away."

Tera regarded her a while. "You sought to be rid of it, then."

"Of course."

"How?"

"I tried—oh, what I hoped might serve, whatever I could think of. But what did I know, I a stranger in the Roman city? Afterward—" Nemeta's voice halted.

"Afterward," Tera followed, "you stayed with Princess Runa."

Nemeta compressed her mouth.

"Trust me." Tera reached for a hand lax on the coverlet and cradled it in hers. "Think you yours is the first woe like this that ever I kenned? I'll keep silence. But sometimes yon leechdoms wreak lasting harm. If you'll tell me what you tried, I'll better know how to help you."

Nemeta considered. When she spoke, her tone was hard with resolution. "Do you swear secrecy? That without my leave you'll utter no breath of whatever I may say here?"

"I promise."

"Nay, you must give oath. Silence about every single

167

thing you heard or saw in the whole while you've been with me."

Tera grimaced. "That's a heavy load. But—Aye." She took a knife that hung at the cord around her waist, nicked her thumb, squeezed a drop onto the floor. "Hark. If I break faith with you, let the Wild Hunt find me, let its hounds lick my blood, let my ghost stray homeless between the worlds. Cernunnos, You have heard."

Nemeta sat up in bed. She shivered with sudden ardor. "You know the old lore, then. Teach me!"

Tera shook her head. "I know just enough to fear how spells can turn on us. Lie back down. Tell me what I asked."

Grudgingly, Nemeta obeyed. She spoke of bitter or nauseating herbs she had taken, of casting herself belly first on the ground, of searches for a witch or wizard or renegade physician. Nothing availed. Outsider, pagan, therefore object of suspicion despite the money Evirion left her after he departed, she dared not inquire forthrightly, even among the poor of Gesocribate. Christian law forbade doing away with the unborn as well as the newborn.

"Runa gave me sapa to drink," she finished. "It only made me weak and ill. At last she said I'd best stop. Presently I felt better. But I was being kicked within my body. As a rider kicks his animal."

Tera frowned. "Sapa?"

"A Roman brew, Runa said. They make it by boiling grape juice in a lead vessel. 'Tis thick, sweet, commonly added to their wines. I took it pure."

"Hm. In Ys they thought lead a slow poison. Belike that's soothfast."

Nemeta raised her eyes. "Runa told me Roman whores are wont to drink sapa. It whitens their skins. Ofttimes it sloughs out their unwanted young. How right, I thought, if I drink a whore's potion against this maggot in me. But it failed."

Tera sat silent before she answered, "Well, keep the child till we find him a foster home, your father and I."

"Does *he* want it?"

"I've a feeling he'd be happier had it died in the womb.

168

And yet . . . 'tis his grandchild, and Queen Forsquilis's. I think he cared for her as much as he did for any of the Nine, aside from Dahilis the mother of Dahut. But Dahilis left us ere I was grown. I knew her just by hearsay. I've seen Forsquilis, though, beautiful, strong, and strange. Aye, Grallon will do whatever he can for the grandchild."

"I will endure, then," Nemeta mumbled. When Tera brought the infant over, she bared her breast and held him close. He suckled with savage eagerness.

—In the time that followed, she showed him neither love nor cruelty. Nursing him, learning from Tera how to care for him, were things she did. Otherwise she gazed afar, spoke little and distantly, fingered the magical objects she was collecting. As strength returned, she first paced the cabin like a cat in a cage, later went off by herself to walk in the woods and bathe in the river.

Those were brief whiles, but increased rapidly. On the third day, Tera said, "Well, I can leave you and go tell your father you're up and about. He'll be glad. When can he come see you, or you come to him?"

Nemeta's answer was low and cold. "I'll send word."

"Men of his will still look in on you daily for a span." Tera's tone softened. "Keep him not waiting much longer. He'd laden and lonely."

"He shall hear. Thank you for your help."

Tera drew a sign in the air. "May They be with you, dear."

—When the woman was gone, Nemeta began to tremble. It worsened till she crouched in a corner hugging herself while the teeth clattered in her jaws. The babe cried. She threw a curse at him. It drowned the noise he made. She howled aloud for a long time.

Thereafter she had mastery of her flesh. Rising, she busied herself. There were things to pack together—knife, a stake she carved, the scribed shoulderblade of an aurochs, flint and steel, tinder, bundle of kindling wood— and a distance to go while daylight wore away toward sunset. As she worked, she muttered, sometimes prayers she had learned as a vestal, sometimes scraps of what she had heard were spells. It helped curb rage at the clamorous creature. She would have gotten silence by nursing

169

him, as well as relief from an ache in swollen breasts, but she could not quite bring herself to that.

At last she donned a clean white shift and hung her filled sack across her back. Quickly, she stooped to lift the infant from the basket Tera had brought to be his crib. He struggled before she got him firmly held on her left hip. With her right hand she took the staff twined with a snake's mummy; and she set forth.

Heat, stillness, odors of wet mould hung over the game trails down which she padded. The babe's yells dropped to a whimper and to naught; rocked by her pace, he slept within the bulwark of her arm. Now and then she heard wings whirr or a cuckoo call. Through the few gaps between boles, sunbeams slanted ever more long and deeply yellow. Finally they went out and shadows closed on her.

She reached the place that people shunned. Here too was a narrow opening in the forest, looking west. Heaven smoldered red where Ys had been. Overhead it arched wan behind leaves; eastward, night filled all spaces. The pool burned with sunset. Swifts darted noiseless in pursuit of mosquitoes that swarmed above it. Chill seeped from the earth below the fallen leaves. They rustled and scratched at her bare feet.

She set her loads before the boulder at the water's edge. It bulked high as her waist, black athwart sundown. The babe started crying again, a sound that sawed the air. Nemeta scuttled about gathering deadwood dry enough to burn. She must lay and light her fire while she could see what she did.

It was never an easy task, making needfire, but she had skill. Her father had taught her. He had taught her whatever he could that she wanted to learn when she was a little girl, ere the rift between him and his Queens denied him to her. How she had missed the big man with the knowing hands.

Her child screamed on and on. "Be quiet," she snarled. "Oh, soon you shall be very quiet."

The fire flickered up. She made sure it would burn untended for a space. The western embers were turning to ash.

She stood, lifted arms, spoke aloud: "Ishtar-Isis-Belisama,

I am here. I call on You, Maiden, Mother, and Hag; Lady of Life and Death; Comforter and Avenger. See, I make myself pure before You."

She stripped off her garment and waded into the pool. Withes caught at her. Slipping along her nakedness, they lashed and stung. Roots made her stumble and bruise her feet. She went on until she stood at the middle, ooze cool around her ankles, water to her waist. Thrice she scooped a double handful and poured it over her head. "Taranis," she called as she did, and "Lir," and "Belisama."

The fire sputtered low when she returned. She squatted to build it anew, feeding it until the glow quivered as far as the lightning-blasted beech nearby. A burning brand in her left hand, the knife in her right, she danced slowly three times around the great dead trunk while she named her Gods.

The babe wailed, kicked, reached arms up from the blanket whereon he lay. Nemeta came back to stand above him. For an instant she found herself moveless, muscles locked together. With a gasp and a shudder she broke free. She plunged the torch into the soil; its flame went out. Her left hand caught the child by a leg and lifted him. He was so small, he weighed scarcely anything.

She took him to the boulder and stretched him on its flat top. He writhed. His cries had grown thin. She held him down and looked aloft. Day was altogether gone. Stars blinked.

Her words rushed forth, half-formed, falling over each other. "Taranis, Lir, Belisama, behold the last of Your worshippers. Men fled in terror of Your wrath, sought a home with the new God of the Romans or the doddering old Gods of the Gauls. I, Nemeta, born to the King of Ys by Your Queen Forsquilis, I alone keep faith with You. Hear me!"

The knife gleamed in her right hand. It was big, heavy-bladed, almost a sword. She had bought it in Gesocribate from a shopkeeper who said it had, long ago, made pagan sacrifices.

"Ys lies drowned," Nemeta yowled. "The Wood of the King has burned. Take what I give you!"

The knife flashed and struck. The cries ceased.

Nemeta lifted the dripping tiny head alongside the blade. "Blood of my blood I give You, flesh of my flesh, I Your worshipper. Now give me what I want!"

Her voice sank to a rasping purr. The flames snapped louder at their back. Their light turned the smoke to a living presence.

"Lir: May those four who made prey of me beside Your sea never win free of it. Let her who haunts the ruins torture their souls forever.

"Taranis: May their kin, in the city Audiarna, perish like vermin. Let this blood of theirs which I have shed to You drain wholly out of Your earth.

"Belisama: May I gain the powers that belonged to my mother, Queen Forsquilis. Let me never again be captive and helpless, but witch-priestess unto You.

"It is spoken."

The fire sank. By its uneasiness she found her way back to the pool, wherein she cast the body, and to the tree, in whose charred cavern she laid the head and pegged it fast.

She prostrated herself, got to her knees, rose to her feet, arms uplifted. "Be always with me," she implored.

Having gathered her things, she set off homeward. It would be impossible to find her way through the dark, but how could she linger here? She would come on a glade where she could see the stars and take shelter there. At dawn she would seek the cabin, wash herself clean in the river, dispose of the bloodied shift. When Gratillonius's man arrived she would have her tears ready. "I went out after berries. I came back and the door stood open and the crib lay empty. Did a wolf steal my babe, or the elves, or, oh, what has become of him?" Her father would believe, he must believe, and console her as best he was able.

3

The feast of St. Johannes had taken unto itself the ancient rites of Midsummer, but otherwise they had changed little. Even many Aquilonians left the city on the eve to dance around bonfires such as blazed from end to end of

Europe, or leap across them, or cast the wreaths they had worn and the pebbles they had gathered into them. Burning wheels rolled down hills while besoms, set alight and waved around, showered the night with sparks. Wild revelry followed, and hasty marriages during the next few months. Relics, partly burnt sticks and the like, were kept till the following summer as charms against misfortune. Brotherhoods and sisterhoods existed to prepare for these gatherings, lead them, and dispose of the remnants lest those fall into the hands of sorcerers.

Bishop Corentinus could not have stopped this, nor did he wish to. Rather than hold the Church aloof from something that dear to her children, he would bring her into it. His priests went about blessing the piled logs before they were lit and conducting prayers for a good harvest. Everyone who possibly could was supposed to attend Mass the day after; confession was encouraged. As for misbehavior, he must hope that in the course of generations it would die out. His duty, and vital, was to purge the observances of their openly pagan elements.

In this one year, however, he saw an opportunity to reinforce the Christian aspect. Among the Confluentians was a large and growing proportion of wedded couples. In some cases man and wife together had escaped the destruction; in other cases they mated with fellow Ysans or with Osismii after reaching these parts. Such knots had generally been tied in heathen wise, if there was any sanctification at all. As yet, rather few members of the widespread tribe had been converted. Corentinus meant to imitate his mentor, holy Martinus, and evangelize the countryside. While any union honestly entered into was doubtless only venially sinful, God's ministers alone could make it truly valid, eternally secure. If it be done at the very Midsummer, it would help the folk understand whose day that truly was. This in turn should give the unbaptized cause for thought and thus guidance toward the Light.

Accordingly, the bishop occupied himself for a pair of months in advance, persuading and arranging. The occasion was a triumph crowned by Julia, daughter of the leader Gratillonius, and Cadoc Himilco, scion of Suffetes, when they joined in Christian wedlock.

They had gone side by side beforehand to make their intention known to her father. He had consented, with a brevity and reserve that slightly diminished her joy, and asked the young man to see him alone later at his house.

It was a simple, white-painted building of squared timbers with a few utilitarian rooms, though it did posses glazed windows and a tile roof. The main chamber, which could scarcely be called an atrium, was for receiving guests. It held little more than some articles of furniture. The plaster of the walls was undecorated and the floor, clay, covered merely with rushes. Gratillonius gestured Cadoc to a stool, gave him a cup of wine, took one for himself, and sat down too.

For a space they took each other's measure. Cadoc saw a burly man, plainly clad in Gallic shirt and breeches, grizzled auburn hair and beard close-cropped after the Roman style, face weathered and, of late, heavily graven around the gray eyes and high-arched nose. Gratillonius noted features also darkened by the sun that had bleached blond locks, but still smooth, clean-shaven; the shabby clothes decked litheness.

"Well,' he said at length, in Latin, raising his cup. "Your health. You'll need it."

"Thank you, sir." The reply was deferential without being servile.

"On the whole, I'm pleased," Gratillonius said. "You come of good stock. Your father was a fine man, and my friend."

"I'll try to be worthy of your kinship, sir."

Gratillonius regarded Cadoc over the rim of his goblet. "That's what I want to talk about. This is not much of a surprise, you know."

The visitor smiled. "Julia warned me you observe more than you let on."

"I keep my thoughts to myself till they're wanted. How do you propose to support a family?"

Startled, Cadoc said, "I have em-em-employment, sir."

"As a carpenter. Not a gifted one. And the demand is dropping as we fill our most urgent needs. What else can you do?"

Cadoc bit his lip. "I've considered that, believe me, sir.

174

I am educated, can read, write, figure, have knowledge of literature, history, philosophy. In Ys I w-was acclaimed for . . . horsemanship. I brought down game in Osismiic woods—"

"You learned what it became a Suffete of Ys to learn," Gratillonius interrupted. "That didn't have much to do with what concerns Rome. Nor was it in any way unusual. Confluentes has a glut of people who could be scribes or tutors. The best of them might make fair-to-middling amanuenses, but Apuleius and Corentinus already have theirs, and who else hereabouts wants any?"

Cadoc flushed at the bluntness. "I'll earn my keep."

"Evirion Baltisi's venture bids fair to prosper. Maybe he'll take you on."

"No!" snapped anger. Then: "I'm sorry, sir. Y-you may not be aware there's bad blood—no, not that, I suppose— call it, uh, ill feeling—between him and me. I'm willing to forgive, b-but will he accept?"

"He may think the forgiveness is owing him," said Gratillonius dryly. "I was aware, and only probing you. I have thought of something, but it calls for wit, strength, and boldness."

Cadoc's countenance brightened. "What, sir? Please!"

Gratillonius rose, set his cup on a table, paced to and fro with hands behind his back. "Exploring and surveying. See here. Aside from a few Roman cities, Gallic settlements, the croplands and meadows around, the roads between, most of middle Armorica is wilderness. Hunters, charcoal burners, and so forth, they know their own parts of it, but nobody knows the whole. To all intents and purposes, it's impassable. If you wanted to go from, say, Venetorum to Fanum Martis, you'd have to travel around through Vorgium or Redonum, adding days you could maybe ill afford. It didn't matter when Rome guarded the coastline and you could go by sea, but that's past. The barbarians ravage one section and are off before soldiers can arrive from another. For a while I got Ys to take the lead, and a naval force kept our waters safe, but now that's gone too. Besides, the Germani are pressing on Rome's eastern land frontiers. Again and again they break through.

Before many more years, they may well be spilling this far west.

"Whatever defense we can raise—I'm looking into the matter—it's got to have mobility, interior lines of communication and transport, or it's no real use. What I have in mind is ways through the forests and over the heaths. No proper roads, we haven't the manpower to build them; just trails, but suitable for men, horses, maybe light carts on some. First we have to learn the country and decide what the practical routes are. Then we clear, grade, bridge where there isn't a ford, maintain—You follow me?"

Cadoc stood. "Oh, wonderful! I am to pioneer this?"

"We'll try you out. It'll be a trial of the whole idea. I'll teach you the basics of surveying, requirements of terrain, and so forth. Rufinus and his men will give you some companionship and guidance, but that's necessarily limited. You'll be largely on your own. Not the same as roving afoot in search of small game, as I know you've done hereabouts when you had free time. Deeper in are outlaws, woods dwellers hostile to strangers, wild beasts—trolls and spooks, for all I know—as well as nature's traps, swamps, streams, storms, sickness. You can easily die, and your body never recovered. You'll get no glory, because we have to do this quietly; the Imperium won't, and doesn't like being bypassed. I wouldn't have told you about it if I didn't have reason to think you can keep your mouth shut. On the other hand, you'll be pretty well paid, in honest money, out of the Aquilonian treasury. I've settled that with Apuleius. You'll be helping secure your family's future. What say? Are you interested?"

"Of course!" Impulsively, Cadoc embraced Gratillonius. "Thank you, thank you!"

The older man smiled a bit. "Save your gratitude till you come home from your first field trip. You may find it in short supply then."

'I won't. I know I won't. And—I'll be meeting those backwoods folk—I can bring them the Word."

"What?"

"The good news. Tell them about Christ. N-not that I'm an apostle or anything like that, I'm not worthy, but if God wills, I can open a way for those who are."

"Hm." Gratillonius frowned, shrugged, and grunted, "If it doesn't antagonize the natives, or otherwise hinder your work, all right."

"Oh, I wouldn't let it do that." Cadoc beamed. "I'll have my Julia to care for, and our children. Your grand-children, sir." He saw the other visage freeze and ex-claimed, "I'm sorry. I d-didn't mean—It was tragic what happened."

"Not altogether," Gratillonius answered curtly. "Sit down and I'll tell you more about what I'll expect of you."

—Midsummer noontide was warm and clear. Fragrances from the forest breathed over fields where grain ripened. A lark caroled on high. Finches twittered near the ground. From Aquilo's eastern gate streamed and chattered Con-fluentians, homeward bound for festivities after the mass avowal and service at the church. Breasting their tide, Gratillonius entered the city and made his way among people equally cheerful. It was a day for rejoicing. Apuleius had invited him to a banquet in honor of his daughter and her new husband. The last thing she had done for him was to wash and pipe-clay a tunic, mend his one colorful cloak, and wax his best sandals, that he might make a little of the showing she told him he deserved.

Citizens hailed him respectfully and tried to give way, but inevitably he was sometimes jostled. Passing the church, he felt a contact and ignored it until that person took his arm. Looking around, he saw Runa, clad in a dark green gown that set off the fair skin and raven hair. "Why, greeting," he said.

"Hail." She smiled. "Shame on you, that were not here for the wedding."

"I am not Christian."

"You could have been with the catechumens like me, to watch ere the Mysteries commenced."

He wondered why she had hung around after the door to the sanctum was closed, and then after the service was over. With some difficulty, he explained: "I thought best not remind Julia of what I am, on this day of her days. It distresses her."

"Yet you come to the feast."

"That's different. You too?"

177

She nodded. Light shimmered in the tortoise shell comb that held her locks coiled and piled. The gesture presented him with a view of her throat, swanlike, perhaps her best feature. "The senator was kind enough. He likes my work for him."

He could think of no more conversation.

"But it grows wearisome," she went on as he failed to respond. "When 'tis done—Mayhap you'll put in a word for me. I know I can stir his interest myself. Yet he may feel shy of maintaining me for what I propose, when there are so many demands on the city's coffers and his own purse."

Gratillonius sympathized. He could imagine few tasks more dismal than copying books. "What is it?"

"A history of Ys, from the founding to the end. They should be remembered, those splendors and great deeds."

He wondered at the vividness with which there came back to him a girl who sang beneath the moon. *I remember Ys, though I have never see her*—"

"Should they not?" Runa persisted into his silence.

He shook himself. "Aye. And you ought to find the work interesting."

"We can hope for the bishop's approval, I believe. He may even be willing to underwrite it. The fall of the proud city holds a powerful moral lesson." She sensed his distaste and hurried on: "But really, what I want is to keep what we loved alive in the minds of men. Save our dear lost ones from oblivion."

"A vast undertaking."

" 'Twill require years. First I must talk with every survivor, and whoever else has recollections—soon, lest death hush them. You foremost, Gratillonius. Though I pray you'll long abide to ward us."

He winced. "Speaking of that . . . will be hard."

"But you owe your Ys, your Queens, children, friends their memorial. I'll go gently. We can do it a little at a time."

He sighed, looked straight before him, and said, "First get Apuleius's agreement."

"You will help me win that? We've worked well together, you and I. We can again. Say you will."

He nodded. "Aye. Though best wait till the hour is right for broaching it."

"Certes. And by then your wounds may have healed more. Gratillonius," she said softly, "you must not remain fast bound in misery. You have a life before you."

"I have my work."

"And happiness to regain." Her fingers tightened the least bit on his arm.

They reached the tribune's house. Skirts flew white around slenderness as Verania, heedless of propriety, darted forth onto the portico. "Oh, you're here!" she cried. "I'd begun to fear you were sick or, or something."

"Why, your father told me to come about noon," he replied, smiling. A chill within him seemed to thaw.

The maiden flushed. "It felt later," she whispered. "I haven't seen you for so long." Confused by her own forwardness, she stood in his path on the stairs. He halted before her.

"I've been busy," he said. "Today—"

"Your host and hostess await you," said Runa firmly, and guided him on past.

X

1

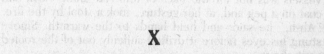

Late on a drizzly day, Bannon of Dochaldun reached the cabin. Beyond its guardian oak the forest faded off into grayness. Amidst that quiet, the Stegir seemed to run loud past reeds and over stones; yet the sound came somehow muffled. Bannon shivered a bit in the dank chill. Water dripped from leaves, the bridle of his horse, the ends of his mustache. His clothes hung heavy.

Dismounting, he knocked. At first he thought the one who opened the door was a boy, gracile in tunic and breeks; then he looked into the thin face and at the hair that tumbled past the shoulders, the hue of flame, like a shout through the gloom all around. Why should a witch who lived by herself not dress like a male, at least for getting about in the woods? he thought. It was better than skirts. . . . Behind her glowed a couple of lamps and a fire banked on the hearthstone.

"Greeting," he said awkwardly, and named himself. "You are Nemeta, daughter of King Gradlon?"

"I am," she replied in his own Osismiic. "If you come in peace, enter. If not, go." She touched a leather bag on a thong around her neck. It must hold charmstuffs. To its outside was sewn the skull of a vole.

"Peace, peace, lady," Bannon said in haste. "Let me but care for my beasts." He had been leading a remount.

"I must have a shelter put up for their kind," Nemeta remarked. "You are the first to arrive riding. Bring your gear in where 'tis dry."

Bannon tethered the horses at a spot with grazing and entered the cabin. It was snug but murky. He glimpsed household wares and stores at the rear, food hung from crossbeams, an ale keg. Closer by was a shelf whereon stood objects from which he averted his glance; staring at sign-carved sticks and bones or at queerly shaped clay vessels was not for the likes of him. He hung cloak and coat on a peg and, at her gesture, took a stool by the fire. "Ah-h," he said, and held hands to the warmth. Smoke stung his eyes before it drifted sullenly out of the roofed vent above.

"Drink," invited Nemeta, and dipped him a wooden cup of ale. She perched herself opposite. The big green eyes caught what light there was and glimmered. He thought of a cat watchful at a mousehole.

A draught or two cleared his throat. "I am the headman of my village," he began.

"I know," she said.

Had she heard? Dochaldun was a mere cluster of dwellings, off by itself in some acres cleared around a hill, a long day's ride from Aquilo. Its folk mainly kept pigs, which mainly lived on mast, though they also had cows and poultry and raised oats. They seldom went anywhere, save at certain times of year to the gatherings of several

180

communities like their own. A person come from magical Ys less than two years ago seemed unlikely to remember even the name, if it had happened to cross her ears.

"They say you know much," Bannon ventured.

"Your kine are falling sick," Nemeta declared coolly. "You wish me to cure them, as I did for the herds at Vindoval and Stag Run."

He could not tell whether fear or gladness made his heart rattle. Sure it was that a chill pringled through his backbone and out into his fingertips. "You are indeed a witch," he breathed.

Her smile was wry. "I may have guessed. Murrains go about. I am not all-wise. How did you learn of me?"

He summoned courage. If the stories were true, she had wrought well and harmed nobody. They told of each animal led to a fire into which she had cast several herbs; the touch of a wand; a snippet of hair cut off and burnt while she spoke in an unknown tongue; within a day the creature recovering, and those that were healthy staying so.

" 'Twas a rumor," Bannon explained. "I had a son of mine track it down. Along the way he heard of lesser deeds you've done. You'll soon be famous, lady."

"Are you Christians yonder?" she asked.

"We are not," he answered, taken aback. "Would you have us be?"

She snickered. " 'Tis easier when you're not, though it hasn't barred some from seeking my help."

"They know you for King Gradlon's daughter—"

"I'm done with that," she cut him off. "I take no more alms of anyone."

Her tone became crisp: "Well, now, these are my terms. For coming to your kine and treating them, you shall send back with me a barrel of well-ground oats, sufficient for a year. If the herd grows well, and it will, each month for thirteen months you shall send me a large ham or the same weight in smoked chops. Have I your pledge?"

"That is . . . much to pay," he demurred.

She grinned. "From elsewhere am I already supplied with wheat flour, butter, and cheese, besides small things for small services. As yet, I have need of more clothing and other woven goods. You may give me those if you'd liefer, but it must be to the same value. I do not haggle. Agree or take your leave."

He had had enough forewarning to sigh, "Be it so. The oats and meat. By my honor."

He had half feared she would require a stronger plighting, but she accepted his word, as well she might. "Good. We'll be off in the morning. I see you meant to guide me back—no magic; you brought a second horse. But take your ease. I'll soon have a meal ready."

With deft hands she fetched a skinned and drawn hare from her larder, cut it in pieces which she rubbed with fat and salt, roasted it on a spit. He wondered whether she had snared it in the ordinary way or sung it to her knife. Also on his trencher went a boiled egg, leeks, roots, and hardtack, while she kept his cup filled. It was strange, having a princess and witch serve him as any housewife might. His head began to buzz in the smoky air.

She kept mostly silent until at the end she said, "You will clean the things tomorrow ere we leave."

Briefly he was astounded, he reached for his dagger, then the meaning of it went into him and he laughed. "Very well, she-chieftain!"

"Your saddle blanket isn't rightly dry," she said, "but I'll lend you covering. Wait here."

She went out. When she came back he took his turn, letting his water in the dark and the rain. As he reentered, he saw her beside the narrow bed, naked. Light flowed tawny over small breasts and subtly rounded flanks.

Desire upwelled. "Lady—" He moved toward her.

She raised a hand. "We will sleep." A drawn sword might have spoken. "Step no nearer, or you will weep for it throughout the rest of your days."

Terror smote. "I'm sorry. You're b-beautiful, and—I'm sorry."

"Blow out the lamps when you've undressed," she said indifferently. With a nod at his bedroll on the floor: "You shall sleep soundly tonight, Bannon."

To his astonishment, he did, quickly drifting off into dreams. Weird, full of music, afterward half remembered, they haunted him until next the moon was new.

182

That summer was cruel to sandy Audiarna. An outbreak of the Egyptian malady wasted it, especially among its poor. Victims turned feverish and strengthless; they grew leathery membranes in mouth and throat, could scarcely swallow, and were apt to bleed heavily from the nose; pulse was weak and rapid, the neck swollen, the face waxy. Most died within a few days, while those who recovered took long to regain full health and in the meantime often suffered paralytic attacks.

This caused ships and overland traders to stay away, thus cutting tax revenues when they were most needed. Hinterland peasants must feed a city which they entered reluctantly. Then at harvest season a new terror struck them.

Gratillonius heard about it from Apuleius, to whom the tribune of Audiarna had sent an appeal for help. The two men discussed it at the senator's house. "A great beast of unknown sort prowling about," Apuleius reported from the letter received. "It's killed and devoured not only live-stock, but lately men—twice. When they didn't come home from outlying fields, searchers found their broken, scattered bones. There's a talk of pugmarks like a lynx's, and sight in twilight of a shape that seemed feline—but enormous. They fear it's a creature from hell, loosed on them for their sins, and huddle in their hamlets with the crops left untended, waiting for the first heavy rains to ruin the harvest."

"Hm . . . a bear?" Gratillonius wondered. "No, not with such a track. Nor've I ever heard of bears behaving that way. . . . Are all men in the city too sick to go after the thing?"

"Or too demoralized. Their prayers and the prayers of their clergy have availed nothing. They ask the spiritual help of Bishop Corentinus and the temporal help of those whom God has spared."

Gratillonius nodded. "They remember how the King of

Ys brought former Bacaudae into these parts to keep the woods safe."

Apuleius looked closely at his friend. "I can understand your bitterness toward the Audiarnans, after they denied a place to your fugitives last year," he murmured. "But in the name of charity—"

Gratillonius laughed. "Oh, never fear. I'll have Rufinus whistle up a gang of huntsmen in short order. And I'll lead them myself."

"What? No, you can't be serious. This may truly be a demon. And whether or not, your life is too valuable to risk."

Gratillonius uttered a rude soldier's word. "I've been dealing with one petty squabble after another, or scarcities or regulations or—It's like wading through a bog of glue. By Hercules, here's a chance to get out and do something real! I'm bound away as soon as I have my men, and that's that."

"A small cry brought his attention around. Verania had entered. "No, please!" she begged. "Not you!"

"And why not, my dear?" asked Gratillonius with a smile.

"I've tried to tell him why not," sighed Apuleius. "Well, I daresay you came in to announce dinner."

She nodded. Her lip quivered. Gratillonius rose with her father. He wanted to pat her on the head, or better hug her, and speak reassurances. Of course, decency forbade. "I don't send men out on hazardous duty I wouldn't take myself," he said to her. "Though I hardly think this compares with a war. It's just a hunt, Verania."

"Adonis w-w-went hunting," she stammered, and fled the room.

Perforce she waited in the triclinium, beside Rovinda and Salomon. She had blinked back tears, but Gratillonius still wanted to console her. Having a pretty girl fret about him felt so warm. The best that occurred to him was to say to her brother, "You've heard too? I'm off after the beast that's been preying around Audiarna. Shall I bring you its tail?"

Worship looked back at him.

3

The devil was elusive. Gratillonius, Rufinus, and their ten followers quested for three days. They found the merest traces, and trails too cold for their hounds.

Each morning they went forth in groups of three, each evening returned to camp. Gratillonius had had the tents pitched upstream from Audiarna, well out of sight and contagion. Fields greened deserted, silent but for the cawing of crows that unhindered robbed them. Forest hemmed and darkened the northern horizon. Likely that was where the brute laired, and the men coursed its tracklessness daily. However, Gratillonius chose to base himself in the open; there a sentry could see whatever was coming. Also, that was the way the creature must fare if it would again have human flesh.

Ranging about or idled at night beside the fire, Gratillonius found his thoughts slipping their moorings. They would not abide by the question of what the thing was that he hunted or how to slay it. Instead, against his will they drifted to his own fate. No longer could he keep himself busy enough in his waking hours that sleep fell straightaway upon him. What did he hope for? Chief of a colony founded in desperation, he lacked any vision of its future by which to guide it. Ninefold widowed, he lacked any son to carry on his name, and of his two living daughters, one had made herself an outcast. Celibate as Corentinus, he lacked any God Whom the sacrifice might please. Among men he found companionship, and two or three good friends, but always some barrier, faith or purpose or something less clear, between their hearts and his. Among women—

He needed a hand-graspable achievement.

Rufinus's sardonic wit and the banter of the company provided a little distraction. They had been chosen for cockiness in the face of man, magic, or mystery. Gratillonius wished he could join in their japes, as once he did with his legionaries, but his mood was too heavy.

The end of the search came in a rush. He, Rufinus, and a woodsman named Ogotorig were on their way back from yet another sweep. Leaving the forest, they started toward the river, careless of trampled grain. At the water they would drink before following it on south to camp. Wearisome hours lay behind them—endless trees, brushwood that fought, flies, mosquitoes, stinging ants, heat, thirst, silence broken only by their curses or the mockery of a cuckoo—and they plodded mute, their dogs droop-tailed behind them. Going in deeper than before, they had emerged late. The sun was down. Dusk drifted westward through coolness that still smelled green. The stalks rustled softly. Swifts darted half-seen across violet-gray heaven.

Suddenly a hound growled, then gave tongue. At once the rest were clamorous. They darted forward, fast lost to sight. "Ha!" Rufinus exclaimed. "Has *he* stumbled on *us?*" He broke into a lope. Gratillonius pounded alongside. Their boar spears bobbed to their haste. Ogotorig stopped to string his bow and nock an arrow.

A deep growl coughed through the baying of the hounds. A yell tore loose, ended in a rattle, the voice of death. The dogs barked, shrill and afraid. Gratillonius heard how they milled about. What a damnable time and place to meet the quarry. How could you see where it was, what it did?

He tripped over the ripped body of a hound. The blow that killed it had flung it yards off. " 'Ware charge!" Rufinus called. Gratillonius saw the grain wave before him, like water when an orca attacks from beneath. Rufinus half moved to get between him and it, but the onslaught was quicker. Gratillonius barely had time to ground his spear.

The thing that rushed at him was dim in the gloaming, huge, he felt the soil shiver beneath its weight. He had a glimpse of shagginess, a mane, eyes agleam and cat-gape open. The shock came.

It knocked him down. The beast had not plunged at him like a boar, but veered. A clawed paw slashed air as he fell. It could have shattered his skull. Rolling over, he bounced to his feet and drew sword.

Blood ran black where his spearpoint had furrowed. That was a flesh wound, and the brute had turned on Rufinus. The man danced aside, jabbing. Did he laugh

186

into the snarls and the brief, thunderlike roar? Gratillonius heard him: "Back, Grallon! Stay clear! Give the archer a shot!"

Ogotorig's bow twanged. A shaft smote; another, another. The monster retreated. Wrath rolled in its throat, but it swung about. Making for the wood, it went slowly, the off hind leg lame. "After it!" Gratillonius bawled, and took the lead.

Exultance leaped in his breast. He never thought how readily he could die. He stayed wary, though, senses alert until the fading light could have been noontide. To breathe the rank smell was to drink wine.

In—thrust home—the blade grates past a rib, meets heaviness beyond, twists back out—spring aside—blood pours off steel—emboldened, the hounds bay, rush in, tear at legs and flanks—the tormented giant shakes itself, drops fly like slingstones from its gashes, and turns around again to do battle—Rufinus drives his spear in from behind and cackles laughter as he shoves deeper—Gratillonius stabs near a shoulder—the beast sinks to earth, the hounds are upon it, it smashes one and maims another before the men can drive them off—Ogotorig looses arrow after arrow—the creature shudders, blood bubbles around a snarl—Gratillonius steps recklessly close, looks into the dimming eyes, and gives the mercy thrust, for this has been a valiant foe. Nonetheless, it—no, he—takes a while to die.

The wrecked hound yammered till Rufinus ended its pain, the last hale one flopped down and panted. The men stood amidst flattened stalks and peered through the darkness that rose and rose. Early stars were out.

"What *is* it?" whispered Ogotorig.

"A lion." Awe hushed Gratillonius's tone.

"First I've seen, aside from statues and pictures," Rufinus said.

"Same for me," Gratillonius answered. "But he's a sign of strength and courage, you know."

"How on earth did he get here?"

"I don't suppose we'll ever know. Escaped from a cage somewhere. I've heard that rich patrons in big cities can get animals from afar for the games, though not often any more. Maybe this one was bound for Treverorum after being shipped through Portus Namnetum when he got free and wandered this way."

"He limped, did you notice? From a fight with a bear, or what? Anyhow, not fit to live off deer. When he started taking cows and sheep, the peasants drove their stock into byres or pens. No wonder he snatched a couple of men when they happened by. Poor creature. Poor lost, lonely, unsurrendering lion."

In the exhaustion that now welled up within him, Gratillonius had dropped into Latin, and Rufinus had responded likewise. "What do you speak of?" Ogotorig asked in his native language. "How on earth did he get here, you wondered." He bent, smeared a little of the spilled blood on his forefinger, daubed his breast with it. "How off earth, I'd say. Wizardry at work. Cernunnos, hunter God, keep us from harm."

The man could be right, Gratillonius thought. What had come was freakish: first pestilence in the city, then this in the hinterland. It was as if a vengeful spell were cast on Audiarna.

4

The bridge boomed underhoof, triumphal drums, and Gratillonius rode through the gate into Aquilo. Sunlight slanted along the road behind him and made a glory of his tousled hair. Soon enclosing houses had him and his followers in shade, but women and children spilled out of them to mingle with their men in the streets. The cheers surfed around, before, everywhere through town. "He's won, he slew the demon, God be praised!" For riding at his back came Rufinus, who bore on a spearshaft the clean-boiled skull of the lion.

Thus Verania saw him from the portico of her father's home. She had dashed out at the sounds of jubilation and nearly fell. Salomon caught her in time. She squeezed her hands together above her bosom and erupted into tears.

He must swallow hard before he could stand in manly wise.

There Gratillonius drew rein. Apuleius and Rovinda came forth. Gratillonius waved. "It's done," he called. "We made an end of the manslayer." When had such joy last fountained in him? At the overcoming of the Franks? No, that had already lain beneath the shadow of strife in Ys. This was wholly clean and brave.

Apuleius barely curbed a whoop. Wrapping himself in Roman gravity, he walked down the stairs. "A marvelous deed," he said through the din. "Yet we of this household will give the most thanks that you have returned unharmed. Enter, you and your band."

Such of the woodsmen as understood looked abashed, except for Rufinus. They were strangers to life among the prosperous. Their chief grinned, though, and licked his lips. "They set a grand table," he said in Gallic.

"Thanks, but we're dirty and sweaty from traveling," Gratillonius replied. "We wanted to relieve any anxiety, but what say we go on to Confluentes—tell the people there, make ourselves presentable, and then come back?"

His glance fell on Verania. "Ho, little lady," he called on impulse. "What are you weeping about?"

"I am, am, am so happy," she stammered.

The brightness waxed within him. "Salomon," he shouted across the hubbub to her brother, "you'll get the tail I promised you. Verania, how'd you like the skin for a rug when it's cured?"

Apuleius reached his foot and looked upward. The countenance, lined and graying but still handsome, had gone grave. "No, best give that to the church in thanks for God's help and mercy," he said. Before Gratillonius could protest: "As for Confluentes, I'll send word. Please don't spoil your well-earned pleasure at once, but wash and borrow clean garments from us, enjoy the best meal Rovinda can provide on short notice, tell us your tale over wine, and take a good night's rest. Trouble can wait."

It was as if a knife stabbed. Gratillonius felt muscles grow taut. At the abrupt pressure of his knees, Favonius whickered and curvetted. He needed a moment to quiet the stallion. The people jamming the street seemed also touched by sudden unease. The chatter ebbed from them and they stood staring.

"What's this?" Gratillonius barked. An inward groan: What now?

"No immediate business," Apuleius said. "It can wait." Distress flitted over his features. "I should have kept silent till tomorrow. Truly, your safety, what you've done, overweighs entirely this other thing. It was inevitable, anyhow."

Gratillonius bit back a curse. "Will you kindly tell me what the devil it is, or must I go ask them yonder?"

Apuleius sighed. "Very well. The procurator has appointed a new agent for this region. He came while you were gone. A former Ysan himself—one Nagon Demari—ah, you remember?—become a Roman citizen. He went about looking at all persons and property, and estimating assessments. We can pay what we must in Aquilo; I've always been careful about keeping reserves and persuading my populace to do likewise. But Confluentes and its dwellers have never been on the tax rolls, of course—"

A surf roared through Gratillonius. He seemed to swim in it, barely keeping above, while it whelmed everything else. Whenever he broke above a wave, his mouth full of its bitterness, he would hear amidst the noise:

"—land tax—" How many husbandmen had it dragged from their homes, down into serfdom? "—quinquennial—" The levy each five years, less in amount but in its workings worse yet, for it emptied the coffers of artisan and merchant alike, crippling where it did not bankrupt. "—indiction next year—" The Imperial decree every fifteen years which set the rates on property and polls; and Confluentes had no record of past payments from which to argue for moderation. "—naming of your curials—" His father had been made into such a beast of burden.

"—irregularities and outright illegalities—" They had no designated overlords in Confluentes. There had been exemptions for Maximus's old soldiers, because they were veterans, but abruptly their right to have land in freehold or to engage in trade was questioned, in view of the fact that it was a usurper under whom they last served. The folk from Ys were not even citizens.

"—fines and other penalties—" Ruin; bondage.

"—compounding—" Besides overt payment to the state, bribes with no limit other than what the officials decided was obtainable, nor any warranty that in after years someone else would not smell out the transactions and demand his own price, unless in zeal he denounced the whole thing to the Imperium itself.

"—suggestion that children have market value—" Gratillonius remembered a young girl who reached between bars to lay her hands in his and ask if he could take her home.

He grew aware that Apuleius was tugging at his ankle. From the portico above, Rovinda and her children watched with horror on them. People began to slip out of the crowd and go elsewhere. The huntsmen glared around. "Gratillonius," the senator called across the surf. "In God's name, man! You look like a Saxon about to start off on a killing spree. Calm down!"

Gratillonius stared at the sword he had drawn. Its blade gleamed dully through evening shades. The tide within him ebbed away. What it left was as cold and sharp as the steel.

"Dismount, come inside, have a beaker, calm down," Apuleius pleaded. "He's gone, I tell you. Nothing has happened yet. I interposed my authority—kept a few armed men at his side to forestall violence; that would have been disastrous—bad enough, the taunts your Ysans flung at him—But he was not actually here to collect anything. Corentinus and I sent him off with a flea in his ear. He'll be back, we can't stop that, but we do have time for appeals to higher authority, time we can stretch into months, I think, if need be. Come, old friend, let's consider how we can work together."

Gratillonius looked toward Rufinus. "Ride ahead, you and the boys," he ordered. "Tell them in Confluentes to meet outside the basilica—the manor house, you know. I'll be there shortly and speak to them."

His henchman dipped the shafted skull and raised it again, as a cavalry trooper might salute with a battle standard. "Aye, my lord," he answered in Ysan. The lean visage had gone wolflike. "After me!" he shouted in Gallic, and clattered away at the head of his hunters.

"I've done what I can to reassure them," Apuleius said. "They're still terrified; no, I believe some are furious, though they don't confide in me, the Roman. You can do better. But plan what you'll say. This was by no means unanticipated, you recall. We knew there would be problems with the government."

Gratillonius remembered vaguely. Later he could summon up those talks between him and the Aquilonian tribune. They might be less than clear to him. He hadn't given them the attention they rated, with everything else he had on his mind. Well, Apuleius could repeat, add detail, stand true as Apuleius had done throughout the years. First, though—"I didn't expect it would be this bad," Gratillonius retorted.

Apuleius shook his head. "We are not alone. I fear it will be difficult for all Armorica."

"Well, . . . we'll get together later. Tomorrow?" Gratillonius breathed deeply. "I must go and meet with them. It can't wait. They are my people."

He touched heels to Favonius. The horse stamped eagerly, wheeled, and broke into a trot. Gratillonius glanced back. Dismay was gone. His will had hardened and he was off again to battle, for the family at his back as much as for anyone. He waved. "Goodnight!" he called. When he smiled, he was looking at Verania. She straightened and waved too.

He forced himself to keep an easy pace, also after he had passed through the east gate and was bound up the river road. The sun stood on the horizon. Fields reached dim, but water and the crowns of trees glowed golden beneath a sky where light would prevail for an hour. Birds flocked homeward. The stream made a cool music around hoofbeats. Leather creaked. The odor of the stallion was warm and sweet. He touched the sheathed sword. This was his land. He lived to nurture and defend it, that his blood might have it in heritage.

Give Rufinus's crew time to halloo around in the colony and the dwellers time to assemble. Meanwhile he would seek his house—care for Favonius, of course—scrub and groom himself—aye, put on the armor Apuleius had had made for him, because tonight he must be warmaster of this tribe.

5

Twilight deepened, the same dusk as at his victory over the lion. Westward a planet shone like a lamp against royal blue. Beyond the manor and off to the east, forest raised a battlemented wall. Stars glimmered there, and a curve of moon aloft. From the steps of the house, Gratillonius saw his Ysans in a mass, shadowed, become one great expectant animal; but above them a few rush-lights lashed to poles flamed defiance. He would have been well-nigh invisible, save that Runa had set lanterns on stools right and left of him. Their luminance sheened off his coat of mail, helmet with centurion's crest, sword once more in his hand. He caught the hot scent of their burning. She stood in the gloom behind.

"—hold fast." His voice rolled out and out across the darkening world. "To those who would break us, we answer Nay. We bid them be off and let us get on with our lives. Best for them if they heed!

"I promise no swift end of troubles. Surely we shall have to make accommodation with the Roman law; and it is proper that we pay our fair share of costs for the state, Rome who is now your mother also. It will not be easy, getting our rights. But we shall, and while the fight is fought, your best service is to go on about your daily business, unafraid.

"Unafraid. Hearken. You've heard talk of men and women made chattels, aye, parents forced to sell their children into hopeless toil or what is worse. I've seen it happen. But I say to you, it shall not happen again . . . while we stand fast. Those things are limited by Roman law.

"Now we may or may not be wise to seek citizenship for ourselves. As foederates, clearly recognized by treaty, we would be better protected in some ways. On the other hand, we have little to bargain with. I will get counsel

193

about this. But while these questions are before the Imperium, we can hold all else in abeyance. That, and everything that follows, needs the guidance of men wise and strong. Else it will fail. But we have such men on our side: Apuleius, senator and tribune; Bishop Corentinus, prince of the Church. Trust them."

"You too, Grallon!" rang from the gathering.

He chuckled. "Nay, I'm naught but an old soldier." His tone deepened as the sword rose. "But I do myself still hold tribune's rank. Mine is the right to speak directly for you—to the praetorian perfect Ardens in Augusta Treverorum, who is friendly toward me and surely toward you; above him, to the Imperial counselor, consul and Master of Soldiers, Stilicho, who must know what it means to Rome, a strong folk bulwarking this far end of her realm. I stand to ward you.

"For I am the King of Ys."

Tumult hailed him, cheers, laughter, and tears.

—The tall torches swayed away through night. Stillness descended. There were many stars.

Runa came to him. She had thrown aside the black cloak that hid her. A silken gown flowed close about her stride, like the hair down past her shoulders, and shone in the lantern light, like her eyes. She reached forth both hands. He took them before he thought. Thinking was beyond him anyhow. The power of what he had done throbbed through his body and radiated into the air around.

"You *are* the King," she said. Her voice shook.

The narrow face seemed to float before him, a cameo. How fair was her skin. "Once I'd have told myself, aye, he is Taranis on earth," he heard. "That's forbidden, and you'd deny. But you were more than mortal this evening, Gratillonius."

He shook his head, blindly. "I did but hearten them."

"Such power comes from outside the world. You cannot at once return to mortality. 'Tis too far below. You are a God . . . a demigod, a hero. Your will be done. Abide the night."

She pressed close, she was in his arms, their mouths strained together. The high tide roared back, but upbearing him on its arrogance.

194

For an instant, a freezing current passed. "The Queens," he mumbled into the fragrance of her locks.

"You've left the Gods of Ys. They've lost all hold on you. Come."

The surge carried him forward.

—In her bedroom, she barely set aside the lantern she had carried along before he seized her. "Nay, wait," she began. He bore her down onto the blankets and hauled up her skirts. The light slipped smoothly over slender legs, rounded thighs and haunches, till it dived into the sable between. She smiled. "I said, your will be done, King."

Almost, he cast himself on her then and there. His mail rustled. Fleetingly he remembered how she had caught her breath as he drew her against it. That must have hurt. He unbuckled his helmet and threw it clanging to the floor. His sword belt dropped on top. The coif came off with the chain links he pulled over his head. Breeches next! She spread her legs and reached to embrace him.

—Afterward he said, "That was too hasty. I'm sorry."

She ruffled his hair. " 'Twas a long time alone for both of us. We have the night."

"Aye." He roused from the peacefulness of release and they undressed entirely, helping each other. Her breasts were small but firm, with brown nipples already again rising. "What pleasures you?" she asked.

"Whatever you like." As yet he felt shy about telling her what he had enjoyed with—Forsquilis, and Tambilis, and—the manifold ways of his Gallicenae. Nor did he dare call them back to him.

She kissed him savoringly. "Well, let's seek the bed and—You've had no supper. Are you hungry?"

"Not for food," he laughed.

"We'll wake Cata later and have her feed us. She can scarcely be more shocked than she already is. It does the complacent old biddy good. But this hour belongs to us and none else."

6

They went afoot to Aquilo. Noontide brimmed with sun, warmth, and harvest odors. Bees buzzed in clover. The view over the Odita was of men, women, and animals busy across the fields, children following to glean. "They gather more briskly than they did yesterday," Runa said.

'They've hope 'tis for themselves they do, Ysans and Gauls alike," Gratillonius answered.

She closed fingers on his arm. "Your work, man of mine."

Somehow those words wakened a misgiving in him, but it was faint and he sent it away.

They entered the town. Clad as befitted dignitaries going to conference, they stood doubly out among ordinary people bound on ordinary occupations. The whole place felt alien to Gratillonius, half a dream. Most of his mind tarried in the night before.

Realizing that, he hauled it back and gave it marching orders. Urgent business was on hand, the initial discussion of strategy and tactics with Apuleius. Simply composing a letter to the praetorian prefect would require much thought; and it must be on its way soon, by the fastest of couriers.

A slave admitted them to the senator's house. He met them in the atrium. Brightness filled it too, shining from the purity of walls and their delicate murals. Apuleius wore a white robe worked with gold thread; Gratillonius thought of a lighted candle. Brows lifted slightly. "Hail," said the gentle voice. "I had begun to fear something was amiss."

"I'm sorry I'm late," Gratillonius replied. "Overslept." A luxurious looseness perfused him.

Apuleius smiled. "Well, you earned the right. I've heard about your speech. We've held the meal for you." He inclined his head toward Runa. "You give us a pleasant surprise, my lady, but you are very welcome to join us."

Verania flitted in from the rear of the house. Joy sparkled from her. "You're here!" she said to Gratillonius. "I have something special for you on the table."

Apuleius frowned indulgently. "Quiet, girl. Mind your manners."

She halted at the inner door, spirits undampened. Gratillonius smiled at her and raised his hand. Her lashes fluttered down and back up again. Rosiness came and went in her cheeks.

"I brought the lady Runa along," Gratillonius told Apuleius, "because her advice should be valuable. She knows, understands things about the Ysans that, well, a man, an outsider like me never really could."

"Subtleties." Apuleius nodded. Immediately he turned solemn. "I wonder, though, if that isn't premature. And . . . the bishop will arrive later today."

"I'll absent myself," Runa offered with a meekness new to her listeners.

"Oh, he's no woman hater," Gratillonius said.

"But he would doubtless feel . . . awkward . . . especially given the circumstances," she pointed out.

Apuleius's glance went from one to the other and back. Runa drew close beside Gratillonius and took his arm. Together they returned the look.

The Roman became expressionless. "Well, well," he said low. "It appears you two have an understanding."

"We do," Gratillonius declared. Glee broke forth. "In all honesty, I brought her because I wanted you to know right away, my friend."

In the doorway, breath tore across. Verania covered her mouth. Her eyes widened till they seemed to fill her whole face. Apuleius turned his head. "Why, daughter, what's wrong?" he asked. Concern dissolved the reserve he had clamped on himself. "You're white as a toga. Are you ill?"

"F-f-forgive me," she choked. "I can't dine—today—" She whirled. They heard her footfalls stumble down the corridor beyond.

197

7

Autumn blew gray from the north. Wind bit. White-capped, iron-hued seas trampled its shrillness beneath their rush and rumble. The air was full of salt mist. It hid the tops of the mountains behind the firth. They lifted stark, ling-clad, with a few gnarly dwarf trees clinging amidst boulders; streams plunged toward the sea. Eochaid had heard that those heights sheltered deep glens and mild vales, but at the prow of his ship he saw none of it. There was haven here, though, and smoke in tatters from a great rath ahead.

Rowers put out a last burst of strength to drive their galley boldly forward. Currachs accompanying her skimmed like gulls. Eochaid had donned a cloak he otherwise kept locked away from weather, of the six bright colors which he as a king's son might wear. It took eyes off the faded and mended shirt, sea-stained kilt, worn-out shoes.

Spearheads glimmered in front of the earthen wall. Men of the rath had come out to see what strangers drew nigh. "A goodly muster," said Subne at his captain's ear, "and, for sure, more of them alert inside. I think we've found the king where he will be spending this Samain tide."

"May we be finding what else we seek," Eochaid said, more to Manandan maqq Léri and whatever other Gods were listening than to any man. He had already promised sacrifices if They were kindly.

Approaching, he raised hands and cried peace. The warriors ashore stood warily while galley and currachs ran onto the strand. When the crews jumped out to secure them, clearly not hostile, the watchers let weapons droop and smiles arise. Their leader advanced to greet Eochaid in the name of Aryagalatis maqq Irgalato, his king.

His speech had the burr of the Ulati. This Dál Riata was a settlement from the land of that same name in northern Ériu. Nonetheless, it was the language of the home island the wayfarers heard, after three years of roving. More than the wind stung tears from their eyes.

Yet Eochaid must enter not as a gangrel but as a chieftain in his own right. Proudly he walked, and behind him his men bearing gifts of Roman gold, silver, jewelry, cloth, the choicest of their plunder.

The ringwall enclosed a number of buildings: barn, stable, workshops, storehouses, cookhouses, lesser dwellings, and the royal hall. Nothing was nearly as grand as Eochaid remembered of his father's holdings in Qóiqet Lagini, let alone what Niall of Mide and his sons possessed. This house was long but low, poles and daub weathered, thatch overrun by moss. However, it was the present seat of a king, and he a man with many spears at his beck.

A runner had told Aryagalatis who was coming. He lifted the knee in salutation and bade Eochaid take a stool before him, Eochaid's followers to settle themselves where they could find places in the smoke and dimness. He was a stoutly built, rugged-featured man with a black bush of hair and beard. His clothes were more for warmth than show, but gold shone on his breast.

Women brought ale for the warriors, hoarded wine for him and Eochaid. Much seemly talk passed on both sides, giving honor, mentioning forebears and kin, exchanging news. When he received his gifts, Aryagalatis could do no less than offer lodging for as long as his guests wished. His chief poet made verses in praise of Eochaid. They lacked the polish heard among the high ones of Ériu, but hallowed fellowship equally well.

"I will speak openly, lord." Eochaid said at last. "You know what misfortune has made me homeless."

Aryagalatis looked hard through the firelight at the marred, once beautiful face. "I do," he answered carefully. "Your deed will keep you from your motherland forever."

Eochaid held his voice steady. "Injustice and mistreatment drove me mad. It is not the first time such has happened to a hero. Myself and these loyal men have proven on the Romans that we keep the goodwill of the Gods."

"I think that may be true. But say on."

"We are weary of wandering. Thin is the comfort in a camp on an islet or with a woman wrenched from her

199

home. We have homes of our own to make, wives to wed, sons to beget and rear. It is land we ask of you and troth we will give you, Aryagalatis."

The king nodded. "Sure and that comes as no surprise. Well, Alba has land aplenty, once the Cruthini are cleared from it. And since they do often come back, we have always need of fighting men. Let us talk more about this during the winter, Eochaid maqq Éndae."

A sigh as of a wave went through the house.

The exile doubled a fist on his thigh. "You may well also want all the spears you can find," he said, "when Niall of the Nine Hostages attacks your folk across the water. He may not stop there—though surely you will be crossing over to give help and take revenge."

Aryagalatis frowned. "This we will not talk of. That could be bad luck. I know he is your enemy; but while you bide among us, you and your men, you will not be provoking his wrath. Do you understand?"

"I do." Eochaid forced sullenness from his voice. "You will find me grateful, lord. Then, if ever the time does come—But now we want only to wish for your good fortune. May you feed fat the ravens of the Mórrigu!"

XI

1

Midwinter's early darkness had fallen before Gratillonius got his horse properly stabled. Under a thick overcast, Confluentes was a still deeper huddle of black. Though he knew every house, street, lane, almost every rut, he stumbled often enough to make him swear at himself for not bringing along a groom with a lantern. There was too much night within him as well as without.

At last he found his own door and passed through into light of a sort. Tallow candles in wooden holders burned around the main room. They mingled their reek with the closeness that a couple of charcoal braziers laid in the air. Nonetheless a tinge of dank chill persisted. Summer felt ages agone.

His manservant took cloak and coat from him and said the maid, who was actually a middle-aged widow, would set forth a meal as soon as might be. Not knowing when to expect his return, she had perforce let preparation wait. "Bring me a stoup of wine," Gratillonius said. "Nay, mead." If wine was worth drinking, it had gotten sufficiently scarce in these parts and at this season—what with piracy, banditry, and the fear of them cutting away at commerce— that he'd rather save it for happier occasions.

Runa entered from the inner house. She wore a shapeless dress of brown wool, thick socks beneath sandals, and a wimple, under which he knew her hair was coiled in tight braids. "Well, you've come," she said. They had taken to speaking Latin in the presence of his servants, who were Ysan countryfolk with scant grasp of the language. Neither of them liked having words of theirs bandied about. "Where were you?"

"I went riding."

Her arched brows lifted higher still. "Indeed? All day, when you've been telling me you haven't half the hours you need for guiding your people?"

He checked an angry retort. That was not what he had declared, and well she knew it. Crises, most of them petty but important to those concerned, had a way of springing up in bunches, like weeds. Otherwise he had undertakings to supervise, military instruction and drill to maintain, dickerings with Osismii and Aquilonians to carry out. But much of his time he spent standing by, passing it with wood and leather in his little workshop.

"A day is very short, these months," he said. "I needed to get out by myself." —use his muscles, gallop along empty roads, range afoot into leafless woods.

"You might have had the goodness to stop at the basilica and tell me you'd be late." She spent her own days in the former manor house. Sometimes she visited the homes of settlers, gathering their memories of Ys and its history,

201

but oftenest she summoned them to her. The habit of deference to a priestess remained in them.

His patience ruptured. "Damnation, must I always be spoke to your hub?"

The manservant brought his goblet. He raised it and swallowed. The mead was well brewed, dry, flavored with woodruff, a pungency recalling meadow margins where cornel bloomed. His mood mildened. This was no easy life for her either. "Well, I should have told you," he admitted, "but the news I'd gotten—Apuleius had the letter passed on to me at sunrise—that drove everything else out of my head." It flitted through him that formerly Apuleius would have come in person, or invited him to Aquilo, and they would have talked.

"Oh." She also gentled. Somehow that made him aware of her pallor, even in this dull light. She had been ill for several days of late, keeping to herself in the manor house as if too proud to let him see her thus. Recovery advanced, but as yet she didn't quite have her full strength back. "Bad. From the South?"

He nodded. She came to him, took his elbow, guided him to a bench built against the wall. They sat down together. Straw ticking rustled beneath them.

He gestured an order that the servant bring drink for her, and stared into his as he dragged forth: "The Visigoths broke down every defense. They're looting and burning all through northern Italy."

It was a minor wonder, perhaps, that couriers had brought the word this far, this soon. Only last month had King Alaric invaded. The war was not much older than that, it had broken out with such stunning swiftness and ferocity. Before, Emperors Arcadius in the East and Honorius in the West—rather, their ministers—seemed to have made peace with those warriors. Alaric had become Master of Soldiers in eastern Illyricum. The thought was like poison in Gratillonius, that quite possibly Constantinople had then secretly persuaded him to fall on Rome.

Be that as it may, "The Imperium has to call in reinforcements," he said. "The letter mentioned troops on their way from the Rhenus. Come sailing weather, if the war is still going on, I wouldn't be surprised but what

202

they're hailed out of Britannia too. And then what about the barbarians along those frontiers?"

"Horrible." Runa's tone stayed level and she did not reach for his hand as Tambilis, say, would have. "But what can we do except continue in those tasks God has set us?"

He grimaced. "Mine is to hurry up the reconstruction of our defenses. If only those sh—those donkeys in Turonum would so much as answer my letters about it!"

"Don't start pacing again. You know how I dislike that. In a year's time, ten years, a hundred, this will be past."

"Like Ys," he said bitterly.

"Well, Ys had its woes too, century after century. Just the same, what I am writing will be glorious as long as the world endures."

The man brought her mead. She sipped as she talked on about her book. It could not simply be written from beginning to end. Her education came back to her in pieces; suddenly she would remember something that happened generations ago, and record it before she forgot again. The other survivors had minds less orderly. "And you must be more forthcoming yourself, Gratillonius. I really must insist you tell me things, tell me in full. I know it hurts you, but you should have the manhood to do it, considering what this means. Oh, and if you'd only trouble yourself to make notes, how much toil you'd spare me, instead of puttering at your bench like a common carpenter."

He refrained from remarks about duties—promises, at least—owed on her part. When Apuleius and Corentinus agreed to jointly sponsor her history, it had been with the understanding that she would continue copying books as well, but thus far she had not again touched that task. When Gratillonius once brought the matter up, she flared that the work was fit for any slave who had had a year's schooling.

Tribune and bishop abstained from reproaches. Indeed, the latter had said little to her and nothing to Gratillonius about their unblessed union. She was just a catechumen, her man an unbeliever. Yet he hated to suppose Corentinus and Apuleius had dismissed them from their hearts. He hoped they hoped the pair would repent and reform.

However that was, he rarely saw the churchman these days.

"—scrawling on wretched wooden slabs. When will you get me a proper supply of papyrus? Or parchment. You said you would."

"It's not that easy," Gratillonius told her. How many times already had he done so? "Traffic from the South goes by fits and starts. Skins have more urgent uses. Besides, scraping them and the rest of the preparation, that's long labor."

"You can find idle hands aplenty to train. Let your hunters bring in deer to replace the sheepskins. Talk to Apuleius. He can arrange such things. He'll scarcely give me a civil word."

No, thought Gratillonius, that family had likewise drifted apart from him. Not that there was a breach, anything like that. He and the senator continued to meet, confer, work as a team. Sometimes when they had been at it till late he stayed for supper. But the conversations didn't range around as they used to, and he didn't get invitations simply for pleasure, and he seldom encountered Rovinda or the children.

Had he given offense? That wasn't reasonable. They had taken him for what he was before, the nine times wedded King of Ys. He did nothing now that they wouldn't expect of such a man, or of many a Christian. Now and then he thought he glimpsed sorrow in the eyes of Apuleius or Corentinus. Of course, in those eyes he was debauching Runa, the convert. . . . Whatever the cause, a constraint had come upon them, and begotten its like in him. Not knowing what to say or do, he kept as withdrawn as possible.

"—if we moved to a city, a real city, Treverorum or Lugdunum or Burdigala, someplace with intelligent people, books, supplies."

"I have my duty here," he snapped. And no wish whatsoever to become one more drop in a bucket.

"A decent house, at the absolute least!"

That had ignited their first quarrel, and others afterward. She refused to leave the manorial one. True, she could far better work in its well-lighted and hypocaust-

204

heated rooms. But for his part, he would not move in with her. He declared that his proper station was inside Confluentes, readily accessible to his people, quickly able to reach any trouble. His private self knew it would feel wrong, like some sly betrayal. They settled on her spending her days there, most of her nights here; but she hated these rough quarters and kept trying to change his mind.

"My lord and lady, your meal awaits you." The servant came as a deliverer, Gratillonius thought wryly.

His mood grew mellower as he went in with Runa, sat across from her—in the other place they would have reclined side by side, Roman style—and shared food and drink. She too seemed glad to have escaped a fight and anxious to let the newest scratches heal. They could converse interestingly, as he could with few men. This evening she asked him to tell her what he knew about the Goths.

That was not a great deal. Their tribes were divided between a western and an eastern branch. Wandering down from Germanic lands, they had settled in regions north of the Danuvius and the Euxinus. Later the thrust of a wholly wild and terrible breed, the Huns, caused them to seek refuge among the Romans. They proved to be formidable soldiers, especially as cavalrymen, but untrustworthy subjects, apt to rebel. Most became Christian, though of the Arian persuasion. . . . This led on to Gratillonius's experiences with other barbarians, Scoti and Picti, in Britannia, and thus to recollections of his boyhood.

Aye, he thought in Ysan, I ought to stand grateful for the good she does. 'Twas not only loosing me from the dread of the King's ancient captivity. However, that was wonder enough, and—She's fair to behold, like a dark-eyed ivory hawk; and if she lacks such ardor as certain of the Queens gave me, still, she is a woman.

At the end, he smiled and asked, "Shall we to our rest? The hour is indeed late, and I'd liefest not be overwearied."

She looked away. "I'm sorry," she replied in Latin. "The moon forbids."

He sat straight up on his bench. "No, wait. That was—a dozen days ago, I think."

"You know what I mean," she said.

205

He did. She wanted no child to weigh her down, endanger her life, and burden her for years afterward. So she had told him, one night during which his anger grew flame-hot and hers snow-cold.

Resentment lifted afresh. "Go back to the manor, then. I'll send Udach along with a light for you."

She met his look almost calmly. "Not that either," she murmured.

We draw too near the edge, too often, Gratillonius thought, and accompanied her to their bedroom.

She set down the candle she had borne from the dining table and turned around toward him. Has she decided otherwise? he wondered. Gladness came to a glow. He stepped closer. "Earlier I talked of being spoke to your hub," he laughed. "Suddenly I see how right that was."

She raised a palm. "No. Not thus." The thin lips curved. "But I do want you to be happy."

He could have forced her. That would doubtless have been the end of their association. Ysan women were seldom submissive. He stopped and let her approach him.

What followed slaked the flesh but left him feeling unfulfilled. He slept lightly, several times waking from dreams where someone kept calling him.

—The slightest wan glimmer showed through a crack in a shutter. He knew he would sleep no further. Runa did, and for a little while he lay by the warmth of her, but restlessness drove him to his feet. Fumbling in murk, he found his tunic on its peg and slipped it over his head against the chill. Knee-length, it would serve. He wanted fresh air.

Beyond the door he saw houses nearly formless among shadows. The east had barely lightened. No sunrise could break through such cloud cover. It was the Birthday of Mithras. Gratillonius rarely saw a calendar, but everybody knew when solstice happened, and from that he could reckon this day.

How leaden it was. Not that that mattered. He had forsaken Mithras as Mithras had forsaken him. Yet his mind flew off across years, to a young man on the Wall, and another who hailed the same dawn and met him at sunset for prayers. O Parnesius, comrade of the heather, it's been so long. Where are you now? Are you now, any more?

<h1 style="text-align:center">2</h1>

Spring cast green over the low land around Deva. Trees budded and bloomed, sudden amazing whiteness, as if bits of the clouds that wandered overhead had drifted to earth. Birdflocks were returning. Showers left rainbows, sparkles, and clean new smells.

On a small and sparsely wooded hill, men fought. Shouts, yells, footfalls, blasts on horns, rattle and clash of metal, hiss of arrows, thud of slingstones frightened robins and finches from their nests. Carrion crows flapped watchful. A mile away, the city walls mirrored their rose hue in the river gliding past them. Round about, smoke stained heaven where villages lately sacked and torched still smoldered.

Far outnumbered, the Romans made the hill a strongpoint whence they cast back wave after Scotic wave. They made the trees their fellows in the shield-rank, as if they had grown roots of their own. When a man sank, one behind dragged him dead or alive inside the square and took his place. Mail-clad bodies nonetheless sprawled or, hideously, moved and moaned on the torn sod farther down. Most of the fallen wore much less, coat and breeches or only the kilt, some among them naked. Blood seemed twice red on their lily skins. Sweat and death bestank the air.

Again Niall shouted to his warriors and led them in a rush. Bones broke under his feet. Once a loop of gut from an opened belly wrapped about his ankle. He kicked it off without slowing. Helmets gleamed ahead. His blade leaped up, down, right, left. A hostile point struck into his targe. Before the hand behind could pull it free, that hand dangled from a wrist cut halfway through. Niall drove the screaming creature before him, onto its back. He was into the Roman line. A banner on a pole hung before his eyes. He would hew his way there and cast it down.

Shields pressed against him. Swords reached from around

them. The sheer weight forced him off. The line closed anew. Breath quick and harsh in his throat, he backed down the slope. The men of Ériu washed past him.

They rallied as before in the swale below, killed accessible enemy wounded, did what they could for their own, clustered around their tuathal chiefs. A certain quiet fell. Their will and courage stayed high, but again they had taken hurts and losses without victory, and needed a rest. They sat or lay widespread on the damp ground. Waterskins went among them.

"I got a look this time," said Uail maqq Carbri. "They haven't much left to call on. A few more charges, and we'll open gaps they can't fill."

"Those will be costly, darling," Niall warned, "and may take us past nightfall." He scowled at the westering sun. No moon would rise until a sliver did shortly before daybreak. He would be unwise if he made any assault in the dark. It would give the Romans, who worked together like arms and legs on a single man, too much advantage. Moreover, the bravest among his lads was prone to terror at night, when anything might stalk abroad. Let fear take hold of the host, and at best they would stumble over each other as they fled wailing back to camp. At worst they would scatter blindly and morning would find most of them alone, ready prey for the Britons.

Was it mere bad luck that had brought that troop here? The word from his spies had seemed a promise from the Gods. The legion that, time out of mind, had lived in yonder city was to leave. As soon as the season allowed, it would march out, across Britannia to a southern seaport, and embark for war across the Channel. Already depleted, the two that stayed behind could hardly garrison Deva too. Until the Romans got together a new force, if they were able, that whole rich countryside, hitherto almost untouched because of the legion, lay like a virgin defenseless. Niall would be the first man there.

And so he had been, with hundreds at his back. Daring the treacherous tides and sands at the rivermouth, they brought their currachs upstream. From the tents they pitched they ranged forth, raping and reaping. Horsemen with bows and spears slowed them, but they drove those off and had not seen any for a pair of days. Niall cherished thoughts of taking the city itself, which seemed as weakly held as you might hope. But then the soldiers came down the highway from the east.

Uail's voice broke in on him: "See! I do think they are sending out a herald."

The man who trod from the enemy line wore no proper garb for that holy office, nor did he carry the white wand in his right hand and sword in his left. However, he walked slowly, mail-clad but weaponless, arms lifted. Behind him, two others winded long horns to show this was not flight or stealth.

The Scoti stared. Such of them as had snatched bow or spear let it drop. Yet those were three bold men. Where the slope began to level off they stopped and waited.

"I will speak to them," said Uail, who knew Latin well. He took time to cut and peel a branch for carrying along. A hornet buzz of voices followed him.

The exchange was brief. Uail sought back to the King and told that the Roman captain did indeed ask for a talk. Niall's heart thumped. He kept his dignity, striding unhurried over the grass, ahead of his henchman, until he met the one newly arriving from among the foe. His torn, grimed clothing, stiff with dried blood and sweat, might have been sacral raiment.

The defender was, at least, just as smelly—and as uncowed. For a few slow breaths the two stood silent, look against look. The soldier was a strongly built, medium tall man of about forty. His face was square and somewhat hooknosed, brown-eyed, stubble black on the big chin. Niall recognized the vinestaff and sidewise crest of a centurion. Chased with silver, the lamellar cuirass told of senior rank.

His voice was hoarse from the day's fighting, but resonant: "Hail. Shall we give oaths that whatever comes of this, both parties return unharmed?"

Niall could follow the Latin in part, though he was glad to have Uail's help. He showed more anger than he really felt. "Do you suppose I would be violating the truce of heralds? That gives me small cause to believe *you* will keep faith."

209

When Uail had made the response clear, the officer flashed a grim grin and said, largely through the interpreter, "Very well. We'll trust each other that far. I command the vexillation. My name is Flavius Claudius Constantinus." He uttered it in full, which Romans seldom did, as if it meant something special.

Since he gave his foeman due honor, agreement might be possible. "I am Niall maqq Echach, called he of the Nine Hostages, King at Temir in Mide, lord over my northern conquests in Ériu."

Thick brows rose. "That man? We know your name, all too well. I'd give much gold and many prayers to bring you down. Maybe I should cut the parley short and start the battle over, in hopes."

Pleased by the recognition, Niall answered, "You are free to do that. But it's we who will overrun you, and I who'll take your head home with me."

Constantinus barked a laugh. "Insolent rogue! . . . Render that 'Proud swordsman,' translator, or we'll get nowhere. . . . How battle goes is in the hands of God. He's more than once cast down the high and raised up the low. But I have my men to think about. And you have yours, King Niall."

"Men of mine scoff at death."

"No doubt. However, wouldn't you rather bring them back whole, with their gains, bring them back to fight another day and breed sons for your sons to lead to other battles—rather that than leave all your bones here for the crows? That's the choice I offer you."

"Say on."

Constantinus's mouth tightened. "Ah, you're no witless animal, worse luck. Well." He put on ease, tucked staff under arm, hooked thumbs in belt, and drawled, "I'll explain. We're not such fools either. When orders came for the Twentieth to pull out, we knew pretty much what would happen shortly after it did, and prepared as best we could. That included keeping our hillman allies ready. You've bounced off them before, you Scoti. Their king, Cunedag, with his cadre of Votadini, he threw your settlers out of that country once, and those who've since

210

returned haven't done it anywhere close to him. Now he lives near Deva—d'you understand?

"The Second Legion is away south at Isca Silurum, and has that whole territory to guard. But my Sixth is at Eburacum, on the eastern side of the island. We've got our own watch to keep, against Saxons and Picti, but we can spare this many men. When we heard of your arrival, we sent to Cunedag at once. Not that he wouldn't have heard too, but we let him know we were ready to work with him. While he raised his warriors, we dispatched cavalry to harass you, and I led my infantry here by forced marches. The legions may be shrunken and weak everywhere else, but by God, we Britons can yet soldier like Romans!

"Well. Here we are, our two forces. While you fight me, you're pinned down; and the Votadini and Ordovices are on their way. I expect them any hour. You can grind us down *almost* to the last man, but you'll pay for it, and what's left of you will be staggering half asleep when our foederates strike.

"Or you can withdraw, pack up your plunder, and escape. The choice, I've said, is yours."

Niall stood silent after Uail had rendered the last of the speech for him. A breeze ruffled and cooled his hair. It brought him the noises of the crippled and dying where they lay.

Did Constantinus lie? Niall thought not. He had known a greater host than his would come from the uplands with much of its own to avenge. He meant to be gone before then. He had not awaited it this soon. Yet if it were not so, why would the Romans have squandered soldiers they could ill afford? The only reason must be to keep the men of Ériu engaged until the reinforcements appeared.

A question remained. "Why have you warned us?" Niall asked. "Had you kept silent and stood fast, the net would have closed on me."

Constantinus's iron smile passed again over his face. "If I'd known beforehand whom I dealt with, I might well have chosen that," he answered. "The news took me by surprise. Too late now. And we have carried out our orders, limited the harm you did. It's not our fault Cunedag's

211

been slower than we hoped. He's growing old. In any case, my orders also were to spare as many of my command as possible. Rome has need of them. How do you feel about yours?"

He could take that head, Niall thought. Maybe he should. Power was in this man, a smell of fate about him; if he lived, many a woman would weep. But so would they keen in Ériu for their men whom Niall had led to death afar.

Across twenty years, the King remembered the onslaught on the Wall in the North and what that had cost. With the ashenness in his hair had come a measure of ash-cold wisdom to his soul. And this was nothing but a raid. The plan from the first had been to depart when the Britons brought too much strength. Let the Scoti carry off honor and a goodly load of booty.

"You will have fame after this day, Constantinus," Niall said. "Maybe we shall be meeting again."

Meanwhile his fleet could harry farther up the coast. Then he must turn back and quell unrest at home. Throughout, he must stay bold but never reckless. He felt his own fate, whatever it might be, still upon him, still to be lived out. Next year— More and more, a song haunted his dreams. He had been too long away from Ys.

3

Governor Glabrio summoned Procurator Bacca to a private meeting. There he gave him the news that had arrived by special courier. The Visigoths were leaving Italy. After the Imperial relief of besieged Mediolanum and a drawn battle fought on Easter Sunday, they had retreated into Etruria. The Romans continued to press them and now, with members of his family captured, Alaric had made terms and his army was bound back toward Histria.

"You must confer with Bishop Bricius about arrangements for a suitable thanksgiving," said Glabrio. "The festivities that follow should emphasize the enduring power of the Roman state, under God."

"No doubt," replied Bacca. "It would be unkind to make any mention of the loose ends."

Glabrio showed irritation, as he often did at remarks by this man. "Oh? Just what do you mean by that, pray tell?"

"Why, it's obvious . . . to one of your perspicacity."

"I prefer frankness. Openness. Fewer of your equivocations, *if* you will be so kind."

Bacca shrugged. "The letter says nothing about the barbarians returning their loot, let alone paying reparations for their ravages. They withdraw in peace, probably not very far, to live off the country and wait for—what? One should think the redoubtable Stilicho would handle them somewhat more vigorously."

"Ah, I daresay, ah, the Master of Soldiers has his reasons."

Bacca nodded. "This isn't the first time, you recall, when he might have crushed Alaric and didn't. Does he nurse a deep plan for the longer term, in which the Visigoths are to be his allies? He's always shown a partiality to barbarian foederates that some Romans find disquieting. Of course, considering his ancestry— Another conceivable explanation is that he vacillates and cobbles together hasty improvisations, like most mortals. His preoccupation with the Ostrogothic threat in Rhaetia seems to have been what allowed Alaric to enter Italy in the first place."

"Have a care." Glabrio lifted a finger. "Indiscretion can prove costly. I will not be party to subversive talk."

"Too much discretion can be even more dangerous," Bacca said. "Men who value their necks should try to see situations as they are, not as one would prefer them to be. And," he added on a proper note of solemnity, "as a patriot one necessarily considers where the best, the strongest governance of the state may be found."

Glabrio's jowls flushed. "You speak of decisiveness. You are very fond of speaking of it. But where is yours? I must say, I expected you would join me in rejoicing and prayers— this great deliverance—not sit there with your sour naysaying. Have a care. I cannot continue indefinitely, weighted and obstructed by persons—persons who are—I refrain from calling them timid. No, they are too proud of their cleverness. They are too clever by half."

213

"Oh, but I share your elation, Governor. Pardon me if I gave the wrong impression. You know I am not a demonstrative man by nature." Bacca smiled. "If I keep silent while hosannahs are sung, it's because I cannot carry a tune. My station in life lies with the grubby details, none of them singly worth the attention of a leader, but collectively adding up to mountains in his path. I can then show where the passes over those mountains are, and offer suggestions as to how and when it is most expeditious to proceed. But the decision is always the leader's."

Glabrio grunted in the way that showed he was mollified. "You have something to propose," he said. "I know you."

"As a matter of fact, I do," replied the procurator. "It concerns this colony of Ysans at Aquilo." He saw fresh vexation rising, and hurried on: "Hear me out, I beg you. You've been after me to move—"

"High time. It's been two years now since I told you something must be done. And how long—more than half a year since the agent *you* chose went there and returned empty-handed."

"He was not sent as a collector," Bacca reminded. "The curials at Aquilo have been rendering the normal amounts, in both money and kind, on schedule. So the situation is ambiguous, and this is what frustrates us.

"I acknowledge, Governor, you've been a saint in your patience, especially compared to Nagon Demari. He drips venom like a viper. I've all I can do sometimes, restraining him from rash, even violent action. You understand what that could bring on. Gratillonius does have powerful . . . friends? At any rate, men who think they see value in him, potential usefulness. If nothing else, they want to wait and see what the decisions are on the highest level."

"None!" fumed Glabrio.

"The Imperium has other things on its mind."

"Nevertheless— Well, I should not have entrusted you with the business. You phrased your letters far too weakly. They conveyed no sense of the urgency and importance of it. Meanwhile Gratillonius does whatever he chooses, without regard to the law, like—like a foederate. An uncurbed

214

foederate. An Alaric. How long must I endure it? Not much longer, I tell you. I will not."

"You need not, God willing," said Bacca fast. "As I've tried to explain before, I've gone ahead cautiously because of the possible consequences, should some mistake occur among all the incalculables. Despite this, I instructed Nagon to be harsh and menacing at Confluentes. That did drive the people there closer than ever to Gratillonius. He seems their only hope. But we need not fear a rebellion, like the Gothic uprising against Valens. Confluentes is a mere village. We can bide our time.

"Today, I believe, that time has come. I've been thinking hard about the matter, throughout the months when you supposed I was neglecting it. I have talked quietly with various people, such as our new bishop, and corresponded with others, and in general laid a foundation. What I waited for was an opportune moment—this moment."

Glabrio's eyes bulged. "What do you propose? When?"

Bacca made a soothing gesture. "A little more waiting, Governor, a little more patience. Today's news means that the situation will shortly be propitious for us. Stilicho will be ready, anxious, to look at countless questions he and his subordinates have perforce postponed. That includes preparing the indiction, this being the year for it. We control the local census takers; and in our report, we can make recommendations.

"The Emperor Honorius, too, will want to follow *his* victory over the Goths by a show of other actions, preferably benevolent. But as I suggested earlier, Stilicho can scarcely feel himself omnipotent. His enemies at court must be raising the same arguments I did, with far more force. He will want allies. He will be prone to agree with the proposals of important men—such as the governor of Lugdunensis Tertia. He will not examine them too closely.

"Let us compose letters to the appropriate persons. Stilicho will be among them, but we don't want anyone to feel slighted. Let us state that the Confluentian question really must be resolved. No hostility toward the good Gratillonius or his unfortunate people. None. On the contrary, we recommend an immediate grant of citizenship."

Glabrio opened his mouth to object. Bacca headed him

215

off: "The more they depend on him, the more helpless they'll be when we break him loose from them. Because, you see, the decree we request from the Emperor will include certain details, each single one entirely legal and reasonable—"

4

They were making a furnace at the top of Mons Ferruginus, where winds could blow free to help charcoal burn the fiercer, and Gratillonius was up there as often as the claims on him allowed. It was a chance to work with his hands—things were so much more forgiving than men and women—as well as to see a hope abuilding.

Iron ore was not far to seek, but no one since the Roman conquest had gone after it. Purchase from slave-manned works elsewhere was easier, cheaper. Now you could rely on importation no more, unless by yourself. Best would be to make your own, and trade off the surplus at a profit. Olath Cartagi, who had been apprenticed to a dealer in metals in Ys, got the idea. He found a man who knew the art to be his partner. Apuleius lent them money and Gratillonius gave all the support he was able.

This went beyond a single enterprise, Gratillonius knew. A ready supply of iron would call up blacksmiths, whom Confluentes needed. Their products would serve other new industries. The colony would in time become a city—not mere inhabitants herded together.

He supposed sufficient ground had been broken to feed them, clothe them after a rough fashion, buy minimal necessities and pay taxes in kind. But with nothing else, it meant a peasant's existence, presently a serf's, never better than an animal's and ofttimes worse. Into oblivion would go every skill, dream, memory, freedom that had formed the soul of Ys. And Julia's first child was swelling within her, his grandchild that he could dare to love.

Take hands off ards, spades, sickles, aye, women's hands too when the power of creation dwelt within them. Do it before toil irreparably thickened fingers and blunted minds.

Coppersmiths, goldsmiths, jewelers—masons, sculptors, glassworkers—weavers, dyers—merchants, shippers, seamen, fresh growth in the trade Aquilo already did—civilization, and the strength to ward it!

Here on this height was a beginning.

Olath straightened, rubbed the small of his back, blew out breath like a weary horse. "Enough for today," he said.

Gratillonius nodded. With surrounding trees cleared away, he had a view down wooded hillside whose green glowed transient gold, across the flat strip along the Odita, over the burnished surface of that water and croplands beyond. After a warm day, mistiness obscured the western horizon and turned the sun into a huge ruddy shield. Air cooled fast; sweaty garments clung clammy. Smoke from fires smothered their acridness, though, and muscles, relaxing, felt less exhausted than sated. It had been a good day's work.

Olath waved and shouted: "Pack it away!"

The gang grinned and busied themselves preparing the site for abandonment till tomorrow. Most of them had been engaged in the various jobs of cleaving and dressing stone to line the smelting pit and its drains. Earlier they had hauled the raw material in, a couple of menhirs which had stood nearby since ages that myth had forgotten. At first such disregard for the Old Folk shocked Gratillonius, then he realized how his years in Ys had wrought on him. The claims of the living outweighed any by the dead. Confluentes would need stone too as it burgeoned, for pavement, better buildings, stouter defenses, the cathedral church that Corentinus planned.

"I should stay and help," Gratillonius said, "but must go bathe and change clothes ere dark. Maeloch's leading several headmen on the tide, from fisher villages. He sent a runner this morning. We're to speak of joint undertakings, in work as well as patrol against pirates. 'Twill keep me occupied a day or two."

"You honor me in explaining, lord King," said Olath, "but 'tis needless. You're no common laborer."

"He has the shoulders for it, he does," laughed another Ysan who overheard.

217

Gratillonius smiled and started down the trail. How splendid that such a man, after everything he had lost and endured, could again crack a joke.

His mind ran ahead of him. Food, drink, lodging for the guests—the better he entertained them, the more willingness he could hope for. As yet, Confluentes could not carry a full share of the load he wanted borne; and Apuleius was not free to commit Aquilo even to so loose an alliance. Well, sailors should be content with heartiness at a feast. It was doubtless for the best that Runa refused to take part. ("Shall I be matron—head servant—to a pack of stinking tribesmen?") Julia had stepped in, dear dutiful Julia.

Gratillonius sighed. More and more he wondered why he continued the union. A woman in his bed; lively conversation sometimes, when otherwise he would be lonely or among dullards, but only sometimes; counsel that might prove worth heeding, but when he deemed it was not, he got an icy tirade and days of sulking. She'd resigned herself to the manual work he did; at least, she'd stopped saying it demeaned her, or anything at all about it.

He came down to the riverside and the road toward Confluentes bridge. Half a dozen men were walking the other way. They were strangers, Celts by the look of them, dusty, shabby, wayworn. For an instant he wished he had a sword rather than an everyday knife. But no, the horrors that prowled these years were still remote. Watchers along the routes satisfied themselves that travelers were harmless before allowing them to go on. Thus far Apuleius had turned aside complaints about it from Turonum.

"Hail," said Gratillonius politely as the newcomers drew near.

"Hail," replied a man who seemed to be the leader. He peered through the sunset light. "Uh, by your leave." His Gallic dialect was of the Redones. "We seek the King of Ys. They told us at the bridge he was yonder. You'd not be him, maybe, your honor?"

"Ys is gone." That hurt to say, and always would. "I am Gratillonius, tribune of those who live." Everybody halted. "What would you with me?"

They made gestures of respect which were clumsy except on the part of a blond young fellow. With a sudden thrill, Gratillonius recognized that particular salute—and the cut of the tunic, the faded patterns in the wool—this was a Durotrigian, from Britannia, neighbor to his Belgae!

"Vellano son of Drach," the leader introduced himself. He named the rest. The Briton was Riwal. "Honored to meet you, my lord."

"I've small time this evening," Gratillonius warned. "Say what you want."

"Why, leave to be your men, lord. We'd serve you faithfully, we and our kin who'll come join us. See, we're strong, healthy, we can show you our skills, and we can each of us fight also, if need be. We ask for a home, lord. For that we'll give you our oaths."

"What, have you no roofs of your own?"

He had heard the story before and learned how to draw it out. Not that he inquired too closely. Displaced farmers and unemployed artisans or laborers were one thing. They weren't supposed to move without permission which was hard to get, but when they did, quietly, as a rule the authorities mounted no search. Those who survived usually ended in servitude, which was preferable to their remaining restive, occasionally riotous freemen. Or else they became Bacaudae, altogether out of reach.

Runaway serfs and slaves were another matter. Gratillonius didn't ask, and had his ways of steering them from telling him. As yet, no census taker had visited his community.

These travelers seemed to be just what they claimed. "However, I shall have to talk further with you ere I decide," Gratillonius told them. "You understand we can't let in thieves, murderers, lepers, any such folk."

"We're none like that, lord."

"For your part, you must know clearly beforehand what's expected of you. This is not a nest of barbarians."

"We know that, sir," said Riwal the Briton. " 'Tis why we've come our long, hard way."

"Longest for you." Gratillonius considered the weathered, hunger-gaunted face. "What drove you from your tribe?"

"The Scoti," Riwal said roughly. "One legion's gone, the other two spread thin and undermanned. When raiders from the sea sacked and burned Vindovaria, we wondered in our own village who'd be next. I vowed my wife and youngsters should not sit and wait our turn. We'd heard tales about safe havens in Armorica. The Gods blew a fisher from there off course and brought her, short of crew, to our little bight. I got a berth on her."

Gratillonius wondered if the man, once among the Redones, had inspired his companions to seek here or had chanced to learn of their plans and persuaded them to let him join. It seemed impossible that the fame of tiny Confluentes had drifted on the winds as far as Britannia.

No, but wait; tales of Ys; and after the city foundered, people would ask whether there had been any survivors, and pass the story—

Gratillonius would find out. Hercules! To talk with a Briton again! This was not the first one to seek refuge in Armorica. There were even some small settlements of them. But this was the first such immigrant he had met. Why, Riwal might know what had become of the Gratillonius estate back there, the Gratillonius blood. It was hard holding that blood cool, it leaped so in his veins.

"I'll get you a place for the night," the tribune said, "and somewhat to eat on the morrow. Barn straw and beggar's fare; but later we'll see what more can be done. Come with me."

5

Having returned from a voyage to Hivernia where he did a profitable trade along the southern shores, Evirion borrowed a horse and rode off to call on Nemeta. It was a relief to arrive at her cabin after a few hours and find no one else there. More and more folk were seeking aid of her.

Summer weighed heavy on the land. Rainfall the day before had not eased its heat, only thickened the air. Leaves hung listless, their green dulled, beneath a stone-

220

blue sky. New clouds were massing in the west and thunder muttered afar. Muddy smells and thin haze smoked above the river, whose purling was almost the single sound going in or out of forest shadows. Garments clung to skin dank and rank with unshed sweat. Flies pestered the mount, mosquitoes the man.

Nemeta's hair seemed to burn the sullenness out of the day. Evirion sprang from the saddle as she came forth and strode to take both her hands in his. "How have you fared?" he exclaimed.

"Well enough." She looked upward into his eyes. Crinkles radiated from them; they had squinted against many weathers. "But you?"

"I likewise. No troubles, though we heard rumors of marshalling to the north. How good to see you again."

She smiled in her way, which always held something back. "The pleasure is mine. You're kindly, that you come so often."

"What else could I? You must be lonely. Will you never heed your father or me and move back into town?"

Nemeta shook her head. The unbound locks rippled over her tunic. "Nay. I have my companions here."

Once more he wondered what those were. Surely not human. While she received visitors and might go off to their homes to cast a needed spell, every tale told about her buttressed his belief that he was the nearest thing to a friend that she had among mortals. Formerly there had been Runa, but she was now leman to the King of Ys, above consorting with a little woodland witch. Briefly, Evirion's lip lifted.

"What matters most, I have my freedom," Nemeta went on. When he had tethered the horse, she took his arm. "Come, let's go within where 'tis cooler. I've lately earned a cask of very good mead. Can you stay a while?"

Her slenderness, bowstring-taut, filled his vision. "As long as you will have me," he said, and felt the blood beat in his face.

She stopped, regarded him carefully, at last sighed, "I meant for hours. Best you start home ere sunset."

"Home?" broke from him. "That hovel?"

With a slight pressure, she moved him onward. "You do

221

your house an injustice," she said, forcing a bit of merriment. " 'Tis larger than this. And soon you'll be able to afford a Roman mansion."

"Why should I want one?"

They entered the cabin. Its darkishness embraced them. She gestured him to take a stool and herself flitted to the storage end of the room. "Why, you ought to be marrying and starting a family," she replied with continued cheer. "Already, I daresay, the maidens of Aquilo daydream about you and their mothers think what a fine catch you'd be."

He tried to match her mood, or at least her pretense. "Oh, I'm too much away. We'll be gone again, my crew and I, after we've refitted *Brennilis*. And 'twill be a longer faring this time. We may have to winter abroad."

She twisted on her heel and looked wide-eyed at him. "Whither?"

"Across the German Sea, to the Cimbrian peninsula and thence, I think, up toward Thule. Amber, furs, slaves, walrus and narwhal ivory. I went there before, you recall. 'Tis a well-rewarded venture if one outlives it."

She hung her head. "But the dangers—"

He shrugged in his manliest wise. "The gains. For Confluentes too. I've talked with curials of Aquilo. They think I can sell most of what cargo I bring home, mayhap all, here. Outsiders will be drawn by it, and so we build up an emporium."

"You are . . . a patriot, is that the Latin word? I will try . . . what I can do." Hastily, Nemeta filled two cups and carried them back. "Now tell me about your newest adventures," she said with great sprightliness.

He had begun when footsteps sounded outside and a form filled the open doorway. Both of them rose. "Is it you?" Nemeta called, and made a mouth.

Cadoc Himilco entered. He was clad in Gallic style—shirt, coat, breeches of sturdy material dyed green, low boots, pack on shoulders—and armed with spear, short-sword, and bow: the outfit of a ranger in the wilderness, such as Gratillonius was making him into. "Hail," he greeted. Recognizing Evirion, he stiffened. "What do you want?"

The seaman showed the same dislike. His height and

breadth hulked against the newcomer's slim frame. "Or you?" he challenged. "Help in finding your arse without a periplus?"

"Hush!" said the woman. "You're both guests. You've each visited me erenow. Sit down and we'll drink together."

Neither man listened. "I am her friend," Evirion growled. "Like a brother, d'you understand? But what are you? Or what do you hope to be, your wife not knowing?"

Thinly sculptured features flushed beneath the freckles the sun had laid over them. "Curb your tongue," Cadoc snapped. "Julia d-does know. She's half-sister to this poor lost soul, after all. She'd come herself, were she able."

"Cadoc wants to win me from heathendom," Nemeta explained. "He's thrice preached Christ, these past months."

"Would that I'd oftener been free to do so," Cadoc said.

Nemeta tossed her head. "Thanks be you weren't! I've suffered it for old times' sake, but frankly, now, you've become a nuisance. Sit, and we'll talk of better things."

"Naught is better than Heaven." Cadoc turned back to Evirion. "I asked you wh-wh-what you seek here."

"And I command you stop your prying," the other man answered. His fists doubled. "Or do you want a dunk in the privy?"

Cadoc stood straighter yet. His weather-bleached hair shone like a pale lamp in the gloom. "Aye, you've the s-s-strength of body to beat me as you did aforetime. But you're soft in the spirit, Evirion Baltisi, too weak for the Faith. Else why would you bid for the help of d-demons?"

"I do not—" The mariner choked on his words. Nemeta had in fact chanted charms for him in advance of his voyages. He had expected she would again. He didn't believe they had much power, but there was a certain comfort in them, as there was in any lucky token. And it was a gift she gave him.

"I am her friend," he declared. "She's glad to see me. She's not glad to see you. Be off."

"N-n-nay. You're the one m-must go."

"What?"

Nemeta laid a hand on Evirion's arm. He stood shivering with rage.

An anger more cold, an indignation, rang through Cadoc's

223

words and drove the stutter from them: "We know ignorant peasants come here. We pity them and mean to guide them toward the Light. What sort of example is it when you—baptized, educated, a man of means—do like them and seek out a pagan sorceress? You're derelict in your duty. Were it your soul alone in danger, I'd be tempted to turn a blind eye, Christ forgive me. But you're leading others to Satan. This must end. Now."

"And if not?" rumbled from Evirion's gullet.

"Then I've no choice but to inform the authorities. You'll be excommunicated. No Christian may have dealings with you. Think upon that, if your salvation is of no concern to you."

"Evirion, hold!" Nemeta cried. "Don't stir!"

Cadoc looked at them both. "I'm t-truly sorry," he told them, and it was in his tone and gleamed on his eyelids. "Believe me, I've no wish to p-play spy, nor any ill will. Oh, Nemeta, would you but hearken and understand, how joyfully we'd welcome you home! And you, Evirion—we've quarreled, but you are a good man at heart, and I pray you be saved from doing evil."

"Go," the seaman rasped, "ere I kill you."

"Very well. N-n-not in fear, but to keep the peace. I'll hold my lips shut too. None shall learn from me where you've been. If you come here no longer. Don't!" Cadoc pleaded, and stumbled from them.

As the sound of him died away, Evirion drained the vessel he had been gripping like a weapon. "Arrgh!" he snarled. "Give me more, lass, or I must needs smash something."

Nemeta hastened to serve him. He gulped that as well, and shuddered toward self-control.

Glowering into a shadowy corner, he said in a voice gone colorless, "The main question is where and how to kill yon insect."

"Nay, you speak madness," she protested.

"What? You'd have me obey him?"

"Not that either. My friend, dear friend, my—my brother—" She clutched his free hand. "Only be careful. And stay your wrath, I beg you. For your own sake and, aye, for Julia's and my father's. And even mine."

224

He set the cup down and fingered his knife. "Hur-r, I suppose I can come afoot and see you unbeknownst. 'Tis a short while till I leave, anyway. But how 'twill gall!"

She nodded. "I'm angry myself. I'll be casting the wands to see whether— Yet because of those others, and simple prudence, we'll do naught harmful, either of us. Will you swear to that?"

He shook his head. "I'll give you my word for this span of time. After I return, what I do will hang on what happens. If that sniveler stays in my way, I'll smash him."

"Or I will make an end of him myself, should he force me to it," she said, a hiss in the words.

XII

1

"**Y**ou are most hospitable, Senator," said Q. Domitius Bacca. "It encourages. In all candor, the governor and I had feared a certain amount of . . . reluctance. But clearly everyone present has the interests of Rome paramount in his heart—or hers, my lady. Excellent. They are the interests of civilization itself, you know."

Wind hooted and dashed rain across roof tiles. Though the hour was at midafternoon, murkiness filled windows and sneaked around the flicker of wax candles. The hypocaust in Apuleius's house had overheated the triclinium. Gratillonius longed to be outside, alone with the honest harshness of autumn.

Shadows deepened the lines in Bacca's gaunt visage. His glance went to and fro around the party reclining, antique fashion, at the dining table: Apuleius, neat gray man nearsightedly squinting; Corentinus, whose rawboned length fitted ill into a gold-trimmed robe suitable for this occasion; Gratillonius, who looked trapped in his own best garb; Runa, modestly clad and given to fluttering her

225

lashes downward, but with hair upswept in such wise as to show off swan throat and ivory complexion, the blue-blackness of it caught by a shell comb inlaid with nacre.

"We are delighted ourselves," said Apuleius without warmth, "that the procurator has deigned to visit us in person."

"Ah, but you deserve the favor." Bacca took a sip of wine. "Aquilo is by no means insignificant; and after the tragedy of Ys, Christian charity requires that the government take Confluentes under its special, loving ward."

Corentinus cleared his throat. Gratillonius suspected that was to head off an oath from his seafaring days. "The Church might best judge what's charity and what isn't," said the bishop. "Suppose we get straight to business."

Bacca raised his brows. "At our meal? That scarcely shows respect for the tribune's generous welcome." He smiled and nodded toward Runa. "Nor for our lady."

In this light it was hard to tell whether she flushed or not. Gratillonius knew how she resented being patronized, and admired the restraint of her reply: "Since the procurator has done me the honor of requesting my presence, as if I were a man, I should take whatever my share may be in the discussion—though God forbid I go beyond what beseems a woman."

Maybe he didn't admire, Gratillonius thought. This was no time to toady. What had become of the independence she claimed so often from him? Anger boiled acrid in his belly.

"Well, perhaps I should make my reasons for that quite clear," Bacca said. "The word I bring—the Imperial decree concerning Confluentes, and the governor's intended measures for carrying it out—it means great and sudden changes in people's lives. You leaders must guide them, keep them in paths of virtue and obedience. This will admittedly be difficult. I have come to explain, aid, and oversee the beginnings. Ysans were used to consulting with their wives, and believed their Queens had supernatural powers. Now, of course, they know the truth. But old habits die hard; and I am sure the women do have counsel as well as influence to lend us. My information is that you, my lady, stand highest among them in both rank and regard. Therefore we need your help."

Apuleius cast a glance at Gratillonius. "Two others were princesses," he reminded.

"I know," said Bacca. "But—correct me if I am wrong— my understanding is that one of them is very near her time. If nothing else, it would be unkind to make demands on her beyond the holy ones of motherhood. The second is . . . unavailable. Is that right, Gratillonius?"

How much have his spies told him? swept through Nemeta's father. Too damned much, for certain. If I could run a sword through that slippery windpipe!

It would be useless. Worse than useless. Gratillonius sagged onto his elbow. He made his head nod.

"Well, then," Bacca continued, geniality undiminished, "I think a preliminary conference between myself and you, the key persons in these little communities, is desirable. I can spell out the terms of the decree and answer questions. Together we can plan how to proceed. For it will, I repeat, be difficult at first. Beneficent in the long run, as the Emperor in his wisdom well knew; but in the early stages, a test of your capabilities and, may I say, your loyalty." He found his target across the table. "Yours especially, Gratillonius."

2

Once, beyond the Wall of Hadrianus, a detachment he had led forth on a scouting mission marched into ambush. The Romans fought their way to a hillcrest and formed up, but the wild men were many and the centurion could hope for no more than to take a number of them with him. While the enemy swirled and howled about, gathering for a rush, he looked through rain at the painted bodies and wet iron, and wondered where the years of his life were gone.

Providentially, a larger band from the Sixth, under Drusus, heard the racket and quick-stepped toward it. All of a sudden a Roman standard blew brilliant above the heather, a tuba sounded, and the javelins flew. Gratillonius took his men back down, and the squadrons cut themselves free.

Now he stood on another high place and yonder stood Drusus, but there could be no rescue, not for either of them, ever again. They had not even any foes they could kill. And where had the years gone?

This market day shone bright. Clouds scudded over the blue, wavelets ran upon rain puddles, the woods tossed and distantly roared as wind bit into them, leaves broke free of yonder red-brown-yellow minglement and scrittled across fields, the last migratory birds trekked aloft with cries ringing as cold as the air, all the world seemed to be in departure. That, at least, was right, thought Gratillonius.

From the top step of the old manor house, his basilica that had been, he saw his people that had been. Here and there a face leaped from the crowd into his vision, like a blow on the shield he no longer carried.

Those were Suffete Councillors of his in Ys—Ramas Tyri, who spoke for the artisans; Hilketh Eliuni of the carters; master mariner Bomatin Kusuri, he of the Celtic tattoos and sweeping mustaches, who had fared overland with his King. Close to them was Amreth Taniti, captain of marines, lately grubbing the soil and the bitterness of it eating him away. Olath Cartagi, ironmaker, nourished a cheerfulness that was about to be taken from him. Maeloch and his woman Tera had elbowed to the front, as near Gratillonius as they could get. Cadoc Himilco was at their side, forgetful of status, half of him off with Julia where she lay in labor.

They trusted their King. And so did others. He made out new settlers, Vellano of the Redones, Riwal from Britannia, and more. He recognized Bannon, headman of Dochaldun, with fellow Osismii who had heard that this day's market would deal in omens. Even the numerous Aquilonians stared expectant.

Some persons were missing. Gratillonius didn't know whether he wished they were here or not. Nemeta, off in her pagan hermitage. Evirion Baltisi, supposedly among the Northmen if he lived. Rufinus, whom Maeloch had ferried to Mumu in Hivernia, where he would spend the next months gleaning intelligence on Niall of the Nine Hostages—for whatever good that might do now—

Bacca leaned slightly toward Gratillonius and said in his ear, "I suggest you commence." The latter forced a nod. Bacca assumed an erect stance. In his toga he was like a marble pillar. Did Runa watch from within the house? No doubt. She'd been so gracious to the procurator, so attentive to his every word. Gratillonius had gone riding, chopped firewood, busied himself in his workshop.

Well, get it over with. He raised his right arm. The buzz and stir before him died out. His voice rolled forth.

Surprised, he found it hurt less than the rehearsals in his mind. He felt himself almost outside the thing that spoke.

"People of Confluentes—" He must use Latin while Bacca listened, who had no Ysan nor, likely, Gallic; for Bacca would report. "—of the whole municipality of Aquilo—" How far did those bounds go? The Imperial will was that this entire region come under close control. "I have the honor to present to you the procurator of your province—" That was the proper form, wasn't it, for a lord of state? "—decided I should give you the news, rather than one of your officials, because you're most familiar with me—" They must hear it from his mouth, which had made such brave noises earlier, that he surrendered.

"Rejoice! In his wisdom and compassion, the Emperor Honorius has been pleased to receive us wholly among the Romans. By his decree, we are all of us, men, women, and children, formerly mere foederates from Ys—we are full citizens of Rome."

Shouts. Groans. A few cheers. Much stunned silence. Hurry on, hold their attention, keep them in hand.

"—I am dismissed as tribune. That title has become meaningless—" Not really.

"Nor, of course, can I or any citizen be King, in this great Republic. You may no longer call me that. Please don't embarrass me and break the law—" Maeloch spat on the ground in plain sight of Bacca.

"—I am a curial of Aquilo, by appointment. My special responsibility is to those citizens who were once Ysan subjects. Under the tribune Apuleius, as directed by our

229

Governor Glabrio in Turonum, I have many duties for your well-being—

"—collect the taxes—

"—maintenance of public order and legality—

"—runaway serfs and slaves identified and returned to their proper places—

"—no more illicit relationships with outlaws in the wilderness. The government intends to rid Armorica of them. We must do our part—"

Bomatin folded arms and glared at his old friend. Bannon clutched the haft of his knife; he had spears at home.

Gratillonius stretched a smile across his face. "Now none of this can happen fast," he said, and heard his tone grow nearly natural. "Go on about your daily lives. Thanks to the Emperor, you have a security you didn't before. True, the taxes are high, but the needs of the state are pressing. Senator Apuleius, Bishop Corentinus, and I, we'll see to it that nobody is destroyed. We'll arrange terms, grant loans, that sort of thing. You know us; you know we'll look after you. We don't plan to make any immediate arrests, either. Everybody who wants to square himself with the law will have his chance. Stay calm. You're Romans, with the rights of Romans."

He cast a glance at Bacca. The man remained impassive. Gratillonius had won permission to add this slight comfort to his speech—he never would have if Corentinus and Apuleius hadn't thrown their weight on his side—but he'd departed from the prepared text, because he felt sure it would have driven the wedge between him and the people deeper yet. Not that he'd said anything forbidden; but Bacca might object to how he said it.

He caught no hint either way. Looking back to the assembly, he finished, "That's all. I'll hear whatever you want to tell me in future, and if you have a legitimate complaint I'll try to do something about it, but for now, this is all. Hail and farewell." The wind scattered his words with the dead leaves.

230

He shut it out when he closed the door of Cadoc's house behind him. His son-in-law was already in the foreroom, having sped there immediately after the meeting. Fine raiment, though rumpled and sweat-stained, was garish amidst rush-strewn clay floor, roughly plastered walls, thatch above ceilingless rafters. Tallow candles guttered against twilight seeping in through the membranes across windows. A charcoal brazier gave some warmth but strengthened the stench.

Cadoc sprang from his stool. "Welcome, sir," he greeted unevenly, in Latin. "G-good of you to come."

"She's my daughter," Gratillonius answered in Ysan. "How fares she?"

"It goes, the midwife said, it goes." Cadoc smote fist in palm. "But so slowly!"

"No more than usual for a first birthing," Gratillonius told him, and hoped he spoke truth. "She's a healthy lass."

"I've been praying. I've made vows to the saints." Cadoc mustered determination. "If you did likewise—"

Gratillonius shrugged. "Would the saints heed an outsider? It might turn them hostile."

Cadoc shuddered.

"Be at ease," Gratillonius counselled. "Men perforce abide these times." He grinned a bit. "Well do I know."

The stare he got made him realize his mistake. "See here," he continued at speed, "you should take your mind off what you can't help, and we've this moment alone. I'd have come sooner, but folk thrust around me, plucked my sleeve, gabbled and sobbed and yelled. 'Twas like being a wisent set on by a pack of hounds."

Cadoc ran tongue over lips. "They w-were wrathful, then?"

"Not at me. I misspoke myself. I meant that they . . . clung." Through Gratillonius's head growled Maeloch's voice, *"By every God there may be, ye be still the King of Ys."* And Maeloch's Tera had flung her stout arms about him and quickly, savagely kissed him on the mouth. He gusted a sigh. "How can I make them wary? We're off on a foreign road."

"The road of Rome," said Cadoc slowly. "I understand. They must learn the way to walk it, and . . . you must be their teacher."

"If I can." Gratillonius began pacing, side to side, fingers clenched against each other at his back. Footfalls thudded, rushes rustled. "I fear that what Rome orders me to do will slay what faith most of them seem yet to have in me—a faith I suspect surprised Bacca, and one he will seek to make me destroy."

"You have experience, sir, in . . . in balancing demands against each other—you, the K-k-king of Ys."

"No more. And that was different. We were sovereign, the Nine and I. Oh, we must take Rome into account, most carefully into account; and of course I bore my duty toward her, I, an officer, a son of hers. But still, we were free in Ys. How do they handle it here?"

"They do as their superiors bid. Nay?"

Gratillonius barked a laugh. "I know better than *that*." His small levity flickered out. "Well, we can't allow rebellion."

"What would you have me do?" Cadoc asked.

Gratillonius stopped before him. Out of turmoil, decision crystallized. "Why, carry on your survey, along with such other rangers as we can trust to be quiet about it. Naught unlawful there. However, we'd liefer they don't hear of it in Turonum, eh?"

Cadoc opened and shut his mouth before he could reply, "Then you mean to g-go on weaving your net of defense? But you can't! It calls for the outlaws in the wilderness, and—and you, we, we're to hunt them down."

"I have no plan," Gratillonius snapped. "Everything may well come to naught. But I said we're not forbidden to keep exploring the woodlands. Nor are we yet commanded to take positive action against their free dwellers; and I doubt any such orders will be forthcoming soon." Memory of army days bobbed from the depths. He seized on it as a man overboard might grab a plank. "If they do, well, belike I'll find myself unable to execute them fast or

232

thoroughly. Meanwhile, soldiers at war may parley. I'll be talking with those old bandits—through Rufinus, when he gets back— Ere then, I can only sit still. Agreed?"

Cadoc traced a cross in the air. "You run a terrible risk, sir."

"Blind obedience holds a worse one. Think. You know what's begun happening again along our coasts. Nay, you don't really, you've not seen it—I have in the past—but you've heard tell. Unless we ready ourselves, one day barbarians will come up this river too. What then of your wife and children, aye, your precious church? Are you with me?"

"I'm not afraid."

Gratillonius heard the offendedness and admitted it was justified. Cadoc had totalled months, oftenest by himself, in the country of wolves.

"B-but prudence, sir," the young man went on. "God's will. Th-those men He has chosen to set above us—"

The inner door opened. The midwife entered. Her hands were washed but her apron speckled with red, that looked black in the candlelight. At her bosom she carried a swaddled bundle.

"Christ help us!" Cadoc beseeched.

From the burden lifted a tiny wail. The woman smiled. "Here's your son," she said in Ysan. "A fine boy. His mother is well."

The men crowded close. Ruddy and wrinkled, the infant sprattled arms outward. His hands were like starfish.

"God be praised," Cadoc moaned.

"Go see her if you will," said the midwife. "Be not affrighted by the blood. 'Tis no more than you'd await. I'll cleanse and make the bed fresh and she can rest till she's ready to nurse. A brave girl, she, hardly ever cried out, aye, true daughter to the King of Ys—"

The men scarcely heard, being already on their way inside.

The bedchamber was a cubicle set off from the main room by walls, or curtains, of wickerwork in the rudest Celtic manner. It stank from the hours of labor. Shadows fell thick over Julia where she lay, but sweat gave her face a sheen. Reddish-blond hair was plastered lank across it.

Her eyes were half shut. Cadoc bent above. "Darling," he breathed. "I'm s-s-so happy. I'll make devotions for us both and, and when you're churched, we'll hold a feast of thanksgiving."

Gratillonius stood aside. He didn't think he quite belonged here. But her gaze found him and she gave him a drowsy smile.

The midwife bustled in. "Now, out, out," she fussed, "and let me care for the poor dear. Go admire your get. But handle him not, d'you hear, till I've shown you how. . . . Oh, but my lord, you'll know. I'm sorry."

Back in the main room, Cadoc leaned over the infant. "My son," he murmured. That had been forever denied the King of Ys. He straightened. "Your grandson, sir."

"Aye, so he is," Gratillonius said, because he must say something.

"I shall give thanks. Many thanks to Heaven. Would you—" The question trailed off.

"Nay, I'd best be on my way. I'll call tomorrow. When you find time, think upon what we've spoken of. Goodnight."

It was a relief to step out into the cold and the wind of dusk. The lanes between houses were blessedly empty. Gratillonius started toward his dwelling.

How wonderful that Julia had come through her battle unscathed—though you were never certain till days afterward—and she had known her father and smiled at him. She always was a sweet child. He'd done well to name her after his mother. Did that Julia look down this night from the Christian Paradise she'd yearned for, and reach a hand in blessing above her son's grandchild?

The parents were going to christen him Johannes, weren't they? Aye, Julia had told Gratillonius that a while ago, awkwardly. "If 'tis a boy, we'll call him after the Baptist. His day was our wedding day, you know." Gratillonius had silently hoped for a Marcus, his own father's name. He doubted the reason for the couple's choice was pure sentiment. Julia would have made that up after the fact. Cadoc simply wanted a powerful patron. Or so Gratillonius believed.

A grandson, honestly begotten, appearing sound in every way. Rejoice. Gratillonius couldn't. Aside from being glad, in an exhausted fashion, that his daughter lived, he felt vacant. Well, he'd seldom had a worse day. Later his heart might awaken. Although, in full frankness with himself and nobody else, he didn't quite like his son-in-law. Cadoc meant well, he was a kind and faithful husband, a brave and able man, but that super-piety of his— We'll see how the kid turns out, Gratillonius thought.

Light glimmered dull from his house—the front room only, one or two candles his servant had kindled. Runa was at the manorial building. She'd spent her nights there since word first arrived that the procurator and his entourage would come in person. "We must have the place worthy of him," she said. "We cannot let him think us barbarians or peasants." Gratillonius had swallowed the implication that that was how he lived. It didn't matter. He'd be too busy himself to pay her the attention she considered her due.

A man got up from the wall bench as he entered. "Good evening to you, your honor," he said in Osismiic. "God grant all is well."

Gratillonius nodded. "It is that, we think. A boy."

"A boy, is it? God be praised. May the angels watch over his crib."

Gratillonius looked into the weathered face. This was one of the deacons Corentinus had chosen, a trusty fellow who otherwise was a boatman on the Odita. "What brings you here, Goban?"

"The bishop sent me. He'd like you to come talk with him—confidentially, you know, if your honor's not too tired."

A thrill tingled some of the grayness out of Gratillonius. He understood what this meant. Corentinus and Apuleius had both absented themselves from the assembly. Bacca had as much as told them to. "This is a matter for common workers and tribesmen. I must be on hand to impress them with the seriousness of it, but your dignity could be compromised."—and their presence could be taken as moral support of the speaker. When guests were leaving the senator that day, Corentinus had found a chance to

235

draw Gratillonius aside and mutter, "We'll discuss this after you've endured it, we twain," in Ysan.

"I'm ready," Gratillonius said.

"He told me the hour don't matter, and he'll have a bit of supper waiting. I'll head back to my lodgings, if it please your honor." Goban winked. "Just so nobody sees us together and gets the wrong idea, right, sir?"

Right, Gratillonius thought as he went forth again. Not that any conspiracy was afoot. Corentinus merely wanted Bacca's nose out of it. Therefore Apuleius, who was hosting the procurator, couldn't be on hand. However, no doubt senator and bishop had gone into the matter today in private.

How to cope with the new order of things. First and foremost, Gratillonius supposed, how to keep the taxes from grinding Confluentes away. The rates Bacca brought were out of all proportion to what the colony was as yet able to produce. Apuleius could stave off ruin for a space—appeals which wouldn't be granted but which would consume time, loans from the Aquilonian treasury or his own purse, lean though both were getting—but sooner or later, one way or another, payment must be dug up. And he, Gratillonius, the curial, must do the digging. From the land and the flesh of his people? No, he was their leader, their defender; but the state had forbidden him to work for their defense; but somehow—

Wind flapped the edges of his cloak and streamed chill over his skin. It brawled in trees along the river road. The water ran darkling. Light flickered across it, cast by a near-half moon that fled between rags of cloud above the western fields. Shelter waited in the bishop's house. Corentinus would surely start by asking after Julia. He'd give thanks for the safe birth, but in a few words, man to man with the saints; then he'd lead the way to his table, rough fare but hearty, and fill the mead cups, or maybe wine for celebration and defiance. It might be like old days in Ys, or at least like the time afterward when they'd worked together for the survival of the folk, before this miserable breach opened between them.

The gate of Aquilo stood wide as usual. Bacca had tut-tutted at that, the first night. Gratillonius explained there was nothing to fear, so far. Bacca made remarks about not allowing people to go in and out freely after dark, lest they be tempted to lawlessness.

The streets were, in fact, deserted save for the wind. Gratillonius passed Apuleius's home. Every pane was aglow. Nothing too good for the procurator. Runa meant to give him a banquet herself before he left. Gratillonius had been inventing excuses for not attending.

A white form flitted out of the portico shadows and down the stairs. For an instant his heart recoiled from ghosts, then he told himself sharply that no matter how weary he was, he had no business being a fool, and then she reached him and he saw, barely, by what light the moon and the windows cast, that it was Verania.

"Hoy, what's this?" he exclaimed.

Tears glistened. "I waited," she gasped. He saw how she trembled in her mere gown, how her hair was gone disheveled. She had not dared take a cloak. Somebody might have noticed.

"Whatever for?" When had they last met, except in passing on his infrequent visits?

"T-to tell you—Gratillonius—"

How had she known he'd come by tonight? She must have overheard her father and Corentinus. Or had she listened beyond the door?

"You're *still* the King of Ys!" she cried, and whirled and ran back. He heard the weeping break loose.

Bewildered, he stood where he was. The house took her into itself and closed up again.

What a girl, he thought after a moment. Something wild dwelt within that quietness. But no, not a girl any longer, a young woman, and fair to see. What was her age now— sixteen, seventeen? More or less the same as Dahilis's when Gratillonius came to her.

Or Dahut's when she died.

It was as if the wind blew between his ribs. He hastened onward.

"You humiliated me," Runa said. "You disgraced yourself. Begging off from my feast for the procurator— You might at least have considered how that damages your position with the state. You claim so much concern for my people. But no, nothing counted besides your own wishes."

Because she had chosen to speak in Latin, Gratillonius did likewise. "I tell you again, it was urgent I go reassure those two important headmen who weren't at the assembly."

"You lie." She kept the same monotone, colder than the rain which roared outside and made blindness in the windowpanes of the old manor house. "It could have waited till he was gone."

It could have. Gratillonius had flat-out judged he'd be unable to spend any more hours deferring to Bacca. A fight would have spelled disaster.

"You simply didn't care," Runa said. "Not about me or the people or anything other than getting back among the oafs you feel comfortable with."

Despite lamps, the room was gloomy. A saint on a wall panel—big-eyed, elongated, stiff, centuries and a world removed from ancestral Rome—stared through shadows whose dance in the draft made him seem to move also, as if pronouncing an anathema. The hypocaust kept floor tiles warm, but cold air slunk around ankles and even at head level you breathed dankness.

Today Runa resembled the saint, narrow face, upright stance, implacable righteousness. "I have borne with you," she said. "I have suffered your arrogance, your brutishness, your utter lack of any consideration, hoping God would unseal your eyes as He was pleased to unseal mine. But no. You keep them shut, willfully. All that matters to you is yourself."

Gratillonius looked down at his hands and sought to curb his temper. He could slap her, but what was the use? "You're not like your mother," he told her. "She consigned me to hell in a few words. How long do you mean to go on?"

"Oh! Now you insult my mother! Well, knowing you, I shouldn't be surprised."

Somehow he felt a sudden tug of pity. We were quite close, he thought while he said the same words aloud. "Have you really turned altogether against me?" he added.

She brought fingers to bosom. "It hurts me, it hurts me more than you can possibly know. But you have already given me so many wounds. This has only been the latest of them. The last, God willing."

"Then you're breaking with me." He was about to voice the hope that they could still work in tandem.

"I am leaving this wretched place," she said.

He gaped. "Huh? How—where—"

"Procurator Bacca has most kindly invited me to accompany him to Turonum."

"What?" Too taken aback for thought, he heard his tongue: "How's he in bed? I'd guess he spends the whole night explaining this will be for the good of the state."

She reached claws toward him, withdrew them, and clipped, "That will do. For your information, I'm finished with sin. In Turonum I'll be baptized and join the community of holy women."

Gratillonius recalled vaguely that Martinus had founded such a thing, corresponding to the monastery.

"And I shall be with civilized persons."

Aye, the tale was that Martinus's successor Bricius held that total austerity was outmoded; it became a master of the Church to live somewhat like the masters of the world with whom he dealt. Runa should do well enough—she wasn't addicted to luxury—and find congenial company in the magnates, especially as she rose to a commanding position among her women. She'd do that, he felt sure.

"The celibacy oughtn't to be any hardship," he said. That might be unfair, though in fact she had responded less and less to his attentions as time went on, and found more and more occasions to avoid them.

Color tinged those sharp cheekbones. "It is a sacrifice I pray will be acceptable to God. I have so much to atone for. Satan was everywhere. Heathendom—fornication, out-

239

right incest, with you—lending your daughter my agreement to her running off, with everything that that led to—seeking the death of her unborn child for her—and doing away with yours, Gratillonius!"

Her look challenged him. She strained arms back and breasts forward, like a Trojan woman before an Achaean sword.

Maybe later he'd be appalled. In this hour he felt nothing beyond . . . a vague sense of release? "I suspected," he said tonelessly. "But I never pursued the thought, I let it skulk aside, because you were my mate and I'd cause to be thankful to you, most of all that you freed me from the ghosts of the Nine, but for other things as well."

"And you didn't care," she said after a minute. "You wouldn't. You can't. I wonder if you haven't been a penance God set me."

Derision: Is that sound Christian doctrine? Doesn't baptism wash every past sin away? It's the ones afterward that count.

"I will try hard to forgive what you've done to me," she said. "I will pray for your salvation. But I'll pray more that God not allow you to lead others astray."

"Goodbye." He turned and walked out.

He heard her follow. "What?" she yelled. "You depart like that? You haven't the simple courtesy to listen?"

"The law doesn't require it," he replied over his shoulder.

"You haven't the courage, that's what! You don't dare hear about the harm you've done me."

I am afraid, he refrained from saying. If I stayed longer I might well strike you, and that could break your neck.

The first breath of regret touched him. "I wish things had ended differently," he confessed.

Still he didn't look behind. In the entry he retrieved his drenched paenula and pulled it over his head. The wind caught at the door as he opened it. He pushed it back shut and went off through the storm toward Confluentes.

XIII

1

Winter heaven hung featureless gray. Trees could well-nigh snag it in their twigs. Mists drifted through raw air. The drip off boughs was the only sound there was, save when dead leaves stirred soddenly underfoot.

Then Bannon said, "Here it is."

He did not call Gratillonius "lord" as aforetime, but it was Gratillonius whom he had sought. "I came to you myself, 'stead of sending the hunter who found the thing, because 'tis a matter for chiefs," he had related in the house. "You know about the outside world, what the Romans might make of this if they hear, maybe even who could have done it—for surely no Osismiic man would, unless he be mad." The pair of them had gone off into the forest without telling anyone else.

Folk shunned the spot they came to, believing it a haunt of vengeful wraiths and what was worse yet. The man from Dochaldun had only dared them, by daylight, when helping to search the woods for two children missing from the village. What he saw sent him running home while he clutched his lucky piece and babbled charms against horror.

Amidst osier and sedge crowding a pool, a boulder that looked like an altar for trolls heaved up its mass. Nearby stood a great beech. Lightning had blasted it long ago, and fire gouged out a hollow. Gratillonius squatted to peer inside. He spent a few heartbeats finding what Bannon pointed at, for it was very small, discolored nearly as dark as the char, and begrown with some of the fungus that clustered on the bark outside. In a few more years it would molder quite to nothing.

He stared into the eye sockets. "This is naught of the little ones you've lost," he said low. "They were old enough

241

to walk. This is the skull of a suckling babe, maybe a newborn. And 'tis been here a while."

"It has that," Bannon answered grimly, "for 'tis pegged in place. No wolf does such a thing."

Gratillonius saw and felt for himself, nodded, and rose. "A human sacrifice."

"Not by any of us, I tell you!"

"Of course." Stories of bloody rites in olden times might or might not be true, but the Romans had certainly exterminated the druids in Gallia. The pagan Gods whom most rustic Armoricans still worshipped were content with fruits of the earth, the mightiest of Them with an animal on Their high holy days.

"Some madman in the past, or a stray barbarian, or who knows what?" Gratillonius said. "I'll see to the burial of this poor shard if you wish. Why should you care?"

"The children we've lost—"

"Children are forever wandering off, and not always found again. I'm sorry, but so 'tis. It has naught to do with this."

Bannon seized Gratillonius by the wrist. "*Does* it? Can you swear no black wizard goes abroad, stealing our young for his cauldron? My thorp will be wanting more than words."

Gratillonius understood. The knowledge was heavy as the sky. "You'd fain talk to Nemeta," he said.

Bannon nodded. "I'd not be recklessly accusing of her. She's done well by us in the woods." His features tightened. "But we must make sure."

"And I—"

"If she's guiltless, maybe she can find out the truth. We've hardly anything to pay her with at this season, though. I asked you along also for coming with me to her. It may help. You are a just man. We have few just men any more."

Unspoken was the likelihood that, if the tribesmen thought she was a murderess after all and her father was trying to shield her, they would kill both.

—Flames flickered in lamps. Brightest burned a Roman one. The bronze and oil were witch-wage lately earned. Darkness had fallen as the two men reached the oak by

242

the Stegir which Gratillonius remembered so well. Nemeta bade them come inside her cabin and spend the night before starting back.

Seated on stools, wooden cups of mead in their hands, they looked up at her where she stood. Barefoot despite the chill, she nonetheless wore a gown of finely woven wool, close-fitted to her litheness. The red hair smoldered, the green eyes gleamed through shifting shadow. It came to Gratillonius that his scrawny girl had become a woman to kindle desire; but the beauty was somehow more hawk or vixen than it was human.

"Epona hunt me through hell if I lie." Her voice moved cat-soft around the things that hung on the walls. "Never have I harmed child of yours or of any living man."

Bannon looked toward Gratillonius. Someone must say it. Gratillonius lifted the load, he felt as if it were about to break his bones, and answered, "Your own was lost, a year and a half agone."

Her gaze scorned him. "It was. Would you make trial of me? I will meet the hounds, or whatever ordeal you name, and the Gods will uphold me."

"Nay, I meant not that!" he croaked in Ysan.

"You are a witch—" Bannon stopped short. Nemeta played her glance over him and fleetingly grinned. Unless a Power intervened, she would be safe in any test that called on the World Beyond.

The chief cleared his throat. "None of us want to blame you," he said. " 'Twould be ill for us too." Again she grinned. If the Romans heard of manslayings to pagan Gods, they might well send soldiers to strike down men and burn down homes. "But must we go in dread this'll happen afresh, or has happened? Can you find our little ones for us, wisewoman?"

Nemeta shook her head. In the uneasy light, Gratillonius could not make out whether compassion crossed her face. "I've been asked the same erenow," she said. "Maybe in later years; but as yet my arts are slight, and—the forest Gods keep the secrets of Their beasts."

"The killer, then. Can you track him for us, that we may make an end of him?"

243

She stood still a while. Through the shutters they heard an owl hoot, once, twice, thrice.

"He's a dangerous one to deal with," she said slowly, "for an offering like that, if made aright, feeds strange strengths. I've doubt I can cast a net over such a man. Yet surely we should rid the land of him. And soon, ere his might grows more."

Gratillonius read meaning in her tone. Fear stabbed. Bannon understood too, in fierce joy, and exclaimed, "You know who he is?"

"I do not," Nemeta answered. "I only know who he might be, and I could be mistaken."

"Who?"

"Cadoc Himilco, the trailmaker from Confluentes."

Gratillonius dropped his cup and leaped to his feet. "Nay, this is moonstruck!" he roared in Ysan. "Have done!"

Bannon rose beside him, to say with hand on knife, "Let her speak."

"But he—I know him, you do yourself, Nemeta, your own sister's husband," Gratillonius stammered. "And a Christian."

"He has indeed plagued us with his Christ, has he not?" Nemeta said to Bannon.

The Gaul nodded. "He has. A pest. A threat, maybe; he talks of overthrowing the shrines. But—"

"Men have lied about their faith often enough," Nemeta said. "Some did out of fear, others—well, Cadoc does range the wilderness wherever he likes. Who knows what he does there, or why? I've had feelings about him that crawled within me."

"Why, you need only talk with him to know him sinless," Gratillonius protested.

"Unless you are Nemeta and have witch-sight?" Bannon growled.

She lifted a hand as if to ward her father off. "I say naught for certain," she reminded. "He may be harmless. You should hear him out."

"He's away." Sickness caught Gratillonius by the throat. "We run the survey in all seasons."

"When he returns, we will ask of him," vowed Bannon.

Nemeta smiled. "Meanwhile, best keep silence about this," she proposed.

Gratillonius knew that would be impossible, once Bannon brought home the tidings.

2

Daily the rumor grew. Gratillonius became fully aware of it when Julia came to him weeping, half crazed. "They mutter those things about Cadoc—one loyal maid warned me, one—I listened when they knew not I was nigh— What will become of him? Of our Johannes? Oh, father—"

He held her close, consoled her to the pitiful degree he was able, at least got her quieted by his promises, then went to Corentinus.

"I've heard," the bishop said. He had ears in many places. "Of course it's baseless. Those children simply fell prey to misfortune, and as for the babe that was sacrificed, Christ Himself would testify to Cadoc's innocence. But pagans live without His comfort, you know. They're all too apt to see magic and malice at work when anything goes wrong. These endless winter nights drive everybody a bit crazy, too. Hatred is easier to live with than fear; it gives you someone to attack. And . . . I'm afraid Cadoc has made himself disliked among the backwoodsmen. He's been too zealous. Evangelism isn't his proper calling. I'll speak to him about that."

"If you get the chance," Gratillonius replied. "How can we even protect him, let alone clear his name?"

Corentinus sighed. "I myself have hardly any voice among the pagans. What you could do—" The eyes beneath the tufted brows pierced. "You could search out the true guilty party, hiding nothing. If you will."

Gratillonius left as soon after that as possible, and turned to Apuleius. The senator received him kindly enough, though somewhat abstractedly. The latest news received was of still another setback in his effort to have the taxes on the Confluentians lowered. The Germanic menace smothered it. Official alarm had redoubled since Emperor

Honorius, after the Visigothic invasion of Italy, moved his capital from Mediolanum to Ravenna, where landward marshes gave added security and the sea offered ready escape to Constantinople. Not but what the danger wasn't real. With the defenses of the Rhenic frontier weakened and the tribes beyond it ever more restless, the praetorian prefect had grown impatient with lesser claims on his attention.

"My heart goes out to your daughter," Apuleius said. "And her husband, when he returns to this grisly business. But what can I do? Keep him under guard, day and night? We haven't the guards to spare, you know. Best we send him, them, to live elsewhere. I can try to arrange that."

"If he isn't murdered in the woods on his way back," Gratillonius said.

"God forbid. I'll pray. If you would also—"

Again Gratillonius made an early farewell. Since Runa departed, constraint had diminished between him and the other two men, but the old cordiality had not risen from its grave. It would be hard having Julia move away. Hard on her too. What roots she had left were in Confluentes. And what kind of living could Cadoc make, out among the Romans? Lacking status, money, or skills that anybody wanted to hire, he might well end by selling himself and his family into slavery.

If only Rufinus were here. How sharply Gratillonius missed the rascal. There was a barrier there too. Somehow, in spite of all they had been through together, they were never really near each other in the way that Gratillonius and Parnesius had been. It was as if Rufinus somehow feared complete openness. Because he felt guilt about the catastrophe of Ys? Gratillonius had told him over and over to forget that. Maybe he couldn't. Or maybe what happened to him in his early youth had forever scarred his heart.

He was always ready with counsel, though. He'd find some fox-trail out of this trap, if anybody could. But what?

My mind is so slow, Gratillonius thought. Well, if it keeps plodding along, it may finally get somewhere. Up on your feet, soldier.

246

That night he lay awake till the east whitened, and this was around midwinter. Back and forth he trudged through the blindness, about and about, to and fro, from thing to thing, and found no answer. A couple of times he wished Runa were at his side, or any woman, that he might lose himself in her and afterward sleep. Otherwise he had decided he didn't miss her. And he had no right to go rutting indiscriminately like a common roadpounder on furlough. He was on duty, he the centurion. . . .

When he woke from a doze, at midday, he had no revelation. He merely opened his eyes and saw something that might work. He mulled it over while he made his preparations by what sunlight was left, and then got a good night's rest. Stars were still brilliant overhead as he left Confluentes.

He would rather have ridden Favonius, but his way led him by paths that were often barely useable by a man on foot, into the forest. Darkness was grizzled when he reached the hut of Vindolenus.

The former Bacauda and his wife made the visitor welcome. They brought forth the best food and drink their meager stores held. A couple of years ago they'd begged the King of Ys to lay hands on their oldest son, and the boy had indeed recovered from his fever. Gratillonius doubted his blessing had anything to do with that. Nevertheless, now he called in the debt.

"You've heard the tale about my son-in-law being a sorcerer who steals children and offers them to his demons?" he asked.

The backwoods dweller reached uneasily for a small thunderstone, spearhead-shaped, such as folk sometimes found and believed to be lucky. He rubbed it. "I've heard a little, lord," he mumbled.

"It's false. Do you hear? I, the King of Ys, swear it's false."

"Well, if you do, lord, then surely it is."

"He should be on his way home from his latest scouting. I must find him ere anybody else, bring him to safety, and show the folk he's blameless. Can you guide me?"

"M-m-m." The lean countenance drew into lines of thoughtfulness, the faded eyes looked afar. "If you've a

247

notion whereabouts he may be, north or west or east o'
here—m-m-m, the trails, the streams—" Cautiously flickered the eagerness of a hunter. "I can try, lord."

"And afterward keep silence, you, your woman, your
children. By the Gods of the land and the Gods of hell,
you shall."

Vindolenus seemed almost affronted. "Lord, I learned
from the Romans how to hold my tongue, and I've taught
my household. Think you we'd blab to a herd of scruffy
tribesfolk?"

Gratillonius saw no reason to tell how much he himself
needed secrecy. He was dealing with one of the men
whom Rome commanded him to hunt down. His hope had
been that thus far they didn't expect he would. Must he in
fact, later, break faith with them?

3

His hounds roused Drusus in the middle of the night.
They bayed, deep ringing threat, and strained against the
staves of their pen. He took his old military sword from
the wall, a tallow candle in his left hand, and went forth
into the drizzling dark. Men of his had already surrounded
the newcomer. Their weapons were lowered. Drusus saw
why. "Gratillonius!" he exclaimed. "What the devil are
you doing here at this hour? Where've you been, anyway?
I heard you were gone from town these past ten days."

"That long?" said the unkempt, travel-stained man. "I
wasn't counting. No matter. I came out of the woods not
far from here and thought my friend would give me a doss
till tomorrow."

"Of course, of course. Come on in. We'll heat up some
wine, how about that? And talk, if you're not too tired.
Plenty of night to sleep in afterward, this time of year,
eh?"

—In the morning Drusus told his wife that he and their
guest would take a few hours' walk into the forest as far as
the Stegir. While on his errands, Gratillonius had seen

spoor that looked promising of big game. They'd bring two hounds, otherwise go alone.

After they returned, Drusus said that he had been shown traces of wisent. The beasts had long since grown rare and, in spite of their size, shy. He didn't want people hallooing around scaring these two or three off. "Stay out of the woods for now, everybody, you hear? I'll go by myself during the next few days and see whether the dogs turn up anything. No grumbling. You heard me. If the buffalo really are still hereabouts, we'll get up a hunt."

Gratillonius returned to Confluentes next morning on a horse lent him. When he was gone, Drusus told his wife: "He didn't want to talk about it much, but the reason he went off alone like that was this business of the child killings. He couldn't stand any longer hearing—no, not hearing, but knowing about the whispers. His daughter's husband!"

"It is horrible," she said. "Do you think Cadoc is guilty?"

"I hate to suppose so, but—well, where there's smoke, there's fire, eh?" Drusus shook a fist. "Body of Christ! Whoever the murderer is, I'd feed him to my hounds!"

"But if he is a magician as they say, can't he stop them?"

"Not when God binds him and his spells. We'll do this like Christians."

In the following several days Drusus said more in the same vein to the household, the neighbors, and on a visit to town. His vehemence surprised those who had known him as easygoing in matters of faith. Well, naturally, black witchcraft was a different thing; and Drusus had children of his own, two of them quite young. . . . Otherwise he continued his searches for the wisents, trying a different brace of hounds each time, until at length he sighed that they had evidently left the area.

Any word concerning Cadoc spread far and fast, as tensely as everyone awaited his homecoming. Pagans found themselves as ready as Christians to accept a trial by ordeal, an idea that somehow came into circulation. Their Gods no more drank human blood than did Christ. If properly asked, They would surely not let such an evildoer work defensive sorcery. Many muttered that Gradlon was bound to protect his son-in-law and whisk him beyond the reach of justice. Best would be if right-minded men found Cadoc first, alone in the wilderness. Yet magic, unchecked by religious rites, might wilt a sword before it could strike. Terror closed in like the winter nights.

Thus astonishment was twofold at the next word that went forth. The suspected one had appeared in Confluentes. Not a single hunter had glimpsed him on his way. Had he flown through the air? But he met no welcome. The tribune immediately ordered his arrest on charges of murder and diabolism. The penalty was death.

Aquilo seethed at the news. Cadoc had pleaded his innocence. There were no witnesses. Sent to a Roman court, he would most likely get off. But Apuleius and Bishop Corentinus had too much care for their people. They would let their God—or the Gods—judge this case, that doubts might once for all be laid to rest.

Julia and her infant had moved in with her father. The three stayed in seclusion.

They emerged for the trial. It took place outside the wall of Confluentes. The day was bleakly bright. Ground had frozen hard and trees bore a thin, glittery leafage of icicles. Breath smoked startlingly white under the blueness above. Townsfolk, farmfolk, woodsfolk ringed the field in. They had been required to leave their weapons, and guardsmen stood about to keep order. Low in the south, the sun cast a sheen over helmets, mail, and uplifted pikes.

A shout arose. Solemnly, Bishop Corentinus led his priests out into the middle of the space. Mass had already been offered at the church; now they called on God beneath His heaven. On this day, it had been announced, pagans might also invoke their deities here, if they did so inconspicuously.

The clergymen withdrew. Apuleius conducted Cadoc forth under guard. The young man wore a peasant's smock frock, whose brown made his hair seem to glow silver-gold. He stood straight and agreed fearlessly that he would submit to the test. Senator and soldiers left him standing alone.

A breath went like a wind through the crowd. From a tent pitched by the wall, Drusus paced. He wore his legionary armor, the first time that most who were there had seen it, a vision out of the mighty past. His right hand gripped tight a leash which held his lead hound. The rest of the pack came after, brindled gaunt beasts larger than wolves. The setting had put them on edge; they growled, snarled, snapped air as if it were prey.

Julia gripped Gratillonius's hand. The nails dug deep. He stayed mute.

Drusus slipped the leash. His call ripped aloud: "Halloo! Kill!" He pointed at the solitary figure of Cadoc.

The hounds clamored and bounded forward. Cadoc waited.

The hounds reached him. They slowed, stopped, walked around. Several whined in puzzlement. The chief of the pack licked his hand. He bowed and ruffled the terrible head before he prostrated himself in prayer.

Like a breaking wave, a shout rose from the watchers. They sought to storm into the place of the miracle. Pikeshafts held them back. That was as well, for the hounds had lost no ferocity. A man who slipped by the cordon was badly slashed before Drusus, with whip and ungodly words, got them under control. Cadoc remained lying.

The crowd surged off toward Corentinus, Apuleius, Gratillonius. Men wept side by side with their women, or laughed or cheered or sang. A few begged for baptism.

Julia fell into her father's arms. Headmen and tribesmen pushed through the Confluentians who milled about him and cried for his touch, for his wonderworking heed, he, their lord, the King of Ys.

4

A light snow fell. Against the blanket it laid, trees looked black. Sight soon lost them in the sifting gray-white. Murmur and gurgle of the Stegir made an undertone to silence. The air had turned almost warm. It was as if the year had finally begun to await spring.

Nemeta had swung window shutters aside and left her door open, so the stenches of the night could leave her cabin. That let in the dove-hued day. Its softness washed

251

shadows from corners and made the instruments of witch-craft into simple, rudely fashioned things of wood, stone, skin, bone.

She and Gratillonius sat on stools opposite each other. Between them glowed a brazier to which they held their hands.

"I know what you did," she said in Ysan.

"You would," he replied as quietly.

She shook her head. "Nay. Not by magic. Mere reason. What must have happened."

"Tell me."

"You got a man of Rufinus's to help you find Cadoc. You left the two of them in a brushwood shelter not far from Drusus's farm and went to seek his help. He's your old soldier comrade, you got him his home, he'd never refuse you. Together you planted the seed of the thought that Cadoc be tried by ordeal—by having the hounds set on him, as the Osismii do to the worst of their criminals—and those hounds would be Drusus's. Meanwhile he brought them piecemeal to Cadoc and taught them this was a person they must not attack. When that was done, Cadoc took down the shelter and Drusus smuggled him into Confluentes. Corentinus and Apuleius already knew what parts were theirs to play. That is how it went."

"You are a clever girl."

"Not truly. What I cannot understand is why anybody would swallow the claim of a miracle. Why did they not reason too?"

"They wanted to believe. Folk are not logical about matters that touch them deeply. You should be more among them, child. 'Tis ill to live alone."

A thrust of bitterness: "I thought Corentinus and Apuleius were honest."

"The bishop says merely that God's will was done. The three of us, with Drusus and Vindolenus, did what we deemed necessary."

"To save yon ranting pest— Forgive me, father. But to me and the tribesfolk, he is."

"He's learned his lesson. He'll stop trying to push others about in their lives." Sternly: "Therefore put down your malice against him."

252

"If he does leave me in peace. . . . But 'twas a risky thing you did. It could have gone awry, and he'd have died. Why didn't you just send him afar?"

"That would have been cruel for him and his. But mainly, I think, I hope, mainly we had the people in mind, Corentinus and Apuleius and I."

"How?"

"By letting the frenzy about Cadoc grow unchecked, we choked off wonderment about who else might have slain the babe. That could have riven kindred asunder. Then by . . . showing him innocent in a remarkable way, we emptied the fury out of them. It will not return. They accept, now, that their own children were lost in ordinary sad wise."

She stared long across the coals at him. "You *are* the King," she finally whispered.

He sighed. "I must not be." Starkness came back upon him. "But I do command you, master your spite. Keep silence about what we have spoken of this day. Let memory of that dead infant fade away with his little ghost. Else it could prove the worse for you, Nemeta."

She caught a sharp breath. "Do you believe I—"

He lifted a hand. "I don't want to hear more. But beware those Gods you serve."

Forlorn defiance: "You have none."

"I know."

"Oh, father," she cried, "you are the one of us that's all alone!"

She jumped to her feet and came around the smoldering fire. He rose to meet her. She laid her face against his breast and held him tightly while she shivered. He embraced her, stroked her hair, and made noises, the meaningless noises of love he had crooned above her cradle.

5

Willows had leaved, oak and chestnut were beginning to, plum trees bedecked themselves in blossom. Other petals colored the sudden vividness of grass, among them

253

borage like small pieces of sky. Migratory birds were coming home.

Rufinus was back. It had been a hard journey for him, by currach from Mumu to Abonae, by ship from Dubris to Gesoriacum, and haste overland across both Britannia and Gallia. But he had not chosen to wait till later in the season when skippers would venture a passage straight over Ocean. He would bring the news to his master as early as might be.

They walked east on the river road, a place to talk unheard; and still they used Latin. On their left the Odita gleamed on its way toward Confluentes, Aquilo, and the sea. Forest rose greening beyond. On their right stretched fields also coming to life, men and oxen at work in the distance, a sight sometimes veiled by flowering dogwood. A lark piped above.

"I've adventures aplenty to relate from this winter, especially when I slipped into Niall's country. Some of them could be true," laughed Rufinus. "But they can wait. What matters is that he will most certainly be back among us this year."

Later Gratillonius would ask precisely what his man had heard and seen. However, it was clear that no barbarian king could ready a campaign in secret. Niall must have made his will known months ago and bidden warriors be ready. A chill tingle went along Gratillonius's spine. "When?" he asked.

"They'll set out very shortly after Beltene. That's what they call their spring festival, do you remember?" Rufinus's humor dropped from him, his voice harshened. "His intent is to ravage northwestern Armorica. Not that he'll have a huge fleet—nothing like the one I've heard about, that you broke—but picked crews. They'll strike and be off elsewhere on the same day. I'm sorry, but I couldn't learn much more than that. His kind generally make up their plans as they go along."

Everything we got restored during those years at Ys, thought Gratillonius. Pain twisted. "We'll warn the Duke, of course," he said with the same roughness. "Maybe he'll pay attention, though all the authorities in Turonum dis-

254

like and distrust me. It won't make any great difference, what with the condition of defenses these days."

"Wait. I do have this," Rufinus told him. "The end point of the Scotic raid will be Ys."

The pain became a sharp thrilling in the blood. "Why? To loot?"

"Mainly to destroy. The whelming didn't drown his hatred of the city. He's vowed to bring down the last stone if he can. Pirates and even traders of the clans he rules over, they have standing orders to put in whenever they come by and do some more demolishing. He himself— We can make a fair guess at when he'll arrive there."

Gratillonius nodded. "You confirm what I already thought. Tales scuttle around. You, though, you've brought the information we need about the one man we want. Good work."

"Will you tell the Romans?" Reluctance was in Rufinus's question.

Gratillonius shook his head. "Not about this. You keep your mouth shut too, so word can't drift to them. They wouldn't dare tie soldiers down, waiting to spring a trap. From their viewpoint, they'd be right. Also, Ys is nothing to them, or worse than nothing. They'd consider it a favor, getting rid of that reminder on these shores."

Rufinus waited. Gravel scrunched beneath hobnails.

"Besides," Gratillonius finished, "if they knew what I have in mind, they'd forbid it. In fact, it could give them the excuse they want to haul me off on charges of treason and behead me. Military action is reserved to the army, you know. For ordinary people to band together against their enemies, that's prohibited. I'll be calling on tribesfolk, and such Ysans as I can trust, and especially on your men, Rufinus, who are now outlaws again."

On which account he must dissemble before Apuleius and, he supposed, Corentinus. That hurt as badly as anything else. Since their conspiracy with him on behalf of Cadoc, they had quite put aside the matter of Runa. She was saved; he was not, but they could cherish hopes and meanwhile, day by day, like the land itself, friendship came back to life.

They might well admit his cause was worthy. But he could not put Verania's father at hazard.

She loved the springtime so, he recalled. After the Black Months, she broke free into joy with the dogwood and the larks. How clouded it would become if she knew what he intended. He must not let on when they saw each other, which was pretty often. That would make him gruff, for he lacked Rufinus's gift for masking himself with mirth, and she would be wounded and wish she knew what was troubling him.

He squared his shoulders. This wasn't really the wrong kind of day wherein to plan bloodshed. It was the exact same time of year, back when Verania was in her mother's womb, that he had slain the King in the Wood.

XIV

1

Strange it was to be again at Ys. Three years had not diminished the longing for what was lost, nor had three days hardened the heart. Standing atop what had been the amphitheater, Gratillonius found he must once more punish himself with a westward look.

The sun was low, dulled by haze, but cast a steel-gray glimmer across the waters. Cold and salt from the south, a breeze had lately stiffened and begun to raise whitecaps on them. They drummed afar, an incoming tide that burst and spouted over the rocks, surfed against cliffs, roiled about the ruins. The mist should have scattered but somehow it lingered, even thickened. Sena lay hidden beyond the vague worldedge it made. The horns of land bulked murky, decked with pale grass that rippled to the wind. A few seabirds cruised above.

The watchman who had sent after him touched his arm. "They *are* the enemy, lord! They must be!" His voice cracked apart. He was a stripling, a backwoods Osismian clad only in a piece of wool, armed only with a spear. You took whom you could get and believed you could trust, if you would make war on the barbarians.

Gratillonius started out of his moment's trance and brought his gaze around. It left Cape Rach, where nothing remained of the pharos and little but tumbled stones of the tombs. The road out to them was nearly obliterated, gravel washed away by rains, bed invaded by weeds. Vision swept across the bight where Ys once stood. What pieces of the city had survived at first were mostly gone, collapsed and rolled off down the sloping sea bottom; against the sun, he glimpsed only formless blacknesses. Waves and scavengers had long since picked the beach clean. The canal which bore the sacred water from a Nymphaeum lately burned to the ground (by chance, Christian torch, thunderbolt of a God?) had silted and fallen in on itself. Without that drainage, the low ground of the amphitheater was becoming a marsh. Sight flew onward—a shadow tracing where Redonian Way had run; the end of Point Vanis, where somebody had dug up old Eppillus's headstone and carted it off or cast it into the sea; gutted hillside mansion with windowframes empty as a skull; beneath, brush reclaiming those charred acres which had been the Wood of the King.

The heights blocked view of Lost Castle. Gratillonius had seen that the Celtic fortress remained untouched save by weather. Older than Ys, it would endure uncounted centuries longer. He stared past, northward over the great sweep of Roman Bay.

Aye, a fleet. What the boy and his fellows on the wall barely glimpsed through the blurry air had drawn close enough to be unmistakable. He could not yet be sure how many leather boats coursed the waves—about a score— but two galleys of the Germanic kind walked on their oars amidst the pack. Standing well out, it beat west along the Gobaean Promontory; and around the shores behind it were surely wreckage, misery, and death.

At that instant Gratillonius felt simply a liberation. All was done with, the furtive preparations, the fears and squabbles and things going wrong, the wait here as men chafed and groused and neared mutiny, the wrench whenever a beacon flared on the horizon or a courier sped in to gasp that the pirates had landed again. He had awakened from his slow nightmare, he had come through the swamp of glue to firm ground, and the freedom to fight was his.

"The Scoti," he said. "Stand fast, lad. We still need eyes aloft."

He remembered to stride, not run, as befitted the commander—over the wall, past the crude platform on it that held the pyre of his own beacon, down the inside stair. Level by level, the signs of destruction thickened, a statue wantonly smashed, an inlay pried out, an upper tier broken and lower bench scarred by stones thrown down them, the spina gone from the arena and that ground turned to mud under inches of stagnant water. Apuleius had learned that Governor Glabrio actively encouraged the plundering of Ys. Its remoteness, the stories about what haunted it, the danger of brigands did not hold off everyone who wanted fine construction material. Looted of treasures, the remnants were a quarry.

Nonetheless Gratillonius wondered at how fast the demolishment by both man and nature went. Did the Veil of Brennilis reach out beyond the grave? Did Lir, Taranis, and Belisama pursue Their vengefulness yet?

He forced the mystery from him. This was the day of battle. Mithras grant—fate, or whatever ruled the world, grant the revenge he himself wanted, for Dahut.

Shadows filled the bowl of the amphitheater with dusk. Men dashed about like the sea in the bight. They shouted and swore, they clashed metal together, their feet thudded on the benches, echoes flew. Gratillonius saw Drusus across yards. The veteran was assembling those like him who had joined the force. They were aging, their armor didn't fit so well any more, but they would be steady, the core of strength.

Amreth yelled at men from Confluentes. His marines were a cadre among them, but few. Most had no knowledge of warfare nor any but the barest gear for it—some merely sickles, woodman's axes, sledge hammers, pruning hooks. Yet a ray of wan light through a hole broken in the

258

wall showed a kind of joy on Amreth's face. No longer was he a peasant.

Bannon and a couple of other headsmen herded their Osismii together. Those knew a little about fighting, not much but a little. They lacked discipline but probably wouldn't panic unless others did first.

Rufinus and his outlaws crouched in a group. Ill clad, disheveled, armed as each saw fit, insolent as wolves, they would be the deadliest part of Gratillonius's ragtag legion.

He made his way around to the box that had been for the King and the Nine, and entered. It had been savaged worst of all. Marble splinters crunched beneath his feet. From this location a speaker could make himself heard throughout the space around. He must not remember games and gaiety, music, dance, the flash and the long human roar as racing chariots rounded the spina, most especially the women with him, the mothers of his daughters. He must fill his lungs and bellow:

"Hear me! Silence! Listen! Your commander has your orders for you.

"Those are the Scotic raiders. They're headed by Point Vanis. They should cross the mouth of the bay and reach Scot's Landing in another hour. Make ready! Meet outside in your different units. You know what to do. You know what we will do." It took repetitions to get their full heed. Then: "Death to the barbarians! Vengeance and victory!"

He pushed through the ruckus toward the cubicle he had occupied, to arm himself.

2

The galleys dropped anchor. They had grounded on many a strand this springtime; but heavy with booty, they would be in peril here. Cobbles covered a strip which the tide made ever narrower, beneath red-brown ramparts of cliff, while the rising south wind churned water about the remnants of Ghost Quay and sought to drive hulls hard against it. Currachs could ferry the crews ashore. The bit of beach having room for few, most boats would thereafter lie empty, tethered to the ships or each other, watched by a few men left aboard the big vessels under captaincy of Uail maqq Carbri.

Calls and laughter rang through the sea noise. Too loudly, Niall thought, too merrily. They denied forebodings about this sinister place where nothing further was to be gained, gold or silver or gems or wonderful weapons, only the toil of breaking stone from stone and dragging it off to push from the heights into Ocean. Well, they knew when they embarked that the King would require it of them; and had he not led them first to riches and glory? He would not keep them long, just tomorrow and the next day, then ho for home; and there he would reward them from his own share of the plunder, as richly as beseemed the high King at Temir.

Three nights to walk from camp to the dead city and be with her who sang. If she came. He believed she would. Foreknowledge must be hers. Ranging through the depths and across the waves, she could have spied him, followed him. On one night, which they spent at sea, he had had glimpses. . . . The moon was gibbous. It would be there after dark for him to see by—see what?

He felt a thrill of dread that was half rapture. It was not fear for himself. She had plighted him her troth if he paid her the honor price she wanted, and he had been doing that. His sense was of going beyond the world. It was like when he had been a boy about to have his first woman, a youth right before his first battle, a man abroad on the night of Samain Eve; but it went deeper than any of those, flowed through him quieter but stronger. He knew not what would become of him, and that was daunting, yet he could not wait for the meeting.

"I've been away from you too long, I have," he whispered down the wind.

The eagerness was real with which he sprang into the lead currach and stood erect as the oarsmen brought it bounding to shore. To hearten his men—and, breathed an inner voice, himself—he wore his bravest garb, helmet ablaze with gilt on locks that were formerly as bright, seven-colored cloak flapping like wings about red tunic and plaid kilt, spear on high and shield faced with polished bronze. Everybody was outfitted for combat, but none to match him.

Not that he looked for trouble. Last year a Scotic wrecking crew had found a band of Gauls come after building stone, subdued them without loss, and borne the survivors off for slaves. Niall counted on no such luck. It didn't matter. Tonight, pulsed within him, tonight, the waves and the moon and the white one who sings.

The ledge on which the fisher houses had clustered was largely crumbled, the upward trail a bare trace. Niall led the way. Supple as any of his followers, he skipped from rock to niche to treacherous slope. Gulls dipped and soared about him. He made the last leap to the top so as to land in a crouch, ready for battle.

The headland stretched empty. Its grass tossed wan under the wind. The heights that reached eastward and the valley between were a thousand shades of green. Little sign of man abided—the amphitheater, dwellings half hidden by the growth that was overrunning them, marks and scraps of roadway. The moon stood pale above distant hills. Clouds scudded. There were no shadows, because the sun was low in the west behind mistiness that despite the wind was encroaching on the rocks and skerries outside of Ys.

Niall led an advance slantwise across Point Vanis. He would camp near the ancient tombs, or what remained of them. Not much did. His warriors might well finish them, with time left to break down shells of homes and set fire to whatever would burn. He needn't be impatient about that, however. The years—weather, roots, rot, humans who enjoyed destruction or wanted to clear the sites for themselves—would more slowly wipe them away. But he should not make her wait for that if he could help it.

He had heard Ys itself was gone beyond ruination by mortal hands. The city hove in sight. He stopped to look. His sailors had spoken truly. Ragged snags of wall or tower still rose above the water, farther out than a work party could wade even at low tide, but they had become very few. Most of what showed were formless rubbleheaps, not yet brought down below sea level. Things closer inshore, some beyond high water mark, had taken less battering;

yet they too were almost all down. Men had smashed at them for the stone or in hopes of finding treasure. Storms, unhindered by a city rampart, cast monstrous billows at them. The earth slid from under their foundations as the soft sandstone at the bottom of the bay came apart. Niall could barely recognize that which had been the gate of the Brothers.

I did this, he thought. I let the sea in over Ys.

I believed that would be the end. I would turn home with my vengeance taken, the ghosts of Breccan and my men who died here set at peace. But the strife wears on. She will not let me go free.

A horn sounded, so faint at its distance and against the wind that he might never have been aware. His eyes told his ears of it. Tiny at their remove, men swarmed from behind the amphitheater. Blink of metal bespoke others hurrying down from the houses where they had laired.

Ambush.

The warriors saw too. They milled about and shouted. Niall's glance swung past them. They'd be outnumbered. Retreat to the currachs—deadly slow. The enemy would arrive before more than a handful could escape, and trap the rest on the cliff edge. He raised his spear for war, his shield for silence. "We'll hold fast where we are, lads, and reap them as they come!" he cried. Smoke rose thick from the amphitheater wall. His illwishers had kindled a beacon.

3

Six or seven miles thence, a watcher on a hilltop spied the signal. Wind tattered it, but surely yonder fire burned for a single reason. Shouting, he sped down the path that twisted among trees, to his village.

It was half a dozen huts on a tiny inlet where a stream ran into the sea. Its boats were gone. Men were out fishing. They would not return till sundown, if then. War or no, they had a living to haul out of the water.

Yet several craft like theirs lay drawn ashore. On the cove a larger smack rode at anchor, eyes painted forward on the black hull. Farther out was a merchantman, magnificent and awesome to simple folk.

The boy yelled and pounded on doors. Men came forth. Others stirred from boats or beach where they had idled away their days. Weathered countenances worked. Oaths rattled. "At last, at last. . . . Is it true, now? . . . Lir, I promise You the best of my every catch for a year. . . ."

"Avast!" bawled Maeloch. "We'll go see!"

A number pounded after him up the hill. "Aye," he panted, "no mistaking that. The King's fighting. Quick and go to him!"

When they got back, Evirion Baltisi had had himself rowed in from his ship. He had spent the weary time of waiting there, often wishing he had stayed longer in Thule and come home too late for this. Better a bunk aboard than a smoky hut so crammed with visitors that a man couldn't leave at night for a piss without stepping on them. Now eagerness blazed in him.

Maeloch was more matter-of-fact. They conferred briefly while the crews gathered whatever weapons they owned, launched their boats, hastened out. Women and children watched from the village. Most stood mute. Some waved, farewell, farewell, luck fare with you.

Evirion's boat took Maeloch to *Osprey*. Her crew numbered more than the fishermen of old. She carried as many fighters as had been willing to ride with the skipper. Hence rations had grown short, tempers vicious, while yonder summons tarried. He'd begun to wonder if the damned Scoti would ever arrive. Staying here like this would hardly have been possible if it weren't in territory which had been Ysan. To these uncouth and impoverished folk also, the city was their life. These days they hoped for protection by Audiarna; but they remembered.

The vessels stood out to sea and started west. They scarcely made a fleet, nine boats with five or six men apiece, *Osprey* with a score, and *Brennilis*. The ship was good-sized, her crew trained in arms, and a number of landsmen had joined them. As they traveled, two more boats slanted in to take part—fishers from the village who happened to see. It was their war too. Still, the force seemed a puny thing to throw at Niall of the Nine Hostages.

"A single slingstone 'ull do for bringing any wolf down," Maeloch growled into his beard.

He stood in the bows, watchful. Waves chopped leaden, streaked and crested with white. The smack rolled, plunged, groaned to their thud and splash against her. Oars creaked on thole pins. Wind thrummed mast stays. It was a south wind, but bitter and steadily rising. Starboard the land loomed dark and ever more sheer. Surf foamed at its feet. Mist ahead, which should not be in air like this, dimmed sight of its western end. The sun had become a sallow shield low above an unseen horizon. Cormorants wheeled in hueless heaven, blackness aflight. With only sail, *Brennilis* kept well out, lest she be driven around. Seeing her thus dwindled was a lonely thing.

"We'll do it, regardless," Maeloch muttered. "Don't s'pose I can bring ye Niall's head, but how'd ye like a gold ring off his arm, Tera?"—Tera, who after two years was fruitful with their child, first of his children since Betha and all theirs drowned with Ys. "Ye'll have your revenge, little Princess Dahut, we'll give ye your honor back."

4

Dusk fell early in the forest. The sun was beyond the trees and the moon had not yet risen above them. Heaven reached gray-blue over the stealthily flowing Stegir, but beneath the king oak gloom deepened.

Within the cabin was nearly full night. Nemeta put aside the bowl into which she had stared unwavering for hours. She could no longer make out the water within it, drawn from the witch-pool and tinged by drops of her own blood. Whatever visions had drifted there must now form themselves from the half-shapes behind shut eyes. She did not think they would be any more clear.

Wind soughed outside, a noise as of the sea. Two boughs rattled together like clashing swords.

She rose from her cross-legged position on the floor. It had left her joints stiff and painful. Chill wrapped around

264

her nakedness. Well though she knew this room, she must fumble a while before she found her snake staff.

She stretched herself on her narrow bed, hands crossed over the pole. Its top rested at her throat, the mummified head on her small breasts, the scales down her belly, the rest of the wood against her groin and between her legs. Staring into blindness, she whispered in Ysan, "Mother, I've cast what few, weak spells I know. Help me. Come to me, mother, from wherever you have wandered, come lend me the wings that once were yours. I will fly to my father."

5

Gratillonius knew the battle would be chaos. Combats never obeyed any man's plan; and here he led no soldiers, but a gathering of colonists, rustics, outlaws, barely leavened by some aging veterans and former marines. Working as a whole was beyond their grasp. And they must take the offensive, cast their bodies against sharpened metal, hold down the fear that even legionaries always felt, that told a man to use his common sense and run away. Gratillonius could only form squads of those who knew each other and hope they would hang together and so keep heart in the rest.

The Scoti were warriors by trade, skilled, well-armed, contemptuous of death. They lacked Roman discipline but could keep an eye on the chieftain's standard and each ward a comrade as well as himself. They numbered about two hundred, Gratillonius fleetingly gauged. Against them he had almost twice as many, who fought for their homes— though the enemy fought for life— That was his solitary advantage.

Since he could not oversee and try to guide operations like Julius Caesar, he took sword and shield himself. He went with the old legionaries. While waiting for this day they had drilled, a little of the craft had come back to them from their youth, they tramped side by side and struck the Scotic flank like a single engine. Drusus was

265

their actual officer. Gratillonius pressed forward on his left but held ready to go elsewhere as necessary. On Gratillonius's left, a step behind him, his fellow Briton Riwal carried the banner that marked the commander's place. It was blue, with an eagle embroidered in gold. Julia had made it for him. Her eyes had sometimes been red, but she sewed on and kept silence.

Her man Cadoc was with Amreth and the other Ysans. Nearly all of them untrained and poorly equipped, they were less a unit than a gang of individual men who tried by ones or twos to bring down individual foes. The marines gave a small core of steadiness, though they themselves had scant experience. Still more did the fear of shaming oneself before a neighbor stiffen the will to fight.

Much the same was true of the Osismii. Pacified these past four hundred years, they were brave—no timid man had answered the call that went secretly over the forest trails—but knew nothing of affrays except for private brawls that seldom ended in death. They too rushed, slashed and hacked, fell down or fell back, tried again in the same man-to-man awkwardness, or dithered about dismayed by lifetime friends who lay gruesomely dead or shrieked for pain in the clutter and stink of entrails.

Rufinus and his wolves were the appalling manslayers, murder made flesh. They skulked about, watched for a chance, leaped in with a snap of weapons like jaws, were gone before a return stroke could reach, harried and hooted and grinned. From the sides their archers and slingers coolly waited for a clear target, then let fly and hit as often as they missed. When a band of Scoti made a desperate rush after them, they laughed and faded off on dancing feet.

Once the Confluentians collided with such a sallying party, away from its main group, and cut it to pieces at whatever cost to themselves. The sight brought Gauls to blood lust and they attacked in a mass that almost reached the barbarian lord. His guards drove it back in confusion, and its losses were hideous, but many a Scotian sprawled gaping at the sky. Every islander harvested was a loss Niall could ill afford.

Thus Gratillonius saw the struggle, whenever a respite

266

allowed. A part of him weighed what he learned, gauged how the work went, told him to push onward. Then he must rejoin Drusus's troop, and for the next while forget all reason, all self. It was cut, thrust, parry, feel the shock of a blow given or taken through metal and bone to the marrow, glimpse an opponent's face contorted into a Medusa mask, engage an arm whose owner was a blur behind a shield, let sweat sting eyes and salten lips and make underpadding sodden and hilt slippery, haul air down a dry fire of a throat, shake at the knees and know he was not a young man any longer. Clash, clang, thud, scream, gasp filled the universe. He lost footing on soaked ground and lived because Drusus covered him while he got back up. He recollected vaguely how he himself had saved Riwal when a giant of a Scotian broke through the Roman line. He fought.

Betweenwhiles he would catch sight of his goal. Niall reared high in the tumult, helmet like a sun, cloak like a rainbow, unmistakable. His sword and his voice rang. Surely he had suffered injuries, but nothing showed, no stone or arrow found him, he seemed as far beyond fatigue as Mithras at war. How could his sworn men do other than die at his feet?

Suddenly timelessness tore across and time was again. Gratillonius stood on Point Vanis with only the wind and the plaints of the wounded about him. A blackness swept across his eyes, a whirling, he nearly fell. Riwal caught his arm. Steadiness returned and he looked around.

A remnant of Scoti had rallied and hewn their way out of the trap. The cliff trail being denied them, they were headed the other way, toward Ys. They moved in a band, less than a hundred, ragged, reddened, stiff with hurts and weariness, steel dimmed by blood, but together and defiant. At their head, under his own flamboyant flag, blazed the helmet of Niall.

The battlefield was heaped and strewn with dead men, crippled men—hard to tell which grimaced the more horribly—and shields, arrows, spears, slingstones, swords, axes, daggers, bills, sickles, hammers, clubs, some broken, some bent or blunted, some ready to kill afresh. Blood dripped, steamed, glared bright or darkened with early

267

clotting. Brains, guts, pieces of people littered the grass. Gulls had begun to crowd overhead. Their mewing grew loud, impatient.

Gauls and Ysans, such as could, lay or sat or stood droop-shouldered, exhausted. Gratillonius saw a couple of them vomit; doubtless more had already. A number had shit in their breeks. The veterans rested more calmly about Drusus. Gratillonius felt a rush of relief when he found Cadoc nearby, arms lifted in prayer. Rufinus's woodsrunners were the coolest. Several of them still had vigor to go about cutting the throats of Scoti and trying to do something for casualties of their own side.

That outfit had suffered the least, though its losses were severe enough. Gratillonius tried to count. He couldn't, really, but he estimated he'd spent a hundred men. That much out of four hundred would have cost him his command in any proper army. But he didn't have one, of course. The Scoti had died in equal numbers merely because each man of them had two against him.

And the chief devil among them was still alive.

Rufinus approached. "We're not finished yet," he said.

Gratillonius's gaze followed his finger. They happened to be in view of Scot's Landing. The reinforcements had arrived. Gratillonius recognized Evirion's ship, anchored at a safe distance, and *Osprey* closer in. Smaller craft plied to and fro, bringing fighters ashore. The first were now bound up the trail. Several were aboard the Scotic galleys. Apparently those had been captured without bloodshed.

Rufinus guessed Gratillonius's thought. "No, the enemy didn't try to hold out on the water," he said. "They understood right away it was hopeless and made off. Yonder."

The sun was very low, dull red and deformed behind the mists. Had the battle taken so long? Or, rather, had it taken no longer than this? Things were hard to make out on the heaving gray of the waves. Gratillonius shaded his eyes and squinted. Most of the leather boats were loose. The Scoti must have manned them with skeleton crews and fled as fast as possible. They were bound west along the point. Oars sent the light craft skimming, graceful as flying fish. *Osprey* threshed in pursuit, but heavier, with more freeboard to catch the south wind, had no chance of interception before the fugitives were past the headland. Through Gratillonius flitted an image of Maeloch roaring at his rowers and his Gods.

"Let 'em go," he said mechanically. "They'll carry the tale home."

"No," Rufinus answered. "That kind don't run to save themselves. They'll make for the bay, with the idea of landing and joining what's left of Niall's troop. What they'll actually do is take them off."

Gratillonius stared into the spare, fork-bearded visage. "By Hercules, you're right!"

Rufinus yelped a laugh. "I needn't be. Here's extra men for us, all fresh and hot. We'll corner Niall, and with any luck we'll bag the currach crews as well."

Lightning sizzled through Gratillonius, It flashed the numbness and every hurt out of him. He went about calling for volunteers. "'If you think you can fight one more fight, come with me. You'll get a double share of booty. But if you can't, stay here, and no disgrace to you. We're mortal. No sense in dying, if you're too tired to send a Scotian to hell. Look after your wounded friends. Pray for our victory." That last was hypocritical, he could well imagine Rufinus's lip twitch in amusement, but they expected it.

Evirion had debarked, fully armored, at the head of a formidable team of mariners. Cadoc insisted he was able to carry on. Was that a good omen, those two who had quarreled so much now side by side? The fishers newly come were at least a tough lot. Drusus, Bannon, men of theirs; Rufinus, and those of his who survived— About three to two this time, Gratillonius reckoned; but a fair part of his force was unblooded, whereas the Scoti staggered along.

"You'd better stay, sir," Rufinus said.

"No," Gratillonius snapped. "What do you take me for?"

"You've fought as well as anybody. We need you alive."

"I am damn well going to be in at the kill." There to avenge Ys and Dahut. The eagle banner rippled on Riwal's staff as Gratillonius led his troops downward.

Point Vanis shouldered off the wind. Mist eddied and smoked over the bay. It was cold and smelled of the deeps. The sun was a red smear out in the formlessness that crept across the skerries. Ruins and rubble hunched nearly as dark as the cliffs on either side. Waves tumbled and clashed. When they flowed off the beach, it gleamed wet until they assailed it again, higher each time. Eastward, night drained into the valley. That part of the sky was clear, purplish, moon ashy above the hills.

The Scoti had formed rank on the strand, as if hoping the sea would guard their backs for them. They were an indistinct mass where swords and spearheads glimmered. In fact, no vessel but their own nimble kind could reach them through the wreckage in the bay. However, a man could wade in the shallows.

Gratillonius stopped his followers out of earshot. "I'll lead our main body at the center," he said. "Let us get well engaged with them. Then you, Evirion, on the right, and you, Rufinus, on the left, take your men around and hit them on the flanks, and from behind if you can. We should be done before those boats get here. I daresay they'll turn tail when they see, but we can try to grab some. Is this clear? Forward."

He strode ahead at the Roman pace, sword in hand, shield held just below nose. His sandals smote earth. Grass brushed past his greaves. Mail rustled. Sweat chilled him as it dried, but he'd soon be back in action and warm. A vast calm had taken hold. It was his fate toward which he walked.

Something passed at the corner of vision. He heard a man at his back exclaim, and looked. His stride broke. His heart stumbled. Wings ghosted overhead. Great eyes caught the last daylight. It was a bird, an owl, an eagle owl.

No, Forsquilis was dead, she died with Ys, here was nothing more than a stray! Gratillonius told himself to be at ease. If this meant anything whatsoever, it betokened well, because Forsquilis had loved him. His spirit refused obedience. He went on with a high thin keening in his head.

But he must never show fear or doubt. His was to lead

the attack. He might even have the unbelievable luck that his was the sword to strike down Niall of the Nine Hostages.

The gilt helmet sheened through the twilight. He choked off an impulse to charge and continued at the drumbeat Roman pace.

A cry like a wildcat's ripped from among the Scoti. Others took it up till it outrode the rushing of near waters, the booming of surf more distant. Steel shook against heaven.

Gratillonius and his men met it. Shield smashed on shield. He laid his weight behind, leaned against his enemy while his blade searched. A blade gonged off his helmet, skittered across his mail on the right side. He cut. He felt bone give beneath the edge. The barbarian yowled and lurched back. Gratillonius pressed inward. They were everywhere around him. No, here was a mailcoat, a man of his who grunted and thrust; there was another, near naked, but wielding a blacksmith's hammer, and a skull split before it like a melon. He was in the water, everybody was, the tide lapped around his knees. The flanking assault had worked, the Scotic line was crumpled and crumbled. Niall's banner went down. Rome's hung over Gratillonius. The colors were lost in mist and murk, but men knew it for what it was.

The melee opened up. He spied Niall himself, waist deep. The foeman lord was alone, his nearest warriors slain, the rest swept from him into a millrace of slaughter. Two ragged shapes—Gauls, were they Osismii, were they Bacaudae?—closed in on him. He shouted. His sword leaped. A man was no more. The second tried to slip aside. Niall made a step through the tide and clove him.

"After me!" Gratillonius called. He slogged outward. The bottom was lumpy and shifty, the water surged and sucked, but he pushed on to meet Niall, and behind him was a score of avengers.

A curve of white, a drift of gold sprang in the waves. Even by this half-light, he knew that hair was gold, was amber, was a challenge to the sun that would turn it fragrant. Naked she swam, orca-swift, seal-beautiful, and her laughter lilted as he remembered it. She came about in a surge of foam, stood with her breasts bare—rosiness

271

had left their tips, they were moon-pallid—and held out her arms to him. Her face was heart-shaped, delicately sculptured, with full mouth and short nose and eyes enormous under blond brows. "Father," she sang, "welcome home, father."

The sword fell from his hand. The shield slatted loose on its shoulder strap. "Dahut," he uttered amidst a roar throughout his world.

"Father, follow me, I love you."

She kicked free of the bottom, straightened her slenderness, swam like a moonglade before him. He groped after her. "Dahut, wait!" he howled. This could not be. How had she outlived Ys? Yet every dear shape was there, head, smile, the little hands that had lain in his. "Dahut, come back!"

He did not see how the men behind him recoiled, stopped where they were, gaped and shivered. He fought his way on into the deepening water. She frolicked close by Niall. The Scotian hefted his sword and went to meet the Roman.

6

It is Dahut, flew through Niall, it was always Dahut, I knew but down underneath I dared not name her.

She streamed by him, supple as the water, white in the twilight. Her speed left a wake in the waves. The wet hair trailed like seaweed, but heavy and clinging to the back that once arched against his weight. Her glance crossed his. It smote into him. The bloodless lips parted in laughter. She rolled over. Light washed across her belly. Legs and one arm drove her onward. The uplifted arm beckoned to the man who raved behind.

She plunged and vanished. Niall wrenched his neck around. Yonder foe who had lost his wits wallowed ahead yet, wailing for her. He'd let go his weapon. She had chosen this prey, Niall thought awhirl. He knew not why, but it was her will, and here in Ys that they had slain together he was her slave. And a new killing should bring him back to himself, make him able to save his last few men—somehow, with her aid.

He hefted his sword and went to meet the Roman.

Wings beat, soundless above the sounding breakers. He looked up. The span was great, an eagle owl's. He glimpsed hooked beak and cruel claws. The eyes were glass bowls full of venom. The bird glided straight at him. It could flay his face and gouge his own eyes out.

Witchcraft was abroad. Niall took firmer grasp on his shield. As the owl swooped near, his blade swung.

He should have struck and flung down a bloody carcass. The iron bit into water. The owl veered. Feathers brushed him and he felt just spray off the waves. The owl swept around and came back. He saw the sword pass through. It was like slashing fog. The owl hit him. Nothing tore, but he was blinded. He dropped his shield and with his left hand batted uselessly at the thing that flapped about his head.

It was a wisp, a ghost. It could not strike him nor he it. But it could hold him here, harry him if he fled, keep him fumbling helpless till an enemy found him. "Dahut!" he cried.

She rose from below. The blindness slipped aside. He saw that she had caught the owl by the right wing. It struggled. Maybe it screamed unheard. Claws raked, beak slashed, left wing buffeted. No mark appeared on her white arms. She clung, her strength against its, and dragged it downward toward drowning.

Niall never thought to stand aside, until afterward. You helped a comrade in combat. He lunged. His foot caught on a submerged fragment of Ys. He tripped, splashed, went under. His body collided with Dahut's. It was as solid as his, but even in the water he felt how cold.

Rising, he saw that the impact had jarred her and she had lost hold of the wing. Yet she had broken it. The lamed owl fluttered wildly athwart the moon, fell, was gone. He should have seen it sink, but didn't. He thought it faded, thinned, became a drift of mist, and was there no more.

For an instant, Niall and Dahut confronted each other. Amazement shook him. Real, no trick of the eye but moving flesh, she nonetheless had power to seize a phantom. Half ghost herself, she was.

Sharp teeth gleamed in a snarl that mocked a smile. She kissed him on the mouth. The cold of it burned. She dived. He had a glimpse of her writhing away like an eel.

Dazedly, he looked about him. The Roman soldier had vanished too. Maybe he'd come to his senses and returned to the men of his who roiled in the shallows. The sky was still pale overhead, Niall could see for many yards, well enough to know friend from foe. The enemy had broken ranks, withdrawn one by one from battle into bewilderment. The Mide men were farther out, in disarray but together.

Niall grew aware of shapes slipping inward from between stumps of wall where billows surged and broke. For a skipped heartbeat he supposed them a pack of sea demons. Then he recognized, and gladness lifted stark. Those were currachs of Ériu.

He had lost his shield but never his sword. He raised it on high. His voice crashed through the surf: "To me, lads! To your King! We're going home!"

7

Rufinus guided his master shoreward. Gratillonius lurched as if blind. Rufinus held him tightly by the arm.

"Dahut," Gratillonius sobbed. "The owl, what became of the owl?"

"Easy now, sir, we're almost there," Rufinus said.

Leaderless, terrified by what some of them had seen, the Armoricans milled on the beach in clumps or flattened themselves and moaned out prayers. The Hivernians could have taken advantage of it, but they were few, worn out, most likely also shaken by sight of a mermaid who fought with a bird of prey. Besides, leather boats were arriving to bear them off. The lean hulls rocked as warriors crawled aboard. Most needed help.

"It was Dahut," said Gratillonius numbly. "But who was the owl?"

The tide washed dead men onto the strand.

274

Outside the bay, wind blew hard and waves ran mighty. Their dash around the headland, following a long day's travel, had wearied rowers. Their craft overloaded with fugitives who could only stare emptily at sea and sky, they could not buck against the weather. At best they could keep a northwesterly heading. It bore them to the skerry grounds. Billows crashed and spurted across reefs. Rocks loomed. Riptides swirled between. The last daylight was fading, the moon was less than full, and the mistiness that had already swallowed sight of distances was here thickening from haze to fog.

Niall crouched in the bows of the lead currach and peered ahead. Wind whined, water brawled and hissed, spindrift blew sharp. His whole body ached and throbbed. "Sure and it was a bad thing that we came," he confessed under his breath to his Gods. "There will be keening aplenty in Mide. I'm sorry, Lir. I should have left Ys to You."

Something gleamed in the froth. A slim shape with a wondrous roundedness of breast and hip swam before him. She waved, she summoned, her song mingled with the wind. Follow me, follow me.

"You will guide us?" he whispered out of the maze wherein he wandered.

Follow me, follow me.

Fresh joy leaped forth. He rose, balanced himself against roll and pitch and yaw, gave his tattered cloak to the nearest man and said, "Lash this to a spear for my banner." His helmet, too, caught the last wan light. He would be the beacon for his handful of boats, while Dahut led them through rocks and shoals to open sea. "Follow me, follow me!" he shouted.

A vessel hove in view from behind Point Vanis. She was plank-built, bigger than any currach, an Ysan fisherman. Steel agleam crowded her deck. The black hull swung about on oars till the eyes at the prow found the wayfarers from Ériu. A sail flapped up on her yard, filled, and drove her swiftly ahead.

9

"**S**kipper, ye're daft!" Usun protested. "Into yon hell, strong wind, high tide, night falling and fog rolling in 'gainst every law o' nature—nay!"

"Aye," said Maeloch. "Daft 'ud be to let him go free and work more harm on our folk."

"How can ye tell he be there?"

Maeloch pointed. Through the dusk and brume, across half a mile, a helmet glinted like a star. "Who else? From what we've heard, he'd be the last o' the lot to fall, and 'twould be on a heap o' slain. But the pirates ha' taken off such as lived at the bay. He'd be in the lead, cutting his way through and bringing them back to their lairs. Sure as death he would."

"But—"

Maeloch slapped Usun's back. "Brace up, man. We can overhaul them well ere full dark. The moon'll help. They'll nay be far inside the skerry grounds—which we know like the way to our women's beds, and they nay at all. I think the rocks will catch most ere ever we can. As for the rest, we've bowmen and slingers, we've a good stout forefoot to ram with, and our rail's too high for them to beswarm. Ha, they've been given into our hands. Ye wouldn't scorn the gift, would ye?"

His voice trumpeted: "Revenge for Ys! Kill yon sharks or they'll be back for your wives and kids! Haul away, ye scuts!"

The men howled answer. They too were become hunters. Blood was on the wind. Usun shrugged and went aft to take over the helm. Oars poised ready to help. Rigging sang, timbers creaked. *Osprey* dashed forward with a bone between her teeth.

Maeloch took stance in the forepeak. He gripped his battle ax hard, though odds were that he'd have no need of it. Despite the furiousness in him, he strained to see, he loosed every sense to keep watch. Better let the barbarians escape than suffer shipwreck. But he didn't think either would happen. Aye, there was Torric's Reef and there towered the Carline, passage between them was tricky but if you kept alert for surges—"Right oars, pull!" —you could slide straight through instead of going around— "Up oars! Port the yard a tad . . . so. . . . Make fast."

The gap closed. He saw that the tall man in the golden helmet now had a flag of sorts. It fluttered in the wind like a bird caught by one wing.

Ahead, seas raged around the Wolf and her three Cubs. Steer wide, starboard. Close beyond were the currachs.

"Little Princess Dahut, tonight ye'll sleep sound," Maeloch said.

Whiter than foam, a shape darted from under the prow. He had barely time to see an arm lift, a hand crook fingers in summons.

Portside aft, fog rivered out of the bank that hid Sena. Suddenly it was there, Maeloch blind on his deck. He heard men yell, oars rattle. Wind dropped nearly to nothing. The sail slatted and banged.

With the speed she still had, *Osprey* drifted across the tide and struck.

It was a monstrous blow. Maeloch fell and rolled. He caught the rail and heaved himself to all fours. The hull slanted crazily. Again and again billows drove it onto stone. Timbers broke with a crack like thunder. The sea came aboard.

Maeloch saw a man reel past, and reached to catch him. The weight was too much. The man wore iron rings sewn to a leather jacket. He went over the side and straight down.

Wind sprang forth anew. It battered *Osprey* as the waves did. She broke apart.

Maeloch found himself swimming. The water trumbled him about. Whenever he got mouth in air, he snatched a breath. Then he was back in swirling darkness. He swam on. Fear was forgotten. He stood outside himself, watched the struggle, gave redes which his body tried to obey. Meanwhile he remembered Betha, their children, Tera, the child of his that she bore. By every God there was, will They or nill They, he was coming home to them.

Stone scraped him flensingly. He caught hold, clung, crawled.

When he got up onto hardness, the fog had blown away. Early stars flickered in the wind. The moon tinged the breakers that brawled around. Strakes and spars dashed among the rocks. He saw nobody else.

Well, he'd hang on. Save in storms, the Wolf was never quite under water. Tomorrow boats would arrive in search. He beat arms across his chest. That might flog some warmth into him. Oh, Usun, old shipmate. . . .

The woman rose. She mounted the reef and walked toward him. Naked she was, dead white but for the deep hair, and smiling. She held out her hands.

He knew her. He was in a nightmare, he must wake, he stumbled back. "Dahut, nay!" he screamed.

At the water's edge he could flee no farther. She reached him and embraced him. Her strength made naught of his. Her flesh was more cold than the sea. She bore him backward and downward. The last thing he saw before he went under was her smile.

Presently she rose anew and swam toward the currachs, to guide them on until they were safely out into Ocean.

XV

1

The bishop's house in Aquilo was modest, and under Corentinus had become austerely if not ascetically furnished. One room in it, small, whitewashed except for a Chi Rho on a wall, held a few things that were his own, mostly gifts of love given him over the years—a ship model, a conch shell, a glass goblet, a flower vase, the doll of a little girl who had died—as if to lend him comfort. It was a room that heard much pain.

Gratillonius leaned forward on his stool. It was low; he sat hunched above lifted knees. The fists on them opened up beseechingly. "What have I done?" His words were thick with unshed tears.

Face to face with him, Corentinus answered gently, "You did what was right. Thank God you were able to do it."

"But the cost. Maeloch; every man there who trusted me and died."

"It was heavy. Not your fault. You didn't have the proper professional force you needed."

"Just the same—"

"Just the same, think what you have gained for us." Corentinus counted off on knobbly fingers. "A loss to the barbarians at least as great. We may hope they take the lesson to heart and don't come back here soon. That means, even in homes now grieving, a better life ahead. Also because of this, that you brought about, the people have a new sense of their own worth. Under you, *they* broke the wild men. I don't believe Our Lord frowns on that kind of pride. And the booty. Since there's no way to return it to its former owners, most of whom must be dead or fled anyway, you're making a righteous division. Men, or their widows—good of you to remember the widows— have hard need of some money; and those who share with the truly poor will have boundless reward in Heaven. As for the bulk of it, you said something about your intentions before your misery crushed you." He leaned over and clasped Gratillonius's shoulder. The seamed and craggy visage softened. "They're worthy of a Maccabaeus."

The other man dropped his gaze to the floor. "That may be. Though I wonder if the gold isn't cursed." A shudder racked him. "The horror we met—"

Corentinus tightened his grasp. "That's what's shaken you so badly. You've only told me so far that a terrible thing happened at the end. What was it?"

Gratillonius fought for breath.

"Speak," Corentinus urged. "You've already met the thing itself. Today you only have to name it."

Still Gratillonius panted.

Corentinus laid both arms about him. "I'll find out from others, you know," he said quietly. "Better straight from you. What, old friend?"

Into the beard and the coarse robe, Gratillonius coughed, "It was, it was, it was Dahut. My lost daughter Dahut there in the sea. She called me. She led me toward her lover Niall, who murdered Ys. An owl tried to stop him, she rose from the water and tried to drag it down, I don't know any more myself, but, but, but Niall couldn't have escaped, Maeloch couldn't have been wrecked—w-w-without her—could they?" He clung tight.

Corentinus stroked his hair. "We've heard evil rumors," he said. "This confirms them, I suppose. Except that the truth is worse. You've got to bear it, man. You can, soldier."

"What can I *do*?"

"I think you have done it already. Won a victory for your people. Now hold your spirit fast."

After a while Corentinus could let go. He got up, poured two cups of diluted rough wine from a jug—this was a room that heard much pain—and brought them back. Gratillonius clasped his almost hard enough to splinter the wood. "Drink," said Corentinus. "Our Lord did, the evening before His agony began. You are in yours."

Gratillonius obeyed. Having taken a couple of swallows, he said dully, staring before him, "Dahut. She was a dear child. Like her mother."

Standing above him, Corentinus shook his head and signed himself, unseen.

"How could it happen to her?" Gratillonius wondered. "How was it possible she could turn into this? Why?"

"That is a mystery," Corentinus replied, "perhaps the darkest mystery of all."

Gratillonius looked up, startled. "What is?"

"Evil. How it can be. Why God allows it."

"Mithras—" Gratillonius stopped at the word.

"I know the Mithraic belief. It gives no real answer either. Oh, it claims to, the cosmic struggle between Ahura-Mazda and Ahriman. But that doesn't really make sense, does it?"

"I left Mithras when Ys foundered."

Corentinus smiled very slightly. "You did the right thing for the wrong reason, my son. Who are we men, that we should hold the Almighty to account? And why *should* we understand such things as evil? The Christian faith is honest about it: we don't and we can't."

"Then what?"

"You've heard, but refused to listen. What we do know is that in Christ is rescue from evil, and only in Christ. Not in this world, unless it be inside us, but the promise of salvation for us all."

"All?" whispered Gratillonius.

"Who will accept it," Corentinus finished for him.

Gratillonius rose. "Dahut also?"

For a moment Corentinus was caught off guard. He looked well-nigh daunted. Then he answered as mutedly, "I don't know. I can't see— But how could I dare set limits on God's mercy? I'll pray for her too if you truly wish."

"I do," Gratillonius said. "And . . . will you teach me more?"

2

Nobody now forbade that Evirion visit Nemeta.

The day was bright and the forest rejoiced. In green depths, sunlight speckled shadow and sweetnesses drifted. Doves cooed like a mother above a cradle. Swollen by recent rains, the Stegir rang and gleamed on its way to the Odita. Swallows and dragonflies darted lightning-blue above it.

He drew rein at the old oak and dismounted. She came out of her cabin. The fieriness of her hair set off how haggard her face had grown. She walked draggingly to meet him.

In his glee he did not notice until he hugged her. She responded with a slight pressure of her left arm. Stepping back, he saw how the right dangled. "What's wrong?" he asked. "Did you hurt yourself?"

She twisted a grin. "In a way."

281

"But this—" He pointed. "What did it?"

"A might greater than mine," she said. "Never again will I fly."

He did not understand at that moment. Later he would recall tales that had gone about concerning the battle of the bay, happenings he had been too busy fighting to witness. "Oh, poor darling!" Tears blurred sight of her. Men in Ys had not thought that unmanly. He blinked hard and reached to take her left hand between both his. "How can I help you? You've but to tell me."

"Thank you," she replied in the same monotone, "but I've no need. My father offered too, when he heard of this lameness."

"You refused?"

She shrugged her left shoulder. "I'd have had to move back to Confluentes. What use, there, is a one-armed woman? Here I'm at least a small wood-witch. Men will come do what work I can't myself, in return for my craft."

He was always impetuous, but felt no surprise at his next words. They had been within him for some time. "Wed me! You'll be a fine lady, with servants and, and my love."

She smiled and shook her head. The green gaze mildened. "Nay. You're kind and true, but you're a Christian and I'd have to make pretense of that. Better to keep what freedom is mine."

"Well, the devil with marriage, then. Come live with me."

"What of your standing in the city?"

He let go her hand and raised a fist. "That for the neighbors!" After a space, levelly: "They need me too much, the trade I bring them, for meddling in my affairs."

"You're away more than half the time."

"Aye, your life could become wretched meanwhile. Sail with me."

The idea would have shocked a Roman woman. Hope sparked in him when she regarded him quite calmly. It died out at her sadness: "I have lost all desire for men. Nor would I so fare, did I wish it. You'd have the worst of luck."

"I can't believe that. Why do you say it?"

"My Gods are angry with me. I told you I've crossed a power beyond aught I'll ever command. They bestowed it. She who bears it would know and come after me."

Rage flared. "And yet you serve those Gods!"

"I'll make terms with Them if I can," she said. Her look upon him turned hard. "By Them I keep my freedom. So They are still my Gods."

Again he was silent a while. "And you are still your father's daughter," he said at last.

3

Window glass made greenish and somewhat dimmed the daylight in the room to which Apuleius took Gratillonius. It was like a patina of age on the wall panel paintings, and in fact they went back generations, to the building of this house—the formal woodlands and meadows, decorous fauns and dryads, cheerful shepherds and milkmaids. The air was grotto-cool and quiet.

Gratillonius had excused himself from sitting down— "I'm too restless"—so Apuleius courteously kept his own feet as the other man prowled. He had already had an account of the fight, heartily approved, softly offered sympathy at the way it ended. Today they both had work on hand.

"You're right, we must move fast," Apuleius said. "I can find three or four reliable agents; can you name one or two more? . . . Good. The captured galleys, I think we'd better resign ourselves to selling dirt cheap in Gesocribate."

"No, I want to keep them," Gratillonius answered. "I've a notion they may come in useful."

"Hm? Well, as you like. But leave them in some obscure place, a cove or stream or whatever, well away from here. We don't want to be found in possession of them. Those few Scoti you took alive are less urgent, since they don't speak Latin or Osismiic. I know a dealer who'll take them on consignment. Don't expect to get rich from that sale, either. The breed is considered too fierce for domestic service."

"I wasn't counting on much there," Gratillonius said

283

impatiently. "What about the gold and silver, though? Coins, jewelry, plate. We found expensive cloth stuff too, and spices and wine and that sort of thing."

"It can be stowed in private places. We want to move it rather slowly, piecemeal, so as not to attract attention."

"But damnation, we need the money! I've given the men or their heirs their parts."

"I know. That's all right, because it's thinly spread among unnotable persons. If their lot suddenly betters a little, who's to notice?"

"The Imperium has its eyes. Postal couriers, for instance."

Apuleius stroked his chin and smiled. "Of course. But our local observers report first to me. Over the years, I've seen to it that their stations are filled by . . . trustworthy men. An elementary precaution, commonly taken."

Gratillonius held to his purpose. "You and I can't help being noticed. And we've expenses we've got to meet. First and foremost, the fu—the bloody taxes. Half the reason I organized that operation was the hope of getting the means to pay them for the next several years."

"Oh, we will, never fear. It's simply that we can't hand over a bag of solidi. That would raise questions, especially since the assessments are normally paid in kind. We'll dispatch Evirion down the coast—Portus Namnetum comes to mind—where he'll buy what's required. It will surprise them in Turonum. However, they'll have no way of proving the Confluentians didn't grow most of it themselves and that a wealthy wellwisher who prefers to remain anonymous—God does not like us to make a show of our charities—came up with the shortfall."

An oath escaped Gratillonius's teeth. "All this to go through, because we dared fight a pack of barbarian robbers!"

Apuleius signed. "So it is. We must be most careful, you and I, about what we admit to. The fact of the battle cannot be concealed. There must be no evidence that you planned and organized the movement."

"Certainly not."

"How have you meant to protect yourself and your men from charges of forming a local militia?"

"Well, you see, it wasn't; it isn't; not really. The ordinary man who was there—if the authorities interrogate him, all he knows is that the word went around that something must be done about those pirates, and he decided to join in. As for me, I'll say that when I learned this was afoot, I thought I'd better provide leadership, or the fellows would be slaughtered."

"A weak story."

Gratillonius halted in his tracks and glared. "Well, what would you say?"

"I would obfuscate." Apuleius smiled afresh. "Let me be your mentor and generally your spokesman. A man in my position learns how to misdirect unwelcome attentions and bog down unwanted proceedings. You needn't pack for flight nor lose any sleep. Whatever investigation takes place will be undermanned and perfunctory, because in fact there is nothing clear-cut to find. People were desperate; you stepped in to mitigate the emergency; you have not subsequently maintained any kind of private army. Believe me, Glabrio won't complain to the praetorian prefect. The risk is too high that he would be reprimanded, perhaps demoted, for letting the things happen that did. However, preserving you depends on keeping the details of actual events vague. Don't talk about it more than you absolutely must, not even to your Ysans. Above all, don't boast."

"I've no wish to do that," said Gratillonius grimly.

Relief and thankfulness burst through. He held out his hand. "By Hercules, Apuleius, I thought I could count on you, but this—you're a *friend!*"

The senator took his arm in the old Roman manner and murmured, "What else? Praise God I can again be what I've longed to be."

"We'll work out details. But right now, it's like . . . coming home from exile." Horror and grief came along, but hushedly, things he could set aside most of the time as a man sets aside the pain of an unhealable wound while he goes about his proper business and daily life the best way he is able.

"It's grand of you— Oh, I understand how it must hurt, playing this kind of tricks with the law you've always honored," Gratillonius said awkwardly.

285

The response was grave: "That law conflicts with a higher one."

Gratillonius nodded. "The Church's. Christ's. It is . . . better, surely, than the state's. So it must be higher."

Apuleius caught his breath. "I expected you'd talk only of honor."

"Where does honor spring from? I've asked Corentinus to explain. This time I'll listen."

"Oh, my beloved friend. My brother." Apuleius embraced Gratillonius, who returned the clasp.

Presently they left the room to get a bit of food and a stoup of the best wine in the house. They joked and laughed a great deal, nothing maudlin about them! Verania entered the triclinium just when they did. It was as if she brought the summer day inside with her.

4

News from the South that year had people back on the hook. Once more Alaric and his Visigoths invaded Italy. At Verona they took a resounding defeat and withdrew. Once more Stilicho failed to follow up his victory and do away with them. Instead he arranged for their settlement in the Savus Valley, astride the border of Dalmatia and Pannonia. Emperor Honorius gave himself a triumph in Rome, the first that that city had witnessed in more than a century.

Procurator Bacca secretly called his agent Nagon Demari to his house in Turonum. They met alone at night. Without Glabrio they could sit over drink and talk more or less freely.

"An interesting communication has arrived," Bacca said. Candlelight filled the hollows of his face with darkness.

Nagon leaned over the table. "What?" he rasped.

"Tribune Apuleius of Aquilo writes, largely on behalf of his associate, the curial Gratillonius, that we should cancel confiscation proceedings. The taxes from Confluentes will be paid in full."

The stocky man sat back, aghast. "Name of God! How?"

"You'll try to find that out when you go to collect, of course. I doubt you'll learn much or that the source will be anything we can lay hands on. It will be the same as with identifying runaways who've settled there or going after the Bacaudae in the woods. Nobody is disobedient, but nobody is competent either, or able to attend to the matter at this moment, and so nothing gets done. I'll pass on to you what little I've discovered."

Nagon smote the tabletop. "Is Satan at work?"

"Shrewd minds are, at least. Backed by strong arms. And . . . I hear the natives thereabouts are feeling their oats since the Scoti were trounced. Be very polite and circumspect when you call on them. We don't want to stir them up further. Besides, I'd be sorry to lose you."

Nagon gnawed his lip and ran fingers through his sandy-gray hair.

"Not that I propose to leave them in their contumacy," Bacca went on. "We both know that Confluentes is a tumor that must be excised for the health of the state. Unfortunately, certain highly placed men have not seen this for themselves. They would deny our diagnosis and refuse to allow the surgery."

Nagon caught the other's drift. He straightened on his bench and thrust out his jaw. "I am ready, sir."

Bacca smiled. "I knew you would be. Careful, though. Discretion is of the essence. I have a tentative plan. While you are there, you will study the layout, the whole situation, from the viewpoint of how feasible my idea may be. Report back fully and frankly. It would not do to go ahead with a procedure that is likely to fail and possibly bring grave consequences on us. Nor to rush. If you find it worth attempting, we shall have to wait for the season when it will have maximum effect." He put elbows on table and fingertips together. "Surgery requires both neatness and proper timing, you know; and the surgeon must hold himself deaf to the screams of the patient."

5

Rain fell in serried silver. Wind dashed it against walls and windowpanes. The first breath of autumn was in it. Gloom and chill filled the bishop's house, for he scorned such worldly comforts as hypocausts; but candleglow made his private room a cave of light.

"You tell me Christ walked the earth as a man," Gratillonius said. "I've been thinking what manhood was His, to die on the Cross when He could have called the legions of Heaven down to save and avenge Him."

Corentinus smiled. "We each of us see our own Christ," he replied.

Gratillonius pushed on toward that over which he had lain wakeful. "He stood by His vows and by those He loved. Would He want me to do less?"

Corentinus looked hard from beneath his brows. "What do you mean?"

Gratillonius shifted on his stool, swallowed, and blurted: "You know. My daughter Nemeta. You've warned me I've got to give up, forswear, heathen things. But she will not. And there she is, alone with her withered arm."

"God may well have smitten her," said the stern voice. "Yet still she won't heed."

"She can't. Nor can I forsake her."

"Not even for your salvation?"

"No." Gratillonius sighed. "Am I beyond hope? I'll go."

"Stay!" rapped Corentinus. He made as if to seize his vistor, drew his hand back, and spoke quickly, in a milder tone: "Surely you didn't suppose I meant you could have nothing to do with pagans. That's nonsense. We have to deal with them all the time. There's nothing wrong with feeling friendship. Our Lord Himself did. Or love—it is commanded. I meant ungodly rites, that sort of thing."

"Of course. I understood that. But she . . . practices them. Her house holds a store of witchy tools."

"I know. Certainly I could never forbid you to call on

her, as long as you don't take part in any abominations. But can't you bring her the truth?"

"I tried. She came near showing me the door. I won't try again."

"Ah, well." Corentinus sighed like wind spilling from a sail. "I'll pray for her. And you do the Lord's work anyway."

"Hm?"

"A man as widely admired as you. You must be aware. Salutary example. More and more pagans come to hear me when I preach, or make welcome the priests I send out to evangelize. Some have already asked for baptism."

Gratillonius frowned, hesitated, finally said, "I don't think I should myself, yet. I couldn't live up to it."

"None but a saint can, my son."

"I, though, I can't try as hard as I ought. I can't even wish I could. Too much anger in me."

"Vengefulness. But also honesty."

"I've been wondering what I should do. Look, I can't go off for forty days and pray, anything like that. Too bloody much work here."

Another smile flickered through Corentinus's beard. "After these sessions we've had—" He donned solemnity. "Well, answer this truthfully. Do you believe in—no, I won't throw the formula at you. Do you believe in the one God, Who sent His only begotten Son to earth—the Son Who with the Holy Spirit is Himself—that we might be saved from our sins and live forever with Him?"

"I do." I must. I think I must.

"Then you would call yourself a Christian, Gratillonius?"

"I'd . . . like to."

"That will do for now. Frankly, I have my doubts whether this new style of early baptism is always a good idea. Be that as it may, what you have just said makes that brand of Mithras on your brow no more forever than another scar. You are a catechumen, my son, not ready to take part in the Mystery, but a brother in the sight of God."

"A Christian." Gratillonius shook his head in bemusement. "It feels strange, and yet it doesn't. I've come to this so gradually, after all."

"If the job went slowly, may it prove the sounder for that. I expect it will."

289

Gratillonius was silent for a space, until, in a rush: "Could I, as I am, could I marry a baptized Christian?"

Laughter gusted from Corentinus. "Ho, thought you'd surprise me, did you? I've only wondered when you would. You sluggard, Verania's already gotten up the pluck to ask me the same."

6

"**H**ere we are," said Cadoc harshly. "Why did you want me to come?"

Rufinus's house in Confluentes made him uneasy, not because it was small and rudely made, but because of its owner. Worse than a pagan, he professed complete unfaith; his friends were mainly former Bacaudae like himself, out in the woods; his secretiveness, beneath the genial mask, gave rise to uncanny rumors. This dark space, crowded with oddments, hardly reassured. Cloud shadows made the window membranes flicker as they came and went. The wuthering of the wind recalled tides around a skerry, such as two shipwrecked men might be alone on.

Rufinus's teeth glistened in the fork beard with his quick, disturbing smile. "I've been bracing different men," he said in Latin. "Today it's your turn." He gestured at a stool. "Won't you sit down? I can offer wine, ale, mead. The mead is far and away the best."

Cadoc ignored both invitations. "Why do you do it?"

"Why invite you, do you mean? Well, you showed courage at the battle, but naturally, that by itself isn't enough. It might be a disqualifier if not coupled with a measure of wits. Gratillonius is your father-in-law and, lately, your fellow Christian. You've been working to further his plans, what with surveying the wilderness for future roadways—oh, of course I know what you're at. I would known even if Gratillonius hadn't told me. What I'm trying to get together, very quietly, is a syndicate to start making those notions of his come real."

"Hold on!" exclaimed Cadoc, alarmed. "I don't— There's

290

n-n-nothing illegal about exploration. I don't want to flirt with . . . with outlawry."

Rufinus raised a brow. "Like me?"

"You said it."

"You're not afraid to hear me out, are you?"

"Go on," Cadoc snapped.

Rufinus went into a corner, squatted, took forth a jug, opened it, and poured into two cups. Meanwhile he talked. His tone was even but unwontedly earnest. "Rome or no Rome, we've got to organize some kind of defense. We can't rely on the army. You must know that. The Scoti would have gobbled our local garrison and reserves up and picked their teeth with the shinbones if they'd come up the Odita instead of along the coast. Gratillonius raised a force—between us two, we can say right out that he raised it—and it gave them a drubbing. But at what a cost! Nothing like that can work again. The ordinary man who was there or who's heard about it is glad of the victory. However, if he's not a fool, he now sees what sort of casualties untrained, undisciplined clutters of people are bound to take. He'll see that this one survived only because of special circumstances that won't repeat themselves for his benefit. Come the next menace, he'll do the sensible thing and hotfoot it for the timber. I would myself. Wouldn't you?"

He returned with the cups full and pressed one into Cadoc's hand. "We must accept what God sends us," the visitor argued.

"Did He send us the Scoti?" sneered Rufinus. "The Saxons? You were a man of Ys once. You remember those Franks. What if Gratillonius had meekly yielded to them?"

"But we can't—set ourselves in defiance of Rome—W-we'd simply have two sets of enemies."

"We'll find ways," Rufinus said in more amicable wise. "Today I only want your agreement in principle."

"Why isn't Gratillonius asking it?" Cadoc demanded.

"He can't so well. Still too much under the Roman eye. Nor does he have a gift for this sort of thing. He foresaw the need, but not the nasty little difficulties." Rufinus laughed. "Besides, these days he's preoccupied."

"With his betrothal?"

"What else? Let the poor man have what enjoyment he can. He hasn't gotten much, these past several years."

Relaxing a trifle, Cadoc drank. It was a good mead, dry, pungent with thyme and rosemary. "She is a sweet girl," he said, "and pious."

"With steel underneath, I think. Rejoice for him."

"Do you?"

"Why, of course," said Rufinus, surprised. "It isn't right for a man to live alone, the way he mostly has since the whelming."

"You do," said Cadoc slowly, gaze fixed on him, "and not because of holiness."

Rufinus scowled. The scar on his cheek writhed. "That's my business. Better for you to think of your own wife and child. If the barbarians come, no doubt you'll die heroically defending them, after which they'll gang-rape her and toss the kid around on their spears. Wouldn't you rather keep them off in the first place?"

"What *are* you getting at?" Cadoc curbed his temper. "W-we could try to have more men enlist."

"Ha! A whole extra ten or twenty? I'd guess that's about the number the army could and would accept out of this entire region. If you don't know how such things work, I suggest you learn."

"Then what do you propose?"

"It isn't clear yet," Rufinus admitted. "I told you, all I'm after is agreement in principle. I've been thinking, however. Gratillonius and I have had a couple of talks since the battle, too. It did give us some experience, something to base our thinking on. The rough units we formed, townsmen, tribesmen, seamen, woodsmen, were natural ones, that we seized on in our haste. But by that same token, they look promising as the kernels of a future standby force. You're right, we can't organize an actual army. What we can do, I suspect, is form associations within those groups—brotherhoods, benefit societies, whatever names they want. The avowed idea will be to foster cooperation in a number of matters, among them the maintenance of law and order. This will obviously require training in weapons, formations, maneuvers, and so on. Everything quite loose, each brotherhood independent of the rest. But the amount and quality of training and the kind of weapons, at least among those who live off the highways, needn't be publicized. Such people don't circulate so much that gossip would likely come to the ears of the mighty in Turonum or wherever. Besides, it wouldn't be actual soldierly drill or equipment. Just hunters honing their skills, say, or sailors practicing to contend with pirates. Nothing to alarm any Roman. But . . . the leaders of the groups would know each other, and meet from time to time. In the event of an emergency, they could quickly assemble a mixed but pretty effective collection of fighters."

He had taken sips as he talked. Now he drained his cup.

Cadoc had listened with increasing attention. "Conspiracies are apt to leak, aren't they?" he warned.

Rufinus grinned. "You're not altogether the dewy infant you sometimes act. Correct. But this isn't really a conspiracy either. Let's call it discreet. If we can form a club of men who're possible leaders, and it agrees on a general plan, then we can approach Gratillonius. That'd make a nice present for him, wouldn't it?"

"We'd still be taking a chance," Cadoc persisted. "And, and the cost is certain, time and effort we need for other things. Would the force you're imagining—could it become good enough t-to warrant this?"

"Absolutely. Because the risk and the cost of doing nothing are sky-high more."

"And of failure? We failed at Ys, you know. We won booty and lost lives, but we failed in what was Gratillonius's main purpose. He told me about it. The Scotic King Niall remains alive and . . . free to work fresh deviltries."

"He won't for much longer," said Rufinus, abruptly stark. "I swear it. After what he did to Gratillonius—to Ys, he shall not live."

Cadoc looked closely at him before murmuring, "You're very concerned for Gratillonius, aren't you? As if that was the foremost thing in your life."

"He's my master," said Rufinus. Briskly: "Well, what about the idea? I don't expect you to decide at once. But offhand, how does it seem to you?"

Cadoc shook his head and stared afar. "It may be the only hope we have," he answered low, "God help us."

7

After the swearing to the marriage contract—on the porch of Apuleius's and Rovinda's home, that everyone in the crowd taking holiday for this might be witness—the wedding party proceeded to the church. There Bishop Martinus blessed the union and held a Mass to celebrate and consecrate it. Gratillonius must wait in the vestry when the door closed behind communicants in the Mystery, and he knew this hurt Verania, but she came forth to him radiant.

Thence the numerous invited guests walked to the old manor house outside Confluentes. They let the bridal pair go first, and themselves bore torches. Most of both populations followed behind. Song rose, sound of harp and horn, mingled with laughter. It was a brilliant day, fire well-nigh lost in its light. Leaves blazed with red, russet, gold, the reminding hue of evergreens. Many birds had departed, but blackbirds, crows, sparrows flew from the din in their sober garb, while a hawk aloft caught splendor on its wings. They were no brighter than Verania's hair, a lock or two fluttering from beneath a garland of autumn crocus and the veil, with the color and vividness of a maple leaf, that she had now drawn back from her face. She held Gratillonius's arm tightly.

Trestle tables had been set up in a nearby field, well laden so common folk could make merry too and drink to the couple's good fortune. For the wedding party, the manor house was swept and garnished. If flowers were scarce, there was abundance of juniper boughs, fiery rowan berries, clustered nuts.

Gratillonius thought briefly that it was as if the place denied every memory of Runa, poor Runa. And today it was not a basilica either, it was an ancestral home of the Apuleii, bidding him welcome into the family.

The feast was not lavish, which would have been beyond the father's and bridegroom's thin-stretched means, but it was excellent, served forth on snowy linen and fine ancient ware. Polite, the company was also in a mood for enjoyment. Afterward musicians played, men and women talked, watched a performance of classical dances, talked, mingled, talked, helped themselves to refreshments, talked, while the atrium grew hot and the newlyweds waited.

Everyone offered Gratillonius congratulations. He'd already gotten those that meant most to him, from persons who were outside or not here at all, Rufinus, woodsrunners, tribesmen, sailors, their wives. . . . Well, the prosperous husbandman Drusus was present; and then Rovinda whispered to him, "How glad I am, how thankful to the kind saints;" and later Apuleius, a trifle in his cups, therefore extremely dignified and honest, said, "I've waited a long time for this, you know."

And finally the sun set and the guests made their farewells. It was maddening how often they lingered at the exit, talking, but the last of them did finally go. They left behind Gratillonius, Verania, her brother, her parents, and household slaves. Also, Drusus had posted several armed men around the walls for the night. Nobody would make a disturbance.

Bearing candles, the few went down the corridor to the bridal chamber. At its door, Salomon uttered with the enormous gravity of youth, "God be with you, my new brother," fell into flame-faced confusion, and shuffled his feet. The slaves said no more than, "Goodnight," though tenderly, for they had always been kindly treated. Nor did Apuleius and Rovinda, but they two each kissed Verania and Gratillonius on the cheek.

The groom stooped, gathered the bride in his arms, lifted her. How slender, firm, warm she was. He carried her past the open door. Rovinda shut it. Gratillonius set Verania down. She did not let go of his neck until she was standing.

Here the air was fresh and rather cold, sweet with arrays of juniper. On one wall hung a tapestry—Ulysses and Penelope when she first knew him on his return—that was traditionally brought forth for nights such as this. Multitudinous candles burned. Drapes did not entirely cover the windows, whose glass reflected the light like big stars.

For a while the pair stood looking at each other. He thought that in her saffron gown she was like a candle herself, aglow above, holding darkness at bay. His heart thudded.

Her smile trembled to a sigh. "I am so happy," she said at last.

"Me too," he answered in his clumsiness. He could not have gotten a lass more dear. How long Dahilis had rested under the sea. But Dahilis would not want him dwelling on that. If her ghost could come tonight from wherever such as she went, she would bless them.

"I waited many years for this," Verania said, while the color ebbed and flowed in her face. She hadn't been in hearing when her father gave Gratillonius the like words. "I think it's been as long as I can remember."

"Oh, now," he mumbled.

"You came riding and striding so gallantly. You were like a wind fresh off the waves that I'd never yet seen."

"Ordinary soldier man. I don't deserve this."

Suddenly her laughter trilled. "What, shall we contend in humility? Haven't we better things to do?"

It sang through his blood. He made a step toward her.

She lifted a small hand. "Hold, please," she said in quickly descending seriousness. "Before we—I should offer thanks, if I may."

His own hands dropped to his sides. "Of course. I was forgetting."

She went to stand by the richly covered bed, lifted arms and eyes upward as if there were no ceiling, and crooned in a voice not quite steady, "Our Father, Who are in Heaven—"

Blindingly came back to him his wedding night with Tambilis. He stood for a moment at the bottom of Ocean among its dead.

He thrust himself from it, all of that from him, and joined Verania. "I should offer thanks too," he said. The glance she cast him was ecstatic.

The formula pattered from his lips. He thought that now if any time he ought to feel what he was speaking. But no awe arose, no sense of Presence, nothing like that which had come over him when he was consecrated a Mithraic Father. Did Christ not care to hear him?

Help me, blessed Virgin, he found himself appealing. Maria, Mother of God, lead me to Him.

Somehow that brought peace to his breast.

Verania took his hand. Her lashes dropped, till she forced herself to level those hazel eyes at him and say, "We've paid our thanks. Shall we . . . take the gift?"

She's braver than I am! he thought. Joy rushed free. He drew her to him.

In Ys they would have left the candles burning through the night. Verania went around gently blowing them out. After that, though, she held nothing back; and enough moonlight stole in to bewilder him with beauty.

8

In the dark of the moon before winter solstice, Confluentes burned.

Verania sensed the first smoke and crackle in her sleep. She roused and shook Gratillonius. He opened his eyes on thick night and sat up, instantly ready for battle. "Darling, I think we have a fire," she said, almost calm. Even as his nostrils drank the acrid whiff, he was aware of her warmth and woman-fragrance close against him.

"Out!" He swung his legs around, got feet on floor—its covering shifted and rustled—and surged erect. Familiar with the layout of his dwelling, he found the door, unbarred and opened it. His first sight was of stars, numberless in crystalline black above roofs and lanes. A thin hoarfrost shimmered over earthly things. His breath steamed before him. Shouts from elsewhere reached his ears. They swelled to a clamor.

Verania appeared. She had fumbled her way to the clothes pegs and taken a tunic for him, a shift for herself, to throw across their nakedness. He ignored them while he jumped forth and stared at the house from outside. Flames crawled yellow and blue at a corner below the eaves. A breeze from the north fanned them. Feeding on dried turf, they were quick to gain size and strength.

He looked around. In moments, other fires leaped tall; those roofs were thatch. He saw them each way he gazed. "Out!" he said again. Verania hesitated. He stepped back, seized her wrist, hauled her from the doorway. "Come along. I've got to take charge, if I can."

She handed him the tunic. Laughter broke against his teeth. What a time for modesty. But no, she was right, it was bitterly cold. "Hang on," he said and, while she was pulling the gown over her head, ducked back inside.

"Gaius!" he heard her scream, and roared: "Stay where you are. You're carrying more than yourself." Just a few days ago she had joy-deliriously told him of reasons to believe she was with child. He found sandals for them both and returned.

Garbed and shod, they started off hand in hand. He cried to everyone he saw—dashing in and out with ridiculous little possessions, moaning and stumbling along in blind funk, standing stupefied— "Leave off that! Go straight to the rivers. Pass the word." If obedience was not immediate, he added, "I order you, I, the King of Ys." That usually worked.

Somewhere a roof fell in. Sparks and embers fountained above the black outlines of its neighbors and splashed on them. They caught fire too. A growling as of an angry surf waxed; above it went a sizzling, spitting, and whistling; Confluentes keened for its own death. Red flickered in smoke. Where it did not hide them, the stars watched indifferent.

Gratillonius and Verania came out in the open close to the meeting of the streams. Water sheened darkly through gray-white reaches. Beyond the Odita, Mons Ferruginus hunched into heaven. People were gathering, more of them by the minute. He dared hope everyone had escaped. They milled around, wept, cursed, prayed, implored, babbled. "Keep them off me, will you?" he requested of Verania. Young though she was, she had an inborn dower of giving heart and solace.

"Can we fight this, sir?" asked a guard. "I've seen a few men with buckets."

Gratillonius shook his head. "Good for them, that they thought of it. But no. Look. It's not a single fire, it's a score or worse. More every minute. Let's get the crowd to shelter."

Rufinus appeared. He spent the winters in town, except when he went off on one of his solitary and unannounced, unexplained long rambles. In the uneasy red light, he might have been a demon from hell. "This isn't accidental," he said. "It was set. Somebody crossed the ditch and the wall—about the middle of the east side, I'd guess— and went around with a torch."

Verania heard. Anguish wrenched her mouth out of shape. "Why?" she wailed. "Who would do such a thing? A man possessed?"

"I suspect not," said Rufinus bleakly. "Sir, may I take a party to try tracking him down?"

Gratillonius nodded. "Go." He thought Rufinus must share his guess as to who had sent the arsonist.

He had more urgent business. With those men and women who showed themselves capable of it, he pushed his way into the throng, bullied, cajoled, bit by bit imposed a ragged sort of order.

People in Aquilo were aware; their own watchmen had seen and called them. Several arrived to offer help. Gratillonius got most of his homeless across the bridge and onto the road leading there. A number of able-bodied men he kept. The basilica manor house and its outbuildings could shelter them. Once again those stood vacant except for caretakers. Verania might have lived there with her husband in much more comfort than his dwelling afforded, but had said of her own accord that his place was among his Ysans and hers at his side.

He set about roughly organizing his gang. "We'll try to save what can be saved," he told them. "We won't get reckless; nothing is worth a life. But it'll mean a lot if we can keep the town granary from burning, for instance, and I think maybe we can."

Verania caught his arm. "You *will* be careful?" she pleaded.

Even then, he could smile down at her. "Certainly. I want to meet my son, you know."

"That manuscript—I forgot it, God forgive me, but could you possibly—not to take any chances, oh, no, but it is a precious thing—"

He had forgotten too. Memory jolted him. She had lately carried from the basilica what there was of Runa's Ysan history, mostly notes, to study at home in her rare moments of leisure. Otherwise she never mentioned Runa, nor did he. At that time, though, she had said, "I have her to thank for all this about your city. Maybe we can find someone who'll carry on the work."

By flamelight and starlight, he shook his head. "I'm sorry. That's bound to be impossible."

And it drummed within him: The Veil of Brennilis, the revenge of the Gods, whatever it is, casts its shadow yet, and always shall, until Ys is wholly lost and forgotten. We'll never find time to write that chronicle, nor will anyone else. The story of Ys will die with the last of us who lived the last days of it; and our city will glimmer away into legend.

He turned to his men. "Let's go," he said.

—Rufinus came back about dawn. Gratillonius was awake in the basilica. The sleep of exhaustion held the others. They had kept the blaze from spreading to granary and warehouse. Those Gratillonius had originally directed to be built near the Stegir, with space between them and adjacent structures. Some houses had survived as well, some valuables were pulled out of others before they caught fire. It was no great victory.

Under the pale east, Confluentes was ash heaps. Dwindling flames gnawed at charred timbers. Most walls had collapsed as the wood weakened too much to hold clay. A few stood black, like boles after a forest has burned. Smoke lay in a stinging, stinking haze.

"We found tracks in the frost, a couple of fellows and I," Rufinus reported. "Three sets. They'd sneaked out of the woods and returned. There they dispersed. We couldn't follow two. They'd taken care to leave no trail we could see by night once they reached the trees and brush. The third was a dunderhead. He'd actually made a campfire and rolled out a blanket for a rest before daybreak." His curtness dissolved in a sigh. "Unfortunately, when we appeared he panicked and bolted. Before we could run him down, one of us put an arrow through him. I'd rather not say who. He's young, hot-headed; the damage is done, and he's loyal and promising. When I dressed him down, he cried and asked to be whipped. A month's worth of the silent treatment will drive the lesson home better than that."

He must be an adorer of yours, Rufinus, thought Gratillonius. Aloud: "Are you sure the party you found was guilty?"

"His clothes were freshly stained with oil. How'd that happen, except when he was pouring it out of a jug onto the wood he was going to set alight? Good clothes, too; he well fed, and barbered within the past few days; so, no landlouper. What else would he be doing in the wilderness at night in the dead of winter?" Rufinus studied Gratillonius. "Do you want to come with me for a look at the corpse? We'd better cover it up, just in case, but it might be somebody you'd recognize. Somebody who—let's say—was with tax agent Nagon Demari on his last visit to us."

"I think likelier not," Gratillonius replied. "They aren't stupid, those who ordered this thing. They'd guard against the chance of their bully boys getting caught at it."

"And mine wringing the truth out. M-hm. A middleman hired them." Rufinus pondered. "Not common alley lice. You couldn't rely on that sort, especially to get through the forest. Maybe the middleman paid their gambling debts and told them he had a long-standing grudge against Ys. If we'd gone to Turonum with his name, we'd have found he'd left for the far South, leaving no address, and no underling of the governor's had any knowledge of him."

"It doesn't matter," said Gratillonius.

Weariness overwhelmed Rufinus. "No, it doesn't, does it?" he croaked. "Confluentes, your colony, your hopes, they're gone."

Gratillonius put a hand on his man's shoulder and tightened the grip till Rufinus met his eyes. The windows in the atrium came awake with the first wan light of day. "Wrong," Gratillonius told him. "We have that treasure Apuleius is keeping for us. We have friends who'll help us again, more willingly this time when they know what we're worth. We have ourselves.

"Those maggots won't eat us away. We're going to build Confluentes over; and we'll make it too strong for them."

XVI

1

Springtime dusk. The air was soft, odors of greening and blossoming not yet cooled out of it. A moon close to fullness had cleared Mons Ferruginus. It looked like old silver afloat in an ever deeper blue sea. The earliest stars trembled forth. Sunset's ghost still lightened the western sky. After the tumult of day—hoofs, boots, wheels, hammer, saw, chisel, trowel, shovel, hod, shout, grunt, oath, banter, the trudging off at day's end—quietude rested enormous over the land. Through it drifted little save belated bird-cries, ripple of the Odita, occasional tiny splash when a fish leaped, footfalls on the river road.

Gratillonius had been gone half a month, traveling about to make his arrangements. He wanted to see how the work had fared meanwhile. At this hour he could get an overview; tomorrow he would watch it in progress. His wife accompanied him from her parents' home in Aquilo, where they were living until their new dwelling was ready. The manor house was full of engineers and other directors. Mostly hired from elsewhere, they naturally expected better quarters than the shacks and tents that served common laborers.

Verania's brother Salomon had asked if he could accompany her and her man. They gave leave, for they had talked about him earlier, when they were alone and after they were at peace with nature.

He pointed. "See," he said importantly, "they've begun on the new wharf."

Gratillonius made out pilings planted just above the juncture of the rivers. The ground beyond was trampled, muddied, heaped and littered with lumber, equipment, scraps, trash. In the end this was supposed to become facilities for ships. Then the bridge at Aquilo would be demolished, so they could come here to the actual head of navigation, a better site in every respect.

A new bridge would span the Odita at Confluentes, stone, with towers at either end for its defense "Wait," requested Verania, halfway over the old wooden one. "The evening is so beautiful." They lingered a few minutes, watching light shiver and fade on the stream, before they continued.

The same light touched the pike of a guard on the opposite side. A number paced their rounds, for the legionary embankment had been levelled, the ditch filled in. Stakes marked where a real wall of the Gallic sort was to be. It would make a complete circuit, east of the Stegir and north of the Odita. That would give room for proper streets and large buildings, as well as a population growth Gratillonius hoped would prove rapid.

The sentry challenged the newcomers. When he recognized the man among them, he snapped a Roman salute. It was crisp, though his outfit was homemade. Drusus and his veterans had long since stopped counselling the local reservists—that came to be frowned on in Turonum—but they were instructing Osismii who had formed an athletic association.

"How goes it?" Gratillonius asked.

"Right well, my lord," replied the guard.

"He speaks truth," said Salomon as the three walked on. "It really does go apace, now when rain and darkness don't hamper us so much. There's no trouble to speak of with thieves. Rufinus's scouts stop any that try to sneak here from outside, and we inspect outbound loads for stolen goods."

"We?" teased Verania. She had been bubblingly light-hearted since Gratillonius returned; but he sensed that it cost her an effort.

"Aw, well," muttered Salomon, abashed. He had grown taller than she, close to the height of Gratillonius, but was

303

as yet reed-thin; under a shock of brown hair, his face continued, for days after he had been shaved, as smooth as hers.

Gratillonius took pity. "He worships you, not far short of idolatry," Verania had told him. "Well he might."

"You stick by your studies," Gratillonius said. "That's your share of the work, making ready for when we'll call on you."

Dim in twilight, Salomon nonetheless glowed.

They wandered about. Order had begun to emerge from confusion and ugliness. Scaffolding and cranes loomed where masonry climbed. Elsewhere were only sites marked off or foundations partly dug, but space and ambition prevailed—for a real basilica, for the big church that Corentinus would make his cathedral, for workshops and storehouses and homes, for a town whose bones were not clay and turf but brick and stone—a *city*.

Northward and eastward, greenwood no longer crowded close. Axes had slain trees across a mile or more in either direction, to make room and timber. Cookfires glimmered yonder, throughout the encampment of the workers. It was a huddle of the rudest shelters, hog-filthy, brawling, drunken, whorish. Dwellers in the neighborhood were too few, and generally bound down by their own occupations. Gratillonius's agents had ranged from end to end of Armorica during the winter, recruiting muscle where they found it. Many of the hirelings were doubtless runaways, claiming to be laborers with a right to take jobs elsewhere. As word spread, no few barbarians who had wandered into Roman territory joined the force. But stiffened by armed men at their beck, the supervisors kept it disciplined in the workplace, without strength left at day's end for much riotousness. And . . . there was life in the camp, a gusty promise as in an equinoctial storm. The new Confluentes would remember.

Not that Gratillonius meant to keep that lot of boors here. For those who proved themselves desirable and wanted to stay, he'd make what arrangements he was able. The rest must go, once the basic task was finished. It might be hard to get rid of some, he might have to bloody heads, but he wasn't going to allow more rabble than he could help. The immigrants he hoped to attract were steady, civilized men, seeking a chance to build a better life for their families. Gallia must hold many such, who would find ways to reach him. And more were in beleaguered Britannia. If he sent word across the channel—

That was a thing to think seriously about, and maybe do, in years unborn. Tonight he walked in peace with his wife, who carried their child within her, and the boy to whom he was like a second father. Distance dwindled noise from the camp to a bare murmur beneath the hush. A bat swooped by. The last light from the west shone through its wings. "Look," Verania said. "Like an angel flying."

"A sign unto us?" marveled Salomon. He gestured at the murky heaps around. "How splendid this will soon be."

Gratillonius smiled. "Easy, there," he cautioned. "It'll take a while."

"The work goes fast."

"Because we're pushing with everything we've got. The city has to be habitable and defensible before winter. But afterward things will slow down. It'll be mostly up to individual people, and they have their livings to make. We'll have spent every last nummus in our present treasury."

Verania sighed. "The cost—" She checked her voice. He heard a gulp, and laid his left hand over hers, which rested on his right arm. Gently, he pressed it.

"You know how we'll meet that," he said.

Since he revealed his plans to her, secretly, last month, she had been fighting desperation. She did so wordlessly, but he knew, and wished he could find reassurances that wouldn't sharpen her fears. They burst through for an instant: "You can't change it?"

He shook his head. "No. That'd break faith with a good many men. With the whole people."

She tensed her clasp on him. "God watch over you, then."

They had stopped in their tracks. "With you to pray for me, what have I got to worry about?" he responded, the weak best he could think of.

305

"What's this?" asked Salomon.

Gratillonius drew breath. "We've been meaning to tell you," he said. "Here we're safe from eavesdroppers. Your father and your sister both believe we can trust you to keep silence, absolute silence."

The skinny frame quivered and grew taut. "I s-swear. By God and all the saints, I do."

Verania too was relieved a little by speaking forth. "You've heard the talk about Gratillonius going along when Evirion Baltisi makes his first voyage of the season, soon after Easter," she said.

"Of course. To look for markets. Oh, sir, I've asked you before. Take me! I'll earn my keep, I promise I will."

"I'm sorry," Gratillonius answered. "An ordinary trading trip would be risky enough these days. This won't be one."

"What will it be, sir? What?"

Gratillonius held hands with Verania while he spoke in his most carefully measured tones: "We're building Confluentes again, and building it right. That's a huge and expensive job. Doing it in a hurry makes it more expensive yet." Finish before Glabrio and Bacca hit on some means of forestalling it. Apuleius was already contending with their objections and legalisms. "We're employing as many Ysans and Osismii as we possibly can, you know. That means farms and other businesses neglected. We'll have to bring in food, most necessities. By autumn, when we've paid off the outside experts, contractors, laborers, we'll have emptied the treasury of Confluentes, everything we took from the Scoti. How then can we go on with what remains to be done? And the city will have to keep paying the people's taxes for them, for the next several years, till farms and industries are solidly on their feet. How?"

"I don't know," Salomon admitted with a humility rare in him. "I should have thought about it."

"Well, nobody gave you any figures," said Gratillonius, smiling at him through the dusk. "We keep such things confidential. I don't want to discuss why, though I think probably you can guess."

"He's bound forth to get what we need." Pride and

306

dread warred in Verania's voice. "I've begged him—he shouldn't go himself—but—"

"But without me, it'll fail," Gratillonius said flatly. "A matter of leadership."

"Yours," breathed Salomon.

Gratillonius turned his gaze back on him and continued: "Evirion and I will rendezvous up the coast with picked men. They'll fill his ship and those two galleys we capture last year. We'll make for the Islands of Crows. You've heard of them, pirate haunts off the Redonic coast. Barbarians often spend the winters there, so they can start raiding again as soon as weather allows. Scoti, Saxons, renegade Romans, every kind of two-legged animal, in lairs stuffed with loot. Rufinus has had his spies out, he's heard a great deal on his missions to Hivernia, he knows where the big hoards are likeliest to be. We'll strike, cut the scum down or scatter them, and bring the treasure back."

No wisp of a thought of danger was in the cry: "Oh, sir, I've got to go!"

"You do not," said Gratillonius. "You're far too young."

Salomon doubled his fists. Did a trembling lower lip stick out? "I'm f-f-fifteen years old."

"You will be later this year," said Verania sharply.

Gratillonius let go her hand and laid both his on the youth's shoulders. He looked into the tearful eyes and said, "You'll have your test of manhood, I promise. It will be harder than you know, keeping silence."

"I w-w-will. I've sworn. But I can fight too."

"Carry out your orders, soldier. I told you already, you've got your share of duty and then some. I'm afraid you'll see plenty of fighting later on. Meanwhile, we can't squander you on a simple raid."

Salomon gulped. "I don't understand, sir," he pleaded.

"I believe you are the future leader of our people—of all Dogwood Land, maybe all Armorica. Your father is beloved; they'll be ready to follow his son, come the day. You've done well in your studies, I hear, and very well in the lessons about soldiering you got me to give you. You have the fire. I won't let some stupid encounter blow it out."

307

"No, you, sir, you're the King."

Gratillonius released his hold. "There's too much of the uncanny—of Ys—about me," he said. "Those who haven't known me before, they'd never feel the way they must about their leader, the way I think they will feel about you. But I'll be at your side as long as I'm on this earth."

Overwhelmed, Salomon sank down onto a baulk of timber and stared before him at the stars above Mons Ferruginus, beneath the moon that rose and waxed toward Easter.

Verania drew Gratillonius aside. She held him close and whispered in his ear, "Come back to us, beloved."

"To you," he replied as low; and, since nobody watched, he kissed her. She returned that with a passion he well knew, and only he.

Like the bat at sunset there flitted through him: She's not Dahilis. Nobody could ever be. But she is mine, and here are no heathen Gods to break us from each other.

2

The men from the currach reached holy Temir a few days after Beltene. They had heard that King Niall was there yet.

Their captain and spokesman Anmureg maqq Cerballi stood before him to say: "The Romans took us unawares. They must have gotten pilots, islanders who knew those waters and shores even better than we do. Suddenly, there they were, two Saxon galleys out of the fog and onto the beach. Men jumped from them and started hewing. It was butchery. Oh, sure, brave lads rallied and I think must have taken some foes with them, while others among us escaped inland, but most died and we lost everything, all we had won in two years of work."

Rain roared on the thatch of the King's House. Wind shrilled. Cold and darkness gnawed against the fires inside. It was wrong weather for this festival time.

Nonetheless Niall sat benched in state, with his warriors well-clad around the walls, their shields catching the

308

flamelight above them. Servants scurried over fresh sweet rushes to keep filled the cups of mead or ale or, for the greatest, outland wine. Smoke thickened the air and stung eyes, but soon it would be full of savory smells, when the tables were set up and the meat brought in from the cookhouse.

Niall leaned forward. The light limned his face athwart shadow, broad brow, straight nose, narrow chin. It showed little of the ashiness in locks and beard that once were primrose yellow, nor of scars and creases or how the blue of the eyes had faded. In richness of fur, brightly dyed wool, gold and amber, his body now verged on guantness; but the thews had not shrunk, the movements remained steady and deft. "Why do you call them Romans?" he asked.

"Some were so outfitted, lord," Anmureg replied. "Others appeared to be Gauls, though from elsewhere than Redonia. We heard Latin as well as their own language, when their chiefs were egging them on against us. Then when my crew was at sea—we happened to be together near our currach, making a small repair, the only ones, for the which we have promised Manandan sacrifices—the fog thinned and we saw a ship of the Roman sort anchored offshore, and one of the galleys drawing close to her in peaceful wise."

Another of the men who stood there dripping from the rain said slowly, "She looked much like what I'd seen earlier, King, that galley did."

Niall held himself unmoving. "How was that?" he inquired. Beneath the crackle in the firepit, stillness deepened around the hall.

"You bought a Saxon galley for yourself, King, shortly before I went off a-roving. Black she was, with a yellow stripe, twenty oars, the sternpost high and spiralled at the top and gilt."

"Such as you lost at Ys," declared Cael maqq Eriai. He, an ollam poet, could dare.

"Did you see the other your enemies had?" Niall asked, his voice deadly quiet.

"Not really well, any of us," Anmureg said. "Yourself will understand what wildness ruled on that beach. We here barely stood off an attack till we had our currach launched. Better, we thought, come back and tell your honor about this, than leave our bones there unavenged. The Gauls call those islands the Islands of Crows."

"You did leave two ships behind at Ys," said Cael.

"Ys-s-s," hissed from Niall. "Forever Ys."

"The men who took them may have sold them off," suggested a brithem judge nearby.

Niall shook his head. "They would not," he said; a gust of wind keened at the words. "Over the years I have gathered knowledge of the King of Ys, that Grallon. His city is fallen but he will not rest in the grave where he belongs. This latest is his work too."

"It is that," the druid Étain told him. "A fate binds you two together, though you have never met and never shall. It has not yet run to its end." Because of her calling, she was the sole woman there. Save at Brigit's Imbolc, usage on Temir was that a Queen entertain female guests in her own house. Étain's long white dress made her a ghostly sight among the shadows.

Cael saw how much heartening everybody needed. He stood up, jingled the metal that hung on his staff, reached for the harp he had tuned beforehand. Rain drummed to the strings. Created as he uttered them, the words rang forth:

"Valiant lord of victories,
Avenge your fallen men!
Heroes rise throughout your hall,
Hailing you their King.

"Goddesses Whose birds you've gorged,
Grant that you may fare
Windborne, fireborne, laying waste
Widely, Roman land.

"Sail upon the southbound wind.
Set your foot ashore,
Letting slip from off his leash
The lean white hound named Fear.

"Swords will reap when they have soared

310

Singing from the sheath
Heavy may your harvest be
Of heads and wealth and fame."

Shouts drowned out the weather. Men pounded fists on benches and feet on floor. Niall climbed erect, raised his arms for silence, loomed above the company, and cried:

"Thanks be to you, poet, and good reward shall you have. You too, warriors who bore us this tale—first, dry clothes, full bellies, and lodging in brotherhood; later, your share in the revenge we will take. I swear by Lúg and Lir and the threefold Mórrigu, for what you and your comrades have suffered, Rome shall weep!"

—But that evening he walked from Temir, and with him only the female druid Étain. Four guards followed, well out of earshot, the least number the King could take and not demean his name.

The storm had blown over. Grass lay rain-weighted, air nearly as wet. Clouds ringed the horizon. Eastward they towered in murky masses, off which whiteness had calved into the deepening blue. Westward they glowed with sundown, molten copper and gold run together across that whole quarter of the sky. Hush and a soft sort of chill lapped earth.

Niall made his way down from the heights of Temir and up again to the ancient hill-fort sacred to Medb. It was empty of men, because he had enough in this train for any trouble. So there he could speak freely, and maybe likewise Those Who brooded over it. Étain came along in shared muteness. She was a woman tall and thin though sightly, her hair thick and red and the first frost of her years in it.

Atop the ringwall they looked vastly over the western plain, the forest and Boand's River to the north. Niall kept his gaze yonder while he leaned on his spear and said, "I wish your counsel."

"You do not,' replied the druid. "You wish my comfort."

He cast her a glance and a troubled grin. "Well, have you any for me?"

"That is for you to know."

I felt easier with old Nemain, he thought. And Laid-

311

chenn's poems had wings, where Cael's walk. Well, time slips through our fingers till at last we hold no more of it.

"A name can abide," she told him.

Startled at being answered, he said in his turn as steadily as he was able, "I would have mine stand always with its honor."

She nodded. "Will you or nill you, that is so. Else power must also fall from it."

"That will surely outlive me. Sons of mine are now kings across the breadth of Ériu."

"But the one of them who is to have Temir and Mide from you— and he will, after your tanist falls—is a little child still. To his heritage you must add terror among his enemies; and for that, you must redeem what happened last year, against which today's news was no more than a spark on fuel. Say how you mean to do it."

He looked again at her, and now did not look back away. Sunset colors welled up behind her. "I think you already know," he murmured; "yet the speaking may help me."

"One-and-twenty years ago, while Rome writhed at war with itself, I gathered a fleet and the finest of my warriors. We set course for the River Liger that flows to the sea through rich lands and past gleaming cities. Boundless could our winnings have been. But the witch-Queens of Ys raised a gale that drove us onto the rocks; and their King slew most of us who made it ashore."

He drew breath to quell an undying pain and went on: "Well, Ys is no more, and yonder stream flows as of old. From travelers and scouts I know how stripped are the garrisons that hold Gallia, with the lower end of the river in the hands of strangers. Soon I will make known my intent, the which is to fare with the same strength to the same hunting ground. Men who follow me will win booty, glory, and revenge for their fathers. Afar in Rome, its King shall bewail his loss, and until the heavens fall they will remember us."

His lifting bravado sank when she asked, "You will not be calling at Ys, though, will you, now?"

"I must steer wide of it," he said harshly, "or the men would cast me overboard to her who haunts that water."

"It is you that she haunts, and after you, him whom she also loved."

"What do you then see for us?" he whispered.

"In the end, you shall not go down to her. That fate is for him."

He scowled. "You speak darkling words."

"As the Gods do to me." Étain reached to stroke his cheek. There was sadness in her smile, but it was undaunted. "Come to my house, darling," she said, "and I will give you the best comfort that is mine; for it is what any mortal woman has power to give."

3

Laden with plunder, *Brennilis* and her companion ships—*Wolf* and *Eagle*, for the emblem creatures of Rome—left the Islands of Crows and steered for Hivernia. There, in Mumu, they set Rufinus off. Once more he would range about gathering intelligence on King Niall, returning to Gallia by some fisher or merchantman making that passage late in the season. "Have no fears for me," he laughed. "I've become an old Ériu hand."

A hand to strike down the enemy, Gratillonius hoped.

Homebound, the ships stood well out to sea. Not only were the waters around Ys dangerous, sight of that land was almost unbearable for some aboard. When they felt sure they were to the south of it they would turn east. That would doubtless mean doubling back along the Armorican coast to the Odita mouth, but was amply worth the added time and effort.

On their second day from Hivernia, a west wind sprang up. Rainsqualls and driving clouds hid every star or scrap of moon that night; in the morning, the position of the sun was a matter of guesswork. With the sky went knowledge of bearings. The ships wallowed on through ever heavier seas, through wet and cold and clamor.

"What foul luck," growled Gratillonius when the next day brought no surcease.

"I wonder if luck is all it is," replied Evirion.

313

"You've said what I did not want to say."

Late that afternoon they saw white spouts and sheets to port. Evirion nodded. "The Bridge of Sena," he reminded landsman Gratillonius—rocks and reefs strung out for miles west of the island. "We should clear them, going close-hauled, but 'twill be a near thing. The galleys will need hard rowing."

Gratillonius snorted a laugh of sorts. "Naught like yonder kind of sight to put force in a man's arms." A jape was a shield.

Wind raved. Spindrift flew bitter. Pushed near the grounds, the farers saw billows crash on skerries and churn between them, foam turning their gray backs into snow-swirls. Spray dimmed sight, a flung-up fog under the hastening smoky clouds. It roared, snarled, hissed, as if dragons ramped within.

And yet the ships clawed off. Beneath strained sail or on straining oars, they lurched and pitched their way south. The dread that had grown within him began to loose its hold on Gratillonius's heart. Soon, he thought, sometime in the endless hours before dark, they'd be past the trap.

Evirion cried out. The galleys were to port of the large ship. Shallower of draught and lower of freeboard, they let their crews see rocks that the waves half hid, in time to veer off and thus warn *Brennilis*. The one farthest in, *Wolf*, had abruptly turned east. She was bound straight for the surf.

"What in Lir's name are they doing?" Evirion yelled. "Come back, you clodheads! Come back, Taranis thunder you!" The wind shredded his call, the breakers trampled it underhoof.

Eagle swung about and bore west. Her oars flailed the water. Whatever they'd seen or heard aboard *Wolf*, the other crew had caught just enough of it to make them flee.

Gratillonius remembered what Maeloch had told him, and later Nemeta. He remembered the fight in the bay at dusk. For an instant the horror stopped his heart. Then he was again the commanding officer of his men. Amreth Taniti, the whole squad of marines from Ys, was in *Wolf*.

He grabbed Evirion's arm. "They've been lured," he said above the skirl and thunder. "If we let them go,

314

they'll drown." And with them a goodly part of the treasure that could save their people—but it was the men, the
men who filled his head.

"Christ have mercy," the captain groaned. "What can
we do?"

"Get me rowers for the lifeboat. Launch it. I'm going
after them."

Evirion gaped. "Have you gone mad too?"

"God damn it, don't piss away what little time we've
got!" Gratillonius snapped in Latin. "Jump to it, if you
haven't lost your balls overboard!"

Evirion's face darkened. Gratillonius knew it was touch
and go whether the young man would strike him or obey
him.

Evirion was off along the deck, shouting into the wind.

Gratillonius came after, likewise bawling forth words.
"Eight men for the rescue! Eight brave Christian men!
You scuts, will you let that demon have your mates?
Christ'll ride with us!"

He was not at all sure of that. But Dahut, Dahut—when
she was little he'd kept her from games that might be
dangerous—she must not play at the bottom of the sea
with the bones of men she murdered, because that could
become her doom forever.

The eight were there. Gratillonius recognized a couple
of pagans among them. Did they want to show they were
as bold as anybody else? No matter. Unlash the boat, drag
it over a wildly rolling deck, tilt it across the rail, lower it
when that side swings toward the waves, slide down a
rope into a hull awash, fend off, bail while the rowers took
their oars and threw the strength of their backs against the
sea.

Gratillonius emptied out a last bucketful, crawled over
the thwarts to the forepeak, braced himself and stood half
crouched, peering ahead. Wind savaged him and his waterlogged garments. Waves loomed wrinkled and clifflike
on both sides, rumbled past, became surges up which the
boat climbed till it poised in spume and shriek before
plunging into the next trough. The galley grew in sight.
Her crew had shipped their oars. He saw them dimly
through the spray, crowded forward, while the wind chiv-

vied *Wolf* toward the breakers. Those were a tangle of mist and violence. Were the men blind, deaf? What gripped them?

Through the noise, a voice; through the chaos, a vision. Somehow the ghastliest of everything was a sunbeam that struck through, blinked out, struck through to gleam on her wet whiteness. Naked she was, save for wildly blowing long hair and the same gold aglow at her loins, white and slender and entrancingly rounded; aye, her beauty had blinded them, and she held out her arms and sang to them. Unhearable in the fury around, the song's clarity streamed forth to encoil the spirit; and what it promised, no man but a saint could flee.

Desire came ablaze in the blood. Gratillonius's member leaped to throbbing stiffness. She was Belisama, she was Dahilis, she was there and he'd have her!

No, she was Dahut, and the vessel that he neared was drifting to shipwreck.

Had he watched and listened an instant longer, she would have caught him. To break free was like ripping his manhood out. His rowers had their backs to her, they had not seen, but they faltered. "Row!" he bellowed. "Row, you scoundrels! Stroke, stroke, stroke!" He drew his knife, wedged himself between the nearest, slashed whenever a head turned around. Twice he bloodied a cheek. Meanwhile he hurled noise out of his lungs, commands, oaths, snatches of prayer, lines from a marching song—"Again the tuba, the tuba calling: 'Come, legionary, get off your duff!'"—anything to ram between that song and his men.

The boat thudded against the galley. He seized a rail and sprang across. Inboard, he stumbled over the benches to the crew. They stared before them. At the very bow was Amreth. The marine captain leaned far out, strained toward her who beckoned and sang.

Where the foam runs white on my breasts,
  White, sparkling, beloved,
    Your kisses course hot—
Where the sun strikes up to your eyes,
  Blue, sea-flung, beloved,
    My gaze clings with joy—

316

Come you here, as the sun joins the foam,
  In all splendor, beloved,
    Come cleave to me now—

Let kissing join gazing, join splendor
With all that's most fierce and most tender
Until our joined souls we both render
    To Lir in His deep.

Gratillonius shouted. He struck with fists, feet, knees, brutally hard, whatever might shock them out of their daze. When he cast them down onto the benches, they sat hunched, shaking their heads. He wrestled oars back into place, clamped hands about them, hallooed deafening into ears: "Row! Row! Row!"

Did the song ring with victory? The galley sprang toward it. Gratillonius bounded aft. He seized the tiller and put it hard over. He should have had rowers on one side only, to make the turnaround fast. He dared not give the order. The men were stunned. They worked like oxen at a millstone. He must not risk their coming fully aware. The slowness raked him.

But then *Wolf* was headed back out. Gratillonius's bulk blocked off sight of the one on the reef. "Stroke, stroke, stroke!"

In the bows, Amreth howled. He sprang. A wave bore him past the stern, toward Dahut.

"Stroke, stroke, stroke!" Gratillonius glared right and left. The lifeboat was also bound for safety. He hazarded a glance behind. Did he catch a last sight of him who swam, or was it seaweed or a piece of wreckage? No more sunlight kindled the foam-haze. There were only rocks and breakers.

The rhythm of the oars clattered to naught. Men gaped at each other. Emptiness in their eyes gave way to bewilderment. "What happened?" Gratillonius heard in tatters through the wind. "What came over me? A dream. . . . I can't rightly remember—"

Eagle coursed to join her sister and give help. *Brennilis* sailed on. Men crowded her port rail to cheer.

Gratillonius sagged at the rudder. He could let go of himself now.

317

Christ, if it was You Who stood by us, thank You. I wish I could honestly say more than that. Maybe later. I'm so tired, so wet, so wrung. All I want to do is crawl off and sleep. If I can. Maybe first, once I'm alone, I'll weep. Forgive me, if You please, when I don't weep for those we lost fighting in the islands or for Amreth my friend, but for Dahut.

4

"**N**o doubt of it, sir," Nagon Demari said.

Bacca raised his brows. "Oh? Just what are your sources?" he inquired. "You can't be exactly beloved in those parts."

Taken aback when the procurator did not at once hang on what he had to relate, Nagon answered sullenly, "I've got my ways."

"Of course. In a position like yours, one must. But what do you yourself employ?"

Nagon stood before the seated man with his legs planted apart, shoulders hunched, head thrust forward, as if under a load. "Well, a couple of fellows who escaped from Ys, common dock workers they were, they've not forgotten what I once did for them and their kind. The great Grallon isn't so wonderful in their eyes. For a little money, they're glad to tell me things. Others—really need money, or they've got a grudge, or I've learned something about them they'd rather nobody knows."

"The usual methods. You had experience in Ys. What is this latest news?"

"Not mere rumors. I went myself when I first heard those, and asked around. Not into town, you understand. The farms, the villages, places where they don't always know who I am."

"Nor are rustics apt to have much first-hand political knowledge of any kind. But what did you find them abuzz over?"

"Grallon's back with another load of loot. This time he went and took it off pirates in—seems to've been the Britannic Sea."

Bacca's lips shaped a soundless whistle. "Indeed?"

"That's the word, sir." Exultation danced in the flat face, the small pale eyes. "You've got him! He's finally overreached himself. Deliberately organized a military expedition, a civilian armed force. You can behead him!"

Bacca sat still for a minute or two. Nagon dithered.

The procurator sighed. "I'm afraid not," he said. "You can't have heard from anybody who took an actual part."

"No, but word's leaked out like through a sieve."

"He's known it would, and allowed for it."

"Arrest a few men who did go, interrogate them under torture—"

"You're an able man in your fashion," Bacca said, "but statecraft is beyond you. Think, however. If we moved openly against Gratillonius, at this hour when he's come home as a savior, why, we would quite likely have a rebellion on our hands. Do *you* want to explain that to the praetorian prefect? Do you imagine the lord Stilicho would praise our handling of the case? Meanwhile, Gratillonius and his worst troublemakers will have slipped off into the wilderness; and his friends the tribune and the bishop will insist this is all an unfortunate misunderstanding.

"No, we cannot act on a basis of gossip, no matter how well-founded it appears to be. You will speak no further of this to anyone whatsoever. Is that clear?"

Nagon's countenance purpled. He lifted fists in air. "Was my work for nothing?" he cried. "Is that devil going to keep on his merry way and, and make a joke of us? Can't you get it into your head, he's *dangerous?*"

Bacca held up a palm. "Softly. Watch your tongue, especially in the presence of your superiors."

Nagon slumped. "I'm sorry, sir," he got out.

"That's better." Bacca rubbed his nose and stared long at the opposite wall. Finally he said, "I do appreciate your efforts, and they do have value. I would have gotten wind of this one way or another, but belatedly and in much less detail than I imagine you can supply. What's important, I think, is the knowledge that Gratillonius does now have at his beck a force capable of carrying out such an operation. Thus far it must be small. Being warned, we can take steps to prevent its further growth, until such time as we are ready to eradicate it. . . . Success like his feeds on itself. We must insure that there are no more successes—no more missions for him and his irregulars. This requires— m-m, some very tactful discussion with . . . the Duke of the Armorican Tract. . . . Not to provoke him into ill-advised action against Confluentes. But to make clear to him that the help of such people is more to be feared than the onslaught of the barbarians. . . . Courage, Nagon. You've done well. Sit down, give me your full report. In due course you shall have an appropriate reward."

5

Harvest brought wholeness.

"I'm not sleepy yet," Gratillonius said. "I'll go for a walk first."

Verania yawned. She always did so in a way that made him think of a kitten. "Well, I'm quite ready for bed," she admitted.

He chucked her under the chin. "I won't be gone long. As soon as you're healed, I won't be gone at all."

She gave him a heavy-lidded glance. "Speed the day."

They kissed, less strongly or lingeringly than they desired. She was warm and supple against him. Memories of a skerry glimmered away for this while. "I'll leave a light burning, of course," she said. "Enjoy your walk. It is a beautiful evening."

He stooped above the tiny, homely miracle in the crib. "Goodnight, Marcus." He looked over his shoulder. "Ungracious rascal. I do believe he snored at me."

She wrinkled her nose. "Takes after his father, he does." In haste: "Not really. Not in that way. You don't often."

His son, he thought. Bearer of the name. Her parents had supposed he chose "Marcus" for the Evangelist, and were pleased. Except for Verania, who went cheerfully along with the conspiracy, he wouldn't disenchant them. His father in Britannia had been Marcus. Strange how this new life strengthened its own wellsprings, even those that had long since flowed into quietness.

He took his cloak and went from the bedroom, down the corridor, out the atrium and front door of Apuleius's house. A few months hence, he and Verania would have their own home; and it wouldn't be a cob-and-turf hovel. In the meantime, the older couple couldn't be kinder. Salomon sometimes got brash, but the boy meant well and . . . already, as easily and naturally as a seed becomes a sapling, was the leader of his age contingent in Aquilo.

May the sapling grow to a mighty oak.

Not far past full, the moon lifted above Mons Ferruginus. Light speckled streets and frosted roofs. Air was still warm and full of earth odors, once Gratillonius had left the city behind. He found a path leading to the heights. Along it he was frequently in darkness cast by trees or by the hill itself, but his feet knew the way.

Years ago, he thought as his tread whispered upward, a few days after the whelming of Ys, he had climbed this same track, in flight from emptiness. It ran him down and brought him to the ground. Or, rather, he had borne it with him while he fled it. Why was tonight otherwise? Why should he dare be happy?

The last of his people were striking new roots, but Rome could well rip them out again. The East might stand firm—he couldn't tell from what confused and fragmentary accounts reached this far—but the walls of the West crumbled before the wild men. Christ was strong; Christ was strange. Nemeta dwelt alone and crippled. What loneliness was Dahut's?

Verania had given him a son.

He reached the top, near the iron smelter where wood had been cleared away, and looked across the land. Fields were hoar, forest crowns dappled, rivers atremble with moonlight. Stars glinted in violet-blue.

Gratillonius raised his hand. *This will be yours, Marcus,* he vowed. *Nobody shall take it from you, ever.*

Aloud into the huge silence: "For your sake also, I am going to make Niall dead. Christ be my witness."

XVII

1

"—*duly noted.*

"Your interest, if sincere, is commendable. However, the value of your report is questionable at best. Your alleged agent in Hivernia has provided nothing more than his own word about what rumors and boasts he heard. The fickleness of barbarian will is notorious. This story of a seaborne raid on the scale of an invasion is in all likelihood some petty chieftain's fantasy.

"Defense is adequate around the Liger estuary. Your recommendation that the Saxon laeti there be reinforced, implying as it does that Christian soldiers go under pagan command, approaches profanation. To strengthen the garrisons upstream, as you also propose, shows you are quite ignorant of the peril at the Germanic frontier, not to mention policy considerations that require maximum troop strength in the South and East.

"Your scheme of raising native forces is totally unacceptable. Law forbids, and this office is not so foolish as to request an exception be made. We have received accounts of such activities on your part, and hereby warn you in the strongest terms that they must stop at once. Otherwise the consequences will be grave for everyone concerned in any violations. Most certainly, the appearance of armed and organized civilians in the Liger Valley will constitute insurrection. Claims of emergency will not excuse it, and punishment will be condign.

"Your obedience to the Imperial decree and your cooperation in suppressing rash attempts at action are required. Copies of this letter are being sent to—"

Gratillonius tossed it down. He had been reading it

aloud. "Never mind," he said dully. "There's more, but I'm about to gag."

"What can Apuleius do?" asked Rufinus.

"Nothing. Understand, this is directly from the Duke of the Armorican Tract."

"The man in command of all our defenses. So Glabrio's finally gotten to him. And he in his turn to whoever's in charge among the Namnetes and Turones." Rufinus tugged his beard. "M-m, it's not quite that simple, I suppose." A grin flickered over the vulpine face. "Rome has reasons to keep weapons from its citizens."

"In God's name!" groaned Gratillonius. "What do they imagine we're plotting? We only want to help."

Winter's rain brawled on the roof and sluiced down window glass. For all its newness and bright paint, the atrium of his house was full of the day's gloom and chill. One could barely see a wall panel that Verania was decorating in her scant spare time. It would show sprays of tall flowers. At first she had intended a picture of Ys, but he replied that the city should rest in its grave, after which she sought to kiss away the pain she heard.

"Well, they distrust us, and we'll have to lie low," Rufinus said. "Maybe after the Scoti have struck—because they will, as surely as fire will burn you—then the lords of state will listen."

"I wonder about that. And anyway—the whole valley sacked? Dead men in windrows, cities torched, Gallia slashed open right through its heart. How long can *we* survive that?"

"I know, master. Your hands are tied." Rufinus straightened. "But mine aren't."

Gratillonius stared at the lean, leather-clad form. "What do you mean?"

"Give me a ship and crew in early spring. Niall won't leave till after Beltene. I'll have time to brew up something."

Gratillonius's heart slugged. "By yourself? Are you out of your head?"

"No more than usual," laughed Rufinus. Soberly: "I can't promise a thing, of course, except that I'll try. I've been half expecting something like this letter, and thinking, but it's vague in my mind. Has to be, what with every

323

single piece in the game a shadow—a shadow thrown by a guttering lamp. . . . No, I shouldn't say more, even to you. Please don't ask me. Just let me try."

Gratillonius reached an unsteady hand toward him. "By Hercules, old friend, you are a man."

Rufinis barely clasped the arm. He turned on his heel. "I have to go now," he said to the one at his back.

"No, wait, stay for dinner, at least."

"Sorry, but I have—things to do—out in the woods. I'll likely be gone several days. Have it well, master." Rufinus strode from the room.

2

Eochaid maqq Éndae held an islet in a narrow bay of the Alban Dál Riata coast. Skies were low when the galley from Armorica arrived; underneath their gray, mists held the tops of the mainland mountains. A cold breeze ruffled the water. Its murkiness made rock, sand, and gnarly dwarf trees on the holm doubly drear. Smoke blew ragged from hearthfires inside a rath. A shed ashore, near a wooden dock, must hold a small ship, and several currachs lay above high-tide mark.

Warriors had hastened out of the stronghold and formed a line before it. Rufinus's rowers brought his vessel to the pier without showing any weapons, and he himself sprang forth, his hands lifted empty. He had donned fine clothes, red cloak above saffron-dyed wool tunic, breeches of blue linen, kid boots. An ornate baldric held his longsword, a belt studded with amber and garnets his knife and pouch. "Peace!" he cried in the tongue of Ériu. "A friend of your chieftain seeks him."

Eochaid stepped from the rank, his own blade lowered. He was coarsely clad. Winter indoors had paled him, so that the three blotchy scars marring his face stood forth in full ugliness. "Who is this?" he asked; and then, looking closer: "Is it you, truly you?" He dropped his sword and ran to embrace the newcomer. "A thousand welcomes, my heart, a thousand thousand!"

Rufinus returned the gesture. Eochaid released him and called to his men, "Here is himself who got me free of Niall's bonds—six years ago, has it been? Were it six hundred, I'd remember him. All that I have is yours, Rufinus."

"I thank you," said the Gaul, "my crew thanks you, my King afar thanks you."

"Come, disembark, come inside. What God has brought you to me, darling?"

"Whichever deals in vengeance," Rufinus answered low. "We've much to talk about alone, you and I."

—Within the earthen wall were houses, byres, cribs, pens, everything meager and crowded together. It was no great estate that King Aryagalatis had bestowed on the fugitive prince. He and his followers might have done better inland; but that, he explained, would mean endless trouble with the displaced Cruthini, and keep him from the sea. "Here we fish, trade, sometimes make a raid southward, otherwise keep our bit of livestock, and always bide our chance," he said. "The day will come for us. It must."

His dwelling was the largest, of the same turf and dry-laid raw stone as the rest but fitted inside with things of gold, silver, and glass. Like most of his men, he had acquired a staff of workers, male and female, generally slaves though a couple of them hirelings from poor families of the nearest tuath. The showpiece was a woman captured from the Brigantes; she knew Latin and was still comely in spite of the hard life and bearing him two children thus far, neither of whom lived long. He offered Rufinus the use of her, or any other of his household.

The guest declined gracefully. "This voyage of mine, seeking you out, my dear, is so important that I took a gess as part of the price for its good outcome. While the feast is being made ready and my men settling in amongst yours, could we go off by ourselves?"

"We can that, if it be your wish." Eagerness quivered in Eochaid's voice. "The boatshed is at least shelter from the wind, and I'll have a cask of mead brought us. I've slept in there twice, when I sought presaging dreams; and they

325

came to me, though double-tongued as sendings from the Gods so often are."

Within were dank dimness and a smell of tar from the galley filling most of the space. The two men sat down with cloaks between them and the ground. They broached the cask and drank from Roman goblets.

"I have heard tales of you," said Rufinus: "how, after you got away from Niall, misfortune still dogged you—"

"It has that," Eochaid declared grimly.

"—but you won through to this."

"Little enough for a son of King Éndae."

"Great enough for me to hear about, and ask my way till I found it."

"Even here, Niall reaches." Eochaid tossed off his cupful and dipped another.

Rufinus nodded. "I know. He readies for a mighty faring south, and calls on every king who is under him or allied to him. But how does he command Aryagalatis?"

"Through the motherland, Dál Riata in Ériu. A son of his has wrung tribute, obedience, from that far corner of Qóiqet nUlat. Agreement was better than invasion."

"M-m-m . . . I've heard tell that Aryagalatis is by no means unwilling."

Eochaid bared teeth. "He is not. The loot and glory bedazzle him as they do everybody."

"Other than yourself."

"What do you think I am?" Eochaid flared. "Never would I follow Niall maqq Echach! May pigs devour my corpse if ever I do!" He drank again and calmed a little. "Aryagalatis understands. I am free to stay behind."

"You chafe, though."

Eochaid sighed. "This is a cheerless place."

"I've come to tell you," said Rufinus weightily, "that you can indeed follow Niall to his war."

The marks stood lurid on Eochaid's skin. "You are my guest, but have a care."

Rufinus smiled. "Sure and you don't think I'd be insulting of you, my heart, do you?" he purred. "A hunter follows an elk that he may bring it down."

Eochaid's hand jerked. Mead slopped from his goblet. "What's this?"

"Listen, please. It's what I've sought you out for, and a weary voyage that was." Rufinus waited until the Scotian was thrummingly still, then said:

"If you tell King Aryagalatis you would like to come along after all, as it might be out of loyalty to him your befriender—as well as for a share in the gains—it's glad he'll be, I'll wager. You and your men are proven warriors. At the same time, he should heed your wish that he say nothing about it to Niall. That could only bring trouble."

"How shall Niall stay unaware?"

"Why, if Aryagalatis makes no mention of it—and Aryagalatis will see very little of him—then talk between crews will scarcely come to the ears of the great King. He'll have so much else to think about and do. I daresay he's well-nigh forgotten you. True, you plundered about in his country once, and later killed the son of his chief poet, but both were avenged in dreadful ways, and—saving your honor—you will be just one small skipper in a fleet from much of Ériu."

Eochaid gripped his dagger. Knuckles stood white above the hilt. "I am no more than that," he said hoarsely, "I, a son of the Laginach King, because of Niall maqq Echach."

"Then make his sons grieve for it."

"How?"

"We shall see. I will travel with you." Rufinus paused and drank before he locked eyes with his host and said: "This is needful. It's why I've sought you out. Going by my own ship, I'd be a marked man. Everybody would ask who I was and where I hailed from. In your crew I'll be hidden. As far as they know, I'm simply your outland friend who's joined you for the adventure. There must be many such in so big a band. Word of me will be lost in the racket of weapons."

Eochaid gave him stare for stare. "Why do you do this?" he asked, deep in his throat.

"I am a man of King Grallon's," Rufinus answered, "and he too has much to avenge on Niall. Oh, endlessly much."

"The King of Ys." Awe shook the words. "What is your plan, man of his?"

"I told you, none. We must wait for our chance. In the

327

welter of such an expedition, it's bound to come, the more so when there are two of us to watch for it and seize it."

Eochaid looked away, into darkness. "This is no real home for me," rustled from him, like dead leaves blowing. "If I must become a roofless wanderer again, or die, after striking Niall down, why, it's joyous I'd go to my doom." He shook himself. "But the hope is so far-fetched. We could die for naught, we two."

Rufinus reached in his pouch. "At the feast this evening we'll exchange such gifts as befits our honor," he said; "but here is one I've brought to give you in secret, and the most precious of the lot."

He undid protective wrappings and held out his hand. Eochaid took the thing he offered and brought it close, the better to see in the cold dimness. It was the skull of a falcon, held together by sinew cords. Graven in the bone was an arrow.

"This winter past, I went to a witch who dwells in the forest," Rufinus told him. "I asked her help. She cast what spells she was able, and made this, though she has the use of but one arm. She said it ought to bring you luck."

Uneasily, Eochaid turned the charm over and over. "What did you give her?"

"Nothing," Rufinus answered, forgetting his tale of the gess. "She thanked me. She also has Ys to avenge and . . . and Grallon to love."

3

That year Beltene in Mide was the greatest and most magnificent ever heard of since the Children of Danu held Ériu. To Temir swarmed men who would fare south with Niall after the rites and the three days of celebration that were to follow. Their tents and booths overran the land round about, a sudden bloom of colors and banners and blinking metal. Their tuathal kings and the wives of these packed the houses on the sacred hill.

Guests were all the more crowded because they must yield place to the mightiest yet seen here, other than Niall himself—Conual Corcc, up from Mumu to keep the feast with his foster-kinsman. Beautiful and terrible were the warriors who accompanied their lord. Chariots rumbled, riders galloped and reared their horses, spears rippled to the march like grain ripe beneath the wind, shields flashed, horns roared when that company appeared; and most wonderful was that it came in peace.

Disquieting to thoughtful folk was that it would depart in peace likewise. King Conual had no wish to sail against the Romans. Rather, he had come in hopes of stopping the venture, the tale of which rang from shore to shore of Ériu.

In this he failed. "I feared my words would be useless," he admitted at the end. "But for the sake of the old bonds between us, I must in honor speak them."

"I thank you for your care of me," said Niall; "but better would be if you laid your strength to mine."

They were side by side in the Feasting Hall on the last night before men went home or went to war. The meat was eaten, the tables cleared away, now servers flitted about refilling cups. A savor lingered in the smoke which firepit and lamps tinged pale red. Elsewhere throughout that cavernous space it gleamed off hanging shields and the gold, silver, bronze, amber, gems upon the men benched around the walls. Talk and laughter boomed between. There was an edge to its roughness, for omens had been unclear and word of that had gotten about. Everyone worked hard to keep good cheer alive. Close by the two great Kings they sat quiet, listening.

"I have my own land to think of," said Conual. "We prosper by trade with the Romans."

"As you did with the Ysans—" Niall stopped short. "I would never be calling you afraid, darling."

Conual lifted his head. The locks were still flame-hued. "I try to be wise," he said. "Why should I offend the Romans and their God? He has ever more followers in Mumu."

"And this makes you hang behind?" Niall's sneer was meaningless, as he himself well knew. They had been over and over the grounds for Conual's counsel against the expedition—recklessness, the gains not worth the risk—

and Niall's for going ahead—glory, wealth, binding closer to him his allies here at home, the fact that he had uttered his intention and could not now back down.

"It does not," said Conual evenly, "as you know. However, I think the morrow is His. I will go to the Gods of my fathers, but it may well be that after me the Rock of Cassel upbears His Cross."

Niall cast a glance at the druid Étain, the sole woman present. Her face remained shut and she said nothing. Thus had it been since she cast ogamm wands and kept silence about what she read.

In sudden cold fury, Niall spat, "He'll have a harder time in Mide!" He turned and beckoned to Laégare, youngest of his living sons, heir to this Kingship; so the tanist Nath Í had sworn beside the Phallus. At six years of age, the boy was reckoned ready to join men at their board. He had sat quietly, for he was of such a nature, though fierce enough in sports and battle practice to gladden his father.

"Come here, my son," Niall bade.

Laégare obeyed. Straight he stood, his hair a brightness amidst leaping shadows. Niall leaned forward and laid hands on his shoulders. "Tomorrow I go from you," Niall said. A hush spread like ripples from a stone thrown into a pool, as others heard.

"If only I could too!" Laégare cried.

Niall smiled. "You're a wee bit young for that, my dear." He grew somber. "But I will take an oath of you, here and now."

Laégare's voice barely trembled. "Whatever it is, father, I swear."

"This: that never in your life you make sacrifice or give pledge to the God of the Romans."

"That is heavy gess to lay on a King," said Conual, troubled. "Who knows what will come to him and his people?"

"At least he shall keep the pride of old Ériu," Niall told them all. "Do you take this last command of mine, my son?"

"I do that," Laégare replied. His voice was still childish, but it rang.

As Niall rode toward the sea, a hare darted across his path and a fox in pursuit of it. At once he called to him those men nearby who had seen and ordered silence about this. "Many would lose heart if they heard of such a sign," he reminded them. His head lifted against heaven. "I go where the Mórrigu wants me."

His old henchman Uail maqq Carbri said nothing to that, but bleakness took hold of the gaunt face.

A generation ago, the mouth of Boand's River had seen as great a fleet as was gathered there now. Currachs drawn up ashore or bobbing in the water seemed beyond counting, as did the warriors who milled around them. At anchor in the shallows lay over a dozen Saxon-built galleys. Once more Niall's bore a Roman skull nailed to the stempost; but this hull was painted red, for blood and fire.

The day was cloudless. Light flared on weapons aloft as men shouted greeting to the King. Color on shirts, kilts, cloaks, shields made a whirlpool rainbow. Gulls soared a hundredfold, a snowstorm of wings. Niall sprang from his chariot and strode toward his ship.

Uail squinted upward, shook his head, and muttered to Cathual, the royal charioteer, "The last time, you remember, a huge raven came down and perched on his shield. What have we today?"

"I fear I shall never be driving him again," said Cathual. Hastily: "Because I am not the lightfoot youth I was. It was kind of him to let me hold the reins on this final trip of his." He winced. Somehow he seemed unable to speak his meaning; the words came out unlucky.

He was not alone in his forebodings. Things had been happening for months which betokened trouble. They could be as slight as a cuckoo heard on the left or as terrifying as groans from the graves at Tallten on Beltene Eve. Old wives wove amulets for their sons to carry. Druids made divinations and shook their heads.

Yet somehow there was no portent of utter disaster, of

anything like the ruin suffered at Ys. The feeling in the air was more akin to a sorrow, though none could name that from which it welled. Niall, conqueror of the North, showed no trace of sharing it. Warriors must therefore deny it in themselves and follow him with good cheer. They dared not open their hearts to each other about it. Thus nobody knew how widely and deeply the cold current ran. The clamor at his back was as of wolves and wildcats.

He waded out to his ship, laid hand on the rail, and boarded in a single leap. Tall he stood at the prow. The light touched his hair with a ghost of the former gold. To Manandan son of Lir he offered a red cock, slashing its head off with his sword and laving the skull with its blood. "And white oxen shall You have when I bring home my victories!" he cried.

Men went to their craft. Oars rattled into place. They bit the ebb tide, and the fleet walked out over the sea.

Never did Niall look back at his country.

He passed it on that first day and made camp for the night south of the Ruirthech outflow, in Qóiqet Lagini. No fighters came to trouble them, nor did they find cattle or sheep to take. The coast stretched desolate. Not yet had the Lagini recovered from the woe that Laidchenn's satire brought on them. When they did, Niall knew, vengefulness must kindle the marches. Well, he would deal with that then; Nath Í would after him; Laégare would when his day came; such was the fate of a King.

At dawn the camp roused and the voyage went on. Weather stayed fine in the next days while the vessels worked their way down the side of Ériu. Their last evening on it, Niall called the tuathal leaders together at his fire. They were many, as diverse as their homelands, some fair as he, some dark, some redhaired, some gray, clad in linen or wool or skins, a few with hair drawn into horsetails like Gauls or with tattoos like Cruthini—subjects, allies, all the way from Condacht's western cliffs to Dál Riata's colony beyond the Roman Wall.

"You see how the Gods are with us," he said; "but they only want us to run mad in battle. First we must get there, the which will take both cunning and patience." While they knew more or less what he intended, he now laid it out at length and answered questions with unexpected mildness.

They would not cross over to the Dumnonic tip of Britannia. The Romans must have gotten at least a breath of what he had afoot. They would look for such a layover. Weakened though their forces were, they, with help from the fierce hillmen north of the Sabrina, might have readied an ambush. "We could doubtless fight them off and get away, but we'd take losses without any gain of booty," Niall said. "Don't belittle them." His mind harked back to a combat near Deva, three years ago, and the strangely impressive centurion with whom he spoke. "Rome is an aged beast, but she still has fangs. We'll get enough of her at the Liger."

He would go on without further stops. That was a long way across open sea; and he would make it longer still by steering very wide of the headlands where Ys had been and the hungry skerries were yet. The Scoti must keep together. Let fog or storm scatter them, and they were foredone. "It is for us to dare," Niall finished, "and undying will be the honor we win."

He overbore objections. They were scant. Everybody knew that their lives were his, and his alone. It seemed to them that he had taken power over wind and wave as well as war; or so they must needs believe.

Therefore, at sunrise they departed due south. This day was also bright. A favoring wind raised whitecaps on the glittery sea, and sails blossomed. Unutterably green astern lay Ériu. To watch it fall from sight was like waking from a dream of someone beloved.

Niall did not. Always he looked ahead.

Sunset smoldered on the rim of vast loneliness and went out. The night was moonless. He had planned things thus. The Romans would reckon on a force like his waiting till it had light after dark, for skippers to keep track of each other. To catch the enemy unawares, he had his galleys spaced well apart, lanterns burning at their rails. By these beacons the currachs would steer.

The wind continued friendly. It filled the sail and yet did not much chill the flesh; it lulled through the undertone of the seas, the seething at the prow, the slight creak of timbers and tackle as the ship rolled onward. Gentle as it was, it did not make the stars gutter. They glinted uncountable around the frosty River of Heaven, almost drowning out the pictures they made, Lúg's Chariot, the Salmon, the Sickle—but high astern stood the Lampflame by which men know the north; and as it sank night by night, it would tell him when to turn east for his goal. Yellow gleams swayed in strings out on Ocean's unbounded night, the riding lights of the galleys.

Niall stood by himself in the bows of his ship. Save for the steersman and two on watch at the waist, sleep filled her hull. With his back to the lanterns he had some vision of mysterious shimmers and foam-swirls under the stars. The skull nodded gray above him.

I am bound for that which I was robbed of, these many years agone, he thought.

It was a quiet thought. He felt beyond hope or anger; his mind was like the wind, steadily bearing south. I am going at last to my luck.

A surge passed through the water. A white and rounded slenderness lifted half out of the bow wave. It swam alongside, or it flew or it was borne, softly and easily as the wind. He saw how the heavy hair streamed behind. She turned toward him, raising her right arm—to greet, to beckon?—and he saw starlight wash over the wet breasts. Her face was ice-pale, her eyes two nights with each its own tiny star.

"Manandan abide!" he choked. Somehow the men on watch did not hear. Was the cold that flowed over him from her or from within himself?

She smiled. Her teeth were the hue of bleached bone. In a way unknown to him he heard: I have said that never will my love let go of you, nor will it ever, Niall, my Niall.

Dahut—But we are so far from Ys where you died.

Across the width of the world can I hear your name, Niall, my lover. It has flown on the wind and the wings of the gulls. Tide had carried it along, and the secret rivers of Ocean, and the whispering of dead men in the deeps. The Gods Whose vengeance I am have told me. Your name was a song and a longing. I followed it, blind with my need; and now again I behold you.

His desire terrified him. —Why can you not rest peaceful?

That which we did in Ys, the work of the wrathful Gods, binds us together and always will. My doom is to love you.

That dooms me too.

Fear not. For you I am the blessing of the sea. I give you fair winds, sweet skies, starlight and moonlight and radiant days. I guide you past rocks and shoals, I bid the storm swing wide of you, I bring you to safe harbor. I wreck the ships of your foemen, I drag them down below, I cast what the eels have left of them ashore for their widows to find. I am your Dahut.

But you cannot free me from the dread of what you are, nor from the sorrow of it, that this is because of me.

Aye, you betrayed me then, and left me alone. You shall betray me again, and leave me alone.

Not willingly, haunter of mine.

Nay. But by dying, as all men must. Unless your death be at sea—

Niall shuddered.

She reached toward him. Her fingers brushed his, which clutched the rail. Cold stabbed through. She lowered herself back into the starlit water and told him sadly:

I cannot bring that about. I can only wish for it, while I strive to make your years on earth as long as may be and your death as happy as may be, old and honored among your own kindred; for I love you. Let me fare by your side, Niall. Your men shall not know. They shall merely wonder at how easy a voyage is theirs. By day I will look at you from the covert of the foam. By night—all I ask is that you stand like this a little while before you seek your rest, that I may feel your gaze upon me and smile at you. You will hear my songs in your dreams.

The fear left him. There grew in its stead a gentleness toward her yearning, and a sense of the strength that coursed in his blood, and a sly hankering for King Grallon to learn of everything. "I give you that, Dahut," he said.

5

Mightily swept the Liger to the sea. Where Corbilo
guarded it on the right bank, its mouth gaped more than a
league from shore to marshy shore. Sandbars in late summer, swollenness in late winter made navigation tricky;
and at every season the Saxon laeti of that neighborhood
were ready to fight for their new homes.

Sight of the Scotic fleet sent the few ships they had on
patrol rowing back at full speed. More would be marshalled at Corbilo, and warriors flocking in from the countryside. The city was a husk of its ancient self, inside walls
hastily and clumsily raised, but the only sure way to go
past it was to take it first, and that meant a hard battle.

Beyond it, though, were nothing but Gallic reservists
and legionary garrisons too depleted to put any stiffness in
them. The valley lay open for ravishing.

Niall's achievements stemmed from his ever having been
more than the ablest and boldest among fighters; as much
as the wildness of his followers allowed, he gathered knowledge and laid careful plans beforehand. According to orders, galleys and currachs made landing just north of the
estuary, in a sheltered bay which spies had come to know
very well during the year that was past. There he would
establish himself unassailably before taking the bulk of his
forces on foot against the city.

A Roman road led to it through lands that had otherwise
largely gone back to forest in the past century or two. A
couple of fisher hamlets and a nearby farmstead stood
empty, their dwellers fled. Aside from some livestock they
had nothing worth reaving and were soon burnt. The
smoke of them blotted the sunlight streaming from the
west.

Vessels necessarily put in over a lengthy stretch of that
shoreline. In case of an alarm, skeleton crews were to take
them off the beach while most men ran to the King's
encampment and formed a war-host. Eochaid's small galley had kept near the tail of the fleet throughout the

journey. He brought her to rest farthest north of any, along with her accompanying boats. "Make things ready here," he ordered Subne. "Rufinus and I will go scouting a while."

His henchman peered into the marred face. He saw how tightly it was drawn and how the lips quivered within the beard. "You have been strange on this faring, my heart," said Subne; "and the strangest is that you came at all. Is it wise what you are thinking, whatever that may be?"

"It is what I have thought for these long years," Eochaid answered.

Subne sighed. "Come what may, I will keep faith with you." He glanced around. The crew were abustle unloading, seeking firewood, shouting to other gangs on the strand. "I cannot speak for every man here. Some could remember too well that they have women and little ones in Dál Riata."

"You borrow trouble, my friend," said Rufinus smoothly. "We're just off for a look around, this lovely evening."

Naturally they went armed. He wore his woodsman's leather, with knife and short sword, sling tucked into belt, spear in hand. Among the stones in his pouch he had, unobserved, put some coins. Eochaid's litheness was in kilt of somber green, a sheathed dagger tucked into it. On his back were a longsword and quiver. He carried a hunting bow.

They left the tumult and went in among the trees. "Likely we *are* only scouting," said Rufinus. "Don't get rash, my dear."

"Nor dither and dawdle," Eochaid grated. "Now, while all is in turmoil—" He snapped his jaws shut.

Brush rustled about legs, old leaves beneath feet. These woods were not yet high or thick. Between the boles was a sight of Ocean, still and burnished-bright. A faint sound of waves mingled with the silence here, a tang of salt with the warm odors. Leaves glowed golden overhead. Rays streamed through to cleave the shadows around.

Having gone a ways inland, the companions turned and went south. Presently Rufinus gestured and moved right. He had taken note of landmarks, a beech standing above

337

its neighbors, a coppice of dogwood likewise visible from the water. They gave him his bearings. Noise waxed as he neared the strand. He stopped, laid finger to mouth, squinted against a sunbeam, finally drew Eochaid aside into the cornel.

From its shade and densely growing stems they looked upon the King's ground. Drawn up where wavelets lapped shore was the red galley. The Roman skull grinned above a pack of currachs nestled on either flank. At hover on Ocean's rim, the sun cast their shadows long upon Gallia. Men scuttered and bawled, making ready for night. They had pitched a tent and started a cookfire, now they claimed places for themselves and sought the best spots to post guards. Spearheads and axes blinked athwart the shining reach of the bay. Banners fluttered brave in a light breeze. Shouts, laughter, lusty song flew with the seabirds on high.

Rufinus heard the breath hiss between Eochaid's teeth. His gaze followed the other's. A man had come into sight from the left, where he must have been talking with chieftains. Like the beech in the wood, he towered over the rest. His powerful frame was as roughly clad as any, but across his shoulders he had pinned a cloak of seven colors. The sunset light passed by it and made a golden torch of his head.

"Niall," Rufinus heard, both name and curse.

How beautiful he is! the Gaul thought.

Movement drew his heed away. At his side, Eochaid strung the bow.

Rufinus grabbed the Scotian's arm. "Wait, you," he warned.

Eochaid shook the grasp off. "I've waited too long already," he snarled. "May he choke on the blood he has shed."

Rufinus stood motionless. Any struggle would give them away.

Eochaid finished stringing the bow and reached for an arrow. "May the winds of winter toss his homeless soul for a thousand years." He nocked the shaft, raised up the bow, drew the string to his ear. Niall had stopped by the galley. He waved aside a man who wanted to speak to him and looked out across Ocean as if in search of something. "May he be reborn a stag that hounds bring down, a salmon on the hook of a woman, a child caught in a burning house where its father and mother lie slain." The bow twanged.

Niall flung his arms aloft, staggered, fell down on his face, feet in the sea, head beneath the skullpost. Red poured out into the water.

Rufinus seized Eochaid's arm again and yanked the man around. "Quick!" he said through the sudden uproar. "Go how I tell you! Else we're dead—" and, unless they were lucky, not soon dead.

You couldn't run through these thickets. At first Eochaid lurched ahead like a sleepwalker. Rufinus followed, giving orders that got awkward obedience, covering the trail as best he was able. It would have been much easier and safer to make off by himself. If necessary, he would. Gratillonius needed him, and this tool had served its purpose. Yet he'd rather not toss Eochaid aside and forget him.

Whatever pursuit there was came to naught. The Scoti could not tell just where the shot had come from; they were witless with grief and rage; Eochaid regained his share of the woodcraft of which Rufinus was a master. Dusk veiled them.

—Eochaid sank to the ground. It was chill and wet beneath him, the verge of marshland. Rufinus remained standing. Trees gloomed around them; they could barely see one another. Between the leaves above, blue deepened slowly toward black. A star or two shivered forth.

"Well, this will be a comfortless camp," said Rufinus, "but we should be in the way of getting a little rest before morning."

"What then?" asked Eochaid.

"Why, I'll be off home, reporting to my lord, and I counsel you do the same. Sure and it's a grand welcome your father ought to give the man who rid the world of that old bucko."

Eochaid shook his head, which hung heavy as a stone. "I cannot be forsaking my men. Nor is it to my honor that I sneak from my deeds like a thief."

Rufinus sighed. "I was afraid of this. You're a mortal danger to those men, once word gets about—and it will, whether or not you speak, because people know you were Niall's foe and out of sight when he fell. Of course, you are free to blame me. I'll not mind that."

"Never, and I wish you had not said it."

"Well, steal back there if you must, then flee before dawn with such of them as may still call themselves yours. Niall's sons will be scouring the seas and every land they can reach, in quest of revenge. I forbid myself the risk of being your guide, but if you can get to Confluentes I'll find a place for you among my foresters."

"Nor that, though I suppose I should be thankful to you," said Eochaid dully. "I won't be calling you a man without honor, but whatever you have of it is something unknowable to me. This that you've brought about—I thought my vengeance would be a flame of glory, but I shot him unseen and they will only remember me as his murderer. Go away, Rufinus. You freed me once, but now leave me alone."

The Gaul was silent a while before he murmured, "I freed you because it was wrong to keep a proud and splendid animal caged. Afterward I took you hunting with me. Well, things change, and this is the hour between dog and wolf. Goodbye." He slipped off into the twilight.

6

There was not enough dry wood in these parts for a balefire worthy of Niall of the Nine Hostages. Those of his sons who had come along ordered his ship dragged fully ashore and set alight. He lay before it on a heap of green boughs. They had taken the arrow from his breast, washed him, dressed him in his finest, combed his hair, closed his eyes, folded his hands over a drawn sword.

High roared the flames, white where they devoured, blue and red and yellow above, streaming away starward in sparks. The water seemed ablaze too. Night leaped in and out but never quite reached to the King. The steel in his clasp outshone the gold on his arms, at his throat, around his brows. Spears fenced him in flashing fire, held by the tuathal kings of Ériu who stood around garbed for a battle they could never fight. Beyond them, the length of the beach, darkness prowled between torches lifted throughout the host of warriors. Ocean whispered underneath their weeping.

Eógan maqq Néill, eldest of the sons who were there, trod forth. He carried the arrow. So close he came to the burning ship that it scorched his hair while he cast the shaft in and cursed him who had sent it.

He withdrew, and Uail maqq Carbri left the ranks and went to stand by the King. He was no poet—there would be many of them to make laments, the foremost Torna Éces himself—but this gray man had been handfast to Niall since they both were boys, and the sons gave him the right to speak for all.

"Ochón," he wailed, "Niall is gone! The stag whose antlers touched heaven, the salmon whose leap was silver in the cataract, the child whose laughter filled earth with music, has left hollowness in our hearts.

"Ochón, Niall is fallen! The hazel whose boughs were a snare for sunlight, the rowan whose berries were fiery as love, the yew whose wood was strong for bows and spearshafts, has left emptiness on our horizon.

"Ochón, Niall is dead! The warrior whose blade sang terror, the King whose judgments were just, the friend whose hand was open, has left ashes on our hearths.

"Niall, you were our strength. Niall, you were our hope. Niall, you were our soul. Farewell forever. Ochón for Mother Ériu, ochón for—"

He faltered, stared down and then around, stammered, "For-forgive me, I can't go on," and stumbled off with head in hands and shoulders shaking.

The host howled their sorrow to the fire and the stars. From the sea beyond the light rose a sound more shrill, as of a winter wind although the air lay moveless. Someone out yonder was keening too.

—In the morning, the chieftains held council, soon ended. None cared to go on. After what had happened, and upon remembrance of warnings over the months, it seemed clear that this faring was doomed. Craftsmen made a long box for the body of Niall and put it aboard Eogan's ship. The fleet set homeward.

Weather stayed gentle. Breezes from the south kept sails filled. Strangest, maybe, was how no stench rose from the coffin. Sometimes at night men glimpsed a whiteness alongside. It seemed to be showing them the way.

Their grief remained boundless. When they came back at last, they buried their King not where lesser ones rested, but in earth of his own. They called it Ochain, the Place of Mourning.

7

Rufinus could not sleep.

Hour by hour his bed had narrowed, like the soil of a grave settling inward. When he twisted about, the sheet tightened around him. Windowpanes were blank with moonlight. It hazed the blackness and dappled the floor. The air hung dead. He heard a faint sharp singing at the middle of its silence and knew this was from himself, a night-wasp he had hatched. Pieces of dream drifted by. They were gone before he saw their faces.

He should be at ease. The Lord, or the Gods, or Whoever, knew he'd drunk enough. Gratillonius had been in such a gusty mood. He often was, ever since Rufinus brought the news. "Not that everything's over with," he said, a little slurrily, when the candles were burning short. "The Scoti'll be back. You've bought us some years, though, some years, at least. We'll make ready. And now Ys can rest. Can't it? And Dahut, if that wasn't an evil spirit in her shape haunting the rocks, surely now Dahut too—I'll ask Corentinus. When he returns. He's off in Turonum, arguing with Bishop Bricius. Swears, if need be, he'll carry the matter as far as Rome. Our right here to grant asylum—Oh, I've told you before, haven't I? Well, here's to you, old buddy. Best investment I ever made, leaving you your life there in the Wood. Paid me a hun-

342

dred times over, you have. A thousand, if Dahut's free. Here's to you."

His beaker clashed against Rufinus's. How those gray eyes shone! The drinkers had gotten merry and bawled out a couple of songs and at last hugged each other goodnight.

Rufinus remembered the arms, beard rough against his cheek, wine-breath and also the sweat-smell, which had the cleanness of a man's who is much outdoors.

Moonlight inched across the floor.

"Oh, hell take this," ripped through him. He sat up and swung his legs out of bed in a single sweep. Tiles were hard and cool underfoot. He rose, stretched, shook nightmare off.

No reason to fumble with striking fire for a candle. He knew his way around this room as well as did the house cat, and it was her favorite in the house. He spoiled her rotten, as he doubtless would young Marcus. His hands knew how to fetch ranger's garb from the chest and slip it over his body. Weapons, bedroll, pack of provisions he always kept ready. He made them fast and opened the door.

The corridor beyond was a tunnel where he was blind. Fingertips brushed a wall which by day would look pretty; Verania was well along with decorating it. Rufinus missed the freedom and casual clutter of his own house, but he'd been too much gone, and too indolent in town, to see about replacing it; you couldn't put up another wattle-and-daub shack in phoenix Confluentes. Someday he'd take care of the matter. Meanwhile it was kind of Gratillonius and Verania to give him a room in their home.

And they didn't meddle. When they found him missing, they'd simply smile. "Off on another of his rambles, is he?"

He passed through the atrium and entry and out the unbarred front door. It gave directly on the street; luxuries like a portico were for years to come, if ever. The wall reared sheer at his back, white with moonlight. How the moon shone, and it still a day short of being full. He wished he could have bidden Gratillonius—and Verania—farewell, with thanks; but of course they were asleep.

His sandals padded over cobblestones. Confluentes might never boast Roman paving blocks. Well, only cities old and rich had ever had them, and this was certainly better than dirt lanes. Rufinus dodged around horse dung and offal heaps. Though Gratillonius fumed about it, there was likely no hope of enforcing such cleanliness as had been on the streets of Ys.

Nor would such towers again soar above the sea. Rufinus hastened on between shadowing houses.

The pomoerium opened before him. It was unpaved, hard-packed, its dustiness pale beneath the moon. He had followed Principal Way and ahead of him lifted the earthen wall, moss upon it full of dew, wooden towers squat above the south gate. It stood ajar; he saw the bridge and river beyond. The moon sailed high. To him the markings upon it had always looked like an old woman who grieved. But elsewhere stars glinted, and a breeze wandered through the gate bearing a scent of wild thyme.

Rufinus drank it. He would go hence into that land from which it blew.

He started across the open space. "Hold!" cried a sentry on the north tower. "Who's there?" The sound was lonesome in the night.

"Friend," gibed Rufinus. "Enemies come the other way, have you heard?"

"Ha, you," laughed the man aloft. "The moon-cat. Well, go with God, wherever you're bound."

I'd liefer not, thought Rufinus as he passed between the massive iron-bound timbers of the doors. Or He'd liefer not. Shall we agree on it, You and I?

Moonlight flowed with the river. Past the bridge, plowland stretched dim toward the sea. On the left, though, a ribbon of road followed the stream, toward the highway to Venetorum. Striding along it, gravel acrunch, he would soon find woodland; and soon after that, a trail which most travelers never noticed led into its depths.

He started across the bridge. The planks felt somehow soft. Perhaps that was because on his right was the new one, half-finished masonry, and behind it a sprawl of docks still under construction. The night blurred shapes. Water clucked and purled, sliding past stone.

344

In the forest lived one who loved him—too humbly, maybe, but Rufinus hoped to teach him pride. His hut lay within a sunrise's reach. Afterward they could sleep late, and then range the woods for days.

And I will raise your image before me, Grallon, thought Rufinus. He smiled with half his mouth. Poor old fellow, you'd be so shocked if you knew, wouldn't you?

She came from downstream up a pier onto the bridge. Small and cold on high, the moon made shimmer the water that ran off her nakedness.

Rufinus halted. He stood wholly alone with her. The shout of the guard, who saw, might have been in a dream or from the Otherworld.

She grinned. Her teeth were shark-white. Did you think I would let *you* go free? he heard.

She glided close. He drew his Roman sword and stabbed. It would not bite, it slid off and fell from his hand. She laid arms around him. They were freezingly cold.

"Oh, Dahut—" Rufinus had no strength to break loose. Locked together, he and she toppled into the river. He caught a taste of the incoming tide. Her lips and her tongue forced him open to her kiss.

XVIII

1

Clouds drifted low, heavy with rain. The breeze rustled leaves. They cast no shadows today, but dimness under their arches grew purple-black as vision ranged into the forest. No birds were calling. The Stegir mumbled lusterless.

Gratillonius halted at the oak and dismounted. Favonius nickered. He secured the stallion. Nemeta must have heard, for she came out of her dwelling. Her hair bore the only bright color in the landscape. She stopped before Gratillonius and regarded him silently. It was as if neither quite dared speak.

345

"How are you?" he asked at last in Ysan. They had not met for months. Summer freckles spread healthily over her arched nose, but she seemed thinner than ever. The sleeves of her plain gray shift were a trifle short; he saw that her right arm had shriveled nearly to the bone.

Her brusqueness told him that she remained herself: "I know why you've come."

It boded ill, though. "I thought you would," he replied. "But how?"

She chuckled without mirth. "Not by any spell. I do get news here." The frigidity broke open. She blinked against tears, shivered, abruptly cast herself against him. "Oh, father!"

He held her close, stroked her mane, let her burrow into his bosom. Her breath rattled. "You liked Rufinus too, did you not?" he murmured.

"Aye, he w-was kind and jolly—when I was a little girl—and—and he was good to you, when all the rest of us had turned on you—" She wrenched free. Her left hand swiped angrily at her eyes.

He could no longer hold his question inside him; yet it resisted coming forth. "Was it, then—The sentry isn't clear about what he saw. It seemed him 'twas a woman, moon-white, but—We know not. We've searched the shores and dragged the river, but haven't found the body."

Nemeta had mastered herself. "You never will," she said in a cold small voice. " 'Twas borne to the sea."

"You've gone into these matters. Can you tell what— what was that thing?"

"Dahut."

"A demon in her shape?"

"Herself. She drowned with Ys, but They would not let her stay dead."

He had awaited this, and prayed it not be, and now that it was he must fight it still. "Who are They?" he challenged.

"The Three. She is Their vengeance on the city."

"You can't be sure! How do you know?"

"By my dreams. By the wands I have cast. By things half seen in a pool and in the smoke of a sacrificial fire."

"You could be mistaken. You could be crazed, huddling alone for years."

346

Pain shook her tones. "Would you have sought me if you didn't believe I could tell you the truth? Father, I know those Gods. I am the last of Their worshippers."

His throat thickened and burned. "Gods like that—you serve, you whose mother They killed—why?"

She made a faint, one-sided shrug. They had been over this ground before. "There are none other for me. Epona and the rest are shrunk to sprites, phantoms; nor do I think they would heed me if I called, as far as I have gone from Their ways. Wotan and His war-band are aliens. I must have some few powers if I am to live as anything better than a slave. From Lir, Taranis, and Belisama I have them."

"Christ has more."

She stiffened. "He'd deny me my freedom."

Hatred sank within him. In its place came sorrow for her, and a weariness he could feel to his marrow. "I've heard this too often," he said. "For the dozenth time I beg, bethink you. Is Verania a slave? Come back with me. She'll be like a sister to you, and I—while I live, you'll be your own woman. And afterward too, if God lets me build what I'm trying to build. Come home, Nemeta, daughter of my Forsquilis whom I loved."

The sudden fear he saw on her slashed through him. Her eyes widened till white ringed the green. Her left hand made a fending gesture. "Nay," she whispered. "Dahut would find me."

"What, you?"

"I counselled and helped Rufinus on his mission to get Niall killed."

For my sake, he understood, and wanted to hold her again but seemed unable to stir.

" 'Tis become Niall that she chiefly exists to avenge. And she knows where they are who were his bane." Nemeta clutched at her breast. She turned her head to and fro, looking. The violence of the motion made her useless arm swing. "I don't think she can swim this far up the Stegir. No tidewater here. She's wholly of the sea now. I dare never go near the sea again. But she can follow the tide through the Odita to Confluentes."

She steadied. He groped in the dark after common

sense. "Rufinus was a pagan; nay, he held by no Gods whatsoever. You—Christ will protect you."

"If I accept Him." The red head shook. "That's not in my heart."

Somewhere at the back of his soul, he wondered about his own faith. Why had he sought Christ? Was it merely for power against evil—at best, because He stood between the world and chaos, like a centurion between Rome and the barbarians? Gratillonius knew Christ lived, but in the same way that he knew the Emperor did. He had never met either. He admired Christ; but did he love Him?

"He will accept you if you ask," Gratillonius said.

The brief pridefulness crumbled. Nemeta looked away, into the dusk of the forest. "Will He ever?" he barely heard. "Can He? Father, you know not the things I have done."

The grimness that that awakened was somehow strengthening. "I may know more than you think," Gratillonius told her. "His waters wash every sin from us." *And that is why I haven't yet dared be baptized.*

"Well, talk to your bishop—about Dahut," she said in forlorn defiance. "I've told you all I've learned."

"Nemeta," he pleaded, "you mustn't suffer this any more, loneliness, poverty, fear. Let those who love you help you."

Her courage lifted anew. "Oh, now, in truth 'tis not so bad. I have my house, my cats—" She even smiled. "You've not met them. They're inside. Three kittens. And I do have my freedom, and these deep woods—" The mood broke. "Father, 'tis you I sometimes weep for."

Wind moaned in the trees. The first raindrops fell down it.

2

Gratillonius was at work several miles from Confluentes when Salomon found him. A man must work, no matter how hollow he felt within.

A curial, responsible for the lives of many, required a suitable livelihood. You couldn't forever spend pirate gold;

besides, it was earmarked for public purposes. Since his marriage he had gone into partnership with Apuleius. Without talent for the management of land, the latter had never been able to make the fundus pay, and Confluentes had taken over that ground. Broad new acres being cleared and claimed, the senator financed operations which Gratillonius—farm boy, soldier, ruler—knew how to run. Sharecroppers were established and this year producing their first, excellent harvest. Meanwhile Gratillonius was properly organizing the horsebreeding Apuleius had begun. Favonius would be the prize stud, but he meant to get more, for the servicing of the finest brood mares he could find. There ought to be a boundless market. Rome needed cavalry.

On this day he was overseeing the fencing of a meadow, taking a hand himself. He didn't enjoy that as erstwhile, he no longer enjoyed anything, but at least it got the cramp out of his muscles. Salomon rode up at his usual breakneck pace, reined in his mount and made it curvet. "Hail!" he shouted.

Gratillonius squinted against the sun, which haloed those locks the hue of Verania's. At sixteen, Salomon was still smooth-cheeked but otherwise a young man, tall, his gangliness filled out and become both hard and supple. His tunic and breeks were striped in the gaudiest Gallic style. "What brings you?" Gratillonius grunted.

Salomon winced a bit. He had, though, resigned himself to his brother-in-law's recent curtness. "You wanted to know when Corentinus returned. Well, he has."

It gave an excuse for a gallop, Gratillonius thought. However, the announcement let him meet with the bishop today rather than tomorrow. That might or might not prove a kindness. "Thanks," Gratillonius remembered to say. He left instructions with his foreman and got onto Favonius.

Radiance poured from above. The clover sown this year bloomed white. Bees droned about, gathering its riches. A stand of wild carrot filled the warmth with pungency. Its filigree was like sea foam. . . . What was the weather at Ys? He imagined fog, the breakers crashing unseen on rocks and remnants. Evil creatures hated sunlight, didn't they? It hurt them.

At the grassy wall of Confluentes, Salomon bade him goodbye and went off, doubtless in search of company more cheerful. Gratillonius continued around. The church there was still abuilding. Corentinus hoped to dedicate it as his cathedral before winter. Enlargement and beautification might continue for generations. That had been an idea strange to Gratillonius; but the world was moving into a different age.

He found the bishop at home in Aquilo. Corentinus met him in the doorway. A minute passed, during which the street traffic seemed remote, while eyes beneath shaggy brows ransacked the visitor. Finally Corentinus said gently, "Welcome, my son. Come in where we can talk."

Gratillonius followed him to the room in which secrets were safe. Corentinus gestured at a stool. Gratillonius slumped onto it. Corentinus mixed water and wine in two cups.

"How did it go?" asked Gratillonius. His words were flat.

"Unseemly strife," Corentinus answered. "I had to get mightily stiff-necked. Not so much with Bricius. He only thought he had more authority than me. I set that straight in short order. But he clung like a limpet to Glabrio's arguments when we carried the matter before the governor."

"I don't understand."

"Really? I'd supposed you did. The question is what right of sanctuary the Church—any church—has. You probably weren't aware of it at the time, and Heaven knows you've had plenty else on your mind since, but seven years ago the Emperor actually abolished the right of sanctuary. That provoked such resistance that he restored it a year later."

Honorius! thought Gratillonius. Had that half-wit any constancy at all? Last year he'd closed the Colosseum, banned gladiatorial games: undeniably a good deed, but why had he let them go on until then, until he'd given himself a triumph in Rome for the victory Stilicho won?

It didn't matter.

"The law is unclear," Corentinus continued. "It can be read as limiting the right in many ways. What kind of fugitives can we take in? Must they be Christians?" He offered his guest a cup.

Gratillonius drank without noticing the taste. "I remember now," he mumbled. "Pardon me. My head is fuzzy these days. You want freedom to use your own judgment in every case, is that it?"

"Exactly." Corentinus stayed erect, looming above the man who sat hunched. "The governor doesn't like that any more than the Emperor ever did. It sets the Church above the state: as is fit and proper, of course." He tossed off a hefty draught. "Matters came to a head like this because it was me involved—meaning you. Confluentes is drawing new people from as far as Britannia. They don't knuckle under easily. Having the Church to appeal to encourages this. Well, I upheld my sovereignty, but I and those clergy who think the same have a long struggle before us. Clear to the Pope in Rome, I'm sure, and to the Emperor, whoever and wherever he is then."

Wherever indeed, Gratillonius thought. Honorius had his seat in Ravenna, from which escape by sea to Constantinople was easy. Stilicho had lately moved the praefectural capital of Gallia from Augusta Treverorum, south to Arelate, also near the sea. It was as if the frontiers were closing in. Or falling in?

"But you didn't come about that, Gratillonius," he heard.

"No." He stared into the cup between his knees. "Have you gotten the news yet?"

"Certainly. Poor Rufinus. A ghastly ending. I'll pray for him. He just may have had time to see the Light. Or, anyhow—Well, we can ask there be mercy for him, if possible. We owe him that much."

Gratillonius barely had strength to force out: "It was Dahut that killed him."

Corentinus reached down to grasp his shoulder. "You've feared something of the kind since your battle at Ys. I have too. But it could be . . . a demon, or sorcerer's work, or . . . *creature*."

Gratillonius shook his head. "I know now. It's Dahut."

Corentinus was silent for a space. "I won't ask you how you know," he said at length, heavily. "I'm afraid you're right. Satan is aprowl in Armorica."

351

"She—" Gratillonius couldn't go on.

"Is surely lost," Corentinus finished.

Gratillonius looked up at him. It was like looking up at an ancient oak behung with gray ivy. "Can't we, can't you do anything?"

"We are free to pray for a miracle," said the compassionate, implacable voice. "Otherwise—It's not simple demonic possession. Exorcism—I can only guess, but I think an exorcism would have to be done in her presence. And she can steer clear of the Cross, or flee it and jeer from afar."

Gratillonius jumped to his feet. The stool clattered one way, the winecup spilled its redness another. "But we can't forsake her!" he yelled.

Corentinus spread his big sailor's hands. "What would you have me do, if I could? An exorcism will cast her down into hell, eternal torment."

"Oh, no, no. Can't she be saved?"

Corentinus seemed, all at once, aged. "I don't see how. At least now she isn't burning. She's taken her revenge. She may in future be content to haunt Ys. Leave her alone with the sharks, and with God."

"That's . . . hard to do."

Corentinus embraced and held him, much as Gratillonius had embraced and held Nemeta. "I understand. But you've got to stop brooding over this. You're man enough to stare it down and get on with life; or else I've terribly misjudged you."

"I've tried," said Gratillonius into the coarse cloth.

"Try harder. You must. My son, my friend, you are not the first father in the world whose little girl turned wicked, nor will you be the last. It gives you no right to pull away from those who need you, who are worthy of your love.

"Let's pray together. In Christ is help."

And afterward: "In Christ is joy. And so there is in your darlings. Go home to them."

—At his house Verania met him, their son beside her.

352

On a day in autumn when the wind went loud and sharp over stubblefields and sent leaves whirling off trees in little scraps of color, folk at Drusus's farm were surprised to see a big man ride up. This was a busy season, as they readied for winter. "The master is in town, sir, the cattle market," said the steward. "He'll not be back for another day or two."

"I know," replied Evirion Baltisi. "I met him there, and he gave me some news that's brought me here."

He dismounted, went inside, paid his respects to the lady of the house. She made him welcome, but had such work on her own hands that she was soon glad to direct him to Tera, who had been the woman of his fellow skipper Maeloch; and it was Tera whom he had come to see.

He found her in the cottage she occupied with her children. Newly built, simple but snug, it stood at some distance from the other buildings, behind it a kitchen garden and pigpen. Fowl wandered about. She was indoors, pickling flesh; the very air in the single room tasted of vinegar. Her youngest offspring played in a corner, the rest were at tasks of their own on the farm itself. "Why, Cap'n, how wonderful!" she cried when he trod in. "What brings you this far from the water?"

"To learn how you fare," he answered.

"What, me? Quite well, thank'ee. And you?"

"I'm home again," he snapped. " 'Twas a long voyage." Mildening: "Yesterday I heard you'd sold Maeloch's house—your house in Confluentes, and moved back hither. Is aught wrong? He was my comrade. I'd fain do what I can for his widow."

She laughed. "Good of you to give me that name. Sit down." She waved at her two stools, set her things aside, wiped her hands, dipped wooden cups full of mead from a small cask, and joined him. Meanwhile she explained: "You're sweet, but fear not for me. 'Twas in town I grew

353

unhappy after Maeloch was gone, me now a nobody, unchristened, offered naught but the meanest of jobs. Here I am free again, with the woods and their landwights not too far off to walk to when there's a break in the work."

"You're not a hireling of Drusus's?"

"Nay, more like a tenant. The kids and I could not go live alone. That would be unsafe, when Ys is no more."

Evirion looked abruptly grim, then thrust his thought aside and made admiring noises about the boy, Maeloch's son, as the mother expected. "How was all this arranged?" he inquired after a time.

"Through King Grallon," said Tera. "I turned to him when the narrowness of streets and spite of neighbors got more than I could bear. Should have done it earlier. He made a deal for me. Drusus took the house, to sell or rent. In return, he built me this dwelling and gives me the use of this plot. Mostly we work for him, me and the kids, getting paid in kind and in protection." She sighed, not unhappily. "Also in open skies and leave to be myself. Oh, I've cause to make my small spells for the welfare of Grallon and Drusus, but don't you be telling them that. It can do no harm, can it? Mayhap a wee bit of help to them. And Grallon, at least, that overburdened man, needs all the help he can get."

"Know you how he is these days?" Evirion asked anxiously. "What I've heard since I came back has been scant and confused. He chancing to be away, I could not call and see for myself."

"He was gruesome downcast after his man Rufinus perished. The rumors about that are eldritch, nay? 'Tis no wonder he grew so forbidding at any talk about it, but thus he only drove the mutterings into corners."

Evirion nodded. " 'Twas a bad business, whatever it was. Aye, when we put to sea I was troubled about him."

"Ease your mind. Over the months, he's gained back heart. Not that I was watching over him, but word gets about—and I've overheard Drusus and his wife speaking of him, they care too—and I've had my whispers from the landwights. . . . Thanks be mostly, I think, to his Verania, he is himself again. There's a lass!"

"Good!" gusted from Evirion.

Tera cocked her head at him. "I recall you as being less than his friend."

"That was straight after the whelming. Later—above all, since the battle at Ys—well, we need him."

"And you've grown inchmeal fond of him to boot, I daresay." A teasing note: "Him and his pretty, unwedded daughter."

At once Tera saw she had gone too far, and went on in haste, "But how has your life been? A long journey, you said. Whither? What happened?"

Evirion's mood stayed darker than before. "Niall being fallen, I reckoned the sea lanes he'd plagued would be clear. And so they were, for a span. We did fine business in southern Hivernia, western Alba and Britannia. But then, as we were homebound, though 'twas uncommonly late in the sailing season, we met Saxons on the water—twice—good-sized packs of their galleys that set after us. For all the size and armament of *Brennilis*, naught saved us but speed. Had the winds been otherwise, I'd lie this day on the bottom. I think a great movement of wolves is again getting under way, and next year we'll hear them howling at our thresholds."

Tera gripped her cup hard. "Despite what befell this spring?"

"Oh, we'll not have Scoti and Saxons together," said Evirion. "Maeloch helped see to that."

Tera looked long into his eyes before she asked low, "Did he? Niall fell not at Ys, but this year. We've all heard tales of it, no two the same. So what did Maeloch really do? What did he die for?"

Evirion chose to misunderstand her. "He was pursuing the Scotic boats, as well you know. Surely Niall was in one of them. Maeloch well-nigh had him overhauled. But a flaw of wind and fog—The weather was very strange that twilight."

"Strange indeed." Her gaze went beyond him. "I've cast my spells, hearkened to my omens, trying and trying to know what went on there at the end. But naught will come to me. Alone, I am helpless against . . . whatever it was." She straightened. "Well," she said almost briskly, "what use in fretting? Each gladsome day we have lived is the one treasure that nobody can rob us of."

4

The Black Months need not be dark. Rather, they could fill with ease and pleasure. Summer's labor was over and winter's was mostly light. Small festivities twinkled before and after the great celebrations at solstice. Occasionally Gratillonius and Verania shocked their servants by staying in bed till the late sunrise.

A pair of candles burned soft, an Ysan practice she had learned from him. The chamber lacked a brazier, but it was not very cold outside and the house was solidly built. Her sweet sweat had anointed the air.

She sat up amidst rumpled blankets, reached for a cake of wheat and raisins on a table, broke a piece off and handed it to him. "Here," she said.

"Thanks," he replied, "but I'm not hungry yet."

"Eat this anyhow. Maintain your strength. You'll need it."

He nibbled from her fingers. "Already again?" he marveled. "And everybody says how demure you are."

She wrinkled her nose. "Ha! You don't know women as well as you think you do. I'm the envy of Armorica, I am."

She leaned over his pillow. Her hair fell in a tent around him. The candlelight glowed along her arm, illuminating the fine down. He reached, cupped a breast, felt milk start forth across its fullness. It was astonishing how one so slender could still nurse a child as lusty as Marcus. Maybe that was why she hadn't conceived anew, more than a year after the birth. They both hoped that was why. It wasn't for lack of trying, once he had put grief behind him.

Her free hand roved impudently. "Well, well," she laughed.

"Oh, give me a while longer."

She raised her brows. "If you're tired, you can keep lying there and—"

"No, no. How could I feel tired with somebody like

you, till the moment I collapse in a cloud of dust? It's only that we were in such a hurry at first." He laid hold of her at the delicate shoulderblades and drew her downward.

"And what would everybody say if they knew how the rough, tough Gratillonius likes to cuddle, and how well he does it, too? Fortunately, I like it myself."

"And do it superbly."

She laid her mouth to his. "R-r-r," she purred.

It racketed at the door. "What the devil?" he growled. The knocking was frantic. None of the staff would interrupt without urgency. "Coming!" he called. His feeling was mainly anger at the wretched mischance, whatever it might be.

Verania drew blankets to chin. Gratillonius didn't trouble to throw anything over himself. That was a man yonder, as hard as he'd struck. Gratillonius opened the door.

Salomon stood there. He wore merely a tunic, hadn't stopped to bind on sandals, must have kicked off indoor slippers and set forth at his full long-legged speed. He still panted. It was in deep, shuddering sobs. Tears coursed from his eyes.

"Father is dead," he reported.

—The sky arched clear, magnificent with stars. The lantern Salomon now carried—he hadn't thought to bring one, and his feet were bruised where he had stubbed them—brought hoarfrost into sight. Here and there a window shone or a man walked, but after the three left Confluentes they were wholly alone. The sound of their stumbling stride rang loud above the river's susurrus.

"We'd finished breakfast," Salomon said. His voice had gone empty. Breath puffed spectral. "A courier had arrived yesterday before dark, but father was keeping a vigil at the church. Mother and I were asleep when he got back, and nobody else thought to tell him. He sent at once when he heard this morning." Of course, Gratillonius realized. Apuleius was an early riser and immediately with his duties. "The man wasn't at the hostel, he'd chosen to stay with somebody he knows here and it took a while to find him. Father was fuming a little. You know how he is—was when he got angry, soft-spoken as ever but the words came out clipped. It didn't seem worth a fuss to me.

357

He'd been feeling poorly the last couple of days, though; didn't say much, but when he mentioned pains you always knew they were real. Well, the courier finally brought him a letter from the governor in Turonum. Father opened it and stood there reading. I saw him frown, purse his lips—then, oh, God, he buckled at the knees and fell. Just like that. He hit his head, not too hard, it barely bled, but he lay there gasping—quick wheezes, and in between them he didn't breathe at all—and his eyes, his eyes were rolled back, blank. I saw the pulse in his throat. It was going like a hailstorm. We gathered around, tried to help, wanted to get him to bed. Mother sent a boy off after the physician, and then suddenly he didn't breathe and his pulse didn't beat and he was dead."

"What was in that letter?" asked Gratillonius, the single thing he could think of to ask.

"Who cares?" Salomon cried. "Father's dead!"

Verania clutched her man's hand very tightly.

—Lamps and candles burned everywhere in the house in Aquilo. Rovinda had gotten Apuleius lifted to a couch and a blanket laid over the foulness of death. She had herself closed his eyes and cleansed the froth from his mouth. As Verania came in with Gratillonius and Salomon, Rovinda quickly drew the blanket across his face.

"Mother, can't I see him?" Verania sounded like a bewildered child.

"Wait a while, dear," the woman answered.

Wait till the grimace has smoothed out and he's expressionless, Gratillonius thought; but not till the corpse-bruises begin to show.

Verania went to Rovinda's arms. Salomon stood numbly aside. Slaves gaped in the background. The physician plucked Gratillonius's sleeve. They withdrew to a corner.

"God must love him," said the physician low, "as well He might. I doubt that he felt or knew of his dying."

"It's cruel for his family," Gratillonius replied in the same undertone. "No warning. Struck down, senselessly; the end of their world, like *that*."

"God's will—"

Gratillonius's hand chopped air. Then he remembered he must not brush the saying aside. Who was he to accuse

358

the Lord? Apuleius was wanted in Heaven. His kin and friends should be happy. Why was that never possible?

"I'll take over," Gratillonius said. "Thanks for your concern. Rovinda's brave, she'll bear up."

She and Verania were murmuring between themselves. The mother beckoned Salomon over. Gratillonius felt hurt. Verania cast him a glance and it was healed. Naturally they needed a little time to themselves.

His gaze drifted about. It caught a pair of wax tablets bound together, which somebody had picked up and put on a table. The dispatch. Gratillonius stepped over to read it. He saw terror on Verania as she observed, and cast her a reassuring smile. Ill-omened though the thing was, it could not be what had slain Apuleius.

The message stood clear in shadows and highlights. It was a communication such as the governor's office sent in multiple copies to local officials when important news had been received.

A fresh horde of Germani was on the move. They were chiefly Ostrogoths out of those lands at the Danastris into which the Huns were pressing. At their head was the infamous warlord Radagaisus. They had crossed the Danuvius. Terrified swarms fled before them as they advanced on Italy.

5

In perfectly chaste wise, Procurator Bacca and the lady Runa had become well acquainted. He enjoyed her conversation and she his: much superior to any else in this provincial city. She was often a guest at his home, and he sometimes visited her to look at her work, calligraphic copying varied by desultory efforts to compile the annals of the Turones.

After all, she was a lay sister among the nuns; furthermore, under Bishop Bricius the rules were considerably relaxed for both male and female religious communities. Runa lived comfortably enough for a person of her tastes, which had never run to sensuousness.

359

"I asked you over this evening because I need your advice," Bacca said after they had dined and gone to his scriptorium. They left the door open for propriety's sake, but everybody knew better than to pass near. The room within was more plain than might have been awaited. Its only special contents were several handsome books, writings of Aristophanes, Ovidius, Catullus. Rain brawled through the murk outside.

"Oh?" murmured Runa. Seated on a cushioned bench, she smoothed her skirts. The gown was simple and modestly cut, as became a woman of her dedicated standing, but its rich dark material set off her white skin and complemented the high-piled raven hair. "I am honored. What is this about?"

Bacca lowered his lankness to a stool facing her. "About the counsel I'll give Governor Glabrio and, I trust, make him heed."

Runa kept an expectant look on him.

"Have you heard?" he said. "Apuleius Vero, the tribune at Aquilo, has died."

"Really? Well, he was getting on in years, wasn't he?" She inquired no further, though she added, "God have mercy on his soul."

"The question is, who should his successor be?"

She flushed faintly. Her nostrils dilated. "A strong man, in that nest of troublemakers."

"Precisely. What would you say to Gaius Valerius Gratillonius?"

"You joke!" she exclaimed, astounded.

"For once, I do nothing of the sort," he replied gravely. "See here. In view of the situation there, the mingled peoples, relationships, tensions, grudges, and factors unknown to us—wouldn't any man of ours find himself in an impossible position? I wouldn't want the job."

"Make them obey. Apuleius was always on Gratillonius's side. A new tribune wouldn't delay, argue, obstruct. If necessary, he'd call in troops."

Bacca sighed. "It isn't that easy. Aquilo—Confluentes—is more important than you may realize."

"Because Gratillonius has made it a thorn in your side."

"That. But also because, in spite of everything we've

done—I say this candidly, confidentially—he's made it
flourish. It grows. It's a magnet for industrious immigrants; one way or another, legally or illegally, they're
coming in, and won't meekly let themselves be displaced.
A thorn? It should be a bulwark. God knows we need
that."

She scowled and bit her lip.

"He preserved us from the Scoti this past summer,"
Bacca said; "but now the Ostrogoths are ravaging into
Italy, and I wonder if He will vouchsafe us another mira-
cle. He may have taken Apuleius away—without warning,
I gather—as a sign that He won't."

"Would you trust Gratillonius?" Runa demanded. "Dare
you?"

"What do you think? You've . . . known him well." She
dropped her glance and doubled her fists. "Set grievances
aside," Bacca urged. "Give me a totally honest opinion, no
matter how it tastes in your mouth. This is for Rome."

She looked back at him. "How earnest you've become."

"Not a comedian tonight, my lady. Rome is my Mother.
Is she still his?"

Runa sat silent, as if listening to the rainstorm, until,
grudgingly, she said, "He never caused me to think
otherwise."

Bacca offered a flicker of a smile. "Thank you. I thought
so myself, but wanted your confirmation."

"He's . . . too stubborn. Utterly self-willed."

Bacca nodded. "It's led him to the verge of insubordination, or beyond, over and over. But outright rebelliousness? Among his merits, set his lack of political experience
and subtlety. He wouldn't conspire against us, would he?"

"No," she fleered. "He isn't that bright."

Bacca stared at the rain on the windowglass. It made
the reflected lamplight shimmer. "I almost wish he would.
What an Emperor he'd be."

She drew back on her seat. "Are you serious?"

"Perhaps. Consider what he accomplished in Ys, and is
accomplishing in Confluentes. I suspect that if he tried for
the purple, I'd support him."

She peered at the door. Nobody stood in the corridor.

Nevertheless she leaned forward and dropped her voice. "This is dreadfully dangerous talk."

"I trust you," he said.

Touched, she could only gulp and tell him, "Thank you."

Bacca's fingers twitched. "We desperately need a leader strong, able, and—honest. Stilicho's double games with the barbarians aren't working." He straightened. "Well," he asked, "do you then think we can get along with Gratillonius as our tribune?"

"It would be difficult at best," she warned. "You'd have to make concessions to him."

"That's clear. In fact, we'll have to give up our efforts to destroy him, and instead try convincing him we aren't actually such bad fellows." Bacca laughed. "I hope Nagon Demari won't be too disappointed."

XIX

1

Spring returned, made green the graves of winter and strewed them with flowers. Days grew longer than nights. Migratory birds trekked home.

The Ostrogoths and their allies were devastating Italy. Where they did not reach, the fear of them did. Imperial agents went through the provinces, frantically seeking military recruits. They offered a bounty of ten solidi, three on enrollment, the balance on discharge after the peril was quelled—if it could be. Slaves got two solidi and their freedom.

Few accepted in northern Gallia. Their own homelands were under attack. Saxon fleets swarmed oversea to loot and burn along the coasts; many crews went deep inland, and some began work on strongholds where they could stay through the year or beyond. The Picti and Scoti harried Britannia. Fugitives who got to Armorica said that

King Niall's successor stood high among the latter. Otherwise hardly any civilized ships stirred from port. Even fishermen dared not venture far; their poor catches joined with lost crops to spread hunger.

A while after Easter, Nagon Demari arrived at Confluentes.

Gratillonius ordinarily received visitors at home. It made for a congenial atmosphere as he talked with Osismiic chiefs, travelers from outside, or common folk who had problems. Besides, the large new basilica in Confluentes was only partly built. He thought it too risky to continue using the manor house outside the wall, no matter that nothing within approached its graciousness. As for the basilica in Aquilo, it was full of the homeless and the orphaned. Corentinus supported him in the idea that their needs outweighed the government's.

"I will not have that man in my house," Verania said. She could be immovably decisive when she chose—occasions rare enough to warrant respect. Moreover, Gratillonius shared her feelings. He ignored her possessive pronoun. Between them such questions were meaningless.

Thus he sent a message to the hostel. It was written, not verbal, so he could be sure it carried his exact words. "You will meet me in the basilica of Confluentes at noon."

Sounds of ongoing construction racketed in the room he employed. It was starkly whitewashed, with a concrete floor that was supposed to be tiled sometime. Its furnishings were a table with writing materials—wooden slabs, ink and quills, wax tablets, styluses—and a few stools. He did not rise when Nagon entered, and waited for the other man to give the first "Hail." Thereafter he gestured at a seat.

Nagon took it. Rage mottled his flat face. "Is this how you receive an officer of the Imperium?" he rasped.

Gratillonius grinned. "You see for yourself that it is."

"Have a care. Be very careful."

"Watch your language. As tribune, I outrank you by quite a bit."

"That can be changed."

"Not by an errand boy. I won't warn you again about curbing your tongue. What do you want?"

Nagon's lips moved and his Adam's apple bobbed several times before he said, trembling, "I'm here about the taxes, of course."

"They'll be paid."

"In the proper kind and amount, I *trust*."

Gratillonius had expected something like this. "In gold of, uh, equivalent value, as we've been doing in part."

"Oh, no. No, sir! You've gotten too much leniency already. The basic payments are to be in kind as the law requires."

"The procurator's office knows we aren't yet prepared to spare that much food and manufactured goods. We can't import them this year as we have done, when pirates bedevil the sea lanes and supply is short everywhere. It was a silly exercise anyway. What with the refugees we're getting, we'll skirt the edge of famine ourselves."

Glee glittered in the little pale eyes. "No excuse. The army can't eat your gold. If you do not tender your lawful share, I shall have to institute collection proceedings."

"Such as rounding up children for the slave market? Will the army eat them?"

"That's enough."

"It certainly is. Now listen to me. Where are the solidi coming from to pay those enlistees the Imperium is trying to attract? We can help substantially with that. As a matter of fact, I mean to order an extra contribution from our treasury, if the procurator will accept the tax in money. You wouldn't understand patriotism, Nagon. I can't say whether your superiors do or not, but they understand business. They'll agree. If the poison in you hasn't addled your wits, you must know they won't let you do your viper's work among us. What did you come here hoping for? To scare a few women and children? To provoke men into rashness? You can't. I'll write to Turonum this afternoon, but I won't trust you with the letter. Go away."

Nagon sprang up. Gratillonius rose too and bulked over him.

"I'll go," Nagon chattered. "You're happy, aren't you? Oh, you're enjoying yourself, persecuting me. You want to take my livelihood from me, don't you, and laugh when my family starves. You want to drive me out of the world like you drove me out of Ys."

"Too bad I succeeded in that," Gratillonius drawled. "You'd have gone down with the city."

Tears came forth. Nagon waved his fists. He shuddered and sobbed. "I'll go. And Glabrio will scorn me and Bacca will patronize me and I'll be a whipped dog. But not for long. Not for long. I'll return, Gratillonius. And when I do, it will be your turn to howl. You'll be sorry for your cruelty, but it will be too late. I'm not stupid, you know. I have a great deal of information about you and your friends. You'll be helpless, Gratillonius. The whip will be across your heart then. Think about it—till I return." He stormed from the room.

2

Flavius Vortivir, tribune at Darioritum Venetorum, was a hard man but righteous in his fashion. It had been said that he and Apuleius were the only senators in Armorica not corrupt; but Armorica didn't have many. Though Gratillonius was only a curial, Vortivir received him on equal terms. He spoke for Confluentes and Aquilo, communities growing when others were shrinking, the see of one of Armorica's few bishops.

"We can set aside the old rivalries, I hope,"—those between the Osismii and the Veneti—said Gratillonius with a smile.

"The newer ones are more difficult," replied Vortivir with his usual lack of humor.

Because it was a beautiful day in a year that was turning out generally cold and wet, they sat on the portico of his house. It was high enough on its hill to look over roofs, the southern city wall, and a mile to the landlocked, island-studded gulf into which the river emptied. Haze gave that water a mysterious shimmer, like a lake in a dream. Tales and songs among the tribespeople told how this had been dry land once, back when the Old Folk raised those avenues of tall stones which still brooded near here. But the sea had broken in. . . . Gratillonius strove not to remember Ys too keenly.

"What do you mean?" he asked.

"You lure commerce and—worse, much worse—men away from us, when they are sorely needed."

Gratillonius picked his words with care. "Sir, we do not lure. Whoever comes to us does it of his own choice."

"Not a choice the law always allows."

"We're accused of harboring runaways. All I can reply is that we aren't magicians, to hear men's inner thoughts. Idlers, thieves, and ruffians don't get leave to stay. If someone believes he can identify a person among us who belongs elsewhere, he is free to come try."

"Ha, I know how likely that is. A hard trip, considerable expense, and the man in question will have disappeared . . . till the searcher leaves, having met a hedge of pretended ignorance and a quagmire of pretended incompetence. You can uphold the law better than that."

"I have more urgent business than looking into private lives, and damned little staff to handle any of it for me. I admit we are taking in outsiders, refugees."

Vortivir nodded. "True. That much is well done of you. I'm not seeking a quarrel, Gratillonius. You are my guest, and your letter said you wanted to discuss a matter of public concern."

"I do. It touches on a big reason why we seem to be lucky in Confluentes, and so draw settlers. That's not happenstance."

"Your enlightened administration?" asked Vortivir, not quite sarcastically.

"I make no claims about that. Also, please remember I've been the tribune for less than half a year. It's longer than that since any raiders hit Osismia. Even the plague of them Rome's now got hasn't reached us yet."

Vortivir's look grew somber. The Veneti had suffered. "Do you think that setback they took at your hands—four years ago, was it?—frightened them off for good? That's not their way."

"Of course not. However, it's given them a healthy respect for us. Saxons too; they heard what happened to the Scoti. Why should they walk into a bear's den, when the rest of the Empire is easy pickings?"

Vortivir studied Gratillonius for a space before he said,

"They're bound to test you again. Will the same . . . spontaneous gathering of wildly diverse groups . . . meet them?"

"It could," Gratillonius answered.

"The law keeps the tribes disarmed. It has to, or they'd soon cut the Empire apart, feuding with it and each other."

"A citizen has a right to defend himself against a robber. I see nothing wrong with encouraging him to learn how to do it."

"That depends." Abruptly Vortivir spat off the portico, turned squarely to the other, and snapped, "How long shall we chop words? It's obvious why you're here. You've sounded me out in the past, and inquired about me, same as you have everybody else you approached or will be approaching."

"I wouldn't want . . . to speak sedition, sir. Nor tempt anyone to."

"Well, I'm not the kind who'd tempt you! I'll state the facts myself. You have these irregular reserves, or whatever you call them. It's debatable whether their existence quite violates the law, and if so, how much. But the question had better not come before the Imperium. Their activities have spread well into the rest of Armorica, mostly the back country but also a number of small coastal settlements. You want to weave men of all the tribes into this loose network of yours. You hope for my sanction, or at least for my blind eye turned your way. Correct?"

"Correct, sir. The aim is purely defensive. That includes suppression of domestic banditry. Together the tribes can do what none can do separately. For instance, you Veneti are a race of seamen." (As the Ysans were.) "You've got boats to keep watch well offshore and carry back warning. You've got ships to bring help to where it's needed. Most of that help could come from inland. For instance, if you were in touch with Redonic members of the association—"

Vortivir lifted a hand. "That's clear. Let's spare the time it takes. There will be plenty of details that are not clear. This doesn't come as any staggering surprise to me, you know. I keep reasonably well informed about events, and about the men who make them happen. If anything, I'm a little surprised you haven't seen me earlier."

"There was a dispute with a couple of Namnetic headmen—"

"Never mind. Tell me about it later. For the moment: Gratillonius, you not only have my sanction. Provided you can settle a few remaining doubts in my mind, and I'm pretty sure you can, you will have my active cooperation."

Gratillonius's hard-held breath burst from him. "Sir, this, this is wonderful!"

"I regard it as my duty," Vortivir said. "That law about armament tamed the old savages. Today it's letting new savages at the throat of Rome."

3

A Saxon flotilla forced the passage of the bay where Gesocribate stood. The barbarians overwhelmed the garrison, scaled the walls, looted, raped, killed for two days, finally set fire to the city and vanished back up the Britannic Sea.

There was nothing the Osismii could do except tender help afterward. A seaport populated largely by mariners who came and went, therefore under closer than ordinary official surveillance, Gesocribate had been outside the native defense movement; and it lay alone at the far end of the peninsula. Its example did jolt many Armoricans into joining the brotherhoods, and these grew more openly militant.

In Confluentes, Evirion raged. It was bad enough that he was penned there, his ship idled, himself likewise as well as tortured equally by boredom and by fretting over the future of his business. What had now happened was a blow to one of his most important harborages and marts. If the home guard could have been there! If he could have been in the front line, splitting enemy skulls!

Occasional paramilitary drills gave him something to do, but redoubled his frustration. He could find no work unless it be as a common laborer, and he would not stoop to that. Nor could he, without fatal damage to his authority over his crew, should *Brennilis* ever put to sea again. He drank too much, got into fights, consorted with whores, lay hours in his own bed staring at the ceiling, slouched sullenly around the towns or along the roads. For reasons obscure to himself he shunned the forest. Yet that was at last where he went.

Summer was then well along, a bleak one this year, chill rains and fleeting pale sunshine. However, for a time it grew hot. Through several days the weather smoldered with never a cloud; folk at night tossed sweating under the weight of air, while crickets outside shrilled mockery. Finally thunderheads massed in the south. Their bases were caverns of purple darkness, their heads noonday white until the sky dimmed. Slowly the overcast thickened. As yet no wind stirred on earth. In heat and silence, the land lay waiting.

Four mounted men rode past Aquilo and up the river road to Confluentes. They led one horse whose saddle was empty. Hoofs clattered on the new stone bridge. They did not enter the city, but passed around and took the dirt road along the Stegir.

That drew remark from onlookers. Their hails got no response. The party trotted onward from the northwest tower, by the old manor and its orchard, through the lately cleared fields beyond, until they reached the present edge of the woods in that direction and disappeared within.

A man came into a tavern, excited, and told his friends what he had seen. The place was tiny, a room in the owner's home; everybody heard. "Two soldiers they were, armored, and two civilians, one of them pretty well dressed, the other a monk or something. Been traveling hard, from the look of them. What could they want?"

"Government business?" wondered a drinker. "But why didn't they stop off at the hostel in Aquilo? My brother works there, and he was telling me this very morning how they haven't had anybody except postal couriers for—I forget how long. So those fellows just got here, and if you saw aright, they didn't even stop to freshen up."

"Ah, these be strange times," muttered a third man. "Holy Martinus, watch over us."

369

Evirion put down his half-emptied cup, left his bench, and hurried out. "Hoy, what the devil?" sounded at his back, but he simply broke into a run when he reached the door.

At his house he shooed away the servant who was cleaning it. Once alone, he took from a chest a pair of knives, his sword, a crossbow such as mariners favored, and a case of bolts for it. A long cloak concealed them while he thrust his way through traffic. A wake of indignation and profanity roiled behind him.

Outside the east gate clustered a number of shops denied space within because they were noisy or smelly or the owners could not afford it. Among them was a livery stable. Evirion selected what he deemed was the least jaded of its three horses, and did not haggle but paid over at once the asking price of a day's rent, in coin. "That should make you outfit her fast," he told the groom. "Failing it, I have the toe of my boot."

If he pushed the sorry nag hard, she might well founder on him. He made the best speed that prudence, not mercy, allowed. It was some slight help for the seething in him that the Romans wouldn't expect pursuit. You couldn't generally gallop along the woodland trails anyway. Their gloom was dense this day, except where the twisting course brought him near the Stegir.

4

Thunder rolled down the sky. Cold gusts went like surf through the treetops. Clouds decked the sun with darkness, but a weird brass-yellow light came through, pervasive as if without any one source, and sheened on the river.

Nemeta stepped from her cabin as the men drew rein. For an instant she surveyed them, and they her. Two were soldiers, cavalry, though not heavy lancers. Helmets and coats of ringmail shone hard above leather breeches and boots. Their swords were long. Axes were sheathed under their saddlebows and shields hung at their horses' breechings. One led a riderless animal.

On their left a lean man with an undershot jaw sat awkwardly, not used to riding and sore from it. He too was trousered, in cloth, but had sandals on bare feet and a brown robe that must be his only everyday garment, pulled up past his knees. Above a short beard, the front half of his scalp was shaven, the hair making a ruff behind. He pressed a small casket close against his side.

The fourth, on the right and somewhat in the lead, wearing blue linen beneath a fine tunic, unarmed aside from a knife—

"Nagon Demari," she said. Dismay shook her voice.

The stocky man skewered her with his gaze. "You are Nemeta, daughter of Gratillonius," he snapped.

"Aye," she replied unthinkingly in Ysan. "What would you of me?"

"Answer me, in Latin."

She braced her thin frame. "Why should I?"

"Obduracy will make matters worse for you," he told her, unrelenting as the thunder. "Name yourself to these men."

She moistened her lips before she uttered, "I am . . . Nemeta," in their language.

"Bear witness," Nagon ordered his band.

Nemeta half raised her useable hand. The wind tossed stray red locks around the white face. "What is this?" she cried. "How do you know me, Nagon? I was a young girl when—when—" She faltered.

He smiled with compressed lips. "You know *me*."

"All Ys knew you. And since then—"

"I have gathered information, piece by piece in these past years. I am a patient man when there is need to be."

"What do you want?"

They stared and stared at her. Nagon squared his shoulders, drew breath, and intoned against the wind: "Nemeta, daughter of Gratillonius, you are a pagan and a witch. Your unholy rites are banned by the law. Your diabolical practices have endangered souls for far too long. Some may already be in hell because of you. By authority of the governor of this province, I arrest you, for conveyance to trial at Caesarodunum Turonum." Thunder followed, louder and nearer.

371

She took a step back, halted, stiffened, and stammered, "This, this is . . . preposterous. I am the daughter of the King—of the tribune."

A laugh slapped at her. "He has indeed been negligent." Sternly: "Make no more trouble for him and yourself. Come. Here is a horse for you. Will you need help in mounting?"

"Hard rain any minute now, sir," a soldier said. "Why don't we wait it out in the cabin?"

His companion flinched and exclaimed, "Not in a witch's house!"

"We go straight back," Nagon commanded. "We are on the Lord's business. Come, woman."

"No, I won't!" Nemeta yelled. She forked the three middle fingers of her hand and thrust it at them. "I *am* a witch! Begone, or I'll strike you down! Belisama, Lir, and Taranis, hear!"

"Witness," Nagon told the others. His voice crackled with exultation. The soldiers stirred uneasily in their seats. He turned to the fourth member of the group. "Brother Philippus."

"I am a priest, my child," said the tonsured man to Nemeta. It was hard to hear him through the rising storm. "An exorcist." He opened the casket and took forth a scroll. Without a grasp on its reins, his horse stamped and tossed its head. "Your poor wickedness has no power against the Lord God and this, His holy word. Attempt no spells. They can only bring a punishment more severe."

Nemeta whirled and sprinted aside. "After her!" Nagon shouted. The soldiers spurred their mounts. Before she reached the brake, they were on either side of her. She was lost between cliffs of height. One man nudged her roughly with his foot. She stumbled back from between them. Nagon and Philippus closed in too.

She slumped. "Again, four of you," she whispered. Her head sank till they saw just the fiery hair.

"Resist no more," said the priest, "and none shall harm you."

"That is for her judge to decide," Nagon crooned.

Lightning flared. Hoofbeats answered thunder. A horse came around the bend of the trail, lathered and lurching.

When its rider yanked on the reins, it halted at once and stood with head a-droop. Breath wheezed in froth.

"Hold on, there!" bellowed he who sat it.

They gaped. Nemeta raised her eyes and gave a kind of moan. "What is this?" Nagon demanded.

"They're . . . taking me away." Nemeta's words blew frail on the wind.

"Oh, no, you don't," said Evirion. He brought up the crossbow he had had on his left arm, cocked and loaded. "Stop right there."

A soldier cursed. Philippus called on God. Nagon reddened and whitened with fury. "Are you mad?" he choked. "We're agents of the state."

"Has she summoned a demon to possess you?" quavered the exorcist.

Nemeta reached resolve. She took a pair of steps from her captors toward the mariner, stopped, and said almost quietly, "Evirion, don't. Go. You can't help me this time."

Death was on his countenance. "The hell I can't. Come here, woman. You others stay back. The first of you that moves, I'll drop."

Nagon grinned his hatred. "And what about the next?" he challenged.

"Please, Evirion," Nemeta begged. "I don't want you beheaded too."

"It could be worse than that, from what I've heard," the big man said. *"Come here."*

She shook her head.

"All right," Evirion snarled. "I'm coming after you."

He sprang from his horse and advanced on her.

"Get him!" Nagon screamed.

The cavalrymen drew blade. A charger neighed. Both boomed past the prisoner and down on the seaman.

Evirion pulled trigger. The bow rang and thumped, the bolt whistled through the wind. The man on the left let go of his sword and toppled. He struck soddenly and lay still in an outwelling of blood. Lightning made his mail shimmer. His horse galloped on, crashed into the brush, was gone.

The second was already at Evirion. A stout crossbow could put a shaft through armor, but took time to load and set. Even to a trained infantryman, a mounted attack was a terrifying sight. Evirion barely dodged aside. He threw his bow. The heavy stock struck in the midriff. The rider did not fall. For a moment, though, he lost control. Instead of taking the chance to run, Evirion darted in. His sword hissed free. A hoof nearly smote him. He got behind and swung.

Hamstrung, the horse screamed, kicked air, plunged and scrabbled. "You swine!" its master shrieked, and threw himself off to the ground. The horse reeled aside, fell, lay thrashing and screaming. Its rider had kept hold of his sword. Evirion pounced like a cat before his opponent was afoot. They went down together. The heel of Evirion's left hand smashed the soldier's nose from beneath. Suddenly that face was a red ruin. The man jerked once and died.

Evirion bounced to a crouch. The encounter had passed in a whirl. The priest clung to the neck of his panicky, rearing mount. Nagon was in little better case. His eyes darted, found Nemeta still frozen. He writhed from the saddle, thumped to earth in a heap, was immediately up and on the run, toward the woman. His knife gleamed forth.

"Nemeta!" Evirion roared, and plunged toward her. She came aware and leaped. Nagon was almost there. He meant to take her hostage or kill her, Evirion knew; no matter which. Nagon's left hand snatched out and caught her by the hair. She jerked to a halt. With a whoop, he pulled her into stabbing distance. She caught that wrist in the crook of her left arm and her teeth. She fell, dragged it down. Her skeleton right arm flopped at his ankles.

Evirion arrived. His sword sang below the lightning. It thwacked as it bit into the neck. Blood spouted. Nagon went to his knees. "Oh, Lydris," bubbled from his mouth—the name of his wife. He crumpled on his face and scrabbled weakly for a while. Blood flowed from him slower and slower, out into an enormous puddle whose red caught the lightning-light.

Evirion knelt and held Nemeta close. The blood that had gushed over her smeared across him. "Fare you well?" he asked frantically in Ysan. "Are you hale, my darling?"

"Aye." The answer came faint. "Not hurt. But you?" Her eyes found his.

374

"I was the quickest of them." He helped her to rise. She leaned on him, tottered, and sank down once they were out of the pool.

"I'm well, but—but my head swims—" She lowered it between her knees.

The exorcist's horse had thrown him. Dazed more by horror than impact, he groped backward from the red-painted man who turned his way. He lifted his arms as if in prayer. "Please, no," he begged. "I belong to the Church."

Evirion pointed. "Go," he said. "Upstream. Don't turn around till . . . till sundown."

"No, not alone at night in the wilderness!"

" 'Twon't hurt you. Use this house if you like." Evirion's laugh clanked. "You shouldn't fear witchcraft, should you, priest? But I don't want you here before dark. Tomorrow, if you can't remember the trails, follow the river to Confluentes. Go!" He made one threatening stride. Philippus whimpered and scuttled off.

Evirion went about securing things. His jade had stood numbly throughout. He cut the throat of the crippled charger. The priest's gelding and the remount were still close by, somewhat calmed. They shied from him, but he caught the reins of first one, then the other, as thickets slowed their escape, and they let him tie them to branches. He collected weapons, washed them in the river, bundled everything in his cloak. The wind blew still stronger and louder. Lightning went in flares and sheets, thunder crashed, a deeper rushing noise told of rain oncoming.

By the time he was through, Nemeta had recovered. She went to him and laid her cheek against his breast. His arms enclosed her. "Evirion, what now?" Her tone still shook. "My father—"

"He's gone on one of his trips," the man told her. "I'd guess Nagon knew he would be, and timed himself for it."

A ghost of joy lilted. "Well do the Gods stand by us! Nobody can accuse my father of aught."

"They'll be after you and me. Let's begone. Here we've two good steeds."

"Whither?"

"I know not. The forest?"

She looked up. A steadiness to match his came into her. "Nay, not at once. We needn't blindly bolt. In Confluentes may be some help. At least, he—my father has the need and right to learn what truly happened."

"Hm—Aye. A sound thought. Well, come, then. 'Tis a long ride, and the earlier we begin, the better."

She disengaged from him, moved toward the horses, stopped. "My cats!"

He blinked. "What?"

"I cannot leave my three cats behind. Who'd care for them?"

Laughter cataracted from him. When its wildness was past, he knuckled his eyes and said, "Very well, fetch them along. I should in honor return this Pegasus I hired, too."

She went to her dwelling. "I'll take them in a basket, to shield them from the rain."

"What about us?"

At her door, she looked back, across the sprawled dead men. "It will wash us clean."

5

The storm passed over. Eventide rested mellow. It tinted the battlements of Confluentes with gold. Swallows darted along the Odita.

Having brought them to Gratillonius's private room, Verania regarded her two drenched, hollow-eyed visitors and asked softly, "What is this?"

"A terrible story," Evirion said. "Best we tell your brother Salomon."

"It happens he's here. I'll go for him if you like. But— Nemeta, dear, we haven't seen you in years. Be welcome. We'll have a bath and a bed for you—oh, and supper, of course. Can you stay till your father returns? He'll be so happy."

Nemeta shook her head. "I must be off." Her glance went fearfully to the window. Low light made its glass shine sea-green. "Never can I spend a night here." The cats she had released from the basket ceased sniffing about the room and sought her. "But can you take these from me?" she requested. "They're housebroken and sweet."

"If you wish it, certainly. I'll call Salomon." Skirts rustled as Verania went out. Nemeta squatted down to stroke and reassure her pets. Evirion prowled.

Verania re-entered. "He'll be here shortly," she explained. "He was asleep. He stays with me when my husband is away. Not that I need be afraid of anything. Gratillonius wants to mark him out as—an heir to leadership. Our mother agrees." Proudly: "People have started bringing disputes before him, and he's active in the guard. But today he went hunting, the weather caught him, he came back exhausted."

"Thank you, my lady," said Evirion. "Maybe you'd best withdraw."

Verania looked at him. "Nemeta will stay, won't she?" When he nodded: "Then it shouldn't be talk unfit for a woman to hear."

"It's dangerous to know."

She flushed. "Do you suppose I won't share any danger that touches my man? We're close, he and I. Let me stay."

"Or she'll have to get it from her brother," Nemeta divined. "I'm sorry, Verania. We can certainly use your counsel."

Salomon appeared, hastily tunicked, hair uncombed and fuzz on his cheeks. But his youth had shrugged fatigue off and he was alert. "Nemeta! Evirion!" he cheered. "Why, this is splendid." He paused. "No, it isn't, is it?"

"Close the door," his sister told him.

They heard the story. Never did they call the deed a crime.

"Holy Georgios, help us," Salomon prayed.

"That horrible creature, Nagon," sighed Verania. "Sick with his own venom."

"He was that, I suppose," Evirion said. "He should have escaped while he could. But he went after Nemeta, and naturally I chopped him."

"God help me, I don't think I can pray for him."

377

Salomon folded his arms and stared downward. "Never mind that now," he said. "What should *we* do?"

"We, Nemeta and I, we won't stay," Evirion promised. "Whether or not that fool priest makes it back, and he will, they'll soon have a pretty good idea in Turonum of what went awry. We mustn't get you fouled in their net. Give us a rest, a bite to eat, dry clothes, some provisions we can carry, and we'll be off as soon as it's dark."

"Nobody will know we were here," Nemeta added. "We were two more wet people among the few in the streets. Your doorkeeper didn't get a good look at me, and never met me before anyway." She had, after all, brought a cloak for herself, and used the cowl to screen her face and distinctive hair. "Who'll think to question him? I suppose he knows Evirion a little, but why should he remember what day he last saw him?"

"Besides, he's loyal," Verania said. "My family's treated its slaves like fellow children of God. . . . But into the wildwood, you two?"

Salomon lifted his head. "Give Gratillonius time, and he may be able to negotiate a pardon," he declared. "In any case, you've got shelter where the state can never find you."

"Where?" coughed Evirion.

"With one of our brotherhoods. Rufinus's old Bacaudae. They'll be glad to take you in."

"How can you be sure?"

"I've been among them enough. Gratillonius wants everybody to get to know me, and me to know them. Come night, I'll guide you."

XX

1

"**Y**ou know why I'm here," said Gratillonius. "Let's get on with it."

"By all means," replied Bacca cordially.

They sat alone in his room of erotic books in Turonum.

Outside, wind blustered. Glass panes flickered with cloud shadows.

"My daughter—"

"And her murderous accomplice."

Gratillonius's eyes stung. "It never had to happen. She harmed nobody. I think she helped many. The country's full of good little witches like her."

Bacca's gaunt visage assumed sternness. "Your duty is to put a stop to that."

"Then every Roman official is derelict," Gratillonius retorted. "I could find witches within five miles of here. So could you, if you'd take the trouble."

"We have more pressing concerns."

"Me too. I thought you wanted my goodwill."

"We did. I still do." Bacca sighed. "Let me give you the background. Nagon was clever. He waited till I was out of the city, then approached the governor. Glabrio has never liked or trusted you."

How true, thought Gratillonius. That was why he had sought audience with the procurator instead. Not that Bacca was a friend either, but he seemed reasonable in his rascality.

"He was quite willing to be persuaded," the smooth voice continued. "One can imagine Nagon's exhortation. 'End the scandal of paganism and sorcery in the very family of a Roman tribune. It's not only his flouting of law and religion, it's his intransigence. Give him a sharp reminder that he must mend his ways. Humble him. Undermine him.'

"They didn't tell me about the decision. Glabrio says he wanted to avoid a futile dispute when his mind was made up. Confidentially, I suspect he was afraid I'd change it for him."

That also sounded true, Gratillonius thought. Glabrio had spite of his own to vent. Weak men are often vicious.

"Once Nagon brought her back, publicly accused, it would be too late," Bacca finished. "We would have no choice but to proceed against her. It was a poor return Nagon made me for my protection, I grant you."

Gratillonius's heart thumped. "Well, how about repairing the damage?" he pressed. "Issue a civil pardon. Bishop Corentinus is ready to give absolution."

379

Bacca's lips pinched together before he answered, "Impossible. That man murdered two soldiers and an officer of the state."

"She was innocent, helpless." Heavily: "Let him stay outlawed." It hurt Gratillonius to the point of nausea, but he had cherished no real hope for Evirion.

"You have not been precisely zealous in organizing pursuit of him," said Bacca.

"How can I ransack the wilderness?"

"You have men who live in it."

Gratillonius shook his head. "No, I don't," he declared with a slight, malicious pleasure. "I'm not allowed to, remember? I have been given no authority over those squatters."

"Very good!" laughed Bacca. "Then why are you so sure the girl is even alive?"

"Let's say I'm confident of God's mercy and justice."

Gaze met gaze. Gratillonius knew that Bacca knew he got word from the forest. For the procurator to state it forthrightly would mean scrapping the policy he had been at pains to get adopted.

Bacca's wry smile faded. "Corentinus cannot reconcile a pagan with Him," he pointed out.

"She would accept baptism."

"I suppose she would, as a matter of expediency. Later—who knows?—His grace might touch her. But it cannot be. She would have to appear in public. Otherwise, what practical difference would these maneuvers make? When she did, we would have to seize her. The case is that notorious. There is much rebelliousness in Armorican hearts these days. Sparing her would feed it like nothing else. No, reprieve is a political impossibility."

Gratillonius bent forward, elbows on thighs, hands clasped between knees, head low. "I was afraid of that. But I had to come try."

"I understand," said Bacca gently. "Courage. Perhaps in a few years, when the sensation has died down, if things in general look less precarious, perhaps then—" He let the words die away.

Gratillonius straightened. "You dangle that bait before me?"

"It may be honest. We shall have to wait and see. At the moment, I cannot give you any promises other than—taking the pressure off you about this business . . . provided you cause no further questions about your loyalty to be raised."

"I won't." Gratillonius could not quite swallow the insult. "You snake, this is extortion."

Bacca seemed unoffended. "It's for Rome," he replied.

2

Autumn weather came earliest to the high midland of Armorica. First the birches grew sallow and their leaves departed on chilly winds, then red and brown and yellow rustled all over the hills. Ducks left the meres and the reeds around them brittled. The rivers seemed to run louder through gorges filling with shadow. Clear nights were crowded with stars; the Swan soared over the evenings and Orion strode up before dawn.

Nemeta thanked Vindolenus and left him to get a bite of food and some rest in Catualorig's house. It was a thirty-league trek the dour old Bacauda had made from the Confluentes neighborhood—thirty leagues for a bird, two or three times that on twisting trails or through tracklessness. Only once earlier had he been able to do it, carrying gifts and a message. He had his living to make; and Gratillonius did not share out the secret of where his daughter was. Vindolenus had taken her and Evirion there in the first instance, after Salomon brought them to him and asked they be given a refuge safely remote. In Roman eyes, men like this were still felons, unwise if they made themselves conspicuous. Some had scattered very widely, founding homesteads where no Armorican tribe would dispute it; but they kept in touch.

Nemeta carried the letter outside. It was a day of pale sunlight and nipping breeze. Fallen leaves rattled over the clearing around the rude, sod-roofed cabin. Its pair of outbuildings crowded close, dwarfish. Rails marked off a fold. Chickens scratched in the dust. A rivulet gurgled and

381

gleamed. Catualorig's daughter returned sulkily from the excitement of the arrival to scrub clothes on the stones in its bed. From behind the cabin an ax thudded as her mother chopped firewood. The man and his two sons were about their tasks in the forest. It hemmed in the dwelling place and a tiny, hand-cultivated field. Height and hues cloaked the ruggedness of terrain, but the northward upslope was unmistakable.

Nemeta found a log at the edge of the plot, sat down, untied the tablets and spread them on her lap. She had become quite adept in the use of a single hand and bare toes. Words pressed into wax were necessarily spare, and Gratillonius's writing style was less than eloquent. Yet she read over and over:

"My dear daughter, we are all well. Food is short but nobody hungers too much. The barbarians are still bad but have not touched us here. Good news too. In August the Romans broke the invaders of Italy at last. Stilicho had collected many recruits, also Alan and Hun allies from beyond the Danuvius. He cut the barbarian supply lines and then killed them group by group. At last Radagaisus was captured and beheaded. We miss you and hope you are well. Your father."

A finer imprint continued, news of people she knew and of everyday things. It ended: *"We love you. God willing, we will yet bring you home. Greet Evirion. Verania."*

Nemeta rose, tucked the tablets close to her, and hurried off upstream. Somberness had left her face. She hummed a song children in Ys once sang when at play. Along the trail she spied the younger boy, herding the swine, and gave him a hail whose cheeriness astonished him.

Shortly she heard the blunt noise of a mallet on wood. Another clearing opened before her. This one was minute, made where a brookside stand of shrubs could readily be removed. An uncompleted building occupied it. It too was small, of the primitive round form, though it would eventually boast a couple of windows with membranes and shutters. The soil was poor for wattle-and-daub, and Evirion built with stout poles, carefully chinked. The roof would be of turf, smokehole louvered; he was no thatcher, and besides, this would diminish the fire hazard. He stood on

382

a ladder—a length of fir with the branches lopped to stubs, leaned against the wall—and pegged a rafter to a crossbeam. Like her, he wore a single garment of coarse wool, for him a kilt. Muscles coiled in view. His beard had grown out and his hair was a hayrick.

"Evirion!" she cried. "A message—Vindolenus again—this time he brought us warm clothes and, and come read for yourself. 'Tis the most wonderful news."

"Hold," he said, and finished securing the roughly shaped timber. Only then did he drop the hammer and climb down. "Well, well. So there is still a world out there. Ofttimes I've felt unsure."

"Take it. Read." She thrust the tablets into his hands.

He scanned them, laid them on the ground, and muttered, "Italy saved. Doubtless a fine thing, but much of it must lie in wreck by now."

"You don't rejoice," she said, crestfallen.

He shrugged. "Why do you? We remain exiles."

"Oh—my father—"

"Aye. You're glad because this word gave him a little happiness." Evirion smiled. "So should I be. He's a good man—the best. Nor should I whine at my own fate."

Warmth swelled in her tones. "You never do. You're too strong for that."

"In some ways. In others—Well, brooding on such things weakens a man by itself."

She waved at the house. "Behold what you've done. And in all weathers, too, this harsh year."

"Ha, I'd better. Winter draws nigh."

"You'll outpace it. Once begun, you've raced ahead like wildfire." He could accomplish little until Vindolenus had brought the tools he requested from Gratillonius. Catualorig's were few, crude, and often needed by him. The settler and his sons lent a hand when necessary, but for the most part had no time to spare for it. They likewise must prepare for winter.

"Aye, 'twill be ready within another month, if my luck holds," he said. "But I'd fain also make it a little comfortable."

"That can come later. I can scarce wait to move in."

They shared the cabin with the family and, at one end

of it, two cows. The dwellers were friendly enough but had no conversation in them. After dark, they snuffed the tallow candles and went to bed on skins spread over juniper boughs on the earthen floor. Then the only light was from coals in the banked firepit. Air was thick with smells of smoke, grease, dung, beast, man. When Catualorig mounted his wife, nobody could sleep till he was done, though that didn't take long. The daughter was apt to giggle at those sounds.

Nemeta and Evirion had quickly decided they didn't want to be immediate neighbors. Fortunately, the yard lacked much space for another structure. It would have been ill done to offend people who were so kindly and who loved Gratillonius themselves.

" 'Twill never be like what you had in Ys, nor even later by the Stegir," Evirion said, "but let me give you something better than a cave."

"Could I but help!" Her pleasure blew away on the wind that soughed around. "It hurts being useless."

"You're not."

"With this arm? And none of my arts?" She dared not practice her small witcheries. Thinly populated though the hills were, word of it would spread, and in time get to Roman ears. Her whereabouts betrayed, she might flee onward, but Gratillonius would be destroyed, with all that he had labored for. Nemeta had not offered the Three as much as a chant. That could have disturbed the inhabitants, who sacrificed to spirits of wood and water and to whom Ys was a tale of doom.

"You are *not* useless," Evirion told her. "You do well with your single hand. They have gain of your aid. You lighten their lives with your stories and poems. You bring me my midday food as I work, and talk and sing to me. Without that cheer, I'd lag far behind."

"The most I can tender you," she answered sadly, "who lost everything because of me."

"That's just as false," he blurted. "You're enough, and more."

"Oh, Evirion—"

He moved to hug her. It would have been chaste, but she slipped aside. His arms fell.

384

"I'm sorry," he said dully. "I forgot. The curse of what happened that day by the sea."

She hung her head and dug a toe into the earth. "The Gods have not healed me of it," she whispered.

"Those Gods?" He curbed his scorn and attempted gaiety. "Well, anyhow, soon you'll have your own house."

She looked up, half alarmed. "Nay, ours."

He let the mask drop from him. Pain roughened his voice. "So I believed too. But I've thought more, and, and may as well tell you now. This hut—Belike 'twould be too much for my strength, living with you as brother and sister in a palace. In a single space, impossible. This shall be yours alone."

"But what will you do?" she wailed.

He forced a grin. "I'll fettle me. Our present lodging can easily become a merry place."

She stared.

"That's a sprightly young chick Catualorig's fathered," he said, "and she's been giving me a twinklesome eye, and he's already hinted he'd liefer have me than a ruck of woodland louts beget his grandchildren."

"*What?*"

He heard and saw she was appalled. Hastily, he said, "Ah, I tease you," then could not resist adding, "Mayhap."

Nemeta tightened her left fist, gulped, finally uttered, "Oh, I've no right—" A yell: "Nay, you're too good for an unwashed hussy like that!"

"Weep not," he begged, contrite. "Please. I was jesting."

She blinked hard. "W-were you?"

"Not altogether," he admitted wryly. "The desire does wax in me day by day, and there she is. But if naught else, 'twould be cruel of me, when I'm bound to forsake her."

"You are? Where can you go?"

"Anywhere else." Bitterness broke through. "You've called yourself useless, wrongly. But what am I? Once this thing is done, what's for my hands? I'm a blunderer in the hunt. I doubt I could dig a straight furrow or make aught grow save weeds. Nor do I care to. This is no life for a seaman. Come spring, if we're here yet, I'm off."

The green eyes were enormous in a face drained of color. "What will you do?"

385

"Make my way south." He gained heart as he spoke. "Who'll know me, once I've changed my name? Surely I can find a berth as a deckhand. Any skipper so bold as to sail nowadays must reck little of guilds and laws. I think of earning me a passage to Britannia. 'Tis in turmoil, but that means opportunities."

She reached out her hand. "Nay, Evirion," she pleaded. "Leave me not."

"Be of good cheer. You'll be quite safe. Catualorig will keep you fed and fuelled. 'Tis no great strain on him. Game is plentiful and he's a master huntsman, besides having his livestock."

"But reavers, barbarians—"

"They've never come this far inland. Naught worth their stealing. And no man of these parts will dare lay a finger on you. Gratillonius's vengeance would be swift and sure. Moreover, though you've put your arts aside, they've some idea of what you can do at need. Fear not. Bide your time."

"'Tis you I fear for! Out in yon ongoing slaughter—"

"I'll live. Or if I die, the foe will rue the price. At worst, 'twill be happier than this—this—" He stopped.

"What? Speak it."

He yielded. "This emptiness. Endless yearning."

She stood a long while silent. The wind ruffled her hair, like flames dancing. Finally she drew breath and said, "We can end it."

"How?"

She looked straight at him. "I love you, Evirion."

He had no words.

"I dared not say it." She spoke almost calmly. "Now I must. I will be yours. What, shall you not embrace me?"

He reeled to her and gathered her in arms that shivered. "I'd never . . . willingly . . . hurt you," he croaked.

"I know you'll be gentle. I think, if you're patient, I think you can teach me. Can give me back what I lost."

He brought his lips down. Hers were shy at first, then clumsy, then eager.

"Come," she said amidst laughter and tears. She tugged at his wrist. "Now, at once. Spread your kilt under me. Away from the wind, inside these walls of ours."

A sharp summer was followed by a hard winter. Snowfalls, rarely seen in Armorica, warmed air a little for a short while, then soon a ringing frost would set in. Against the whitened steeps where Gesocribate had nestled, its burnt-over shell seemed doubly black.

Brick and tile, the house of Septimius Rullus was among those that had escaped conflagration. It was sacked; the rooms echoed hollowly. Cleaning had removed the shards of beautiful things and the filth, but could do nothing for murals smoke-stained and hacked, mosaic floor wantonly chipped and pried at. The curial survived because he left the city when the Saxons first hove in view. That was not cowardice. Old, a widower, he could only have gotten in the way of the defenders and consumed supplies they needed if the combat turned into a siege. He had taken with him as many of the helpless as he was able to lead, kept their spirits from breaking while they fled across the hinterland and huddled in whatever shelter they found, brought them back to take up existence among the ruins.

Others there had avoided the general massacre in various ways. The barbarians had also overlooked food stores sufficient to last this remnant population a few months, if miserly doled out. Manufactures resumed on a small scale, producing goods to trade for necessities. The nearest thing to a tribune that ghost Gesocribate had, Rullus got all this effort started and held it together. Therefore Gratillonius, who had heard the story, sought him out.

They sat on stools hastily made and held their hands close to a single brazier, in lieu of a hypocaust for which there was not enough firewood. Its glow and a couple of tallow candles stuck to a battered table gave feeble light. Outside was day, but panes had been shattered and windows were stuffed with rags. It was just as well, perhaps; the chamber was no longer a pretty sight. A slave had brought in bread, cheese, and ale. The farm-brewed drink was in two goblets of exquisite glass and a silver decanter;

the raiders had not found absolutely everything. Rullus had remarked that he would sell the pieces when he found a buyer who could pay what they were worth. "My son and son-in-law were both killed," he added stoically. "Their wives and children have more need of money than of heirlooms."

A handsome graybeard with a scholarly manner of speech, he reminded Gratillonius of Apuleius, or of Ausonius. (Christ have mercy, how many years was it since Gratillonius met the poet?) Breath puffed white in the gloom as he said, "This is a poor welcome for you."

"Who can offer more than the best he has?" replied Gratillonius. It had been a saying of his father's.

"Well, you of all men must realize what it means to come down in the world. It was rather different for us, of course. This city flourished when I was a boy. But trade shriveled year by year—revived for a while, then Ys fell—and so our catastrophe has cost humanity less than yours."

"Do you think you can rebuild?"

"Not as it was. Under certain unlikely conditions, we could resurrect something. But only Our Lord had power to bring Lazarus entirely back to life."

"What do you need?"

"Basically, a measure of assurance that it won't be for nothing. Thus, a defense we can rely on."

"That's what I've come about."

Rullus studied the shadows and highlights of his guest's face. "I thought so. One hears, shall we say, rumors."

"They may have been misleading. I do not propose breaking laws." The hell I don't, Gratillonius thought. The risk be damned. We've got to take it. Gesocribate be my witness. "Men of the city and its environs can be taught to defend themselves until . . . military reinforcements arrive."

Rullus lifted his brows. "Suppose they don't."

"Well, given a proper understanding between you people and the rest of us, we can jointly set up a line of communications—beacons, runners—so men from farther inland can arrive in time to help."

"In a strictly civilian capacity, of course."

"Of course." Gratillonius's tone was equally dry.

Rullus sighed. "A beautiful fantasy."

"It's become real."

"I know. The deadly surprise the Scoti got at the Gobaean Promontory. Other incidents subsequently." Rullus shook his head. "But you see, Gesocribate can't meet the conditions. You presuppose a viable city, worth saving, able to take a share in the common defense."

"It can be built. Meanwhile, for the sake of the future, we'll mount guard over it. You can have a going concern again in a year or two, I'd guess. I can find some of the necessary manpower for you."

Rullus lifted a finger. "Ah, but the defense you are thinking of will be insufficient."

"I tell you, we can hold off the barbarians."

"I mean the tax collector." Rullus's voice became bleak. "There is no prospect of remission, merely because we've had a disaster. The government is insensately desperate for resources, like a starving man who eats the seed corn. When payment falls due next year, I shall be wiped out, together with every so-called free man down to the lowliest fisher."

"Appeal to Arelate. If need be, to Rome—Ravenna. I can help. I've gotten a few influential associates."

Rullus remained skeptical. "I fear the chance of success is negligible. And imagining we do get a little leniency, why should we rebuild? As soon as we have anything again, we'll be wrung dry of it. Better to seek some great landholder's protection. Not that I'd make a serf he'd want; but the monks at Turonum may take me in. . . . No matter. These are not times when we should pity the aged. It's the young we must weep for."

"Hold on!" exclaimed Gratillonius. "I've considered this too. If nothing else works, well, Confluentes can spare Gesocribate enough out of its treasury to keep you afloat till you're back on your feet." And what would Ausonius have thought of that figure of speech? flickered through him.

Rullus was silent a minute before he said slowly, "This—is a rather overwhelming charitableness."

Gratillonius smiled. "We have our selfish reasons. Armorica, which includes Confluentes, needs your port. It's been a main link with Britannia."

389

"Would that be of any use any more?" asked Rullus, puzzled.

"What do you mean? Of course it would. Trade, mutual defense—"

"You haven't heard?"

Dread struck deep, as if the cold around had turned into a single knife. "I've been . . . on the road a spell. Tribal chiefs to see along the way."

"Ah." Rullus nodded. "We got the news three days ago, from yet another boatload of people hoping for a better life in Armorica. The pirates have gone home or into winter quarters, and—These waifs put in here because they knew it was the nearest safe anchorage, if no longer a real harbor."

"Hercules, man! Don't torture me. What'd they have to tell?"

"I'm sorry. It's so painful. The legions in Britannia, what's left of them, have risen. They've deposed the diocesan government and proclaimed a man of theirs, one Marcus, Emperor."

"Marcus," Gratillonius whispered. In that stunned moment he could only think: *The name of my father, the name of my son.*

"So the immigrants may discover they were unwise," Rullus continued. "When Marcus crosses over to Gallia, we'll have a new civil war."

4

As the year spun down to solstice, cold deepened. The Odita and Stegir lay frozen between banks where the snow glittered rock-hard. Icicles hung from naked boughs, eaves, battlements, like spears turned downward. When a man had been outdoors a while, his mustache was rimed. Skies were cloudless, the sun a wan disc briefly seen low in the south, the nights bitterly brilliant. The occasional traveler from the east related that it was thus over the whole breadth of northern Gallia, and beyond.

After the meager harvest, midwinter festivities were lean.

In Confluentes and its region they had, though, a hectic exuberance, as bright and loud and dancing as the bonfires lit to call the sun back home. Folk had outlived that spring, summer, autumn. They had enough to see them through the winter if they husbanded it. The Saxons had steered wide of them and ought not to be a danger again till after the thaws. They and those they loved could draw into their snug little dens and be at ease, at peace.

Gratillonius and his family had moved back to the house in Aquilo, and meant to abide there till about equinox. It had a hypocaust, whereas they feared what their own place, ill heated by open fires, might do to Marcus, *their* Marcus. Rovinda and Salomon received them happily. They had a bedroom to themselves; the child slept with his nurse.

One evening about a score of days after the solstice, father and son were romping as usual, until Verania said, also as usual, that that was ample ride-horsey and a certain young man was much overdue for his rest. Gratillonius went along and sang over the crib, which had become another of his customs. This time it was the three or four decent stanzas in an old legionary marching song. He had explained that all too soon small children developed a sense for music and, like their elders, requested him to stop.

He returned laughing to the atrium. "That boy's going to be a great cavalryman!" he said. "Did you see how he sits? Might almost have grown out of my back. Any time, now, I expect he'll reach down and make reins of my ears."

Verania smiled at him from the stool where she sat embroidering. A five-branched brass candelabrum, on a table beside her, gave adequate light. Tapers elsewhere keep the rest of the room bright and brought out the soft hues of its murals. The household could afford clean-burning wax; this area was rich in honeybees. The light caressed her as Jupiter had caressed Danaë, golden in hair and on cheeks and along the slight fullness that had begun proclaiming to the world that she was with child anew. The air was warm, but because he liked it she had had a small amount of charcoal kindled in a brazier and laid a pine cone there. Its smoke was like vanished summers.

Rovinda was the sole other person present, seated nearby with distaff and spindle. Apuleius had taught that work with the hands beseemed patricians—Ulysses, Cincinnatus, not to mention the Saviour—though he himself was manually awkward. Salomon was out carousing. At his age you couldn't be forever serious, and he never let it get the better of him. The slaves had been dismissed for the night.

Trouble touched the older woman's face. She was, still, often hard put to maintain serenity. "Must he become a soldier?" she asked mutedly.

"Oh, perhaps a merchant or landholder," Verania said.

Gratillonius didn't feel like sitting down yet. He stood before them, several feet off so they needn't crane their necks up, folded his arms, and replied, "I'm afraid he'll have to know his weapons whatever he becomes."

"Not if it's a churchman," Rovinda pointed out. She sounded wistful. Since her husband's death she had turned extremely pious, as if to make amends for past religious lapses and earn hope of rejoining him in Paradise.

The idea quenched Gratillonius's already dampened mirth. Nothing really wrong with the clergy, no, no; in fact, Corentinus was a fine fellow, and Martinus had been admirable in his odd fashion; an able man could rise to bishop, even Pope, and make his mark on history; nevertheless, his first-born son—

Verania read the distaste on him and told her mother, "No, I don't think that's in Marcus's blood. He's such a lively little scamp. Maybe our next will be more the sort."

"Then the future is his," Rovinda said.

"M-m, it could as well be a girl, you know."

"And as welcome," said Gratillonius. He wanted strong sons, but a couple of new Veranias would certainly lend sparkle to his days. She cast him a fond look, which he sent back.

Rovinda's spindle twirled to a stop. She stared away, as if through the wall into the darkness outside. "God forgive me, I almost hope not," she murmured. "Women are too weak."

"I wouldn't say that," Verania answered. "Each time we go in childbed, we do battle."

Across the years, his Queens and their daughters in Ys rose before Gratillonius; and Julia; and Nemeta, Nemeta. How fared Nemeta this cruel night?

"We haven't the strength to wield swords nor the right to be priests," Rovinda said.

Gratillonius cleared his throat. "Any girl of ours will marry a man who can protect her," he declared loudly.

Verania smiled. "I did."

Gratillonius felt soothed. "I try."

That quick fierceness which she mostly kept asleep flashed through Verania. "We'll hold what is ours."

"God has been good to us," Rovinda said, "but by the same token, we have much to lose. Be not proud. In Heaven alone is sureness."

Gratillonius could not let that go by. "Therefore, here on earth we need cavalrymen."

Rovinda shook her graying head. "If only we didn't. These are terrible times we live in."

Verania turned grave. "The hour between dog and wolf," she said low.

"What?" asked Gratillonius. Recollection came; it was a Gallic phrase for the twilight. "Oh. Right. They are wolves, the barbarians, two-legged wolves. I could have put it that what we need is watchdogs. Hounds for hunting, too."

"It isn't that simple, dear," Verania told him with her father's earnestness and love of discourse.

"Why not?" He spread his hands. "Look, I don't want to spoil the evening. We've gotten way too serious all of a sudden. But I've seen the work of the barbarians, and the single thing to do with them is kill them, hunt them down, till the last few skulk back to the wilderness that bred them. Stilicho thought he could tame them. I pray he's finally learned better, because Mother Rome has!"

"They are human beings," Verania argued. Not for the first time, it crossed his mind how bored he would be with a wife who never did. "Each king of theirs is a hero to his people. He surely thinks of himself as responsible for their well-being, their lives."

"Ha! He thinks of his own glory and how much he can rob."

Verania took her man aback: "Are civilized rulers different? In any event, our ancestors were wild Celts. Or Homer's Achaeans—how did the Trojans see them?"

"Are you telling me we're all the same?"

"We are all of us sinners," Rovinda said.

393

"No, there is a difference, a very real difference," Verania granted. "But it's not in the blood. It is—hard to put into words. I tried, four years ago when you went off to war against the Scoti, and in the end found I'd only made a verse."

"Let's hear it," Gratillonius said, interested.

A certain shyness brought Verania's lashes fluttering downward. "Oh, it's nothing. Just a few lines. You see, I was trying to understand *why* you were out there, you, the one I loved, setting your life at stake."

"Let's hear it," Gratillonius repeated. "Please."

"Well, it's—If you insist. Let me think. . . . *Would you know the dog from the wolf? You—*"

A banging resounded. "Hold," Gratillonius said. "Somebody at our knocker." He strode across the room to the entry and the front door. Unease prickled his skin. Who could this be? It wasn't barred till the last person went to bed. If Salomon for some reason came home earlier, he'd simply walk in. If later, as was likely, he'd thunder the porter awake, unless it was when the house was again astir before dawn. The aged slave was yawning and creaking out of the alcove where he slept.

Gratillonius opened the door. Keen air flowed in across him. A full moon had cleared rooftops and made the snow on them gleam, more radiance than what trickled into the entry from the atrium. A man wearing breeches, boots, heavy tunic, cowled cloak stood in the portico. He was short, with bow legs bespeaking a life on horseback. "Imperial courier," he said wearily. "I have a dispatch for the tribune Gratillonius. They told me at the hostel he's here."

"Come in," Gratillonius invited, and led the way back to the atrium. The porter closed the door behind them. "I am the tribune. You've ridden hard."

"We all did, sir. Epona be thanked for the clear nights. I understand this message is from the frontier."

It would have gone first to Turonum, while other copies were galloped in relays to Arelate, Ravenna, wherever they must get the bad news as fast as possible. It could only be bad news. At Turonum, more copies were made and directed to regional authorities. It could only be bad news that concerned all Armorica, urgently.

"Can you get this man something hot to drink, or at least

a cup of wine?" Gratillonius asked the women. They had risen and stood stricken, waiting. "Let's have the letter, fellow."

He brought it to the candelabrum where Verania had been embroidering, untied it, and read. Considering distances and road conditions, he decided that the information was about ten days old.

A horde of barbarians had crossed the ice on the Rhenus, uncounted thousands of them. It was as though entire Germanic nations were on the move together; scouts had certainly recognized the standards of Alamanni, Suevi, Vandals, Burgundians, with Alani whose fathers had migrated from Scythian reaches where now prowled the Huns. Moguntiacum had fallen to them almost at once, stood plundered and ablaze, while their tide rolled unstoppable, strewing to their death-Gods any feeble opposition that it met, over the snow into the lands of Rome.

Gratillonius stood a long while unmoving. His silence spread outward from him till it brimmed the house. Deep within it he thought—scarcely felt; no shock or horror; those could cry out in him later but at this moment he was entirely watchfulness and thought. The thing that was happening was foreordained, not by God or the stars but by the blindness of men, since he lay in his mother's womb. His response to it was equally ineluctable.

"We must call up the brotherhoods," he said.

XXI

1

Augusta Treverorum, the splendor of the Roman North, seethed with looters, murderers, rapists, like a corpse with maggots. That news reached Confluentes as Gratillonius was about to ride forth. It redoubled the urgency with which he and his companions hastened to Vorgium.

There, near the middle of the Armorican peninsula, the leaders met. They were poorly housed and ill fed. The city had dwindled to an impoverished village amidst the wreckage that repeated sacks a generation or more ago had left. It was needful to clear from the council chamber of the basilica those people who slept there. Straw from their pallets littered the floor, smoke from their fires blackened walls and ceiling. Windows were rudely boarded up, choking the space with gloom as well as rime-frosting chill. Handy men among the delegates got pine torches started, lashed to improvised holders. Fixed stone benches provided seating, if you didn't mind dirt and a numb butt.

Corentinus and Gratillonius mounted the dais. While the bishop gave an invocation, Gratillonius's gaze probed the uneasy murk. They were a mixed fifty-odd who confronted him, city dwellers with cloaks drawn tight around riding garb, tribal headmen in thick woolen tunics with breeches or kilts, wilder-looking backwoodsmen wearing mostly leather and pelts, farmers, herders, fishers, artisans—and in the front row, pipe-clayed white and purple-bordered, the archaic senatorial toga in which Flavius Vortivir had arrayed himself. Eyeballs glistened, breath sounded harsh in the echoful emptiness. Memory of the Council of Suffetes in Ys was suddenly almost unbearable.

He forced it from him and trod forward as Corentinus finished and stood aside. Raising his right arm, he said: "Greeting. We know why we are here," at this place, which he had chosen partly for its location and partly for its reminding ruins. "It was short notice, and I thank you for arriving within the days I allowed you. Now let's waste no further time. If nothing else, the inhabitants need their room back by nightfall."

Corentinus rendered it into Gallic for such as had little or no Latin. The dialects of Armorica were mutually comprehensible.

Vortivir signalled for attention and Gratillonius acknowledged him. "Nevertheless, it is necessary to spell things out," said the tribune of Venetorum. "We are no gaggle of tribesmen, to go honking off at the first noise we hear." Several Gauls showed offense, and Corentinus gave a translation more tactful. Vortivir, who knew both languages, registered displeasure of his own. Gratillonius frowned at him, but needed him too much to reply with other than:

"Please state your meaning, sir. Maybe we'd better thresh this out between us, and then the bishop can render the gist of it."

"Undeniably," said Vortivir in measured tones, "we face a terrible threat. By all accounts, this irruption is the largest and worst yet visited on Gallia. However, it is still a good three hundred leagues from here."

"Less from the edge of Armorica," interrupted the old mariner Bomatin Kusuri, who spoke for the Ysans. "And moving west."

"We have our garrisons and their local reservists," Vortivir answered.

Gratillonius could not entirely hold back the bitterness: "We know what those are worth. Look around you. Vorgium was once the first city in Armorica."

"After Ys," said Bomatin in his mustache.

The veteran Drusus gestured, got the nod, and added: "Or think of the cities that fell this month. They had their garrisons and reserves, with catapults on high walls to boot."

"If we stay as we are, the barbarians will devour us piecemeal," Gratillonius said.

Vortivir: "You want to assemble those irregular guard units—'societies,' 'confraternities,' 'sport and exercise clubs' —that you've gotten formed, and try to hold the line."

Gratillonius shook his head. "No, sir. We have to be mobile. We can't maintain an army" (there, he thought, I've said it) "like that for more than ten or fifteen days. We lack the organization. Every man will have to bring his own rations and bedroll and whatever else he'll need. If we let him forage, our force will be just a gang of bandits. You and I and others like us can do something about extra supplies, baggage animals, maybe a few wagons— surgeons—a commissariat of sorts that can *pay* for what food and stuff we requisition—such things, if we're lucky; but it'll be strictly limited.

"No use waiting in a stronghold till we starve. The barbarians could easily bypass us. The brothers will know this. They aren't stupid; they can figure it out for themselves. They won't come in the first place. Better stay home, prepared to flee with their families. I would myself.

"No, we have got to show that the force will be effective."

Vortivir: "Also, since your army's action, its very existence, will be illegal, it must do whatever it does quickly and disband, melt back into the general population, before the government sends troops against it."

Gratillonius nodded at Corentinus. This appeared a strategic moment for a summary. The bishop's was concise.

Bannon, headman of Dochaldun, lifted a fist. "That shows you what Rome is worth!" he roared in Osismiic.

Doranius, a young man from Gesocribate who represented aged Rullus, spoke in Latin: "That is what we pay our taxes for."

Gratillonius: "Wait, wait. I'll have nothing to do with rebellion. Bad enough, what's going on in Britannia."

Vortivir: "You are already in rebellion, sir. I am merely calling the fact to everyone's attention. Let us clearly understand what it is we propose to do before we go ahead with it. Otherwise we'll reap panic and disaster."

Doranius: "What is it, then? We meet somewhere—oh, Gesocribate still has a few hale men—and march against the horde? Is that really your intent, Gratillonius? We'll be annihilated."

Vindolenus, former Bacauda, who knew Latin: "We'll take plenty of them along to serve us in hell."

Bannon, who had gotten the drift: "We'd never get that far before we ran out of food and starved. Not that the lads would go much beyond Armorica. They want to defend their homes, not a lot of fat Romans." A growl of assent went among the native chieftains.

Gratillonius: "Hold on. Of course I know our limitations. I don't imagine we can mount an expedition. But remember, those Germani aren't a single army like a Roman force. They can't be; not their nature. They're a swarm of war bands, each following one of several score, maybe two or three hundred, lords. I'll bet fights break out every day between groups, and men get killed, and this brings on more fights. The Germani must be dispersed and their coordination ramshackle. Some are surely going to feel squeezed out by others more powerful, and scatter west to pick up what they can. A part of them, traveling fast, going by cities they haven't the manpower

398

to take, could get as far as Armorica. That wouldn't be a full-scale invasion of us, no. But it'd leave desolation where it came, and might well give the rest the idea of ravaging their way in the same direction.

"My hope is that if we—taking advantage of scouts, couriers, beacons—if we find such a band or two, we'll cut them up. If we don't meet any, well, then we haven't lost much except our time, and have gained experience I believe will be invaluable in future. If we do, if we encounter Germani and win, word will get back east. It may decide those kings, in their gravelly little brains, to sheer off from the far West. They'll see it would be costly; it'd give the Romans added time to mobilize against them; they could find themselves boxed in this peninsula; and Armorica is poor country compared to the South."

Doranius: "Especially after what barbarians have already done to it, in this past century."

Bomatin: "Thanks to Rome, that was supposed to protect it."

Gratillonius: "I said no seditious talk! By Hercules, the next man speaks any such word, I'll gag him with his own teeth."

Corentinus: "Peace, brothers. In God's name, don't go off on side paths."

Vortivir: "Yet you, Gratillonius, are the one who called this meeting—who begot the brotherhoods themselves."

Gratillonius: "Of necessity." It began so gradually, when I was King of Ys. I didn't really see what was happening or where it was headed. Do I now? "Later I'll put our case before Stilicho—before the Emperor." He had reached the resolve on his winter journey here: "He can behead me if he will."

Vortivir: "Oh, no. We need you far too much, my friend."

Corentinus: "It is God's ship you steer. You may not take your hand from the helm." Into the rising hubbub, he again reported in Gallic.

Uproar followed. I am committed, Gratillonius thought. There's no way back. But where is it we're bound?

Corentinus got the turmoil quieted. Then Vortivir's voice carried sharp: "I spoke as I did because we must consider

399

the aftermath before we act. I was not speaking against the action itself. It has my full endorsement."

Drusus: "And we won't all be rank amateurs, sir. I know a good many reservists will join us, once they see what we're up to."

Vortivir: "I have been looking into that myself. Most of mine will."

More cries rang out.

"Quiet!" ordered Gratillonius. "Very well, the senator has made an excellent point and we must reach a decision about it. First, though, we have to talk war."

2

Skies hung heavy, low above old snow and skeleton trees, a world of grays and whites. The hues men brought into it were dulled; banners hung listless in the cold.

"Will they never come?" Salomon fretted. "We could freeze to death, waiting like this."

"Most of a soldier's life goes in waiting," Gratillonius told him.

They sat their horses before such other men as rode this day, on the crest of a long hill. It dropped ahead of them into a broad trough between it and another ridge. A dirt road ran through, over one, down into the dell, up the next, and beyond. On their left was a wood, tangled second growth on abandoned farmland. From where the hill slanted downward in that direction, across the road, and onward to the right, the country opened up, except for hurdles and rail fences. In the distance that way, a village squatted under its thatch. No smoke rose; the people had fled, driving livestock along. This was the ground Gratillonius had chosen for his battle.

Scouts had brought news of the enemy; skirmishers had gone forth to draw him; now it was to wait. Not to hope, unless you were young like Salomon, nor to fear: only to wait, composing your soul because that helped conserve your strength.

Gratillonius sighed, with a rueful smile. "What is it,

sir?" asked Salomon. Since first they fared off, he had set intimacy aside and striven to be military.

"Nothing. A stray thought." A remembrance that he, Gratillonius, approached the half-century mark. It seldom entered his awareness. He still had most of his teeth and the skill in his hands. Speed and wind weren't what they had been, but they were there and sufficient when he called on them, and the mail coat rested lightly. While things extremely close got blurred, his vision was otherwise keen. Even in this weather, he suffered no aches or coughs. But—Verania had contracted for a long widowhood. It might begin today.

Favonius snorted and stamped. "Easy, boy." Gratillonius reached past the dear coarseness of the mane to stroke the warm neck.

Presently he'd learn how well the stallion did in combat. They had practiced together, as had the men and horses at their back, but it was unschooled and restricted. A real cavalry mount required raising to it from colthood. Likewise did its rider. The best that might be awaited of these was that they wouldn't balk or bolt—most of them.

In front, about halfway down the hill, were the foot, the vast majority, about three thousand, as motley as their captains. The line, four deep, was rough. Men shifted position, hunkered down, trotted in place to keep warm, talked, altogether unsoldierly. The best outfitted had a cap and breastplate of boiled leather. In rare cases, pieces of iron had been sewn to especially vulnerable spots. Many had nothing but the clothes of workaday life, greasy and stenchful after these past days, with perhaps a wooden shield. However, axes and spears were bright, as would be blades when unsheathed. Bows and slings rested ready.

And those troops were better organized than they looked, not as a single army but as brotherhoods of neighbors, each man known to his comrades and his leader. They had come from their widely scattered homes to rendezvous a little east of Condate Redonum in orderly wise and with various answers to the problem of provisions—parched or smoked food, mules, noncombatant bearers, light carts, or whatever. A few units, arriving belatedly, had quickened their steps and caught up with the rest. The standards were of every size, shape, and material, but each bore an emblem that meant much, embroidered tree or fish or horse or Cross or the like, unless it was a bundle of evergreen boughs or a pair of aurochs horns on a pole. . . . The local reservists who had joined them should help provide stiffness.

A block of men stood separately on the far right at the bottom of the hill. They were those Gratillonius deemed his best, Drusus and whatever other of Maximus's veterans were able to campaign, the Ysan marines, the much larger number of younger fighters trained by these, and a band of Frankish laeti from Redonum who had gotten wind of the enterprise and, astoundingly, showed up to join. Well, if they could lay old grudges aside in the face of a common danger, Gratillonius could too. He didn't have to like them.

Hidden in the woods on the left were the foresters Rufinus had shaped into a force. (God, how he missed Rufinus, and Maeloch, and Amreth, and more and more gone down before him into the dark!) Also hidden, by the bulk of the hill, were the supplies, wagons, animals, traces of encampment. He hadn't left a guard there. He didn't expect the barbarians would flank him and take possession. If they did, small difference. The army had pretty well used up its rations, and could not keep the field more than a few days past this. At that, the trek home would be a hungry one.

Gratillonius and those who met with him in Vorgium had given themselves a month prior to rendezvous. He reckoned it would take any invaders longer than that to reach Armorica. They'd have a lot of miles to cross, pillaging as they went, maybe once in a while overrunning some pathetic attempt at resistance while bypassing any real strongpoints—whose garrisons wouldn't dare try taking them in the rear. Since the time available to his troops would be short, they shouldn't start off until the earliest date at which it was reasonable to look for an incursion. Besides, a month gave opportunity to accumulate additional stuff, get together a small baggage train, recruit a few physicians and such.

Of course, it also gave opportunity for Glabrio to learn

what was going on and take measures. You had to keep things as quiet as possible, and nevertheless rumors were bound to reach Turonum. Inquiries went off to him. He stalled them. It helped that governor and Duke had other worries to occupy them. In Britannia the legions had cast down the Marcus they raised, killed him, and proclaimed one Gratianus Emperor. Ill-omened name, that. . . .

Then the hour came when Gratillonius sent forth his summons, and after that it was too late for anybody to stop anything.

Horns lowed, shouts ripped, faint across distance but growing. On the crest of the opposite hill, men appeared. A kind of sigh went through the Armoricans. Here came the battle.

The die is cast, Caesar said. Gratillonius knew that for him it had been cast earlier—but when? At the departure from Redonum, an open and irreparable breach of Imperial law; at the meeting in Vorgium, when the decision was made; at the moment in Confluentes when he resolved to call that meeting; or earlier, out on the Gobaean Promontory, or far back when he reigned in Ys, or when he marched off at the behest of Maximus, or—No matter. He had these Germani to deal with, and later those Romans.

He'd hoped more than he'd feared that there would be no action after all. The men grumbled at tramping about in winter between comfortless bivouacs, but they'd have returned home alive. Bacca might thereupon have agreed, and gotten Glabrio and the Duke to agree, that this episode was best smoothed over, that it could actually prove useful toward convincing the Armoricans of their folly. There would be no way to overlook an armed engagement, not small and off at the end of the peninsula, but major and in the heart of Lugdunensis Tertia.

Well, Gratillonius thought, I've been spared the worst horror, that we went back and *then* the barbarians arrived.

His skirmishers were running down to the bottomland. They'd taken bad losses, he saw, and now fled helter-skelter; but they'd done their job.

"Shall I go?" cried Salomon. His mount sensed his impatience and whinnied. That made Favonius curvet.

"No, I told you I want you here with me where you can

403

see what's happening," Gratillonius snapped. "You may learn something. You owe that to the men you'll lead."

"Sir." The tone, half mutinous, became a gasp and a shout: "There they are!"

The Germani poured over the crest. They weren't dashing, but went along at a steady, mile-eating wolf-lope which would in the end have overtaken their quarry. When those in front saw what awaited them across the dell, they checked for an instant, and the surge flowed back through them as it does through a breaker striking a reef. Horns winded, yells lifted, spears tossed in the air like stalks in a storm. Yet they must have known that those men who harassed them came from some larger company; and however that might be, their hearts were always battle-ready.

"If they stop and hold their hill, we're in trouble," Gratillonius told Salomon. "A charge is about the hardest thing in war even for seasoned troops. But I don't expect—Ah, no, they're moving again."

In a spindrift of roars and howls, the wave rolled on. They were mostly big, fair men with long mustaches and braided hair. Many wore coats of mail, many more at least had iron helmets. Some in the van had been on shaggy little horses—the riders' feet nearly touched the ground—but sprang off and let their mounts go or turned them over to boys who'd run alongside. Only the Goths among Germani were cavalrymen.

"Pay attention," Gratillonius instructed. "That advance isn't as pell-mell as it looks. They train from childhood. Notice the standards," as varied as the Armorican. "See how they're spaced. See how the whole is shaping into a kind of wedge as it proceeds. The usual Germanic formation. They can't coordinate themselves any better than that, though." Not that he had much personal experience with this race; but he had learned from men such as Drusus, who did.

Salomon leaned forward in the saddle as if straining toward the dark mass. "How many are they?" he wondered. "Countless. I feel the ground shake under them."

"A common bit of imagination. As for their number, m-m, I make it about two thousand, possibly a bit more.

We have the advantage there. It may or may not outweigh armor and practice. Don't underestimate their leadership. That petty king—I suppose that's what he is—had to have a certain amount of shrewdness as well as boldness, and a firm hold on his followers, to get this far."

An ambitious fellow, no doubt, who struck off to scoop up the easy cream ahead of the rest. Somewhere he'd call halt, establish a base, stake out as large a territory as he thought he could hold against the Romans and the later-arriving Germani. Likeliest he did not intend to settle down there. It was for the widest and most thorough spoliation, the utter ruining of the land round about, before he moved on.

Behind his warriors would be stolen animals—horses and mules, no cumbersome wagons—laden with plunder and maybe with food. The food would be particularly welcome, supposing the Armoricans won.

"Take your shield, Salomon. Up across your face; look over the top. They're getting into arrow range."

A command rapped. With a monstrous whistle, Gratillonius's archers loosed their volley. And their next, and their next. On higher ground slings whipped and spat.

Attacking, the barbarians could but slightly reply in kind. Some missiles flew from the sides of their wedge. Gratillonius saw a couple of his men drop. Neither was killed, both were taken off, their comrades stood firm. Good; the first river had been waded. The others that must be crossed would be in furious spate. But quite a few Germani fell, and were trampled under onrushing feet.

"Hold steady," Gratillonius ordered Salomon. "Control your mount. Stay calm. Watch close, and *think* about it."

He signalled. That evoked more commands. Pikemen lowered their weapons.

The enemy struck.

Thunder and earthquake erupted. The Germanic host turned into a roil of creatures that snarled, yelped, struggled to get at the defenders, got there, smote, died, sank under those behind. Four deep, the Armorican line held firm. When one of its front rankers went down, the man at his back took his place. Swords, axes, knives, spears, clubs hewed, sliced, thrust, hammered. Shield thumped against

405

shield, weight strained against weight. A man stared into the eyes of a stranger and strove to kill him. It was as though a mist of blood and sweat blurred the hillside.

If the enemy broke through, that was the end. Make him commit himself beyond retreat; yet watch for the time when your own line began to waver and buckle. It would. These were not lifetime fighters, they were simply men defending their hearths. Gauge the right moment—

Gratillonius turned to a lad on a pony. "Go tell them to come out of the woods," he said. The boy sketched a salute and trotted off, wide of the combat.

Gratillonius bit back terror and said calmly to Salomon, no louder than needful to carry through the hell's clatter and clamor below: "All right, son, be on your way. But do not attack till you hear the trumpet. Understand? When you hear the trumpet." He clapped the young shoulder. "God be with you."

"And you, Gradlon." There was no solemnity in Salomon's response. Eagerness flamed. He spurred his horse and cantered off to the right and downhill. Beside him rode his standard bearer, carrying on a pole the insigne Rovinda and Verania had made for him: upon blue silk, a golden A, for Aquilo and Apuleius and a new beginning.

Salomon's cloak fluttered red from his mail. On his helmet tossed a white plume. The shield in his left hand was blue, a gold Cross upon it. Like Favonius and the few other horses meant for combat, his bore chamfron and pectoral of leather. A youthful God he might have been, Apollo's lyre singing him onward. But, oh, Christ, how easily made into a twisted, gaping, discolored corpse!

The danger had to be. He would have it so himself. His need was to learn warfare, leadership, and to gain a name that kindled fire in men. It was the need of his people.

The Armorican line had gone ragged, in places seemingly melted together with the foe, in places only a single man deep. Reserves came down from the rear, but those were the untrained, the unstrong, doomed if they were in action very long, unless they panicked and thereby dissolved their whole army.

Salomon joined the veterans in the plowland on the right. Their square had sent assaults reeling back. At the feet of those soldiers dead men sprawled and the snow thawed red, smoky from blood-heat. They had resisted the temptation to pursue and held fast as ordered. The barbarians gave up on them for the time being and pressed wholly forward, except for a contingent that glowered watchful some yards distant. The newcome riders and banner now gleamed above their heads.

Out of the woods sped the foresters, old Bacaudae, their elder sons, hunters, trappers, loggers, charcoal burners, solitaries. At their front, brightly armored, trotted Cadoc. They formed a wedge of their own and pierced the Germanic one in flank and rear. Men mingled, a whirlpool of slaughter that chewed its way inward.

"Sound the charge," Gratillonius told his trumpeter. The brazen call slashed through voices, thuds, clash, dunting of horns. Salomon and his standard bearer led the soldiers against the barbarian left. Briefly, faintly, there came to Gratillonius their shout, "Salaun, Salaun!" It was the Gallic softening of their new leader's name.

War receded from the hill, not at once but in waves, eddies, retreats, rallies, retreats, vast hollow roars, like ebb tide in the bay of Ys. Man by man the Germani grew aware of the onslaughts and went confusedly to meet them. The Armorican infantry stood, or flung themselves to the ground, behind windrows of killed and wounded. They gasped for air. That sound was lost in the noises from the hurt.

Gratillonius clucked to Favonius. To and fro he rode along the line. "Good lads," he called in their language, "brave lads, it's grandly you've done. A last great push, now, and we'll take them, we'll have them and reap them. In Christ's name, by Lug and Epona and Cernunnos and Hercules, we go!"

And finally, when he had them marshalled and a direction chosen, he went to the van with his fellow riders. His standard bearer lifted his banner. It was Verania's work, black on gold with a red border. At first he had wanted an eagle, Rome's bird, but they decided that was impolitic and he bore a wolf, the She-Wolf who nurtured the founder of the City.

He drew sword, raised it, brought it down, and touched

407

spurs to sides, most gently. Favonius trotted, cantered, drummed in gallop. The other horsemen came on his right and left. A few had made modern lances and taught themselves the use, but most wielded blades. It would take long for Armorica to breed cataphracts. These were a handful, mere captains and symbols and terrifying sight; but at their backs the men of Armorica paced down to battle.

They struck.

After that everything was chaos, riot, no more plans, no more formations, man against man, a blow taken, a blow given, then somebody else there, slash, guard, stab, keep your saddle or lose it, keep your feet or die. Gratillonius stayed mounted. Favonius did not go runaway like some, but he went mad, screaming, lashing with hoofs, slashing with teeth, havoc made flesh. Gratillonius kept him well clear of friends. Foes were plentiful enough.

And then they weren't. They were slain or crippled or broken apart. Survivors dashed singly over the field in chase of their lives. A few formed into desperate little knots. The Armorican archers and slingers collected missiles off the bloodied snow and butchered them at leisure. Armorican foot and horse bayed in pursuit of the fleeing, caught them, chopped them down, glared round and went after the next nearest. The corpses were many before the hunters quit, exhausted, and turned back.

From a rough count, Gratillonius estimated later that perhaps a hundred Germani won free. Scattered as they were amidst a revengeful populace, most would surely die. Knives, wood axes, pruning hooks, sickles, flails, cudgels, flung stones were peasant weapons, and town garrisons would sally forth in search of any stragglers reported. A very few would bring to the horde the tale of what they had met in the West.

3

Twilight deepened fast. The world had fallen quiet. Germanic wounded had been silenced and left with the already slain for the crows. Armorican wounded had been cared for as well as might be and rested, slept, or sank into stupors from which they would not awaken. Words mumbled and flames crackled across spaces where the torn, drenched soil was freezing hard. Some brotherbands had collected firewood; others, less lucky or more weary, had merely settled down together. Now and then an abandoned dog howled on a farmstead. It sounded much like a wolf.

The dispersal was rotten military practice, but hardly any of the men were real soldiers, all were bone-tired, and nothing would attack them during the night. Guards stood posted around a shadowiness which was the gathered Armorican dead, awaiting burial in the morning before the living turned home.

Salomon, Cadoc, Drusus, and several more from their area sat around one fire. Bomatin Kusuri was missing; he lay in yonder ring of spears. Cadoc's left hand was wrapped, the little finger lost after his shield got knocked from his grasp, but it hadn't bled too badly and he remained alert in a glassy-eyed fashion. Salomon wore a dressing on his right forearm, over a minor cut—nothing worse, though he had ramped among the enemy till his mount was disabled and his standard bearer pierced, then taken to the ground and continued hewing while the banner swayed and fluttered in his grasp.

Exuberance left no room in him for fatigue. He gesticulated wildly. "I tell you, their baggage is cram full of gold and silver and gems!" he gloated. "Every man of ours can bring back a good year's pay, and we'll have a hoard left over for the public treasury."

"Think of those from whom it was robbed, in churches and storehouses and homes," Cadoc mumbled.

Salomon bit his lip, a brief gleam of teeth in the wavering ruddy light. "Oh, true, but done is done, we can't ever find the rightful owners if they're even alive, and this gives our men a share of the victory, solid in their hands."

"It'll help morale, sure," grunted Drusus. "What'll help more is the armor and weapons we collected. Next time we won't take near the casualties we did here."

Cadoc covered his face. "Christ have mercy, shall there

409

be a next time?" Quickly, he looked up. "Understand, I'll be there. What were our losses?"

Gratillonius trod out of the dusk. "I've been going the rounds getting information about that," he said. His voice was hoarse and without timbre. "About three hundred dead or seriously hurt." He sat down, crossed his legs, held his palms toward the fire. Like the rest, he wore leather breeches that wouldn't take up too much wet or cold before he rolled into his cloak for the night. "Bad. Under normal conditions, Pyrrhic. But no worse than I expected, frankly. And we gave so much better than we got that I don't think many among us have lost heart, if any have. Instead, most ought to have learned the lesson."

"What lesson, Gradlon?" asked Salomon. He and Verania were slipping into the Armorican usage for his name; it made a kind of endearment.

"The need for better organization, training, and discipline. We only prevailed today because we had some of that, together with terrain and other circumstances favorable for the tactics I picked. At the same time, our men have now been blooded, and taken it well, and that means a great deal. It works both ways, naturally. I, our officers, we've gotten a lot to mull over, about how to handle an army of this kind. And it'll be our responsibility to build the organization and do the teaching."

"We'll never build a legion, though," Drusus said.

"No." Gratillonius sighed. "The time for that is past. We don't live in the same world any more."

"I understand, sir. Just the same, it's too bad we can't hold—oh, not a triumph for you, I suppose, but at least a parade. Come home together, in formation, standards high, before the women and kids and everybody. That always did wonders for our spirits . . . in the old days."

Gratillonius smiled, a wolfish withdrawal of lips from teeth. "As a matter of fact, I mean to offer a fair-sized body of picked men exactly that chance to show themselves off. You're invited."

They stared. "What, sir?" asked Drusus.

"They'll follow me when I report to the authorities in Turonum."

410

No Roman could be sure why the barbarians did as they did. Perhaps they themselves did not know, perhaps they were more a natural force than a human thing, their impulses as blind as a storm.

They sacked Durocotorum and Samarobriva. That was as far west as the bulk of them got. From there they lumbered northeast, laying waste Nemetacum and Turnacum, with the hinterlands of those cities. That entire corner of Gallia was a desolation.

They had stripped and burnt it bare. It could no longer support them, nor anyone else. But why did they not bear southwest, till they found the rich valley of the Liger and raged down it to the sea? Had something that way given them pause?

Rome knew only that from Turnacum the horde moved almost due south toward Aquitania.

They were three who sat behind a long table in a room of the basilica: the Duke of the Armorican Tract, the governor of Lugdunensis Tertia, and his procurator. Gratillonius stood before them, alone. None desired witnesses to this meeting. That would have made impossible the saying of certain things.

The room was still for a while. Outside, the wind wuthered across brown fields and piped between city walls. Clouds scudded. Earth drank warmth from the sun, and snowdrops blossomed under newly budding willows.

Flaminius Murena, the Duke, cleared his throat. He was a large man, as Gallic in his blood as Gratillonius was Britannic, but from the darker tribes of the South. Like Bacca, he wore a robe. Glabrio affected a toga. Gratillonius was in his riding clothes.

"So," Murena said, "you raised your own army after all. Now you've come here with an armed force capable of overwhelming our garrison. Are you about to reach for the purple?"

"No, sir," Gratillonius replied levelly, "I am not."

Glabrio showed purple himself, on his jowls. "It isn't even a proper military unit," he fumed. "A rabble, a rabble in arms!"

Bacca's tone remained soft. "This is the most alarming prospect," he said. "Gratianus in Britannia could conceivably turn into another Constantinus. But you have raised the Bacaudae against Rome."

"I have not," Gratillonius said, "and my followers are nothing of the sort. They are decent, hard-working, ordinary folk who ask nothing except to be left in peace." Never mind what leather-clad woodsmen and shaggy tribesmen slouched about among those fighters who occupied the streets of Turonum and, without making it totally blatant, surrounded the basilica. "The Germani wouldn't give them that; and the Romans couldn't stop the Germani . . . by themselves." To Murena: "Sir, what we did was save this military district of yours for you."

"And what do you mean to do next?" the Duke demanded.

Gratillonius shrugged. "Go back to our everyday lives. Stand by to come to your side again whenever need be. No, I have no intention of rebelling. Let Gratianus cross over from Britannia and he'll have us to deal with."

Bacca stroked his chin. "Since you have such respect for the law and our Emperor," he purred, "it's curious how you kept his ministers waiting this long until you condescended to visit them."

Glabrio: "Outrageous. Repeated refusals to obey my summons. Unheard of."

Gratillonius: "My replies explained the reasons, over and over. First we had to go home, care for the injured, let our men pick their lives back up. Then it was time to start working the farms. It still is. I have my own, as well as everything that's had to be postponed in my tribuneship."

Glabrio: "Tribuneship! You arrive with that pack of bandits and dare call yourself an officer of the state?"

Gratillonius: "I did it for your sakes, sirs."

Glabrio: *"What?"*

Murena: "Easy, Glabrio. Say on, Gratillonius."

Gratillonius: "If anything untoward should happen to me, that would be unfortunate. It could well unleash the selfsame revolt you fear. I thought that bringing a bodyguard was a sensible precaution."

Bacca: "Against hotheads?"

Gratillonius: "I'm sure the procurator is not among them."

Bacca: "What do you propose?"

Gratillonius: "I told you, I'll go quietly home and take up my work and my public duties." Slowly: "But the men who saved Armorica—all of them, everywhere, serfs, reservists, everybody, they must have amnesty. No harm shall come to a single soul of them. Otherwise I can't answer for the consequences."

Bacca: "I daresay you'd quickly learn about any . . . incidents."

Gratillonius: *"They* will. The brotherhoods."

Murena: "You refuse to disband them, then?"

Gratillonius: "Sir, I couldn't. Men are flocking to join. Isn't the only sensible thing to allow this, encourage it, help improve it, and so keep it at the service of Rome?"

Murena: "Under you."

Gratillonius: "I offer my counsel."

Bacca: "You mean your good offices."

Glabrio: "Offices? Impossible! Absurd! Your commission was revoked the moment I learned of your deeds."

Gratillonius: "That's in the governor's power, but please remember that my petition is on its way to the Emperor. Not for myself, but for the people of Armorica, asking for a rescript granting us the right to defend ourselves. Meanwhile, if the governor chooses to replace me as tribune, I'll cooperate with the new man to the best of my ability."

Murena: "Ha! Glabrio, don't waste anybody on that nest of vipers."

Gratillonius: "If we have to govern ourselves in Aquilo and Confluentes, we will. We'll maintain law and order. The taxes will be paid on schedule."

Glabrio: "And when your petition is denied, when the order comes from Ravenna for your arrest and execution, what then?"

Gratillonius: "I'm not sure that it will, sir. Lord Stilicho may well advise his Imperial Majesty that what we have in Armorica is the foundation of a Roman fortress."

Bacca: "If he does that, then, bluntly put, he's a fool who can't see past the end of his Vandal snout. The precedent—"

Gratillonius: "Times change, sir."

Bacca: "And Stilicho . . . is given to improvising."

There was another silence. The wind blustered.

At length Murena asked, "Has anyone anything else to say?" Throttled fury trembled in the words.

"Just putting our agreement in plain language that none of us can forget or misunderstand," Gratillonius answered.

"Because it can't very well be recorded, can it? We must connive with you at gross illegality to avoid what is worse." The smile on Bacca's lips was a grimace as of a man in great pain. "You're right, times do change. A strong Emperor with some sense of statecraft—But let us get on with our distasteful business."

"Then I'll go home," said Gratillonius.

6

"**H**ail, Caesar!" boomed the deep young voices.

From the towertop where he stood, Constantinus saw widely over those domains that were his. The river sheened beneath soft heaven and brilliant sun. On its opposite bank reached the roofs of the civilian city, red tile, neat thatch, and beyond them a landscape of hills and vales grown vividly green, white where fruit trees and hawthorn blossomed, the breeze from it laden with odors of earth and flower. So had the springtime been five years ago, at Deva on the far side of Britannia, that day when he turned back the mighty barbarian Niall.

"Hail, Caesar!"

His gaze dropped between the walls of the fortress. So had they stood for centuries. Here had come the Emperor Hadrianus, who built the Wall; here had died the Emperors Severus and Constantinus; here the legions had proclaimed that man's son, another Constantinus, their Augustus, he who first conquered in the sign of Christ. This countryside had prospered peaceful throughout the wars that tore the Empire, lifetime after lifetime, because Eboracum abided as the home of the Sixth Victrix. Strange to think that he, Flavius Claudius Constantinus, would end its long watch.

"Hail, Caesar!"

The cry was antiquated. Caesar had come to mean simply the Imperial associate and heir apparent. The troops were making him supreme Augustus. They would march and sail and march at his beck to enforce it—or, if he failed to lead them, kill him and name another. Below, at the front of the armored men massed and shouting, the head of Gratianus gaped on a spear.

Constantinus lifted an arm. Across the shoulders of his own mail he had thrown a purple cloak. His brows bore a laurel wreath. Swords drawn, his elder son Constans stood proud on his right, his younger son Julianus on his left.

Stillness fell, till he heard the murmur of the breeze and a lark song on high. Faces and faces and faces stared upward. Sunlight gleamed on their eagles. Elsewhere in the world, horsemen had become lords of the battlefield. Only in Britannia did something remain of that unbreakable fighting machine which had carried the power of Rome from Caledonia to Egypt. Oh, the machine had corroded, he'd need plenty of cavalry himself, but the Sixth and Second, the Britannic infantry, set down in Gallic soil, would be the dragon's teeth from which his armies grew.

He filled his lungs. When he spoke, it rolled forth over the ranks. He'd learned how to do that, as common soldier, centurion, senior centurion. Thence he went to camp prefect, but that was a short service. Already the troops were ill pleased with Gratianus, who was doing nothing, like Marcus before him. Constantinus had known how to steer that discontent. . . .

"Hail, my legionaries! Great beyond all measure is this honor you have done me. Next after God, I thank you for it. Under Him, I will prove myself worthy of it.

415

"You are soldiers. I am a soldier, one among you. I too have marched and fought, endured rain and snow, hunger and weariness and the loss of dear comrades. I too have eaten bitterness as barbarians pillaged and burned along our shores, killed our men, ravished our women, dashed the brains of our little children out against walls that our forefathers raised. And Britannia is not alone in her wretchedness. Again and again, Goths break into the Southern lands, even into Italy. How long till Rome herself burns? And now the Germani spill across Gallia, right there over the narrow sea. And a weakling Emperor with a witling councillor lies idle.

"The time is overpast for action. Rome needs a strong man, a fighting man, an Emperor who sits less on the throne than in the saddle. If God will give us such leadership, we shall yet prevail. We will crush the heathen; but first we will crush the fools and traitors who let them in.

"This I promise you. I promise it by Christ Jesus, Our Lord and Saviour. I promise it by my great namesake Constantinus, whom your forebears hailed within this very stronghold, and who went forth to restore the Empire and establish the Faith. I promise it by my kinsman Magnus Maximus, who likewise went from here to redeem; he fell, but his spirit lives on, immortal. By my own soul and hope of salvation, I promise you victory!"

He paused for cheers.

7

The sun drew nigh to midsummer. This was a beautiful year, as if to atone for last. Croplands burgeoned, kine sleekened in lush pastures, forests teemed with game and rivers with fish. Armoricans kept watch over their coasts, but seaborne raiders were few and all were beaten off. It was as though Saxon and Scotian bided their time until a certain word should reach them. Meanwhile folk made ready for the solstice festival.

In a private room of the basilica in Turonum, Duke Murena stood before seated Governor Glabrio and Procurator Bacca. A letter was in his hand, hastily scrawled on a wooden slab. His phrases fell like stones. "That is the news."

Glabrio ran tongue over lips. His features hung tallow-white. "Nothing more?"

"Not yet," Murena said. "Weren't you listening? He was in the process of landing when this went off to me. I expect he'll guard every road out of Gesoriacum, take control of communications, while his Britons finish crossing and his Gallic allies gather."

"Which way will he move, then?" The question quavered.

"South, surely." Impatience edged Murena's heavy tones.

"Those Germani—"

"They're down that way, but more to the west. If I were Constantinus, I'd strike for Arelate. Of course, before venturing that far, he's got to consolidate his position in the North."

Bacca rose. "A new Constantinus, come from Britannia," he said low. "A new age?" Wonder transformed the sunken countenance.

"What shall we do?" Glabrio cried.

Morena shrugged. "Whatever seems advisable."

"Could we stay neutral?"

"That may prove inadvisable."

"Armorica did wh-when Maximus struck."

Bacca's tartness returned. "This isn't Armorica," he pointed out. "Turonum was as involved with Maximus's campaign as any place was, and afterward fully under his rule. Besides, Armorican aloofness was largely the work of Gratillonius, who had Ys for his tool kit, and he did the job on behalf of Maximus."

Color mottled Glabrio's skin. Fury elbowed fear aside. "Gratillonius! Will he declare for this usurper too?"

"I rather think not," replied Bacca. "He denied any such intention to us, and he is a man of his word. I made a mistake when I recommended him for tribune—though an inevitable mistake, mind you—but that much I'm still certain of. Also, I know, he grew disillusioned with Maximus."

"And today he's no King of Ys," Murena growled. "Nothing but a mutinous scoundrel with a lot of Bacaudae on call."

"And a much larger lot of ordinary Armoricans," Bacca said. "They won't likely want any part of this new quarrel."

"Gratillonius, Gratillonius!" puffed Glabrio. He pounded a knee. "Must he forever obsess us? Armorica's only a military district, an outlying part of my province. I have my whole province to think of."

"And Rome," added Bacca, quietly again.

Glabrio blinked up at him. "Well, of course, but—"

"If you mean that sincerely, then you'll declare for Constantinus."

Glabrio swallowed. "Would that be . . . prudent?"

Murena paced a turn around the room. "My guess is that we won't dare not, unless we start for Hispania tomorrow morning," he said. "I've been keeping track of events in Britannia as best I could, you know. It's hard to see what can stop him this side of the Pyrenaei Mountains. Stilicho stripped Gallia of regular troops, as well as volunteers, to meet the Goths. Those that've come back— and my intelligence of such things is good—they mostly feel disgusted. They think their absence was what invited the barbarians into their homeland. No matter that they'd returned by then, this is how they feel. And there is some justice to it. Their losses were heavy, and the Gallic military has been disorganized ever since. Meanwhile Italy is a wreck and Stilicho spars with the East. No, I think pretty soon men of Constantinus's will be here in Turonum, and soldiers everywhere in western Gallia going over to him."

Bacca pounced. "Therefore we should declare for him at once. Win the favor of our future Augustus."

"That—is an unnecessary risk?" Glabrio's indignation had faltered. He plucked at his robe. "Constantinus may fail. In that case, we must be able to show we had no choice."

"And afterward be political eunuchs," Bacca retorted scornfully. Ardor followed: "Whereas if we join the cause early—the cause of him who does look like the man with the power, the mission, to save Rome—God Himself will smile on us."

"You speak more surely of Him than is usual for you," Murena gibed.

"I speak from the heart."

"M-m—"

"Consider also this matter of Armorica."

"What of it?"

"Insubordinate. Defiant. Here we have an opportunity sent from Heaven."

Glabrio straightened his bulk. "How?" he piped.

Bacca waited, making attention come full upon him, before he said: "Without special incentive, Constantinus will pass Armorica by, won't he? It's just a thinly populated peninsula. If he doesn't expect it'll menace his rear, he'll ignore it till later. Maximus did—because Gratillonius made it safe for him."

Murena scowled. "Do you think Gratillonius would incite the Armoricans to fight for Honorius?"

"Scarcely," answered Bacca. "I don't believe he could if he wanted to, nor do I believe he does want to." He raised a forefinger. "What I do think is that we, as Constantinus's early friends, can show him the advantages of making Armorica positively his. Immediately, for manpower and revenue, both of which he'll be wanting in quantities as vast as possible. In the longer and more important run, to eliminate this armed peasantry, this cancer in the state, before it spreads further. That alone will make the magnates throughout the Empire see him for what he is, the deliverer, the guarantor. And the demonstration, at the very beginning, of his determination to rule—that will bring submission and support like nothing else."

"Can he spare the troops?" Murena asked doubtfully.

"It won't take but a handful. Not barbarian wolves, Roman soldiers: *Roman*, protecting Imperial officers in the performance of their duties. I suspect they'll only need to occupy Confluentes. Then everything falls apart for Gratillonius, and soon Armorica is ours."

Glabrio stared at a vision of glory. "To break Gratillonius," he crooned. "To destroy Gratillonius."

419

XXII

1

To Gratillonius it was like a storm he had seen afar, gigantic bruise-dark cloud masses thundering and lightening over the hills toward the ridge where he stood. Yet he was surprised when at last it broke over him—at how quietly the thing went, and how its bolt did not strike at him but into his heart.

Light spilled from a sky where only scraps of fleece drifted above thousandfold wings. Summer brooded in majesty on ripening grain and fragrance-heavy forests. There often the only sounds were bees at work in clover and the call of a cuckoo. Air lay mild over earth, as might a benediction or a woman's hand.

He was out among his mares and stallions when a boy galloped up with word from Salomon. At once Gratillonius resaddled Favonius and made racetrack speed back to Confluentes. At the south gate he saw the strangers across the Odita on his left, coming along the road from Venetorum. For an instant a surf of darkness went through him. It was as if he were again at the whelming of Ys.

"Romans," the boy had said; and across the fields and down the woodland trails, word had already scuttered to him of squadrons out of the east. Closer than that it did not speak of them, for the time was long and long since Armorica had seen anything of quite this kind.

Two men rode at the head. One wore civil garb. The other was helmeted, beneath the transverse red crest of a centurion. Behind them tramped thirty-two afoot. Sunlight gleamed fierce off mail, shields, javelin points. At their rear, three led the pack horses. At their front, one had a bearskin over his armor, and from the staff in his hand rippled an eagle banner.

Legionaries as of old, as of Caesar or Hadrianus, as of Gratillonius's youth when Britannia still bred them, not mounted lancers nor barbarian auxiliaries nor peasant levies but Romans of the legion; O God, he knew that emblem!

The dizziness passed. He grew aware of those who trailed, a hundred yards or more to the rear, Osismiic men, perhaps fifty, a sullen, wary pack, their clothes gray with grime but spears and bills slanting forward, axes and bows on shoulders. And he knew without seeing that shadowy forms had flitted along through the woods and now waited at the edge of cultivation. And city dwellers were on the walls at his back, beswarming the pomoerium, choking the gateway. He heard them mutter and mumble.

The soldiers never looked right or left or rearward. A single proud being, they advanced on Confluentes. Dust flew up to the drumbeat rhythm of their hobnails. Their centurion held his mount to the same rate, the Roman marching pace that once carried the eagles across half a world. So had Gratillonius led his vexillation to Ys, four-and-twenty years ago.

A pair of his guards kept uneasy watch at the far end of the bridge. Gratillonius rode across. Hoofs thudded on stone. "Get back there," he instructed the men. "Call the sentries down from the wall. I want that gateway and the street cleared. I want everybody orderly. Go!"

Relief washed over them. They had something to do; he had abolished formlessness. They hastened in obedience. He cantered on.

Nearing, he made out faces. Family faces, not of anybody he knew but unmistakable. Some twenty of them could only be Britannic. The insignia grew clear in his sight. They were of the Second Augusta. His legion.

Their ranks came on against him. He lifted his right arm in Roman salute. A strange figure he must be to them, he thought, a big man with gray-shot auburn hair and beard, in rough Gallic tunic and breeches that smelled of sweat, smoke, horses, but riding a superb animal and at his hip not a long Gallic sword but one like their own.

The centurion returned the gesture. Gratillonius reined

421

his stallion in, wheeled, and drew alongside, so that he and the centurion rode almost knee to knee. A small, homely squeak of saddle leather wove itself through the footfalls at their backs. The centurion was lean and dark-haired, but with skin that would have been fair if less weatherbeaten. The civilian on his farther hand was gangly and blond, well clad for travel, bearing somehow the look of a city man though obviously fit for a journey like this.

"Hail," Gratillonius said, "and welcome to Confluentes."

"Hail," the centurion replied brusquely. Both men gazed hard at the newcomer.

"I am Valerius Gratillonius. You might call me . . . the headman here. When I heard of your approach I hurried to meet you."

"You, Gratillonius?" exclaimed the civilian. He collected his wits. "This is unexpected, I must say."

"I'm sure you're aware the situation here is, hm, peculiar in many ways."

"Starting with that weapon of yours," the centurion said.

"These are dangerous times. Most men go armed."

"I've noticed. That's part of what we've come about."

The pain of it jagged through Gratillonius. *My brother of the legion, our legion, do we have to spar like this? Why? How have they fared all these years in Isca Silurum? Do you know if my father's house still stands and who holds the land that was his? What has it meant to you, bearing your eagle from Britannia after four hundred years? Couldn't we sit down over a cup or twenty of wine—I have a little of Apuleius's Burdigalan left, I'd gladly break it out for you, centurion—and tell each other how it's been, how it is?*

"On behalf of Constantinus," he said coldly.

"The Augustus," replied the civilian.

"Let's try not to quarrel," said Gratillonius. "May I ask your names?"

"Valerius Einiaunus," the civilian answered, "tribune of the Emperor for affairs in this part of Armorica."

My gens, Gratillonius thought. *It doesn't mean anything, of course, hasn't for centuries, except—except that*

422

when Romans were newly settling into Britannia, a man of the Valerii became the patron of our ancestors; and both their houses bore his name ever afterward, along with Belgic names they tried to make Latin; and now we have both forsaken Britannia.

"Cynan," the centurion introduced himself, and blinked. "What's wrong?"

"Nothing." Gratillonius brushed air with his hand and stared elsewhere. "Surprise. I used to know somebody of that name. Are you by any chance a Demetaean?"

"I am." As Cynan who marched to Ys and died there had been.

Gratillonius forced himself to meet the blue gaze. "What's your cohort, centurion?"

"The seventh."

It would be. My own. It would be.

"Well, I've had reports of your vexillation for a while," Gratillonius said. "You've not met much friendliness, have you? It's a touchy business. I'll do my best for you, and hope we can talk frankly and reach agreement."

Cynan jerked a thumb backward. "Rustics like them have dogged us since we left Redonum," he said. "They turn back at the next village, but always there's a fresh bunch of louts, and nothing but surliness from anybody. Often jeers, pretty nasty ones, and even rocks and offal thrown at us. It's been a job, keeping my men from retaliating."

Einiaunus's look lingered on Gratillonius. "They're as many as the Emperor felt he could spare for this mission," he said. "If necessary, they should be enough to cut their way back to him."

"I wouldn't count on that," Gratillonius replied around the fist inside his throat. "The Armoricans— But we'll talk." He regained fluency. "First let's get you settled in. I'm sorry I can't offer you hospitality myself, but my wife is very near her time, and besides, it's better that all of you keep close together. That strikes out the hostel in Aquilo too, I think. It couldn't hold near this many, and there's no campground nearby. I've arranged for you as best I could, and—if you don't mind—we'll improvise quarters in the basilica of Confluentes. It's unfinished, but

423

a solid block. I've had boughs brought in for men to sleep on, and a couple of real beds in rooms of their own. As soon as you're ready, we'll talk."

"You seem more reasonable than I'd been led to expect," Einiaunus said. "That augurs well for everybody."

Abruptly Gratillonius could no longer keep up the pretense. He snapped off a laugh. "Put down your hopes," he said. "I mean to tell you the truth."

2

The long day of Armorican summer wore on. Men and women of Confluentes went about their work. The crowd that gathered around the basilica was mostly from outside, yeomen, tenants, tribesmen, a number of forest dwellers. They stood, or sat on the cobbles, or wandered about, hour after hour. They spoke mutedly among themselves, ate and drank what city folk brought them, sometimes tossed dice or arm wrestled or listened to someone who made music. As their toil ended, more and more Confluentians and Aquilonians joined them, and seemed to take from them the same implacable earthy patience. The westering sun cast beams that flared off weapons.

In the monastically austere room that Gratillonius used for private conferences, Einiaunus met with him, Bishop Corentinus, and youthful Salomon Vero. Cynan was there because Gratillonius insisted. At the same time Gratillonius had declined a suggestion that he and Einiaunus speak alone. Though the western window was blank with radiance, twilight crept up over them.

Einiaunus straightened. "The documents, the decree, I have brought for you to inspect," he said. "But since you asked, I'll first deliver the message orally. That won't be hard. The requirements of the Augustus are simple and just."

Blood throbbed in Salomon's countenance. "Merely that we take a hand in his usurpation," he sneered.

Einiaunus and Cynan bridled. "Hush, my son," admonished Corentinus.

Einiaunus eased a little. "Thank you, your reverence," he said. After drawing breath: "For you Armoricans, obedience is only prudent. In fact, this is such an opportunity that you should be filling your churches to thank a generous God. You'll gain pardon for past offenses and be at the forefront of glory." Into skepticism: "Everywhere Constantinus is victorious. As I left Turonum to come here, he and his main body were departing for Lemovicium. The garrison there, that far ahead of his advance, it had already expelled Honorius's government and called on him to reign."

Corentinus shook his shaggy head like an old bull. The shaven brow glimmered among shadows. "We saw Maximus come and go," he sighed, "and before him Magnentius, and—God alone knows what the outcome of this will be. But I cannot believe He looks kindly on the warfare of brother against brother."

"It is not!" Einiaunus denied. "It's to raise up the one man who can save Rome."

"And therefore he pulled the last legions out of Britannia," Gratillonius said. The words coughed forth like vomit, and as bitter. "Therefore he left his homeland, and yours, and mine, naked to the wolves."

"The legions will return, redoubled in strength," Einiaunus vowed.

"I think not. The Twentieth never did. It's the Saxons who'll return, the Picti, the Scoti, the darkness."

"Enough of your nightmares. Let me state my message."

"Hear him," Corentinus said.

Encouraged, Einiaunus smoothed his tone: "You especially should be grateful, Gratillonius. When the governor of Lugdunensis Tertia exchanged letters with the Augustus, and later when they met in Turonum, what he urged was your arrest and execution as a rebel."

Gratillonius snorted contempt. "And he got disappointed."

Corentinus frowned and made a warning gesture.

"The Emperor was merciful," Einiaunus persisted. "He was prepared to believe you were driven to desperate measures by the failure of Honorius and Stilicho to protect Armorica—precisely the failure that Constantinus Augustus will correct. He's willing to grant you and those who follow you complete amnesty."

"And in return," Gratillonius growled, "I give over to him our treasury, and disband the brotherhoods, and order the Armoricans to go along with his conscription of them for his war."

Einiaunus showed surprise. "How can you know this?"

"Word reaches me. Constantinus has sent out a few parties like yours to other areas. Smaller and less well-armed, to be sure."

"The Armoricans blocked the roads as soon as they knew, and turned them back," Salomon exulted. "One party that refused to go away is dead."

Einiaunus and Cynan sat speechless.

"You see," Gratillonius hammered, "our men don't want to leave their country unguarded, like Britannia, while they fight on alien soil for a usurper, like you."

Cynan opened his mouth and snapped it shut again.

"I hoped you could bring them to reason," Einiaunus said slowly.

"To submission, you mean," Gratillonius answered. "Well, if I wanted to I couldn't. Not any more. They've had their fill. And I don't want to. I've had my fill."

Corentinus leaned forward. "Has it occurred to you, Einiaunus," he asked softly, "that Governor Glabrio knew this is how things are, and misled your Emperor?"

"Why on earth would he?" the tribune retorted.

"For revenge on us in Confluentes."

"—Maybe." The tone crispened. "But you are in a state of insurrection here, you and your Bacauda army. Constantinus can no more tolerate that than Honorius can. And Constantinus is stronger."

"He is not," Gratillonius said.

Einiaunus stared. Cynan sucked in a breath, narrowed his eyes, leaned forward.

"You came with your legionaries in the hope you'd frighten us into submission," Gratillonius began to explain.

"Or shame you into it," Einiaunus interrupted.

"God will judge where the most shame ought to lie," Corentinus said. "But did I hear you forcing that indignation into your voice, my son?"

Gratillonius decided to ignore the exchange. He went on: "Glabrio and Bacca suppose that we, in this community they suppose is a backwater, don't understand the true situation. They expect the appearance of a legionary vexillation will overawe us." My legion, twisted within him. It was my legion once. "Well, they're mistaken. We're quite adequately informed."

"How?" asked Cynan. Did the sound betray pain of his own?

Gratillonius spoke starkly. "Armorica is still attached to the rest of Gallia, and Gallia to the rest of the world. People still go to and fro, traders, couriers, ordinary folk on their private affairs, and others less respectable. They're apt to observe more, with more shrewdness, than their overlords imagine. Over the years, I've made my connections among them." Mostly, Rufinus made them for me. "And then there is the Church, a network from end to end of the Empire. We have our friends in the Church, we Armoricans.

"So we know what maybe Constantinus himself doesn't really know, that he isn't an advancing conqueror, he's a reckless gambler. Only look at everything he has to take into account, prepare for, try to cope with as he meets it.

"The Germani are in Gallia, in huge and growing numbers. We've turned them southward, but that just makes matters worse for anybody whose fate depends on controlling what happens. Constantinus has got to maintain strength against them. He has got to come to some kind of terms with them. That alone will take half or more of his attention, his resources.

"Arcadius in Constantinople is a sluggard, a fool, and an invalid who's not likely to live much longer. His Empress—daughter of a Frankish general—supplied the backbone, but she's dead now and he's the puppet of his praetorian prefect, who hasn't got Stilicho's forcefulness. Stilicho hasn't dropped his old ambitions. He's negotiating with the Goths again, and my sources don't believe it's anything straightforward. My guess is that he wants them to occupy Greece while he invades the Eastern Empire farther north. What will come of that, if it happens, God alone can foretell. Constantinus certainly can't. But he'll face the consequences.

427

"And will Stilicho forever continue the fiction that he acts on behalf of Honorius? Rumors fly that he means to seize the throne of the West—the thrones of West and East both—in the name of his son. If he does, Constantinus will have that problem. If he does not, or if his enemies at court bring him down, Constantinus will have a different but equally dangerous problem.

"No, your self-proclaimed Emperor has far too much else on his hands to pursue this matter of Armorica's denying him. You were sent with the idea that we don't know this and you could take charge here. You've already seen how the mass of the people feel about that. Now I've told you what we, their leaders, know, and what we intend to do and not do.

"Take your soldiers back, Einiaunus. You'd have had to quite soon anyway. Your Constantinus needs every man he can scrape up."

Gratillonius's throat felt rough, his mouth dry. His heart thudded. He longed for a strong gulp of wine. But he must keep his Roman stoicism until he could be by himself.

Einiaunus had turned white. "You forget one thing," he thrust forth. "Law. Over and above any single Emperor, the state. I call on you in the name of the law, at least to lay down your arms."

Corentinus cast a glance at Gratillonius and replied for him, "Let us not waste time disputing which party is in the worst violation. Without righteousness, justice, the law has lost its soul. It's no more than a walking corpse."

Gratillonius rallied. "Never mind catchwords," he said. "The fact is that this last demand has broken us of tameness. We *will not* give up our right of self-defense. We *will not* take part in your damned civil war."

"Then you support Honorius." Einiaunus slumped.

"Call it what you like," Gratillonius said, suddenly weary.

Corentinus lifted a hand. "Our trust is that we support Rome, and Christendom," he said.

"You and your pagans?" Einiaunus gibed in his despair.

"Let's have done," said Gratillonius. "Go home. . . . No, go back, back to your Emperor. You've left your home to the barbarians."

Cynan stirred. "Watch your tongue, fellow," he rasped.

428

Gratillonius cast him half a smile. "I'm sorry," he murmured. "This isn't so easy for you, is it?"

"I have my duty, sir."

"And I have mine. . . . I'll go, now, and talk to the people outside, and have rations brought you. Tomorrow you start back. I'll give you an escort as far as Redonum, one that ought to act as a safe conduct. Salomon."

"Sir?" said the young man.

"You collect a squadron for this and lead it. Show your standard in the van, every mile you go."

Reluctance: "That's hard duty, sir. Not the danger, I don't suppose there will be any, but—"

"You have your orders," Gratillonius declared. "It's part of learning to be a king."

3

That night Verania was delivered of a daughter. Her husband kept watch at her door till he heard it was well with them, then went in and kissed her.

He returned a few hours past sunrise. This year workmen had completed the addition of a solarium to their house. Glass had become costly, but the gift rejoiced her, she who was so much a child of light. Gratillonius found her there, resting in a chair with arms and reclined back and soft upholstery which he had made for her himself. He had also made the crib beside her, and carved it with birds and flowers. A maid sat in attendance, spinning yarn. Marcus was outdoors playing, as beseemed a healthy three-year-old.

Verania had a book on her lap, her beloved *Georgics* of Vergilius; she had inherited her father's library. The brightness of the small airy room found its center in her hair. She hadn't yet gotten it done up in matronly wise, it was damp from washing and flowed like a maiden's across her white gown. When Gratillonius entered she laid the book down and smiled as had the little girl who skipped forth to meet him, he riding from Ys.

He bent low till hazel eyes blurred in his vision and the

sweetness of her filled his nostrils. Lips brushed across lips. Standing back, he asked, "How are you?"

"Most wonderfully well," she answered.

He studied pallor in cheeks, dark smudges beneath lids. "You would say that."

"She speaks truth, lord," ventured the maid. "This wee slip of a thing, she's tougher than most peasant women."

"Nevertheless you ought to be in bed," Gratillonius fretted.

"I'll go back soon," Verania promised. "But the weather's lovely, and I felt quite able to walk this far and sit."

Somehow she always got her way, and he had decided that that led to the best for him too. He stooped above the crib. The newborn slept, a wrinkled red miracle, incredibly tiny. "Maria," he murmured. Verania had wanted that name, should it be a girl, to honor God's Mother. He agreed, feeling inwardly that it honored every mother.

Verania's gaze dwelt on him. "You're the one to have a care about," she said. "Have you slept at all? You're emptied out, poor darling."

He shrugged. "It's a busy time."

"What's happened since yesterday evening?"

He lowered himself to a stool facing her. "I've just sent the Romans off, with Salomon for escort." The last of my legion.

Gladness had yielded to concern in her. Now something else took possession. So quiet was it that he could not tell whether it was dread or sorrow. "You have cast the die," she said slowly.

He grimaced. "It was cast for me. Again and again and again, always coming up the same. When Constantinus landed in Gallia, that was the final throw."

"You play on."

"It's become a different game."

"And Salomon also a marked man."

Though he heard nothing of reproach in her tone, he must plead, "How could I have stopped him? And we need him. I've told you before. Everybody loved Apuleius and remembers him. They'll rally around his son as they would around nobody else."

Pride suddenly pulsed: "Except you."

430

"I won't be here forever." He saw her stricken, jumped to his feet, laid hands on her shoulders. "Easy there, sweetheart. I intend to last for many years yet, annoying the devil out of those who'd prefer it otherwise." A smile trembled briefly on her mouth.

He straightened, turned, paced to and fro before her. "But I've got to think beyond," he said. "Come my time, Marcus will still be too young. Not that I could ever be King, or leave the kingdom to my son. Too much of Ys clings to me."

Her eyes widened. She brought hand to lips. Her whisper came appalled. "King—!"

Trying to explain, knowing how awkwardly he did it but unable to find any better words, he plowed on. "What I can do is take the immediate leadership. Forge the sword. Lay the foundation. The rest will be for Salomon after me."

"Do you really mean to break from Rome?" The voice shuddered. "You, my husband? He, my brother?"

Aghast, he could only halt and stammer, "Oh, darling, the pain in you!"

She steadied. "I hear it worse in you," she told him sadly.

"I don't necessarily mean we rebel," he said. "Except against this rebellion, this Constantinus who deserted Britannia for his own ambition. I was wrong about Maximus, long ago when I was young. I can't make the same mistake twice, can I? Afterward, when Armorica has the strength to bargain, then maybe—" He didn't know what then.

She nodded. Her calm deepened. "I see. You say 'King' as a short word for something infinitely complex and changeable."

"It may come to real kingship in the end," he confessed. "I can't foresee. Pray for a good tomorrow. God will hear you more willingly than me."

"He hears all who speak to Him." She looked away for a while, out at sunlight and sky. He stood silent. The spindle whirred at his back.

Verania returned herself to him. "No, I don't imagine you could have done anything but what you are doing," she said.

431

He spread his hands, closed them into fists, dropped them slack at his sides. "I thought about it. My thoughts ran around and leaped and dashed themselves against walls like a wolf in a pitfall. Should I take you, Marcus, Maria, and run? Where to? No place in the Empire. Changing our names wouldn't help. What work could a masterless man my age find, among those guilds and laws, unless as a field hand, serf or slave? Settle in the wilderness, or with the barbarians? What sort of life would that be for you and our children?" Unconsciously, he came to military attention. "No, Verania, we'll live and die as Romans."

Her voice caressed him. "I understand. The chiefs, the people will rise regardless. That can only bring ruin on them—without you and Salomon. You can make things better rather than let them go on getting worse. Do what you must, with my blessing. And I think with God's," —her smile flowered—"my dear old watchdog."

She reached out and took his head between her hands as he bent down to kiss her. A wave of healing went through him. And yet below it, like an undertow, passed memory of her poem. *"Would you know the dog from the wolf?—"*

He stood up. "Thank you," he said. "I will go get a little sleep."

"And then?"

"Send out my summons. Also to Nemeta and Evirion. They can come home now."

And also, he thought, seek out a certain smith, the best in Osismia, perhaps in all Armorica. Confluentes had drawn men like that. He would bid him lay other work aside and make a sword befitting a king.

4

Rain came, not cruelly slashing as in last year but a mildness that swelled the crops to full ripening. It made earth a shadowless cool gray haunted by its whisper on the leaves. When the sun broke through, mists curled beneath spiderwebs turned to jewelry strung with stars. Dwellers in a land always wet, the Armoricans paid these showers scant heed while they went about their labors. Earlier they had joked that seven clear days in a row were a dangerous drought; the moss on them was dying.

One afternoon a cry from Verania brought Gratillonius out of the workshop in a rearward room where he had been releasing some of the tension in him through his hands. He found her and a gaggle of chattering servants in the atrium. The front door stood open on dim silver. The air that drifted through it mingled with city odors of smoke and horse dung the richer scents from beyond, of soil and growth. Two had entered, man and woman. Water dripped off them and puddled on the floor.

Coarsely garbed as they were, in wool stiff with grease and smelling in this weather like a sheepfold, for an instant he thought them woodfolk of the most primitive sort. The man was big, shock-headed, full-bearded; he was ferociously armed, bearing knives, sword, crossbow, and a staff with a fire-hardened point on top. The woman was wrapped in a cowled cloak, but the ankles above her deerhide shoes showed her to be fine-boned.

Then Verania sped to embrace her, and the hood fell back and unkempt locks made a flame in the chamber. "Nemeta!" Gratillonius bellowed, and plunged to take her for himself.

How thin she was. He thought he could feel the arch of every rib, and her poor dead arm dangled loose though the left clung hard and dug fingers into his back. But when he stepped away he saw skin clear, eyes cat-green, and after her trek she stood firm-footed beside Evirion.

"Welcome, welcome, welcome," Gratillonius babbled, foolish with delight. "A long, hard walk, wasn't it? But here you are. How we'll feast!"

Nemeta looked from him toward Evirion, and edged nearer the young man. He let his shaft clatter to the tiles and took hold of her searching hand. "Damp days, and pretty hungry." Why did he sound so gruff? "Vindolenus wanted to hunt, but we made him push on. We lived on cheese and hardtack we'd packed, and berries, and whatever his hook or traps caught overnight."

433

"You must be ravenous," Verania said. "Which do you want first, a bite to eat or a bath and dry clothes?"

They ignored the question. "How fares it?" Evirion asked Gratillonius, remembered the wife, and inquired again in Latin.

"You're barely in time," Gratillonius told him. "Day after tomorrow, Salomon and I are off to Vorgium. Come along if you're able. You'll be important to us in the time ahead. Did I write to you that you still have your house and ship? Everything was confiscated, sold for the public treasury, but . . . Salomon was the only bidder."

Evirion blinked, smacked his thigh, whooped a laugh.

"And you, Nemeta, must stay with us," Verania said. "We've ample space."

The red head shook. "I thank you, no."

"She's with me," Evirion stated half defiantly.

Gratillonius felt less jarred than he might have expected. They'd been a year alone in the wilds, those two—the settler and his family could not have counted for much—and both were young, attractive, bound together by the same danger and thus, at last, by the same need.

"We are going to be married," Evirion said.

Verania clapped her hands. "Oh, Nemeta, wonderful! And you, Evirion. Everybody will be overjoyed for you—" Happiness faded. "No. I'm afraid—the bishop says—"

Nemeta lifted her head to look straight at her father and stepmother. "I am a Christian now," she told them. It rang like a challenge. "As soon as Corentinus will baptize me, he may."

Verania broke into tears and hugged her all over again. Gratillonius barked clumsy good wishes until he turned about, seized Evirion's hand, and choked, "Thank you. You've g-given me back my daughter."

The other's grin masked a diffidence which his voice betrayed. " 'Twasn't easy, sir. I'm no missionary. It's just that, well, there we were, the Black Months holding us, talking and talking and— She wanted to learn about me, my life, everything. I the same for her, of course, but hers had been so terrible." His words dropped low. "She was afraid. Not in any cowardly way, nobody's braver than Nemeta, but deep inside, as dreadfully as she'd been hurt and, and the things that'd caused her to do. But the hurting started to go away and she began to understand she'd be *welcome.*"

"And the Gods of Ys lost Their last worshipper," said Gratillonius in a rush of savage glee.

"Well, I'm no holy man, sir, but it is true that baptism washes out every sin, isn't it?" The question was not humble. Evirion stood with hand on sword haft as if to say it had better be true.

Gratillonius nodded. "The bishop tells me that pretty often. He wants me baptized. And I will be, but I don't yet feel quite right about it. Nemeta, though—" Eyes met eyes. An undertone: "The sooner the better. You know why, I suppose. Corentinus will have to know also, if the old fox doesn't already. Nobody else need ever."

His daughter's lover gripped him by the arm. They stood a minute thus.

Verania had let go, and Nemeta was saying in reply to her: "We can't. I'm sorry, we must leave at once."

"For where?" asked Verania, shocked.

"My old cabin in the woods, if it remains. That's a long way. We can't reach it till after nightfall. Could we borrow lanterns, or even a pair of horses?"

"In God's name, why?"

"Not for witchcraft. I'll cleanse it of that, I swear. But—" Nemeta gathered courage. Her gaze locked with her father's. "You know," she said.

Memory stooped on him—a day in the forest outside that dwelling—and struck. The talons broke his joy apart. Little feathers and blood drops of it rained around him. "Dahut," he uttered.

"I dare not linger near tidewater," Nemeta told Verania. The listening servants shrank from her and made signs against evil. "She came this far upstream for revenge on Rufinus, who got Niall killed. I helped him in that. She'll know I'm here—already she knows—and she'll come after me too."

"She hasn't shown herself to me in these parts," Gratillonius said out of his hopelessness.

"I don't know why," answered the unmerciful terror. "I

can only guess. You weren't directly part of the death. Or else it is that—that— No. I don't know why."

Or else it is that I am her father.

"But this is horrible!" Verania nearly screamed. "That you have to go in fear of that, that unclean thing—" She saw the look on Gratillonius, went to him, laid her face to his breast and wept. He consoled her as best he might.

"I've wondered if the bishop could protect her," Evirion said.

Gratillonius shook his head above his wife's tears. "No," he replied. "I don't see how. Not without exorcising Dahut. He's moved here to Confluentes, but—well, we don't know how far she can come up on land, but he has to be out of his house most of the time, and anyway, you two couldn't simply cower in there." A dreary chuckle. "He can't allow carnal relations under his roof, can he?"

"We've got to be on our way soon."

"*You* can't hide in the woods any more. We need you! I'll explain why in a minute. And, and haven't you had enough of that? I'm surprised you stood it this long."

"I couldn't have without Nemeta."

An idea bobbed up, like flotsam from a sunken ship. "Wait. You can stay closer. I've built a house out by my horse pastures, less than three leagues from here. It's only a shieling for the watchman and whoever else may have to spend a night there, but it's warm and tight and we can bring some things along for you. You may as well keep guard; he'll be glad of a chance to come to town. Later we'll see what better we can do."

"Water," said Nemeta. Her eyes stood huge in the white face.

"A burn. It feeds a pool where the horses drink, then runs on to the Stegir, a league or so away. No trace of salt." Gratillonius ordered up a laugh. "I repeat, the place is nothing much, but surely a palace compared to where you've been. You can make of it whatever you like."

Verania disengaged from him. She gulped and dabbed at her eyes, but it lilted from her: "Why, that's right, Gradlon. Of course."

"Meanwhile," he reminded them, "we have plenty of daylight left for celebrating in."

His cheer was a lie. Before him wavered Dahut—strangely, not as he had last seen her, a swimmer in bloodied surf around the ruins, but the living girl who cried for his help while the sea swept her from him in sundering Ys.

5

A pair of candles and a banked hearthfire brought Nemeta and Evirion out of the night for each other, highlights on countenances, along the angles of his body and the delicate curves of hers. The air smelled of smoke and lovemaking. Rain chuckled at the eaves of the shieling.

He raised himself to an elbow and looked down at her. The straw in their pallet rustled beneath him. She reached up her good hand to stroke his newly smooth cheek. He caught the wine scent on her breath, wild and sweet.

She smiled at him and said drowsily, "There will be no more witchcraft."

"What?" he asked in gentle startlement. "I thought you—"

"Oh, I forswore it when I gave myself the name of Christian. And yet . . . 'twould have been unwise for me to become fruitful, nay? Off in the wilderness, with naught of knowing what would befall us or when we must flee onward. I cast certain small spells at certain times between moon and moon, and they seem to have worked as I hoped. No more than that, I swear, beloved. And now not even that. We are come home. Tonight I have opened my womb for you."

6

That year they kept the Feast of Lug in Armorica without their chiefs. They held what fairs and festivals a tribe could afford in this troubled time, they plucked flowers and herbs on grounds that were anciently holy, they met

437

on hills and by streams and springs and sought with apprehension to divine the future. In churches the Mass was more than commonly prayerful.

Most leaders were at Vorgium, those who had been there earlier and the many who came freshly, hammering out the compact by which they would live or die. As the full moon rose, they went forth from the ruined city to swear to it.

One man, and a Christian priest he was, had garlanded a menhir beyond the walls: as his forebears had done at the Feast of Lug since first the Celts rolled their chariots into Armorica, and maybe the Old Folk before them. Nearby hulked a dolmen. They had kindled needfire between, and built it up to a tall, booming blaze. Under the moon, first with mistletoe, second with drawn blades, last with blood from themselves, by Lug and Christ and the threefold Mother, they plighted their faith.

Standing above them on the capstone of the dolmen, hands resting across the pommel of a naked Gallic sword, Gratillonius wondered what the civilized men present—and those were not few—thought of this. Were any repelled, did most hold it a necessary concession to allies, might it catch some by their hearts? Flamelight cast iron, clan emblems, wild faces in and out of shadow. The moon limned treetops ghostly against a sky where the Dragon coiled far aloft around the Pole Star. Its light upon dew beyond the fire's dominion made a phantom also of the open land, fields gone back to grass and brambles which lapped around broken walls he could no longer descry. When the shouts rang away into silence, he heard an owl calling. Rome of the law that he would fain uphold seemed as remote as yonder stars, Rome that he had never seen nor ever would.

The gathering waited for his word.

He lifted the sword before him, kissed the blade, brought it around and sent it hissing into the sheath. "I thank you," he said in the cadenced tones of a centurion addressing his men; but tonight his language was the language of Armorica. "I thank you for the honor you have given me, and the patience you have shown,"—he would not say anything about endless wrangling, pettiness, anger, bloodshed barely averted a couple of times—"and above all for your loyalty to the people and the law. With everything that is in me, everything I am, I will strive to be worthy of your trust."

He couldn't help it, he was no orator, his words turned plain and hard. "You've chosen me to be your war lord, your duke. My charge is nothing more or less than to see that you, your wives, your children, the old and the young and those not yet born, shall be free to get on with their lives untroubled by robbers, murderers, slavers, within and without. For that we'll have to fight. I was a soldier once. I'm taking up my trade again. You must be soldiers too. I'll have work out of you and your followers, sweat, long dull days where nothing happens, wounds and death when we need to spend men. You will carry out orders with no back talk. I'll be free with my punishments, and as for rewards—as for rewards—why, those will be your wives and children and the roofs above them. Is that clear?"

They shouted. Nonetheless, he knew, this night called for something that was not in him to give, he, rough old roadpounder. They wanted one who could not so much speak as sing to them, a young God, a dream become flesh.

"I am only the duke," he said. "I'm your leader for now, but just a soldier. Not your King. Here we can't name any such man. There's no foreknowing what will happen, what will be wise. All we can do for years ahead is defend our hearths. But you have a right to hail my deputy—him who'll take my place if God or the luck of battle calls me away—who after I've stepped down, if I live, will carry on—Salomon Vero."

It was no surprise. Everyone had understood beforehand. Yet blades flashed and shouts crashed until birds of day flew crying from their nests. "Salaun! Salaun! Salaun!"

The son of Apuleius swung lithely onto the dolmen and trod into firelight. Gratillonius knelt, picked up what had rested at his feet, unwrapped it. Steel shimmered like rippling water. Bronze plated the guard, silver coiled in the haft, and on the pommel smoldered a ruby, for the star of Mars. He lifted the weapon on high. "Take the sword of Armorica," he called, and laid it in Salomon's hands.

XXIII

1

Harvest was done, the last sheaf consecrated as the Maiden, the wether chosen as Wolf of the Fold sacrificed, a branch hung with ears of grain brought into house or barn. Much remained to do, but the wise-women said this glorious weather would hold for another month or better, and the chiefs said that meanwhile more urgent was the business of war.

Suddenly, there the host was, down out of Redonum to Portus Namnetum and its neighbor Condevincum. Badly outnumbered, threatened by uprisings between the walls and dissension in their own ranks, the garrisons yielded without a fight. Gratillonius left a force sufficient to hold the gains, under Vortivir, who understood how to govern a city and make warriors respect pledges of no looting or violence. The bulk of his men started up the Liger Valley, commanded by Drusus. Gratillonius himself led a picked detachment rapidly ahead on horseback, with remounts. Most of them lacked the art of fighting in the saddle, but that didn't matter now. As formidable as they were, the troops at Juliomagus made no move when they passed, nor did anyone disturb them at night.

On the third morning they clattered by the monastery across the river—the brothers scarcely had time to call on God and holy Martinus before the armed men were again out of view—and reached Caesarodunum Turonum.

To watchers on the ramparts, they were a dismaying sight. The stones of the bridge rang under the hoofs of their horses. Standards rippled to their speed until they drew rein; on the foremost banner grinned a she-wolf. Spears swayed like stalks before a rising wind. Sunlight flashed darkly over helmets and mailcoats, most taken off

440

slain Germani. Barbarically bright were many cloaks or Gallic breeches; but it was the wilderness that had yielded those furs and lowing aurochs horns.

Three hundred strong, they massed on the riverside just out of ready bowshot. One cantered from among them holding up a green bough. Stentor-voiced, he called for truce and parley. Duke Gratillonius—surely the big man of middle age, outfitted like a centurion, who dispatched him—wished no harm on the city. If he must, he would take it. This company alone could get over its weakly manned defenses. However, he would wait for his army. The Romans were free to send riders under safe conduct who could verify its strength. If caused to spend added days away from home, where it was needed both for warding against barbarians and for help with the winnowing and other vital tasks, it would be an angry pack of men. Duke Gratillonius would still forbid a sack, but he could not warrant that any of the garrison would survive. Better that the Imperials promptly negotiate terms.

—In the event, Bacca and Bricius were the delegates who came forth, accompanied by half a dozen scribes and assistants. Gratillonius received them in a large tent he had had pitched. Camp life brawled around it, rough tones and laughter, fire-crackle, footfalls, clash of iron, occasional shout or neigh or snatch of a song old when Caesar came and went through Armorica. The blue-and-white sailcloth gave shade but scant shelter.

Gratillonius, armored yet, said, "Hail" and gestured at some saddles. "I'm afraid that's the best I can offer you to sit on," he told the guests, "and river water the best drink. We've traveled light, so as to travel fast."

Bricius, his portly form attired in a red silk robe, a golden cross hung on his breast, puffed indignantly, "I will not demean my sacred office by squatting down like a savage."

Bacca's smile was wry. "We may as well stand," he said. "I doubt this will take long. What do you want, Gratillonius?"

A gem glittered as the bishop lifted a forefinger. "Beware," he warned. "You rebel against God's anointed. Satan makes ready a place for you."

Bacca dissolved the scowl on Gratillonius by remarking, "There are some who consider God's anointed to be Honorius."

"Mother Church takes no side in earthly quarrels between her children," Bricius said hastily. "She can but sorrow, that they are proud and hard of heart. God will give victory to the righteous. You, though, Gratillonius, defy any and all authority. I say to you that unless you repent and make amends for the damage you have done, God will cast you down, and your torment shall be eternal."

"Bishop Corentinus tells me differently," the leader snapped. "If Christians can't even agree on what they believe, the Church has no business in their worldly affairs."

"I have the impression that Bishop Corentinus does not quite accept that proposition either," Bacca said, crumpling his cheeks with a second lip-shut smile.

"Well, I'll take my ghostly counsel from the man I know to be honest," Gratillonius said. "You've wasted your time coming out, your reverence. Please don't waste ours too."

"Oh, the insolence!" Bricius groaned. "Scribes, are you noting this down in full?"

"It won't be much use to anybody. Naturally, your reverence and the monks, all clergy, can stay. No one will lay a hand on you or anything of yours, and we'll maintain order and allow trade as usual, so that the city needn't suffer either." Gratillonius turned to Bacca. "But the officials of the state—Governor Glabrio, Duke Murena, and you, Procurator, together with your underlings—you shall go. Officers of the garrison likewise, unless they swear obedience to those we'll put in charge. Same for ordinary soldiers; but I expect, since they're almost entirely local lads, they'll choose to stay. That happened at Namnetum."

Bricius gobbled in dismay. Bacca regarded Gratillonius coolly and said, "We weren't sure, but the cutoff of communications suggested you'd occupied the port. What else?"

"We'll do the same at Juliomagus, but that's a minor job. I wanted to secure Turonum first."

"Expelling the Imperium, as you've done throughout Armorica. But you're a considerable way from Armorica, my friend."

"Listen." Gratillonius softened his tone. "I remind you

442

that when we sent those people packing, it was bloodless."
Well, almost. Despite his orders, some grudges got paid
off. He couldn't be everywhere, but must rely on the
patchwork confraternities and on tribal bands awakened to
remembrance of the fact that their forefathers had been
warriors. "They've mostly come to you, including such
officers and troops as refused to join us. Those aren't
many. Armorica has never been well defended, which is a
main reason she's in revolt today. Murena's been trying to
make those soldiers a kernel for a force that will retake our
country. He's written to Constantinus, asking for reinforcements. Don't deny it. We've intercepted a letter.
This countryside is also full of disaffected folk, and I've
had agents among them for a long time." Rufinus accomplished that. "Murena has doubtless sent appeals that did
get through. We cannot allow such a threat to be built up,
six easy days' march from Redonum."

Bacca lifted his brows. "Ah, but can your impetuous Gauls hold a position six days' march distant from
Redonum?"

Gratillonius chuckled. "You're a shrewd devil, you are.
Care to join my staff? I promise you an interesting life."

"Were I young, I might consider it. But I fear I value
my comfort, books, conversations, correspondence too
much. My hope was, and perforce continues to be, that
Constantinus will guarantee them. Are you not the least
bit afraid of his vengeance?"

"He's busy in the South, Romans ahead of him, Germani
on his flank. If we neutralize the lower Liger Valley and
make accommodation with the Saxons at the estuary—that's
in train—then he'll have no base here. He won't send
troops to bog themselves down in a war that serves no
strategic purpose. I credit him with better sense than that.
Supposing he does win out at last over his present enemies and gets things well enough in hand in the South
that he can turn his attention back to the North—that
can't be for years, and meanwhile we'll have been making
ready."

"You do not actually propose to hold the valley, then?"

"We might hang onto Namnetum. I'd like to, but it
depends on how the next several months go and what

443

arrangement we finally make with the Saxons at Corbilo. Otherwise, once you officials are out, we'll simply keep an eye on Juliomagus and Turonum. It'll be to everybody's interest to leave them in peace. Tell Constantinus that."

"You assume I will . . . be seeing the Augustus again soon."

"What choice have you? Listen, I am not going to dicker with you, or Glabrio, or Murena, or anybody, about anything except the practical details of how to start you headed south. I want it to happen fast. Understood?"

"In short, you demand capitulation. Have you thought that this might put, say, Murena on his honor to refuse?"

"I'll leave you to handle Murena's honor," Gratillonius drawled.

The procurator laughed. "You're a fairly shrewd fellow yourself, in your fashion. Damn, I wish we could have worked together. I'm actually going to miss you. Well, let's get busy."

Bricius had smoothed himself and maintained a politic silence.

2

Next morning the Emperor's men departed. With them traveled their families, sympathizers, most paid subordinates, and some slaves. Others refused obedience and stayed behind, expecting to become free. Gratillonius hoped that wouldn't bring undue grief on them or on innocent civilians. He could not take up their cause, or any but Armorica's.

The Romans showed nervousness at first, unsure what the Gauls who lined both sides of the highway would do. The soldiers among them surrounded a richly curtained litter which doubtless carried Governor Glabrio. The Duke of the Armorican Tract rode in armor, astride a tall horse, at their head, looking straight before him, his face locked into fury. More horses and mules followed, carrying people or possessions. Oxcarts creaked heavy-laden; here and there a gleam from below the canvases or within the tilts showed how much treasure was loaded aboard. Gratillonius had advised against that. Well, what escort the caravan had could probably discourage bandits; it was only sixty or seventy miles to Pictavum, the nearest substantial city.

The Armoricans neither molested nor mocked. They watched, swapping occasional soft words, perhaps a little awed by what they had so easily done, perhaps a little frightened at seeing empire ebb away like this.

From his saddle Gratillonius spied Bacca on an easy-paced gelding, quite self-possessed. Beside him trundled a canopied cart in which sat a plump woman, well gowned, with two half-grown children. The driver was a youth slightly older. Gratillonius realized in vague surprise that he had never thought of the procurator as having a family.

Several yards farther in the dismal parade, another woman came alone. She sat lightly on a gray palfrey. The breeze fluttered a cowled black cloak away from an enveloping dress of good brown material and a small pectoral cross. Again Gratillonius felt surprise brush him. Did Roman women ride horses, even sidesaddle? He'd seen ladies do it in Britannia when he was young, but they were provincials, and not among the wealthier ones.

Recognition shocked.

"Stay where you are," he told his guards, and trotted Favonius out onto the pavement. Eddies of alarm swerved some outcasts in their course. He heard gasps, mumbles, a squeal. Ignoring them, he drew next to the woman. She had glanced about, seen him, and at once looked forward, as stiffly as Murena.

"Runa," he said in Ysan, "Runa, I awaited not this. Methought you dwelt among the religious women. They'll take no harm, I swear."

She held her vision to the south. His traveled over the sharp profile and ivory skin, down to the slender hands. They had held him close once, those hands. Veins made a faint blue tracery on them, and he had never seen any other fingers or nails as finely formed as theirs. They had wrought much beauty on parchment and papyrus, those hands.

"Have you fared so ill here that you would liefer hazard a journey into war?" he asked. "Come back with me then

445

to Confluentes. You shall have a decent home and due respect. Aye, you'll have friendship. We who remember Ys—"

"I'm going to civilization," she interrupted in Latin, still keeping her face from him. "You've destroyed it here."

"Now, wait!" he protested in the same language. "We're behaving ourselves a sight better than Romans do when they take a city—no, their barbarian hirelings and allies. Turonum could well be an ash heap if we hadn't stopped the Germani in Lugdunensis Tertia. It wasn't me who ordered away the last defenders of Britannia to fight against fellow Romans. Destroy civilization? All we want is a chance to save it!"

She did finally give him a steadfast glare. Words ran forth, cold as a river in winter spate. "Oh, you're quick with your excuses. You always have your noble-sounding plans for the public benefit. It frees you to ride roughshod over mere human beings, doesn't it? Not that you dismiss their cries. You don't hear them. You never hear anything you don't want to hear. Nor see, nor feel. You don't suppose you ever hurt me, because you cannot imagine how you might ever. You're more alien than the bloodiest barbarian. At least he has a heart, though it be a wolf's, where you have a stone. Go back to that simpering little wife I hear you've taken. Poor creature, I hope she likes pain; I hope she is very happy with you. Go back—"

"Thank you, I will," he said, and rode off.

She wouldn't be pleased if she learned that his sole feeling was of relief. She'd closed a wound in his conscience which had sometimes bothered him, and he need give her no further thought.

3

Salomon was at Confluentes, in charge while Gratillonius took the army away, when a boy on a spent horse galloped in from the west. Morning was young, shadows long across meadows where dew still sparkled and heaven startlingly blue over city roofs. The prince, as Latin speakers were

446

already calling him, had just come up from Aquilo to his matutinal duties at the basilica: conferences, mediations, judgments. He found most of the work unspeakably tedious, but Gratillonius insisted it was part of being a ruler. Later he'd go hawking.

Hoofs stumbled over cobblestones and stopped his feet on the stairs. Men stared at the desperate lad on the lathered animal. His cry seemed to echo through an immediate silence. "Help, the Scoti are at Audiarna, they're enough to overrun us, in God's name help!"

Salomon ran down to meet the messenger and conduct him inside. Gratillonius had instituted the practice of posting two sentries at the basilica during the hours it was open. Salomon told them to keep the gathering crowd orderly and as calm as possible. He led the boy on into the private room, sat him down, sent a housekeeper off for mead, and said with a control that amazed himself: "All right, you reached us, you're safe. Catch your breath and cool off a bit first."

The slight frame shuddered. A wrist rubbed eyes that stung from sweat. "Sir, they, they—Scoti, hundreds and hundreds—at Audiarna—"

Eeriness thrilled through Salomon. He had gotten no hint of pirates anywhere closer than the north coast, off toward Fanum Martis and Saxons at that. Fishers who spied strange ships on the horizon would promptly have put in and delivered a warning. Gratillonius's network of beacons, runners, riders would carry the news to him before the crew got ashore.

The servant brought the mead. A long draught brought balance. "They came up the river about moonset, when dawn was barely in the sky. By the time the watch had seen and roused us, they'd landed and were spilling around our walls. We counted forty leather boats. The commander ordered a sally just to get me through them and away. I heard the roaring and screaming for a long while afterward. That was . . . more than an hour ago? How has the battle gone? Sir, can you help us?"

Forty Scotic vessels. Salomon's reckoning went meteorswift. If they were large, that meant some four hundred barbarians, maybe even five hundred. Gratillonius had not

447

stripped Armorica of fighters for his expedition—by no means—but he had taken the best of them, or nearly so. There remained a great many members of the different brotherhoods, scattered in their daily occupations, plus a leavening of crack troops left behind against contingencies that had seemed unlikely.

Now that ordinary men were openly taken into the guard and drilled, Audiarna might give a better account of itself than the Scoti expected. On the other hand, those men were, as yet, largely raw recruits; and the city had never regained the population it lost to the epidemic six years ago. The Scoti had no skill at siegecraft; they would take the place by storm or not at all. Whatever happened, tomorrow morning at latest would see it finished.

Salomon beckoned. "Come," he said, and led the messenger to the council chamber. People waited there, impatient at his delayed arrival, a couple of chiefs, various yeomen, artisans, merchants, sailors, woodsmen, three women such as Gratillonius encouraged to bring their grievances before him. They grew quite still when they saw the face of Salomon. He mounted the dais. "Put your business aside and hear this boy," he told them. "Meanwhile bring me my couriers."

—Evirion answered the summons at a dead run from his home in the pastures. He still gulped for air as Salomon drew him aside and described the situation. That rekindled him. "Michael and Heavenly host!" he exclaimed. "What would you have me do?"

"How quickly can you take your ship to Audiarna?" the prince asked.

Evirion started, recovered, moved his lips in calculation. "No pledges, of course," he said. "I can board my crew in time to catch this outgoing tide, but travel's always slow on the river. If you can provide plenty of strong backs for the towboats— You can? Good. Once we've cleared the bar, the wind is anybody's guess, but mine is for a rather light, steady sea breeze. We'll have to work well southwest, which'll also be slow, but then we should have a run almost straight downwind. Before sunset is about the best I can say, and when we get there we'll have the tide against us."

"God grant you better luck. Your cargo will be the keenest men from these garrisons."

"I never bore any more gladly." Evirion looked beyond the walls. "Grallon was right. My seamen and I chafed when he made us stay behind, but he was right. We careened *Brennilis*, you know, cleaned her bottom, made everything shipshape, and became a crew again after that long year on the beach. Did he foresee this need?"

"Hardly, or he'd have left us more strength," Salomon replied. "But—the way he puts it—he hedges his bets."

That was not in the nature of a young man afire to go fight. Salomon hoped fleetingly that in the years to come he would learn. If those years be granted him and his mentor.

—They were not a real cavalry force whom he led west, though all went mounted. Some had mastered the lance, more could strike from the saddle without risk of losing their seats or having their steeds panic, a few had trained themselves into horse archers. The choicest such were afar in the Liger Valley. Most of Salomon's were fighters afoot, who rode in order to reach the scene quickly. He made them, too, vary the pace, spare the animals. A long afternoon lay ahead in which to spend four-legged strength.

4

Smoke and soot drifted from burnt-out farmsteads. Thrice had the Scoti hurled themselves at the city. Thrice had men on the walls sent them back, but at a cost to their own ranks that they could ill afford. Each wave came higher than the last.

A cheer lifted thin when the oncoming armor blinked into view. The attackers abandoned their improvised scaling ladders and swarmed snarling, yelping, turbulent, to meet the newcomers.

Salomon leveled spear. The standard of blue and gold flapped furiously in the van of his charge. A warrior stood before him, half naked, sword awhirl over a face contorted by a wildcat scream. Salomon's point went in with a dull impact. The man stumbled against another. Blood spouted from his belly. Salomon hauled the lance out. Loops of gut snagged it. He shook them free while he clubbed the next enemy with the shaft. A tug on the reins, a nudge of the spurs, and his horse reared, appallingly tall, blotting out the sun. Bones splintered under descending hoofs. Salomon pressed inward. An ax chopped his spear half across. He dropped it, grabbed sword, hewed around him.

Not very far in, though. The Scoti were too many. His riders could drown in the whirlpool of them. He signalled the trumpet at his back to sound retreat. The troopers beat their way out of the crowd. They rejoined the larger number of comrades who had jumped to earth and fought as infantry—a barely organized infantry, armed and out-fitted in wildly diverse fashion, but stark in its determination.

The barbarians fell away, disordered. They rallied fifty yards off, shouted and glowered and threatened, but made no move at once to counterattack. The dead who sprawled and the wounded who writhed on the red sod between held far more of them than of Armoricans.

Their living remained vastly the superior. A concerted rush would drag down Salomon's band as hounds drag down an elk. The price would be high, though, even to men who disdained death. It could well end any hope of capturing the city. Salomon saw a lean gray wight lifted on a shield in the ancient Celtic manner. He seemed less to harangue the war party than address it. There followed lengthy, often florid argument, also in the ancient Celtic manner. Excellent, Salomon thought. Every minute that passed was a minute in which to rest, a minute wherein friends drew a bit nearer.

The sun trudged down the sky. Decision came. The mass of the foe turned back to Audiarna, leaving about a hundred to deal with the Armorican reinforcements.

That was as Salomon had hoped. The Scoti evidently didn't know how many more he had on call. Unless sheer thirst for blood and glory made them indifferent. You never really knew what went on in those wild heads. What he must fight was a delaying action.

His immediate opponents howled and attacked. They had the numbers but he had the horses and, in his foot, at least the seed corn of legionary discipline. Those men closed ranks and held fast. His riders harried flanks and rear. The charge broke up, bloodily.

After that the battle became a series of skirmishes. Salomon's command beat off assault after assault. In between, it struck at the main body of the Scoti, now here, now there. The tactics were simply to reap and retreat. That alone was confusing to warriors who knew of nothing but headlong advance, except when "the dread of the Mórrigu" stampeded them altogether. It blunted their onslaughts against walls to which a heartened garrison clung tighter than before.

Though the Armoricans took losses, their count swelled. Osismii who had gotten the word arrived in groups, hour after hour, to join the blue standard. At last the core of the Confluentians appeared. They were not fresh, after their forced march; but by then, neither was anyone else on the field.

The Scoti left the walls. They collected into a single huge pack and moved toward their foe to tear his throat out. Quite likely they could do that much, a consolation to them for the survival of a city they would thereafter be in no condition to take. "We are in the hands of God," Salomon called to his troops. "Know that and keep your hearts high. Let our battle cry be—" not religious, with all the pagans here—"*Armorica and freedom.*"

Should he have said "Osismia" instead? The idea of Armorica as a nation was barely in embryo. . . . No, let him nurture it, let him feed it with his blood.

A shout lifted. Among the enemy it turned into a screech, wail, death-dirge.

Up from the sea and into the river mouth came a ship. Her sail spread like a wing on the evening wind that drove her majestic against the tide. Black with a red stripe, her hull flaunted a scrolled bowsprit whose gilt blazed in the long sunbeams. From her stern reared the head of a gigantic horse, as if Roman cavalry also rode over the waves. Yet somehow she was not of Rome. She might have been a ship of Ys risen from that drowned harbor to carry Nemesis hither.

Her deck pulsed with men armed and armored. She

451

grounded among the boats, crushing two of them under her forefoot. A catapult near the prow throbbed. Its bolt skewered three men of Hivernia. The crew sprang out or slid down ropes, waded ashore, formed and moved forward, a walking thicket of pikes. A few stayed behind and began demolishing the rest of the boats.

That broke the Scotic will. Warriors turned into a shrieking blind torrent. It gushed past the city, down to the riverbank, to get at those craft and away before every man of it was trapped into exile. The Armoricans pursued, smiting.

Their harvest was large. It cost them. Even demoralized, a barbarian was a dangerous beast. The wrecking gang must scramble clear, and several were too slow. The squadron from the ship barely held its ground while the escapers poured around it. The sailors left aboard were hard put to fend off valiant savages who tried to climb the sides. In the end, perhaps two-thirds of the Scoti crowded into what boats were left, bent to their oars, and vanished seaward.

Well, Salomon thought, they would bring back a tale that should give pause to future pirates. And Audiarna had been saved. The story his followers told would be of hope reborn. He wiped and sheathed his sword, lifted his hands aloft, and from the saddle gave thanks to the Lord God of Hosts.

5

Clouds had risen on the rim of Ocean and a vast sunset filled the west, layered flame and molten gold, smoky purple slowly spreading as night moved out of the east. The moon lifted enormous above trees as black as the battlements close by. Heaven overhead preserved for a while a greenish clarity. Across it winged a flight of cormorants, homeward bound to the skerries outside Ys. Waves and the river went *hush-hush-hush*. Wind had lain down to rest in the cool.

Before he sought his own sleep behind yonder gates,

Salomon had much to do. He must see to quartering and feeding his men, as well as what horses they had left; the badly wounded required special conveyance into town; the dead wanted care too. Fallen Scoti could wait where they were for a mass grave in the morning, but the Armoricans should rest together under reverent guard until their brethren bore them home.

There were words to speak, praise, encouragement, condolence, shared prayer. Finally there were words to exchange with the enemy. Those maimed lay still, knife-stuck; but a dozen or so had been captured, hale enough to seem worth binding. They sat on the trampled grass near the stream, hobbled, wrists lashed behind backs, in a dumb defiance. Equally weary, their keepers leaned on spears whose heads glimmered in the dying light. The hull of *Brennilis* made a cliff blocking off the sea.

Salomon approached with Evirion, who understood the Scotic language. "I don't know what information, if any, we can get out of them," the prince explained, "nor what use, if any, it may be. However, Gratillonius believes in gathering all the intelligence he can."

Hardly had the skipper begun to say that this was their conqueror who had come, than one among them crawled to his feet. He was aged for a warfarer, the gray hair sparse on his head, beard nearly white. Scars won long ago intertwined with gashes and clotted smears from to-day. His tunic hung a rag on the gaunt body. Yet gold shone on neck and arms, and his look made Salomon think of a hawk newly taken from the wild.

"Sure and is it himself you've brought?" he said in Latin. Hivernian lilt and turn of phrase made music of it. "I'll met, your honor." He smiled around the teeth left to him. "But 'twas a grand fight you gave us. No shame in defeat at hands like yours."

Astonished, Salomon blurted, "Who are you?"

The seamed visage registered offense. "It is unworthy to mock a man in his grief. The Gods mislike that."

Verania had said barbarians were more than witless animals. Someday such as these might be brought to Christ. "I'm sorry," Salomon replied. "You've worn me out, and I forgot myself."

453

The man laughed, a clear sound, like a boy. His friends raised their heads to behold him athwart the sky. "Ah, that's better. I am Uail maqq Carbri of Tuath Caelchon in Mide, and fortunate you are, for I it was who led this journeying from Ériu."

"What?" Incredible luck, maybe. No, likely not; his people would never disgrace him by offering ransom. Just the same—"I command the Armoricans here, Salomon, son of Apuleius. Our lord, uh, our lord Gratillonius is away or he would have met you himself."

"I knew that," said Uail. "It was a reason why we came. We did not await the young wolf fighting as stoutly as the old, saving your honor."

"You knew? How, in God's name—by what sorcery?"

Uail's smile grew sly. "Ah, that would be telling."

"Tell you will!" Evirion snarled.

Uail gave him look for look and said quietly, "Your Roman tortures would only close our mouths the harder." To Salomon: "But you and I might strike a bargain, chieftain with chieftain."

His face was blurring as dusk closed in. "Go on," Salomon urged, and felt how suddenly the eventide was chilling off.

"I will answer your questions, so be it they touch not my honor or the honor of my King, until—" Uail glanced east. "Until seven stars are in the sky. That is generous of me, for the moon will make the little ones slow tonight. Then you will strike the heads off us you have bound."

"Are you mad?" Or a barbarian.

"I am not, and I know I speak on behalf of these lads with me, young though they are while I am long past my time, I who outlived my King. You will make slaves of us otherwise, will you not? You will put us to digging in your fields and turning your millstones. Because our owners will fear us, they may first blind us—or geld, and we may be so unlucky as not to die of that. I bid you my answers in return for our freedom. We shall swear to it by each his Gods and his honor. Is this not fair?"

"Make the deal," Evirion whispered in Salomon's ear. "It's the best we can do. But don't let him blather on till the time's run out."

Salomon swallowed a lump of dryness. His pulse

454

thuttered. "It is fair, Uail," he said. "I swear by Christ Jesus, my hope of salvation, and, and my honor."

"And I by the heads of my forefathers, the threefold Mórrigu, and my honor, the which is the honor of my King Niall."

"Niall!" exclaimed Salomon.

Uail's voice rang. "I was his handfast man these many years. He was my King, my father, my dearest brother. It was for the avenging of him that I called the young men to sail with me: not for plunder or fame, though that lured them, but for vengeance upon his murderers. Ochón, that we failed! Ochón for the dead! Ochón for the righting of the wrong, now when none abide who remember Niall as does this old head soon to fall! But we gave him a pretty booty of newly uprooted souls, did we not?"

"But Niall died—south of us—at the hand of another Scotian."

Hatred flickered. "Ah, you would be knowing of that, wouldn't you?" After a breath, Uail spoke half amicably. "Well, I do not believe you, Salomon, with your honest face and all, had any part in that work of infamy. Nor quite did your King Grallon, though the Gods know he had much of his own to avenge and I do not think he forbade—"

"How did you reach us like this?" Evirion interrupted. "Nobody saw you before dawn."

"Ah, we stepped masts and sailed straight across," Uail said blandly. "By day and by night the wind was fair for us, the waves gentle, and we unafraid though everywhere around us was only Lir's Ocean. I knew that our course held true, and from me the lads took courage—"

"None of your damned talking the time away!" Evirion broke in again. "Where did you make landfall?"

'Why, just where we wished, at the headlands of Ys. In among the rocks we threaded, cat-sure, never endangered, and there we took the first small part of Niall's revenge for him. Men were at work ashore, breaking what still stood. We put in and ran them down, like foxes after hares, and laughed as we slew them. You may go find their bones and the bones of their oxen above Ys. The oxen we roasted and ate; the gulls will have feasted on the men."

455

Salomon remembered sickly that despite the terror that misted yonder bay, bold scavengers made forays yet. The gold and gems were gone, but dressed stones remained. They called to need more than greed. Folk built houses, often where raiders had destroyed wooden ones; they decked paths against winter's mire; they raised shrines or chapels—Gesocribate required much building material to repair and heighten its shattered defenses—

"Then you rowed by moonlight to Audiarna," Evirion was saying. "What would you have done if you'd taken it?"

"Why, looted, killed, and left a waste, a memorial pyre to Niall," Uail said. "After that, ah, well, that would have been as the Gods willed, and a fickle lot They are, as every sailor and warrior well knows. We bore hopes of going on upstream, not this river but your Odita, as I understand you call it, to seize Grallon's very rath, and him returning to no more than what Niall found at Emain Macha. We might not have chosen this attempt, for I am not as rash as you may be thinking, but if not, then we would have raged up and down your coast until—"

"Hold!" Salomon cried. Twilight deepened. Moonlight tinged the grass and the dead. The cold was within himself, he knew, and shuddered with it. "Who told you Gratillonius was away?"

"She did," Uail answered. "She rose from the sea and sang to me while I walked by night mourning for my King. That was where the Ruirthech flows into its great bight, and across it the land of the Lagini to whom he gave so much sorrow, but who in the end—"

Salomon seized the ripped tunic in both fists. His knuckles knocked on the breast behind. "Who is she?" he yelled.

"The White One," Uail said, "she who swam before our prows to guide us and—" He looked over his shoulder at the night-blue east, beyond the moon, and finished triumphant: "And now, your honor, behold the seven stars."

XXIV

1

There was a man named Catto who was a fisher at Whalestrand, a hamlet clinging to the shore near the eastern edge of the territory that belonged to Ys. After the city foundered, the Whalestrand folk allied themselves with the nearest clan of Osismii and brought their catches to Audiarna. There Catto, embittered at the Gods of Ys, soon learned to call on Christ.

He saved what he could, and was at last able to get a small vessel of his own, which he named the *Tern* and worked with his grown sons Esun and Surach. Their affairs prospered in the meager fashion of their kind. They were ashamed when they learned the Scotic raiders had gotten past their watchfulness, though that was at night; but first they had rejoiced to see currachs full of wild men fleeing scattered back oversea.

Once sure that the danger was past, Catto hoisted sail and left home behind him again. The season grew late; fishers must toil until storms and vast nights put an end to it, if they were to have enough to last them through the winter. *Tern* was not a boat for venturing out far and staying long, but her sailors knew the shoals around Sena. There the nets often gathered richly, and few others cared to go near that haunted island.

The vessel had just passed Cape Rach when a fog bank to the south rolled on a suddenly changing wind over her—whereupon the wind died away and left her becalmed. For hours she floated blind. The gray swirled and smoked so her crew could barely see past the rail to slow, oily-looking swells that rocked her before them with hardly a whisper. The sound of water dripping off yard and stays

457

was almost the loudest in the world. Cold and dankness seeped through to men's bones.

Then, blurred by faintness but ever stronger as time crawled along, came the rush and boom of surf. "We're in a bad way, lads," Catto told his sons. "The Race of Sena is bearing us where it will, but never did I know it to flow just like this." He peered out of his hood, forward from the steering oars whose useless tiller he gripped, into the brume. "Pray God—nay, He'll ha' no ear for the likes of us—ask holy Martinus if he'll bring us in safe, for 'tis out of our hands now."

"Can he see us where we are, or walk over the water to us?" Surach wondered.

"There's them that could," Esun said, and shivered.

Darkness thickened, but they made out a reef that they passed, a lean black length around which the waves grunted and sucked.

"I'll give the Powers whatever they want for our lives," Catto said.

He thought those might be unlucky words, and fumbled after better. All at once a breeze sprang up, sharp and salt on his lips. The mist streamed away before it, lightening around the boat though low and murkful yet overhead. To starboard and port the noise of breakers deepened but also steadied. Among the vapors, dim and mighty shapes began to appear. Closer by, lesser ones lifted jagged, turbulence afoam at their feet.

"Christ ha' mercy, 'tis the bay of Ys," Catto cried. "We've drifted this far and the wind's blowing us in."

"What'll we do?" Esun called back through the roiled gray. Surach clutched an amulet of seal bone hung from his neck and mouthed half-remembered spells.

"Steer on," Catto answered grimly. "Stand by to fend off, ye twain."

Both younger men fell to. Soaked and heavy, airs slight to belly it out, the sail gave *Tern* little more than steerage way, about the same as Esun and Surach had they been at the sweeps. Thus they could wield boathooks when she was about to collide or scrape, while their father kept the helm. Here the rocks were not natural, but remnants of what human hands once wrought. Several years had brought

458

most low and eroded the sandstone of what still reached above water. Nonetheless they could tell what tower yonder snag had been, see a piece of wall below which they used to walk, glimpse a broken pillar drunkenly leaning, stare into a sculptured face trapped in a skerry of tumbled marble blocks. Not labor alone made the breath sob in their throats.

The tide was in flood, close to full, but this evening its violence was at the cliffs and it went up the beach almost gently. Ground grated under forefoot and keel. "Heave anchor!" Catto ordered. His shout was muffled in the emptiness around.

"We'll camp ashore," he told his sons. "There'll be another high in the morning to float her." They were glad of that. Here a night aboard would have been cheerless indeed. The three waded up through the shallows carrying food, gear, and a line for making their craft doubly secure and aiding them back.

Wind strengthened. It shredded fog and drove clouds over the headlands that gloomed right and left. Westward past the ruins and the rising restlessness beyond, sunset glowered sullen red and went out. Eastward the valley filled with a night which had already engulfed the hills at its end. The wind whined and flung briny cold at the men. " 'Tis swinging north," Catto said. "If it stays like that, Point Vanis 'ull break it for us tomorrow and we can row till we're clear and then catch it for a run to our fishing grounds. Thank ye, holy Martinus."

"If 'twas him," Surach muttered.

They ventured not to whatever shelter the partly demolished amphitheater afforded. Ghosts might house within. However, while some brown light lingered they sought among the grasses and bits of pavement that way, and made a find. Bones of oxen lay strewn about ashes of the fires that had cooked them. The wagons those animals drew had mostly been hacked up for burning, but fragments were left.

"Scotic work," Catto thought aloud. "I suppose Prince Salomon sent a party to fetch the slain drivers for rightful burial. Well, poor fellows, they'll nay grudge us what warmth we get from this." He and his sons filled their arms with the wood and carried it back to the beach, where they had hitched their line to a rock above high-water mark. Such nearness to their boat gave a little comfort. By the last of the dusk, Catto used flint, steel, and tinder on what Esun and Surach split for him. Flames licked up to flap yellow on the wind.

The men spread their bedrolls and hunkered by the fire with hardtack, cheese, dried fish, water jug. Its light brought leathery faces flickery into sight. Night prowled, whistled, mumbled close around. "Aye, an eldritch haven," Catto said, "but we'll gi' thanks for it natheless, and tomorrow 'ull see us where we ought to've been."

Laughter sang in the dark. The food dropped from their hands. They leaped to their feet and stared outward. The high, sweet music jeered:

"Fishers who would fain put forth
As the wind is shifting,
Spindrift-bitter, to the north,
Where will you be drifting?
Low beyond this loom of land,
Rock and reef await you.
Wives at home shall understand
That the congers ate you."

Catto lifted his arms against the blowing blackness. "Holy Martinus, help us, help us," he groaned.

The song danced nearer.

"Thunder-heavy in His wrath,
God Whom you've forsaken,
Lord Taranis walks your path,
And the seas awaken.
Where His graybeard combers break
While the rigging ices,
As of old, comes Lir to take
Ancient sacrifices."

They saw her at the edge of sight, the White One risen out of Ys, and whirled and fled inland. The song pursued. It seemed to ring from Cape Rach to Point Vanis and back again, up the valley between the hills under the wrack, it filled the world and their skulls, it echoed within their ribs.

"Belisama leads Her Wild

460

Hunt of unforgiving
Women once abed with child,
Torn away from living.
Vengeance winds you in your flight.
Hounds of Hers will follow,
Howls resounding through the night,
Hollow, hollow, hollow."

—They ran until they dropped beneath the weight of dread and their senses whirled from them. So did they lie when day broke. Unbelieving, they blinked at each other, crept painfully to their feet, limped off in search of humanity.

Later they returned with some reckless young companions they had found, they themselves unsure what had happened, save that it had been horror beyond anything the priests had to say of hell. After all, *Tern* was their livelihood. But she was gone. Nobody who fished those waters ever saw her adrift.

They plodded back to Whalestrands. By that time Catto had a fever. He raved on his bed in their hut till the tide of thick fluid in his lungs drowned him. Esun got work as a deckhand but Surach must become a dock walloper in Audiarna at starvation wages.

Word flew around. After they heard, no more fishers put to sea that season, and many talked of staying ashore next year. It would mean suffering for a land that depended heavily on their catches, and desperation for them, but they feared Dahut more.

2

The storks had long since departed, and now skies were full of other wings trekking south. Through nights when hoarfrost settled on stones and on grass going sallow, cries rang, plover, dunlin, lapwing, swan, wild goose and duck. Birch leaves turned pale gold and drifted to earth. Stags in forests made ready their antlers. Huntsmen's horns bayed through wet reaches where green had begun to fade.

Rowan berries flamed. Apples fell with a sound as of someone knocking on the door of the year.

Gratillonius walked with Evirion and Nemeta from their hut in his pastures. It was a cool day, windless, diamond-clear. Down its quietness drifted the call of the geese passing over in their long spearheads. Low above woodlands outside the rail fence, the sun washed with light an eagle at hover. Horses grazed, lifted their heads as the three came near, sometimes broke into a gallop across the broad spaces he had given them, manes and tales flying.

He had found it impossible to say what he must in the smoke and gloom of the shieling. His words were for Evirion, but as close as Nemeta was to them both, she went along. They followed a footpath by the rails. It had width only for him, so Evirion paced on his left and Nemeta beyond, the forage dampening the men's breeks and the woman's bare feet and ankles.

"A late time for sailing, I know," Gratillonius said. "But we're barely past equinox, and can reasonably hope the autumn will be as mild as spring and summer were. You're a crack mariner and command a well-found ship. Salomon's chastened the Scoti for a while; news of what he dealt out will have reached other tribes of theirs. The Saxons have gone home or into winter quarters from which they won't range far if at all. Besides past experience, I've some confirmation of that from the king of those at Corbilo. He's become fairly friendly to us, but keeps in touch with his kinfolk elsewhere. I wouldn't ask this of you if I didn't believe you'll be safe." He hesitated. "Or as safe as most men these days, which I admit isn't saying much."

Evirion's blunt features showed still less doubt. "To Britannia, eh?" he replied. "What for?"

"I've an idea we can reach agreement with several leaders in the West. Think what it's meant to them, Constantinus pulling out the last legions. Oh, he left skeleton garrisons behind, but from what I've learned, they are exactly as useful as any skeleton. Some Britons must be in despair; some may still cling to belief in his promises; but surely some are furious. They'll feel as betrayed as we in Armorica, and mightily interested in what we're doing about it. God knows we need every ally we can get."

462

"What help can they give us?"

"That, we'll have to explore. I can imagine things like joint patrols at sea and even joint expeditions to clean out the ugliest barbarian infestations there and here. It will take time to organize, prepare—years, most likely. But the sooner we start, the better. We have the advantage for a while that Rome's whole attention is off us. That may not last."

"Well, I have some acquaintance with people in those parts. I can try sounding them out."

"That's the purpose of this trip. I'll give you letters to several leading men who look like good prospects, and you'll have Riwal and a couple of other reliable natives along to advise and assist."

"How long will this take?" asked Nemeta. Her voice was small.

"Not too long, I trust," Gratillonius reassured her. "This isn't really a diplomatic mission or anything like that. Unless he gets weatherbound, you should have him back well before solstice."

"I can trade," said Evirion eagerly. "That'll give me a cover, and be worthwhile in its own right. Wares have been piling up in our dealers' storehouses, what with trouble and fear emptying the sea lanes. I'll bring you home a healthy profit, darling. We'll build us a proper house."

"Right," said Gratillonius. "How soon can you go?"

"A very few days. My men are as impatient as I for a whiff of salt water and a sight of new shores."

"Dahut."

The name from Nemeta stopped them in their tracks. They turned to look at her. She stared past them, beyond meadow and horses and forest, to that which distance hid in the west. Fiery hair and jade eyes were like autumn colors above early-fallen snow. The bones in her face stood forth well-nigh as sharp as those in her dead arm.

"You'll be rounding Sena." Her whisper trembled in Ysan. "She will know."

Evirion took her left hand in both his. "Now, beloved, be of brave heart," he urged loudly in the same tongue. "We'll stand far out to sea."

"She can swim wheresoever she lists that the tides flow. Wherever she scents ruin to be wreaked."

He scowled. "Aye, she has strength, strength enough for dragging men under to their deaths. But 'tis not such as would avail against a ship, nor drive her through the waves swifter than a dolphin."

"The fishers—"

"They've let themselves be terrorized. What really happened that night at Ys? Had yon men stood fast, she'd have slunk back to her eels and sunken wrecks. My crew helped choke her on her malice at Audiarna. We'd welcome a fight against her own self!"

Remembrance came to them both of who stood at their side. The look on Gratillonius struck them mute.

The older man swayed a little on his feet. Fists clamped together as if he would strangle the air. Words grated out of him: "I've not forgotten her. Evirion must be right about her powers. Else would she have slain us all when we fought her Niall at Ys, her lair. She does have other might than of the body—"

Evirion drew Nemeta close to him.

"But that too must lie within bounds," Gratillonius went on. "A certain command of the weather, meseems. Yet if you do indeed steer very wide of Sena, no storm can force you onto the skerries. Can it? Are you of a mind yet to fare, Evirion?"

"I am," said the captain.

"Good. We will talk . . . more . . . later. I leave you now. You twain will have your . . . farewells to say."

Gratillonius stumbled off alone, back toward the place where Favonius was tethered. His daughter and her man moved to follow, then stayed where they were, holding each other, watching him leave them. A new flock of wild geese cried overhead on its way south.

3

Salomon dispatched a note to Verania requesting she pay him a discreet visit at his and their mother's home in

Aquilo. She left the children in care of their nurse and walked. That day was cold and gusty after a night of rainshowers. Clouds smoked in haste above tossing, soughing treetops. Wind ruffled the steely-gleaming Odita. Crows in the fields flattened their wings before it like hens before a cock. The first fallen leaves scrittled across the land.

Rovinda was attending Mass, which she did whenever possible. Salomon received his sister at the door, helped her remove her cloak, led her to the room where their father used to read his books and write his letters. The walls bore the same gentle, slightly faded pastoral frescos, but instead of codices and papyrus the table held the sword of mastery in its sheath, while behind it a staff on a pedestal displayed the battle banner.

"Have a seat," Salomon invited. "What refreshment would you like?"

"Nothing, thank you," she replied, and remained standing. He did likewise.

Silence fell, except for the wind's bluster outside, until he said awkwardly, "I want to ask you—about Gradlon."

"I thought so." Her look upon him steadied.

"Why is he doing this?" broke from him.

"You should know better than I," she answered as softly as before. "The newest revolt—"

"Certainly I know!" he snapped. For a moment his weather-darkened countenance flushed red. The thought rang between them: The western Caletes taking fire from us and declaring themselves also free of Rome. Northern Gallia broken out of the Empire between the mouths of the Liger and the Sequana. Salomon checked his temper and said with care, "I realize he must go there and show himself, his best troops, tell them what we've done here and that they can do likewise but only if they'll work with us. Of course. This soon, though?"

"It is a short time. Hardly more than, m-m, ten days since he returned from Turonum."

"And the news didn't reach us till after that."

Verania sighed. "I confess it's hard to bear. But I must, because he must."

"What do you mean?" Salomon demanded. "I asked you, This soon? Why? It's insane. He's like a whirlwind.

465

Evirion left for Britannia only the other day. Can't Gradlon be satisfied with that for a while? The men he's taking—I tell you, they're not happy at being hauled off again at once from their firesides, for another two or three months on the road."

Verania's hazel gaze widened. "Didn't he explain the reason to you, of all people? Those are Celts too. Even in an important city like Rotomagus, they're still Celts. If he doesn't get them bound together—by persuading, wheedling, bargaining, bullying, till he has their sacred oaths—they'll soon be at each other's throats. Some will pledge Pseudo-Constantinus allegiance if he'll help them against their neighbors. There goes any hope of holding him off after he's through in the South."

Salomon whistled. "Pseudo-Constantinus! Sister, you do have our old man's gift for phrases." It diverted indignation and he continued levelly, "Of course Gradlon's explained to me. We talked about it already before he went to the Liger Valley, because he thought other secessions were likely. But he never said his part in it would be this urgent. Surely it can wait till, oh, Beltane. The tribes, the clans won't stir during the Black Months. Why must he?"

"Why are you so concerned?" she responded. "What harm if he does it early rather than late?"

His glance went around, to the window, the wall, the sword, back to her, like a newly caged bird. "It's . . . everything." His tongue moved heavily. "I fear for him. Something's gone terribly wrong. He arrived home so cheerful. He'd done so much, and talked about our getting a well-earned rest, and— Not that I ever imagined him sitting idle. But he has a pile of matters needing attention here, and—and his own family!"

She smiled the least bit. "Well, you know him. Old duty horse."

"This isn't duty," Salomon maintained. "He's driven. Almost since he came back, he's been caught in a pit of gloom. He tries to hide it, but, well, when he suddenly grows short-spoken, or outright unmannerly—when he goes off on those long gallops—and this, this demonic haste—" Fear shivered. "Could it be a demon?"

"It is," Verania said low.

"What?" he croaked.

"Oh, not as you suppose. Not possessing him. But it's why he must go. He hasn't told me; I don't believe he can tell anyone. But I know. In work is his hope of healing, work from the moment he wakes till the moment he drops, so he can sleep through some of the night."

Salomon braced himself. "Tell me."

She must summon will of her own. "Dahut. This evildoing of hers. He shoved it aside at first, wouldn't think of it, or anyhow didn't speak of it, but in the end—he'd just broached his plan to Evirion—she, Dahut, broke through the wall he'd raised. Now he has to escape her."

"I see . . . ," Salomon breathed.

Verania struggled against tears. "His daughter. The child of his Dahilis, whom he never stopped loving." She seized both her brother's hands and hurried on: "No, no, he's happy with me—he has been—and I'm the mother of two children he adores, but there will never be another Dahilis. It's all right. I am content. I simply pray that someday he'll be free of Dahut."

Salomon stared before him. "He thought after Niall died and . . . she avenged him . . . she'd only brood over the sunken ruins of Ys. Instead—"

Vigor came back to Verania's tone. "Instead, her malignancy hounds us. It's too much to ask that he face at once. Let him go off and be among men, ride hard, meet challenges, risk his life if need be. A good farewell is the single gift we can give him, you and I."

"And a glad greeting when he returns."

"Pray God he does, heartened."

He stood for a space quiet, until he shook himself and said with half a smile, "I think, before he leaves, I can jolly his men somewhat. They are the best we have, our chosen few. I'll remind them of that—Celts do love flattery—and speak of new places they'll see, adventures, celebrations, willing girls—It'll help Gradlon's spirits, having theirs high."

"God bless you," Verania murmured.

He turned grave. "And you, sister mine. Thank you for this."

—When he reached the parade ground north of Con-

467

fluentes, near his family's old manor house, a squadron of infantry was at drill. To and fro they marched, wheeled, countermarched. Their boots struck earth together, dust flew and thud racketed up into the wind. Each man was outfitted however he or his kin could provide, a wildness of mail, leather, kilts dyed in gaudy clan hues; but a ripple as through a ripening wheatfield went in the pikes that flashed aloft, and the officer who watched from horseback had no reason to shout commands. It was they who set their cadence, singing together, one of the many new songs that went about the country; and while the tune had been old among the legions, the language today was not Latin.

"When the Scoti come a-raiding, or the Saxons or the Franks,
It's the horn of Gradlon calls us—Take your weapons! Form your ranks!

"Pound the road to Audiarna, sail Odita to the sea,
Be a tribe what you may name it, all Armorican are we.

"For we're done with belly-crawling to beseech the lords of state
That they please defend the people from the reaver at the gate.

"Where were all the mercenaries when the Vandals ran in rout?
In the barracks gulping senseless till they spewed the wine-juice out.

"Where were all the tax collectors when we saved them from the sack?
In the privy shitting rivers, thinking how much gold to pack.

"Let the legions make their Caesars. We must guard the fields of home.
We will follow good King Gradlon and we'll stand no more with Rome."

468

Sunset smoldered among the ragged dark clouds. For a while it reddened wave-crests, to bridge the waste between worldedge and *Brennilis*, but Ocean kept shattering the work. Then it died out and the west deepened from ice-green toward purple and thence black. Eastward the waves took a sheen more pale, also broken and fugitive, off a hunchbacked moon three days short of the full. Clouds yonder made it seem to fly, yet it stayed over the starboard rail, as if the ship too were rushing at windspeed across endlessness.

The clouds were merely a wrack, fleet moon-tinged scraps. The brighter stars flickered visible, Eagle, Swan, Lyre, Dragon, a glimpse of the Bears sufficient to mark Polaris, by which Evirion steered. He fared thus through night, twenty miles or more from any land, not in recklessness but because the fortunes of wind and current brought him abeam of Ys, as nearly as he could gauge, at this chosen time. Every man agreed that the only wisdom was to pass those evil headlands as soon as might be.

Sharply heeled, *Brennilis* creaked; her forefoot hissed and smacked, cleaving water; lines aloft thrummed to the skirl of air; sometimes the leach of the straining spritsail snapped or its spar shifted about and boomed against the mast. The seas had a thousand voices of their own, deep drumroll, torrent, splash, whirr, growl, while their surges pitched the hull that rode them. Spray off their manes fell bitter on lips. The cold of them was a live thing that coiled and tugged and bit.

The wind was from the moon, though, not the sunset as men had dreaded. It thrust the ship off the reach of rocks beyond Sena, out onto the deeps where there were simply billows to do them harm. Powerful, it was not too much to beat across, holding a course that ought to make landfall somewhere on the west coast of Britannia. That was another reason Evirion had decided to sail on in the dark.

Standing lookout at the prow, Riwal the Durotrigian

gazed homeward. He saw little more than the vague gray of the artemon, until across murk his vision met stars; but yonder lay the country of his birth, the fields and folk of his tribe, an upwelling of memories . . . the downs shouldering into a vast summer sky, chalk cliffs tumbling to water utterly blue, himself small and gorging on blackberries (the prickliness was part of the joy) with honeybees abuzz around him. . . . No. Home was no longer there. In five years since he made his way to Armorica, and saved earnings till he could send after wife and children, they had struck new roots; and it was in a better place, in the lee of Gradlon, safer than most from the storms that savaged the world. Yet maybe his sons would remember together with him, maybe they would keep the dear music of the old speech and something of the old ways. For more and more Britons came over in search of refuge.

Nevertheless—

He felt mass betread the deck behind him. Turning his head, he recognized Evirion's tall form. "How goes it?" asked the captain.

"All's well, sir," Riwal said. "I thought you were asleep."

"I'll sleep in the morning, when I know we're clear of the Gobaean. We can't hope to pass West Island by then, but any dangers will be natural ones."

Riwal wiped his drenched mustache, cleared his throat, and ventured, "I've been wondering, sir. This isn't too late in the year, but if we aren't so lucky with the weather when our business is done and have to winter in Britannia—"

"We won't," Evirion vowed. "I'm going home—" He peered starboard. "Hoy, what's that?" And in a roar: "Sheer off, you! Helmsman, hard a-lee!"

Riwal barely saw what came out of the night. A large fishing boat, sail filled with the wind that drove her straight at *Brennilis*, a last great leap, he had not quite understood when stem smote strakes and the doomsday crash hurled him backward.

He struck the port bulwark and grabbed after any handhold. The deck canted. It spilled men elsewhere into the sea. Sail flapped thunderous, masthead wavered crazily across the stars and then swept downward like a spear

470

dropped by a warrior who has taken an arrow in the belly. Now the deck slipped about and canted forward. Riwal lost his grip and tumbled back into the bows. There the starboard bulwark stood splintered above timbers torn loose from their fastenings. Through it he saw the boat. Her prow was deep in the hull of *Brennilis*. Impact had sheared loose her own mast, it lay in a tangle of rigging and sailcloth alongside, waves made it a ram to batter the ship. One billow cataracted across him. He heard a huge noise of water pouring in. Ballasted and laden, the ship was going down by the head.

From the helm of the boat flitted a whiteness that might have been foam. Riwal lost sight of it. Then suddenly it was over the rail and aboard with him.

Clouds broke from the moon. By its wanness he spied a couple of men amidships. They clung to the lashings of the lifeboat, which they were trying to cut. The nearer man was big—Evirion? The white thing passed up the slanted, sluggishly rolling deck. Wind blew the long hair from the shape of a naked woman.

Riwal screamed. The brawl of sea, the groan and sundering of wood smothered it. He cowered into the angle where he clung, and the mast cut off sight of what happened yonder. Maybe, whirled in his nightmare, maybe she wouldn't notice him. Maybe she would swim off, sated; and at least a part of the ship might float a derelict till it washed ashore, Epona, Christ, give this, make it be!

A wave overran him. He got it in his open mouth and strangled. Somehow he coughed the water out and caught a breath before the next whelming.

The next, the next, the next, each deeper and wrenching harder than the last.

A weight ground its way along the splintered planks. He looked and saw the lifeboat, free of its moorings, somehow turned right side up. It slid forward at every pitch, cutwater aimed at him where he lay tumbled and trapped in the bows.

Blindly, he clawed himself up and went over the side. The sea swallowed him. He could swim, he flailed through the swirls of the dark and broke out into moonlight. In a black-and-white blur he saw waves heave, spindrift fly,

471

Brennilis with stern aloft, a last bit of the craft that had gored her, and the boat, the boat. As the ship rolled, the boat slipped through a gap in the bulwark and floated free.

It floated toward him where he threshed.

She leaned forth and laid hold of his tunic. By the gibbous moon he saw her smile. She hauled him aboard, he fell into the bilge, and for a spell nothing was but a blackness that wailed.

When he crept back to himself he found mast stepped and sail full of wind. The boat bounded easily over long rollers where foam sparkled. They rushed and lulled. The moon shone ahead. Wind had swung clear around and now bore for Ys.

The woman sat at the helm. Moonlight quivered on her wet whiteness. She saw him see her and smiled. She was wholly beautiful, but he still burned from the cold of her touch.

He huddled where he was, afraid to stir or cry out.

Clouds blew away. The Milky Way shone across the great wheel of the stars. The moon climbed until it was crooked and tiny on high, then sank toward Ocean aft. Winter's Orion strode gigantic up from the east. Wind boomed softly. Riwal began to feel no more chill, no more fear. Finally, corpse-numb, he felt no more time.

Point Vanis and Cape Rach followed Orion into heaven. The boat glided between their bulks and wove among the remains of Ys. Faint as a gnat's football, Riwal heard its keel plow into the shore. The wind fell, the sail dropped lifeless. The moon was sunken but waters were metallic with the earliest dawnlight above eastern hills.

She left the tiller, stood up, beckoned to him. His cramped legs would barely move. He lurched to the rail, fell over, sprattled for a moment before he could reel to his feet.

She was gone. He blinked in dim puzzlement. Where was she? What did she want of him? He was hers. The sea had washed everything but obedience out of him.

She appeared from behind what had been a gateway and flowed over sand, cobbles, weed, shells, pieces of wreckage, to him. There was now enough light that he could see the gold of her hair; but no color was in lips or nipples or nails, and the blue of the eyes had no depth, it was blank as Ocean under a dead calm. Though the air lay murmurous, pierced by the mew of an early wakened gull, silence and cold enclosed her.

In her right hand she held something which she reached toward him. He stared. It was a small carving in wood, long since water-logged and gone to the bottom. Paint was worn off and worms had riddled it, but the thought trickled through him that this was once a prancing horse, playfully shaped, with jointed legs, toy for a child.

She thrust it at him. His fingers closed on its soddenness. Hers brushed them, and the chill jagged to his heart. It shocked him back into terror. She gestured imperiously. He turned and shambled off inland as she commanded. Never did he dare look back to see if those empty eyes gazed after him. But as he, having passed the amphitheater, climbed to what was left of the eastbound road on the heights, his glance fell over the bay, and all he saw move there in the strengthening light were waves and a flight of cormorants.

5

Equinox almost a month behind them, nights drew in fast. The sun was down when Tera reached the shieling at the meadows. Autumn colors in the woods had gone dun, though as yet crowns were limned sharp against a sky where a yellowish glow lingered. A breeze sighed bleak over the grass. Fallen leaves rustled.

Candleglow spilled around Nemeta's slight figure and burned in her tresses as she opened the door to the newcomer's knock. "Welcome, oh, welcome." Her tones shook. "Come in. My house is yours."

"We'll have scant need of it, I think," said the stocky woman. Nonetheless she entered. Smoke off the hearthfire stung her at first; she sneezed and wiped a hand below her pug nose while she leaned her staff against the wall. Otherwise she carried an emptied water bag and a sack with lumpy things in it, tied to her back. Her weather-

473

whitened mane was the brightest sight among the shadows. The years had begun to dull it.

"I have wine, food," Nemeta offered.

Tera shook her head. "We'll eat otherwise this night. Have you brought the foal I wanted?" After Nemeta had sent a runner to her, carrying simply the spoken appeal, "Please let me hear from you," messages more confidential had gone between them on the tongue of her oldest son.

"Aye. He's tethered behind the house. The horses are in winter quarters nearer Confluentes—But how have you fared? We've not met for long and long."

"Since Maeloch's death."

"I should have sought you out," Nemeta said contritely. "You earned my abiding thanks once."

"Well, you've had full days of your own, dear, and—" The round face tightened briefly into a frown. "Some signs made me believe 'twere best to leave you to yourself." A sad smile. "But that's all past. We who remember Ys should stand together."

"How *have* you fared?"

"Well enough. Drusus is a kindly man. My children are not ill content either, save that 'tis plain the son of Maeloch will never make a farmer." Tera looked hard at Nemeta. The fire wavered and sputtered. "But you, lass, you're more gaunt than ever, and you tremble as you stand there. What is it?"

"I want—I need—" Nemeta twisted her head right and left. "You know why I asked you here!"

"Somewhat," Tera answered slowly. "News does reach us, though drop by drop and often muddied. A madman came back to Confluentes from the sea. You'd have me help you divine what it means because . . . he'd sailed with your man."

Nemeta's neck stiffened. She stared before her into the darknesses that wove over the cob wall and said fast: "Riwal, he is, or was, a Briton who moved hither several years ago. He was with a mission my Evirion led to his country a score of days past—less two—oh, I've counted, I've counted every one. A shepherd found him rambling aimlessly in the high pastures some leagues east of Ys. He was half dead and could only mumble and moan. Folk nourished a little strength into him and brought him to Confluentes, where he was known—family, friends—When I heard, I dared go there myself, by day. He was under care at the church, but no physician could mend his wits, nor could Bishop Corentinus drive any demon out of him. All he can tell is that 'she' gave him something he must bring back. When pressed to say more, he falls into a weeping, whimpering fit. Otherwise he's quiet, aye, sits unstirring for hours on end and gapes at the air. He knows the names of wife and children and likes it when they are nigh; he has a few words of his own and obeys simple commands as a dog might; Corentinus thinks he may in time be able to do rough labor for his keep.

"*And he sailed with my man!*" she yelled, flung herself on Tera's broad bosom, clung tight with her good arm, and let the sobs shake her.

"Poor lamb. Easy, easy. Come, let's sit." Tera guided her to the bed, where they could be close.

In sawtoothed fragments, the story came out. Tera had only heard rumors of Dahut's doings after the battle at Ys where Maeloch drowned. "Aye," she said starkly, "she killed him and more, she lamed you and keeps you afraid, now you fear what she may have done to your Evirion, aye, aye. The dead bitch that will not lie down, can your Christian priests do naught against her?"

"I asked the bishop." Nemeta had regained will. She sat straight in the circle of the other woman's arm and spoke in a hard, low voice. "I begged of him. He told me these things are forbidden Christian souls to ransack. His God has sent him no vision. He cannot, may not conjure, and from the power that is in his prayers she need merely swim away. He bade me abide, with my trust in Christ. Then I bethought me of you."

"But you and, and Evirion are Christian yourselves, nay?"

Nemeta nodded. "We are, and for what I seek to do, I must answer heavily to God. Yet I cannot wait and wait, alone each night in this bed we shared, not knowing what—she—has done to him. Nor what she may do to us all. Tera, I carry Evirion's child. Lately I've been sure of

475

it. Evirion's child, Grallon's grandchild. What shall *his* lot be in a land where she haunts the shores?"

"I am no Queen of Ys, darling, nor even a witch like what you were."

Nemeta looked at her. "But you serve the old Gods yet," she whispered. "Not the Gods of Ys but of your own people, Cernunnos, Epona, Teutatis, Those Who once were mighty here and may still keep a little, little strength to help Their last few worshippers. And I forswore my witchcraft, but for this, for Evirion and the damning of Dahut, I will call back what I can of it. Together we may do something. I know not what, but—for your own children, Tera, and for Maeloch's ghost, wherever he wanders this night—will you stand by me?"

—It was the dark of the moon, as it must be, but crystalline, star-thronged, the River of Tiamat frozen to bright ice. Light edged the upper blackness of forest and made the rime on turf and stones shimmer. Maybe Tera could have done without the torch that Nemeta held for her while she squatted at a stacked pile of wood and, with a drill whereon signs were carved, kindled the needfire. Flames burned quietly, standing tall now that wind had died away. The faint blood-tinge of them rose high in the smoke until it lost itself among stars.

From the shieling she fetched a cauldron, too big for a one-armed woman to carry, but it was Nemeta who went to and fro bringing water from the pond while Tera sat cross-legged and shut-eyed, lips forming ancient unspoken sounds. When at length the water seethed and steam lent its whiteness to the smoke, they both paced around and around. Tera had brought the dried borage, nettle, mandrake root that they cast in, but the chant, high and ululating, was Nemeta's.

It hurt her when they led the foal to the fire. He was a fine young stallion, roan with a silver blaze, get of Favonius. She felt she betrayed her father's trust. Gratillonius had left her here after Evirion departed, rather than returning the former watchman. She fought back the tears. Beneath her heart she carried his grandchild.

The colt tossed his head, rolled his eyes, whinnied, alarmed by this strangeness. She gripped the bridle tightly, rubbed her head against his neck, crooned comfort, soothed him.

"We call," said Tera, and Nemeta stepped aside. Her companion raised a sledge hammer in both strong hands. Old stains were on haft and head. She smashed it forward. The horse screamed and went down. Tera leaped on him, knife drawn, and struck. The blood spouted. A while he struggled, then shivered and lay still. The blood that pooled around him steamed like the kettle. The women marked themselves with it.

Did a shadow of antlers rise athwart the stars? Did hoofs gallop? A wolf howled. Not for years had men heard wolves this near their city.

Tera butchered the sacrifice quickly and roughly, and cast the meat in the cauldron, while Nemeta cursed the Gods of Ys and summoned the Old Folk from their dolmens. They did not cook the food long before they forced down as much of it as they were able. Afterward they ate the holy toadstools, rolled themselves in blankets by the waning fire, and invoked sleep. It thundered upon them.

—Stars glimmered yet in the west, but had fled the pallor of the east. Hoarfrost crusted every blade of grass. Ice had formed on the stiffened blood around guts, hide, half-stripped bones. It made a skin over the stew in the kettle. Dust drifted on a dawn breeze from the ash underneath.

The women huddled close in their coverings, as if a wraith of heat lingered for them. They shook with weariness. Breath smoked at each hoarse word.

"So we know," Tera said. "Dahut brought my Maeloch onto the rocks, and herself bore him below. She rammed *Brennilis* with a craft she'd robbed from some fishers she drew to Ys for this, and herself bore Evirion below. Everyone aboard was lost save for Riwal. Him she ferried ashore. We know not why that was."

"And we know," Nemeta joined in, "that she bore Rufinus below, but her vengefulness was unquenchable and so she led the Scoti to Audiarna. We know of other wreck and ruin she has wrought among humble folk whom nobody mourned but those that loved them. We know the evil of

477

her can only end with herself; for the Gods of Ys have made her Their revenge on the world."

"But how can we seek her out?"

"*We* cannot. The One God gives her leave to be. We know not why. By His might alone may her sea take her back to it forever."

Tera shuddered. "Are her powers that great?"

"She swims untiring," said Nemeta's toneless chant, "but she cannot long endure sun, nor be on land more than a very little span. Where she goes, she commands the wind, though she breathes no longer. She lures, enchants, dazzles, terrifies. Nonetheless men have wrenched themselves from her call, and to it a saint would be deaf. With a single prayer he could destroy her."

"She will ken him from afar, and flee."

"She is of the moon. Ever its fullness draws her back to Ys, where she died, that she may drink its light upon that bay. By a gibbous moon she sought out Rufinus on the bridge and led the Scoti to Audiarna, but afterward she left them and returned home, that she might swim in its fullness among the ruins of Ys. There and then can someone find her."

"But still she will know him, and escape into Ocean."

Nemeta slumped before the ashes. Exhaustion dragged down her voice. "More I cannot say. Nor did the Horned One have more to give your dreams, did He? Let us go indoors and seek mortal sleep."

Tera rose. "And what next will you do, lonely dear?" she asked. "Me, I'll trudge back to the farm, but you?"

"I will seek Bishop Corentinus," Nemeta answered. "I will tell him what we have learned, and beg his forgiveness, and Christ's, and Christ's help against yonder thing."

XXV

1

The day before solstice hung still and murky. Breath misted, but there was no real sense of cold, nor of wetness, and noises all seemed hushed. The rivers glided iron-dark under earthen walls of Confluentes where summer's grass was gone sere, and, mingled together, on past Aquilo toward the sea. Folk in the streets and shops went about their work unwontedly subdued, though none could have said why. It was as if the world lay waiting.

Suddenly, far down the Venetorum road, against bare brown fields and skeleton trees, color burst forth. Red-bordered gold with black emblem, the wolf banner flew at the head of a mounted troop. Behind it, cloaks billowed rainbow-colored; tunics and breeks proclaimed clans by their interwoven hues; metal winked, helmets, mailcoats, spearheads that rose and fell and rose again to the rocking rhythm of the horses. Hoofs thudded. Even the baggage mules were eager. A horn sang, a shout lifted, for the men of Gradlon saw home before them.

Sentinels of the city cried answer and winded trumpets of their own. News washed like a wave between the turrets. Men, women, children dropped whatever they were at and swarmed forth. Their cheers defied the sullen sky. "He comes! The King is back!"— not the Duke, as he named himself, but the King, as they did.

Ever louder through hoofbeats, creak of leather, jangle of iron, whoops out of throats, the sound of his cities reached Gratillonius. His vision strained forward. How well he knew each battlement, each timber in the portal and stone in the bridge. Behind them reached the ways he had laid out, the buildings he had watched grow, the people for whom he had been riding, hearthfires and

479

hope. O Verania! What was Marcus up to, how much bigger was Maria?

Ahead laired trouble, toil, much anger, some heart-break. You didn't get away from any of those, this side of Heaven. But he felt ready to meet them. Eastward he left a good job of work, alliances firmly forged. In doing it he had shored up the spirit within himself. Today was the day when he would again embrace Verania.

For an instant Dahilis flitted through his awareness. He thought she smiled and waved. A farewell? She was gone. He signalled his trumpeter to sound gallop. Favonius surged.

His hoofs thundered on the bridge. Gratillonius glanced left. Several boats were moored at the wharf, a couple of them large enough to be called small ships, but mostly the piers were winter-empty.

Brennilis was not there.

The shock made him rein in with needless force. Favonius neighed angrily, reared, went on at a skittish walk. Turbulence erupted as the troopers filed off to cross. Every-body was impatient. Hurrahs gusted from the open gate.

Had the weather proven too fierce around Britannia? It had continued benign on the mainland. Only yesterday, Gratillonius had with a breastful of anxiety inquired of the villagers near whom he camped, and heard that it had also been mild hereabouts. Misfortune? Pirates would scarcely have been out so late in the year; if any were, they'd scarcely attack a craft as redoubtable as *Brennilis*. Evirion would be wary of ambushes ashore. The Britons might reject Gratillonius's offer at once, unlikely though that seemed, but they wouldn't harm the bearer, would they?

He rode through the gate. Guardsmen fenced Principal Way with their pikeshafts, holding back the crowd on either side. The street was clear for him—and there, where it crossed Market Way, on which their house stood, there waited Verania in the middle of the intersection. She carried Maria in her arms. Marcus hopped and shouted on her right. Tall on her left, his cloak a splash of spring-time green, was Salomon. Across the yards between, Gratillonius knew them. He must hold Favonius in. He might trample them if he went too fast. Another minute.

Bishop Corentinus stepped out of Apostolic Way and stopped. "Whoa!" Barely, Gratillonius halted.

The man afoot must look up at the man on horseback, yet somehow it was as if their eyes met on a level: for all at once the walls, the tumult, everything receded from Gratillonius and they two were alone in a strange place. Corentinus wore sandals on his bare feet and a coarse black robe over his rawboned height. He had thrown a cloak across his shoulders and put a wide-brimmed hat on his head. Hair and beard were more white than gray. His right hand gripped a staff, his left was upraised, palm outward, a command to stop. It was eerie how Gratillonius came to think of the Germanic God Wotan the Wanderer, Who leads the dead away.

"Hail," he said. Seeing this confrontation, the people fell piecemeal silent, until they stood staring under the low dark sky.

"Welcome back," replied Corentinus with never a smile. "Did you succeed in your mission?"

"I did, but—"

"That is well; for much here is ill. Listen. You can see for yourself that your family is hale. I'm sorry to bar you from them, but there are tidings I think you'd best have first,—" Sternness fell from voice and craggy face. "—old friend. It needn't take long, then you can rejoin them. Will you follow me now?"

Gratillonius sat hearing the pulse in his head. It felt like a while and a while before he said, "As you will," and turned about to give the troop into charge of his deputy.

Likewise he gave the reins of Favonius, and dismounted. As he left with the bishop, he looked toward Verania. She waved at him, as his memory of Dahilis had waved.

—Corentinus had moved from Aquilo to a house newly erected beside the cathedral in Confluentes. It was a good-sized building and decently, if austerely, furnished, for he received men of importance, on matters temporal as well as spiritual, and his flock would have him do so in such manner as to reflect credit on their community. At the rear, however, he had had made a room that was his alone, for prayer, meditation, and sleep. It was a mere cell, its window a single uncovered slit. The dirt floor held

481

one stool and a straw pallet with a thin blanket. Walls and ceiling were bare plaster. Above the bed hung a small, roughly whittled wooden cross which holy Martinus had blessed. A clay lamp on a shelf burned the poorest sort of fat. Today it flickered alight because else men would have been like moles. Dankness and chill were gathered as thick as the gloom.

"Here we'll talk," Corentinus said, "for I may hope a faintest breath of sanctity is present, and what we have to speak of is terrible."

Gratillonius sat hunched on the stool and regarded the guttering yellow flame. Corentinus loomed above him. In a few words, the tale came out.

"Oh, no," Gratillonius whispered. "No, no."

"So it is, my son."

Gratillonius twisted his neck around and peered upward. He saw only the hair, the beard, a glint of eyes. "Nemeta, how is she?"

"Sorrowful but in health."

"I must go to her. Is she still out at the pastures? What have you done about, about her sin? Do you think she's lost?"

Corentinus shook his head. "No. She's a valiant lass. I've never seen more bravery than was in her when she came to confess to me. She thought she might well be damned, and was ready to take that, if the Church would receive her child." A knobbly hand reached down to squeeze the shoulder beneath. "She did what she did largely for you, Gratillonius."

Unshed tears can fill the gullet. "Wha-what did you do?"

"I told her to sin no more. And yet—she acted less in fear or hatred than out of love. That was why she could not wholly repent." A rusty chuckle. "I asked her if she was sorry she could not, and this she agreed to. So then and there I baptized her."

Gratillonius caught hold of the hand that clasped him, and pressed it hard.

"I'll provide for her, of course," he said when he was able. "She can't stay on alone in that wretched shack."

"She dares not come into town at all any more, now that

she carries Evirion's child," said Corentinus harshly. "And Verania wonders whether your children and she are safe, even within the walls. She will no longer let them out, no, not to the manor house where they've had pleasure, certainly not across the bridge and down along the river to see their grandmother. Dwellers on the coast live in fright, worse than any barbarians ever brought them, for barbarians are at least human and—do not stalk the shores in winter."

As he listened, a tide rose in Gratillonius. He heard it roar, he felt himself drowning in it. "Dahut," he called across the wild waters, "Dahut."

"You cannot keep hiding from this," the relentless voice marched on above him. "We must destroy that hell-creature or perish in trying."

Gratillonius sprang up. "We can't!" he yelled. "There is no way!" He struck his fist against the wall. Plaster cracked apart and fell. The cross shivered.

"There is, with God's help," said Corentinus at his back. "Nemeta staked her soul to discover it."

Gratillonius leaned head on arm and shut his eyes.

The bishop's tone gentled a little. "She did not see this herself, and best we keep the secret between us. I did not either, at first, nor is it entirely clear to me yet. We've a fouled line to untangle, you and I, and afterward a hard course to steer. It may well end in wreck for us too."

Somehow the warning put a measure of strength back in Gratillonius. He turned from the wall.

"Good man, oh, good man," murmured Corentinus. "I need your counsel. Can you give it? Afterward I'll let you go home."

Gratillonius forced a nod.

"I haven't told you quite everything about poor mad Riwal," said the other. "He was carrying something when the shepherd found him, and wouldn't let slip of it. As I tried to speak with him later, he mouthed broken words about Dahut, the White One, bringing him ashore. Well, I've told you that. I thought, as I imagine you do, she did this—for Nemeta's vision declared it was true she did—in refined cruelty. She'd leave no doubt that she, and nothing mortal or natural, had sunken the ship and murdered the crew. But then I looked at the thing in his hand, and the peasant who'd brought him in explained about it. When I asked, he gave it to me, no, forced it on me. 'For Gradlon,' he babbled, 'for Gradlon.' I still don't understand. But here it is."

He stooped with an aged man's stiffness and from beneath the blanket fetched a small object which he proffered. Gratillonius took it and held it near the lamp to see. Rotten wood was damp and spongy between his fingers. Decayed, worm-eaten, battered, the thing had scant form left. And yet he knew it. Suddenly he was cold down into his bones, sea-bottom cold.

"It doesn't seem like a cult object or a magical tool, does it?" he heard across immensities. "Almost a toy."

"That's what it is," he heard inside his skull. "A horse figure I made for her when she was a little girl."

"Why on—earth—would she send it to you? A taunt? A challenge?"

"I think not," said Gratillonius from somewhere outside himself. "My daughter was always glad of my gifts. She was so proud that her Papa could make them. This one was her special favorite. I think she's calling me."

2

Snow began to fall as the couple neared the top of Mons Ferruginus. It dropped through windless quiet in flakes tiny but teeming. Beyond a few yards there soon was white blindness. Ground vanished beneath it and the bare boughs of trees and shrubs bore a new flowering. A measure of warmth had stolen into the air.

Gratillonius halted on the trail. "We may as well go back," he said.

"I'm sorry," Verania replied. "You wanted so much a view over your country."

He glanced down at her. She looked up from within her snow-dusted cowl. The cloak happened to be black, and winter always paled her fair skin, so lips and hazel eyes and a stray brown lock bore all the colors he saw in a world of gray and white.

"Did I say that?" he asked.

"No, not really. But I could tell."

"You notice more than you let on."

She shook her head. "I only pay attention—to you, my dearest."

"Ah, well," he sighed, "I've plenty memories from here." With a grave smile: "Besides, what I most wanted was to get off alone with you."

She came to him and laid her cheek against his breast. For a moment they held each other, then started homeward, hand in hand. The trail being narrow, often one of them must go off it into brush which scratched and crackled unnaturally loud; but neither let go.

"Anyhow," Gratillonius said, "now I'll have more time with the children before we tuck them in."

"They're lucky," she answered. "My father was like you in this, if little else. It's a rare kind."

"Aw," he mumbled.

Her grip tightened. Abruptly her voice grew shrill. "Come back to us!"

He stopped again. Her delicate features worked until she could stiffen them. Tears glinted on the lashes. "Of course I will," he promised.

"How do I know?" The words tumbled forth. "You haven't told me anything except that you're leaving already."

It tore away the visor he had lowered against her. "I haven't dared," he rasped. "Nobody. Nor can I speak till afterward."

"You are going—"

"To deal with a certain menace. It won't take long."

"Unless you're the one who dies."

He shrugged.

"It could be worse than death," she said frantically. "Gradlon, that evil is not of this world."

"You notice too much," he snapped.

She looked from him, and back at him, shuddered within the cloak, finally said low, "And I think about it."

He tugged at her hand. "Come," he proposed. They went on downhill through the snowfall.

485

When he thought she had calmed a bit, he said, "You've always been wise for your age, Verania. Have you the wisdom now to keep silence?"

She nodded.

Her fingers, which had gone icy, seemed pace by pace to thaw in his. At last she gave him a smile.

The snowfall thickened.

"Strange," he said slowly. "All at once I remember. Today is the Birthday of Mithras."

Alarm touched her tone. "You don't follow that God any longer!"

"Certainly not. But it seems to me somehow as though this, everything that matters to me, it began that selfsame day, five-and-twenty years ago. I stood guard on the Wall. . . . And soon, one way or another, it will end."

"It won't!" she cried. "Not for you!" Her face lifted toward hidden heaven. Snow struck it, melted, ran down in rain. "Holy Maria, Mother of God," she appealed, "we've only had four years."

In a way he did not understand but that was like a smith quenching a newly forged sword, it hardened his will for that to which he had plighted himself.

3

Midwinter nights fell early and dwelt late in Armorica, day hardly more than a glimmer between them, but this one was ice-clear. Stars thronged the dark, so bright that he could see colors in some, blue like steel, yellow like brass, red like rust. Their brilliance was also in the Milky Way, which to Ys had been the River of Tiamat, primordial Serpent of Chaos, but which elsewhere was the bridge by which the dead leave our world. Snow on the ground caught the light from above, glowed and glittered. It was a crust frozen hard, crunching underhoof; the earth beneath it boomed. Gratillonius rode easily across a vast unreal sweep of hills above the whitened valley. He was aware of the cold around him but did not feel it; he went as if in a dream.

The moon rose full, immense, over the eastern range as Favonius started down Aquilonian Way. Night became yet the more luminous, dazzlingly; but now there were fewer stars and many crooked shadows. The stallion slowed, for scattered or broken paving blocks, holes, and brambles made this part of the road treacherous. Below the thuds and the vaporous breathing, his rider began to hear the sea.

Tide was about two hours into ebb, water still well up the bay. Radiance ran across it where wave crests caught moonbeams. The wet strand shimmered. He could make out the last few rubble-bulks as blacknesses unstirring amidst that mercury fluidity. Right and left, the cliffs also denied the light. Their brutal masses shouldered into a sky that Ocean walled off afar.

He came down onto level ground and turned again west. The amphitheater huddled in its congealed marsh under a ragged blanket of snow. He glimpsed stars through gaps in the sides. Demolition had continued since he fought his battle here. By the time of his death, likely no trace whatsoever of Ys would remain.

That was supposing he reached a fairly ripe age. He might die this hour. No fear of it was in him. He had dropped such human things on the journey from Confluentes. They waited for him at home.

The amphitheater fell behind. Snow dwindled to patches and then to naught, washed away by sea-spray. Frost sparkled on rocks and leafless shrubs. The murmur he heard from the heights had become deep, multitudinously whispery at the shore, rumbling and roaring farther out. Phantoms leaped where combers broke on skerries.

"Whoa," said Gratillonius, and drew rein. He sprang from the saddle and tethered Favonius to a bush at the rim of the beach. His cloak he unfastened and laid across the horse's withers for whatever slight warmth it might give. It could hamper him. He wore simply Gallic tunic, breeks, soft shoes that let his feet grip the soil. Roman sword and Celtic dirk were at his belt, but he did not think he would have use for either.

Favonius whickered. Gratillonius stroked a hand down

the head and over the soft nose. "Good luck, old buddy," he said. "God keep you."

He turned and walked over sand and shingle toward the water. They gritted. Kelp coiled snakish. Cold such as this deadened most odors, but his nostrils drank a sharpness of salt.

Two hillocks marked where High Gate formerly stood. Passing between, he saw more. On his left, that one had been the royal palace; on his right, that one had been the Temple of Belisama. A vague track and two or three cracked slabs told him that he betrod Lir Way. Moored to a stump of stone lay a boat—aye, the lifeboat from *Brennilis*.

At the water's edge he halted and looked outward. Receding, Ocean nonetheless cast small waves that licked around his ankles. He did not mark their chill. Froth roiled around pieces of wall and a single pillar.

Here I am, Dahut, his spirit called. I have come in answer to your bidding.

For a span that seemed long, nothing stirred but the waves. He was without expectations. How could a mortal man foreknow what would travel through this night? Witchcraft had told that she would be in her Ys, but Satan was the wellspring of untruth. Gratillonius had arrived at moonrise to make doubly sure, and to see as well as might be, little though he wanted to. He was himself burdened with sin, and unbaptized; she ought not to fear him. Though she had knowledge of where those were whom she hated, he did not believe she could hear their thoughts; else she would scarcely have sent her token to him. But what did he know?

His task was to keep her heedful of him; how?

He waited.

A wave, yonder where the gate once opened to the sea? A riptide? Seal-swift it flowed his way. A wake shone brokenly behind. Now he saw an arm uplifted, now he saw the thick, rippling hair. She reached the shallows, a few yards from him, halted, and stood.

The tide swirled around her waist. The light poured over her face, her breasts, the arms she held toward him. White she was as the snow or the waves that shattered on the skerries, save for the mane that he knew was golden

488

and the eyes that he knew were summer-blue. So had he last seen her, demonic at the Bridge of Sena, and the worst horror of it had been the lust that raged aloft in him.

But tonight it was not thus at all. She was merely and wholly beautiful. The whiteness was purity. Her sea had washed her clean; she was renewed, Princess of Ys, and she smiled across the water like that little girl for whom he carved a wooden horse. She was his daughter, born to Dahilis, and she needed him.

Her song went high and sweet over the shout and thunder below the cliffs.

> "Out of this moonlight on the sea,
> Sundered from you ashore,
> Father, I call you, come to me
> And give me your love once more.
>
> "Though I have left your world of man,
> Flung on the wind like foam,
> Do you remember how I ran
> To meet you when you came home?
>
> "Lullaby now is wave on reef,
> Hollow and comfortless.
> Yours was the laugh that healed all grief,
> And there was no loneliness.
>
> "Cold were those years when I at sea
> Longed, and yet could not weep.
> Father, I call you, come to me
> And rock me again to sleep."

By the mercy of Christ. No, he could not judge that. He must not utter it.

She stood waiting for him. If he stayed on the land that was forbidden her, she would soon swim away, alone forever.

He waded forth. The bottom sloped steeply. A few feet past her, he would be over his depth. Salt drops stung his lips.

Joy pulsed from her. She leaned forward, as if she could

go no higher. The hands trembled that reached for him. Her smile outshone the stars that wreathed her hair.

He opened his arms. She fell into them. He held her tightly against him. Her embrace around his neck, her head on his breast, stabbed with chill. "Dahut," he said, "oh, Dahut."

She wrenched herself loose. Her scream clawed. Never had he beheld such terror on any face.

Not looking around, he knew that his follower Corentinus had reached the strand and begun the exorcism.

Dahut dived. She had time to flee.

Gratillonius snatched after her. His fingers closed in the streaming tresses. Her strength hauled him under. Blind, the breath gone from him, he tumbled with her, outward over the deeps. His free hand found solidness, curve of flesh. He locked a leg around those that kicked at him.

Heads came above water. He saw her eyes wide, mouth open, before the struggle whirled him toward the moon and its whiteness dazed sight of her. He gasped air full of froth churned up. Her nails raked him. It smote through his awareness: *Once she cried for me to draw her from the sea. Tonight at last I do.*

The voice resounded through the surf: "I exorcise you, unclean spirit, in the name of Jesus Christ, Who did cast forth demons, and by the power that He gave unto His holy Church, against which the gates of hell shall not prevail. Begone, creature of Satan, he the enemy of God and of mankind, he whose rebellion brought war in Heaven and whose falseness brought death into the world, he the root of evil, discord, and misery. Begone to him. Begone. Amen. Amen. Amen."

Dahut shrieked. It echoed off the cliffs and flew out over Ocean. She writhed and slumped.

Gratillonius felt hardness underfoot, a fallen shard of Ys. He regained balance and stood there on it, the tide up to his heart, in his arms a dead young woman.

4

At dawn the sea was withdrawing anew, gray and white between darkling cliffs and among the rocks. It drummed an undertone to a silence otherwise broken by only the earliest of the gulls. A breeze blew sharp down the valley.

Stiffly, Gratillonius rose. Corentinus did too, and gave him an anxious look. The bishop had built and tended a small fire above the strand. He had gone after his own mount and the pack animal, with dry clothes which he forced his companion to don. Afterward no word passed from one of them to the other. Corentinus prayed through the night while Gratillonius sat beside that which he had wrapped in his cloak.

"You really should get some sleep before we start back," the bishop said.

"No need," Gratillonius replied.

"Food?" Corentinus gestured at their rations.

"No."

"Well, then, let's load our stuff."

"Not that either."

Corentinus raised his brows. "What?"

Gratillonius pointed to the object at his feet. "Dahut. I have to bury her."

"I thought we'd bring her with us."

Now the voice clanged: "Slung over a horse's rump? To be jeered and cursed and lie like a beast in unhallowed ground? No. She's going home to the Queens of Ys."

"But without that shown them, will the people believe?" Corentinus protested. "They may think she haunts these waters yet."

"Let them. Some bold sailors will take our word. When no harm comes, the rest will soon take ship likewise."

Corentinus stood meditative a while before he sighed, "Ah, well. . . . So be it. They'll remember her with Ys, a legend, a hearthside story on winter nights."

Gratillonius stared at the bundle. "That's all that will be left."

Corentinus blinked hard. "My son—" He must try afresh. "I can barely guess, old childless I, what wounds you carry. May they heal in you. The scars of them will be a pledge of your reward in Heaven, my son."

"My daughter—" Gratillonius lifted his head and met those eyes. "There at the end, she told me she loved me."

The response was rough. "Another snare of hers."

"I don't know," Gratillonius said. "I never will, unless after I'm dead myself. *Should* I have held her for you?"

Corentinus nodded. "You should. No matter what. It was your duty."

Gratillonius spread his hands. "If she did speak the truth—if she did—is she in hell? Might God have taken her to Him after all?"

"It is not for us to set bounds on His mercy," Corentinus answered low. What else could he say? Louder: "But in His name, Gratillonius, and for everyone's sake, do not brood on this."

The father grinned. "Oh, I'll have enough else to do. There will be war again in spring."

He bent down at the knees, gathered the body, bore it across the strand to the water. The lifeboat still floated at a few inches' depth. He laid his burden within. Searching about, he found a stone of the size he wanted. It was off the capital of a pillar, the eroded image of a flower. He put it in the boat and hauled himself after. Unstepped mast, yardarm, furled sail, oars were neatly lashed in place. He freed the oars, cast off, and bent to the rowing. The ebb tide helped. Corentinus watched from shore till he must go sit down. His years were heavy upon him.

Past the ruins, over the sea gate, and on outward Gratillonius went. Oars creaked and thumped between their tholes, for the wind stiffened, to make the boat roll and pitch. Waves tramped by, gray-green and wrinkled, spindrift blown off their crests. They snarled and crashed on rocks, flinging whiteness high for the wind to catch. It was a chill morning, the sun wan above the snow.

Presently he reached the funeral grounds of Ys, where the bottom plunged to depths unknown. He shipped his oars and let the boat swing adrift. Far off to the west he spied a streak of darkness that was Sena.

He cut a length from the lashings, made stone fast to ankles, wound the line up the shrouding cloak but stopped short. Ys had had her own service for the dead. *Gods of mystery, Gods of life and death, sea that nourishes Ys, take this my beloved—* But he must not say such words. Nor would he if he might.

A prayer to Christ? Somehow that wasn't right either.

He folded back the cloth. The hours had smoothed her face. With eyes closed and jaw bound, she lay in that inhuman peacefulness which dwells for a time before dissolution begins. He kissed her brow. She was no colder than the wind.

He covered her again, made the cord secure, and on his knees—because to stand would have been dangerous, and he had duties—lifted her up and dropped her over the side. She sank at once. A gull mewed.

He settled onto his thwart, took the oars, and rowed back.

It was a long haul against the flow of air and water, that brought him a blessed weariness. When at last he grounded, he could roll into a blanket and sleep an hour or two.

Rousing, for a moment he was full of gladness. Then he remembered. But miles lay ahead, to Audiarna where he and his companion would rest before going on to Confluentes. When he was at home with Verania he could weep; and she would make all things good.

Favonius pawed the ground, eager to be off. Corentinus had gotten the baggage ready. The men departed. Sundown at their backs, they rode into night.

Would you know the dog from the wolf? You may look at his paw,
Comparing the claw and the pad; you may measure his stride;
You may handle his coat and his ears; you may study his jaw;
And yet what you seek is not found in his bones or his hide,
For between the Dog and the Wolf there is only the Law.

NOTES

Although we hope our story explains itself, it may raise
a few questions in the minds of some readers, while others
may wish to know a little more about the period. These
notes are intended for them.

I

The plight of the Ysans: While the Osismii were friendly
enough, it should be remembered that the concept of
foreign aid did not exist. True, the Roman Empire often
supplied grain (or money) to client states, but this was a
subsidy and depended on their being perceived as useful.

Suffetes: Members of the thirteen aristocratic Ysan families. See the earlier books.

Emain Macha: The central stronghold of the Ulati. See
Dahut.

Gess (now *geas*): A kind of taboo; a prohibition laid upon
an individual or a class. See *Roma Mater*.

Corentinus's warning: As we have remarked before, the
early Christian Church did not deny that most pagan
gods were real, but tended to consider them demons
intent on misleading men. Euhemerism sometimes provided an alternative explanation, as in the *Heimskringla*.

Kilt: This was originally no mere skirt, but a garment—
often a poor man's only garment—ample to cover most of
the body and to serve as a bedroll at night.

Chorepiscopus: In the early Church, a cleric with rank between that of a priest and a bishop. See the notes to *Roma Mater*. Corentinus had been the chorepiscopus at Ys.

Iron ore: This was generally bog iron, collected rather than mined.

Garrison troops: According to an extant record, as of about 425 A.D. there were fourteen units of *limitanei*, totaling less than 10,000 men, in Sequania, Moguntiacum, Belgica, and Armorica. It seems unlikely that there were many more a quarter century earlier. To be sure, they were supplemented by native *numeri* (regulars) and other outfits, but these had nothing like the effectiveness of the old legions.

Comet: The comet of 400 is known to have been visible from 19 March to 10 April (Gregorian dates); the actual span may have been longer.

Robin: The European bird, smaller than the North American and of a different genus, is meant.

Summoning the gods: Gallic beliefs and practices, especially on extraordinary occasions, are scarcely known; one must guess. Besides, they probably varied with time and from tribe to tribe.

Crossbow: Versions of this weapon existed from quite ancient times, though its use did not become widespread until the Middle Ages.

Britannic Sea (Oceanus Britannicus): The English Channel.

The Islands of Crows (in Latin, *Corvorum Insulae*, this word order being preferred in such cases): The Channel

Islands. Almost nothing is known of their history prior to the medieval period. There are traces of Roman occupation, but slight, indicating that it was nominal and came to an end before the Empire did. It is our own idea that they thereupon became a haunt of pirates and so acquired the nickname we use.

German Sea (Oceanus Germanicus): The North Sea.

Celtic languages: Through closely related, these had enough differences from each other to make them distinct. We suppose that a speaker of the Irish tongue could acquire a Continental one fairly easily, and vice versa.

Danes (Dani): For a brief discussion of this people, see the notes to *Dahut*. While the viking era would not commence for several centuries, it is reasonable to suppose that some Scandinavians joined the Western Germanic sailors already harrying the Empire.

Tungri and Continental Belgae: Tribes inhabiting what are now the Low Countries and the adjacent part of France. Belgae had also established themselves quite powerfully in Britain before the Roman conquest.

III

Liguria: A region of Italy which at this time included what is now Lombardy. Modern Liguria is only a seaboard strip.

Mediolanum: Milan. Very little is known of its layout or appearance in Roman times.

Alaric: Visigothic king whose armies repeatedly invaded Italy, beginning as early as 401. In between hostilities there was occasional uneasy alliance with the Romans.

(The next few entries repeat, briefly, explanations made in earlier volumes.)

Ruirthech: The River Liffey. Today it does *not* mark the

border of Leinster, but we suppose that the Tara dynasty carved most of Mide out of the latter.

Kings: Each tuath in early Ireland had its own king, who was little more than a wartime leader and peacetime arbitrator. Such kings generally owed allegiance to more powerful ones, among whom the strongest might dominate a realm; but he was in no sense a monarch.

Mumu: Approximately, Munster. At this time the chief king was Conual Corcc, whom we suppose to have been friendly toward both Niall and Ys.

Temir: Tara.

Women in early Ireland: They had almost as many rights and as much freedom as men, including sexually, even after marriage.

IV

The turf wall: We base our description on the experimental work of Robin Birley and his team. A turf cut to the regulation Roman army size of 18″ x 12″ x 6″ weighs about 2¼ stone, or a little over 30 pounds. Edward Luttwak has pointed out that the real value of the perimeter defense of a legionary camp was its enabling most men to get a good night's sleep.

Darioritum Venetorum: Vannes.

Vorgium: Carhaix.

Gesoscribate: A Roman port on or near the site of present-day Brest.

Jecta: The River Jet (conjectural from Aqua Iactar, "the water thrown in a straight line," thence Jecta, and so on to the modern form).

Postal privileges: The Imperial mails went via frequent relay stations where fresh horses, relief riders, and, at longer intervals, lodging were available. The system was reserved for official communications, but favored persons were occasionally allowed to use it. Ordinary people employed private carriers.

Dumnoniic shore: The Dumnonii inhabited what is now Cornwall and Devon. It seems believable that, under Roman influence, they were sometimes building better boats than their Irish cousins—although the currach is itself very seaworthy.

Egyptians: Egypt was largely Christian by the early fourth century, and remained so until the Moslem conquest.

V

Indiction (Latin *indictio*): The decree issued every fifteen years by the Roman Emperors, establishing property and head taxes on the basis of census reports; also, the taxes themselves, collected annually and for the most part in kind. The indiction was by no means the only levy, and often superindictions were added. The year 402 was one of indiction.

Fundus: A landed estate. See *Roma Mater*.

Gong: Bells were probably not yet known. The earliest date suggested by any evidence is the late fourth century, and the actual date may well lie a hundred or more years later. Certainly bells would not be found in Armorica at the time of our story.

Seating: As we have observed before, chairs were not common (except in Ys) until fairly recent times. People usually sat on benches or stools, though for the well-to-do these might be elaborately made and upholstered. The floor was quite often used, especially by the poor, and to offer a visitor nothing better would be a blunt subordination of him.

Sucat: St. Patrick to be. See *Gallicenae*.

Stories of St. Martin: These two—that Satan appeared to him in the guise of Christ but was identified and dismissed, and that he raised and exorcised the ghost of a false saint—occur in his legend.

Confluentes Cornuales: The Breton name "Kemper," which French renders "Quimper," means "confluence." We have supposed that there was a Latin original with the same meaning, most likely in the plural form as is permissible in that language. Our historical analogue is Koblenz in Germany. The general area in which Quimper lies is known as Cornouaille. This is not a version of "Cornwall," bestowed by immigrants from Britain, as is often said; its source is obscure. That the region came to be called Dogwood Land, Terra Cornualis, in late Roman times, and thus eventually Cornouaille, is our own idea.

VII

The high Mass: This scene represents our reconstruction of a Gallic Mass, which was quite different from forms elsewhere and those that developed later. Much is uncertain about it, and there appears to have been considerable variation from time to time and place to place.

Corentinus a bishop: There is no record of a bishop of Quimper in the fifth century. Yet Breton tradition holds that St. Corentin held the office, having been consecrated by St. Martin. If this is true, as we assume in the story, perhaps it fell vacant for a long time after his death. Alternatively, it may have happened that no bishop of Quimper attended a synod—as Martin himself did not subsequent to the Priscillianist affair—throughout the same period, and hence none is mentioned in what chronicles and lists have survived. Political and ethnic divisions might account for the absences.

A carcass breeds maggots: This belief was widespread before the life cycle was understood.

Vienna: The River Vienne.

Liger: The River Loire.

Death of St. Martin: Our account follows that of Sulpicius, with a few slight adaptations. The date was probably 8 November. (A modern biography gives it as the 11th, but this was likelier the date of burial.) However, a calendrical inconsistency in the chronicle makes the year uncertain. Depending on how one reads, it was either 397 or 400. We have chosen the latter.

VIII

The Biblical verse: Hebrews xiii, 12.

Exorcism: In the early Church, this was repeatedly done over candidates for baptism, at least if they were adult and if time allowed.

Baptism: As we have observed before, the usual practice even in Christian families had been to defer baptism until the person and his bishop agreed he was ready— often quite late in life. This remained common in the East, but in the West the earliest possible christening came to be more and more favored, until by about 400 it was generally done for infants. Most converts were still first given some instruction, which included the exorcisms mentioned.

Piracy: Throughout history, pirates have raided the land much more frequently than they have attacked ships at sea.

Church organization: We have already explained that this was different from what it later became. Priests were essentially assistants to the bishop, ranking above deacons but without certain of the powers, such as independently administering baptism, that later became theirs.

Baptismal rites: These varied considerably from time to time, place to place, and according to circumstances. What we have depicted is a variant of a form commonly employed; the modifications for women are rather conjectural, but may well have been ordered by some if not all bishops. Holy Saturday was the favored time. From the preceding period of instruction and abstinence developed, quite probably, many Lenten practices that later became general.

Drusus's farm: It is not typically Celtic in its layout nor Roman in its legal standing. However, under peculiar conditions such as prevailed around Aquilo at the time, something like this was a logical development among new settlers.

Paganism: Though pagan rites were now illegal, the law was seldom enforceable, except against conspicuous centers; and baptism was not yet compulsory.

IX

Sprit rig: Formerly this was thought to be a Dutch invention of the late Middle Ages, but archeological evidence has come to light that the Romans knew it, as well as a version of the lateen sail.

Artemon: A small square sail hung from the bowsprit to aid in steering.

Roman Bay: Baie de Douarnenez. The name that the Romans themselves gave it is unknown.

501

Goat Foreland: Cap de la Chèvre. We suppose that the Ysans and their neighbors gave it a name with the same meaning.

Sapa: Pliny describes this substance, its preparation and uses. In terms of modern chemistry, the active ingredients were organic lead salts. Lead is an abortifacient; when it lightens the complexion, it does so by causing anemia.

Johannes: Latin form of "John," in this case John the Baptist. His feast day is not now precisely at the solstice, but Midsummer Night rituals connected with it persisted until quite recent times, and in some areas the bonfires are still lighted.

Marriage: Church doctrine and practice with respect to matrimony in the early fifth century are discussed in a later note.

X

The witch: It is unlikely that medieval witchcraft represented a widespread, underground Old Religion, as is often claimed. Granted, there were pagan survivals in the practice of it, but so there were in Christianity. Doubtless some witches and their male counterparts were outright pagans, like Nemeta, though probably more were henotheistic and still more thought of themselves as Christian (or, in some cases, Jewish). Certain monkish chroniclers seem to have greatly exaggerated the significance of magic and passed on the wildest rumors. Despite this, the fact is that for centuries magic was generally tolerated, provided it was not openly blasphemous—which would scarcely have been so if the Church saw it as a threat. There were actually stories of pious wizards such as Merlin. Full persecution of witches and alleged witches was a phenomenon of the Reformation era, and did not succeed in extirpating them everywhere. Within living memory, some parts of southern Europe had their village witches whose spells were supposed to help people with minor problems. This is not to say that *no* witches and warlocks were ever feared, or that horrid rites and malign intent never happened. Evil occurs in all walks of life.

Egyptian malady: Diphtheria, described under this name by Aretaeus in the second century. There is much uncertainty about the epidemiology of the ancient world. The devastating plague in the reign of Marcus Aurelius does not appear to have been bubonic, which is first unequivocally documented in Europe in the sixth century. Smallpox seems to have entered from Asia about a hundred years later than that.

Imperial tax agent: At this period, tax collection was as a general rule the responsibility of the curials of each locality. They might sometimes engage a man to go about the countryside performing the duty, and he might take a considerable rakeoff, thus in a way reviving the tax farming of the Republic and early Empire. Laws, such as those which supposedly forbade the selling of children above the age of ten into slavery, could be ignored when the poor had no access to higher authority and might not even know the laws were on the books. Lugotorix in *Roma Mater* is a publican of this kind. In addition, special tax officers reported directly to provincial or diocesal officialdom. One class of these collected arrears, another oversaw the whole process and kept the curials up to the mark. Or so the theory went; in practice, they often terrorized everybody, screening their peculations and extortions with bureaucratic obfuscation. A common way for them to grow rich was to convert arrears of taxes into private debts at huge rates of interest. Nagon has been appointed to such a provincial office.

Dál Riata: As we have explained earlier, this was the first Irish colony in what is now Scotland, on the Argyll

503

coast, founded by emigrants from an Ulster kingdom of that name and for a long time considered part of it. The date of the settlement is uncertain. Some authorities place it a century or more after the time of our story, but we are here following traditional accounts.

Aryagalatis: The chronicle calls him Gabran, but we follow the suggestion of Alexei Kondratiev as to what the earlier form of the name had been. (Admittedly, we are inconsistent in that we do not do likewise for the name "Niall" and for a few such words as "tuath," but these, like "Rome" and "Constantinople," are familiar enough that we would rather not risk seeming pedantic.) Though he bore that title, he was not a sovereign monarch. Any man of the right descent, leading any group from a tuath upward, was called its king (*rí*). His powers were always strictly limited; see earlier parts of this story for details. Aryagalatis would have been essentially the chief war lord and sacral figure of the colonial tuaths and whatever natives they subdued. The medieval story says he gave Eochaid refuge after the latter must flee Ireland because of having murdered the poet's son. That Eochaid first roamed about as a pirate is our idea, but quite possible.

Alba: The early Gaelic name for what is now Scotland; sometimes it was extended to include England and Wales.

Cruthini: The Irish name for that people, or those tribes, the Romans lumped together as Picts. Prior to the great Irish (Scotic) immigration early in the Dark Ages, they formed most of the population of what the Irish called Alba and we today call Scotland. Smaller numbers of them also lived here and there in Gaul and in Ireland itself.

XI

The first Visigothic invasion of Italy: Dates are not quite certain, but most authorities put it in November, 401.

Illyricum: The political status and official boundaries of this region varied in the course of history, but in general it comprised much of the Balkan area. Around 400 it was a prefecture, divided between the Western and Eastern Empires. (So they were by that time, although theoretically still one.)

Rhenus: The River Rhine.

Danuvius: The River Danube.

Euxinus: The Black Sea.

Deva: Chester.

The legion at Chester: As admirers of the work of Stephen Vincent Benét, we regretted making the discovery that the Twentieth Valeria Victrix was not, after all, the last legion to depart from Britain.

Etruria: Tuscany and northern Latium.

Histria (later *Istria*): The area around what is now Trieste.

Rhaetia (or *Raetia*): An area occupying what are now known as the Grisons of eastern Switzerland, much of the Tyrol of Austria, and part of Lombardy.

Iron ore: This was usually bog iron, collected rather than mined.

Durotriges: A British tribe occupying, approximately, Dorset.

British immigration into Armorica: This is generally supposed to have gone on in the fifth and sixth centuries, but there is evidence that it began earlier. Some modern scholars believe that it had actually become overwhelming by about 400, but we stay with the traditional view.

German Sea (Oceanus Germanicus): The North Sea.

Cimbrian peninsula: Jutland.

Thule: It is not known what Classical geographers meant by this, and they themselves may well have been unsure or in disagreement. We accept the idea that it was in Norway.

XII

The Republic: Even this late, the Western Empire, at least, maintained the fiction that it was a republic, the Emperor its chief magistrate—although sanctified by the office and surrounded by the trappings of Oriental monarchy.

Churching: The rite readmitting a woman to services after she had given birth.

Deacon: As explained previously, clergy of the early Church, below the rank of bishop, had usually had mundane occupations by which they earned their livings. By the time of our story, priests were supposed to receive stipends, but it is doubtful that deacons did, unless perhaps in the wealthiest churches.

Bricius: Now known as St. Brice, this bishop relaxed the strict rules of his predecessor St. Martin. He was later accused of immorality. The Pope absolved him but he never returned to his see, which suggests he had in fact been guilty.

Paenula: A poncho-like outer garment.

XIII

The move to Ravenna: Its date is not certain, but was probably in summer or autumn of 402.

The case against Cadoc: Breton legend relates how King Grallon cleared St. Ronan of a similar charge by similar means. We are supposing that the story derives from an actual incident and was later transferred to the canonized churchman.

Duke: The Duke of the Armorican Tract, director of defense in that district of Lugdunensis Tertia province.

XIV

The obliteration of Ys: Greater cities than this have been lost from the face of the earth. Archeologists in modern times have identified the sites and uncovered traces of a number of them, but not yet all, and this has generally been with historical records to provide clues.

XV

Postal couriers: These frequently doubled as intelligence agents for the civil authorities.

Savus: The River Drava.

Dalmatia: A province occupying, approximately, what is now most of Yugoslavia.

Pannonia: A province occupying, approximately, what is now Hungary with parts of Austria and Yugoslavia (Croatia).

Resettlement of the Visigoths: Stilicho's repeated leniency toward Alaric was most likely prompted by a desire to make an ally of him for a drive that would establish the supremacy of the Western over the Eastern Empire. The policy was to prove disastrously mistaken.

Procedures possible against the Confluentians: If these

seem limited to the modern reader, one should bear in mind that, while the Romans developed many instruments of tyranny with the inevitable social consequences, the idea of income tax as we know it never occurred to them. Besides, they would have lacked the technology to enforce it.

The wedding: To the Romans, until very late in their history, marriage was a civil contract. Since Tertullian, Christians believed the public blessing of the Church was necessary to make it valid (a view somewhat modified today), but not until after St. Augustine did they consider it a sacrament in itself. Then marriages with pagans and heretics came to be disallowed. However, this had not yet happened at the time of our story. (Augustine issued his *De Bono Conjugali* in 401; it would hardly have reached Armorica by 403, let alone become a basis of doctrine.) Observances surely varied from place to place and time to time. Our version derives in large part from ancient customs, but we suppose that the new religion and the special circumstances caused these to be a little altered.

The prayer: As we have explained before, early Christians had not ordinarily knelt to pray. Except when they prostrated themselves, they stood upright with arms lifted. Kneeling, though not folding of hands, presently came into use in church, but individuals alone probably, as a rule, continued the older practice.

The Virgin Mary: Adoration of her seems to have begun in earnest during the fourth century. It was not yet anything like what it became in the Middle Ages, nor could it yet have had much currency in the North; but Gratillonius's impulse seems to us a very natural one under the circumstances.

508

XVI

Head of navigation: As we have explained earlier, today this is at Locmaria (Aquilo), and then only at high tide and for rather small craft; but apparently the Odet and, perhaps, the Steir were larger and deeper in the past, and ancient vessels generally drew less water than today's. A change in the harbor site helps explain how Quimper (Confluentes) came to overshadow and eventually absorb the older settlement.

Bridge of Sena: Pont de Sein. We suppose that this is the French form of a name going back to ancient times.

XVII

Brigantes: A tribe occupying a substantial part of Britain just south of Hadrian's Wall.

Laégare (later rendered *Laoghaire*, now sometimes *Leary*): According to the traditional histories, he was King at Tara when St. Patrick returned to Ireland. He became friendly with the missionaries and put no obstacles in their path. Indeed, he got Patrick to help him reform and write down the Brehon Laws, the ancient Irish code, which continued in effect for centuries thereafter. However, he himself never accepted baptism. When he died he was buried according to his wish, upright in full battle gear, facing his hereditary enemies the Leinstermen.

Fox and hare: Within living memory in Ireland, it was believed unlucky if either of these animals crossed one's path. Galway fishermen bound for their boats would often turn home.

Lúg's Chariot, etc: It is not known what constellations the Irish and other Celts actually invented. We do know that, while ancient mariners hugged the coasts as much as possible, the Mediterranean civilizations had developed means of measuring the altitudes of heavenly bodies with some precision, and so estimating latitude. The voyages made by more primitive sailors such as the Irish and Saxons show that they must have possessed a similar capability, perhaps learned from the Romans.

Corbilo: Mentioned by Strabo as an important maritime city of Gaul, it seems to have occupied the site of present-day St. Nazaire. About the end of the fourth century, when its circumstances must have been much reduced, it was taken over by Saxons, presumably laeti but evidently with effective autonomy, since they were not converted for another one or two hundred years.

The hour between dog and wolf: This French phrase for twilight, *"l'heure entre chien et loup,"* may have ancient origins.

Torna Éces: According to legend, this greatest of the ancient poets was foster-father to both Niall and Conual, and lamented them both after their deaths. The implied lifespan is great, but not impossible.

XVIII

Sanctuary: This issue was an early one in that conflict between Church and state which was to dominate Western history for centuries and shape much of the new civilization. At the time of our story, a bishop was virtually sovereign with respect to ecclesiastical matters within his (religious) diocese, and had great temporal authority and influence as well. The Pope was only *primus inter pares*, the final arbiter of disputes between bishops but otherwise with little power unique to his office.

Arelate: Arles. The date when it supplanted Trier is not known exactly, but 404 is a reasonable guess.

Exorcism: Corentinus's opinion may not seem canonical to a modern Catholic, but it should be remembered that in the fifth century much doctrine was still unformulated, while disagreements and heresies were rife. Moreover, Dahut's case may have been unique in demonology.

Milk: Children were nursed for a long time by modern standards, well after they began to take solid foods—which were not pressed on them in the manner of today. Lactation does in fact often inhibit impregnation.

Danastris: The River Dniester.

Danuvius: The River Danube. It seems likely that the Goths did not slow themselves by much plundering along the way, but pushed on to catch the Romans ill-prepared in Italy.

XIX

Terms of enlistment: These are attested, and help show how desperate the situation was.

Niall's successor: According to the Irish chronicles, he was Nath Í (or Nathi or Dathi), a fierce warrior who perished in 428 when struck by lightning on an expedition into the Alps. This is almost surely a copyist's error for "Alba," Scotland or England. His successor in turn was Niall's son Laégare, in whose reign St. Patrick began his mission.

Gesocribate: Virtually nothing is known of this city. Even its location is uncertain, though at or near the site of Brest. Its oblivion indicates that it was probably rather small, and may well have been repeatedly sacked until at last it was abandoned.

Crossbow: Little is known about the ancient form of this weapon. Apparently it was drawn by hand rather than wound like the medieval arbalest, but by the fifth century it may sometimes have possessed a pawl. Given sufficient pull, arrows can certainly penetrate mail. Although the rate of discharge is low, the crossbow has an advantage in requiring less skill, hence less training, than the straight bow does.

Holy Georgios: St. George, patron of soldiers. While the cult of saints had not yet approached its medieval intensity, unless perhaps in Egypt, the idea of their intercession, implicit in Scripture, was taking hold widely. No doubt the evangelization of the rural Empire strengthened it. Pagan halidoms were rededicated to specific saints, and people continued to seek help there.

XX

Scythia: At this time it was a rather vague designation; but the Alani, an Iranian people with some Altaic admixture, originated north of the Caspian Sea and spread into the steppes of Russia. Some eventually reached Germanic lands and there joined in the Völkerwanderung.

Moguntiacum: Mainz.

XXI

Vorgium: Carhaix.

Brains: Galen, in the second century, taught that the brain is the seat of consciousness, and his medical works became canonical, although doubtless the uneducated in the fifth century clung to older concepts.

Durocortorum: Reims.

Samarobriva: Amiens.

Nemetacum: Arras.

512

Turnacum: Tournay.

Eboracum (or *Eburacum*): York.

Constantinus: Today called Constantine III or Constantine the Usurper. Virtually nothing is known about the events leading up to his try for the purple, except the names of his predecessors Marcus and Gratian, and that the latter reigned for four months (which implies that the former was no more durable). Constantine's origin is equally obscure. Little has been recorded of his character, and that by hostile writers. He is said to have been a common soldier, but this can scarcely mean that he was when the legions hailed him. We have supplied him with a career that brought him up from the ranks. The fact that he had two sons who took an active part in his campaigns gives a clue to his age at the time. A tradition holds that he was himself a son of Magnus Maximus, who had become a folk hero among the Britons (at least, in the West; see *Roma Mater*). This seems implausible to us, but perhaps there was some more distant kinship, such as Maximus's wife having been Constantine's aunt.

Saxon and Scotian: Unlettered, ferocious, and impulsive though they were, the barbarian leaders cannot often have been stupid. Else the migration of whole tribes could not have happened. Spies, scouts, talkative traders, and other such sources must have given them some idea of what was going on in those parts of the Empire that interested them. The Romans can hardly ever have been able to keep events secret. Even the huge alliance that crossed the Rhine at the end of 406 would have had intelligence of what to expect.

Gesoriacum: Boulogne (not to be confused with Gesocribate).

Pyrenaei Mountains: The Pyrenees.

513

XXII

Lemovicium: Limoges. Earlier it was Augustoritum but in the fourth century, like so many other cities, it came to be called after the tribe in whose ancient territory it lay.

The Feast of Lug: As we have observed before, the pre-harvest festival known in Ireland as Lugnasad and in England as Lammas has long been fixed at 1 August. (The customs we mention were Irish until recent times and must have been of very old Celtic origin.) We hypothesize that, like other such dates, this one was established with Christianity and the Roman calendar, and that originally it was determined by the moon.

Salaun: Breton form of the name "Salomon," which belonged to the legendary first King of Brittany. We shall have more to say about him later in these notes.

XXIII

The Armorican revolt of 407: Nothing is really known about the circumstances. The chronicles say merely that Roman officials were expelled and independence declared; they attribute this to Bacaudae. That seems absurd if taken literally. There could not have been that many outlaws, nor would they have been well enough organized, nor does it appear likely they would have refrained from massacring those they looked on as oppressors. "Bacaudae" must be essentially a swear word, though perhaps with more meaning where it comes to things that happened elsewhere or later. We think our reconstruction of events that year in Armorica is plausible. Of course, all the details are fictional.

Pictavum: Poitiers. The older name was Limonum. The Pictones of Gaul were not related to the Picts of Alba, "Picti" being a name bestowed by the Romans on the latter, the "painted people." However, apparently some tribes related to them did live in Gaul and Ireland as well as Scotland.

Prince (Latin *princeps*): Originally an honorific, meaning "first," applied to various persons such as the first senator on the censor's list in the Republic (*princeps senatus*), later under the Empire as a title of various civil and military officials. Thus in our period it did not yet connote superiority or royal blood. Still, Armoricans might very naturally apply it to the associate and prospective successor of the man they regarded as their Duke (*dux*, "leader," especially a military leader, though this inevitably gave him command over certain civil functions as well).

Hawking: Falconry was practiced by the Romans, albeit the slight and vague mentions of it that we have from them, and the lack of artistic representations, indicate that it had nothing like the popularity it gained during the Middle Ages.

Gelding: Given the lack of what we consider basic prophylaxis, the death rate among new castrates—at least, human ones—was extremely high. Moreover, Roman law forbade the operation on citizens. Eunuchs were either prisoners of war or, oftener, imported from abroad, especially Persia. In consequence, they were expensive. The restrictions were later lifted.

XXIV

The Race of Sena: Raz de Sein, between the island and the mainland.

Garrison in Britain: Virtually nothing is known for certain, but there is some reason to suppose Constantine left a few soldiers behind—much too few to be effective, as the course of events shows.

515

British-Armorican alliance: Obviously this did not come to pass in 407, but there is mention (date not deducible, reliability somewhat questionable) of joint action against the Germans in Gaul, and more than this may have taken place. If so, it was probably after 410, when Honorius's rescript gave the Britons leave to defend themselves.

Caletes: A tribe occupying what is now, approximately, Seine-Maritime.

Sequana: The River Seine. Apparently the revolt in Gaul reached at least this far; and areas farther off had their own uprisings.

Rotomagus: Rouen.

Beltane: We use this variant spelling to indicate a difference between the languages of the insular and the Continental Celts.

Infantry: There was no possibility of re-creating anything like the old Roman legions, and the military future for almost the next thousand years belonged to the heavy cavalryman. The independent Gauls could scarcely raise such a corps either; at best, they may have developed some reasonably good light horse. The bulk of their forces must have been foot. Still, given training and equipment, these could meet the Germans and the seaborne raiders on equal terms.

The Gallic revolt: One should beware of identifying the many different rebellions in the ancient world with any revolution in the modern, such as the American, French, Russian, or Philippine, to name just four widely divergent examples. Each case in the period of our story and earlier was probably unique too. Nothing is really known about the Gallic instance. By analogy with events in Britain, we suppose that ancient tribalism awoke and asserted itself among people who had despaired of Rome. In both countries there appears also to have been a certain amount of nascent nationalism, though it never developed into anything as strong as the modern form.

West Island: Ushant (hypothetical; its name in Roman times is unknown).

XXV

Wotan: This god appears to have been originally a conductor of the dead like Hermes or Mercury, with whom the Romans therefore identified him. We suppose that in the fifth century he had not yet gained those other, overshadowing attributes we know of in his late version, Odin of the viking era.

The moon: It was full on 30 December 407 (Gregorian calendar).

The exorcism: This is not the present-day formula, which is of rather recent origin. There does not seem to have been a standard one in the fifth century; ours is conjectural.

The aftermath: In 408 Stilicho married his daughter Thermantia to Honorius, but soon afterward the machinations of his rivals achieved their purpose. He was accused of treasonous dealings with Alaric the Visigoth, his troops mutinied, and he was assassinated in August of that year. There followed such a wave of anti-German feeling and persecution that the soldiers of that origin and their families went over to Alaric. He marched on Rome, and only an exorbitant payment turned him from it. The next year he came back and set up a puppet emperor whom the Senate perforce acknowledged but quickly thereafter disowned. Alaric returned in 410, captured and sacked Rome, and was on his way through Italy to invade North Africa when he died.

Meanwhile Constantine III established himself in Arles and, defeating forces sent against him by Honorius, wrung from the government the consulship of 409 and recognition as an Imperial colleague; he and his older son proclaimed themselves Augusti. He defended the Rhine frontier rather ably and brought the Germans who had invaded Gaul under a measure of control. Intrigues and attacks led to his overthrow in 411. He surrendered to Honorius, who, repudiating a guarantee of safety, had him executed.

The year 410 was also when Honorius sent his famous rescript to the Britons, granting them the right to organize their own defenses because the help for which they appealed would not be forthcoming. It appears they were temporarily victorious about the middle of the century and this is the seed from which the Arthurian legend sprang. Germans continued to enter Roman territory on the Continent and founded independent kingdoms in it, the Burgundians as early as 413. The Huns, sometimes allies of the Empire, became more and more often its ravishers.

Nevertheless a chronicle declares that in or about 417 the Romans regained Armorica and other secessionist parts of Gaul. No details are given. It seems probable to us that, if this did happen, the submission was nominal, the result of a mutually advantageous compromise, and that the Armoricans retained essential autonomy. Honorius could not very well punish an uprising which had, after all, been against the usurper Constantine; nor could he have spared troops to occupy the region and compel subservience. (He died unlamented in 423.) There is mention of later revolts of "Bacaudae" in various areas, but these may have been incidents of jacquerie.

According to the Breton accounts, Salaun (Salomon) reigned as king from 421 to 435; he abolished the Roman practice of selling children into slavery to pay taxes, but was killed by pagans who resented his efforts to Christianize the country. If this can be trusted, and it looks no more unreliable than the Mediterranean sources, it bears out the idea of a free Armorica. Still more does an extant roll of the nations that sent men to join Aëtius in his historic battle against the Huns, 451. "The Armoricans" are listed like any others, implying that they were sovereign allies.

Equally suggestive is the heavy immigration from Brit-

518

ain in this and the subsequent century. It would scarcely have gone in the direction of more oppression and less security. Of course, it resulted in the flooding of the small native population. Armorica became known as Breizh (Bretagne in French, Brittany in English) and the Celtic language still spoken there is of southwestern British origin. A few traditions survive from ancient times— among them, perhaps, the story of Ys.

AFTERWORD

The Breton folk tell many different tales about the sunken city of Ys, its king, and his daughter. Bearing in mind that these often disagree, let us give a synopsis of the basic medieval story.

Grallon (sometimes rendered "Gradlon") was ruler of Cornouaille, along the southwestern shore of Brittany, with his seat at Quimper, which some say he helped found. Once he took a great fleet overseas and made war on Malgven, Queen of the North. In conquering her country he also won her heart, as she did his. They started off together for his home, but terrible weather kept them at sea for a year. During this time Malgven bore a girl child, and died in so doing. When the heartbroken Grallon finally returned, he could deny nothing to his daughter Dahut (in some versions, Ahes). She grew up beautiful and evil.

While hunting, Grallon met a hermit, Corentin, who lived in the forest. This man was miraculously nourished; each day he drew a fish from the water, ate half, and threw the other half back, whereupon it became whole and alive again. However, it was his wisdom that most impressed the king. Grallon persuaded Corentin to join him in Quimper, and there the holy man won the people

519

over to righteous ways. Other legends maintain that he was the actual founder or co-founder of the city, and its first bishop.

Dahut felt oppressed by the piety all around her, and begged her father to give her a place of her own. He built Ys on the shore— Ys of the hundred towers, walled against the waters that forever threatened its splendor. Hung upon his breast, Grallon kept the silver key that alone could unlock the sea gate. Otherwise he gave Dahut free rein and turned a blind eye to her wickedness.

Led by her, Ys became altogether iniquitous. The rich ground down the poor, gave themselves to licentious pleasures, forgot their duty to God, and even blasphemed Him. Dahut herself took a different lover every night, and in the morning had him cast to his death in the sea.

Another holy man, St. Guénolé, was stirred to enter the city and plead with the people to mend their ways. For a while he did succeed in frightening many into reform; but the baneful influence of Dahut was too strong, and they drifted back into sin.

At last God determined to destroy Ys, and gave the Devil leave to carry out the mission. Taking the guise of a handsome young man, he sought Dahut in her palace and was soon welcomed into her bed. Him she did not have killed. Rather, she fell wildly in love. He demanded, as a sign of her affection, that she bring him the key Grallon bore. Dahut stole it while the king was asleep and gave it to her lover. The night was wild with storm. He slipped out and unlocked the gate. The sea raged in and overwhelmed Ys.

It had no power over St. Guénolé, who awakened innocent Grallon and warned him to flee. Barely did the king's great charger carry him through the waters as they surged in between the city walls. Dahut screamed in terror. Her father saw, and tried to save her. The saint told him he must not, for the weight of her sins would drag him down too; and she was swept away from his grasp. None but Grallon and Guénolé escaped, as Ys went under the waves.

Guénolé laid the doom on the city that it would remain sunken until a Mass was said in it upon a Good Friday. Dahut became a siren, haunting the coast, luring sailors to shipwreck among the many rocks thereabouts. Grallon gave up his crown and ended his days in the abbey of Landévennec which Guénolé had founded.

A later story relates how one mariner was borne beneath the water by certain strange swimmers. Somehow he did not drown, and they led him to the sunken city and into a church where a service was going on. He was afraid to give the responses, when no one else did. Afterward his guides brought him ashore and let him go; but first they asked sadly, "Why did you not say what you should have at the Mass? Then we would all have been released."

Ys is still there under the sea.

Thus far the tradition. As for its origin, the prosaic fact is that stories about submerged towns are common along the Welsh and Cornish coasts. Folk from those parts could well have carried the idea with them during their massive emigration to Armorica in the fifth and sixth centuries. In the course of time it came to be associated with Grallon and with several of the host of Breton saints. On the other hand, the tale could conceivably have been a native one which the Bretons found when they arrived, and this we have assumed for our purposes.

Among the disagreements between versions of the legend, conspicuous is that concerning the site. Some accounts put Ys on the Baie de Douarnenez, others on the Baie d'Audierne, still others on the Baie des Trépassés. We have chosen the last of these.

Obviously we have made a good many more choices! First and foremost, we have imagined that there really was an Ys.

If so, when did it perish? Saints Corentin and Guénolé are assigned to the fifth and sixth centuries respectively; therefore they could not both have been involved. We picked the earlier era. (If nothing else, the farther back in time, the more plausible it is that no record would survive of the city and its destruction. At that, we have had to offer some explanation of why the Romans left none.) Therefore Corentin must needs assume the role that folklore gives to Guénolé. Besides, legend associates him with the founding of Quimper and makes St. Martin consecrate him its bishop.

Since no kingdom of Cornouaille existed at this time, our Grallon would have had to begin as the ruler of Ys, which must thus have been flourishing long before his birth. He in turn would have had no reason to start a settlement at what was to become Quimper until after the loss of his realm. The need for a new stronghold, in the chaos that was spreading through Gaul, would be clear to him if he was himself a Roman, as we have supposed.

From the first-century geographer Pomponius Mela we have adopted and adapted the Gallicenae. True, he describes them as vestal virgins, but with his own sources all being indirect, he was not necessarily right about this. The sixth-century historian Procopius gives an account of the Ferriers of the Dead; he says they took their unseen passengers from Gaul to Britain, but we depict men so engaged between Ys and the Île de Sein. The king who must win and defend his crown in mortal combat is best known from Lake Nemi, as described by Sir James Frazer in *The Golden Bough*. However, the practice has occurred elsewhere too, in various guises, around the world, so we could reasonably attribute it to Ys.

Aside from such modifications, logically required, we have stayed as close as possible to the legends. After all, this is a fantasy. Yet we have at the same time tried to keep it within the framework of facts that are well established.

For us it all began one day in 1979, when we were staying on a farm near Médréac in Brittany and Karen, on impulse, wrote the poem with which our story ends. Earlier in the same trip we had visited a number of Roman remains in England and stood on Hadrian's Wall. Now somehow this came together with Ys, of which our surroundings reminded us, and the first dim outlines of the tale appeared. At home we thought and talked about it more and more often, until by 1982 our ideas were clear enough that we returned to Brittany for a look at sites we had not examined before. There followed about a year's worth of book research, and then the actual writing—occasionally interrupted to meet other commitments—lasted into the spring of 1987. The whole business has been a strange and rewarding experience. We hope readers will enjoy what has come out of it.

GEOGRAPHICAL GLOSSARY

These equivalents are for the most part only approximations. For further details, see the Notes.

Abonae: Sea Mills.
Alba: Scotic name of what is now Scotland, sometimes including England and Wales.
Aquilo: Locmaria, now a district at the south end of Quimper.
Arelate: Arles.
Armorica: Brittany.
Audiarna: Audierne (hypothetical).
Augusta Treverorum: Trier.
Boand's River: The River Boyne.
Bridge of Sena: Pont de Sein.
Britannic Sea (Oceanus Britannicus): The English Channel.
Britannia: The Roman part of Britain, essentially England and Wales.
Burdigala: Bordeaux.
Caesarodunum Turonum: Tours.
Caledonia: Roman name of Scotland.
Cape Rach: Pointe du Raz (hypothetical).
Cassel: Cashel.
Cimbrian peninsula: Jutland.
Clón Tarui: Clontarf, now a district of Dublin.
Condacht: Connaught.
Condate Redonum: Rennes.
Condevincum: A small city, now part of Nantes.
Confluentes: Quimper (hypothetical).
Corbilo: St. Nazaire.

523

Dalmatia: A province occupying, approximately, what is now much of Yugoslavia.

Dál Riata: A realm in Ulster, or its colony on the Argyll coast.

Danastris: The River Dniester.

Danuvius: The River Danube.

Darioritum Venetorum: Vannes.

Deva: Chester.

Dochaldun: An Osismiic village (imaginary).

Dubris: Dover.

Durocotorum: Reims.

Eboracum: York.

Emain Macha: Seat of the principal Ulster kings, near present-day Armagh.

Ériu: Early Gaelic name of Ireland.

Etruria: Tuscany and northern Latium.

Euxinus: The Black Sea.

Fanum Martis: Corseul.

Gallia: Gaul, including France and parts of Belgium, Germany, and Switzerland.

Garomagus: A town at or near present-day Douarnenez (hypothetical).

German Sea (Oceanus Germanicus): The North Sea.

Gesocribate: A seaport at or near the site of Brest.

Gesoriacum: Boulogne.

Goat Foreland: Cap de la Chèvre (hypothetical).

Gobaean Promontory (Promontorium Gobaeum): Cap Sizun.

Hispania: Spain and Portugal.

Histria: The area around what is now Trieste.

Hivernia: Roman name of Ireland.

Illyricum: A Roman diocese (major administrative division) occupying, approximately, Greece and much of Yugoslavia.

Islands of Crows: The Channel Islands (hypothetical nickname).

Isca Silurum: Caerleon.

Jecta: The River Jet (hypothetical).

Juliomagus: Angers.

Lemovicium: Limoges.

Liger: The River Loire.

Liguria: A region of Italy including Lombardy and present-day Liguria.

Lugdunensis Tertia: A Roman province comprising north-western France.

Lugdunum: Lyons.

Mediolanum: Milan.

Moguntiacum: Mainz.

Mons Ferruginus: Mont Frugy (hypothetical).

Mumu: Munster.

Namnetum: See *Portus Namnetum*.

Neapolis: Naples.

Nemetacum: Arras.

Odita: The River Odet (hypothetical).

Osismia: The country of the Osismii, in western Brittany.

Pannonia: A Roman province occupying parts of Hungary, Austria, and Yugoslavia.

Pictavum: Poitiers.

Point Vanis: Pointe du Van (hypothetical).

Portus Namnetum: Nantes (in part).

Pyrenaei Mountains: The Pyrenees.

Qóiqet Lagini: Leinster (in part).

Qóiqet nUlat: Ulster.

Race of Sena: Raz de Sein.

Redonia: The country of the Redones, in eastern Brittany.

Redonum: See *Condate Redonum*.

Rhaetia: A Roman province occupying the eastern Alps and western Tyrol.

Rhenus: The River Rhine.

Roman Bay: Baie de Douarnenez (hypothetical).

Rotomagus: Rouen.

Ruirthech: The River Liffey.

Sabrina: The River Severn.

Samarobriva: Amiens.

Savus: The River Drava.

Scandia: The southern part of the Scandinavian peninsula.

Scot's Landing: A fisher hamlet near Ys (imaginary).

Sena: Île de Sein.

Stag Run: An Osismiic village (imaginary).

Stegir: The River Steir (hypothetical).

Tallten: Teltown, in County Meath, Ireland.

Temir: Tara.

Teutoburg Forest: Scene of a Roman military disaster at German hands in the reign of Augustus Caesar.

Treverorum: See *Augusta Treverorum*.

Turnacum: Tournay.

Turonum: See *Caesarodunum Turonum*.

Venetorum: See *Darioritum Venetorum*.

Vindoval: An Osismiic village (imaginary).

Vindovaria: A village in Britain (imaginary).

Vorgium: Carhaix.

Whalestrand: A fisher hamlet in western Brittany (imaginary).

Ys: City-state at the far western end of Brittany (legendary).

DRAMATIS PERSONAE

Where characters are fictional or legendary, their names are in Roman lower case; where historical (in the opinion of most authorities), in Roman capitals; where of doubtful or debatable historicity, in italics. When a full name has not appeared in the text, it is generally not here either, for it was of no great importance even to the bearer.

Aébell: A daughter of Cellach.

ALARIC: King of the Visigoths.

Amair: A daughter of Fennalis by Hoel.

Amreth Taniti: Commander of the surviving Ysan marines.

Anmureg maqq Cerballi: A sea rover from Mide.

Arban Cartagi: An Ysan Suffete, husband of Talavair, father of Korai.

Ardens, Septimius Cornelius: Praetorian prefect of Gallia, Hispania, and Britannia.

Aryagalatis maqq Irgalato: King of Dál Riata in Alba.

Apuleius Vero: A senator in Aquilo and a tribune of the city.

ARCADIUS, FLAVIUS: Augustus of the East.

Bacca, Quintus Domitius: Procurator of Lugdunensis Tertia.

Bannon: Headman of Dochaldun.

Betha: Wife of Maeloch.

Bodilis: A Queen of Ys.

Boia: A daughter of Lanarvilis by Hoel.

Bomatin Kusuri: Former Mariner delegate to the Council of Suffetes in Ys.

Breccan: Eldest son of Niall, killed in battle at Ys.

Brennilis: Leader of the Gallicenae at the time of Julius and Augustus Caesar, responsible for the building of the sea wall and gate.

BRICIUS: Successor of Martinus; known today as St. Brice.

Budic: A legionary in Gratillonius's detachment at Ys, killed by him in combat at the Wood of the King.

Cadoc Himilco: A young Ysan of Suffete family.

Cael Maqq Eriai: An ollam poet at Niall's court.

Carsa: A young Gallo-Roman stationed in Ys, killed by Gratillonius in combat at the Wood of the King.

Cata: A female worker at the Apuleius manor house.

Cathual: Charioteer to Niall.

Catto: A fisherman from Whalestrand.

Catualorig: A former Bacauda.

Cellach maqq Blathmaic: The hostelkeeper at Clón Tarui.

Colconor: A former King of Ys, slain by Gratillonius.

CONSTANTINUS, CONSTANS: Elder son of Flavius Claudius Constantinus.

CONSTANTINUS, FLAVIUS CLAUDIUS: A Roman army officer in Britannia, later a usurper known as CONSTANTINUS III.

CONSTANTINUS, JULIANUS: Younger son of Flavius Claudius Constantinus.

CONUAL CORCC: Principal king in Mumu.

Corentinus: A holy man, chorepiscopus at Ys, later bishop of Confluentes and Aquilo; known today as St. Corentin.

CUNEDAG: A leader of the Votadini, settled in western Britannia to be an ally of Rome.

Cynan: (1) A legionary in Gratillonius's detachment at Ys. (2) A centurion in Constantinus's army.

Dahilis: A Queen of Ys, mother of Dahut.

Dahut: Daughter of Dahilis and Gratillonius.

Dion: A youth from Neapolis.

Doranius: A young man from Gesocribate.

Drach: Father of Vellano.

Drusus, Publius Flavius: A Britannic centurion under Maximus, later a settler in Armorica.

Einiaunus, Valerius: A Britannic official in Constantinus's service.

Éndae Qennsalach: Principal king in Qóiqet Lagini.

Eochaid maqq Éndae: A son of Éndae, exiled for murder of a poet and implacable enemy of Niall.

Eógan: A son of Niall.

Eppillus: A legionary in Gratillonius's detachment at Ys, killed in action there.

Estar: A daughter of Gratillonius and Tambilis.

Esun: A son of Catto.

Étain: A female druid at Niall's court.

Evirion Baltisi: A young Ysan sea captain.

Favonius: Gratillonius's favorite horse.

Fennalis: A Queen of Ys.

Fogartach: A follower of Eochaid.

Forsquilis: A Queen of Ys, mother of Nemeta.

GAINAS: A Roman general of Gothic origin.

Glabrio, Titus Scribona: Governor of Lugdunensis Tertia.

Goban: An Osismiic boatman and deacon to Corentinus.

Gradlon: An Armorican version of "Gratillonius."

Grallon: An Ysan version of "Gratillonius."

GRATIANUS: A legionary officer in Britannia, briefly claimant of the purple.

Gratillonius, Gaius Valerius: A Romano-Briton of the Belgic tribe, centurion in the Second Legion Augusta, later King of Ys.

Guilvilis: A Queen of Ys.

Gunnung Ivarsson: A Danic skipper and sea rover.

Hilketh Eliuni: Former Transporter delegate to the Council of Suffetes in Ys.

Hoel: King of Ys before Colconor.

HONORIUS, FLAVIUS: Augustus of the West.

Innloch: Father of Maeloch.

Johannes: Son of Julia and Cadoc.

Julia: Daughter of Lanarvilis and Gratillonius.

Korai: Granddaughter of Bodilis.

LAÉGARE: Youngest son of Niall.

Laidchenn maqq Barchedo: An ollam poet formerly at Niall's court.

Lanarvilis: A Queen of Ys, mother of Julia.

Lavinia: A lady in Mediolanum.

Lorccan maqq Flandi: A Scotic warrior.

Lydris: Wife of Nagon Demari.

Maecius: Chorepiscopus at Aquilo, presently retired.

Maeloch: An Ysan fisher captain and formerly a Ferrier of the Dead.

Marcus: Son of Verania and Gratillonius.

MARCUS: A legionary officer in Britannia, briefly claimant of the purple.

Maria: Daughter of Verania and Gratillonius.

MARTINUS: Bishop of Turonum and founder of a monastery nearby; known today as St. Martin of Tours.

MAXIMUS, MAGNUS CLEMENS: Commander of Roman forces in Britannia, who later forcibly took power as co-Emperor but was overthrown and executed by Theodosius the Great.

Miraine: A daughter of Lanarvilis and Hoel.

Mongfind: Stepmother of Niall, long dead, said to have been a witch.

Morvanalis: A Queen of Ys, mother of Guilvilis.

Murena, Flaminius: Duke of the Armorican Tract.

Nagon Demari: A Suffete in Ys, self-exiled during Gratillonius's reign and bitterly hostile to him.

Namma: Cook in the Apuleius household.

Nath Í: Nephew, tanist, and eventual successor of Niall.

Nemain maqq Aedo: Late chief druid at Niall's court.

Nemeta: Daughter of Forsquilis and Gratillonius.

NIALL MAQQ ECHACH, also known as NIALL OF THE NINE HOSTAGES: King at Temir and overlord of Mide.

Norom: A crewman of Maeloch's.

Ogotorig: A hunter, formerly a Bacauda.

Olath Cartagi: An Ysan survivor who became an iron-maker.

Parnesius: A friend of Gratillonius in his youth.

Philippus: An exorcist in Turonum.

Quintilius: A courtier in Mediolanum.

RADAGAISUS: A Gothic warlord.

Ramas Tyri: Former Artisan delegate to the Council of Suffetes in Ys.

Riwal: A Durotrigian (from Britannia) who moved to Confluentes.

Rovinda: Wife of Apuleius.

Rufinus: A Redonian, formerly a Bacauda, henchman of Gratillonius.

Rullus, Septimius: A curial in Gesocribate.

Runa: Daughter of Vindilis and Hoel.

Salaun: An Armorican version of "Salomon."

Salomon: Son of Rovinda and Apuleius.

Sasai: Birth name of Guilvilis.

Semuramat: A daughter of Tambilis and Gratillonius.

STILICHO, FLAVIUS: A Roman general, half Vandal by birth, who became effectively the dictator of the West Roman Empire.

Subne maqq Dúnchado: A follower of Eochaid.

SUCAT: A young holy man, later called Patricius; known today as St. Patrick.

Surach: A son of Catto.

Taenus Himilco: Father of Cadoc.

Talavair: A daughter of Bodilis and Hoel.

Tambilis: A Queen of Ys.

Tera: An Ysan countrywoman.

Tigernach maqq Laidchinni: A son and pupil of Laid-chenn, murdered by Eochaid.

Timbro: A follower of Ullus.

Tommaltach maqq Donngalii: A young Scotian living in Ys, killed by Gratillonius in combat at the Wood of the King.

Torna Éces: Greatest poet in Ériu, foster-father of Niall and Conual.

Tronan Sironai: Late husband of Runa.

Uail maqq Carbri: Henchman of Niall.

Udach: A servant of Gratillonius.

Ullus: A bully from Audiarna.
Una: Daughter of Bodilis and Gratillonius.
Usun: An Ysan fisherman, Maeloch's mate on *Osprey*.
Vellano: A Redonian who moved to Confluentes.
Verania: Daughter of Rovinda and Apuleius.
Vindilis: A Queen of Ys, mother of Runa.
Vindolenus: A former Bacauda.
Vortivir, Flavius: Tribune at Darioritum Venetorum.

Here is an excerpt from Heroing *by Dafydd ab Hugh, coming in October 1987 as part of the new* SIGN OF THE DRAGON *fantasy line from Baen Books:*

Hesitantly, Jiana crawled into the crack.

"It's okay, guys," she called back, "but it's a bit cramped. Toldo next—wait! —Dida, then Toldo. I want . . . the priest in back." She felt a twinge of guilt. What she really wanted was the boy where she could reach out and touch his hand when needed.

Dida whimpered something. Jiana turned back in surprise.

"What's wrong?"

"Oh, love . . . are we really going—into *there?*"

"Dida, it's the only way. Are you a mouse? Come on, warrior!" He pressed his lips together and crawled toward her hand. When she touched him, she felt him trembling.

"Don't fear. I came through here, remember?"

The tunnel smelled as fresh as flowers after the stench of sewage. Jiana could breathe again without gagging.

The ceiling of the passage sank and sank, until she was almost afraid it would narrow to a wedge and block them off. But she remembered her harrowing crawl from the prison, her heart pounding with fear, feeling the hot, fetid breath of *something* on her neck, and she knew the passage was passable. At last, they were scraping along with their bellies on the floor and their backs against the splintery ceiling. Jiana wondered how Toldo Mondo was managing with his prodigious girth.

Suddenly, she knew something was wrong. She crawled on a few more yards, then stopped. Dida was no longer behind her. She heard a faint cry from behind her.

"Jiana, help me—please help me . . ."

"Lady Jiana," called out Toldo, "I think you had better come back here. The boy . . . seems to have a problem." Jiana felt a chill in her stomach; Toldo sounded much too professionally casual.

"What's wrong?" She turned slowly around on her stomach, and inched her way back to where the two had stopped. She stretched out her hand and took Dida's; it was clammy and shaking. With her fingers she felt his pulse, and it was pounding wildly.

"I can't do it," he whispered miserably. "I can't do it—I just can't do it—all that weight—I can't breathe! —I can't . . ."

"What? Oh, for Tooqa's sake! What next?"

As if in answer to her blasphemy, the ground began to shake and roll. Again she heard the scraping, grinding noise, only this time much closer. Dida continued to whimper.

"Oh gods, oh gods, oh please, let me out, oh please, take it away . . ."

"Too close," she whispered, trying to peer through the pitch blackness.

"Oh my lord," gasped Toldo Mondo, "don't you hear it?"

Again the ground shook, and this time the scraping was closer yet, and accompanied by a slimy sucking sound.

For a moment all were silent; even Dida stopped his whimpering. Then Jiana and Toldo began to babble simultaneously.

"I'm sorry," she cried, "I'm sorry, o Ineffable One, o Nameless Scaly One, o You Who Shall Not Be Named! I never meant—"

Toldo chanted something over and over in another language; it sounded like a penance. The fearful noise suddenly became much louder.

"Toldo! It's coming this way! Oh lordy, what'll we do? Crawl, damn you, crawl, crawl! And push the kid along—I'll grab his front and drag!"

"You fool! It's here! Don't you hear it? Am I the only one who hears it?!"

"Shut up and push, you fat tub of goat cheese!"

In a frenzy, they began to squirm away from the sound, dragging Dida, and Jiana discovered that the tiny crawlway was as wide as a king's hall, though the ceiling was but a foot and a half off the floor. Dida was no help. He was in shock, as if he'd been stabbed in a battle. He could only move his arms and legs in a feeble attempt at locomotion, praying to be "let out."

After a few moments, Jiana realized she was hopelessly lost. Had they kept going straight from the hole by the river, they would have found the next door. But they were moving to the right, and she did not know how far they had gone in the pitch black. In fact, she was not even sure which way they were currently pointing; the horrible noises had seemed to change direction, and they had concentrated on keeping them to their rear.

"Oh gods, I've done it now," she moaned; "we won't ever get out of here!" A sob from Dida caught at her heart, and she cursed herself for speaking aloud.

"We shall make it," retorted Toldo Mondo. "There must be *something* in this direction, if we go far enough!"

Soon, Jiana herself began to feel the oppression of millions of tons of rock pressing down on her. She had terrifying visions of being buried alive in the blackness by a sudden cave-in caused by the movements of whatever was behind them. With every beat of her heart it got closer, and the shaking grew worse. She could clearly hear a sound like a baby sucking on its fist.

"Jiana, go!" cried Toldo in a panic. "Crawl, go—faster, woman! It's here, it's—Jiana, I CAN SMELL IT!"

"How does it squeeze along, when even we barely fit?" she wondered aloud. *You're babbling, Ji . . . stop it!*

She surged and lunged forward, not letting go of Dida, though he was like a wet sack of cornmeal. And then, there was a rocky wall in front of her. There was nowhere left to crawl.

Coming in October 1987 * 65344-X * 352 pp. * $3.50